THE WORLD OF
MYSTERY FICTION

THE WORLD OF
MYSTERY
FICTION

Edited by
ELLIOT L. GILBERT

Bowling Green State University Popular Press
Bowling Green, Ohio 43403

Illustration Acknowledgments
Page 1—Gustave Doré from *London: A Pilgrammage* by Gustave Doré and Blanchard Jerrold, Grant & Co., London, 1872. Page 99—Sidney Paget. Page 165—John Odam. Page 243—Darrel Millsap. Page 387—M. C. Escher, "Relativity." Used with permission of the Escher Foundation, Haags Gemeentemuseum, The Hague.

The World of Mystery Fiction designed by Jim Crouch.

Published by The Reader's Digest Association, Inc., 1990, by special arrangement with the Bowling Green State University Popular Press.

CONTENTS

INTRODUCTION

I. In the Beginning . . .

What was the first detective story?

In his landmark mystery anthology, *101 Years' Entertainment*, Ellery Queen suggests that the account of Abel's murder by Cain in Genesis 4:8, with its killer, victim, motive, and implied weapon, would make an excellent candidate for the honor except that it lacks the one element essential to all detective fiction—a detective. But there *is* an investigator of sorts in the case, one who skillfully takes advantage of the criminal's confusion and self-consciousness to expose his guilt. God's interrogation of Cain is, in fact, almost a model of the familiar police detective grilling, a combination of aggressive questioning and direct accusation designed to break the will of the most self-possessed murderer. "Where is Abel thy brother?" God begins, and in response to Cain's well-known evasive and incriminating reply continues, "What hast thou done? The voice of thy brother's blood crieth unto me from the ground."

The investigative technique demonstrated here was developed during the examination of a still earlier crime. Indeed, in questioning Adam about the matter of the missing apple, God had already shown Himself to be a masterful sleuth, at one point employing a device for exposing the criminal which mystery writers have used ever since with great success. Walking in the garden in the cool of the afternoon, God misses Adam and calls out "Where art thou?" at which Adam, flustered and obliged to invent some excuse for his absence in a hurry, unwittingly reveals his guilt by mentioning a fact that only the criminal could have known. "I hid from Thee," he says, "because I was naked." God immediately exploits this blunder. "Who told thee thou was naked?" He demands, and then continues at once, allowing Adam no chance to recover just as later He allows Cain none, "Hast thou eaten of the tree whereof I commanded thee that thou shouldst not eat?" Again, the culprit breaks down and confesses.

The strongest argument against considering God a detective in these stories is that, given His omniscience, He necessarily knows all the answers to His questions before He asks them and is therefore not really detecting anything. No doubt this is what Ellery Queen had in mind when he rejected Genesis 4 as the first detective story. But such an objection would not apply to other detective-like characters in biblical and classical literature. In the story of Susanna and the elders, for example, mentioned by Dorothy L. Sayers as an early instance of the genre,[1] Daniel too traps the guilty with a clever question, while Solomon's strategy for determining the mother of the disputed child in 1 Kings 4:16–28 is up to the highest standard of a Sherlock Holmes or a Nero Wolfe. In Sophocles' Oedipus, we not only get a fully worked out murder investigation but perhaps the first appearance of one of the most important of all mystery story themes, the identification of the detective with the criminal. And in an equally famous Shakespearian murder mystery, the central character reveals almost professional investigatory skills in his questioning of a group of witnesses, cleverly leading them into an apparent inconsistency and then pouncing.

Horatio:	My lord, I think I saw him yesternight.
Hamlet:	Saw? Who?
Horatio:	My lord, the king your father.
Hamlet:	The king my father?
Horatio:	. . . A figure like your father
	Armed at point, exactly, cap-a-pe . . .
Hamlet:	Armed, you say?
Horatio:	Armed, my lord.
Hamlet:	From top to toe?
All:	My lord, from head to foot.
Hamlet:	Then saw you not his face.

It is easy enough to multiply examples of this kind as a way of establishing the antiquity of the detective, but such a procedure is based on an obvious fallacy, that of confusing a few characteristics of a phenomenon with the phenomenon itself. For it makes no more sense to say that a person who employs certain clever but universal problem-solving techniques is automatically a detective than it does to suggest that one who can bandage a cut finger or diagnose a head cold is necessarily a doctor. The detective profession is a complex and formal one, and if we define it rigorously as an organized system for the exposure and apprehension of criminals, we can reasonably say that it has not been in existence for much more than 150 years. Indeed, the *Oxford English Dictionary* cites no use of the word "detective" earlier than the nineteenth century, and no even rudimentary professional detective appears

---

1. Howard Haycraft, ed., *The Art of the Mystery Story* (New York: Grosset and Dunlap, 1961), p. 72.

in English or American history before the middle of the eighteenth.

The detective was in large part a product of the growing industrialization of eighteenth- and nineteenth-century society. As masses of people began to move from country villages to big cities to be nearer mills and factories, the old informal police system of night watchmen and part-time constables who were personally acquainted with a small, stable population of neighbors and friends began to fail. Instead, what the larger, more mobile, and increasingly anonymous crowds of industrial Europe now required for the control of crime was a trained and expert corps of professional police.

But such a professional force took a long time to develop. Many of the first eighteenth-century police spies, informers, and thief-takers got their jobs because they were themselves former criminals; as one magistrate of the time put it: "While the present system continues, and while robberies and burglaries are so frequent, without the means of prevention, there is no alternative on many occasions but to employ a thief to catch a thief."[2] Not surprisingly, these earliest detective-like figures often could not be distinguished from the lawbreakers they were hunting. They frequently used questionable and even illegal methods to earn the large rewards offered for important criminals and regularly perjured themselves to get convictions at a time when even minor offenses were punishable by death. Add to this the fact that when they weren't acting as agents of a frequently unscrupulous and oppressive government they were often in the employ of wealthy private citizens bent on personal revenge, and it will be clear why during these years, as one critic has put it, "the aversion to police appeared to be even greater than the aversion to crime."[3] Indeed, the great eighteenth-century folk heroes were much more likely to be thieves and rogues than thief-takers and "detectives."

For the reputation of these first "detectives" to improve, people needed some sign that those chosen to be police officers were themselves morally respectable, that the detective force existed to serve not its own self-interest but something in the nature of an abstract ideal of justice. The government, of course, would have to learn over the years to protect the civil rights of individuals through those fair courtroom procedures and impartial rules of evidence on which true detection and abstract justice depend; but in the meanwhile, separate efforts could be—and were—made to do something about the scandalously bad police systems.

Among the best known of these efforts was novelist Henry Fielding's establishment, in 1753, of the Bow Street Flying Squad. Five years

---

2. Ian Ousby, *Bloodhounds of Heaven* (Cambridge: Harvard University Press, 1976), p. 11.
3. Ibid., p. 8.

before, Fielding had been commissioned a police magistrate, his court located in Bow Street, Covent Garden, at the very center of London's criminal activities. On several occasions, Fielding tried and failed to create a full-time, paid professional police service for the country. (The English feared such a service might become the equivalent of the political secret police systems on the continent and act to undermine civil liberties.) Finally, he decided on his own to train half a dozen of his cleverest constables in criminal law and the basic principles of investigation, and these Bow Street Runners, as they later came to be known, persisted as an organization for more than three-quarters of a century, "the ancestors," E. F. Bleiler calls them, "of detective police in Great Britain," or as he also puts it, "the Scotland Yard of its day."[4]

. The Runners were a colorful group, experts in matters of crime, clever and daring in action, and they did much to improve the image of the police in the public's mind. But they also had their less attractive side. Many of them had joined the force after at least quasi-criminal careers of their own, and the fact that they were paid a fee for each case they accepted inevitably raised doubts about their disinterestedness and objectivity. By the middle of the nineteenth century, Charles Dickens could write in retrospect of the Bow Street Runners:

We think there was a vast amount of humbug about those worthies. Apart from many of them being men of very indifferent character, and far too much in the habit of consorting with thieves and the like, they never lost a public occasion of jobbing and trading in mystery and making the most of themselves. . . . As a Preventive Police they were utterly ineffective, and as a Detective Police were very loose and uncertain in their operations.[5]

Dickens made these remarks in an essay published some twenty years after the establishment of the London Metropolitan Police, a paid professional force created by Robert Peel in 1829 in the spirit of Fielding's earlier proposals. These "peelers," or "bobbies," as they were soon being called, generally came to their new jobs from military rather than criminal backgrounds, and because they drew adequate official salaries, they were less inclined to accept bribes or indulge in other irregularities. The Bow Street Runners continued to perform detective functions for another dozen years, but in 1842 they were finally replaced by the Detective Department, an eight-man professional investigative organi-

---

4. *Richmond: Scenes in the Life of a Bow Street Runner*, ed. E. F. Bleiler (New York: Dover, 1976), p. vi.

5. Charles Dickens, "The Detective Police," in *Reprinted Pieces* (London: Oxford University Press, 1958), p. 485.

zation which further increased the respectability and public acceptance of the police system.

All during this approximately one-hundred-year period, works of literature recorded the changing attitudes toward crime and the police, and if it is true, as Howard Haycraft reasonably puts it, that "there could be no detective stories until there were detectives,"[6] it is among these works we must look for a tale to be designated the first piece of detective fiction. Two eighteenth-century novels of crime and detection, published fifty years apart, reflect the then prevalent public hostility toward the questionable activities of the police, and for that reason alone they could hardly be considered founders of the modern detective story tradition. Henry Fielding's own satiric *Jonathan Wild* (1743) recounts the career of a spectacular private investigator and thief-taker who is at the same time a master criminal and who ends his life on the gallows, and William Godwin's *Caleb Williams* (1794) is a book which, according to Julian Symons, "denies all the assertions to be made later through the detective story. In the detective story, the rule of law is justified as an absolute good; in Godwin's book it is seen as wholly evil."[7] In the words of one criminal in the novel, "We, who are thieves without a license, are at open war with another sort of men, who are thieves according to law."

In the period from 1827 to 1829, two books were published which approach more closely to true detective fiction. Both are really collections of short stories, though presented as memoirs, and both display their detective heroes in a more generally favorable light than either Fielding or Godwin do theirs. *Richmond: Scenes in the Life of a Bow Street Runner*, called by E. F. Bleiler "the first collection of detective stories in English," records the life of a young man who decides to make up for a misspent though not criminal youth by joining the Bow Street Runners. In the book, the Runners are described as an adventurous but essentially honest band of detective police, their cases calling for them to display considerable courage and some cunning. Only a year after *Richmond* appeared, *The Memoirs of Vidocq, Principal Agent of the French Police* was published in Paris and almost simultaneously in an English translation in London. Vidocq's career harks back to the earlier tradition of the thief turned thief-taker, but the book is able to capitalize on its subject's undoubted successes as a detective and his many years as first chief of the French Sûreté. Nevertheless, it would be difficult to argue that the memoirs of either Richmond or Vidocq contain anything that could be

---

6. Howard Haycraft, *Murder for Pleasure* (New York: Appleton-Century, 1941), p. 5.

7. Julian Symons, *Mortal Consequences* (New York: Schocken Books, 1973), p. 21.

properly called "the first detective story." Neither work shows much literary distinction, and though both contain certain features that would later be more fully worked out in police procedural and hard-boiled detective fiction, it is unlikely that anyone could have predicted, on the basis of these two books, the future development of the detective story.

By the middle of the nineteenth century, literature about the detective police had become even more flattering. The hero of William Russell's *Recollections of a Policeman*, though he joins the Metropolitan Police in desperation after a life of "reckless folly," is clearly presented to the reader as a member of a respectable profession, while the depiction of the sleuth in Charles Dickens' *Household Words* articles about contemporary detectives amounts at times to simple hero-worship. It is true that Russell's later book, *The Experiences of a French Detective Officer*, seems at first a return to the earlier disapproval of the detective, but in fact its intention is to praise the English detective force by comparing it favorably with its politically repressive French counterpart, and so it, too, contributes to the legitimation of the police system.

Despite so much support and even celebration of the detective, however, neither the Dickens nor the Russell pieces can be said to qualify as the first detective story. Missing from them is any feeling for the detective as the possessor of an extraordinary mind, any sense of the part which must be played in a model detective story by the imaginative force of intellect. Clearly, Field and Duhamel, like Wild and Vidocq, are remarkable people, but it is no genius of theirs for ratiocination that makes them special, and it is just such genius which the detective story demands. Yet even if the Dickens or Russell works had displayed notable genius of this kind, they would have come too late for either to be considered the first detective story. For nearly ten years before even the earliest of them was published, that memorable first story had already appeared.

II. The First Great Detective

Like all literary professionals who must live by their writing, Edgar Allan Poe discovered early the need to satisfy public taste in poetry and fiction. It was an exercise in which he was sometimes quite successful, as the enormous contemporary popularity of "The Raven" and "The Gold-Bug" makes clear. And the fact that he considerably increased the circulation of the several mass audience magazines he edited is further proof that Poe, though hardly the most practical of authors, understood very well the popular literary market of his time and was both willing and able to work in it and write for it.

One key to popular literary success is the ability to adapt and rework the material of other successful authors, and Poe had a particular genius for this kind of revisionary writing. "The Raven," for example, plainly owes much to the earlier efforts of Thomas Holley Chivers, whose "To Allegra Florence in Heaven" contains such a familiar sounding stanza as

> Thy dear father will tomorrow
> Lay thy body, with deep sorrow,
> In the grave which is so narrow —
> There to rest for evermore!

And "The Tell-Tale Heart" is an obvious "reinventing" of Charles Dickens' "A Confession Found in a Prison in the Time of Charles the Second," which Poe had read and called a story "of remarkable power, truly original in conception, and worked out with great ability."

Poe did more, of course, than merely imitate his models. "The Raven," for example, while echoing the meter and refrain of Chivers's work, uses those elements to express what was for the later poet an original and very personal theme. And a comparison of "The Tell-Tale Heart" with the previous treatment of the same material by Dickens reveals still more clearly Poe's skill at adapting popular literary elements to his own ends. Both stories develop the old and familiar theme of the retributive power of guilt, the idea that "murder will out" already expressed in the words from Genesis: "The voice of thy brother's blood crieth unto me from the ground." Both stories also take advantage of the contemporary reader's fascination with murder and detection as well as with the idea that the criminal and the sleuth are often one and the same person. In "The Tell-Tale Heart," however, Poe moves significantly beyond all his sources, heightening the impact of his tale by locating the whole drama in the mind of his madman/narrator. Even more important, he increases the psychological validity of the story by choosing as the instrument of justice not (as Dickens does) the chance curiosity of an animal but instead the murderer's confusion of his own terrified heartbeat with that of his victim. Plainly, a major subgenre of crime fiction has its origins in "The Tell-Tale Heart."

Poe's talent for giving artistic shape to commercial literary materials is nowhere more clear than in his handling of the popular elements of mystery and detection. The writer knew Vidocq's memoirs well and followed with interest the success other authors were having with crime fiction. In a review of Dickens' serialized novel *Barnaby Rudge*, for instance, Poe tried to solve the murder mystery that is an important part of the novel's plot before the author himself revealed the solution. His considerable success is supposed to have caused Dickens to remark of him that "the man must be the devil."

The extraordinary attraction of the detective story for Poe lay in the fact that it appealed both to his preoccupation with horror and death and his fascination with reason and logic. Poe's tales of pure horror are too well known to need any comment here. Perhaps a little less familiar is his intense interest in codes and ciphers or his clever ratiocinative article attempting to expose the mystery of Maelzel's celebrated chess-playing automaton. So curious a combination of interests was a fateful one for the history of detective fiction, for it permitted Edgar Allan Poe to bring together elements from such diverse literary forms as the Gothic novel, the popular philosophical essay, and the memoir of thieves and thief-takers, to mark them with his own special vision, and to fashion from them the first detective story.

On April 18, 1841, "The Murders in the Rue Morgue" appeared in *Graham's Lady's and Gentlemen's Magazine*, a popular periodical of which Poe was then editor. It is this tale, introducing super sleuth C. Auguste Dupin, which is most often named as the first detective story, the single most influential work in the history of detective fiction. During the next four years, Poe wrote two more stories about Dupin, "The Mystery of Marie Rogêt" and "The Purloined Letter," and two additional stories, "'Thou Art the Man'" and "The Gold Bug," sometimes also included in his list of detective fiction. These five stories may not at first seem an impressive achievement set beside, for example, John Creasey's almost 600 novels of crime and detection, but as a group they anticipated nearly every element employed by mystery fiction since that time, and by themselves formed a virtually complete catalog of the genre's principal techniques and devices.

Robert A. W. Lowndes, in his essay "The Contributions of Edgar Allan Poe,"[8] finds no fewer than thirty-two such elements and devices in the Dupin stories alone, twenty of them in "The Murders in the Rue Morgue." These include the eccentric private detective with a genius for applying pure inductive and deductive reasoning to human behavior, the less acute friend who narrates the story, an extraordinary crime such as, in this case, a locked-room mystery, the open display of clues giving the reader a fair chance to solve the puzzle before the detective does, the need to relieve an innocent person of suspicion, the detective's visit to the scene of the crime, the battle of wits with the official police, and the final summary scene in which the surprising but satisfactory solution is revealed.

"The Mystery of Marie Rogêt" and "The Purloined Letter" contribute,

---

8. Francis M. Nevins, Jr., ed., *The Mystery Writer's Art* (Bowling Green, Ohio: Popular Press, 1971), p. 1 ff.

as Lowndes calculates it, another dozen devices to the list, such elements as the police coming to the detective to implore his help, the detective studying only official data and newspaper accounts of the case and solving the mystery without leaving his "armchair," and the sleuth having a personal score to settle with the culprit. To these items, J. R. Christopher in "Poe and the Tradition of the Detective Story"[9] adds the concept of psychological detection, the ultra-obvious place of concealment, the planned diversion of the criminal, and the involvement of the detective in state affairs, as well as, from "'Thou Art the Man,'" the device of the least likely suspect, and from "The Gold-Bug," the concept of the detective story as a cryptogram. It may be possible, of course, to trace one or more of these elements to sources other than Poe. Indeed, Poe worked, we have seen, by converting just such elements of popular literature to his own uses. But certainly no earlier writer ever thought of gathering these diverse and unusual elements together into a single group of stories, and it was by doing this that Poe was able to create, in little more than a hundred pages, the whole rich and elaborate genre of detective fiction.

III. The Game's Afoot

As influential as Poe's stories were to be, that influence took a long time to make itself felt. Nearly half a century passed between the publication of "The Murders in the Rue Morgue" and the first appearance of Sherlock Holmes in *A Study in Scarlet* (1887), and in the meanwhile, the detectives who continued to appear in contemporary fiction owed much more to the vigor and cunning of Richmond and Vidocq than to the pure ratiocination of C. Auguste Dupin. The considerable improvement in the reputation of the police that we've traced from the middle of the eighteenth century to the middle of the nineteenth reflected, among other things, the period's growing faith in scientific and technological progress. But that faith began to recede during the second half of the 1800s, and the detective began at the same time to lose some of his new glamour.

It was not that he returned to his old role of barely reformed criminal; with the increased institutional controls of the profession, those days were largely behind him. It was rather that writers now began to recognize and depict the limitations of the detective just as they were depicting the limitations of science and technology generally. Even Dickens, who, in his magazine writing, consistently praised the London detective force, frequently used the sleuth in his novels to demonstrate

---

9. Ibid., p. 19 ff.

the narrow boundaries of human reason and will. As early as 1844, for example, he was creating in *Martin Chuzzlewit* the private inquiry agent Nadgett, an investigator remarkably clever and efficient at collecting information and drawing shrewd conclusions from it but entirely impotent in the face of murderous human passion. And in *Bleak House* (1853), even Inspector Bucket, modeled on the much-admired Inspector Field, becomes a symbol of the ultimate futility of detection. After some false starts, Bucket manages to solve the novel's murder mystery, but as he is about to lead the culprit away, the killer turns on him and says, after several sarcastic nods, "Listen, you are very spiritual. But can you restore him back to life?" Bucket's rueful reply, "Not exactly," makes Dickens' point clear. Even where the detective succeeds, his triumph is frequently trivial in the face of the criminal's victory; the murderer may be undone, but never the murder. Mr. Bucket may be a successful solver of puzzles, but true mysteries—like the grand mystery of death—will always elude him.

Other mystery novelists of the period also concentrated on what seemed the necessary failure of the detective. In *The Moonstone* (1868), for example, Wilkie Collins used an actual criminal case as the basis for his fictional one, making an important change, however, in the retelling. In the real murder investigation, the police detective's deductions proved sound, but in the story, the otherwise formidable Sergeant Cuff blunders badly in his interpretation of the facts and is forced to admit that he was wrong. Unsuccessful sleuths also appear in the works of less well-known writers of the period, including James Payn's *Lost Sir Massingberd* (1864), a novel containing a Bow Street Runner who leaves the story without having solved the mystery he was investigating, Mary Elizabeth Braddon's *Henry Dunbar* (1864) in which the detective, Carter, identifies the murderer but is tricked into letting him get away, and Mrs. Henry Wood's *Mrs. Halliburton's Troubles* (1862) in which the detective is depicted as, in the words of one commentator, "neatly disposing of a case of petty theft [while failing] to solve the murder mystery that occupies most of the final part of the book."[10] Incompetent or unimaginative police detectives appear in Poe, of course, but there the failure of the ordinary sleuth is merely a prelude to the success of the great one. In the novels we've been considering, however, no success at all is possible for the detective. The point is a metaphysical one. In a universe ruled by the irrational force of chance, these stories seem to say, the power of human reason to solve mysteries is dramatically limited.

The major French practitioner of the detective story during this period

---

10. Ousby, *Bloodhounds of Heaven*, p. 115.

was Emile Gaboriau, whose sensational crime and mystery fiction was colored by France's continuing suspicion of its own police. Gaboriau plainly modeled the career of his principal detective, Monsieur Lecoq, on that of Vidocq, alluding to Lecoq's shady past prior to his joining the Sûreté and representing him as vain and ambitious, willing on occasion to connive and cut corners in order to get ahead in his profession. At the same time, he portrayed Lecoq as an imaginative and skillful sleuth, expert at disguise and capable of brilliant deductions from such physical clues as the first plaster casts of footprints ever to appear in a detective story. Gaboriau had done considerable research in French police courts, morgues, and prisons before beginning the Lecoq series, and books like *Le Dossier No. 113* (1867) and *Monsieur Lecoq* (1869) are full of the sort of accurate technical details about the legal system and evidence collecting that were later to be employed regularly by writers of police procedural fiction.

Dupin, Bucket, Lecoq, Cuff—these were the literary detectives on whom the young Arthur Conan Doyle could draw for precedents when in 1886 he set out to write his own first mystery novel. Doyle himself particularly mentioned Poe and Gaboriau as authors who had influenced him, and it is possible to read the early Sherlock Holmes short stories as an elaborate homage to C. Auguste Dupin. "A Scandal in Bohemia," for example, is Conan Doyle's reworking of "The Purloined Letter," the detective's failure in the later story constituting the writer's own treatment of that popular theme. "The Red-Headed League," with its device of concealment through prominent display, also owes much to "The Purloined Letter," and "The Adventure of the Speckled Band" is a frank retelling of "The Murders in the Rue Morgue," complete with "Gothic" horror, a locked-room puzzle, and the same uncanny solution.

Gaboriau too contributed to the portrait of Sherlock Holmes, though the Great Detective himself once called Lecoq "a miserable bungler." (He had previously disposed of Dupin as "a very inferior fellow.") Skill at disguise, a Lecoq specialty, is one of Sherlock Holmes' most prominent traits as well, and the French sleuth's ability to draw startling conclusions about people from a few brief observations and deductions is also a memorable Holmesian talent. "You have been in Afghanistan, I perceive," are the young detective's first words to Watson when the two have been introduced. To which Watson replies, setting the familiar tone of their whole future relationship, "How on earth did you know that?"

This ability to draw accurate inferences from close observation was also a notable talent of Dr. Joseph Bell, one of Conan Doyle's medical instructors at Edinburgh University and a man whom the writer always credited with being the principal model for the character of Sherlock

Holmes. Some of Bell's feats of induction and deduction have been preserved, including an instance when the teacher was able to deduce from the red clay on the boots of a patient that she had just visited the botanical gardens and from the dermatitis on the fingers of her right hand that she worked in a linoleum factory.[11] Bell, for his part, modestly declined to take any credit for Holmes, writing to Conan Doyle on one occasion that "you are yourself Sherlock Holmes and well you know it."[12] And it is true that Doyle was quite capable of duplicating some of his instructor's detective-like achievements. Once, visiting a hospital, he paused beside a young baby and almost immediately said to the infant's mother, "You must stop painting the child's crib." Questioned about his instant analysis of the case, Doyle smiled and explained, "The child looked pale but well-fed. He was listless and his wrist dropped as he tried to hold a toy. The mother was neatly dressed, but she had specks of white paint on the fingers of her right hand. Children like to sharpen their teeth on the rails of a crib—so lead poisoning seemed a likely diagnosis."[13]

This talent of Conan Doyle's for putting the principles of pure reason to practical use may help account for the extraordinary success and influence of the Sherlock Holmes stories. We have seen that the detective in literature was almost from the start treated as a historical figure, one who, in the hands of Fielding, Godwin, Vidocq, Russell, and Dickens, could be employed as an instrument of political, economic, and social commentary. For entertainment value, these detective stories generally offered dramatic depictions of the sleuth's courage and cleverness, but even such virtues had their limits, and the stories also portrayed the detective as morally and intellectually fallible, not necessarily superior to the criminals he pursued and sometimes indistinguishable from them.

With Poe, the detective story entered a new phase, one in which the sleuth became the embodiment of pure and abstract reason operating in a world where such reason always triumphed. But the fact that these stories took so long to influence the genre suggests that readers may have found Poe's universe too abstract, too unhistorical to be entirely convincing. The world of everyday reality is, after all, one in which ratiocination seems to fail as often as it succeeds, one in which pure logic is often defeated by chance. Certainly, this is the sort of world that went on being

11. William S. Baring-Gould, *The Annotated Sherlock Holmes*, Vol. I (New York: Potter, 1967), p. 8.
12. Ibid.
13. Ibid., p. 9.

depicted in detective fiction long after Poe had completed his own work. What Arthur Conan Doyle was able to do, with the creation of Sherlock Holmes, was to bring these two strands of the detective story tradition together. As a scientist, a doctor, and a student of Joseph Bell, Doyle firmly believed that the purest and most abstract reasoning was also the most practical, and he set out to invent a detective character who, like Bell, would demonstrate that such reasoning could be successfully employed in the world of everyday reality. Sherlock Holmes clearly inhabits that kind of world, midway between Poe's extravagant celebrations of human reason and mid-Victorian fears about its limits. Dupin lives in a visionary Paris that Poe had never seen except in imagination, while Inspector Bucket patrols a gritty London ultimately beyond the help of detection. Sherlock Holmes represents a remarkable synthesis of his two predecessors. Superhumanly accomplished and yet realistically fallible, he sums up a whole half century of detective fiction and sets the tone for much of the genre's future.

IV. More Great Detectives

If the detective fiction genre developed slowly in the two quarter centuries from Poe to Gaboriau and Gaboriau to Conan Doyle, it virtually exploded into creative activity during the twenty-five years following the first appearance of Sherlock Holmes. That intense activity may in part reflect the growing importance of the short story as a literary form during the period. Short fiction tends to encourage innovation, and major artists like Rudyard Kipling, Joseph Conrad, D. H. Lawrence, Katherine Mansfield, and James Joyce wrote some of their best work in the medium. Sherlock Holmes did first appear in two novels, A Study in Scarlet and The Sign of Four (1890), but it was The Strand magazine short story series, later published as The Adventures of Sherlock Holmes (1892), that was really responsible for the detective's international popularity and inspired so many other writers to produce mystery fiction, much of it in the short form. Of these, perhaps the most important were G. K. Chesterton and Melville Davisson Post, but many other authors and their sleuths also appeared during these years to help satisfy the enormous appetite for detective fiction aroused by the Sherlock Holmes series.

In 1894, for example, The Strand published half a dozen stories about Martin Hewitt, a new detective character created by Arthur Morrison. Morrison, who had previously been known as the author of a group of naturalistic stories collected under the title Tales of Mean Streets (1894), created in Hewitt a detective plainly influenced by Holmes through, as E. F. Bleiler puts it, "the identity of opposites."

Whereas Holmes is tall and gaunt, Hewitt is of medium stature and plump; whereas Holmes is egotistical and arrogant, Hewitt is pleasant and unctuously affable; whereas Holmes scorns Scotland Yard, Hewitt is grateful for its cooperation. . . . Holmes's adventures are set at high key; Hewitt is deliberately low key.[14]

In the introduction to his recent Dover collection, *Best Martin Hewitt Detective Stories* (1976), Bleiler regrets that London's "mean streets," which Morrison knew well from personal experience, were so rigorously excluded from the Hewitt stories, stories which would then have anticipated the *Black Mask* mystery school by a generation. Nevertheless, with just eighteen short tales and a single longer serial, Morrison managed to secure his reputation as one of the major writers of the detective story in the era of Sherlock Holmes.

While Martin Hewitt is portrayed by Morrison as a quite ordinary person, other fictional detectives of the period, again under the influence of Sherlock Holmes, were depicted as memorable eccentrics. Holmes' famous quirks—nonstop violin playing, indoor target practice—clearly have their own origins in C. Auguste Dupin's fondness for the dark or Sergeant Cuff's passion for roses, and by the turn of the century, the notion that a literary detective ought to display certain peculiar habits or character traits had become well established. Among the most bizarre detective figures created during these years was M. P. Shiel's Prince Zaleski, an exiled Russian nobleman who lives in an exotic London apartment with his faithful Ethiopian servant Ham, indulges in an obscure but potent Mohammedan drug, and solves mysteries by combining intense concentration with inductive reasoning and intuition. Of his strange sleuth, Shiel once wrote: "There is no detective but *the* detective and the father of detectives, the 'Dupin' of Poe, of whom this Zaleski is the legitimate son, and the notorious Holmes the bastard son." Other eccentric detectives of the period include Baroness Orczy's Old Man in the Corner, who clears up baffling mysteries from his chair in a London tea shop while tying and untying intricate knots in a piece of string, Ernest Bramah's Max Carrados, the first blind sleuth in literature, and Jacques Futrelle's "Thinking Machine," the most purely cerebral of great detectives. "The Problem of Cell 13," an early "Thinking Machine" adventure, is one of the best known of all detective stories.

Dr. John Evelyn Thorndyke, created in 1907 by R. Austin Freeman, is a criminal investigator who elaborates on another of Sherlock Holmes' notable characteristics: the great detective's skill as a laboratory scien-

---

14. Arthur Morrison, *Best Martin Hewitt Detective Stories*, ed. E. F. Bleiler (New York: Dover, 1976), p. xiii.

tist. It is Holmes, the discoverer of a new test for hemoglobin in *A Study in Scarlet*, with whom Dr. Thorndyke has most in common, and in the eleven novels and forty-two short stories in which Freeman's detective appears, emphasis is consistently placed on the solving of crimes through technologically sophisticated examinations of physical evidence. In such matters as the analysis of dust, the preservation of footprints, or the classification of blood, Dr. Thorndyke, who is never without his well-stocked green research kit, often anticipated actual police techniques of his day, and Freeman was equally careful and accurate in his depiction of courtroom scenes, rules of evidence, and other legal procedures. One distinct innovation in the Dr. Thorndyke series is what Freeman himself called the inverted detective story, a work in which the reader is first shown the crime being committed, with all of the facts, even the identity of the criminal, frankly revealed. "It would have seemed," Freeman wrote in his essay "The Art of the Detective Story,"

that after this there was nothing left to tell, but I calculated that the reader would be so occupied with the crime that he would overlook the evidence. And so it turned out. The second part of the story, which described the investigation of the crime, had to most readers the effect of new matter.

"The Case of Oscar Brodski," in which the technique of the inverted detective story was notably employed, is today considered a significant contribution to the history of detective fiction.

The quarter century following the publication of *A Study in Scarlet* came to a memorable conclusion with the first appearance in 1911 of two major detective characters, G. K. Chesterton's Father Brown and Melville Davisson Post's Uncle Abner. In many ways the two new sleuths were products of the enormous popularity of Sherlock Holmes, but in one very important sense they reached back beyond Holmes to explore issues which had been raised earlier by mid-Victorian pessimism about detection and ratiocination. Conan Doyle himself had dealt with such matters in a small way, matching, for example, the murderer's metaphysical challenge to the detective in *Bleak House* with Holmes' own anguished question at the end of "The Adventure of the Cardboard Box."

"What is the meaning of it, Watson? What object is served by this circle of misery, violence, and fear? It must tend to some end, or else our universe is ruled by chance, which is unthinkable. But what end? There is the great standing perennial problem to which human reason is as far from an answer as ever."

What Conan Doyle did only occasionally in his stories, however, Chesterton and Post did regularly in theirs, quite deliberately exploring the complex relationship between the sort of mysteries that can be solved through the application of human reason and the sort that cannot. The two sleuths were themselves divided over the issue; Catholic priest Father Brown worked hard in his cases to distinguish between secular and theological mysteries, while early American fundamentalist Uncle Abner argued that the attempt to solve any mystery of human behavior inevitably becomes an inquiry into the profoundest religious questions. The effect of both the Chesterton and the Post series, however, despite their differences, was to make of the detective story an instrument for examining serious philosophical questions, and it was clearly this fact that attracted an author like William Faulkner to the genre and helped him to create his own detective, "Uncle" Gavin Stevens, in the spirit of Post's Uncle Abner.

V. The Golden Age

The period roughly following the one we have just been discussing is often called the Golden Age of the detective story, though for a number of reasons no precise definition of that term has ever been firmly established. For one thing, the brief history of detective fiction, together with the gratifying longevity of many mystery writers, has made it difficult to label the several eras of the genre rigorously. "The Casebook of Sherlock Holmes" (1927), for instance, was published by Conan Doyle several years *after* the first appearances of such major Golden Age sleuths as Hercule Poirot, Reggie Fortune, Superintendent Wilson, and Lord Peter Wimsey. In addition, the desire to choose an exact date for the start of the Golden Age frequently clashes with the effort to establish the key attributes of the works published during the period. Sometimes stories and detectives with "wrong" dates perfectly represent the ideals of Golden Age fiction, while just as often writers who belong chronologically to the period display few characteristics of the Golden Age detective story.

Ellery Queen has listed some of the characteristics of Golden Age detective fiction as

ingenuity and complexity of plot; originality of concept, including the "locked room," the "miracle problem," and the "impossible crime"; subtle and legitimate misdirection of clues—poetic license—but always with complete fairness to the reader; and often a stunning surprise solution. In a phrase (R. Austin Freeman's), "an exhibition of mental gymnastics."[15]

---

15. Ellery Queen, ed., *Masterpieces of Mystery: The Golden Age—I* (New York: Davis Publications, 1977), p. 7.

These attributes clearly describe some works of the period more accurately than they do others; many writers during these years preferred, for example, to concentrate on character and atmosphere rather than on pure puzzles. But such variety was obviously good for the genre, and among Golden Age authors can be found an unusually large number of major figures in the history of the detective story.

The publication in 1920 of Agatha Christie's first book about Hercule Poirot, of whom more will be said later, has made that year a convenient one from which to date the Golden Age; it is even more convenient because in the same year a first collection of short stories appeared about a detective who was to become the most popular literary sleuth in Great Britain between the two world wars. The volume was H. C. Bailey's *Call Mr. Fortune*, and the detective was the aristocratic Reginald, or "Reggie," Fortune, a practicing physician and surgeon who advises Scotland Yard on medical matters, solves difficult murder mysteries through intuition and a "simple faith in facts," and between cases likes to spend time in his laboratory or garden. Bailey depicts Fortune as a plump, cherubic, middle-aged gourmet who expresses great sympathy for the "common people" while driving around in a Rolls-Royce, and this characterization of the detective as a snobbish, mannered intellectual was to have great influence on such other famous sleuths of the 1920s as Dorothy L. Sayers' Lord Peter Wimsey, S. S. Van Dine's Philo Vance, and the early Ellery Queen. The complexity of H. C. Bailey's puzzles and the willingness of the author to play fair with the reader make the Reggie Fortune stories prime examples of Golden Age mystery fiction.

To match this collection of affected private sleuths, the Golden Age also produced an assortment of successful if somewhat less colorful police detectives, including Freeman Wills Crofts' Inspector Joseph French, G. D. H. and M. I. Cole's Superintendent Henry Wilson, and Georges Simenon's Inspector Jules Maigret. Of these writers, it is Crofts who is most often identified with the beginning of the Golden Age. He came late to fiction when his career as a railway engineer was interrupted by a serious illness during which he took up writing to pass the time. The book that resulted from this therapy, *The Cask* (1920), quickly achieved the status of a mystery classic, "the definitive novel," Anthony Boucher has called it, "of alibis, timetables, and all the absorbing hairsplitting of detection."[16] Crofts' best-known sleuth, Inspector (later Superintendent) French of Scotland Yard, first appeared in the 1924 novel *Inspector*

16. Chris Steinbrunner and Otto Penzler, eds., *Encyclopedia of Mystery and Detection* (New York: McGraw-Hill, 1976), p. 112.

French's Greatest Case, where he is described as a clean-shaven, easy-going, tweedy man, fond of good food and travel and inclined to discuss his cases with his wife. A number of the parallels here with Simenon's Maigret are striking, but where Maigret succeeds as a detective principally by entering intuitively into the psychological states of the criminals he pursues, Inspector French achieves his remarkable record of never having failed to solve a case through the dogged collection and shrewd interpretation of physical evidence. In this he is clearly the product of an authorial mind formed by the study of engineering and mathematics, and Julian Symons has written rather unsympathetically of the Crofts stories, as well as those about Superintendent Wilson:

They fulfill much better than S. S. Van Dine his dictum that the detective story properly belongs in the category of riddles or crossword puzzles.[17]

Symons is very frank here about defining the detective story, and particularly the Golden Age detective story, as a game, an ingenious diversion having as little as possible to do with the serious concerns of "real" life. Van Dine makes the point even more openly in his essay "Twenty Rules for Writing Detective Stories" where he announces that in tales of detection

there must be no love interest . . . no long descriptive passages, no literary dallying with side issues, no subtly worked out character analyses, no "atmospheric" preoccupations.[18]

But such restrictions clearly disturbed some Golden Age writers, those who, without losing sight of the mystery story's primary obligation to entertain by puzzling, felt that the suppressing of all other literary and social values was a mistake. Dorothy L. Sayers, for one, was ambivalent about Van Dine's description of her craft. Even after writing "The Fascinating Problem of Uncle Meleager's Will," a mystery whose solution depends on the completion of a crossword puzzle, she declared her intention of producing a book "less like a conventional detective story and more like a novel. . . . More a novel of manners than a crossword puzzle."[19] The creators of Ellery Queen developed their work in a similar direction. They moved from a story like "The Mad Tea Party," which cleverly exploits children's literature in the manner of S. S. Van Dine's

---

17. Symons, *Mortal Consequences*, p. 114.

18. Haycraft, *The Art of the Mystery Story*, pp. 189, 191–192.

19. Steinbrunner and Penzler, *Encyclopedia of Mystery and Detection*, p. 354.

The Bishop Murder Case (1929) or Agatha Christie's later *And Then There Were None* (1939), toward the greater seriousness of such books as *Cat of Many Tales* (1949), an exploration of the phenomenon of mass hysteria, and *The Glass Village* (1954), a study of McCarthyism. Rex Stout largely avoided the pitfall of triviality in his detective fiction by concerning himself from the start much more with character than with plot in his Nero Wolfe stories. "Criticism has sometimes been leveled at Wolfe's recorded cases," Otto Penzler has written,

because the plots have occasionally been flawed. . . . But the real strength of the stories is the Wolfe-Goodwin relationship, their repartee, the humor, which is unequalled in any sustained series in literature, and the ambience of their life style.

Meanwhile, the development of the suspense tale and the crime novel during this period provided authors with still other ways of escaping the inevitable sterility of a purely mechanical puzzle story.

VI. The Black Mask School

The most influential literary alternative to Golden Age mystery fiction and all it represented first appeared in the United States with its principal outlet a pulp magazine called *Black Mask*. Founded by H. L. Mencken and George Jean Nathan, *Black Mask* began publishing in 1920, the very year in which Christie's *The Mysterious Affair at Styles*, Crofts' *The Cask*, and Bailey's *Call Mr. Fortune* were inaugurating the Golden Age in Great Britain. Under the editorship of Captain Joseph T. Shaw, the magazine developed what is now familiarly referred to as the hard-boiled detective story: tough, realistic, cynical crime fiction in which believable characterization counts for more than ingenious plotting and from which every element that doesn't contribute to violent physical excitement is excluded. By the 1930s, other pulp magazines, so called because they were printed on cheap, untrimmed wood pulp paper, had arrived to challenge *Black Mask's* near monopoly of the genre and the tradition continued into the 1940s with publications like *Dime Detective* and *Detective Fiction Weekly* presenting stories about the tough, resourceful private eye who was the major achievement of the *Black Mask* school of mystery fiction.

The first of these private detectives to appear in *Black Mask* was Carroll John Daly's Race Williams, a fearless, sometimes brutal figure who lives by a primitive code of good and evil that frequently requires him to act as both judge and executioner in his cases. In this he is a forerunner of Mickey Spillane's Mike Hammer as well as a throwback to the morally ambiguous thief-takers of early detective fiction. Williams' opponents in these stories are often such stock villains as communists and sinister foreigners, a fact which confirms the criticism that Daly's work lacks strong characterization. Full of fast-paced action, however, the Race Williams stories made Daly one of the most popular of all *Black Mask* writers.

The early Race Williams stories preceded by only a few months the first appearance in *Black Mask* of perhaps the greatest of all hard-boiled detectives, Dashiell Hammett's Continental Op. There is no doubt that the extraordinary influence the *Black Mask* school has had on the literary detective is largely the result of Hammett's genius for powerful character studies and lean, Hemingwayesque prose. From the comparatively crude Op stories of the early 1920s, Hammett went on to refine his narrative skills until, in 1929, he published *The Maltese Falcon*, the novel which introduced detective Sam Spade and which, both representing and transcending its genre, has come to be accepted as an important work of American literature. Hammett's influence continues to be strongly felt today in television and films as well as in fiction and has led to the virtual disappearance of the puzzle-solving gentleman sleuth of the Golden Age.

Other writers who contributed to the success of *Black Mask* in its early days were Raoul Whitfield, who published his Jo Gar stories under the pseudonym Ramon Decolta, and Erle Stanley Gardner, now best known for his Perry Mason novels but in the 1920s the proprietor of such miscellaneous heroes as Speed Dash, the human fly, and Sidney Zoom and his police dog, Rip. In the 1930s, a second generation of pulp contributors arrived, including George Harmon Coxe, creator of the Flashgun Casey series, Frank Gruber, who later recounted his experiences as a struggling young author in *The Pulp Jungle* (1967), Cornell Woolrich, whose work emphasizes the terror of the everyday, and the most highly regarded of the hard-boiled writers after Hammett, Raymond Chandler.

Chandler, whose reputation in fact rests on his much admired Philip Marlowe novels rather than on the novelettes that appeared in *Black Mask*, also became the most influential theoretician of the hard-boiled school when, in December 1944, he published an essay called "The Simple Art of Murder" in *The Atlantic Monthly*. The essay, still controversial, describes the principles and ideals of *Black Mask* fiction and compares them with those of the Golden Age detective story. Had Chandler been content merely to list the differences between these two approaches to the mystery, his article would hardly have caused much of a stir. But he went further, vigorously and wittily condemning the majority of Golden Age stories as artificial and absurd. It was this judgment which evoked the long series of critical responses, including the important one in Barzun's and Taylor's A *Catalogue of Crime* (1971), that have helped establish Chandler's ideas as a major force in the study of detective literature.

In his essay, Chandler singles out for particular attention A. A. Milne's *The Red House Mystery* (1922), and in a long analysis reminiscent of Mark Twain's "Fenimore Cooper's Literary Offences," rebukes the British author for reckless inattention to realistic detail. The essence of the criticism is contained in the writer's comments about the novel's principal sleuth.

The detective in the case is an insouciant amateur . . . with a cheery eye, a nice little flat in town, and that airy manner. He is not making any money on the assignment, but is always available when the local gendarmerie loses its notebook. The English police endure him with their customary stoicism, but I shudder to think what the boys down at the Homicide Bureau in my city would do to him.

In this passage, Chandler mocks the implausibility of many Golden Age detectives, and to the extent that he exposes genuine absurdities in the plot of *The Red House Mystery*, his essay is convincing. But implicit in his remarks about Milne's sleuth are two questionable premises: first, the idea that reality is to be defined as whatever may seem real at any given moment to a Los Angeles policeman; and second, the notion that for a work of art to be successful it must limit itself strictly to that reality.

Most critics of the essay have noted the weakness of such reasoning and go on to turn the writer's own arguments against him. Barzun and Taylor, for example, find Chandler's detective, with his carelessness about money and his willingness to absorb frequent beatings and shootings, quite as implausible as Milne's. Others have seen in Chandler's romantic portrait of the private eye as a modern knight "in search of hidden truth" an artificiality as great as anything in Golden Age fiction. Ross Macdonald, who did not begin publishing until *Black Mask* had gone out of business but who is clearly one of the most important heirs to the hard-boiled tradition, has written an essay of his own, called "The Writer as Detective Hero," in which he praises Chandler's stories for a "tender and romantic sensibility" that any L.A. cop might find unrealistic and artificial. What Barzun, Taylor, Macdonald, and the others are saying, at least by implication, is that all literature is artificial, *even when its object is to appear real*. The strength of the *Black Mask* school lies not in the fact that it mindlessly and mechanically reproduces some actual reality, but that like all other successful movements in the history of detective fiction, it creates a world so exciting and authentic as to become a reality of its own.

VII. The Limits of Detection

To the extent that every literary form tries to create its own reality, every literary form is limited, for life, however confusing and unfocused, is always bigger and more surprising than any human reconstruction of it could possibly be. For every invention, every work of art, every idea, the moment inevitably comes when too much is asked of it, when it reaches its limit and can no longer function. Often the study of such a moment can be illuminating. To test the tensile strength of a rope, it is necessary to put enough strain on the rope to break it, and to understand any phenomenon really well, it is important to know not only what that phenomenon is capable of but what it isn't.

We've already seen how mid-nineteenth-century writers studied the detective in this way, constantly pushing him to the point of failure in order to be able to distinguish between the things he could do and those he couldn't. The question "Can you restore him back to life?" in *Bleak House* describes one such limit of detection; at the same time, it reveals the even broader interest of the period in exploring the boundary between science and religion. One reason, then, for examining the limits of detection, as such limits are depicted in mystery stories, is to discover what larger issues people were most concerned about during the time those stories were being written.

The first step in this process is to find materials to study. Writers of popular commercial literature, while not against innovation, usually like to stick to established formats. Sometimes, however, without forgetting about entertainment values or the need to sell their work, they produce a story that breaks some of the rules, a story that takes the usual format as far as it will go, and then further. In the mystery fiction genre, these are often the works that reveal the limits of detection, and a few of them have been collected here.

Robert Barr's "The Absent-Minded Coterie" is an ingenious and delightful detective story in which the sleuth, by failing at his job, reveals the limits of his profession and his society. It is also the least obviously satiric of the eight stories in *The Triumphs of Eugène Valmont* (1906), a book whose ironic title helps to make the humorous intention of the whole volume clearer. Valmont is a French detective living in London, and Barr writes about him with a British contempt for Gallic sleuths that goes back to Russell's *The Experiences of a French Detective Officer* and looks ahead to Inspector Clouseau of the *Pink Panther* films. Still, "The Absent-Minded Coterie" has its serious side, exploring the way in which, with the best of intentions, a person may break the law in the very act of trying to uphold it. The theme is one of the most persistent in detective fiction, the impossibility of distinguishing between criminal and sleuth, and it raises large questions about moral ambiguity in society which clearly go beyond the mystery genre.

The failure of Hercule Poirot in Agatha Christie's "The Chocolate Box" occurs for a different reason. Poirot, too, derives from the tradition of the contemptible French detective, though Christie, by making him a Belgian, seems to be assuring her readers that her detective's absurdities will be only superficial. Still, she places this story of Poirot's failure prominently at the end of her first volume of short fiction, allowing the series to conclude on a curiously negative note. Poirot can be said to fail in "The Chocolate Box" because life is too complex for him. Sherlock Holmes' famous advice to detectives that they reject all impossible solutions and accept whatever may remain, however improbable, as the truth presupposes that at the end of such a process only one solution will be left. But what would happen if two or more answers remained after all the winnowing? Obviously, unable to make any further choice, the detective would be at the end of his resources, would have reached his limit.

This is the issue that Agatha Christie raises in "The Chocolate Box," and though she later retreats a bit from the idea, it continues to hover over the story. It hovers too over much of twentieth-century literature and in particular over the short fiction of Jorge Luis Borges, whose key symbol is the labyrinth and who titled one of his near-detective stories "The Garden of Forking Paths." Borges' fiction is haunted by what the author calls "superfluous symmetries and maniacal repetitions" among which human beings wander without direction. And in "Death and the Compass" he portrays a sleuth who, incapable of dealing with such empty duplication, reaches the ultimate limit of a detective, death at the hands of the criminal he is tracking. But in a world of "maniacal repetitions," even death is not final. Instead, it must be gone through over and over again, always promising a new experience but always the same. Obviously, for a century like the present one, plagued by the nightmare of meaningless growth in a number of forms—urban sprawl, population explosion, cancer—"Death and the Compass" is a representative story and its defeated detective a representative man.

Borges' use of the detective to symbolize the arrogance of any search for final truth has its echoes in the work of such other major contemporary writers as Eugène Ionesco, Alain Robbe-Grillet, and Friedrich Duerrenmatt. In popular literature, meanwhile, the detective has come through all these explorations of his limits with remarkable strength.

According to a recent survey, one out of every four books sold in the United States is a work of mystery fiction, that term covering such subgenres as the detective story, the police procedural, the spy novel, the private eye story, the so-called Gothic, the crime story, and the novel of suspense. *Ellery Queen's Mystery Magazine*, which began in 1941 as a reprint publication, is today almost entirely devoted to new stories, offering some fifteen of them each month, and the popularity of the detective on television and in films is further proof of the continuing vitality of the genre. In the light of such widespread acceptance, the future of mystery fiction seems bright. Both as commercial entertainment and as a vehicle for the most serious literary efforts, the detective story gives strong promise of continuing its long and influential career.

More to Read

From the many books and articles about detective fiction, the following have been selected as among the most immediately useful for the reader of this anthology. Studies of individual writers and works have been listed in the headnotes to the appropriate stories. The titles included here are general reference works and anthologies.

Ball, John, et al. *The Mystery Story*. Del Mar, Calif.: The Mystery Library, 1976. A collection of essays on a variety of subjects by well-known mystery writers and critics. Its bibliographical articles are particularly useful.

Barzun, Jacques, and Wendell Hertig Taylor. *A Catalogue of Crime*. New York: Harper & Row, 1971. Critical comments on literally thousands of works of mystery fiction.

Haycraft, Howard, ed. *The Art of the Mystery Story*. New York: Simon & Schuster, 1946; paperbound, New York: Grosset and Dunlap, 1961. A valuable collection of critical essays including those by R. Austin Freeman, S. S. Van Dine, Dorothy L. Sayers, and Raymond Chandler referred to in the introduction to this anthology.

Haycraft, Howard. *Murder for Pleasure: The Life and Times of the Detective Story*. New York: Appleton-Century, 1941; newly enlarged edition, New York: Biblo and Tannen, 1968. A major history of the detective story.

Landrum, Larry N., Pat Browne, & Ray B. Browne, eds. *Dimensions of Detective Fiction*. Bowling Green, Ohio: Popular Press, 1976. A collection of essays in which the detective story is frequently set in a larger cultural context.

Nevins, Francis M., Jr., ed. *The Mystery Writer's Art*. Bowling Green, Ohio: Popular Press, 1971. Twenty-one essays, several of which are referred to in the introduction and head notes of this anthology.

Queen, Ellery. *Queen's Quorum*. Boston: Little, Brown, 1951; new edition, with supplements through 1967, New York: Biblo and Tannen, 1969. A history of the detective-crime short story told through a discussion of 125 classic volumes of short fiction.

Steinbrunner, Chris, and Otto Penzler, editors. *Encyclopedia of Mystery and Detection*. New York: McGraw-Hill Book Co., 1976. The basic reference work in the field, containing biographies of authors and characters, checklists of books and films, plot summaries, and many illustrations.

Symons, Julian. *Mortal Consequences*. New York: Harper & Row, 1972; paperbound, New York: Schocken Books, 1973. A well-written, informative, opinionated history of detective-crime fiction.

Winn, Dilys. *Murder Ink: The Mystery Reader's Companion*. New York: Workman, 1977. An entertaining collection of brief, mostly humorous articles.

CHAPTER I

IN THE BEGINNING

VICTIMS OF MY CRAFT
By Vidocq

François Eugène Vidocq (1775–1857) was a baker's son born in Arras. After an eventful early life, including a period in the army, he joined a band of criminals and was sentenced to a long term in the galleys for a crime he always denied having committed. Following many years of imprisonment, notable for a number of sensational escapes, he offered his services to the authorities in 1809 as a police spy. For a time, he acted as an informer while remaining in prison. Then he was freed and in 1812 became head of the newly established Sûreté, a job he held for fifteen years while, according to some reports, continuing his criminal activities. In later years, he managed a paper mill operated entirely by ex-convicts, and when that venture failed he opened a private detective agency. After what appears to have been a return to crime, however, he was driven out of his practice and died in poverty at Brussels. "Such in brief was the career of an extraordinary man," writes Edwin Gile Rich, "who started the work of detection in anything like the modern sense of the word and whose writings have been the inspiration of all detective, mystery, and crime stories for the past century or more." The writings Rich refers to were the Memoirs of Vidocq, a rambling and romanticized account of the author's life published both in France and England in 1828/1829. Emile Morice and Louis-François L'Héritier have sometimes been mentioned as the actual authors of the four volumes, and scholars disagree about the reliability of the Memoirs as history, though they all concede their influence on the genre of detective fiction. "Victims of My Craft" is taken from Vidocq (Boston: Houghton Mifflin, 1935), Rich's modern translation. Arno Press reprinted the 1829 English version in 1976.

The names of Baron Pasquier and M. Henry will never be erased from my memory. These two generous men were my liberators. How much I owe to them! They gave me more than the life which I would have sacrificed for them a thousand times, and I think they will believe me when they know how often I exposed it to obtain a word or look of satisfaction from them.

I breathed again, moved about freely, and now that I was a secret agent I had regular duties, in which M. Henry undertook to instruct me. My task was difficult to fulfil. M. Henry guided my first steps; he eased my difficulties, and if in the end I acquired some celebrity in the police, I owed it to his counsels and to the lessons he gave me. Endowed with a cool and reflective disposition, M. Henry possessed to the highest degree that gift of observation which distinguishes guilt under the most innocent appearance. He had a prodigious memory and an astonishing insight; nothing escaped him; added to that, he was an excellent judge of faces. Rarely did a criminal whom he examined leave his office without confessing his crime or giving some clue, unknown to himself, by which to convict him.

As soon as I was installed as a secret agent, I began to pound the pavement in order to become familiar with it and to be able to do my work usefully. These excursions, during the course of which I made a great number of observations, took me twenty days, during which I was only preparing myself to act; I was studying the terrain. One morning I was summoned by the chief of the division. It was about the discovery of a man named Watrin, accused of having made and put in circulation counterfeit money and bank-notes. Watrin had already been arrested by the police inspectors, but as usual they had not known how to keep him. M. Henry gave me all the information he judged proper to put me on his tracks. Unfortunately, this information consisted only of data of his old habits; the places he had frequented were described to me, but it was not believable that he would come to them at once, since in his position prudence prescribed that he flee all places where he was known. So I had left only the hope of reaching him in some indirect way when I learned that he had some of his effects in a furnished house, boulevard Mont Parnasse, where he had lodged. The officials took it for granted that sooner or later he would present himself to demand them or at least that he would have someone else demand them for him. That was my opinion too.

In consequence I directed all my search on that point, and after

From *Memoirs of Vidocq*, translated by Edwin Gile Rich, Houghton Mifflin, 1935. Used by permission of the publisher.

getting acquainted with the mansion, I lay in wait near-by night and day in order to have an eye on the comings and goings. This supervision had lasted nearly a week. Finally, tired of seeing nothing, I conceived the idea of getting the master of the house in my interests and hiring an apartment, where I established myself with Annette. My presence would not be suspect. I had occupied this post for a fortnight, when one evening towards eleven o'clock I was warned that Watrin had just appeared, accompanied by another individual. I was slightly indisposed and,had gone to bed earlier than usual. I got up hurriedly and went down the stairs two at a time, but with all my diligence I could only reach Watrin's companion. I had no right to arrest him, but I foresaw that if I intimidated him, I might be able to obtain some information. I seized him, threatened him, and soon he told me, trembling with fear, that he was a shoemaker and that Watrin lived with him, at rue des Mauvais Garçons Saint-Germain, No. 4.

That was all I needed to know. I had thrown only an overcoat over my shirt, but, without stopping for other garments, I ran to that address and arrived in front of the house just as someone was going out. Persuaded that it was Watrin, I tried to seize him. He escaped me; I dashed after him up the staircase, but, just as I was reaching for him, a kick in my chest sent me down twenty steps. I dashed after him again and with such speed that, to get rid of my pursuit, he was obliged to get into his quarters through a window on the landing. I then knocked on his door and summoned him to open. He refused.

Annette had followed me. I ordered her to go in search of the police, and, while she went to obey, I imitated the noise of a man going downstairs. Watrin was deceived by this feint, and wanted to assure himself that I had really gone. He put his head out of the window.

That was what I wanted, and I at once grabbed him by the hair. He seized me in the same way, and a fight started. Clinging to the dividing wall which separated us, he opposed an obstinate resistance; however, I felt that he was weakening. I gathered my strength for a last jerk; already he had only his feet left in the room; another effort and he was mine. I pulled him out vigorously and he fell into the corridor. To deprive him of the shoemaker's knife with which he was armed and drag him outside was the work of a moment.

Accompanied only by Annette, I led him to the Prefecture, where I received the felicitations of M. Henry, and then those of the Prefect of Police, who gave me a pecuniary reward.

Watrin was a man of rare address; he practised a rude profession, yet he executed forgeries which demanded the greatest delicacy of touch. He was condemned to death, but he was reprieved an hour

4

before he was to be led to punishment. The scaffold had already been erected; it was taken down; the virtuosi had made a useless change of base. The report spread that he was going to make revelations, but, as he had nothing to tell, some days later the sentence was executed.

Watrin was my first capture and it was an important one. The success of my début aroused the jealousy of some of the police; some inveighed against me, but in vain. They did not forgive me for being more skillful than they were; on the contrary, my chiefs had a decided liking for me. I doubled my zeal to deserve their confidence more and more.

About this time a large number of false five-franc pieces had been put in circulation. They showed me several, and on examination it seemed to me that I recognized the work of my denouncer Boudin and his friend Doctor Terrier. I resolved to get at the truth. In consequence I spied on the movements of these two individuals, and, as I could not follow them closely without being recognized and so arousing their distrust, it was difficult to get the light I needed. However, by force of perseverance, I became certain that I was not mistaken, and the two counterfeiters were arrested in the act of manufacture. Some time after they were condemned to death and executed.

In a city as populous as Paris the number of evil resorts is rather large; and in them all the men of tarnished reputation meet. In order to see them and watch them, I assiduously frequented these places of ill-fame, sometimes under one name and sometimes under another, changing my costume often as a person who needs to escape the eyes of the police. All the thieves whom I saw habitually would have sworn that I was one of them. In the persuasion that I was a fugitive, they would have been quartered to hide me, for not only did they have full confidence in me, but they liked me. As a result they told me about their plans, and, if they did not propose that I co-operate with them, it was for fear of compromising me, in view of my position as an escaped convict. However, all were not so delicate.

I had been at my secret investigations for some months, when by chance I met Saint-Germain, whose visits had so many times filled me with consternation. He was with a man named Boudin whom I had seen as a restaurant keeper in rue des Prouvaires, and whom I knew as one knows a host to whose place one goes from time to time to take a meal and pays for it. Boudin had no trouble in remembering me; he even bordered on a sort of familiarity, to which I pretended not to respond.

"Have I done something to you," he asked, "that you don't seem to want to talk to me?"

"No, but I've learned that you have been a police spy."

"Well, if that's all! Yes, I was a spy, but when you know all, I'm sure you will bear me no ill-will."

"Certainly," said Saint-Germain, "you'll have no ill-will; Boudin is a good fellow, and I'll answer for him as for myself. Things often happen in life which one can't foresee. If Boudin accepted the place you speak of, it was only to save his brother. Besides, you ought to know that if he had bad principles, I should not be his friend."

I found Saint-Germain's guaranty excellent, and I made no more difficulty about talking to Boudin.

It was natural that Saint-Germain should tell me what had happened since his last disappearance which had given me so much pleasure. After he had complimented me on my escape, he told me that, since I had been arrested, he had recovered his old place, but that he had quickly lost it again, and was now reduced to expedients. I asked him for news of Blondy and Duluc. "My friend," he said, "the two who did in the carter with me have been cut down at Beauvais." When he announced that those two scoundrels had paid the penalty for their crimes, I had but one regret: that the head of their accomplice had not fallen on the same scaffold.

After we had emptied several bottles of wine, we separated. As he left me, Saint-Germain remarked that I was rather poorly dressed and asked me what I was doing. As I told him that I was doing nothing, he promised to think of me if ever a good occasion presented itself. I observed that as I rarely went out for fear of being arrested, it might be that we should not meet soon. "You can see me when you want to," he said. "I even demand that you come to see me." When I had promised, he gave me his address, without learning mine.

Saint-Germain was not so formidable a being to me now; I even believed that I should not lose him from sight, for if I was to watch malefactors, no one was more worthy than he of my attention. In the end, I conceived a hope of purging society of such a monster. While I waited, I waged war on the whole herd of crooks who infested the capital. At the moment robberies of all kinds multiplied in a frightful manner; one heard only of railings carried off, doors forced, leads stolen; more than twenty street-lamps were taken one after another, in rue Fontaine-au-Roi, without the thieves who took them down being arrested. For one whole month inspectors had been on watch to surprise them, and the first night they relaxed their vigilance, the street-lamps again disappeared, as if it were a defiance to the police. I accepted the job for myself, and to the great disappointment of the Arguses of the Quai du Nord, in a short time I delivered to justice these impudent thieves, who were all sent to the galleys.

I made new discoveries every day; all those sent to prison went on my indication. Nevertheless, none of them had the slightest idea of accusing me of having them sent to jail. I arranged things so well that nothing transpired either inside or outside; the thieves of my acquaintance considered me the best of comrades; the rest thought themselves fortunate to be able to initiate me into their secrets, either for the pleasure of entertaining me or to consult me.

It was especially outside the Barrier that I met this world. One day I was going over the outer boulevards when I was accosted by Saint-Germain; Boudin was still with him. They invited me to dinner; I accepted, and at dessert they did me the honour of proposing that I should make a third in a murder. Two old men were in question; they lived together in the house where Boudin had his habitation in rue des Prouvaires. Shuddering at the confidence which these scoundrels made me, I blessed the invisible power who had urged them toward me. At first I hesitated to enter the plot, but in the end I pretended to give in to their keen and pressing solicitations. It was arranged that we should wait until a favourable moment to put this abominable project into execution.

When this resolution had been taken, I said au revoir to Saint-Germain and his companion, and, resolved to prevent the crime, I hastened to make a report to M. Henry, who sent for me at once in order to obtain the fullest details on the revelation I had just made to him. His intention was to assure himself that I had really been solicited, and that in a badly understood duty I had not had recourse to provocations. I protested that I had in no way taken the initiative, and, as he believed he recognized the truth of this declaration, he announced that he was satisfied, which did not prevent his making a speech on *agents provocateurs* that touched me to the depths of my being.

Although I did not need the lesson, I thanked M. Henry, who advised me to stick to the heels of the two murderers and to neglect nothing to prevent the execution of the deed. According to his instructions, I did not let a single day go by without seeing Saint-Germain and his friend Boudin. As the *coup* they planned was to bring in some money, I concluded that it would not seem extraordinary if I showed a little impatience.

"Well, when is the famous affair?" I asked every time we were together.

"When?" Saint-Germain answered. "The pear isn't ripe. When the time comes," he added, pointing to Boudin, "there's the friend who'll warn you."

Several meetings had taken place and nothing was decided. I again addressed the usual questions to Saint-Germain.

"Ah, this time," he said, "it is for tomorrow. We'll wait for you to talk it over."

The meeting-place was outside of Paris. I was careful not to fail in attendance, and Saint-Germain was no less prompt.

"Listen," he said to me. "We have thought over that affair which cannot be pulled off for the present, but we have another one to propose, and I warn you in advance that you must be frank and answer yes or no. Before we take up the project which brought us here, I owe you a confidence which was made us yesterday. A fellow named Carré, who knew you at La Force, pretends that you got out on condition of serving the police and that you are a secret agent."

At the words "secret.agent," I felt almost suffocated; but I soon recovered. It was necessary that nothing should show, as Saint-Germain was watching me and waiting for my explanation. That presence of mind which never deserts me found itself immediately.

"I am not surprised," I answered, "that I am represented as a secret agent. I know the source of that story. Perhaps you don't know that I was to be transferred to Bicêtre, and that I escaped on the way. I have stayed in Paris because I could not go anywhere else. One has to live where he has resources. Unfortunately, I have to stay in hiding; I escape the search by disguising myself; but there are always some who recognize me, those, for example, with whom I lived in intimacy. Among the latter are some who would like to have me arrested, either to injure me or through self-interest. Well, to get rid of that desire, every time I have thought them capable of denouncing me, I have told them that I was attached to the police."

"That's good," Saint-Germain replied. "I believe you, and to give you a proof of my confidence in you, I am going to let you know what we are going to do this evening. At the corner of rue de'Enghien and rue Hauteville lives a banker whose house looks out on a rather large garden, which will be a help in our expedition and to our flight. The banker is away today, and his strong-box, in which he keeps a lot of gold and silver, as well as bank-notes, is guarded by only two persons. We have decided to take it this very evening. Until now we are only three to execute the plan, and you must be the fourth. We count on you; if you refuse, you will confirm our opinion that you are a police spy."

As I did not know the mental reservations of Saint-Germain, I accepted eagerly; Boudin and he seemed pleased with me. I soon saw a third man appear whom I did not know, a cab-driver named Debenne.

He was the father of a family and had allowed himself to be drawn in by these wretches. They began to talk of one thing and another; I was already thinking of what steps I could take to arrest them in the act, but to my great astonishment, when the moment came to pay the scot, I heard Saint-Germaine address us in these terms:

"My friends, when one risks his neck, he should look closely. Today we are going to play a game which I don't want to lose. That luck may be on our side, I have decided as follows, and I am sure that you will applaud my measures. At midnight all four of us are to get into the house in question. Boudin and I will look after the interior, and you two will stay in the garden, ready to help us in case of surprise. If this operation succeeds, as I think it will, it ought to give us enough to live quietly for some time. But it is important for our mutual safety that we do not leave each other until the hour of fulfilment."

This final word, which I pretended not to have heard well, was repeated. This time, I said to myself, I don't know how I shall get out of the business or what means to employ. Saint-Germain was a man of unusual rashness, avid of money, and always ready to shed blood to get it. It was only ten o'clock in the morning, and the time till midnight was long. I hoped that during the time we had to wait, an opportunity would present itself to slip away adroitly and warn the police. Whatever might happen, I agreed to Saint-Germain's proposition and made not the slightest objection to this precaution, which was the best guaranty of everyone's discretion. When he saw that we agreed with him, Saint-Germain, who through his energy and conception was really the leader in the plot, spoke a few words of satisfaction. "I am pleased," he told us, "to see you in such sentiments. For my part, I will do all that I can to deserve to be your friend for a long time!"

It was arranged that we should all go together to his place, rue Saint-Antoine. A cab took us to the door. When we arrived, we went up to his room, where we were to be detained until the moment of departure. Confined within the four walls, face to face with these brigands, I did not know to what saint to dedicate myself. To invent a pretext to go out was impossible; Saint-Germain would have made me out immediately, and at the slightest suspicion, he was capable of blowing out my brains. No matter what happened, I had decided to resign myself to events; there was nothing better to do than to help gracefully in the preparations for the crime. They began immediately. Some pistols were brought to the table to be unloaded and recharged. We examined them; Saint-Germain noticed a pair which did not seem to him to be of further use; he put them to one side.

"While you dismount the batteries," he said to us, "I'm going to change these." And he started to go out.

"One moment," I said; "according to our arrangement no one should leave this place unaccompanied."

"That's true," he answered. "I like one to be faithful to his agreements; so come with me."

"But these gentlemen?"

"We'll shut them up under a double lock."

We did what he said; I accompanied Saint-Germain. We bought some bullets, powder, and flints; the poor pistols were exchanged for others, and we returned. Then we finished our preparations, which made me shudder; the calmness of Boudin, sharpening two table knives on a stone, was horrible.

However, time passed; it was one o'clock, and no expedient for salvation had presented itself. I yawned, I stretched, I simulated boredom, and, going into the next room, I threw myself on a bed as if to rest. After a few moments I seemed still more tired from this inactivity, and I saw that the rest were not less so.

"If we had something to drink," Saint-Germain said to me.

"An admirable idea," I cried, jumping with pleasure. "Appropriately I have at my house a basket of excellent burgundy if you want to send for it."

Everyone agreed that nothing could be more to the point. Saint-Germain dispatched a porter to Annette whom I advised to come with the provision. We agreed to say nothing in front of her, and while they promised to do honour to my largesse, I threw myself on the bed for a second time, and traced these lines with a pencil: "Get out of here, disguise yourself, and do not lose track of us, Saint-Germain, Boudin, and me; be careful not to be noticed; take care to pick up anything I let fall, and take it down there." Although very short, my instructions were sufficient. Annette had received similar advice before, and I was sure that she would understand the full meaning.

Annette was not slow to appear with the basket of wine. Its appearance brought gaity. Everyone complimented her; I waited to celebrate until she was ready to go, and then, as I embraced her, I slipped her the note.

We dined copiously, after which I offered the opinion that Saint-Germain and I should go alone to reconnoitre the place, and examine it by daylight in order to provide against all accidents. This prudence was natural. Saint-Germain was not astonished; only I proposed to take a cab, while he thought it better to walk. When we reached the place, he pointed out the most favourable spot to scale, and I noted it well enough so that there should be no mistake. When our reconnaissance was completed, Saint-Germain told me that we needed some black crêpe to cover our faces, so we went to the Palais Royal to buy some. While he went into a shop, I made a pretext and closed myself up in a lavatory, where I had time to write all the information which would put the police in a way to prevent the crime.

Saint-Germain had kept me in sight as much as possible and he took me to a taproom, where we drank some bottles of beer. When we were about to re-enter our retreat, I saw that Annette was watching for our return. Sure that she had seen me, near the threshold I let the paper drop, and abandoned myself to fate.

It is impossible for me to convey all the terrors which preyed on me while we were waiting for the moment of the expedition. In spite of the warning I had given, I feared that the measures would be too late, and then, when the crime was consummated, could I alone undertake to arrest Saint-Germain and his accomplices? I recalled that in many circumstances the police had abandoned their agents, and that in others they had been unable to prevent the tribunals confounding them with their guilty. I was in such cruel apprehensions, when Saint-Germain charged me to go with Debenne, whose cab was to be stationed at the street-corner to receive the bags of gold and silver. We went down, and as I went out I saw Annette, who made a signal that she had delivered my message. At the same time Debenne asked me where the rendezvous was. I do not know what good genius then suggested to me the thought of saving this wretch. I had observed that he was not bad at heart, and it seemed to me that he had rather been pushed toward the abyss by want and perfidious advice than by a fatal propensity for crime. So I assigned him a post at another spot than the one indicated, and rejoined Saint-Germain and Boudin at the corner of the boulevard Saint-Denis.

It was still only ten-thirty. I told them that the cab would only be ready in an hour and that I had given Debenne his orders to be at the corner of rue du Faubourg Poissonnière. He would come at the agreed signal. I made them understand that if he was too near the place where we were to operate, the presence of the cab might arouse suspicions, so I had judged it more proper to keep him at a distance. They approved this precaution.

Eleven o'clock struck; we took a drink in the Faubourg Saint-Denis, and we headed for the banker's house. Boudin and his accomplice walked along smoking their pipes; their tranquillity frightened me. Finally, we were at the foot of the post which was to serve as a ladder. Saint-Germain asked me for my pistols. At that moment, I thought he had made me out and wanted to take my life. I gave them to him. I was wrong; he opened the fire-pan, changed the cap, and returned them. After he had done the same to his own and Boudin's, he set the example by climbing the post, and both, without stopping smoking, jumped into the garden. I had to follow. Trembling, I gained the top of the wall. All my apprehensions returned. Had the police had time to set an ambush? Such was the question I asked myself; such were my doubts. Finally, in this terrible uncertainty, I made a resolution—to prevent the crime even if I succumbed in the unequal struggle.

Just then Saint-Germain saw me astride the coping, and, impatient at my slowness, cried, "Come on, get down." He had hardly finished these words when suddenly he was assailed by a number of men; he and Boudin made a vigorous resistance. Shots were fired on both sides; bullets whistled, and after a battle of some minutes the two assassins were taken. Several agents were wounded in this action; Saint-Germain and his assistant were too. As a mere spectator of the engagement, I should have met with no grievous accident. However, to play my part to the end, I fell on the field of battle, as if I had been mortally hit. An instant after, they wrapped me in a quilt, and in this way I was carried into a room where Boudin and Saint-Germain were. The latter appeared deeply touched by my death; he shed tears, and they had to use force to prevent his falling on what he believed was only a corpse.

I remember no event in my life which has brought me more joy than the capture of these two scoundrels. I applauded myself for having delivered society from two monsters, at the same time that I felt happy at having kept the cabman Debenne from the fate which was reserved for them.

THE
PRISON MAZAS
By William Russell

Little is known of William Russell, partly because he chose to publish his many detective adventure books under pseudonyms. Like the anonymous author of Richmond: Scenes in the Life of a Bow Street Runner, *another early account of detective experiences, Russell was anxious to preserve the illusion of his stories being historical records of actual police activities rather than the fictions they really were. His first book was* Recollections of a Detective Police-Officer *(1856) by "Thomas Waters," a group of short stories about the London Metropolitan Police first serialized in* Chambers' Edinburgh Journal *beginning in 1849. In 1852 they were published as* The Recollections of a Policeman *in the United States, and after their appearance in Great Britain four years later, they were translated into French and German. This book was followed by a number of other short story collections including, in 1861,* The Experiences of a French Detective Officer, *in which "The Prison Mazas" is the last chapter.* Experiences *is offered as an adaptation by "Waters" of a manuscript by French secret agent Theodore Duhamel and is intended to establish the moral superiority of the English police over the French. The book is now available in a reprint from Arno Press (1976). For an extended discussion of Russell's contribution to the detective story, see Ian Ousby's* Bloodhounds of Heaven *(Cambridge: Harvard University Press, 1976).*

Near the site of the ancient Bastille stands the modern Bastille Mazas, into the long before prepared cells of which the Paris Police on the morning of the 2nd of December, 1851, thrust a *"fournée"* of the most distinguished men in France—Statesmen, Savants, Generals— many of them surprised in, and stolen out of their beds.

The formality of "lettres de cachet," was not observed upon that occasion. The Prince-President's verbal order conveyed to us through De Maupas, the Prefect of Police, would have been quite sufficient warrant to shoot as well as seize the proscribed men. It will be the same again whenever the Senate or Corps Législatif shall presume to abuse, in their master's opinion, the week or so's liberty of speech graciously accorded to them. "Do not be alarmed," wrote an acquaintance of mine from Paris on the 16th of March last, to a Bonapartist *pur sang.* "Do not be alarmed by Plichon speeches. There are always Mazas and Cayenne."

Yes, Mazas and Cayenne are always there, and I have now to relate how it happened that I, a Detective Officer, whose political creed might have been summed up in one sentence—"zealous obedience to the power capable of enforcing obedience," incurred and escaped the hazard of being found incarcerated in the prison, and next shipped off to the pestilential penal settlement.

To do so, I must go back to 1849, towards the close of which year I engaged a lodging in the Rue Neuve, Saint Eustache. In the same house dwelt Madame Colbert, her twin-sons, Albert and François Colbert, and Louise, wife of Albert. François was a working-goldsmith; Albert a watch-maker, skilled in a branch of the manufacture much better re- munerated than other portions of watch-work. Their age was five or six and twenty, and as the families boarded together, and the young men were expert workmen, industrious and frugal, their united earnings supported them all in creditable.competence. In colour of hair, com- plexion, height, figure, François and Albert Colbert closely resembled each other, as they also did in character, temperament, and opinion. Ultra-Republicans, and at the same remarkably devout—children of the Crusaders, not of Voltaire, as they used to boast—they were the most attached and duteous of sons, and well entitled was the excellent Madame Colbert to that filial love and duty. Madame Louise Colbert was a pale, delicate young woman, not pretty, perhaps, but a person of the sweetest disposition. She had been married over four years, and had two charming children, named Albert and Louíse.

I was honoured with the friendship of this amiable family, upon whom I became the innocent cause of inflicting a cruel calamity. I was engaged in carrying on an enquiry, in the result of which a very young widow was deeply interested. One day, when I was suffering from a severe cold, a piece of intelligence reached me, which rendered it necessary for me at once to personally communicate with the widow. I dispatched a note requesting her to call upon me. She arrived, when I happened to be in consultation with an officer from the Prefecture. She was shown into a room by Madame Louise, where the two children, Albert and Louise were playing, and requested to wait there till I could see her. Madame Louise noticed that the young person looked flushed, excited, but naturally attributed that to anxiety caused by my message to her. It might have been half an hour before I could wait upon the widow, who I found fondling the children, one upon each knee. Our conference did not last more than ten minutes, and she was about to leave, when Madame Colbert entered the room. The moment her glance rested upon the widow, an expression of intense alarm flashed over her pale features. Instantly she hurried the children away. Returning in a few minutes she sternly remarked, addressing the young woman—"Your coming here, Madame, is a criminal imprudence, which may have terrible results. Permit me," and without waiting for permission, Madame unfastened the widow's dress at the throat. "It is a fever—you are in the first stage of scarlet-fever!"

"Grand Dieu!" exclaimed the woman. "But no—it is not possible! I have a bilious head-ache—nothing more," she added, shivering nevertheless, in every limb, and sinking down upon a sofa.

"It is the scarlet-fever, I tell you," repeated Madame Colbert. "I know the symptoms but too well. Send for a *fiacre*, M. Duhamel. This poor woman must be sent home at once."

"God grant that the children have not taken the infection," said Madame Colbert, when we were alone together. "I will send for Dr. Petit, at once. And you, too, should take precautions. Not a word of this to my sons, or Louise."

The precautions taken did not avail to save the children, who before a week had passed, were buried in one grave at Perè La Chaise. The stroke of death is never so severe, so cruel, as when it descends upon the cradle of a child.

The bereaved family did not reproach me. It would have been sovereignly unjust on their part to do so. Yet I could not bear to be a daily witness of the young mother's agony of grief for her lost little ones; and I quitted the house. The woman who had unwittingly brought death into that before happy home, survived the children a few days only.

This may appear to be a strange introduction to the "The Prison Mazas." Nevertheless, without it, my conduct in that prison, necessitating my flight from France, would be without intelligible motive or excuse.

I frequently met the Colbert family afterwards in the streets and other places of public resort, and was always kindly recognised by them. Madame Louise bore no more children. The cradle remained empty, the void in her own and her husband's heart unfilled. I could not express in words the remorseful regret I felt for having, however innocently, brought such a remediless calamity upon an amiable family from whom I had received every kindness. Madame Colbert nursed me as a mother nurses her son through a sharp and dangerous illness. True, I was completely blameless as to intention, but it was equally true that if I had not lodged in the same house with them, little Albert and Louise would, in all human probability, be still alive. This grew to be a morbid sentiment with me, utterly irrational in its exaggeration.

The complete success of the *Coup d'Etat*, on the 2nd of December, 1851, never for an hour really doubtful, with such satanic skill and irresistible force was the blow dealt, was assured beyond question when the massacre of an unarmed crowd of men, women and children on the 4th of December, after the spasmodic, feeble resistance of Paris had entirely ceased, stamped the conviction upon the palpitating brain of every Frenchman and Frenchwoman that once more *"La Terreur Armée,"* was enthroned in France. To finish the work, there only remained to make up the list of the proscribed, arrest such as were not already in custody, and hand them all over for formal condemnation to the Courts-Martial, sitting *en permanence* in every chief town of France.

Upon my list of "men of action," whom it had been decided ought, in the interests of the public safety, to be sent to Cayenne, was one Etienne Delaporte, a young man of soul so ardent as to be kindled to flame by the false fire of a spurious socialism. He was already a recognised *chef* of the Reds, and the last time he was seen in public was when fighting by the side of Doussoub, at the barricade where that representative of the Haute Vienne, and member of the Mountain, was killed.

A man of courage and resource, Etienne Delaporte was not a man to be easily captured. He could not, however, have left Paris, and I believed myself to be close at his heels, when a note reached me from Madame Colbert, which gave the hunted man a respite by engaging my services in quite a different cause than that of capturing a so-called criminal.

Madame Colbert's son, the husband of Louise, accused of homi-

16

cide, with premeditation, had been seized and lodged in the prison Mazas. No one, not even a lawyer, would be permitted to see him till the judge had completed the "Instruction"; but it being well-known to Madame Colbert that the political police were invested with exceptional privileges in such cases, she entreated me to communicate with her son, who would be in sore need of sympathy and counsel, without delay.

No second request was needed; and within an hour of receiving Madame Colbert's note, I was myself, *"au secrèt,"* with Albert Colbert, the readily-received pretence for the interview being private instructions from the Prefecture of Police.

I listened with mingled surprise and consternation to a narrative of the chain of circumstance that had led to the crime of which he was accused, and would, he felt a bitter conviction, cause his head before many days had passed, "to fall into the basket"—meaning his death by guillotine. The shadow of that death had already settled upon his haggard countenance, which was that of a man who had aged, in appearance, full ten years, since I last saw him. He had received a flesh wound which, though not serious, had caused considerable loss of blood, adding to the pallor of a face which gleamed whitely out of the gloom of the dungeon, one of the gloomiest cells in the prison, like that of a spectre.

"It is kind of you, Duhamel, to visit me, at considerable risk, I can have no doubt, to yourself, considering the position you hold, but you are too clear-headed to hold out any hope to me, after you shall have heard what I have to say. I am a lost man, and must accept the gift of a stern fate as best I may. For me the stroke of death will be brief as sharp; the prolonged agony will be the loving mother's, wife's, brothers. And it is I, the well-loved son, husband, brother, that shall have inflicted upon them that life-long grief. Death in all his quiver has no sharper sting than that!

"You cannot remain very long, and would learn all the facts of the case, which, to calmer judgments than mine, may not, you say, appear so desperate. You *shall*, since you so strongly urge the request, know all—all without reserve, or false colouring.

"I love my wife Louise—you will need no assurance of that. Yes, and with a profounder tenderness since the loss of our children. We seemed to clasp each other more closely in the solitariness of our path through the world than when it was gay with the laugh, the prattle of children. Enough. The subject is, I know, a painful one. Pardon me, my friend.

"But my wife was not the idol before which my young heart bowed

17

down. Nor have I—let the truth be spoken—the ear of Louise will never be wounded by it—nor have I felt for her the transporting passion with which Adrienne—, her sire-name need not be mentioned inspired me, inspired me before I discovered that the master-passion of her soul was to acquire fortune, position, to be uplifted from the humble condition into which the downfall of her father had precipitated her. The awakening from my dream was a bitter one, and attended with humiliating circumstances, the sting of which has never ceased to rankle in my proud French heart. The recollection even now fires my blood: I can only glance at what occurred, and it will be enough to say that in Adrienne's presence, I was treated with brutal personal indignity by a man, a rich man, I understood, whose name I could never discover—and whom I never again met with till the day before yesterday. Nor did I again see Adrienne, till within a few minutes of the time I chanced to encounter *him*. She had become his mistress, and his regiment—he was then a captain in the line—has not till lately been quartered in Paris."

"His name?"

"Achard."

"Achard—Chef de Bataillon, in Carrelet's division?"

"Louis Achard, Chef de Bataillon, in Carrelet's division."

"I have heard of him. He is to be a great man under the new régime. He was a prime favourite at the Elysée, and has a brilliant career before him."

"His career is finished. It is Achard whom I am accused of having killed with pre-meditation."

"*Diable!* That is bad news. How did it happen?"

"I will tell you in a few words. Both myself and brother, notwithstanding the ardour of our principles, well-known to you, abstained from taking any part in the late conflict—partly restrained by the tears and prayers of our mother and my wife, partly because aware of the futility of attempting to cope with the overwhelming military force concentrated in Paris. It happened, unfortunately, that I had business in the Rue de la Paix on the fourth, and was endeavouring to push through the unarmed crowd of men, women, and children who were looking on, as at an ordinary military spectacle, upon the masses of troops echeloned there, when in a handsomely dressed woman near me, I recognized Adrienne. A mist came before my eyes—my heart beat with terrible violence—a storm of rage—indignation—pity, for her vocation could not be mistaken—swept through my soul. She was alone, if any one could be said to be alone in such a closely packed crowd, and did not see me. Recovering myself, I followed the eager

18

direction of her eye. It was fixed upon a mounted officer—upon the man by whom I, seven years since, was treated with brutal indignity—Louis Achard, *enfin*. He, in his turn, had noticed Adrienne, and a sardonic smile replied to the piteous supplication of her look.

"Holy thunder of God!—I verily believe that but for the pressure of the crowd by which I was held as if enclosed by a circle of iron, I should have been mad enough to have made one tiger-spring for vengeance at the smiling, triumphant, mocking villain. As it was, I could only writhe, curse, gnash my teeth with impotent fury.

"Just then a few shouts of '*Vive la République*,' '*A bas le Tyran*,' gave the hoped for opportunity of striking terror to the hearts of the Parisians. Without one word of warning the word was given. The soldiers levelled their muskets,.and a crashing, murderous volley was poured into the dense mass of unarmed people from not ten yards distance. Shrieks, groans, curses, cries for mercy, were the only replies to the soldiers' terrible fire, which was kept up with unabated spirit, not only at the fleeing people, but at any inhabitant of a house who chanced to show him or herself at a window.

"I myself was slightly wounded, and fell on the pavement, thrown down by the hustling, hurrying crowd. As I rose to my feet, a feeble grasp was laid upon the tail of my coat. It was Adrienne's. 'Save me—save me,' murmured the wretched woman—'Save me, Albert.'

"Blood was welling through, and trickling down her showy dress from a bullet-wound in her bosom; and only He who created could, I feared, save her. I snatched her up and hurried her away—so thin, emaciated was she that her weight was nothing—pursued for a considerable distance by the shouts and shots of the inebriated soldiery.

"At last I had placed her in the shop of a shoemaker, with whom I am slightly, very slightly, acquainted, and at his suggestion ran off again at once to procure some wine, whilst he, leaving Adrienne in the care of his wife, hurried away in search of medical assistance.

"Louis Achart had seen Adrienne struck down, recognised by whom she was carried off, and actuated by some capricious impulse, followed. I had not left the shoemaker's three minutes when he arrived, accompanied by several soldiers, and ordered her instant removal. The soldiers were about to do so, when it was discovered that she was dead. Possibly she died in my arms.

"The shoemaker's wife had the prudence to meet me outside the shop, to inform me that the unfortunate young woman was dead, and that soldiers and an officer, who had asked for me—that is for the man who brought the woman there—were within.

"What demon possessed me to rush, as I did, upon destruction!

The officer was gazing, his back towards me, upon the face of the dead; he turned sharply round upon hearing my step, and I was face to face—within arm's length—of Louis Achard. I yelled out a frightful malediction, and struck at him wildly, feebly. He caught my arm—flung me off—he was a man of five times my strength—and drove me with a shower of blows and contemptuous curses out of the shop.

"Certainly I was no longer a responsible being. Carried away by a tempest of convulsing, choking rage, I darted back after him—seized a musket belonging to one of the soldiers—shouted '*Gare scélérat*—assassin!' His sword flew out of the scabbard, and he made a pass at me, inflicting a slight flesh wound, at the same moment that my bayonet went through his body.

"Horrified at what I had done—seized with terror for the consequences to myself—I made off before the soldiers recovered from the stupefaction caused by the suddenness of the deed, and sped away, running for my life. They pursued, but I soon distanced them, and as the shoemaker and his wife did not know my name, nor where I dwelt, a faint hope of escape was dawning upon my mind, when I was stopped by some gendarmes. The soldiers came up, and though I persisted in asserting that I was not the man they were in search of, that I had not been in a shoemaker's shop, and that I was running to get home as quickly as possible out of the tumult of the streets, having been already slightly wounded by an Insurrectionist, they as strictly asserted I was the culprit they were in pursuit of— and—*voila tout!*"

"You have persisted in denying your identity with the homicide to the *Juge d'Instruction?* Yes?"

"I have as yet seen no *Juge d'Instruction*. The agents of 'Justice' have such a mass of business on their hands that I am told it may be a fortnight or three weeks before 'the *Juge*' will visit me."

"In the letter to Madame Colbert, which *must* have been read by the authorities of the prison, you kept up the pretence of innocence?"

"I did. Yet what can such barefaced denial avail at the end of the reckoning? The shoemaker and his wife will prove that it was I who slew Louis Achard."

"That is true! And as you will be tried by a military commission, there will be no chance of 'extenuating circumstances' being tacked to the verdict. This is a terrible calamity. Persist, however, I counsel you, in denying that you are the homicide. Louis Achard is dead. Died he instantly?"

"Yes; the soldiers declared that he did."

"Adrienne is dead—the soldiers could scarcely have taken exact cognisance of you, and in running they lost sight of the man they pursued. The shoemaker and his wife—yes, there is the difficulty. What is their name?"

"Upon my word I am not quite sure. Carlier, or Cartier, a name of some such sound as that. My acquaintance with them, as I told you, is of the slightest kind. Bah! Duhamel, what is this but the catching at a straw by a drowning man? Better throw up the cards at once, and frankly recognise that the game, the grand game of life, is irretrievably lost."

"Persist, I again counsel you, in asserting that you are François Colbert——."

"*Francois* Colbert!"

"You signed the note to your mother A. Colbert, of course. But those who read it will hardly remember whether the initial letter of your baptismal name was A. or F."

"Do you know, M. Duhamel, that all sounds to me like so much——"

"Like so much folly—absurdity! I have no doubt of it. Notwithstanding that very decided opinion, please persist in denying that you, François Colbert, are the homicide. You know I would incur considerable risk to save you from the terrible doom you have unquestionably incurred. An idea has glanced upon my mind, the unformed shadow of an idea as yet, but which *may*, may become clearer, assume a practical shape. If it should, the evidence of the shoemaker and his wife will be invaluable. He is a respectable man, I hope, this Carlier or Cartier?"

"Yes, in circumstances, but a furious Bonapartist."

"So much the better. The shadow is defining itself into shape rapidly. Adieu, my friend. There is always hope, you know? I go to see Madame Colbert, and your wife and brother."

It was not, however, till the next day, when I had fully elaborated the scheme, a faint outline of which had traced itself upon my mind during my interview with Albert Colbert in the Prison Mazas, that I waited upon his mother and other relatives.

Family councils are legal institutions in France, though not exactly of the kind at which I upon that occasion assisted.

I first set forth the exact particulars, omitting only the early love-phase of the affair, and that the Chef de Bataillon had been the successful rival of Albert in the favour of an attractive, worthless girl.

Next I frankly stated my real conviction, that should Albert be brought to trial, he would be condemned to death, and that execution would follow, either by the guillotine or the bullets of a firing party. I added, induced by a sincere friendship for a family upon whom I had unwittingly brought a great calamity, that I was willing to undergo considerable risk to save Albert's life; a feeling which, of course, glowed with much greater intensity in the hearts of his relatives than in mine. Mother, wife, brother, protested, I was sure, truly, that there was no sacrifice they would not make to save Albert.

"I knew I should receive that answer. Now then to explain. I have, like all well-known, and in their vocation, celebrated Detectives, not only the entrée of the criminal prisons of France, but a privilege rarely questioned, of communicating privately with prisoners.

"*C'est connu.* Precisely. That fact I may call the base of the superstructure I propose to raise. We now proceed to the first step of that hypothetical superstructure. You, Monsieur François Colbert, have, doubtless, heard of one Etienne Delaporte, a notability amongst the Reds?"

"*Parbleu!* Who has *not*, during the last week, heard of Etienne Delaporte?"

"No reader of the journals, certainly. Well, Etienne Delaporte, whom I am commissioned to capture, is described to be of your height—the colour of his hair the same as yours. He must resemble you as nearly as you do your brother. Etienne Delaporte also affects a particular dress, which no law, I am aware of, if there can, indeed, be said to be any law just now in France, prohibits being worn by any other individual. Now, I have discovered the said Etienne's haunts; and but for this affair of your brother's, I should have seized him yesterday, and I want this very afternoon to capture you for him."

"*Comment.* . . What? Capture me for Etienne Delaporte?"

"Yes; you will be surprised and seized by myself and three other Police-Agents, neither of whom, myself inclusive, know Delaporte by sight. You will say you are George Duplay, and the papers with which I shall furnish you will be perfectly *en règle.* We, Police-Agents, shall treat all that as nonsense—*blague*-the papers as borrowed. We take you to the prison Mazas, obtain a receipt for you, and the notorious Etienne Delaporte is at last in the hands of justice."

"What does all this mean?" exclaimed poor Madame Colbert. "You propose to put *both* my sons in prison?"

"Yes, Madame, in order to get *both* out. I must, however, in candour, tell you that it will not be safe for you, Mesdames, to remain in Paris, perhaps not in France!"

"That is nothing—absolutely nothing," exclaimed the mother and wife in a breath.

"Albert is an excellent working-watchmaker. I am a fair working-

22

goldsmith," subjoined François; "we shall do well anywhere. In England, for example. But speak of my going to prison for Etienne Delaporte. The doors of a prison open readily enough to let you in, but getting out again, I have heard is——."

"Another affair. That is quite true, under ordinary circumstances. But first, in your mind's eye, survey the situation when you are locked up, as I will manage it, in a cell close adjoining that in which your brother is confined. I have free, private admission into each. What, then, watching an opportunity, but an inconceivable maladroitness can prevent François and Albert Colbert from exchanging cells, exchanging clothes? Ah! ah! you begin to comprehend? But let us continue. To-morrow morning, I, somewhat staggered by Etienne Delaporte's positive assertion that he is not Etienne Delaporte, but one Duplay, visit the prison, accompanied by officers, who know Delaporte well. We discover our mistake; make a thousand apologies; the governor, who has not yet seen your brother, is bamboozled; the accusation treated as *non avenue*; and Albert Colbert passes out of Mazas on his way, without stopping, to England. François Colbert remains in prison awaiting his trial as the assassin of Major Louis Achard. It is delicious—*impayable*."

"I am not so sure of '*impayable*,'" said François, in a tone indicating a considerably cooled enthusiasm. "It is just possible that I may be made to pay for the delicious device with my head. The shoemaker and his wife, you say, were very slightly acquainted with Albert; my brother and I are much alike, and the Military Tribunal may decide that I am really the man who killed Chef de Bataillon Achard. That is serious, *nom de Dieu!* I would incur any risk in reason to save poor Albert, still——"

"Bah! you are scared by the merest shadows. True, you and your brother strongly resemble each other. That is a main element in our chance of success, strengthened by the number of persons suddenly crowded into the prison, with whose faces the officials are not yet familiar. But Carlier and his wife will be sure to recognise the mistake they will suppose the soldiers to have made, the soldiers the same, who will attribute it to your having been stopped whilst running in the same direction the homicide had taken, and that you were bleeding from a recent wound."

"Ah! to be sure, that I was wounded, bleeding," exclaimed François, brightening up; "that now is a reliable circumstance. Mother— Louise, I shall venture."

It was my turn to falter in resolution. Should Carlier and his wife, and the soldiers, misled by the resemblance of the brothers, and a previously formed conviction, depose to François being the veritable culprit, he would, of course, to save himself, appeal to the indisputable fact that he was not wounded on the fourth of December. That might place me in a pretty predicament, for it was quite sure the authorities would not release him till they had ascertained by whose agency the exchange of prisoners had been effected! Such a startling possibility had not crossed my mind.

"True," said I, speaking to myself rather than to the Colberts; "true, you have not been wounded. That will be decisive—if—if— bah! It is certain the witnesses will recognise that you are not the man who killed Achard. The wound, which is already healed, will not be spoken of. Of course you will not appeal to the wound, nor mention it, except in the very last extremity?"

"Certainly I will not."

Our conversation then turned upon minor details of the suggested scheme, and François Colbert having fully mastered them, I left to prepare for my part in the enterprise, which in my eyes did not wear so inviting an aspect as when I first proposed it to the Colbert family. I could not, however, well recede, after swaggering so loudly of my chivalrous determination to serve those persons to whom I was so greatly indebted, and whom I had been the means of plunging into such deep affliction. Had, indeed, the proposition been to make, instead of being made, I should at least have taken some time longer to consider it.

One remark is called for in this place. Was I, a Police-Agent, morally justified in aiding the escape from Mazas, of the homicide Albert Colbert? I could not but think so. The hands of Achard when he was slain, were still red with the blood of the unarmed people of Paris, amongst them the woman whom he had seduced and ruined, and there was poetical justice in the death-stroke having been dealt by Adrienne's former lover. Then, Colbert had been brutally ill-used by a much stronger man than himself; there was, moreover, a real duel, if not one precisely *selon les règles*. A sword would generally be more than a match for a fixed bayonet, and Albert had, in fact, received a wound which, had the thrust been better aimed, might have been a mortal one. Yes, I was morally justified in attempting to save Albert Colbert's life. At least I so persuaded myself.

The gendarmes who were to assist in arresting the pretended Etienne Delaporte having arrived, we were about to depart on our errand, when I bethought me that I had omitted to prepare a dye with which Albert Colbert might tint his white cheeks to the natural hue of health. The ingredients were, however, in my possession, so requesting

24

the gendarmes to wait, I passed into an adjoining room, and folded up a small quantity of each powder in a scrap of paper, upon which I wrote the necessary directions for mixing and using the preparation, adding a strict injunction to destroy the paper.

François Colbert was duly arrested, and spite of his furious assertions that he was not Etienne Delaporte, hurried off to Mazas. The crowded state of the prison, upon which, as the reader is aware, I had to a certain extent relied, gave us an unlooked for advantage.

"Where to place this prisoner," said the officer, who acted as quarter-master of the prison, silencing with an imperious gesture François Colbert's protestations that a frightful mistake had been committed; that he was *not* Etienne Delaporte, or whatever the *scélérat* for whom he was taken, was called; "Where to place this prisoner, I know not. Mazas is already full—more than full."

A bright idea flashed across my mind, which I was ass enough to translate into speech.

"Cannot you," I said, "place him for a short time in the cell with the prisoner Colbert, whom I visited yesterday. It *might be advantageous*," I added with *sotte voce* official emphasis, aside to the officer.

"With Colbert, accused of armed sedition, and the murder of the Chef de Bataillon, Achard?" said the officer, flashing at me a sharp, inquisitive look. "Well, yes," after a brief reflective pause, also in a tone inaudible to the prisoner, "upon *your* responsibility—you who *must* know whether such a companionship is likely to aid or defeat justice."

The necessary order was given to a subordinate, and I said aloud, addressing the officer, "It is just possible, monsieur, that this man may *not* be Etienne Delaporte, and to put an end to all doubt, I will go at once to M. Ambrose Quesnel, Commissaire de Police, by whom I am instructed, and who knows the said Delaporte well. I shall probably return in about an hour," I added. It would require nearly that time to prepare, and apply the dye, I had passed unobserved to François.

"*Tres bien,*" said the officer, "If he be not Etienne Delaporte, we shall get rid of him at once."

"This man is not Etienne Delaporte," said M. le Commissaire Quesnel, after a glance at Albert Colbert, who had exchanged clothes with his brother, and whose cheeks were skillfully touched. "Certainly not. It is a mistake, and we would make you an apology if you had not chosen to dress in that *bizarre* mode. I will see that you are at once discharged."

Less than ten minutes afterwards, Albert Colbert left Mazas a free man. The same day, he and his wife left for London, where they are now domiciled. Madame Colbert remained in Paris till François should be liberated.

I was disturbed in mind during the next three days, much disturbed. "What the devil business is this of mine?" I repeated to myself fifty times a day, as the dismal conviction grew upon me that I, urged by a Quixotic impulse, only excusable in boys, lovers, and maniacs, had run *tête basse* into a frightful danger, and this conviction became a certainty when I learned that although Carlier and his wife, deposed before the *Juge d'Instruction* that the actual prisoner was *not* the man who slew the Chef de Bataillon, Achard, the soldiers, with equal confidence, swore he *was* the veritable culprit.

It was all over, the career of *mouchard* was closed to me forever! and, hundred devils!—that was but a trifle! A rigorous investigation would take place—was at that moment, no doubt, taking place; the whole truth would be discovered; had been, perhaps, already—I sweated *sang et eau* at the thought—had, perhaps, already been discovered. As to François Colbert, his brother's devotion would, no doubt, be generously considered, a few months more or less of simple imprisonment was all he had to fear. But Theodore Duhamel, a paid Police-Agent, who had rescued the assassin of Chef de Bataillon Achard, a petted favourite of the Elysée—of the Prince who had first written his title to supreme power in the blood of Frenchmen—would, as surely as he lived, be visited with condign punishment—"*peine afflictive et infamanto*";—Cayenne or Lambessa, for life, no doubt.

I determined upon instant departure whilst my legs were my own. First, I dispatched by post a note to the Prefecture of Police, stating that before it arrived, I should have left Paris, having obtained information relative to the affair Fleury, which required to be immediately and closely followed up; adding that I should not be absent from Paris more than about four days.

I then made my *pacquet*—two or three changes of linen only—it would not do to encumber myself with luggage; pocketed all the cash and jewels I possessed, and left the house. Just in time: had I remained another hour, I, myself, should have been an inmate of Mazas, with a certainty of Cayenne, etc., in the near distance.

With the assistance of a trusted and trustworthy comrade to whom I immediately hastened, I sallied forth the next morning so well made up as a stout, middle aged gentleman of the glossiest respectability, wearing blue, gold-rimmed spectacles, and carrying a gold-headed cane, that I believed I might defy recognition. I have before said that I was clever at such metamorphoses, and I need not say that I tried my art to the utmost upon that particular occasion. My passport, duly *visé* purported to be that of M. Victor Robinet, of Marseilles. In fact it *was* a genuine document, which M. V. Robinet, having lost, had come into the possession of my friend. My friend kept the passport, and M. Robinet, after much worry and some expense, was favoured with a duplicate. I had choice of several obtained in a similar manner, but M. Robinet's was chosen for the paramount reason that I could dress, with wig, and whisker, well up to the description.

And where does the reader think I, a man in mortal danger of Cayenne, first betook myself? Positively to the Palais de Justice! I had heard that the affair Colbert would come on that day before the military tribunal sitting there, and a kind of fascination—a sort of morbid *entrainement*—impelled me to learn the worst or best with my own ears.

The *salle*, where the tribunal presided over by the colonel of a line regiment sat, was crowded throughout, but I, contrived—swathed, artificially corpulent as I was, sweltering with heat, and presently with terror—to stand out without fainting, the ten minutes which sufficed to effectively settle my little business.

The affair "Colbert," had commenced before I entered the salle. François looking very nervous and excited, was on the *banc des accusés*, and M. le Procureur-General *substitut*, was remarking upon the circumstances disclosed in the *proces-verbal*, to show that the individual at the bar, who there could be no question, it had been ascertained, was *not* the assassin of Chef de Bataillon, Louis Achard, could not be tried for the only offence of which he was accused by a military tribunal. He should be sent before the Cour d'Assises. François Colbert, with the assistance of one Theodore Duhamel, a Police-Agent, effected the escape from the Prison Mazas, and from France, of his brother, Albert Colbert, accused of armed sedition and homicide, for which offence François Colbert could only be tried by a civil tribunal. The proofs of criminal complicity on the part of Duhamel," added the Procureur-General *substitut*, "are irresistible, and to complete the chain of circumstantial evidence, a memorandum in the caitiff's handwriting has this morning been found, instructing Albert Colbert how to mix and apply certain powders so as to colour his face with a brown healthy tint, in order the more certainly to pass out of the prison unrecognised."

"Is Duhamel in custody?" asked the military president.

"Not yet, but there is little doubt he will be before many hours have passed. Numerous active officers are at his heels. His crime is a

27

grave one," added M. le Procureur-General, "and should be visited with signal punishment."

The court cordially concurred in that opinion; also that François Colbert should be sent before a civil tribunal. I may here mention that he was sentenced by the next Cour d'Assises for the Seine to one year's imprisonment.

The affair "Colbert," disposed of, another was called, which I did not stop to hear. I left Paris by the first *convoi* for Havre-de-Grace. My sensations during that terrible journey added considerably to my "detective" experience. I knew what it was to be hunted, as well as to hunt.

Grand Dieu, didn't I mentally anathematise with all the strength of my soul "that noblest achievement of modern science," as I had been in the habit of designating the Electric Telegraph, consign the wondrous wings of fire to their native, bottomless pit! What with weight of clothes and mortal terror, I must have lost two stone in weight during that cursed journey.

Havre was reached at last; my passport was *visé* at the Sous-Prefecture, without remark, and twelve hours afterwards I disembarked at the Southampton Docks. Hurrah!

CONFESSION FOUND IN A PRISON

By Charles Dickens

Charles Dickens (1812–1870), one of England's greatest novelists, turned repeatedly in his writing to the subjects of crime, detection, and imprisonment, the choice of material dictated in part by his own childhood experiences. In his earliest years, the young Dickens was encouraged by prosperous parents to count on a university education and a comfortable life. By the time he was eleven, however, the family finances had collapsed, his father was imprisoned for debt, and the boy was forced to go to work in a blacking factory. Living alone in a London garret, he learned first hand about the grim street life of the city. With no hope of advanced schooling, Dickens studied shorthand and soon made a name for himself as a parliamentary reporter. At the same time, he began writing a series of sketches, drawing on his own close observations of the everyday world of London. The success of these Sketches by Boz (1836) earned the young author a commission to provide texts for a group of sporting prints, a project which grew into The Pickwick Papers (1837) and made him world famous at the age of twenty-four. Amusing as it is, even Pickwick has its prison scenes, and Dickens' next novel, Oliver Twist (1833), makes violent crime and punishment its principal subject. During 1840 and 1841, Dickens worked on a literary project he called Master Humphrey's Clock. This was a weekly series of humorous essays, contemporary comments, short stories, and satires presumably shared by a miscellaneous group of acquaintances gathered around an old grandfather clock belonging to the crippled Master Humphrey. "A Confession Found in a Prison in the Time of Charles the Second" is the tale told by Jack Redburn, one of Master Humphrey's closest friends, and is another example of Dickens' preoccupation with horrible crimes and equally terrible retribution. For a study of the writer's interest in these subjects see Philip Collins' Dickens and Crime (Bloomington: Indiana University Press, 1962). The definitive biography of the author is Edgar Johnson's Charles Dickens: His Tragedy and Triumph (New York: Simon & Schuster, 1952).

I held a lieutenant's commission in his Majesty's army, and served abroad in the campaigns of 1677 and 1678. The treaty of Nimeguen being concluded, I returned home, and retiring from the service, withdrew to a small estate lying a few miles east of London, which I had recently acquired in right of my wife.

This is the last night I have to live, and I will set down the naked truth without disguise. I was never a brave man, and had always been from my childhood of a secret, sullen, distrustful nature. I speak of myself as if I had passed from the world; for while I write this, my grave is digging, and my name is written in the black-book of death.

Soon after my return to England, my only brother was seized with mortal illness. This circumstance gave me slight or no pain; for since we had been men, we had associated but very little together. He was open-hearted and generous, handsomer than I, more accomplished, and generally beloved. Those who sought my acquaintance abroad or at home, because they were friends of his, seldom attached themselves to me long, and would usually say, in our first conversation, that they were surprised to find two brothers so unlike in their manners and appearance. It was my habit to lead them on to this avowal; for I knew what comparisons they must draw between us; and having a ranking envy in my heart, I sought to justify it to myself.

We had married two sisters. This additional tie between us, as it may appear to some, only estranged us the more. His wife knew me well. I never struggled with any secret jealousy or gall when she was present but that woman knew it as well as I did. I never raised my eyes at such times but I found hers fixed upon me; I never bent them on the ground or looked another way but I felt that she overlooked me always. It was an inexpressible relief to me when we quarrelled, and a greater relief still when I heard abroad that she was dead. It seems to me now as if some strange and terrible foreshadowing of what has happened since must have hung over us then. I was afraid of her; she haunted me; her fixed and steady look comes back upon me now, like the memory of a dark dream, and makes my blood run cold.

She died shortly after giving birth to a child—a boy. When my brother knew that all hope of his own recovery was past, he called my wife to his bedside, and confided this orphan, a child of four years old, to her protection. He bequeathed to him all the property he had, and willed that, in case of his child's death, it should pass to my wife, as the only acknowledgment he could make her for her care and love. He exchanged a few brotherly words with me, deploring our long separation; and being exhausted, fell into a slumber, from which he never awoke.

We had no children; and as there had been a strong affection between the sisters, and my wife had almost supplied the place of a mother to this boy, she loved him as if he had been her own. The child was ardently attached to her; but he was his mother's image in face and spirit, and always mistrusted me.

I can scarcely fix the date when the feeling first came upon me; but I soon began to be uneasy when this child was by. I never roused myself from some moody train of thought but I marked him looking at me; not with mere childish wonder, but with something of the purpose and meaning that I had so often noted in his mother. It was no effort of my fancy, founded on close resemblance of feature and expression. I never could look the boy down. He feared me, but seemed by some instinct to despise me while he did so; and even when he drew back beneath my gaze—as he would when we were alone, to get nearer to the door—he would keep his bright eyes upon me still.

Perhaps I hide the truth from myself, but I do not think that, when this began, I meditated to do him any wrong. I may have thought how serviceable his inheritance would be to us, and may have wished him dead; but I believe I had no thought of compassing his death. Neither did the idea come upon me at once, but by very slow degrees, presenting itself at first in dim shapes at a very great distance, as men may think of an earthquake or the last day; then drawing nearer and nearer, and losing something of its horror and improbability; then coming to be part and parcel—nay nearly the whole sum and substance—of my daily thoughts, and resolving itself into a question of means and safety; not of doing or abstaining from the deed.

While this was going on within me, I never could bear that the child should see me looking at him, and yet I was under a fascination which made it a kind of business with me to contemplate his slight and fragile figure and think how easily it might be done. Sometimes I would steal upstairs and watch him as he slept; but usually I hovered in the garden near the window of the room in which he learnt his little tasks; and there, as he sat upon a low seat beside my wife, I would peer at him for hours together from behind a tree; starting, like the guilty wretch I was, at every rustling of a leaf, and still gliding back to look and start again.

Hard by our cottage, but quite out of sight, and (if there were any wind astir) of hearing too, was a deep sheet of water. I spent days in shaping with my pocket-knife a rough model of a boat, which I finished at last and dropped in the child's way. Then I withdrew to a secret place, which he must pass if he stole away alone to swim this bauble, and lurked there for his coming. He came neither that day nor the

31

next, though I waited from noon till nightfall. I was sure that I had him in my net, for I had heard him prattling of the toy, and knew that in his infant pleasure he kept it by his side in bed. I felt no weariness or fatigue, but waited patiently, and on the third day he passed me, running joyously along, with his silken hair streaming in the wind, and he singing—God have mercy upon me!—singing a merry ballad,—who could hardly lisp the words.

I stole down after him, creeping under certain shrubs which grow in that place, and none but devils know with what terror I, a strong, full-grown man, tracked the footsteps of that baby as he approached the water's brink. I was close upon him, had sunk upon my knee and raised my hand to thrust him in, when he saw my shadow in the stream and turned him round.

His mother's ghost was looking from his eyes. The sun burst forth from behind a cloud; it shone in the bright sky, the glistening earth, the clear water, the sparkling drops of rain upon the leaves. There were eyes in everything. The whole great universe of light was there to see the murder done. I know not what he said; he came of bold and manly blood, and, child as he was, he did not crouch or fawn upon me. I heard him cry that he would try to love me,—not that he did,—and then I saw him running back towards the house. The next I saw was my own sword naked in my hand, and he lying at my feet stark dead,—dabbled here and there with blood, but otherwise no different from what I had seen him in his sleep—in the same attitude too, with his cheek resting upon his little hand.

I took him in my arms and laid him—very gently now that he was dead—in a thicket. My wife was from home that day, and would not return until the next. Our bedroom window, the only sleeping-room on that side of the house, was but a few feet from the ground, and I resolved to descend from it at night and bury him in the garden. I had no thought that I had failed in my design, no thought that the water would be dragged and nothing found, that the money must now lie waste, since I must encourage the idea that the child was lost or stolen. All my thoughts were bound up and knotted together in the one absorbing necessity of hiding what I had done.

How I felt when they came to tell me that the child was missing, when I ordered scouts in all directions, when I gasped and trembled at every one's approach, no tongue can tell or mind of man conceive. I buried him that night. When I parted the boughs and looked into the dark thicket, there was a glow-worm shining like the visible spirit of God upon the murdered child. I glanced down into his grave when I had placed him there, and still it gleamed upon his breast; an eye of fire looking up to Heaven in supplication to the stars that watched me at my work.

I had to meet my wife, and break the news, and give her hope that the child would soon be found. All this I did,—with some appearance, I suppose, of being sincere, for I was the object of no suspicion. This done, I sat at the bed-room window all day long, and watched the spot where the dreadful secret lay.

It was in a piece of ground which had been dug up to be newly turfed, and which I had chosen on that account, as the traces of my spade were less likely to attract attention. The men who laid down the grass must have thought me mad. I called to them continually to expedite their work, ran out and worked beside them, trod down the earth with my feet, and hurried them with frantic eagerness. They had finished their task before night, and then I thought myself comparatively safe.

I slept,—not as men do who awake refreshed and cheerful, but I did sleep, passing from vague and shadowy dreams of being hunted down, to visions of the plot of grass, through which now a hand, and now a foot, and now the head itself was starting out. At this point I always woke and stole to the window, to make sure that it was not really so. That done, I crept to bed again; and thus I spent the night in fits and starts, getting up and lying down full twenty times, and dreaming the same dream over and over again,—which was far worse than lying awake, for every dream had a whole night's suffering of its own. Once I thought the child was alive, and that I had never tried to kill him. To wake from that dream was the most dreadful agony of all.

The next day I sat at the window again, never once taking my eyes from the place, which, although it was covered by the grass, was as plain to me—its shape, its size, its depth, its jagged sides, and all—as if it had been open to the light of day. When a servant walked across it, I felt as if he must sink in; when he had passed, I looked to see that his feet had not worn the edges. If a bird lighted there, I was in terror lest by some tremendous interposition it should be instrumental in the discovery; if a breath of air sighed across it, to me it whispered murder. There was not a sight or a sound—how ordinary, mean, or unimportant soever—but was fraught with fear. And in this state of ceaseless watching I spent three days.

On the fourth there came to the gate one who had served with me abroad, accompanied by a brother officer of his whom I had never seen. I felt that I could not bear to be out of sight of the place. It was a summer evening, and I bade my people take a table and a flask of wine into the garden. Then I sat down *with my chair upon the grave*, and being

33

assured that nobody could disturb it now without my knowledge, tried to drink and talk.

They hoped that my wife was well, — that she was not obliged to keep her chamber, — that they had not frightened her away. What could I do but tell them with a faltering tongue about the child? The officer whom I did not know was a down-looking man, and kept his eyes upon the ground while I was speaking. Even that terrified me. I could not divest myself of the idea that he saw something there which caused him to suspect the truth. I asked him hurriedly if he supposed that— and stopped. "That the child has been murdered?" said he, looking mildly at me: "O no! what could a man gain by murdering a poor child?" I could have told him what a man gained by such a deed, no one better: but I held my peace and shivered as with an ague.

Mistaking my emotion, they were endeavoring to cheer me with the hope that the boy would certainly be found, — great cheer that was for me! — when we heard a low deep howl, and presently there sprung over the wall two great dogs, who, bounding into the garden, repeated the baying sound we had heard before.

"Bloodhounds!" cried my visitors.

What need to tell me that! I had never seen one of that kind in all my life, but I knew what they were and for what purpose they had come. I grasped the elbows of my chair, and neither spoke nor moved.

"They are of the genuine breed," said the man whom I had known abroad, "and being out for exercise have no doubt escaped from their keeper."

Both he and his friend turned to look at the dogs, who with their noses to the ground moved restlessly about, running to and fro, and up and down, and across, and round in circles, careering about like wild things, and all this time taking no notice of us, but ever and again repeating the yell we had heard already, then dropping their noses to the ground again and tracking earnestly here and there. They now began to snuff the earth more eagerly than they had done yet, and although they were still very restless, no longer beat about in such wide circuits, but kept near to one spot, and constantly diminished the distance between themselves and me.

At last they came up close to the great chair on which I sat, and raising their frightful howl once more, tried to tear away the wooden rails that kept them from the ground beneath. I saw how I looked, in the faces of the two who were with me.

"They scent some prey," said they, both together.

"They scent no prey!" cried I.

"In Heaven's name, move!" said the one I knew, very earnestly, "or you will be torn to pieces."

"Let them tear me from limb to limb, I'll never leave this place!" cried I. "Are dogs to hurry men to shameful deaths! Hew them down, cut them in pieces."

"There is some foul mystery here!" said the officer whom I did not know, drawing his sword. "In King Charles's name, assist me to secure this man."

They both set upon me and forced me away, though I fought and bit and caught at them like a madman. After a struggle, they got me quietly between them; and then, my God! I saw the angry dogs tearing at the earth and throwing it up into the air like water.

What more have I to tell? That I fell upon my knees, and with chattering teeth confessed the truth, and prayed to be forgiven. That I have since denied, and now confess to it again. That I have been tried for the crime, and found guilty, and sentenced. That I have not the courage to anticipate my doom, or to bear up manfully against it. That I have no compassion, no consolation, no hope, no friend. That my wife has happily lost for the time those faculties which would enable her to know my misery or hers. That I am alone in this stone dungeon with my evil spirit, and that I die to-morrow.

THREE 'DETECTIVE' ANECDOTES

By Charles Dickens

In nearly all of Dickens' novels, crime and punishment are central elements and the detective is a familiar figure under such names as Nadgett in Martin Chuzzlewit *(1844),* Inspector Bucket in Bleak House *(1853), and Dick Datchery in* The Mystery of Edwin Drood *(1870). Dickens also interviewed members of the London Detective Force and accompanied them on their rounds, publishing the results of these experiences in* Houshold Words, *a weekly magazine he edited from 1850 to 1859. "Three 'Detective' Anecdotes" is one of these articles; its "Inspector Wield" is a thinly disguised portrait of the then well-known Inspector Charles Frederick Field, on whom Dickens is supposed to have modeled the character of Bucket in* Bleak House. *Other* Household Words *detective articles include "The Detective Police" and "On Duty with Inspector Field," collected in* Reprinted Pieces *(1858).*

I. THE PAIR OF GLOVES

"It's a singler story, sir," said Inspector Wield, of the Detective Police, who, in company with Sergeants Dornton and Mith, paid us another twilight visit, one July evening; "and I've been thinking you might like to know it.

"It's concerning the murder of the young woman, Eliza Grimwood, some years ago, over in the Waterloo Road. She was commonly called The Countess, because of her handsome appearance and her proud way of carrying of herself; and when I saw the poor Countess (I had known her well to speak to), lying dead, with her throat cut, on the floor of her bedroom, you'll believe me that a variety of reflections calculated to make a man rather low in his spirits, came into my head.

"That's neither here nor there. I went to the house the morning after the murder, and examined the body, and made a general observation of the bedroom where it was. Turning down the pillow of the bed with my hand, I found, underneath it, a pair of gloves. A pair of gentleman's dress gloves, very dirty; and inside the lining, the letters TR, and a cross.

"Well, sir, I took them gloves away, and I showed 'em to the magistrate, over at Union Hall, before whom the case was. He says, 'Wield,' he says, 'there's no doubt this is a discovery that may lead to something very important; and what you have got to do, Wield, is to find out the owner of these gloves.'

"I was of the same opinion, of course, and I went at it immediately. I looked at the gloves pretty narrowly, and it was my opinion that they had been cleaned. There was a smell of sulphur and rosin about 'em, you know, which cleaned gloves usually have, more or less. I took 'em over to a friend of mine at Kennington, who was in that line, and I put it to him. 'What do you say now? Have these gloves been cleaned?' 'These gloves have been cleaned,' says he. 'Have you any idea who cleaned them?' says I. 'Not at all,' says he; 'I've a very distinct idea who *didn't* clean 'em, and that's myself. But I'll tell you what, Wield, there ain't above eight or nine reg'lar glove-cleaners in London,'—there were not, at that time, it seems—'and I think I can give you their addresses, and you may find out, by that means, who did clean 'em.' Accordingly, he gave me the directions, and I went here, and I went there, and I looked up this man, and I looked up that man; but, though they all agreed that the gloves had been cleaned, I couldn't find the man, woman, or child, that had cleaned that aforesaid pair of gloves.

"What with this person not being at home, and that person being expected home in the afternoon, and so forth, the inquiry took me three days. On the evening of the third day, coming over Waterloo Bridge from the Surrey side of the river, quite beat, and very much vexed and disappointed, I thought I'd have a shilling's worth of entertainment at the Lyceum Theatre to freshen myself up. So I went into the Pit, at half-price, and I sat myself down next to a very quiet, modest sort of young man. Seeing I was a stranger (which I thought it just as well to appear to be) he told me the names of the actors on the stage, and we got into conversation. When the play was over, we came out together, and I said, 'We've been very companionable and agreeable, and perhaps you wouldn't object to a drain?' 'Well, you're very good,' says he; 'I *shouldn't* object to a drain.' Accordingly, we went to a public-house, near the Theatre, sat ourselves down in a quiet room up-stairs on the first floor, and called for a pint of half-and-half apiece, and a pipe.

"Well, sir, we put our pipes aboard, and we drank our half-and-half, and sat a-talking, very sociably, when the young man says, 'You must excuse me stopping very long,' he says, 'because I'm forced to go home in good time. I must be at work all night.' 'At work all night?' says I. 'You ain't a baker?' 'No,' he says, laughing, 'I ain't a baker.' 'I thought not,' says I, 'you haven't the looks of a baker.' 'No,' says he, 'I'm a glove-cleaner.'

"I never was more astonished in my life, than when I heard them words come out of his lips. 'You're a glove-cleaner, are you?' says I. 'Yes,' he says, 'I am.' 'Then, perhaps,' says I, taking the gloves out of my pocket, 'you can tell me who cleaned this pair of gloves? It's a rum story,' I says. 'I was dining over at Lambeth, the other day, at a free-and-easy—quite promiscuous—with a public company—when some gentleman, he left these gloves behind him! Another gentleman and me, you see, we laid a wager of a sovereign, that I wouldn't find out who they belonged to. I've spent as much as seven shillings already, in trying to discover; but, if you could help me, I'd stand another seven and welcome. You see there's TR and a cross inside.' '*I* see,' he says. 'Bless you, *I* know these gloves very well! I've seen dozens of pairs belonging to the same party.' 'No?' says I. 'Yes,' says he. 'Then you know who cleaned 'em?' says I. 'Rather so,' says he. 'My father cleaned 'em.'

"'Where does your father live?' says I. 'Just round the corner,' says the young man, 'near Exeter Street, here. He'll tell you who they belong to, directly.' 'Would you come round with me now?' says I. 'Certainly,' says he, 'but you needn't tell my father that you found me at the play, you know, because he mightn't like it.' 'All right!' We went round to the place, and there we found an old man in a white apron, with two or three daughters, all rubbing and cleaning away at lots of gloves, in a front parlour. 'Oh, Father!' says the young man, 'here's a person been and made a bet about the ownership of a pair of gloves, and I've told him you can settle it.' 'Good evening, sir,' says I to the old gentleman. 'Here's the gloves your son speaks of. Letters TR, you see, and a cross.' 'Oh yes,' he says, 'I know these gloves very well; I've cleaned dozens of pairs of 'em. They belong to Mr. Trinkle, the great upholsterer in Cheapside.' 'Did you get 'em from Mr. Trinkle, direct,' says I, 'if you'll excuse my asking the question?' 'No,' says he; 'Mr. Trinkle always sends 'em to Mr. Phibbs's, the haberdasher's, opposite his shop, and the haberdasher sends 'em to me.' 'Perhaps *you* wouldn't object to a drain?' says I. 'Not in the least!' says he. So I took the old gentleman out, and had a little more talk with him and his son, over a glass, and we parted ex-cellent friends.

"This was late on a Saturday night. First thing on the Monday morning, I went to the haberdasher's shop, opposite Mr. Trinkle's, the great upholsterer's in Cheapside. 'Mr. Phibbs in the way?' 'My name is Phibbs.' 'Oh! I believe you sent this pair of gloves to be cleaned?' 'Yes, I did, for young Mr. Trinkle over the way. There he is in the shop!' 'Oh! that's him in the shop, is it? Him in the green coat?' 'The same individual.' 'Well, Mr. Phibbs, this is an unpleasant affair; but the fact is, I am Inspector Wield of the Detective Police, and I found these gloves under the pillow of the young woman that was murdered the other day, over in the Waterloo Road.' 'Good Heaven!' says he. 'He's a most respectable young man, and if his father was to hear of it, it would be the ruin of him!' 'I'm very sorry for it,' says I, 'but I must take him into custody.' 'Good Heaven!' says Mr. Phibbs, again; 'can nothing be done!' 'Nothing,' says I. 'Will you allow me to call him over here,' says he, 'that his father may not see it done?' 'I don't object to that,' says I; 'but unfortunately, Mr. Phibbs, I can't allow of any communication between you. If any was attempted, I should have to interfere directly. Perhaps you'll beckon him over here?' Mr. Phibbs went to the door and beckoned, and the young fellow came across the street directly; a smart, brisk young fellow.

"'Good morning, sir,' says I. 'Good morning, sir,' says he. 'Would you allow me to inquire, sir,' says I, 'if you ever had any acquaintance with a party of the name of Grimwood?' 'Grimwood! Grimwood!' says he. 'No!' 'You know the Waterloo Road?' 'Oh! Of course I know the Waterloo Road!' 'Happen to have heard of a young woman being murdered there?' 'Yes, I read it in the paper, and very sorry I was to read it.' 'Here's a pair of gloves belonging to you, that I found under her pillow the morning afterwards!'

"He was in a dreadful state, sir; a dreadful state! 'Mr. Wield,' he says, 'upon my solemn oath I never was there. I never so much as saw her, to my knowledge, in my life!' 'I am very sorry,' says I. 'To tell you the truth; I don't think you *are* the murderer, but I must take you to Union Hall in a cab. However, I think it's a case of that sort, that, at present, at all events, the magistrate will hear it in private.'

"A private examination took place, and then it came out that this young man was acquainted with a cousin of the unfortunate Eliza Grimwood, and that, calling to see this cousin a day or two before the murder, he left these gloves upon the table. Who should come in, shortly afterwards, but Eliza Grimwood! 'Whose gloves are these?' she says, taking 'em up. 'Those are Mr. Trinkle's gloves,' says her cousin. 'Oh!' says she, 'they are very dirty, and of no use to him, I am sure. I shall take 'em away for my girl to clean the stoves with.' And she put 'em in her pocket. The girl had used 'em to clean the stoves, and, I have no doubt, had left 'em lying on the bedroom mantelpiece, or on the drawers, or somewhere; and her mistress, looking round to see that the room was tidy, had caught 'em up and put 'em under the pillow where I found 'em.

"That's the story, sir."

II. THE ARTFUL TOUCH

"One of the most *beautiful* things that ever was done, perhaps," said Inspector Wield, emphasising the adjective, as preparing us to expect dexterity or ingenuity rather than strong interest, "was a move of Sergeant Witchem's. It was a lovely idea!

"Witchem and me were down at Epsom one Derby Day, waiting at the station for the Swell Mob. As I mentioned, when we were talking about these things before, we are ready at the station when there's races, or an Agricultural Show, or a Chancellor sworn in for an university, or Jenny Lind, or anything of that sort; and as the Swell Mob came down, we send 'em back again by the next train. But some of the Swell Mob, on the occasion of this Derby that I refer to, so far kidded us as to hire a horse and shay; start away from London by Whitechapel, and miles round; come into Epsom from the opposite direction; and go to work, right and left, on the course, while we were waiting for 'em at the Rail. That, however, ain't the point of what I'm going to tell you.

"While Witchem and me were waiting at the station, there comes up one Mr. Tatt; a gentleman formerly in the public line, quite an amateur Detective in his way, and very much respected. 'Halloa, Charley Wield,' he says. 'What are you doing here? On the look out for some of your old friends?' 'Yes, the old move, Mr. Tatt.' 'Come along,' he

40

says, 'you and Witchem, and have a glass of sherry.' 'We can't stir from the place,' says I, 'till the next train comes in; but after that, we will with pleasure.' Mr. Tatt waits, and the train comes in, and then Witchem and me go off with him to the Hotel. Mr. Tatt he's got up quite regardless of expense, for the occasion; and in his shirt-front there's a beautiful diamond prop, cost him fifteen or twenty pound—a very handsome pin indeed. We drink our sherry at the bar, and have had our three or four glasses, when Witchem cries suddenly, 'Look out, Mr. Wield! stand fast!' and a dash is made into the place by the Swell Mob—four of 'em—that have come down as I tell you, and in a moment Mr. Tatt's prop is gone! Witchem, he cuts 'em off at the door, I lay about me as hard as I can, Mr. Tatt shows fight like a good 'un, and there we are, all down together, heads and heels, knocking about on the floor of the bar—perhaps you never see such a scene of confusion! However, we stick to our men (Mr. Tatt being as good as any officer), and we take 'em all, and carry 'em off to the station. The station's full of people, who have been took on the course; and it's a precious piece of work to get 'em secured. However, we do it at last, and we search 'em; but nothing's found upon 'em, and they're locked up; and a pretty state of heat we are in by that time, I assure you!

"I was very blank over it, myself, to think that the prop had been passed away; and I said to Witchem, when we had set 'em to rights, and were cooling ourselves along with Mr. Tatt, 'we don't take much by this move, anyway, for nothing's found upon 'em, and it's only the braggadocia[1], after all.' 'What do you mean, Mr. Wield?' says Witchem. 'Here's the diamond pin!' and in the palm of his hand there it was, safe and sound! 'Why, in the name of wonder,' says me and Mr. Tatt, in astonishment, 'how did you come by that?' 'I'll tell you how I come by it,' says he. 'I saw which of 'em took it; and when we were all down on the floor together, knocking about, I just gave him a little touch on the back of his hand, as I knew his pal would; and he thought it WAS his pal; and gave it me!' It was beautiful, beau-ti-ful!

"Even that was hardly the best of the case, for that chap was tried at the Quarter Sessions at Guildford. You know what Quarter Sessions are, sir. Well, if you'll believe me, while them slow justices were looking over the Acts of Parliament, to see what they could do to him, I'm blowed if he didn't cut out of the dock before their faces! He cut out of the dock, sir, then and there; swam across a river; and got up into a tree to dry himself. In the tree he was took—an old woman having seen him climb up—and Witchem's artful touch transported him!"

---

[1]Three month's imprisonment as reputed thieves.

III. THE SOFA

"What young men will do, sometimes, to ruin themselves and break their friends' hearts," said Sergeant Dornton, "it's surprising! I had a case at Saint Blank's Hospital which was of this sort. A bad case, indeed, with a bad end!"

"The Secretary, and the House-Surgeon, and the Treasurer, of Saint Blank's Hospital, came to Scotland Yard to give information of numerous robberies having been committed on the students. The students could leave nothing in the pockets of their great-coats, while the great-coats were hanging at the hospital, but it was almost certain to be stolen. Property of various descriptions was constantly being lost; and the gentlemen were naturally uneasy about it, and anxious, for the credit of the institution, that the thief or thieves should be discovered. The case was entrusted to me, and I went to the hospital.

"'Now, gentlemen,' said I, after we had talked it over; 'I understand this property is usually lost from one room.'

"Yes, they said. It was.

"'I should wish, if you please,' said I, 'to see the room.'

"It was a good-sized bare room down-stairs, with a few tables and forms in it, and a row of pegs, all round, for hats and coats.

"'Next, gentlemen,' said I, 'do you suspect anybody?'

"Yes, they said. They did suspect somebody. They were sorry to say, they suspected one of the porters.

"'I should like,' said I, 'to have that man pointed out to me, and to have a little time to look after him.'

"He was pointed out, and I looked after him, and then I went back to the hospital, and said, 'Now, gentlemen, it's not the porter. He's, unfortunately for himself, a little too fond of drink, but he's nothing worse. My suspicion is, that these robberies are committed by one of the students; and if you'll put me a sofa into that room where the pegs are—as there's no closet—I think I shall be able to detect the thief. I wish the sofa, if you please, to be covered with chintz, or something of that sort, so that I may lie on my chest, underneath it, without being seen.'

"The sofa was provided, and next day at eleven o'clock, before any of the students came, I went there, with those gentlemen, to get underneath it. It turned out to be one of those old-fashioned sofas with a great cross-beam at the bottom, that would have broken my back in no time if I could ever have got below it. We had quite a job to break all this away in the time; however, I fell to work, and they fell to work, and we broke it out, and made a clear place for me. I got under the sofa, lay down on my chest, took out my knife, and made a convenient hole in the chintz to look through. It was then settled between me and the gentlemen that when the students were all up in the wards, one of the gentlemen should come in, and hang up a great-coat on one of the pegs. And that that great-coat should have, in one of the pockets, a pocket-book containing marked money.

"After I had been there some time, the students began to drop into the room, by ones, and twos, and threes, and to talk about all sorts of things, little thinking there was anybody under the sofa—and then to go up-stairs. At last there came in one who remained until he was alone in the room by himself. A tallish, good-looking young man of one or two and twenty, with a light whisker. He went to a particular hatpeg, took off a good hat that was hanging there, tried it on, hung his own hat in its place, and hung that hat on another peg, nearly opposite to me. I then felt quite certain that he was the thief, and would come back by-and-by.

"When they were all upstairs, the gentleman came in with the great-coat. I showed him where to hang it, so that I might have a good view of it; and he went away; and I lay under the sofa on my chest, for a couple of hours or so, waiting.

"At last, the same young man came down. He walked across the room, whistling—stopped and listened—took another walk and whistled—stopped again, and listened—then began to go regularly round the pegs, feeling in the pockets of all the coats. When he came to THE great-coat, and felt the pocket-book, he was so eager and so hurried that he broke the strap in tearing it open. As he began to put the money in his pocket, I crawled out from under the sofa, and his eyes met mine.

"My face, as you may perceive, is brown now, but it was pale at that time, my health not being good; and looked as long as a horse's. Besides which, there was a great draught of air from the door, underneath the sofa, and I had tied a handkerchief round my head; so what I looked like, altogether, I don't know. He turned blue—literally blue—when he saw me crawling out, and I couldn't feel surprised at it.

"'I am an officer of the Detective Police,' said I, 'and have been lying here, since you first came in this morning. I regret, for the sake of yourself and your friends, that you should have done what you have; but this case is complete. You have the pocket-book in your hand and the money upon you; and I must take you into custody!'

"It was impossible to make out any case in his behalf, and on his trial he pleaded guilty. How or when he got the means I don't know;

but while he was awaiting his sentence, he poisoned himself in Newgate."

We inquired of this officer, on the conclusion of the foregoing anecdote, whether the time appeared long, or short, when he lay in that constrained position under the sofa?

"Why, you see, sir," he replied, "if he hadn't come in, the first time, and I had not been quite sure he was the thief, and would return, the time would have seemed long. But, as it was, I being dead certain of my man, the time seemed pretty short."

CHAPTER II

POE
AND THE FIRST
GREAT DETECTIVE

Edgar A Poe

MURDERS IN THE RUE MORGUE

By Edgar Allan Poe

Edgar Allan Poe (1809–1849), generally considered the father of the detective story, was born in Boston, but three years later he was taken to Richmond, Virginia after his parents died and he was adopted by John Allan. Between his sixth and eleventh years, Poe received a classical education in England and then returned with the Allan family to the United States where he continued his studies, first in a private school in Richmond and then at the University of Virginia. Withdrawn from the university in 1926 because of gambling debts, Poe ran away to Boston and joined the army. In the years that followed, he spent a brief time as a cadet at West Point, published two volumes of poetry, won a short story contest which brought him a job with the Southern Literary Messenger *in Richmond, and married his fourteen-year-old cousin Virginia Clemm. In 1834, John Allan died leaving nothing in his will for his foster son, and Poe embarked on a lifelong struggle with poverty. Though he skillfully edited several important magazines, and though works like "The Raven" and "The Gold-Bug" brought him a national reputation, he earned comparatively little from his literary efforts and constantly undermined his own success through arrogance and dissipation. From his wife's death in 1847 to his own two years later, Poe wrote almost nothing. He became involved in a number of more or less unhappy love affairs, apparently suffered periods of insanity, attempted suicide, and on October 7, 1849 was found on the streets of Baltimore in a delirious condition from which he never recovered. "The Murders in the Rue Morgue," the first of the tales of ratiocination with which Poe inaugurated the genre of the detective story and introduced his detective C. Auguste Dupin, originally appeared in* Graham's Lady's and Gentleman's Magazine *in April 1841.*

The mental features discoursed of as the analytical, are, in themselves, but little susceptible of analysis. We appreciate them only in their effects. We know of them, among other things, that they are always to their possessor, when inordinately possessed, a source of the liveliest enjoyment. As the strong man exults in his physical ability, delighting in such exercises as call his muscles into action, so glories the analyst in that moral activity which *disentangles*. He drives pleasure from even the most trivial occupations bringing his talent into play. He is fond of enigmas, of conundrums, hieroglyphics; exhibiting in his solutions of each a degree of *acumen* which appears to the ordinary apprehension præternatural. His results, brought about by the very soul and essence of method, have, in truth, the whole air of intuition.

The faculty of re-solution is possibly much invigorated by mathematical study, and especially by that highest branch of it which, unjustly, and merely on account of its retrograde operations, has been called, as if *par excellence*, analysis. Yet to calculate is not in itself to analyze. A chess player, for example, does the one, without effort at the other. It follows that the game of chess, in its effects upon mental character, is greatly misunderstood. I am not now writing a treatise, but simply prefacing a somewhat peculiar narrative by observations very much at random; I will, therefore, take occasion to assert that the higher powers of the reflective intellect are more decidedly and more usefully tasked by the unostentatious game of draughts than by all the elaborate frivolity of chess. In this latter, where the pieces have different and *bizarre* motions, with various and variable values, what is only complex, is mistaken (a not unusual error) for what is profound. The *attention* is here called powerfully into play. If it flag for an instant, an oversight is committed, resulting in injury or defeat. The possible moves being not only manifold, but involute, the chances of such oversights are multiplied; and in nine cases out of ten, it is the more concentrative rather than the more acute player who conquers. In draughts, on the contrary, where the moves are *unique* and have but little variation, the probabilities of inadvertence are diminished, and the mere attention being left comparatively unemployed, what advantages are obtained by either party are obtained by superior *acumen*. To be less abstract, let us suppose a game of draughts where the pieces are reduced to four kings, and where, of course, no oversight is to be expected. It is obvious that here the victory can be decided (the players being at all equal) only by some *recherché* movement, the result of some strong exertion of the intellect. Deprived of ordinary resources, the analyst throws himself into the spirit of his opponent, identifies himself therewith, and not unfrequently sees thus, at a glance, the sole

47

methods (sometimes indeed absurdly simple ones) by which he may seduce into error or hurry into miscalculation.

Whist has long been noted for its influence upon what is termed the calculating power; and men of the highest order of intellect have been known to take an apparently unaccountable delight in it, while eschewing chess as frivolous. Beyond doubt there is nothing of a similar nature so greatly tasking the faculty of analysis. The best chess-player in Christendom *may* be little more than the best player of chess; but proficiency in whist implies capacity for success in all those more important undertakings where mind struggles with mind. When I say proficiency, I mean that perfection in the game which includes a comprehension of *all* the sources whence legitimate advantage may be derived. These are not only manifold, but multiform, and lie frequently among recesses of thought altogether inaccessible to the ordinary understanding. To observe attentively is to remember distinctly; and, so far, the concentrative chess-player will do very well at whist; while the rules of Hoyle (themselves based upon the mere mechanism of the game) are sufficiently and generally comprehensible. Thus to have a retentive memory, and proceed by "the book" are points commonly regarded as the sum total of good playing. But it is in matters beyond the limits of mere rule that the skill of the analyst is evinced. He makes, in silence, a host of observations and inferences. So, perhaps, do his companions; and the difference in the extent of the information obtained, lies not so much in the validity of the inference as in the quality of the observation. The necessary knowledge is that of *what* to observe. Our player confines himself not at all; nor, because the game is the object, does he reject deductions from things external to the game. He examines the countenance of his partner, comparing it carefully with that of each of his opponents. He considers the mode of assorting the cards in each hand; often counting trump by trump, and honor by honor, through the glances bestowed by their holders upon each. He notes every variation of face as the play progresses, gathering a fund of thought from the differences in the expression of certainty, of surprise, of triumph, or chagrin. From the manner of gathering up a trick he judges whether the person taking it, can make another in the suit. He recognises what is played through feint, by the air with which it is thrown upon the table. A casual or inadvertent word; the accidental dropping or turning of a card, with the accompanying anxiety or carelessness in regard to its concealment; the counting of the tricks, with the order of their arrangement; embarrassment, hesitation, eagerness, or trepidation—all afford, to his apparently intuitive perception, indications of the true state of affairs. The first two or three rounds having been played, he is in full possession of the contents of each hand, and thenceforward puts down his cards with as absolute a precision of purpose as if the rest of the party had turned outward the faces of their own.

The analytical power should not be confounded with simple ingenuity; for while the analyst is necessarily ingenious, the ingenious man is often remarkably incapable of analysis. The constructive or combining power, by which ingenuity is usually manifested, and to which the phrenologists (I believe erroneously) have assigned a separate organ, supposing it a primitive faculty, has been so frequently seen in those whose intellect bordered otherwise upon idiocy, as to have attracted general observation among writers on morals. Between ingenuity and the analytic ability there exists a difference far greater, indeed, than that between the fancy and the imagination, but of a character very strictly analogous. It will be found, in fact, that the ingenious are always fanciful, and the *truly* imaginative never otherwise than analytic.

The narrative which follows will appear to the reader somewhat in the light of a commentary upon the propositions just advanced.

Residing in Paris during the spring and part of the summer of 18—, I there became acquainted with a Monsieur C. Auguste Dupin. This young gentleman was of an excellent, indeed of an illustrious family, but, by a variety of untoward events, had been reduced to such poverty that the energy of his character succumbed beneath it, and he ceased to bestir himself in the world, or to care for the retrieval of his fortunes. By courtesy of his creditors, there still remained in his possession a small remnant of his patrimony; and, upon the income arising from this, he managed, by means of a rigorous economy, to procure the necessaries of life, without troubling himself about its superfluities. Books, indeed, were his sole luxuries, and in Paris these are easily obtained.

Our first meeting was at an obscure library in the Rue Montmartre, where the accident of our both being in search of the same very rare and very remarkable volume, brought us into closer communion. We saw each other again and again. I was deeply interested in the little family history which he detailed to me with all that candor which a Frenchman indulges whenever mere self is his theme. I was astonished, too, at the vast extent of his reading; and, above all, I felt my soul enkindled within me by the wild fervor, and the vivid freshness of his imagination. Seeking in Paris the objects I then sought, I felt that the society of such a man would be to me a treasure beyond price; and this feeling I frankly confided to him. It was at length arranged that we should live together during my stay in the city; and as my worldly circumstances were somewhat less embarrassed than his own, I was permitted to be at the expense of renting, and furnishing in a style which suited the rather fantastic gloom of our common temper, a time-eaten and grotesque mansion, long deserted through superstitions into which we did not inquire, and tottering to its fall in a retired and desolate portion of the Faubourg St. Germain.

Had the routine of our life at this place been known to the world, we should have been regarded as madmen—although, perhaps, as madmen of a harmless nature. Our seclusion was perfect. We admitted no visitors. Indeed the locality of our retirement had been carefully kept a secret from my own former associates; and it had been many years since Dupin had ceased to know or be known in Paris. We existed within ourselves alone.

It was a freak of fancy in my friend (for what else shall I call it?) to be enamored of the night for her own sake; and into this *bizarrerie*, as into all his others, I quietly fell; giving myself up to his wild whims with a perfect *abandon*. The sable divinity would not herself dwell with us always; but we could counterfeit her presence. At the first dawn of the morning we closed all the massy shutters of our old building; lighting a couple of tapers which, strongly perfumed, threw out only the ghastliest and feeblest of rays. By the aid of these we then busied our souls in dreams—reading, writing, or conversing, until warned by the clock of the advent of the true Darkness. Then we sallied forth into the streets, arm in arm, continuing the topics of the day, or roaming far and wide until a late hour, seeking, amid the wild lights and shadows of the populous city, that infinity of mental excitement which quiet observation can afford.

At such times I could not help remarking and admiring (although from his rich ideality I had been prepared to expect it) a peculiar analytic ability in Dupin. He seemed, too, to take an eager delight in its exercise—if not exactly in its display—and did not hesitate to confess the pleasure thus derived. He boasted to me, with a low chuckling laugh, that most men, in respect to himself, wore windows in their bosoms, and was wont to follow up such assertions by direct and very startling proofs of his intimate knowledge of my own. His manner at these moments was frigid and abstract; his eyes were vacant in expression; while his voice, usually a rich tenor, rose into a treble which would have sounded petulantly but for the deliberateness and entire distinctness of the enunciation. Observing him in these moods, I often dwelt meditatively upon the old philosophy of the Bi-Part Soul, and amused myself with the fancy of a double Dupin—the creative and the resolvent.

Let it not be supposed, from what I have just said, that I am detailing any mystery, or penning any romance. What I have described in the Frenchman was merely the result of an excited, or perhaps of a diseased, intelligence, but of the character of his remarks at the periods in question an example will best convey the idea.

We were strolling one night down a long dirty street, in the vicinity of the Palais Royal. Being both, apparently, occupied with thought, neither of us had spoken a syllable for fifteen minutes at least. All at once Dupin broke forth with these words:

"He is a very little fellow, that's true, and would do better for the *Théâtre des Variétés*."

"There can be no doubt of that," I replied, unwittingly, and not at first observing (so much had I been absorbed in reflection) the extraordinary manner in which the speaker had chimed in with my meditations. In an instant afterward I recollected myself, and my astonishment was profound.

"Dupin," said I, gravely, "this is beyond my comprehension. I do not hesitate to say that I am amazed, and can scarcely credit my senses. How was it possible you should know I was thinking of ——?" Here I paused, to ascertain beyond a doubt whether he really knew of whom I thought.

"—— of Chantilly," said he, "why do you pause? You were remarking to yourself that his diminutive figure unfitted him for tragedy."

This was precisely what had formed the subject of my reflections. Chantilly was a *quondam* cobbler of the Rue St. Dennis, who, becoming stage-mad, had attempted the *rôle* of Xerxes, Crébillon's tragedy so called, and been notoriously Pasquinaded for his pains.

"Tell me, for Heaven's sake," I exclaimed, "the method—if method there is—by which you have been enabled to fathom my soul in this matter." In fact, I was even more startled than I would have been willing to express.

"It was the fruiterer," replied my friend, "who brought you to the conclusion that the mender of soles was not of sufficient height for Xerxes *et id genus omne*."

"The fruiterer!—you astonish me—I know no fruiterer whomsoever."

"The man who ran up against you as we entered the street—it may have been fifteen minutes ago."

I now remembered that, in fact, a fruiterer, carrying upon his head a large basket of apples, had nearly thrown me down, by accident, as we passed from the Rue C—— into the thoroughfare where we stood; but what this had to do with Chantilly I could not possibly understand.

51

There was not a particle of *charlatânerie* about Dupin. "I will explain," he said, "and that you may comprehend all clearly, we will first retrace the course of your meditations, from the moment in which I spoke to you until that of the *recontre* with the fruiterer in question. The larger links of the chain run thus—Chantilly, Orion, Dr. Nichols, Epicurus, Stereotomy, the street stones, the fruiterer."

There are few persons who have not, at some period of their lives, amused themselves in retracing their steps by which particular conclusions of their own minds have been attained. The occupation is often full of interest; and he who attempts it for the first time is astonished by the apparently illimitable distance and incoherence between the starting-point and the goal. What, then, must have been my amazement, when I heard the Frenchman speak what he had just spoken, and I could not help acknowledging that he had spoken the truth. He continued:

"We had been talking of horses, if I remember aright, just before leaving the Rue C——. This was the last subject we discussed. As we crossed into this street, a fruiterer, with a large basket upon his head, brushing quickly past us, thrust you upon a pile of paving-stones collected at a spot where the causeway is undergoing repair. You stepped upon one of the loose fragments, slipped, slightly strained your ankle, appeared vexed or sulky, muttered a few words, turned to look at the pile, and then proceeded in silence. I was not particularly attentive to what you did; but observation has become with me, of late, a species of necessity.

"You kept your eyes upon the ground—glancing, with a petulant expression, at the holes and ruts in the pavement, (so that I saw you were still thinking of the stones,) until we reached the little alley called Lamartine, which has been paved, by way of experiment, with the overlapping and riveted blocks. Here your countenance brightened up, and, perceiving your lips move, I could not doubt that you murmured the word 'stereotomy,' a term very affectedly applied to this species of pavement. I knew that you could not say to yourself 'stereotomy' without being brought to think of atomies, and thus of the theories of Epicurus; and since, when we discussed this subject not very long ago, I mentioned to you how singularly, yet with how little notice, the vague guesses of that noble Greek had met with confirmation in the late nebular cosmogony, I felt that you could not avoid casting your eyes upward to the great *nebula* in Orion, and I certainly expected that you would do so. You did look up; and I was now assured that I had correctly followed your steps. But in that bitter *tirade* upon Chantilly, which appeared in yesterday's 'Musée,' the satirist, making some disgraceful allusions to the cobbler's change of name upon assuming the buskin, quoted a Latin line about which we have often conversed. I mean the line

Perdidit antiquum litera prima sonum.

I had told you that this was in reference to Orion, formerly written Urion; and, from certain pungencies connected with this explanation, I was aware that you could not have forgotten it. It was clear, therefore, that you would not fail to combine the two ideas of Orion and Chantilly. That you did combine them I saw by the character of the smile which passed over your lips. You thought of the poor cobbler's immolation. So far, you had been stooping in your gait; but now I saw you draw yourself up to your full height. I was then sure that you reflected upon the diminutive figure of Chantilly. At this point I interrupted your meditations to remark that as, in fact, he *was* a very little fellow—that Chantilly—he would do better at the *Théâtre des Variétés.*"

Not long after this, we were looking over an evening edition of the *Gazette des Tribunaux*, when the following paragraphs arrested our attention.

"EXTRAORDINARY MURDERS.—This morning, about three o'clock, the inhabitants of the Quartier St. Roch were roused from sleep by a succession of terrific shrieks, issuing, apparently, from the fourth story of a house in the Rue Morgue, known to be in the sole occupancy of one Madame L'Espanaye, and her daughter, Mademoiselle Camille L'Espanaye. After some delay, occasioned by a fruitless attempt to procure admission in the usual manner, the gateway was broken in with a crowbar, and eight or ten of the neighbors entered, accompanied by two *gendarmes.* By this time the cries had ceased; but, as the party rushed up the first flight of stairs, two or more rough voices, in angry contention, were distinguished, and seemed to proceed from the upper part of the house. As the second landing was reached, these sounds, also, had ceased, and every thing remained perfectly quiet. The party spread themselves, and hurried from room to room. Upon arriving at a large back chamber in the fourth story, (the door of which, being found locked, with the key inside, was forced open,) a spectacle presented itself which struck every one present not less with horror than with astonishment.

"The apartment was in the wildest disorder—the furniture broken and thrown about in all directions. There was only one bedstead; and from this the bed had been removed, and thrown into the middle of the floor. On a chair lay a razor, besmeared with blood. On the hearth were two or three long and thick tresses of gray human hair, also dabbled with blood, and seeming to have been pulled out by the roots. Upon the floor were found four Napoleons, an ear-ring of topaz, three large silver spoons, three smaller of *métal d'Alger*, and two bags, containing nearly four thousand francs in gold. The drawers of a *bureau*, which stood in one corner, were open, and had been, apparently, rifled, although many articles still remained in them. A small iron safe was discovered under the *bed* (not under the bedstead). It was open, with the key still in the door. It had no contents beyond a few old letters, and other papers of little consequence.

"Of Madame L'Espanaye no traces were here seen; but an unusual quantity of soot being observed in the fireplace, a search was made in the chimney, and (horrible to relate!) the corpse of the daughter, head downward, was dragged therefrom; it having been thus forced up the narrow aperture for a considerable distance. The body was quite warm. Upon examining it, many excoriations were perceived, no doubt occasioned by the violence with which it had been thrust up and disengaged. Upon the face were many severe scratches, and, upon the throat, dark bruises, and deep indentations of finger nails, as if the deceased had been throttled to death.

"After a thorough investigation of every portion of the house without farther discovery, the party made its way into a small paved yard in the rear of the building, where lay the corpse of the old lady, with her throat so entirely cut that, upon an attempt to raise her, the head fell off. The body, as well as the head, was fearfully mutilated— the former so much so as scarcely to retain any semblance of humanity.

"To this horrible mystery there is not as yet, we believe, the slightest clew."

The next day's paper had these additional particulars:

"*The Tragedy in the Rue Morgue.*—Many individuals have been examined in relation to this most extraordinary and frightful affair," [the word '*affaire*' has not yet, in France, that levity of import which it conveys with us] "but nothing whatever has transpired to throw light upon it. We give below all the material testimony elicited.

"*Pauline Dubourg*, laundress, deposes that she has known both the deceased for three years, having washed for them during that period. The old lady and her daughter seemed on good terms—very affectionate toward each other. They were excellent pay. Could not speak in regard to their mode or means of living. Believed that Madame L. told fortunes for a living. Was reputed to have money put by. Never met any person in the house when she called for the clothes or took them home. Was sure that they had no servant in employ. There appeared to be no furniture in any part of the building except in the fourth story.

"*Pierre Moreau*, tobacconist, deposes that he has been in the habit of selling small quantities of tobacco and snuff to Madame L'Espanaye for nearly four years. Was born in the neighborhood, and has always resided there. The deceased and her daughter had occupied the house in which the corpses were found, for more than six years. It was formerly occupied by a jeweller, who under-let the upper rooms to various persons. The house was the property of Madame L. She became dissatisfied with the abuse of the premises by her tenant, and moved into them herself, refusing to let any portion. The old lady was childish. Witness had seen the daughter some five or six times during the six years. The two lived an exceedingly retired life—were reputed to have money. Had heard it said among the neighbors that Madame L. told fortunes—did not believe it. Had never seen any person enter the door except the old lady and her daughter, a porter once or twice, and a physician some eight or ten times.

"Many other persons, neighbors, gave evidence to the same effect. No one was spoken of as frequenting the house. It was not known whether there were any living connections of Madame L. and her daughter. The shutters of the front windows were seldom opened. Those in the rear were always closed, with the exception of the large back room, fourth story. The house was a good house—not very old.

"*Isidore Musèt, gendarme*, deposes that he was called to the house about three o'clock in the morning, and found some twenty or thirty persons at the gateway, endeavoring to gain admittance. Forced it open, at length, with a bayonet—not with a crowbar. Had but little difficulty in getting it open, on account of its being a double or folding gate, and bolted neither at bottom nor top. The shrieks were continued until the gate was forced—and then suddenly ceased. They seemed to be screams of some person (or persons) in great agony—were loud and drawn out, not short and quick. Witness led the way up stairs. Upon reaching the first landing, heard two voices in loud and angry contention—the one a gruff voice, the other much shriller—a very strange voice. Could distinguish some words of the former, which was that of a Frenchman. Was positive that it was not a woman's voice. Could distinguish the words '*sacré*' and '*diable*.' The shrill voice was that of a foreigner. Could not be sure whether it was the voice of a man or of a woman. Could not make out what was said, but believed the language to be Spanish. The state of the room and of the bodies was described by this witness as we described them yesterday.

"*Henri Duval*, a neighbor, and by trade a silver-smith, deposes that he was one of the party who first entered the house. Corroborates the testimony of Musèt in general. As soon as they forced an entrance, they reclosed the door, to keep out the crowd, which collected very fast, notwithstanding the lateness of the hour. The shrill voice, this witness thinks, was that of an Italian. Was certain it was not French. Could not be sure that it was a man's voice. It might have been a woman's. Was not acquainted with the Italian language. Could not distinguish the words, but was convinced by the intonation that the speaker was an Italian. Knew Madame L. and her daughter. Had conversed with both frequently. Was sure that the shrill voice was not that of either of the deceased.

"—— *Odenheimer, restaurateur.*—This witness volunteered his testimony. Not speaking French, was examined through an interpreter. Is a native of Amsterdam. Was passing the house at the time of the shrieks. They lasted for several minutes—probably ten. They were long and loud—very awful and distressing. Was one of those who entered the building. Corroborated the previous evidence in every respect but one. Was sure that the shrill voice was that of a man—of a Frenchman. Could not distinguish the words uttered. They were loud and quick—unequal—spoken apparently in fear as well as in anger. The voice was harsh—not so much shrill as harsh. Could not call it a shrill voice. The gruff voice said repeatedly, '*sacré,*' '*diable,*' and once '*mon Dieu.*'

"*Jules Mignaud*, banker, of the firm of Mignaud et Fils, Rue Deloraine. Is the elder Mignaud. Madame L'Espanaye had some property. Had opened an account with his banking house in the spring of the year—(eight years previously). Made frequent deposits in small sums. Had checked for nothing until the third day before her death, when she took out in person the sum of 4000 francs. This sum was paid in gold, and a clerk sent home with the money.

"*Adolphe Le Bon*, clerk to Mignaud et Fils, deposes that on the day in question, about noon, he accompanied Madame L'Espanaye to her residence with the 4000 francs, put up in two bags. Upon the door being opened, Mademoiselle L. appeared and took from his hands one of the bags, while the old lady relieved him of the other. He then bowed and departed. Did not see any person in the street at the time. It is a by-street—very lonely.

"*William Bird*, tailor, deposes that he was one of the party who entered the house. Is an Englishmen. Has lived in Paris two years. Was one of the first to ascend the stairs. Heard the voices in contention. The gruff voice was that of a Frenchman. Could make out several words, but cannot now remember all. Heard distinctly '*sacré*' and '*mon Dieu.*' There was a sound at the moment as if of several persons struggling—a scraping and scuffling sound. The shrill voice was very loud—louder than the gruff one. Is sure that it was not the voice of an Englishman. Appeared to be that of a German. Might have been a woman's voice. Does not understand German.

"Four of the above-named witnesses being recalled, deposed that the door of the chamber in which was found the body of Mademoiselle L. was locked on the inside when the party reached it. Every thing was perfectly silent—no groans or noises of any kind. Upon forcing the door no person was seen. The windows, both of the back and front room, were down and firmly fastened from within. A door between the two rooms was closed but not locked. The door leading from the front room into the passage was locked, with the key on the inside. A small room in the front of the house, on the fourth story, at the head of the passage, was open, the door being ajar. This room was crowded with old beds, boxes, and so forth. These were carefully removed and searched. There was not an inch of any portion of the house which was not carefully searched. Sweeps were sent up and down the chimneys. The house was a four-story one, with garrets (*mansardes*). A trap-door on the roof was nailed down very securely—did not appear to have been opened for years. The time elapsing between the hearing of the voices in contention and the breaking open of the room door was variously stated by the witnesses. Some made it as short as three minutes—some as long as five. The door was opened with difficulty.

"*Alfonzo Garcio*, undertaker, deposes that he resides in the Rue Morgue. Is a native of Spain. Was one of the party who entered the house. Did not proceed up stairs. Is nervous, and was apprehensive of the consequences of agitation. Heard the voices in contention. The gruff voice was that of a Frenchman. Could not distinguish what was said. The shrill voice was that of an Englishman—is sure of this. Does not understand the English language, but judges by the intonation.

"*Alberto Montani*, confectioner, deposes that he was among the first to ascend the stairs. Heard the voices in question. The gruff voice was that of a Frenchman. Distinguished several words. The speaker appeared to be expostulating. Could not make out the words of the shrill voice. Spoke quick and unevenly. Thinks it the voice of a Russian. Corroborates the general testimony. Is an Italian. Never conversed with a native of Russia.

"Several witnesses, recalled, here testified that the chimneys of all the rooms on the fourth story were too narrow to admit the passage of a human being. By 'sweeps' were meant cylindrical sweeping-brushes, such as are employed by those who clean chimneys. These brushes were passed up and down every flue in the house. There is no back passage by which any one could have descended while the party proceeded up stairs. The body of Mademoiselle L'Espanaye was so firmly wedged in the chimney that it could not be got down until four or five of the party united their strength.

"*Paul Dumas*, physician, deposes that he was called to view the bodies about daybreak. They were both then lying on the sacking of the bedstead in the chamber where Mademoiselle L. was found. The corpse of the young lady was much bruised and excoriated. The fact that it had been thrust up the chimney would sufficiently account for these appearances. The throat was greatly chafed. There were several deep scratches just below the chin, together with a series of livid spots which were evidently the impression of fingers. The face was fearfully discolored, and the eyeballs protruded. The tongue had been partially bitten through. A large bruise was discovered upon the pit of the stomach, produced, apparently, by the pressure of a knee. In the opinion of M. Dumas, Mademoiselle L'Espanaye had been throttled to death by some person or persons unknown. The corpse of the mother was horribly mutilated. All the bones of the right leg and arm were more or less shattered. The left *tibia* much splintered, as well as all the ribs of the left side. Whole body dreadfully bruised and discolored. It was not possible to say how the injuries had been inflicted. A heavy club of wood, or a broad bar of iron—a chair—any large, heavy, and obtuse weapon would have produced such results if wielded by the hands of a very powerful man. No woman could have inflicted the blows with any weapon. The head of the deceased, when seen by witness, was entirely separated from the body, and was also greatly shattered. The throat had evidently been cut with some very sharp instrument—probably with a razor.

"*Alexandre Etienne*, surgeon, was called with M. Dumas to view the bodies. Corroborated the testimony and the opinions of M. Dumas.

"Nothing further of importance was elicited, although several other persons were examined. A murder so mysterious, and so perplexing in all its particulars, was never before committed in Paris—if indeed a murder has been committed at all. The police are entirely at fault—an unusual occurrence in affairs of this nature. There is not, however, the shadow of a clew apparent."

The evening edition of the paper stated that the greatest excitement still continued in the Quartier St. Roch—that the premises in question had been carefully re-searched, and fresh examinations of witnesses instituted, but all to no purpose. A postscript, however, mentioned that Adolphe Le Bon had been arrested and imprisoned—although nothing appeared to criminate him beyond the facts already detailed.

Dupin seemed singularly interested in the progress of this affair—at least so I judged from his manner, for he made no comments. It was only after the announcement that Le Bon had been imprisoned, that he asked me my opinion respecting the murders.

I could merely agree with all Paris in considering them an insoluble mystery. I saw no means by which it would be possible to trace the murderer.

"We must not judge of the means," said Dupin, "by this shell of an examination. The Parisian police, so much extolled for *acumen*, are cunning, but no more. There is no method in their proceedings, beyond the method of the moment. They make a vast parade of measures; but, not unfrequently, these are so ill-adapted to the objects proposed, as to put us in mind of Monsieur Jordain's calling for his *robe-de-chambre—pour mieux entendre la musique*. The results attained by them are not unfrequently surprising, but, for the most part, are brought about by simple diligence and activity. When these qualities are unavailing, their schemes fail. Vidocq, for example, was a good guesser, and a persevering man. But, without educated thought, he erred continually by the very intensity of his investigations. He impaired his vision by holding the object too close. He might see, perhaps, one or two points with unusual clearness, but in so doing he, necessarily, lost sight of the matter as a whole. Thus there is such a thing as being too profound. Truth is not always in a well. In fact, as regards the more important knowledge, I do believe that she is invariably superficial. The depth lies in the valleys where we seek her, and not upon the mountain-tops where she is found. The modes and sources of this kind of error are well typified in the contemplation of the heavenly bodies. To look at a star by glances—to view it in a side-long way, by turning toward it the exterior portions of the *retina* (more susceptible of feeble impressions of light than the interior), is to behold the star distinctly—is to have the best appreciation of its lustre—a lustre which grows dim just in proportion as we turn our vision *fully* upon it. A greater number of rays actually fall upon the eye in the latter case, but in the former, there is the more refined capacity for comprehension. By undue profundity we perplex and enfeeble thought; and it is possible to make even Venus herself vanish from the firmanent by a scrutiny too sustained, too concentrated, or too direct.

"As for these murders, let us enter into some examinations for ourselves, before we make up an opinion respecting them. An inquiry will afford us amusement," [I thought this an odd term, so applied, but said nothing] "and besides, Le Bon once rendered me a service for which I am not ungrateful. We will go and see the premises with our own eyes. I know G——, the Prefect of Police, and shall have no difficulty in obtaining the necessary permission."

The permission was obtained, and we proceeded at once to the Rue Morgue. This is one of those miserable thoroughfares which intervene between the Rue Richelieu and the Rue St. Roch. It was late in the afternoon when we reached it, as this quarter is at a great distance from that in which we resided. The house was readily found; for there were still many persons gazing up at the closed shutters, with an objectless curiosity, from the opposite side of the way. It was an ordinary Parisian house, with a gateway, on one side of which was a glazed watch-box, with a sliding panel in the window, indicating a *loge de concierge*. Before going in we walked up the street, turned down an alley, and then, again turning, passed in the rear of the building— Dupin, meanwhile, examining the whole neighborhood, as well as the house, with a minuteness of attention for which I could see no possible object.

Retracing our steps we came again to the front of the dwelling, rang, and having shown our credentials, were admitted by the agents in charge. We went up stairs—into the chamber where the body of Mademoiselle L'Espanaye had been found, and where both the deceased still lay. The disorders of the room had, as usual, been suffered to exist. I saw nothing beyond what had been stated in the *Gazette des Tribunaux*. Dupin scrutinized every thing—not excepting the bodies of the victims. We then went into the other rooms, and into the yard; a *gendarme* accompanying us throughout. The examination occupied us until dark, when we took our departure. On our way home my companion stepped in for a moment at the office of one of the daily papers.

I have said that the whims of my friend were manifold, and that *Je les ménageais:* —for this phrase there is no English equivalent. It was his humor, now, to decline all conversation on the subject of the murder, until about noon the next day. He then asked me, suddenly, if I had observed any thing *peculiar* at the scene of the atrocity.

There was something in his manner of emphasizing the word "peculiar," which caused me to shudder, without knowing why.

"No, nothing *peculiar*," I said; "nothing more, at least, than we both saw stated in the paper."

"The *Gazette*," he replied, "has not entered, I fear, into the unusual horror of the thing. But dismiss the idle opinions of this print. It appears to me that this mystery is considered insoluble, for the very reason which should cause it to be regarded as easy of solution—I mean for the *outré* character of its features. The police are confounded by the seeming absence of motive—not for the murder itself—but for the atrocity of the murder. They are puzzled, too, by the seeming impossibility of reconciling the voices heard in contention, with the facts that no one was discovered upstairs but the assassinated Mademoiselle L'Espanaye, and that there were no means of egress without the notice of the party ascending. The wild disorder of the room; the corpse thrust, with the head downward, up the chimney; the frightful mutilation of the body of the old lady; these considerations, with those just mentioned, and others which I need not mention, have sufficed to paralyze the powers, by putting completely at fault the boasted *acumen*, of the government agents. They have fallen into the gross but common error of confounding the unusual with the abstruse. But it is by these deviations from the plane of the ordinary, that reason feels its way, if at all, in its search for the true. In investigations such as we are now pursuing, it should not be so much asked 'what has occurred,' as 'what has occurred that has never occurred before.' In fact, the facility with which I shall arrive, or have arrived, at the solution of this mystery, is in the direct ratio of its apparent insolubility in the eyes of the police."

I stared at the speaker in mute astonishment.

"I am now awaiting," continued he, looking toward the door of our apartment—"I am now awaiting a person who, although perhaps not the perpetrator of these butcheries, must have been in some measure implicated in their perpetration. Of the worst portion of the crimes committed, it is probable that he is innocent. I hope that I am right in this supposition; for upon it I build my expectation of reading the entire riddle. I look for the man here—in this room—every moment. It is true that he may not arrive; but the probability is that he will. Should he come, it will be necessary to detain him. Here are pistols; and we both know how to use them when occasion demands their use."

I took the pistols, scarcely knowing what I did, or believing what I heard, while Dupin went on, very much as if in a soliloquy. I have already spoken of his abstract manner at such times. His discourse was addressed to myself; but his voice, although by no means loud, had that intonation which is commonly employed in speaking to some one at a great distance. His eyes, vacant in expression, regarded only the wall.

"That the voices heard in contention," he said, "by the party upon the stairs, were not the voices of the women themselves, was fully proved by the evidence. This relieves us of all doubt upon the question whether the old lady could have first destroyed the daughter, and afterward have committed suicide. I speak of this point chiefly for the sake of method; for the strength of Madame L'Espanaye would have been utterly unequal to the task of thrusting her daughter's corpse up the chimney as it was found; and the nature of the wounds upon her own person entirely precludes the idea of self-destruction. Murder, then, has been committed by some third party; and the voices of this third party were those heard in contention. Let me now advert—not to the whole testimony respecting these voices—but to what was *peculiar* in that testimony. Did you observe any thing peculiar about it.?"

I remarked that, while all the witnesses agreed in supposing the gruff voice to be that of a Frenchman, there was much disagreement in regard to the shrill, or, as one individual termed it, the harsh voice.

"That was the evidence itself," said Dupin, "but it was not the peculiarity of the evidence. You have observed nothing distinctive. Yet there *was* something to be observed. The witnesses, as you remark, agreed about the gruff voice; they were here unanimous. But in regard to the shrill voice, the peculiarty is—not that they disagreed—but that, while an Italian, an Englishman, a Spaniard, a Hollander, and a Frenchman attempted to describe it, each one spoke of it as that *of a foreigner*. Each is sure that it was not the voice of one of his own countrymen. Each likens it—not to the voice of an individual of any nation with whose language he is conversant—but the converse. The Frenchman supposes it the voice of a Spaniard, and 'might have distin-guished some words *had he been acquainted with the Spanish.*' The Dutchman maintains it to have been that of a Frenchman; but we find it stated that '*not understanding French this witness was examined through an interpreter.*' The Englishman thinks it the voice of a German, and '*does not understand German.*' The Spaniard 'is sure' that it was that of an Englishman, but 'judges by the intonation' altogether, '*as he has no knowledge of the English.*' The Italian believes it the voice of a Russian, but '*has never conversed with a native of Russia.*' A second Frenchman differs, moreover, with the first, and is positive that the voice was that of an Italian; but, *not being cognizant of that tongue*, is, like the Spaniard, 'convinced by the intonation.' Now, how strangely unusual must that voice have really been, about which such testimony as this *could* have been elicited!—in whose *tones*, even, denizens of the five great divi-sions of Europe could recognize nothing familiar! You will say that it might have been the voice of an Asiatic—of an African. Neither Asiatics nor Africans abound in Paris; but, without denying the infer-ence, I will now merely call your attention to three points. The voice is termed by one witness 'harsh rather than shrill.' It is represented by two others to have been 'quick and *unequal.*' No words—no sounds re-sembling words—were by any witness mentioned as distinguishable.

"I know not," continued Dupin, "what impression I may have made, so far, upon your own understanding; but I do not hesitate to say that legitimate deductions even from this portion of the testimony—

the portion respecting the gruff and shrill voices—are in themselves sufficient to engender a suspicion which should give direction to all farther progress in the investigation of the mystery. I said 'legitimate deductions'; but my meaning is not thus fully expressed. I designed to imply that the deductions are the *sole* proper ones, and that the suspicion arises *inevitably* from them as the single result. What the suspicion is, however, I will not say just yet. I merely wish you to bear in mind that, with myself, it was sufficiently forcible to give a definite form—a certain tendency—to my inquiries in the chamber.

"Let us now transport ourselves, in fancy, to this chamber. What shall we first seek here? The means of egress employed by the murderers. It is not too much to say that neither of us believe in præternatural events. Madame and Mademoiselle L'Espanaye were not destroyed by spirits. The doers of the deed were material and escaped materially. Then how? Fortunately there is but one mode of reasoning upon the point, and that mode *must* lead us to a definite decision. Let us examine, each by each, the possible means of egress. It is clear that the assassins were in the room where Mademoiselle L'Espanaye was found, or at least in the room adjoining, when the party ascended the stairs. It is, then, only from these two apartments that we have to seek issues. The police have laid bare the floors, the ceiling, and the masonry of the walls, in every direction. No *secret* issues could have escaped their vigilance. But, not trusting to *their* eyes, I examined with my own. There were, then, no secret issues. Both doors leading from the rooms into the passage were securely locked, with the keys inside. Let us turn to the chimneys. These, although of ordinary width for some eight or ten feet above the hearths, will not admit, throughout their extent, the body of a large cat. The impossibility of egress, by means already stated, being thus absolute, we are reduced to the windows. Through those of the front room no one could have escaped without notice from the crowd in the street. The murderers *must* have passed, then, through those of the back room. Now, brought to this conclusion in so unequivocal a manner as we are, it is not our part, as reasoners, to reject it on account of apparent impossibilities. It is only left for us to prove that these apparent 'impossibilities' are, in reality, not such.

"There are two windows in the chamber. One of them is unobstructed by furniture, and is wholly visible. The lower portion of the other is hidden from view by the head of the unwieldy bedstead which is thrust close up against it. The former was found securely fastened from within. It resisted the utmost force of those who endeavored to raise it. A large gimlet-hole had been pierced in its frame to the left, and a very stout nail was found fitted therein, nearly to the head. Upon examing the other window, a similar nail was seen similarly fitted in it; and a vigorous attempt to raise this sash failed also. The police were now entirely satisfied that egress had not been in these directions. And, *therefore*, it was thought a matter of supererogation to withdraw the nails and open the windows.

"My own examination was somewhat more particular, and was so for the reason I have just given—because here it was, I knew, that all apparent impossibilities *must* be proved to be not such in reality.

"I proceeded to think thus—*a posteriori*. The murderers *did* escape from one of these windows. This being so, they could not have re-fastened the sashes from the inside, as they were found fastened—the consideration which put a stop, through its obviousness, to the scrutiny of the police in this quarter. Yet the sashes *were* fastened. They *must*, then, have the power of fastening themselves. There was no escape from this conclusion. I stepped to the unobstructed casement, withdrew the nail with some difficulty, and attempted to raise the sash. It resisted all my efforts, as I had anticipated. A concealed spring must, I now knew, exist; and this corroboration of my idea convinced me that my premises, at least, were correct, however mysterious still appeared the circumstances attending the nails. A careful search soon brought to light the hidden spring. I pressed it, and, satisfied with the discovery, forbore to upraise the sash.

"I now replaced the nail and regarded it attentively. A person passing out through this window might have reclosed it, and the spring would have caught—but the nail could not have been replaced. The conclusion was plain, and again narrowed in the field of my investigations. The assassins *must* have escaped through the other window. Supposing, then, the springs upon each sash to be the same, as was probable, there *must* be found a difference between the nails, or at least between the modes of their fixture. Getting upon the sacking of the bedstead, I looked over the head-board minutely at the second casement. Passing my hand down behind the board, I readily discovered and pressed the spring, which was, as I had supposed, identical in character with its neighbor. I now looked at the nail. It was as stout as the other, and apparently fitted in the same manner—driven in nearly up to the head.

"You will say that I was puzzled; but, if you think so, you must have misunderstood the nature of the inductions. To use a sporting phrase, I had not been once 'at fault.' The scent had never for an instant been lost. There was no flaw in any link of the chain. I had traced the secret to its ultimate result,—and that result was *the nail*. It had, I say, in every respect, the appearance of its fellow in the other window; but this fact was an absolute nullity (conclusive as it might seem to be) when compared with the consideration that here, at this point, terminated the clew. 'There *must* be something wrong,' I said, 'about the nail.' I touched it; and the head, with about a quarter of an inch of the shank came off in my fingers. The rest of the shank was in the gimlet-hole, where it had been broken off. The fracture was an old one (for its edges were incrusted with rust), and had apparently been accomplished by the blow of a hammer, which had partially imbedded, in the top of the bottom sash, the head portion of the nail. I now carefully replaced this head portion in the indentation whence I had taken it, and the re-semblance to a perfect nail was complete—the fissure was invisible. Pressing the spring, I gently raised the sash for a few inches; the head went up with it, remaining firm in its bed. I closed the window, and the semblance of the whole nail was again perfect.

"This riddle, so far, was now unriddled. The assassin had escaped through the window which looked upon the bed. Dropping of its own accord upon his exit (or perhaps purposely closed), it had become fastened by the spring; and it was the retention of this spring which had been mistaken by the police for that of the nail, —farther inquiry being thus considered unnecessary.

"The next question is that of the mode of descent. Upon this point I had been satisfied in my walk with you around the building. About five feet and a half from the casement in question there runs a lightning-rod. From this rod it would have been impossible for any one to reach the window itself, to say nothing of entering it. I observed, however, that the shutters of the fourth story were of the peculiar kind called by Parisian carpenters *ferrades*—a kind rarely employed at the present day, but frequently seen upon very old mansions at Lyons and Bourdeaux. They are in the form of an ordinary door (a single, not a folding door), except that the upper half is latticed or worked in open trellis—thus affording an excellent hold for the hands. In the present instance these shutters are fully three feet and a half broad. When we saw them from the rear of the house, they were both about half open—that is to say, they stood off at right angles from the wall. It is probable that the police, as well as myself, examined the back of the tenement; but, if so, in looking at these *ferrades* in the line of their breadth (as they must have done), they did not perceive this great breadth itself, or, at all events, failed to take it into due consideration. In fact, having once satisfied themselves that no egress could have been made in this quarter, they would naturally bestow here a very cursory examination. It was clear to me, however, that the shutter belonging to the window at the head of the bed, would, if swung fully back to the wall, reach to within two feet of the lightning-rod. It was also evident that, by exertion of a very unusual degree of activity and courage, an entrance into the window, from the rod, might have been thus effected. By reaching to the distance of two feet and a half (we now suppose the shutter open to its whole extent) a robber might have taken a firm grasp upon the trellis-work. Letting go, then, his hold upon the rod, placing his feet securely against the wall, and springing boldly from it, he might have swung the shutter so as to close it, and, if we imagine the window open at the time, might even have swung himself into the room.

"I wish you to bear especially in mind that I have spoken of a *very* unusual degree of activity as requisite to success in so hazardous and so difficult a feat. It is my design to show you first, that the thing might possibly have been accomplished:—but, secondly and *chiefly*, I wish to impress upon your understanding the *very extraordinary*—the almost præternatural character of that agility which could have accomplished it.

"You will say, no doubt, using the language of the law, that 'to make out my case,' I should rather undervalue, than insist upon a full estimation of the activity required in this matter. This may be the practice in law, but it is not the usage of reason. My ultimate object is only the truth. My immediate purpose is to lead you to place in juxtaposition, that *very unusual* activity of which I have just spoken, with that *very peculiar* shrill (or harsh) and *unequal* voice, about whose nationality no two persons could be found to agree, and in whose utterance no syllabification could be detected."

At these words a vague and half-formed conception of the meaning of Dupin flitted over my mind. I seemed to be upon the verge of comprehension, without power to comprehend—as men, at times, find themselves upon the brink of remembrance, without being able, in the end, to remember. My friend went on with his discourse.

"You will see," he said, "that I have shifted the question from the mode of egress to that of ingress. It was my design to convey the idea that both were effected in the same manner, at the same point. Let us now revert to the interior of the room. Let us survey the appearances here. The drawers of the bureau, it is said, had been rifled, although many articles of apparel still remained within them. The conclusion here is absurd. It is a mere guess—a very silly one—and no more. How are we to know that the articles found in the drawers were not all these drawers had originally contained? Madame L'Espanaye and her daughter lived an exceedingly retired life—saw no company—seldom went out—had little use for numerous changes of habiliment. Those found were at least of as good quality as any likely to be possessed by these ladies. If a thief had taken any, why did he not take the best—why did he not take all? In a word, why did he abandon four thousand francs in gold to encumber himself with a bundle of linen? The gold *was* abandoned. Nearly the whole sum mentioned by Monsieur Mignaud, the banker, was discovered, in bags, upon the floor. I wish you therefore, to discard from your thoughts the blundering idea of *motive*, engendered in the brains of the police by that portion of the evidence which speaks of money delivered at the door of the house. Coincidences ten times as remarkable as this (the delivery of the money, and murder committed within three days upon the party receiving it), happen to all of us every hour of our lives, without attracting even momentary notice. Coincidences, in general, are great stumbling-blocks in the way of that class of thinkers who have been educated to know nothing of the theory of probabilities—that theory to which the most glorious objects of human research are indebted for the most glorious of illustration. In the present instance, had the gold been gone, the fact of its delivery three days before would have formed something more than a coincidence. It would have been corroborative of this idea of motive. But, under the real circumstances of the case, if we are to suppose gold the motive of this outrage, we must also imagine the perpetrator so vacillating an idiot as to have abandoned his gold and his motive together.

"Keeping now steadily in mind the points to which I have drawn your attention—that peculiar voice, that unusual agility, and that startling absence of motive in a murder so singularly atrocious as this—let us glance at the butchery itself. Here is a woman strangled to death by manual strength, and thrust up a chimney head downward. Ordinary assassins employ no such mode of murder as this. Least of all, do they thus dispose of the murdered. In this manner of thrusting the corpse up the chimney, you will admit that there was something *excessively outré*—something altogether irreconcilable with our common notions of human action, even when we suppose the actors the most depraved of men. Think, too, how great must have been that strength which could have thrust the body *up* such an aperture so forcibly that the united vigor of several persons was found barely sufficient to drag it *down*!

"Turn, now, to other indications of the employment of vigor most marvellous. On the hearth were thick tresses—very thick tresses—of gray human hair. These had been torn out by the roots. You are aware of the great force necessary in tearing thus from the head even twenty or thirty hairs together. You saw the locks in question as well as myself. Their roots (a hideous sight!) were clotted with fragments of the flesh of the scalp—sure token of the prodigious power which had been exerted in uprooting perhaps half a million of hairs at a time. The throat of the old lady was not merely cut, but the head absolutely severed from the body: the instrument was a mere razor. I wish you also to look at the *brutal* ferocity of these deeds. Of the bruises upon the body of Madame L'Espanaye I do not speak. Monsieur Dumas, and his worthy co-adjutor Monsieur Etienne, have pronounced that they were inflicted by some obtuse instrument; and so far these gentlemen are very correct. The obtuse instrument was clearly the stone pavement in the yard, upon which the victim had fallen from the window which looked in upon the bed. This idea, however simple it may now seem, escaped the police for the same reason that the breadth of the shutters escaped them— because, by the affair of the nails, their perceptions had been hermetically sealed against the possibility of the windows having ever been opened at all.

"If now, in addition to all these things, you have properly reflected upon the odd disorder of the chamber, we have gone so far as to combine the ideas of an agility astounding, a strength superhuman, a ferocity brutal, a butchery without motive, a *grotesquerie* in horror absolutely alien from humanity, and a voice foreign in tone to the ears of men of many nations, and devoid of all distinct or intelligible syllabification. What result, then, has ensued? What impression have I made upon your fancy?"

I felt a creeping of the flesh as Dupin asked me the question. "A madman," I said, "has done this deed—some raving maniac, escaping from a neighboring *Maison de Santé*."

"In some respects," he replied, "your idea is not irrelevant. But the voice of madmen, even in their wildest paroxysms, are never found to tally with that peculiar voice heard upon the stairs. Madmen are of some nation, and their language, however incoherent in its words, has always the coherence of syllabification. Besides, the hair of a madman is not such as I now hold in my hand. I disentangled this little tuft from the rigidly clutched fingers of Madame L'Espanaye. Tell me what you can make of it."

"Dupin!" I said, completely unnerved; "this hair is most unusual—this is no *human* hair."

"I have not asserted that it is," said he; "but, before we decide this point, I wish you to glance at the little sketch I have here traced upon this paper. It is a *fac-simile* drawing of what has been described in one portion of the testimony as 'dark bruises and deep indentations of finger nails' upon the throat of Mademoiselle L'Espanaye, and in another (by

Messrs. Dumas and Etienne) as a 'series of livid spots, evidently the impressions of fingers.'

"You will perceive," continued my friend, spreading out the paper upon the table before us, "that this drawing gives the idea of a firm and fixed hold. There is no *slipping* apparent. Each finger has retained—possibly until the death of the victim—the fearful grasp by which it originally imbedded itself. Attempt, now, to place all your fingers, at the same time, in the respective impressions as you see them."

I made the attempt in vain.

"We are possibly not giving this matter a fair trial," he said. "The paper is spread out upon a plane surface; but the human throat is cylindrical. Here is a billet of wood, the circumference of which is about that of the throat. Wrap the drawing around it, and try the experiment again."

I did so; but the difficulty was even more obvious than before. "This," I said, "is the mark of no human hand."

"Read now," replied Dupin, "this passage from Cuvier."

It was a minute anatomical and generally descriptive account of the large fulvous Ourang-Outang of the East Indian islands. The gigantic stature, the prodigious strength and activity, the wild ferocity, and the imitative propensities of these mammalia are sufficiently well known to all. I understood the full horrors of the murder at once.

"The description of the digits," said I, as I made an end of reading, "is in exact accordance with this drawing. I see that no animal but an Ourang-Outang, of the species here mentioned, could have impressed the indentations as you have traced them. This tuft of tawny hair, too, is identical in character with that of the beast of Cuvier. But I cannot possibly comprehend the particulars of this frightful mystery. Besides, there were *two* voices heard in contention, and one of them was unquestionably the voice of a Frenchman."

"True; and you will remember an expression attributed almost unanimously, by the evidence, to this voice,—the expression, 'mon Dieu!' This, under the circumstances, has been justly characterized by one of the witnesses (Montani, the confectioner) as an expression of remonstrance or expostulation. Upon these two words, therefore, I have mainly built my hopes of a full solution of the riddle. A Frenchman was cognizant of the murder. It is possible—indeed it is far more than probable—that he was innocent of all participation in the bloody transaction which took place. The Ourang-Outang may have escaped from him. He may have traced it to the chamber; but, under the agitating circumstances which ensued, he could never have recaptured it. It is still at large. I will not pursue these guesses—for I have no right to call them more—since the shades of reflection upon which they are based are scarcely of sufficient depth to be appreciable by my own intellect, and since I could not pretend to make them intelligible to the understanding of another. We will call them guesses, then, and speak of them as such. If the Frenchman in question is indeed, as I suppose, innocent of this atrocity, this advertisement, which I left last night upon our return home, at the office of *Le Monde* (a paper devoted to the shipping interest, and much sought by sailors), will bring him to our residence."

He handed me a paper, and I read thus:

CAUGHT—*In the Bois de Boulogne, early in the morning of the ——inst.* (the morning of the murder), *a very large, tawny Ourang-Outang of the Bornese species. The owner (who is ascertained to be a sailor, belonging to a Maltese vessel) may have the animal again, upon identifying it satisfactorily, and paying a few charges arising from its capture and keeping. Call at No. —— Rue ——, Faubourg St. Germain—au troisième.*"

"How was it possible," I asked, "that you should know the man to be a sailor, and belonging to a Maltese vessel?"

"I do *not know* it," said Dupin. "I am not *sure* of it. Here, however, is a small piece of ribbon, which from its form, and from its greasy appearance, has evidently been used in tying the hair in one of those long *queues* of which sailors are so fond. Moreover, this knot is one which few besides sailors can tie, and it is peculiar to the Maltese. I picked the ribbon up at the foot of the lightning-rod. It could not have belonged to either of the deceased. Now if, after all, I am wrong in my induction from this ribbon, that the Frenchman was a sailor belonging to a Maltese vessel, still I can have done no harm in saying what I did in the advertisement. If I am right, a great point is gained. Cognizant although innocent of the murder, the Frenchman will naturally hesitate about replying to the advertisement—about demanding the Ourang-Outang. He will reason thus:—'I am innocent; I am poor; my Ourang-Outang is of great value—to one in my circumstances a fortune of itself—why should I lose it through idle apprehensions of danger? Here it is, within my grasp. It was found in the Bois de Boulogne—at a vast distance from the scene of that butchery. How can it ever be suspected that a brute beast should have done the deed? The police are at fault—they have failed to procure the slightest clew. Should they even trace the animal, it would be impossible to prove me cognizant of the murder, or to implicate me in guilt on account of that cognizance. Above all, *I am known*. The advertiser designates me as the possessor of the beast. I am not sure to what limit his knowledge may extend. Should I avoid claiming a property of so great value, which it is

70

known that I possess, I will render the animal at least, liable to suspicion. It is not my policy to attract attention either to myself or to the beast. I will answer the advertisement, get the Ourang-Outang, and keep it close until this matter has blown over."

At this moment we heard a step upon the stairs.

"Be ready," said Dupin, "with your pistols, but neither use them nor show them until at a signal from myself."

The front door of the house had been left open, and the visitor had entered, without ringing, and advanced several steps upon the staircase. Now, however, he seemed to hesitate. Presently we heard him descending. Dupin was moving quickly to the door, when we again heard him coming up. He did not turn back a second time, but stepped up with decision, and rapped at the door of our chamber.

"Come in," said Dupin, in a cheerful and hearty tone.

A man entered. He was a sailor, evidently,—a tall, stout, and muscular-looking person, with a certain daredevil expression of countenance, not altogether unprepossessing. His face, greatly sunburnt, was more than half hidden by whisker and *mustachio*. He had with him a huge oaken cudgel, but appeared to be otherwise unarmed. He bowed awkwardly, and bade us "good evening," in French accents, which, although somewhat Neufchatelish, were still sufficiently indicative of a Parisian origin.

"Sit down, my friend," said Dupin. "I suppose you have called about the Ourang-Outang. Upon my word, I almost envy you the possession of him; a remarkably fine, and no doubt a very valuable animal. How old do you suppose him to be?"

The sailor drew a long breath, with the air of a man relieved of some intolerable burden, and then replied, in an assured tone:

"I have no way of telling—but he can't be more than four or five years old. Have you got him here?"

"Oh, no; we had no conveniences for keeping him here. He is at a livery stable in the Rue Dubourg, just by. You can get him in the morning. Of course you are prepared to identify the property?"

"To be sure I am, sir."

"I shall be sorry to part with him," said Dupin.

"I don't mean that you should be at all this trouble for nothing, sir," said the man. "Couldn't expect it. Am very willing to pay a reward for the finding of the animal—that is to say, anything in reason."

"Well," replied my friend, "that is all very fair, to be sure. Let me think!—what should I have? Oh! I will tell you. My reward shall be this. You shall give me all the information in your power about these murders in the Rue Morgue."

Dupin said the last words in a very low tone, and very quietly. Just as quietly, too, he walked toward the door, locked it, and put the key in his pocket. He then drew a pistol from his bosom and placed it, without the least flurry, upon the table.

The sailor's face flushed up as if he were struggling with suffocation. He started to his feet and grasped his cudgel; but the next moment he fell back into his seat, trembling violently, and with the countenance of death itself. He spoke not a word. I pitied him from the bottom of my heart.

"My friend," said Dupin, in a kind tone, "you are alarming yourself unnecessarily—you are indeed. We mean you no harm whatever. I pledge you the honor of a gentleman, and of a Frenchman, that we intend you no injury. I perfectly well know that you are innocent of the artocities in the Rue Morgue. It will not do, however, to deny that you are in some measure implicated in them. From what I have already said, you must know that I have had means of information about this matter—means of which you could never have dreamed. Now the thing stands thus. You have done nothing which you could have avoided—nothing, certainly, which renders you culpable. You are not even guilty of robbery, when you might have robbed with impunity. You have nothing to conceal. You have no reason for concealment. On the other hand, you are bound by every principle of honor to confess all you know. An innocent man is now imprisoned, charged with that crime of which you can point out the perpetrator."

The sailor had recovered his presence of mind, in a great measure, while Dupin uttered these words; but his original boldness of bearing was all gone.

"So help me God!" said he, after a brief pause, "I *will* tell you all I know about this affair;—but I do not expect you to believe one half I say—I would be a fool indeed if I did. Still, I *am* innocent, and I will make a clean breast if I die for it."

What he stated was, in substance, this. He had lately made a voyage to the Indian Archipelago. A party, of which he formed one, landed at Borneo, and passed into the interior on an excursion of pleasure. Himself and a companion had captured the Ourang-Outang. This companion dying, the animal fell into his own exclusive possession. After a great trouble, occasioned by the intractable ferocity of his captive during the home voyage, he at length succeeded in lodging it safely at his own residence in Paris, where, not to attract toward himself the unpleasant curiosity of his neighbors, he kept it carefully secluded, until such time as it should recover from a wound in the foot, received from a splinter on board ship. His ultimate design was to sell it.

Returning home from some sailor's frolic on the night, or rather in the morning, of the murder, he found the beast occupying his own bedroom, into which it had broken from a closet adjoining, where it had been, as was thought, securely confined. Razor in hand, and fully lathered, it was sitting before a looking-glass, attempting the operation of shaving, in which it had no doubt previously watched its master through the keyhole of the closet. Terrified at the sight of so dangerous a weapon in the possession of an animal so ferocious, and so well able to use it, the man, for some moments, was at a loss what to do. He had been accustomed, however, to quiet the creature, even in its fiercest moods, by the use of a whip, and to this he now resorted. Upon sight of it, the Ourang-Outang sprang at once through the door of the chamber, down the stairs, and thence, through a window, unfortunately open, into the street.

The Frenchman followed in despair; the ape, razor still in hand, occasionally stopping to look back and gesticulate at his pursuer, until the latter had nearly come up with it. It then again made off. In this manner, the chase continued for a long time. The streets were profoundly quiet, as it was nearly three o'clock in the morning. In passing down an alley in the rear of the Rue Morgue, the fugitive's attention was arrested by a light gleaming from the open window of Madame L'Espanaye's chamber, in the fourth story of her house. Rushing to the building, it perceived the lightning-rod, clambered up with inconceivable agility, grasped the shutter, which was thrown fully back against the wall, and, by its means, swung itself directly upon the headboard of the bed. The whole feat did not occupy a minute. The shutter was kicked open again by the Ourang-Outang as it entered the room.

The sailor, in the meantime, was both rejoiced and perplexed. He had strong hopes of now recapturing the brute, as it could scarcely escape from the trap into which it had ventured, except by the rod, where it might be intercepted as it came down. On the other hand, there was much cause for anxiety as to what it might do in the house. This latter reflection urged the man still to follow the fugitive. A lightning-rod is ascended without difficulty, especially by a sailor; but, when he had arrived as high as the window, which lay far to his left, his career was stopped; the most that he could accomplish was to reach over so as to obtain a glimpse of the interior of the room. At this glimpse he nearly fell from his hold through excess of horror. Now it was that those hideous shrieks arose upon the night, which had startled from slumber the inmates of the Rue Morgue. Madame L'Espanaye and her daughter, habited in their night clothes, had apparently been occupied in arranging some papers in the iron chest already mentioned, which had been wheeled into the middle of the room. It was open, and its contents lay beside it on the floor. The victims must have been sitting with their backs toward the window; and, from the time elapsing between the ingress of the beast and the screams, it seems probable that it was not immediately perceived. The flapping to of the shutter would naturally have been attributed to the wind.

As the sailor looked in, the gigantic animal had seized Madame L'Espanaye by the hair (which was loose, as she had been combing it), and was flourishing a razor about her face, in imitation of the motions of a barber. The daughter lay prostrate and motionless; she had swooned. The screams and struggles of the old lady (during which the hair was torn from her head) had the effect of changing the probably pacific purposes of the Ourang-Outang into those of wrath. With one determined sweep of its muscular arm it nearly severed her head from her body. The sight of blood inflamed its anger into phrenzy. Gnashing its teeth, and flashing fire from its eyes, it flew upon the body of the girl and embedded its fearful talons in her throat, retaining its grasp until she expired. Its wandering and wild glances fell at this moment upon the head of the bed, over which the face of its master, rigid with horror, was just discernible. The fury of the beast, who no doubt bore still in mind the dreaded whip, was instantly converted into fear. Conscious of having deserved punishment, it seemed desirous of concealing its bloody deeds, and skipped about the chamber in an agony of nervous agitation; throwing down and breaking the furniture as it moved, and dragging the bed from the bedstead. In conclusion, it seized first the corpse of the daughter, and thrust it up the chimney, as it was found; then that of the old lady, which, it immediately hurled through the window headlong.

As the ape approached the casement with its mutilated burden, the sailor shrank aghast to the rod, and, rather gliding than clambering down it, hurried at once home—dreading the consequences of the butchery, and gladly abandoning, in his terror, all solicitude about the fate of the Ourang-Outang. The words heard by the party upon the staircase were the Frenchman's exclamations of horror and affright, commingled with the fiendish jabberings of the brute.

I have scarcely any thing to add. The Ourang-Outang must have escaped from the chamber, by the rod, just before the breaking of the door. It must have closed the window as it passed through it. It was subsequently caught by the owner himself, who obtained for it a very large sum at the *Jardin des Plantes*. Le Bon was instantly released, upon our narration of the circumstances (with some comments from Dupin) at the *bureau* of the Prefect of Police. This functionary, however, well disposed to my friend, could not altogether conceal his chagrin at the turn which affairs had taken, and was fain to indulge in a sarcasm or two about the propriety of every person minding his own business.

"Let him talk," said Dupin, who had not thought it necessary to reply. "Let him discourse; it will ease his conscience. I am satisfied with having defeated him in his own castle. Nevertheless, that he failed in the solution of this mystery, is by no means that matter for wonder which he supposes it; for, in truth, our friend the prefect is somewhat too cunning to be profound. In his wisdom is no *stamen*. It is all head and no body, like the pictures of the Goddess Laverna—or, at best, all head and shoulders, like a codfish. But he is a good creature after all. I like him especially for one master stroke of cant, by which he has attained his reputation for ingenuity, I mean the way he has '*de nier ce qui est, et d'expliquer ce qui n'est pas.*'"*

*Rousseau—Nouvelle Heloise

THE PURLOINED LETTER

By Edgar Allan Poe

"The Purloined Letter" is the third of Poe's three influential tales of ratiocination featuring detective C. Auguste Dupin, the second being "The Mystery of Marie Rogêt." Dupin, whose name Poe may have taken from the heroine of a story in Burton's Gentleman's Magazine *dealing with the life of Vidocq, was the first of the great analytical detectives, and the three stories in which he appears are meant to demonstrate the triumph of human reason over the problems and terrors of life. At least one critic has suggested that Poe wrote these stories in order to strengthen his own rather shaky grip on sanity, in order—as Joseph Wood Krutch somewhat melodramatically puts it—"that he might not go mad." "The Purloined Letter" first appeared in* The Gift: A Christmas, New Year's and Birthday Present *in 1845. For more about Poe and the detective story, see Robert A. W. Lowndes' "The Contributions of Edgar Allan Poe,"* The Mystery Writer's Art *(Bowling Green, Ohio: Popular Press, 1970), p. 1. See also John Walsh's* Poe the Detective *(New Brunswick, N.J.: Rutgers University Press, 1968) and Daniel Hoffman's* Poe Poe Poe Poe Poe Poe Poe *(Garden City, N.Y.: Doubleday, 1972).*

At Paris, just after dark one gusty evening in the autumn of 18—, I was enjoying the twofold luxury of meditation and a meerschaum, in company with my friend C. Auguste Dupin, in his little back library, or book-closet, *au troisième, No. 33, Rue Dunôt, Faubourg St. Germain*. For one hour at least we had maintained a profound silence; while each, to any casual observer, might have seemed intently and exclusively occupied with the curling eddies of smoke that oppressed the atmosphere of the chamber. For myself, however, I was mentally discussing certain topics which had formed matter for conversation between us at an earlier period of the evening; I mean the affair of the Rue Morgue, and the mystery attending the murder of Marie Rogêt. I looked upon it, therefore, as something of a coincidence, when the door of our apartment was thrown open and admitted our old acquaintance, Monsieur G——, the Prefect of the Parisian police.

We gave him a hearty welcome; for here was nearly half as much of the entertaining as of the contemptible about the man, and we had not seen him for several years. We had been sitting in the dark, and Dupin now arose for the purpose of lighting a lamp, but sat down again, without doing so, upon G——'s saying that he had called to consult us, or rather to ask the opinion of my friend, about some official business which had occasioned a great deal of trouble.

"If it is any point requiring reflection," observed Dupin, as he forebore to enkindle the wick, "we shall examine it to better purpose in the dark."

"That is another of your odd notions," said the Prefect, who had a fashion of calling every thing "odd" that was beyond his comprehension, and thus lived amid an absolute legion of "oddities."

"Very true," said Dupin, as he supplied his visitor with a pipe, and rolled towards him a comfortable chair.

"And what is the difficulty now?" I asked. "Nothing more in the assassination way, I hope?"

"Oh no; nothing of that nature. The fact is, the business is *very* simple indeed, and I make no doubt that we can manage it sufficiently well ourselves; but then I thought Dupin would like to hear the details of it, because it is so excessively *odd*."

"Simple and odd," said Dupin.

"Why, yes; and not exactly that, either. The fact is, we have all been a good deal puzzled beause the affair *is* so simple, and yet baffles us altogether."

"Perhaps it is the very simplicity of the thing which puts you at fault," said my friend.

"What nonsense you *do* talk!" replied the Prefect, laughing heartily.

"Perhaps the mystery is a little *too* plain," said Dupin.

"Oh, good heavens! who ever heard of such an idea?"

"A little *too* self-evident."

"Ha! ha! ha!—ha! ha! ha!—ho! ho! ho!"—roared our visitor, profoundly amused, "oh, Dupin, you will be the death of me yet!"

"And what, after all, *is* the matter on hand?" I asked.

"Why, I will tell you," replied the Prefect, as he gave a long, steady, and contemplative puff, and settled himself in his chair. "I will tell you in a few words; but, before I begin, let me caution you that this is an affair demanding the greatest secrecy, and that I should most probably lose the positon I now hold, were it known that I confided it to any one."

"Proceed," said I.

"Or not," said Dupin.

"Well, then; I have received personal information, from a very high quarter, that a certain document of the last importance has been purloined from the royal apartments. The individual who purloined it is known; this beyond a doubt; he was seen to take it. It is known, also, that it still remains in his possession."

"How is this known?" asked Dupin.

"It is clearly inferred," replied the Prefect, "from the nature of the document, and from the non-appearance of certain results which would at once arise from its passing *out* of the robber's possession;—that is to say, from his employing it as he must design in the end to employ it."

"Be a little more explicit," I said.

"Well, I may venture so far as to say that the paper gives its holder a certain power in a certain quarter where such power is immensely valuable." The Prefect was fond of the cant of diplomacy.

"Still I do not quite understand," said Dupin.

"No? Well; the disclosure of the document to a third person who shall be nameless would bring in question the honor of a personage of most exalted station; and this fact gives the holder of the document an ascendancy over the illustrious personage whose honor and peace are so jeopardized."

"But this ascendancy," I interposed, "would depend upon the robber's knowledge of the loser's knowledge of the robber. Who would dare—"

"The thief," said G——, "is the Minister D——, who dares all things, those unbecoming as well as those becoming a man. The method of the theft was not less ingenious than bold. The document in question—a letter, to be frank—had been received by the personage robbed while alone in the royal *boudoir*. During its perusal she was suddenly interrupted by the entrance of the other exalted personage from whom especially it was her wish to conceal it. After a hurried and vain endeavor to thrust it in a drawer, she was forced to place it, open as it was, upon a table. The address, however, was uppermost, and, the contents thus unexposed, the letter escaped notice. At this juncture enters the Minister D——. His lynx eye immediately perceives the paper, recognizes the handwriting of the address, observes the confusion of the personage addressed, and fathoms her secret. After some business transactions, hurried through in his ordinary manner, he produces a letter somewhat similar to the one in question, opens it, pretends to read it, and then places it in close juxtaposition to the other. Again he converses, for some fifteen minutes, upon the public affairs. At length, in taking leave, he takes also from the table the letter to which he had no claim. Its rightful owner saw, but, of course, dared not call attention to the act, in the presence of the third personage who stood at her elbow. The Minister decamped; leaving his own letter—one of no importance—upon the table."

"Here, then," said Dupin to me, "you have precisely what you demand to make the ascendancy complete—the robber's knowledge of the loser's knowledge of the robber."

"Yes," replied the Prefect; "and the power thus attained has, for some months past, been wielded, for political purposes, to a very dangerous extent. The personage robbed is more thoroughly convinced, every day, of the necessity of reclaiming her letter. But this, of course, cannot be done openly. In fine, driven to despair, she has committed the matter to me."

"Than whom," said Dupin, amid a perfect whirlwind of smoke, "no more sagacious agent could, I suppose, be desired, or even imagined."

"You flatter me," replied the Prefect; "but it is possible that some such opinion may have been entertained."

"It is clear," said I, "as you observe, that the letter is still in possession of the Minister; since it is this possession, and not any employment of the letter, which bestows the power. With the employment the power departs."

"True," said G——; "and upon this conviction I proceeded. My first care was to make thorough search of the Minister's hotel; and here my chief embarrassment lay in the necessity of searching without his knowledge. Beyond all things, I have been warned of the danger which would result from giving him reason to suspect our design."

"But," said I, "you are quite *au fait* in these investigations. The Parisian police have done this thing often before."

"Oh yes; and for this reason I did not despair. The habits of the Minister gave me, too, a great advantage. He is frequently absent from home all night. His servants are by no means numerous. They sleep at a distance from their master's apartment, and, being chiefly Neapolitans, are readily made drunk. I have keys, as you know, with which I can open any chamber or cabinet in Paris. For three months a night has not passed, during the greater part of which I have not been engaged, personally, in ransacking the D—— Hôtel. My honor is interested, and, to mention a great secret, the reward is enormous. So I did not abandon the search until I had become fully satisfied that the thief is a more astute man than myself. I fancy that I have investigated every nook and corner of the premises in which it is possible that the paper can be concealed."

"But is it not possible," I suggested, "that although the letter may be in the possession of the Minister, as it unquestionably is, he may have concealed it elsewhere than upon his own premises?"

"This is barely possible," said Dupin. "The present peculiar condition of affairs at court, and especially of those intrigues in which D—— is known to be involved, would render the instant availability of the document—its susceptibility of being reproduced at a moment's notice—a point of nearly equal importance with its possession."

"Its susceptibility of being produced?" said I.

"That is to say, of being *destroyed*," said Dupin.

"True," I observed; "the paper is clearly then upon the premises. As for its being upon the person of the Minister, we may consider that as out of the question."

"Entirely," said the Prefect. "He has been twice waylaid, as if by footpads, and his person rigorously searched under my own inspection."

"You might have spared yourself this trouble," said Dupin. "D——, I presume, is not altogether a fool, and, if not, must have anticipated these waylayings, as a matter of course."

"Not *altogether* a fool," said G——, "but then he's a poet, which I take to be only one remove from a fool."

"True," said Dupin, after a long and thoughtful whiff from his meerschaum, "although I have been guilty of certain doggerel myself."

"Suppose you detail," said I, "the particulars of your search."

"Why the fact is, we took our time, and we searched *every where*. I have had long experience in these affairs. I took the entire building, room by room; devoting the nights of a whole week to each. We examined, first, the furniture of each apartment. We opened every possible drawer; and I presume you know that, to a properly trained police agent, such a thing as a *secret* drawer is impossible. Any man is a dolt who permits a 'secret' drawer to escape him in a search of this kind. The thing is *so* plain. There is a certain amount of bulk—a space—to be accounted for in every cabinet. Then we have accurate rules. The fiftieth part of a line could not escape us. After the cabinets we took the chairs. The cushions we probed .vith the fine long needles you have seen me employ. From the tables we removed the tops."

"Why so?"

"Sometimes the top of a table, or other similarly arranged piece of furniture, is removed by the person wishing to conceal an article; then the leg is excavated, the article deposited within the cavity, and the top replaced. The bottoms and tops of bed-posts are employed in the same way."

"But could not the cavity be detected by sounding?" I asked.

"By no means, if, when the article is deposited, a sufficient wadding of cotton be placed around it. Besides, in our case, we were obliged to proceed without noise."

"But you could not have removed—you could not have taken to pieces *all* articles of furniture in which it would have been possible to make a deposit in the manner you mention. A letter may be compressed into a thin spiral roll, not differing much in shape or bulk from a large knitting-needle, and in this form it might be inserted into the rung of a chair, for example. You did not take to pieces all the chairs?"

"Certainly not; but we did better—we examined the rungs of every chair in the hotel, and, indeed, the jointings of every description of furniture, by the aid of a most powerful microscope. Had there been any traces of recent disturbance we should not have failed to detect it instantly. A single grain of gimlet-dust, for example, would have been as obvious as an apple. Any disorder in the glueing—any unusual gaping in the joints—would have sufficed to insure detection."

"I presume you looked to the mirrors, between the boards and the plates, and you probed the beds and the bed-clothes, as well as the curtains and carpets."

"That of course; and when we had absolutely completed every particle of the furniture in this way, then we examined the house itself. We divided its entire surface into compartments, which we numbered, so that none might be missed; then we scrutinized each individual square inch throughout the premises, including the two houses immediately adjoining, with the microscope, as before."

"The two houses adjoining!" I exclaimed; "you must have had a great deal of trouble."

"We had; but the reward offered is prodigious."

"You include the *grounds* about the houses?"

"All the grounds are paved with brick. They gave us comparatively little trouble. We examined the moss between the bricks, and found it undisturbed."

"You looked among D——'s papers, of course, and into the books of the library?"

"Certainly; we opened every package and parcel; we not only opened every book, but we turned over every leaf in each volume, not contenting ourselves with a mere shake, according to the fashion of some of our police officers. We also measured the thickness of every book-*cover*, with the most accurate admeasurement, and applied to each the most jealous scrutiny of the microscope. Had any of the bindings been recently meddled with, it would have been utterly impossible that the face should have escaped observation. Some five or six volumes, just from the hands of the binder, we carefully probed, longitudinally, with the needles."

"You explored the floors beneath the carpets?"

"Beyond doubt. We removed every carpet, and examined the boards with the microscope."

"And the paper on the walls?"

"Yes."

"You looked into the cellars?"

"We did."

"Then," I said, "you have been making a miscalculation, and the letter is *not* upon the premises, as you suppose."

"I fear you are right there," said the Prefect. "And now, Dupin, what would you advise me to do?"

"To make a thorough re-search of the premises."

"That is absolutely needless," replied G——. "I am not more sure that I breathe than I am that the letter is not at the Hôtel."

"I have no better advice to give you," said Dupin. "You have, of course, an accurate description of the letter?"

"Oh yes!"—And here the Prefect, producing a memorandum-book, proceeded to read aloud a minute account of the internal, and especially of the external appearance of the missing document. Soon after finishing the perusal of this description, he took his departure, more entirely depressed in spirits than I had ever known the good gentleman before.

In about a month afterwards he paid us another visit, and found us occupied very nearly as before. He took a pipe and a chair and entered into some ordinary conversation. At length I said,—

"Well, but G——, what of the purloined letter? I presume you have at last made up your mind that there is no such thing as overreaching the Minister?"

"Confound him, say I—yes; I made the re-examination, however, as Dupin suggested—but it was all labor lost, as I knew it would be."

"How much was the reward offered, did you say?" asked Dupin.

"Why, a very great deal—a *very* liberal reward—I don't like to say how much, precisely; but one thing I *will* say, that I wouldn't mind giving my individual check for fifty thousand francs to any one who could obtain me that letter. The fact is, it is becoming of more and more importance every day; and the reward has been lately doubled. If it were trebled, however, I could do no more than I have done."

"Why, yes," said Dupin, drawlingly, between the whiffs of his meerschaum, "I really—think, G——, you have not exerted yourself—to the utmost in this matter. You might—do a little more, I think, eh?"

"How?—in what way?"

"Why—puff, puff—you might—puff, puff—employ counsel in the matter, eh?—puff, puff, puff. Do you remember the story they tell of Abernethy?"

"No; hang Abernethy!"

"To be sure! hang him and welcome. But, once upon a time, a certain rich miser conceived the design of sponging upon this Abernethy for a medical opinion. Getting up, for this purpose, an ordinary conversation in a private company, he insinuated his case to his physician, as that of an imaginary individual.

"'We will suppose,' said the miser, 'that his symptoms are such and such; now, doctor, what would *you* have directed him to take?'"

"'Take!' said Abernethy, 'why, take *advice*, to be sure.'"

"But," said the Prefect, a little discomposed, "I am *perfectly* willing to take advice, and to pay for it. I would *really* give fifty thousand francs to any one who would aid me in the matter."

"In that case," replied Dupin, opening a drawer, and producing a check-book, "you may as well fill me up a check for the amount mentioned. When you have signed it, I will hand you the letter."

I was astounded. The Prefect appeared absolutely thunderstricken. For some minutes he remained speechless and motionless, looking incredulously at my friend with open mouth, and eyes that seemed starting from their sockets; then, apparently recovering himself in some measure, he seized a pen, and after several pauses and vacant stares, finally filled up and signed a check for fifty thousand francs, and handed it across the table to Dupin. The latter examined it carefully and deposited it in his pocket-book; then, unlocking an *escritoire*, took thence a letter and gave it to the Prefect. This functionary grasped it in a perfect agony of joy, opened it with a trembling hand, cast a rapid glance at its contents, and then, scrambling and struggling to the door, rushed at length unceremoniously from the room and from the house, without having uttered a syllable since Dupin had requested him to fill up the check.

When he had gone, my friend entered into some explanations.

"The Parisian police," he said, "are exceedingly able in their way. They are persevering, ingenious, cunning, and thoroughly versed in the knowledge which their duties seem chiefly to demand. Thus, when G—— detailed to us his mode of searching the premises at the Hôtel D——, I felt entire confidence in his having made a satisfactory investigation—so far as his labors extended."

"So far as his labors extended?" said I.

"Yes," said Dupin. "The measures adopted were not only the best of their kind, but carried out to absolute perfection. Had the letter been deposited within the range of their search, these fellows would, beyond a question, have found it."

I merely laughed—but he seemed quite serious in all that he said.

"The measures, then," he continued, "were good in their kind, and well executed; their defect lay in their being inapplicable to the case, and to the man. A certain set of highly ingenious resources are, with the Prefect, a sort of Procrustean bed, to which he forcibly adapts his designs. But he perpetually errs by being too deep or too shallow, for the matter in hand; and many a schoolboy is a better reasoner than he. I knew one about eight years of age, whose success at guessing in the game of 'even and odd' attracted universal admiration. This game is simple, and is played with marbles. One player holds in his hand a number of these toys, and demands of another whether that number is even or odd. If the guess is right, the guesser wins one; if wrong, he loses one. The boy to whom I allude won all the marbles of the school. Of course he had some principle of guessing; and this lay in mere observation and admeasurement of the astuteness of his opponents. For example, an arrant simpleton is his opponent, and, holding up his closed hand, asks, 'are they even or odd?' Our schoolboy replies, 'odd,' and loses; but upon the second trial he wins, for he then says to himself, 'the simpleton had them even upon the first trial, and his amount of cunning is just sufficient to make him have them odd upon the second; I will therefore guess odd';—he guesses odd, and wins. Now, with a simpleton a degree above the first, he would have reasoned thus: 'This fellow finds that in the first instance I guessed odd, and, in the second, he will propose to himself upon the first impulse, a simple variation from even to odd, as did the first simpleton; but then a second thought will suggest that this is too simple a variation, and finally he will decide upon putting it even as before. I will therefore guess even';—he guesses even, and wins. Now this mode of reasoning in the schoolboy, whom his fellows termed 'lucky,'—what, in its last analysis, is it?"

"It is merely," I said, "an identification of the reasoner's intellect with that of his opponent."

"It is," said Dupin; "and, upon inquiring of the boy by what means he effected the *thorough* identification in which his success consisted, I received answer as follows: 'When I wish to find out how wise, or how stupid, or how good, or how wicked is any one, or what are his thoughts at the moment, I fashion the expression of my face, as accurately as possible, in accordance with the expression of his, and then wait to see what thoughts or sentiments arise in my mind or heart, as if to match or correspond with the expression.' This response of the schoolboy lies at the bottom of all the spurious profundity which has been attributed to Rochefoucauld, to La Bougive, to Machiavelli, and to Campanella."

"And the identification," I said, "of the reasoner's intellect with that of his opponent, depends, if I understand you aright, upon the accuracy with which the opponent's intellect is admeasured."

"For its practical value it depends upon this," replied Dupin; "and the Prefect and his cohort fail so frequently, first, by default of this identification, and, secondly, by ill-admeasurement, or rather through non-admeasurement of the intellect with which they are engaged. They consider only their *own* ideas of ingenuity; and, in searching for anything hidden, advert only to the modes in which *they* would have hidden it. They are right in this much—that their own ingenuity is a faithful representative of that of *the mass*; but when the cunning of the individual felon is diverse in character from their own, the felon foils them, of course. This always happens when it is above their own, and very usually when it is below. They have no variation of principle in their investigations; at best, when urged by some unusual emergency—by some extraordinary reward—they extend or exaggerate their old modes of *practice*, without touching their principles. What, for example, in his case of D——, has been done to vary the principle of action? What is all this boring, and probing, and sounding, and scrutinizing with the microscope, and dividing the surface of the building into registered square inches—what is it all but an exaggeration *of the application* of the one principle or set of principles of search, which are based upon the one set of notions regarding human ingenuity, to which the Prefect, in the long routine of his duty, has been accustomed? Do you not see he has taken it for granted that *all* men proceed to conceal a letter—not exactly in a gimlet-hole bored in a chair-leg—but, at least, in *some* out-of-the-way hole or corner suggested by the same tenor of thought which would urge a man to secrete a letter in a gimlet-hole bored in a chair-leg? And do you not see also, that such *recherchés* nooks for concealment are adopted only for ordinary occasions, and would be adopted only by ordinary intellects; for, in all cases of concealment, a disposal of the article concealed—a disposal of it in this *recherché* manner—is, in the very first instance, presumable and presumed; and thus its discovery depends, not at all upon the acumen, but altogether upon the mere care, patience, and determination of the seekers; and where the case is of importance—or, what amounts to the same thing in the policial eyes, when the reward is of magnitude, — the qualities in question have *never* been known to fail? You will now understand what I meant in suggesting that, had the purloined letter been hidden any where within the limits of the Prefect's examination—in other words, had the principle of its concealment been comprehended within the principles of the Prefect—its discovery would have been a matter altogether beyond question. This functionary, however, has been thoroughly mystified; and the remote source of his defeat lies in the supposition that the Minister is a fool, because he has acquired renown as a poet. All fools are poets; this the Prefect *feels*; and he is merely guilty of a *non distributio medii* [undistributed middle] in thence inferring that all poets are fools."

"But is this really the poet?" I asked. "There are two brothers, I know; and both have attained reputation in letters. The Minister I believe has written learnedly on the Differential Calculus. He is a mathematician, and no poet."

"You are mistaken; I know him well; he is both. As poet *and* mathematician, he would reason well; as mere mathematician, he could not have reasoned at all, and thus would have been at the mercy of the Prefect."

"You surprise me," I said, "by these opinions, which have been contradicted by the voice of the world. You do not mean to set at naught the well-digested idea of centuries. The mathematical reason has long been regarded as *the* reason *par excellence*."

"'*Il y a à parier*,'" replied Dupin, quoting from Chamfort, "'*que toute idée publique, toute convention reçue, est une sottise, car elle a convenu au plus grand nombre*.' [I'll bet that every popular idea, every set convention, is an idiocy, because it has suited the majority.] The mathematicians, I grant you, have done their best to promulgate the popular error to which you allude, and which is none the less an error for its promulgation as truth. With an art worthy a better cause, for example, they have insinuated the term 'analysis' into application to algebra. The French are the originators of this particular deception; but if a term is of any importance—if words derive any value from applicability—then 'analysis' conveys 'algebra' about as much as, in Latin, '*ambitus*' implies 'ambition,' '*religio*' 'religion,' or '*homines honesti*' a set of *honorable* men."

"You have a quarrel on hand, I see," said I, "with some of the algebraists of Paris; but proceed."

"I dispute the availability, and thus the value, of that reason which is cultivated in any especial form other than the abstractly logical. I dispute, in particular, the reason educed by mathematical study. The mathematics are the science of form and quantity; mathematical reasoning is merely logic applied to observation upon form and quantity. The great error lies in supposing that even the truths of what is called *pure* algebra, are abstract or general truths. And this error is so egregious that I am confounded at the universality with which it has been received. Mathematical axioms are *not* axioms of general truth. What is true of *relation*—of form and quantity—is often grossly false in regard to morals, for example. In this latter science it is very usually *un*true that the aggregated parts are equal to the whole. In chemistry also the axiom fails. In the consideration of motive it fails; for two motives, each of a given value, have not, necessarily, a value when united, equal to the sum of their values apart. There are numerous other mathematical truths which are only truths within the limits of *relation*. But the mathematician argues, from his *finite truths*, through habit, as if they were of an absolutely general applicability—as the world indeed imagines them to be. Bryant, in his very learned 'Mythology,' mentions an analogous source of error, when he says that 'although the Pagan fables are not believed, yet we forget ourselves continually, and make inferences from them as existing realities.' With the algebraists, however, who are Pagans themselves, the 'Pagan fables' *are* believed, and the inferences are made, not so much through lapse of memory, as through an unaccountable addling of the brains. In short, I never yet encountered the mere mathematician who could be trusted out of equal roots, or one who did not clandestinely hold it as a point of his faith that $x^2 + px$ was absolutely and unconditionally equal to q. Say to one of these gentlemen, by way of experiment, if you please, that you believe occasions may occur where $x^2 + px$ is *not* altogether equal to q, and, having made him understand what you mean, get out of his reach as speedily as convenient, for, beyond doubt, he will endeavor to knock you down.

"I mean to say," continued Dupin, while I merely laughed at his last observations, "that if the Minister had been no more than a mathematician, the Prefect would have been under no necessity of giving me this check. I knew him, however, as both mathematician and poet, and my measures were adapted to his capacity, with reference to the circumstances by which he was surrounded. I knew him as a courtier, too, and as a bold *intriguant*. Such a man, I considered, could not fail to be aware of the ordinary policial modes of action. He could not have failed to anticipate—and events have proved that he did not fail to anticipate—the waylayings to which he was subjected. He must have foreseen, I reflected, the secret investigations of his premises. His frequent absences from home at night, which were hailed by the Prefect as certain aids to his success, I regarded only as *ruses*, to afford opportunity for thorough search to the police, and thus the sooner to impress them with the conviction to which G——, in fact, did finally arrive—the conviction that the letter was not upon the premises. I felt, also, that the whole train of thought, which I was at some pains in detailing to you just now, concerning the invariable principle of policial action in searches for articles concealed—I felt that this whole train of thought would necessarily pass through the mind of the Minister. It would imperatively lead him to despise all the ordinary *nooks* of concealment. *He* could not, I reflected, be so weak as not to see that the most intricate and remote recess of his hotel would be as open as his commonest closets to the eyes, to the probes, to the gimlets, and to the microscopes of the Prefect. I saw, in fine, that he would be driven, as a matter of course, to *simplicity*, if not deliberately induced to it as a matter of choice. You will remember, perhaps, how desperately the Prefect laughed when I suggested, upon our first interview, that it was just possible this mystery troubled him so much on account of its being so *very* self-evident."

"Yes," said I, "I remember his merriment well. I really thought he would have fallen into convulsions."

"The material world," continued Dupin, "abounds with the very strict analogies to the immaterial; and thus some color of truth has been given to the rhetorical dogma, that metaphor, or simile, may be made to strengthen an argument, as well as to embellish a description. The principle of the *vis inertiae* [force of inertia], for example, seems to be identical in physics and metaphysics. It is not more true in the former, that a large body is with more difficulty set in motion than a smaller one, and that its subsequent *momentum* is commensurate with this difficulty, than it is, in the latter, that intellects of the vaster capacity, while more forcible, more constant, and more eventful in their movements than those of inferior grade, are yet the less readily moved, and more embarrassed and full of hesitation in the first few steps of their progress. Again: have you ever noticed which of the street signs, over the shop doors, are the most attractive of attention?"

"I have never given the matter a thought," I said.

"There is a game of puzzles," he resumed, "which is played upon a map. One party playing requires another to find a given word—the name of town, river, state or empire—any word, in short, upon the motley and perplexed surface of the chart. A novice in the game generally seeks to embarrass his opponents by giving them the most minutely lettered names; but the adept selects such words as stretch, in large characters, from one end of the chart to the other. These, like the over-largely lettered signs and placards of the street, escape observation by dint of being excessively obvious; and here the physical oversight is precisely analogous with the moral inapprehension by which the intellect suffers to pass unnoticed those considerations which are too obtrusively and too palpably self-evident. But this is a point, it appears, somewhat above or beneath the understanding of the Prefect. He never once thought it probable, or possible, that the Minister had deposited the letter immediately beneath the nose of the whole world, by way of best preventing any portion of that world from perceiving it.

"But the more I reflected upon the daring, dashing, and discriminating ingenuity of D——; upon the fact that the document must always have been *at hand*, if he intended to use it to good purpose; and upon the decisive evidence, obtained by the Prefect, that it was not hidden within the limits of that dignitary's ordinary search—the more satisfied I became that, to conceal this letter, the Minister had resorted to the comprehensive and sagacious expedient of not attempting to conceal it at all.

"Full of these ideas, I prepared myself with a pair of green spectacles, and called one fine morning, quite by accident, at the Ministerial hotel. I found D—— at home, yawning, lounging, and dawdling, as usual, and pretending to be in the last extremity of *ennui*. He is, perhaps, the most really energetic human being now alive—but that is only when nobody sees him.

"To be even with him, I complained of my weak eyes, and lamented the necessity of the spectacles, under cover of which I cautiously and thoroughly surveyed the apartment, while seemingly intent only upon the conversation of my host.

"I paid especial attention to a large writing-table near which he sat, and upon which lay confusedly some miscellaneous letters and other papers, with one or two musical instruments and a few books.

89

Here, however, after a long and very deliberate scrutiny, I saw nothing to excite particular suspicion.

"At length my eyes, in going the circuit of the room, fell upon a trumpery filigree card-rack of pasteboard, that hung dangling by a dirty blue ribbon, from a little brass knob just beneath the middle of the mantel-piece. In this rack, which had three or four compartments, were five or six visiting cards and a solitary letter. This last was much soiled and crumpled. It was torn nearly in two, across the middle—as if a design, in the first instance, to tear it entirely up as worthless, had been altered, or stayed, in the second. It had a large black seal, bearing the D—— cipher *very* conspicuously, and was addressed, in a diminutive female hand, to D——, the Minister, himself. It was thrust carelessly, and even, as it seemed, contemptuously, into one of the upper divisions of the rack.

"No sooner had I glanced at this letter, than I concluded it to be that of which I was in search. To be sure, it was, to all appearance, radically different from the one of which the Prefect had read us so minute a description. Here the seal was large and black, with the D—— cipher; there it was small and red, with the ducal arms of the S—— family. Here, the address, to the Minister, was diminutive and feminine; there the superscription, to a certain royal personage, was markedly bold and decided; the size alone formed a point of correspondence. But, then, the *radicalness* of these differences, which was excessive; the dirt; the soiled and torn condition of the paper, so inconsistent with the *true* methodical habits of D——, and so suggestive of a design to delude the beholder into an idea of the worthlessness of the document;—these things, together with the hyperobtrusive situation of this document, full in the view of every visitor, and thus exactly in accordance with the conclusions to which I had previously arrived; these things, I say, were strongly corroborative of suspicion, in one who came with the intention to suspect.

"I protracted my visit as long as possible, and, while I maintained a most animated discussion with the Minister, on a topic which I knew well had never failed to interest and excite him, I kept my attention really riveted upon the letter. In this examination, I committed to memory its external appearance and arrangement in the rack; and also fell, at length, upon a discovery which set at rest whatever trivial doubt I might have entertained. In scrutinizing the edges of the paper, I observed them to be more *chafed* than seemed necessary. They presented the *broken* appearance which is manifested when a stiff paper, having been once folded and pressed with a folder, is refolded in a reversed direction, in the same creases or edges which had formed the original fold. This discovery was sufficient. It was clear to me that the letter had been turned, as a glove, inside out, re-directed, and resealed. I bade the Minister good morning, and took my departure at once, leaving a gold snuff-box upon the table.

"The next morning I called for the snuff-box, when we resumed, quite eagerly, the conversation of the preceding day. While thus engaged, however, a loud report, as if of a pistol, was heard immediately beneath the windows of the hotel, and was succeeded by a series of fearful screams, and the shoutings of a mob. D—— rushed to a casement, threw it open, and looked out. In the meantime, I stepped to the card-rack, took the letter, and put it in my pocket, and replaced it by a *fac-simile* (so far as regards externals), which I had carefully prepared at my lodgings; imitating the D—— cipher, very readily, by means of a seal formed of bread.

"The disturbance in the street had been occasioned by the frantic behavior of a man with a musket. He had fired it among a crowd of women and children. It proved, however, to have been without ball, and the fellow was suffered to go his way as a lunatic or a drunkard. When he had gone, D—— came from the window, whither I had followed him immediately upon securing the object in view. Soon afterwards I bade him farewell. The pretended lunatic was a man in my own pay."

"But what purpose had you," I asked, "in replacing the letter by a *fac-simile?* Would it not have been better, at the first visit, to have seized it openly, and departed?"

"D——," replied Dupin, "is a desperate man, and a man of nerve. His hotel, too, is not without attendants devoted to his interests. Had I made the wild attempt you suggest, I might never have left the Ministerial presence alive. The good people of Paris might have heard of me no more. But I had an object apart from these considerations. You know my political prepossessions. In this matter, I act as a partisan of the lady concerned. For eighteen months the Minister has had her in his power. She has now him in hers—since, being unaware that the letter is not in his possession, he will proceed with his exactions as if it was. Thus will he inevitably commit himself, at once, to his political destruction. His downfall, too, will not be more precipitate than awkward. It is all very well to talk about the *facilis descensus Averni* [facile descent to Hades]; but in all kinds of climbing, as Catalani said of singing, it is far more easy to get up than to come down. In the present instance I have no sympathy—at least no pity—for him who descends. He is that *monstrum horrendum* [horrendous monster], an unprincipled man of genius. I confess, however, that I should like very well to know the precise character of his thoughts, when, being defied by her whom the Prefect terms 'a certain personage,' he is reduced to opening the letter which I left for him in the card-rack."

"How? did you put any thing particular in it?"

"Why—it did not seem altogether right to leave the interior blank—that would have been insulting. D——, at Vienna once, did me an evil turn, which I told him, quite good-humoredly, that I should remember. So, as I knew he would feel some curiosity in regard to the identity of the person who had outwitted him, I thought it a pity not to give him a clue. He is well acquainted with my MS., and I just copied into the middle of the blank sheet the words—

> "—Un dessein si funeste,
> S'il n'est digne d'Atrée, est digne de Thyeste.

[A plan so deadly is worthy of Thyestes, if not of Atreus.]

They are to be found in Crébillon's 'Atrée.'"

THE
TELL-TALE HEART

By Edgar Allan Poe

"The Tell-Tale Heart" is not generally considered one of Poe's detective stories though it does contain such conventional elements of the form as a brutal murder and plodding but incompetent police. Rather than ratiocination or analysis in the work, however, it is guilt that reveals the identity of the criminal, and this device has since become traditional in the crime story, a genre closely allied to detective fiction. "The Tell-Tale Heart" was first published in the Pioneer in January 1843 and should be read in conjunction with Dickens' "A Confession Found in a Prison in the Time of Charles the Second," a story which preceded it by some three years. For more information about Poe's life see Arthur H. Quinn's Edgar Allan Poe: A Critical Biography (New York: Apple-Century-Crofts, 1941).

True!—nervous—very, very dreadfully nervous I had been and am; but why *will* you say that I am mad? The disease had sharpened my senses—not destroyed—not dulled them. Above all was the sense of hearing acute. I heard all things in the heaven and in the earth. I heard many things in hell. How, then, am I mad? Hearken! and observe how healthily—how calmly I can tell you the whole story.

It is impossible to say how first the idea entered my brain; but once conceived, it haunted me day and night. Object there was none. Passion there was none. I loved the old man. He had never wronged me. He had never given me insult. For his gold I had no desire. I think it was his eye! yes, it was this! One of his resembled that of a vulture—a pale blue eye, with a film over it. Whenever it fell upon me, my blood ran cold; and so by degrees—very gradually—I made up my mind to take the life of the old man, and thus rid myself of the eye for ever.

Now this is the point. You fancy me mad. Madmen know nothing. But you should have seen *me*. You should have seen how wisely I proceeded—with what caution—with what foresight—with what dissimulation I went to work! I was never kinder to the old man than during the whole week before I killed him. And every night, about midnight, I turned the latch of his door and opened it—oh, so gently! And then, when I had made an opening sufficient for my head, I put in a dark lantern, all closed, closed, so that no light shone out, and then I thrust in my head. Oh, you would have laughed to see how cunningly I thrust it in! I moved it slowly—very, very slowly, so that I might not disturb the old man's sleep. It took me an hour to place my whole head within the opening so far that I could see him as he lay upon his bed. Ha!—would a madman have been so wise as this? And then, when my head was well in the room, I undid the lantern cautiously—oh, so cautiously—cautiously (for the hinges creaked)—I undid it just so much that a single thin ray fell upon the vulture eye. And this I did for seven long nights—every night just at midnight—but I found the eye always closed; and so it was impossible to do the work; for it was not the old man who vexed me, but his Evil Eye. And every morning, when the day broke, I went boldly into the chamber, and spoke courageously to him, calling him by name in a hearty tone, and inquiring how he had passed the night. So you see he would have been a very profound old man, indeed, to suspect that every night, just at twelve, I looked in upon him while he slept.

Upon the eighth night I was more than usually cautious in opening the door. A watch's minute hand moves more quickly than did mine. Never before that night had I *felt* the extent of my own powers — of my sagacity. I could scarcely contain my feelings of triumph. To think that there I was, opening the door, little by little, and he not even to dream of my secret deeds or thoughts. I fairly chuckled at the idea; and perhaps he heard me; for he moved on the bed suddenly, as if startled. Now you may think that I drew back — but no. His room was as black as pitch with the thick darkness (for the shutters were close fastened, through fear of robbers), and so I knew that he could not see the opening of the door, and I kept pushing it on steadily, steadily.

I had my head in, and was about to open the lantern, when my thumb slipped upon the tin fastening, and the old man sprang up in the bed, crying out — "Who's there?"

I kept quite still and said nothing. For a whole hour I did not move a muscle, and in the meantime I did not hear him lie down. He was still sitting up in the bed listening; — just as I have done, night after night, hearkening to the death watches in the wall.

Presently I heard a slight groan, and I knew it was the groan of mortal terror. It was not a groan of pain or of grief — oh, no! — it was the low stifled sound that arises from the bottom of the soul when overcharged with awe. I knew the sound well. Many a night, just at midnight, when all the world slept, it has welled up from my own bosom, deepening, with its dreadful echo, the terrors that distracted me. I say I knew it well. I knew what the old man felt, and pitied him, although I chuckled at heart. I knew that he had been lying awake ever since the first slight noise, when he had turned in the bed. His fears had been ever since growing upon him. He had been trying to fancy them causeless, but could not. He had been saying to himself — "It is nothing but the wind in the chimney — it is only a mouse crossing the floor," or "it is merely a cricket which has made a single chirp." Yes, he has been trying to comfort himself with these suppositions; but he had found all in vain. *All in vain*; because Death, in approaching him, had stalked with his black shadow before him, and enveloped the victim. And it was the mournful influence of the unperceived shadow that caused him to feel — although he neither saw nor heard — to *feel* the presence of my head within the room.

When I had waited a long time, very patiently, without hearing him lie down, I resolved to open a little — a very, very little crevice in the lantern. So I opened it — you cannot imagine how stealthily, stealthily — until, at length, a single dim ray, like the thread of a spider, shot from out the crevice and full upon the vulture eye.

It was open—wide, wide open—and I grew furious as I gazed upon it. I saw it with perfect distinctness—all a dull blue, with a hideous veil over it that chilled the very marrow in my bones; but I could see nothing else of the old man's face or person: for I had directed the ray as if by instinct, precisely upon the damned spot.

And now have I not told you that what you mistake for madness is but over-acuteness of the senses?—now, I say, there came to my ears a low, dull, quick sound, such as a watch makes when enveloped in cotton. I knew *that* sound well too. It was the beating of the old man's heart. It increased my fury, as the beating of a drum stimulates the soldier into courage.

But even yet I refrained and kept still. I scarcely breathed. I held the lantern motionless. I tried how steadily I could maintain the ray upon the eye. Meantime the hellish tattoo of the heart increased. It grew quicker and quicker, and louder and louder every instant. The old man's terror *must* have been extreme! It grew louder, I say, louder every moment!—do you mark me well? I have told you that I am nervous: so I am. And now at the dead hour of the night, amid the dreadful silence of that old house, so strange a noise as this excited me to uncontrollable terror. Yet, for some minutes longer I refrained and stood still. But the beating grew louder, louder! I thought the heart must burst. And now a new anxiety seized me—the sound would be heard by a neighbor! The old man's hour had come! With a loud yell, I threw open the lantern and leaped into the room. He shrieked once—once only. In an instant I dragged him to the floor, and pulled the heavy bed over him. I then smiled gaily, to find the deed so far done. But, for many minutes, the heart beat on with a muffled sound. This, however, did not vex me; it would not be heard through the wall. At length it ceased. The old man was dead. I removed the bed and examined the corpse. Yes, he was stone, stone dead. I placed my hand upon the heart and held it there many minutes. There was no pulsation. He was stone dead. His eye would trouble me no more.

If still you think me mad, you will think so no longer when I describe the wise precautions I took for the concealment of the body. The night waned, and I worked hastily, but in silence. First of all I dismembered the corpse. I cut off the head and the arms and the legs.

I then took up three planks from the flooring of the chamber, and deposited all between the scantlings. I then replaced the boards so cleverly, so cunningly, that no human eye—not even *his*—could have detected any thing wrong. There was nothing to wash out—no stain of any kind—no blood-spot whatever. I had been too wary for that. A tub had caught all—ha! ha!

When I had made an end of these labors, it was four o'clock—still dark as midnight. As the bell sounded the hour, there came a knocking at the street door. I went down to open it with a light heart,—for what had I *now* to fear? There entered three men, who introduced themselves with perfect suavity, as officers of the police. A shriek had been heard by a neighbor during the night; suspicion of foul play had been aroused; information had been lodged at the police office, and they (the officers) had been deputed to search the premises.

I smiled,—for *what* had I to fear? I bade the gentlemen welcome. The shriek, I said, was my own in a dream. The old man, I mentioned, was absent in the country. I took my visitors all over the house. I bade them search—search *well*. I led them, at length, to *his* chamber. I showed them his treasures, secure, undisturbed. In the enthusiasm of my confidence, I brought chairs into the room, and desired them *here* to rest from their fatigues, while I myself, in the wild audacity of my perfect triumph, placed my own seat upon the very spot beneath which reposed the corpse of the victim.

The officers were satisfied. My *manner* had convinced them. I was singularly at ease. They sat, and while I answered cheerfully, they chatted familiar things. But, ere long, I felt myself getting pale and wished them gone. My head ached, and I fancied a ringing in my ears: but still they sat and still chatted. The ringing became more distinct:—it continued and became more distinct: I talked more freely to get rid of the feeling: but it continued and gained definitiveness— until, at length, I found that the noise was *not* within my ears.

No doubt I now grew *very* pale;—but I talked more fluently, and with a heightened voice. Yet the sound increased—and what could I do? It was *a low, dull, quick sound—much such a sound as a watch makes when enveloped in cotton*. I gasped for breath—and yet the officers heard it not. I talked more quickly—more vehemently; but the noise steadily increased. I arose and argued about trifles, in a high key and with violent gesticulations, but the noise steadily increased. Why *would* they not be gone? I paced the floor to and fro with heavy strides, as if excited to fury by the observation of the men—but the noise steadily increased. Oh God! what *could* I do? I foamed—I raved—I swore! I swung the chair upon which I had been sitting, and grated it upon the boards, but the noise arose over all and continually increased. It grew louder—louder—*louder!* And still the men chatted pleasantly, and smiled. Was it possible they heard not? Almighty God!—no, no! They heard!—they suspected!—they *knew!*—they were making a mockery of my horror!—this I thought, and this I think. But any thing was better than this agony! Any thing was more tolerable than this derision! I could bear those hypocritical smiles no longer! I felt that I must scream or die!—and now—again!—hark! louder! louder! louder! *louder!*—

"Villains!" I shrieked, "dissemble no more! I admit the deed!—tear up the planks!—here, here!—it is the beating of his hideous heart!"

CHAPTER III

THE GAME'S AFOOT

A SCANDAL
IN BOHEMIA

By Arthur Conan Doyle

Sir Arthur Conan Doyle (1859–1930), creator of Sherlock Holmes, the best known of all fictional detectives, was born in Scotland of Irish parents and attended Edinburgh University where, in 1881, he received a Bachelor of Medicine degree. After a year as a ship's doctor, first in the Arctic and later in Africa, he opened his own practice in the English coastal town of Southsea but attracted few patients and turned to the writing of fiction to fill the time. He had previously published a few short stories and now began to write longer works, beginning with an autobiographical novel never published and now lost. In 1886 he completed A Study in Scarlet, the first book about Sherlock Holmes, basing the character of the detective in part on Poe's C. Auguste Dupin, in part on Dr. Joseph Bell, an Edinburgh surgeon and one of Conan Doyle's medical instructors at the university. A Study in Scarlet was published in 1887 and was followed, in 1890, by The Sign of Four and, in 1891, by the series of Sherlock Holmes short stories in The Strand magazine of London that made the lean, sharp-featured detective world famous. These stories were later collected in two volumes, The Adventures of Sherlock Holmes (1892) and The Memoirs of Sherlock Holmes (1894). "A Scandal in Bohemia," the first published short story featuring Holmes, originally appeared in The Strand in July 1891 and became the opening work in The Adventures.

To Sherlock Holmes she is always *the* woman. I have seldom heard him mention her under any other name. In his eyes she eclipses and predominates the whole of her sex. It was not that he felt any emotion akin to love for Irene Adler. All emotions, and that one particularly, were abhorrent to his cold, precise, but admirably balanced mind. He was, I take it, the most perfect reasoning and observing machine that the world has seen; but, as a lover, he would have placed himself in a false position. He never spoke of the softer passions, save with a gibe and a sneer. They were admirable things for the observer—excellent for drawing the veil from men's motives and actions. But for the trained reasoner to admit such intrusions into his own delicate and finely adjusted temperament was to introduce a distracting factor which might throw a doubt upon all his mental results. Grit in a sensitive instrument, or a crack in one of his own high-power lenses, would not be more disturbing than a strong emotion in a nature such as his. And yet there was but one woman to him, and that woman was the late Irene Adler, of dubious and questionable memory.

I had seen little of Holmes lately. My marriage had drifted us away from each other. My own complete happiness, and the home-centered interests which rise up around the man who first finds himself master of his own establishment, were sufficient to absorb all my attention; while Holmes, who loathed every form of society with his whole Bohemian soul, remained in our lodgings in Baker-street, buried among his old books, and alternating from week to week between cocaine and ambition, the drowsiness of the drug, and the fierce energy of his own keen nature. He was still, as ever, deeply attracted by the study of crime, and occupied his immense faculties and extraordinary powers of observation in following out those clues, and clearing up those mysteries, which had been abandoned as hopeless by the official police. From time to time I heard some vague account of his doings: of his summons to Odessa in the case of the Trepoff murder, of his clearing up of the singular tragedy of the Atkinson brothers at Trincomalee, and finally of the mission which he had accomplished so delicately and successfully for the reigning family of Holland. Beyond these signs of his activity, however, which I merely shared with all the readers of the daily press, I knew little of my former friend and companion.

One night—it was on the 20th of March, 1888—I was returning from a journey to a patient (for I had now returned to civil practice), when my way led me through Baker-street. As I passed the well-remembered door, which must always be associated in my mind with my wooing, and with the dark incidents of the Study in Scarlet, I was seized with a keen desire to see Holmes again, and to know how he was employing his extraordinary powers. His rooms were brilliantly lit, and, even as I looked up, I saw his tall spare figure pass twice in a dark silhouette against the blind. He was pacing the room swiftly, eagerly, with his head sunk upon his chest, and his hands clasped behind him. To me, who knew his every mood and habit, his attitude and manner told their own story. He was at work again. He had arisen out of his drug-created dreams, and was hot upon the scent of some new problem. I rang the bell, and was shown up to the chamber which had formerly been in part my own.

His manner was not effusive. It seldom was; but he was glad, I think, to see me. With hardly a word spoken, but with a kindly eye, he waved me to an armchair, threw across his case of cigars, and indicated a spirit case and a gasogene in the corner. Then he stood before the fire, and looked me over in his singular introspective fashion.

"Wedlock suits you," he remarked. "I think, Watson, that you have put on seven and a half pounds since I saw you."

"Seven," I answered.

"Indeed, I should have thought a little more. Just a trifle more, I fancy, Watson. And in practice again, I observe. You did not tell me that you intended to go into harness."

"Then, how do you know?"

"I see it, I deduce it. How do I know that you have been getting yourself very wet lately, and that you have a most clumsy and careless servant girl?"

"My dear Holmes," said I, "this is too much. You would certainly have been burned, had you lived a few centuries ago. It is true that I had a country walk on Thursday and came home in a dreadful mess; but, as I have changed my clothes, I can't imagine how you deduce it. As to Mary Jane, she is incorrigible, and my wife has given her notice; but there again I fail to see how you work it out."

He chuckled to himself and rubbed his long nervous hands together.

"It is simplicity itself," said he; "my eyes tell me that on the inside of your left shoe, just where the firelight strikes it, the leather is scored by six almost parallel cuts. Obviously they have been caused by some-one who has very carelessly scraped round the edges of the sole in order to remove crusted mud from it. Hence, you see, my double deduction that you had been out in vile weather, and that you had a particularly malignant boot-slitting specimen of the London slavey. As to your practice, if a gentleman walks into my rooms smelling of iodoform, with a black mark of nitrate of silver upon his right fore-finger, and a bulge on the side of his top-hat to show where he has secreted his stethoscope, I must be dull indeed, if I do not pronounce him to be an active member of the medical profession."

I could not help laughing at the ease with which he explained his process of deduction. "When I hear you give your reasons," I remarked, "the thing always appears to me to be so ridiculously simple that I could easily do it myself, though at each successive instance of your reasoning I am baffled, until you explain your process. And yet I believe that my eyes are as good as yours."

"Quite so," he answered, lighting a cigarette, and throwing himself down into an armchair. "You see, but you do not observe. The distinction is clear. For example, you have frequently seen the steps which lead up from the hall to this room."

"Frequently."

"How often?"

"Well, some hundreds of times."

"Then how many are there?"

"How many! I don't know."

"Quite so! You have not observed. And yet you have seen. That is just my point. Now, I know that there are seventeen steps, because I have both seen and observed. By the way, since you are interested in these little problems, and since you are good enough to chronicle one or two of my trifling experiences, you may be interested in this." He threw over a sheet of thick, pink-tinted notepaper which had been lying open upon the table. "It came by the last post," said he. "Read it aloud."

The note was undated, and without either signature or address.

"There will call upon you to-night, at a quarter to eight o'clock," it said, "a gentleman who desires to consult you upon a matter of the very deepest moment. Your recent services to one of the Royal Houses of Europe have shown that you are one who may safely be trusted with matters which are of an importance which can hardly be exaggerated. This account of you we have from all quarters received. Be in your chamber then at that hour, and do not take it amiss if your visitor wear a mask."

"This is indeed a mystery," I remarked. "What do you imagine that it means?"

"I have no data yet. It is a capital mistake to theorise before one has data. Insensibly one begins to twist facts to suit theories, instead of theories to suit facts. But the note itself. What do you deduce from it?"

I carefully examined the writing, and the paper upon which it was written.

"The man who wrote it was presumably well to do," I remarked, endeavoring to imitate my companion's processes. "Such paper could not be bought under half a crown a packet. It is peculiarly strong and stiff."

"Peculiar—that is the very word," said Holmes. "It is not an English paper at all. Hold it up to the light."

I did so, and saw a large E with a small g, a P, and a large G with a small t woven into the texture of the paper.

"What do you make of that?" asked Holmes.

"The name of the maker no doubt; or his monogram, rather."

"Not at all. The G with the small t stands for "Gesellschaft," which is the German for "Company." It is a customary contraction like our "Co." P, of course, stands for "Papier." Now for the Eg. Let us glance at our Continental Gazetteer." He took down a heavy brown voluıne from his shelves. "Eglow, Eglonitz—here we are, Egria. It is in a German-speaking country—in Bohemia, not far from Carlsbad. 'Remarkable as being the scene of the death of Wallenstein, and for its numerous glass factories and paper mills.' Ha, ha, my boy, what do you make of that?" His eyes sparkled, and he sent up a great blue triumphant cloud from his cigarette.

"The paper was made in Bohemia," I said.

"Precisely. And the man who wrote the note is a German. Do you note the peculiar construction of the sentence—'This account of you we have from all quarters received.' A Frenchman or Russian could not have written that. It is the German who is so uncourteous to his verbs. It only remains, therefore, to discover what is wanted by this German who writes upon Bohemian paper, and prefers wearing a mask to showing his face. And here he comes, if I am not mistaken, to resolve all our doubts."

As he spoke there was the sharp sound of horses' hoofs and grating wheels against the curb, followed by a sharp pull at the bell. Holmes whistled.

"A pair, by the sound," said he. "Yes," he continued, glancing out of the window. "A nice little brougham and a pair of beauties. A hundred and fifty guineas apiece. There's money in this case, Watson, if there is nothing else."

"I think that I had better go, Holmes."

"Not a bit, Doctor. Stay where you are. I am lost without my Boswell. And this promises to be interesting. It would be a pity to miss it."

"But your client ——"

"Never mind him. I may want your help, and so may he. Here

he comes. Sit down in that armchair, Doctor, and give us your best attention."

A slow and heavy step, which had been heard upon the stairs and in the passage, paused immediately outside the door. Then there was a loud and authoritative tap.

"Come in!" said Holmes.

A man entered who could hardly have been less than six feet six inches in height, with the chest and limbs of a Hercules. His dress was rich with a richness which would, in England, be looked upon as akin to bad taste. Heavy bands of Astrakhan were slashed across the sleeves and fronts of his double-breasted coat, while the deep blue cloak which was thrown over his shoulders was lined with flame-coloured silk, and secured at the neck with a brooch which consisted of a single flaming beryl. Boots which extended half way up his calves, and which were trimmed at the tops with rich brown fur, completed the impression of barbaric opulence which was suggested by his whole appearance. He carried a broad-brimmed hat in his hand, while he wore across the upper part of his face, extending down past the cheek-bones, a black vizard mask, which he had apparently adjusted that very moment, for his hand was still raised to it as he entered. From the lower part of the face he appeared to be a man of strong character, with a thick, hanging lip, and a long straight chin, suggestive of resolution pushed to the length of obstinacy.

"You had my note?" he asked, with a deep harsh voice and a strongly marked German accent. "I told you that I would call." He looked from one to the other of us, as if uncertain which to address.

"Pray take a seat," said Holmes. "This is my friend and colleague, Dr. Watson, who is occasionally good enough to help me in my cases. Whom have I the honour to address?"

"You may address me as the Count Von Kramm, a Bohemian nobleman. I understand that this gentleman, your friend, is a man of honour and discretion, whom I may trust with a matter of the most extreme importance. If not, I should much prefer to communicate with you alone."

I rose to go, but Holmes caught me by the wrist and pushed me back into my chair. "It is, both, or none," said he. "You may say before this gentleman anything which you may say to me."

The Count shrugged his broad shoulders. "Then I must begin," said he, "by binding you both to absolute secrecy for two years, at the end of that time the matter will be of no importance. At present it is not too much to say that it is of such weight that it may have an influence upon European history."

"I promise," said Holmes.

"And I."

"You will excuse this mask," continued our strange visitor. "The august person who employs me wishes his agent to be unknown to you, and I may confess at once that the title by which I have just called myself is not exactly my own."

"I was aware of it," said Holmes dryly.

"The circumstances are of great delicacy, and every precaution has to be taken to quench what might grow to be an immense scandal and seriously compromise one of the reigning families of Europe. To speak plainly, the matter implicates the great House of Ormstein, hereditary kings of Bohemia."

"I was also aware of that," murmured Holmes, settling himself down in his armchair, and closing his eyes.

Our visitor glanced with some apparent surprise at the languid, lounging figure of the man who had been no doubt depicted to him as the most incisive reasoner, and most energetic agent in Europe. Holmes slowly reopened his eyes, and looked impatiently at his gigantic client.

"If your majesty would condescend to state your case," he remarked, "I should be better able to advise you."

The man sprang from his chair, and paced up and down the room in uncontrollable agitation. Then, with a gesture of desperation, he tore the mask from his face and hurled it upon the ground. "You are right," he cried, "I am the King. Why should I attempt to conceal it?"

"Why, indeed?" murmured Holmes. "Your Majesty had not spoken before I was aware that I was addressing Wilhelm Gottsreich Sigismond von Ormstein, Grand Duke of Cassel-Felstein, and hereditary King of Bohemia."

"But you can understand," said our strange visitor, sitting down once more and passing his hand over his high, white forehead, "you can understand that I am not accustomed to doing such business in my own person. Yet the matter was so delicate that I could not confide it to an agent without putting myself in his power. I have come *incognito* from Prague for the purpose of consulting you."

"Then, pray consult," said Holmes, shutting his eyes once more.

"The facts are briefly these: Some five years ago, during a lengthy visit to Warsaw, I made the acquaintance of the well-known adventuress Irene Adler. The name is no doubt familiar to you."

"Kindly look her up in my index, Doctor," murmured Holmes, without opening his eyes. For many years he had adopted a system of docketing all paragraphs concerning men and things, so that it was difficult to name a subject or a person on which he could not at once furnish information. In this case I found her biography sandwiched in between that of a Hebrew Rabbi and that of a staff-commander who had written a monograph upon the deep sea fishes.

"Let me see?" said Holmes. "Hum! Born in New Jersey in the year 1858. Contralto—hum! La Scala, hum! Prima donna Imperial Opera of Warsaw—Yes! Retired from operatic stage—ha! Living in London—quite so! Your Majesty, as I understand, became entangled with this young person, wrote her some compromising letters, and is now desirous of getting those letters back."

"Precisely so. But how ——"

"Was there a secret marriage?"

"None."

"No legal papers or certificates?"

"None."

"Then I fail to follow your Majesty. If this young person should produce her letters for blackmailing or other purposes, how is she to prove their authenticity?"

"There is the writing."

"Pooh, pooh! Forgery."

"My private notepaper."

"Stolen."

"My own seal."

"Imitated."

"My photograph."

"Bought."

"We were both in the photograph."

"Oh dear! That is very bad! Your Majesty has indeed committed an indiscretion."

"I was mad—insane."

"You have compromised yourself seriously."

"I was only Crown Prince then. I was young. I am but thirty now."

"It must be recovered."

"We have tried and failed."

"Your Majesty must pay. It must be bought."

"She will not sell."

"Stolen, then."

"Five attempts have been made. Twice burglars in my pay ransacked her house. Once we diverted her luggage when she travelled. Twice she has been waylaid. There has been no result."

"No sight of it?"

"Absolutely none."

Holmes laughed. "It is quite a pretty little problem," said he.

"But a very serious one to me," returned the King, reproachfully.

"Very, indeed. And what does she propose to do with the photograph?"

"To ruin me."

"But how?"

"I am about to be married."

"So I have heard."

"To Clotilde Lothman von Saxe-Meningen, second daughter of the King of Scandinavia. You may know the strict principles of her family. She is herself the very soul of delicacy. A shadow of a doubt as to my conduct would bring the matter to an end."

"And Irene Adler?"

"Threatens to send them the photograph. And she will do it. I know that she will do it. You do not know her, but she has a soul of steel. She has the face of the most beautiful of women, and the mind of the most resolute of men. Rather than I should marry another woman, there are no lengths to which she would not go—none."

"You are sure that she has not sent it yet?"

"I am sure."

"And why?"

"Because she has said that she would send it on the day when the betrothal was publicly proclaimed. That will be next Monday."

"Oh, then, we have three days yet," said Holmes, with a yawn. "That is very fortunate, as I have one or two matters of importance to look into just at present. Your Majesty will, of course, stay in London for the present?"

"Certainly. You will find me at the Langham, under the name of the Count Von Kramm."

"Then I shall drop you a line to let you know how we progress."

"Pray do so. I shall be all anxiety."

"Then, as to money?"

"You have *carte blanche*."

"Absolutely?"

"I tell you that I would give one of the provinces of my kingdom to have that photograph."

"And for present expenses?"

The king took a heavy chamois leather bag from under his cloak, and laid it on the table.

"There are three hundred pounds in gold, and seven hundred in notes," he said.

Holmes scribbled a receipt upon a sheet of his note-book, and handed it to him.

"And mademoiselle's address?" he asked.

"Is Briony Lodge, Serpentine-avenue, St. John's Wood."

Holmes took a note of it. "One other question," said he. "Was the photograph a cabinet?"

"It was."

"Then, good night, your Majesty, and I trust that we shall soon have some good news for you. And good night, Watson," he added, as the wheels of the Royal brougham rolled down the street. "If you will be good enough to call tomorrow afternoon, at three o'clock, I should like to chat this little matter over with you."

II.

At three o'clock precisely I was at Baker-street, but Holmes had not yet returned. The landlady informed me that he had left the house shortly after eight o'clock in the morning. I sat down beside the fire, however, with the intention of awaiting him, however long he might be. I was already deeply interested in his inquiry, for, though it was surrounded by none of the grim and strange features which were associated with the two crimes which I have already recorded, still, the nature of the case and the exalted station of his client gave it a character of its own. Indeed, apart from the nature of the investigation which my friend had on hand, there was something in his masterly grasp of a situation, and his keen, incisive reasoning, which make it a pleasure to me to study his system of work, and to follow the quick, subtle methods by which he disentangled the most inextricable mysteries. So accustomed was I to his invariable success that the very possibility of his failing had ceased to enter into my head.

It was close upon four before the door opened, and a drunken-looking groom, ill-kempt and side-whiskered, with an inflamed face and disreputable clothes, walked into the room. Accustomed as I was to my friend's amazing powers in the use of disguises, I had to look three times before I was certain that it was indeed he. With a nod he vanished into the bedroom, whence he emerged in five minutes tweed-suited and respectable, as of old. Putting his hands into his pockets, he stretched out his legs in front of the fire, and laughed heartily for some minutes.

"Well, really!" he cried, and then he choked; and laughed again until he was obliged to lie back, limp and helpless, in the chair.

"What is it?"

"It's quite too funny. I am sure you could never guess how I employed my morning, or what I ended by doing."

"I can't imagine. I suppose that you have been watching the habits, and perhaps the house, of Miss Irene Adler."

"Quite so, but the sequel was rather unusual. I will tell you, however. I left the house a little after eight o'clock this morning, in the character of a groom out of work. There is a wonderful sympathy and freemasonry among horsey men. Be one of them, and you will know all that there is to know. I soon found Briony Lodge. It is a *bijou* villa, with a garden at the back, but built out in front right up to the road, two stories. Chubb lock to the door. Large sitting-room on the right side, well furnished, with long windows almost to the floor, and those preposterous English window fasteners which a child could open. Behind there was nothing remarkable, save that the passage window could be reached from the top of the coach-house. I walked round it and examined it closely from every point of view, but without noting anything else of interest.

"I then lounged down the street, and found, as I expected, that there was a mews in a lane which runs down by one wall of the garden. I lent the ostlers a hand in rubbing down their horses, and I received in exchange twopence, a glass of half-and-half, two fills of shag tobacco, and as much information as I could desire about Miss Adler, to say nothing of half a dozen other people in the neighbourhood in whom I was not in the least interested, but whose biographies I was compelled to listen to."

"And what of Irene Adler?" I asked.

"Oh, she has turned all the men's heads down in that part. She is the daintiest thing under a bonnet on this planet. So say the Serpentine-mews, to a man. She lives quietly, sings at concerts, drives out at five every day, and returns at seven sharp for dinner. Seldom goes out at other times, except when she sings. Has only one male visitor, but a good deal of him. He is dark, handsome, and dashing; never calls less than once a day, and often twice. He is a Mr. Godfrey Norton, of the Inner Temple. See the advantages of a cabman as confidant. They had driven him home a dozen times from Serpentine-mews, and knew all about him. When I had listened to all that they had to tell, I began to walk up and down near Briony Lodge once more, and to think over my plan of campaign.

"This Godfrey Norton was evidently an important factor in the matter. He was a lawyer. That sounded ominous. What was the relation between them, and what the object of his repeated visits? Was she his client, his friend, or his mistress? If the former, she had probably transferred the photograph to his keeping. If the latter, it was less likely. On the issue of this question depended whether I should continue my work at Briony Lodge, or turn my attention to the gentleman's chambers in the Temple. It was a delicate point, and it widened the field of my inquiry. I fear that I bore you with these details, but I have to let you see my little difficulties, if you are to understand the situation."

"I am following you closely," I answered.

"I was still balancing the matter in my mind, when a hansom cab drove up to Briony Lodge, and a gentleman sprang out. He was a remarkably handsome man, dark, aquiline, and moustached—evidently the man of whom I had heard. He appeared to be in a great hurry, shouted to the cabman to wait, and brushed past the maid who opened the door with the air of a man who was thoroughly at home.

"He was in the house about half an hour, and I could catch glimpses of him, in the windows of the sitting-room, pacing up and down, talking excitedly and waving his arms. Of her I could see nothing. Presently he emerged, looking even more flurried than before. As he stepped up to the cab, he pulled a gold watch from his pocket and looked at it earnestly. 'Drive like the devil,' he shouted, 'first to Gross & Hankey's in Regent-street, and then to the church of St. Monica in the Edgware-road. Half a guinea if you do it in twenty minutes!'

"Away they went, and I was just wondering whether I should not do well to follow them, when up the lane came a neat little landau, the coachman with his coat only half buttoned, and his tie under his ear, while all the tags of his harness were sticking out of the buckles. It hadn't pulled up before she shot out of the hall door and into it. I only caught a glimpse of her at the moment, but she was a lovely woman, with a face that a man might die for.

"'The Church of St. Monica, John,' she cried, 'and half a sovereign if you reach it in twenty minutes.'

"This was quite too good to lose, Watson. I was just balancing whether I should run for it, or whether I should perch behind her landau, when a cab came through the street. The driver looked twice at such a shabby fare; but I jumped in before he could object. 'The Church of St. Monica,' said I, 'and half a soverign if you reach it in twenty minutes.' It was twenty-five minutes to twelve, and of course it was clear enough what was in the wind.

"My cabby drove fast. I don't think I ever drove faster, but the others were there before us. The cab and the landau with their steaming horses were in front of the door when I arrived. I paid the man, and hurried into the church. There was not a soul there save the two whom I had followed and a surpliced clergyman, who seemed to be expostulating with them. They were all three standing in a knot in front of the

111

altar. I lounged up the side aisle like any other idler who has dropped into a church. Suddenly, to my surprise, the three at the altar faced round to me, and Godfrey Norton came running as hard as he could towards me."

"Thank God!" he cried. "You'll do. Come! Come!"

"What then?" I asked.

"Come man, come, only three minutes, or it won't be legal."

I was half dragged up to the altar, and before I knew where I was, I found myself mumbling responses which were whispered in my ear, and vouching for things of which I knew nothing, and generally assisting in the secure tying up of Irene Adler, spinster, to Godfrey Norton, bachelor. It was all done in an instant, and there was the gentleman thanking me on the one side and the lady on the other, while the clergyman beamed on me in front. It was the most preposterous position in which I ever found myself in my life, and it was the thought of it that started me laughing just now. It seems that there had been some informality about their licence, that the clergyman absolutely refused to marry them without a witness of some sort, and that my lucky appearance saved the bridegroom from having to sally out into the streets in search of a best man. The bride gave me a sovereign, and I mean to wear it on my watch chain in memory of the ocasion."

"This is a very unexpected turn of affairs," said I; "and what then?"

"Well, I found my plans very seriously menaced. It looked as if the pair might take an immediate departure, and so necessitate very prompt and energetic measures on my part. At the church door, however, they separated, he driving back to the Temple, and she to her own house. 'I shall drive out in the Park at five as usual,' she said as she left him. I heard no more. They drove away in different directions, and I went off to make my own arrangements."

"Which are?"

"Some cold beef and a glass of beer," he answered, ringing the bell. "I have been too busy to think of food, and I am likely to be busier still this evening. By the way, Doctor, I shall want your co-operation."

"I shall be delighted."

"You don't mind breaking the law?"

"Not in the least."

"Nor running a chance of arrest?"

"Not in a good cause."

"Oh, the cause is excellent!"

"Then I am your man."

"I was sure that I might rely on you."

"But what is it you wish?"

"When Mrs. Turner has brought in the tray I will make it clear to you. Now," he said, as he turned hungrily on the simple fare that our landlady had provided, "I must discuss it while I eat, for I have not much time. It is nearly five now. In two hours we must be on the scene of action. Miss Irene, or Madame, rather, returns from her drive at seven. We must be at Briony Lodge to meet her."

"And what then?"

"You must leave that to me. I have already arranged what is to occur. There is only one point on which I must insist. You must not interfere, come what may. You understand?"

"I am to be neutral?"

"To do nothing whatever. There will probably be some small unpleasantness. Do not join in it. It will end in my being conveyed into the house. Four or five minutes afterwards the sitting-room window will open. You are to station yourself close to that open window."

"Yes."

"You are to watch me, for I will be visible to you."

"Yes."

"And when I raise my hand—so—you will throw into the room what I give you to throw, and will, at the same time, raise the cry of fire. You quite follow me?"

"Entirely."

"It is nothing very formidable," he said, taking a long cigar-shaped roll from his pocket. "It is an ordinary plumber's smoke rocket, fitted with a cap at either end to make it self-lighting. Your task is confined to that. When you raise your cry of fire, it will be taken up by quite a number of people. You may then walk to the end of the street, and I will rejoin you in ten minutes. I hope that I have made myself clear?"

"I am to remain neutral, to get near the window, to watch you, and, at the signal, to throw in this object, then to raise the cry of fire, and to wait you at the corner of the street."

"Precisely."

"Then you may entirely rely on me."

"That is excellent. I think perhaps it is almost time that I prepared for the new rôle I have to play."

He disappeared into his bedroom, and returned in a few minutes in the character of an amiable and simple-minded Nonconformist clergyman. His broad black hat, his baggy trousers, his white tie, his sympathetic smile, and general look of peering and benevolent curiosity were such as Mr. John Hare alone could have equalled. It was not merely that Holmes changed his costume. His expression, his manner, his very soul seemed to vary with every fresh part that he assumed. The stage lost a fine actor, even as science lost an acute reasoner, when he became a specialist in crime.

It was a quarter past six when we left Baker-street, and it still wanted ten minutes to the hour when we found ourselves in Serpentine-avenue. It was already dusk, and the lamps were just being lighted as we paced up and down in front of Briony Lodge, waiting for the coming of its occupant. The house was just such as I had pictured it from Sherlock Holmes' succinct description, but the locality appeared to be less private than I expected. On the contrary, for a small street in a quiet neighbourhood, it was remarkably animated. There was a group of shabbily-dressed men smoking and laughing in a corner, a scissors grinder with his wheel, two guardsmen who were flirting with a nurse-girl, and several well-dressed young men who were lounging up and down with cigars in their mouths.

"You see," remarked Holmes, as we paced to and fro in front of the house, "this marriage rather simplifies matters. The photograph becomes a double-edged weapon now. The chances are that she would be as averse to its being seen by Mr. Godfrey Norton, as our client is to its coming to the eyes of his Princess. Now the question is—Where are we to find the photograph?"

"Where, indeed?"

"It is most unlikely that she carries it about with her. It is cabinet size. Too large for easy concealment about a woman's dress. She knows that the King is capable of having her waylaid and searched. Two attempts of the sort have already been made. We may take it then that she does not carry it about with her."

"Where, then?"

"Her banker or her lawyer. There is that double possibility. But I am inclined to think neither. Women are naturally secretive, and they like to do their own secreting. Why should she hand it over to anyone else? She could trust her own guardianship, but she could not tell what indirect or political influence might be brought to bear upon a business man. Besides, remember that she had resolved to use it within a few days. It must be where she can lay her hands upon it. It must be in her own house."

"But it has twice been burgled."

"Pshaw! They did not know how to look."

"But how will you look?"

"I will not look."

"What then?"

"I will get her to show me."

114

"But she will refuse."

"She will not be able to. But I hear the rumble of wheels. It is her carriage. Now carry out my orders to the letter."

As he spoke the gleam of the sidelights of a carriage came round the curve of the avenue. It was a smart little landau which rattled up to the door of Briony Lodge. As it pulled up one of the loafing men at the corner dashed forward to open the door in the hope of earning a copper, but was elbowed away by another loafer who had rushed up with the same intention. A fierce quarrel broke out, which was increased by the two guardsmen, who took sides with one of the loungers, and by the scissors grinder, who was equally hot upon the other side. A blow was struck, and in an instant the lady, who had stepped from her carriage, was the centre of a little knot of flushed and struggling men who struck savagely at each other with their fists and sticks. Holmes dashed into the crowd to protect the lady; but, just as he reached her, he gave a cry and dropped to the ground, with the blood running freely down his face. At his fall the guardsmen took to their heels in one direction and the loungers in the other, while a number of better dressed people who had watched the scuffle without taking part in it, crowded in to help the lady and to attend to the injured man. Irene Adler, as I will still call her, had hurried up the steps; but she stood at the top with her superb figure outlined against the lights of the hall, looking back into the street.

"Is the poor gentleman much hurt?" she asked.

"He is dead," cried several voices.

"No, no, there's life in him," shouted another. "But he'll be gone before you can get him to hospital."

"He's a brave fellow," said a woman. "They would have had the lady's purse and watch if it hadn't been for him. They were a gang, and a rough one too. Ah, he's breathing now."

"He can't lie in the street. May we bring him in, marm?"

"Surely. Bring him into the sitting-room. There is a comfortable sofa. This way, please!"

Slowly and solemnly he was borne into Briony Lodge, and laid out in the principal room, while I still observed the proceedings from my post by the window. The lamps had been lit, but the blinds had not been drawn, so that I could see Holmes as he lay upon the couch. I do not know whether he was seized with compunction at that moment for the part he was playing, but I know that I never felt more heartily ashamed of myself in my life than when I saw the beautiful creature against whom I was conspiring, or the grace and kindliness with which she waited upon the injured man. And yet it would be the blackest treachery to Holmes to draw back now from the part which he had entrusted to me. I hardened my heart, and took the smoke-rocket from under my ulster. After all, I thought, we are not injuring her. We are but preventing her from injuring another.

Holmes had sat up upon the couch, and I saw him motion like a man who is in need of air. A maid rushed across and threw open the window. At the same instant I saw him raise his hand, and at the signal I tossed my rocket into the room with a cry of "Fire." The word was no sooner out of my mouth than the whole crowd of spectators, well dressed and ill—gentlemen, ostiers, and servant maids—join in a general shriek of "Fire." Thick clouds of smoke curled through the room, and out at the open window. I caught a glimpse of rushing figures, and a moment later the voice of Holmes from within, assuring them that it was a false alarm. Slipping through the shouting crowd I made my way to the corner of the street, and in ten minutes was rejoiced to find my friend's arm in mine, and to get away from the scene of uproar. He walked swiftly and in silence for some few minutes, until we had turned down one of the quiet streets which lead towards the Edgware-road.

"You did it very nicely, Doctor," he remarked. "Nothing could have been better. It is all right."

"You have the photograph!"

"I know where it is."

"And how did you find out?"

"She showed me, as I told you that she would."

"I am still in the dark."

"I do not wish to make a mystery," said he laughing. "The matter was perfectly simple. You, of course, saw that everyone in the street was an accomplice. They were all engaged for the evening."

"I guessed as much."

"Then, when the row broke out, I had a little moist red paint in the palm of my hand. I rushed forward, fell down, clapped my hand to my face, and became a piteous spectacle. It is an old trick."

"That also I could fathom."

"Then they carried me in. She was bound to have me in. What else could she do? And into her sitting-room, which was the very room which I suspected. It lay between that and her bedroom, and I was determined to see which. They laid me on a couch, I motioned for air, they were compelled to open the window, and you had your chance."

"How did that help you?"

"It was all-important. When a woman thinks that her house is on fire, her instinct is at once to rush to the thing which she values most. It is a perfectly overpowering impulse, and I have more than once taken advantage of it. In the case of the Darlington Substitution Scandal it was of use to me, and also in the Arnsworth Castle business. A married woman grabs at her baby—an unmarried one reaches for her jewel box. Now it was clear to me that our lady of to-day had nothing in the house more precious to her than what we are in quest of. She would rush to secure it. The alarm of fire was admirably done. The smoke and shouting were enough to shake nerves of steel. She responded beautifully. The photograph is in a recess behind a sliding panel just above the right bell pull. She was there in an instant, and I caught a glimpse of it as she half drew it out. When I cried out that it was a false alarm, she replaced it, glanced at the rocket, rushed from the room, and I have not seen her since. I rose, and, making my excuses, escaped from the house. I hesitated whether to attempt to secure the photograph at once; but the coachman had come in, and, as he was watching me narrowly, it seemed safer to wait. A little over-precipitance may ruin all."

"And now?" I asked.

"Our quest is practically finished. I shall call with the King to-morrow, and with you, if you care to come with us. We will be shown into the sitting-room to wait for the lady, but it is probable that when she comes she may find neither us nor the photograph. It might be a satisfaction to His Majesty to regain it with his own hands."

"And when will you call?"

"At eight in the morning. She will not be up, so that we shall have a clear field. Besides, we must be prompt, for this marriage may mean a complete change in her life and habits. I must wire to the King without delay."

We had reached Baker-street, and had stopped at the door. He was searching his pockets for the key, when someone passing said:—

"Good-night, Mister Sherlock Holmes."

There were several people on the pavement at the time, but the greeting appeared to come from a slim youth in an ulster who had hurried by.

"I've heard that voice before," said Holmes, staring down the dimly lit street. "Now, I wonder who the deuce that could have been."

III.

I slept at Baker-street that night, and we were engaged upon our toast and coffee in the morning when the King of Bohemia rushed into the room.

"You have really got it!" he cried, grasping Sherlock Holmes by either shoulder, and looking eagerly into his face.

"Not yet."

"But you have hopes?"

"I have hopes."

"Then, come. I am all impatience to be gone."

"We must have a cab."

"No, my brougham is waiting."

"Then that will simplify matters." We descended, and started off once more for Briony Lodge.

"Irene Adler is married," remarked Holmes.

"Married! When?"

"Yesterday."

"But to whom?"

"To an English lawyer named Norton."

"But she could not love him?"

"I am in hopes that she does."

"And why in hopes?"

"Because it would spare your Majesty all fear of future annoyance. If the lady loves her husband, she does not love your Majesty. If she does not love your Majesty, there is no reason why she should interfere with your Majesty's plan."

"It is true. And yet—! Well! I wish she had been of my own station! What a queen she would have made!" He relapsed into a moody silence which was not broken, until we drew up in Serpentine-avenue.

The door of Briony Lodge was open, and an elderly woman stood upon the steps. She watched us with a sardonic eye as we stepped from the brougham.

"Mr. Sherlock Holmes, I believe?" said she.

"I am Mr. Holmes," answered my companion, looking at her with a questioning and rather startled gaze.

"Indeed! My mistress told me that you were likely to call. She left this morning with her husband, by the 5:15 train from Charing-cross, for the Continent."

"What!" Sherlock Holmes staggered back, white with chagrin and surprise. "Do you mean that she has left England?"

"Never to return."

"And the papers?" asked the King, hoarsely. "All is lost."

"We shall see." He pushed past the servant, and rushed into the drawing-room, followed by the King and myself. The furniture was scattered about in every direction, with dismantled shelves, and open drawers, as if the lady had hurriedly ransacked them before her flight. Holmes rushed at the bell-pull, tore back a small sliding shutter, and, plunging in his hand, pulled out a photograph and a letter. The photograph was of Irene Adler herself in evening dress, the letter was superscribed to "Sherlock Holmes, Esq. To be left till called for." My friend tore it open, and we all three read it together. It was dated at midnight of the preceding night, and ran in this way:—

MY DEAR MR. SHERLOCK HOLMES,—You really did it very well. You took me in completely. Until after the alarm of fire, I had not a suspicion. But then, when I found how I had betrayed myself, I began to think. I had been warned against you months ago. I had been told that, if the King employed an agent, it would certainly be you. And your address had been given me. Yet, with all this, you made me reveal what you wanted to know. Even after I became suspicious, I found it hard to think evil of such a dear, kind old clergyman. But, you know, I have been trained as an actress myself. Male costume is nothing new to me. I often take advantage of the freedom which it gives. I sent John, the coachman, to watch you, ran upstairs, got into my walking clothes, as I call them, and came down just as you departed.

"Well, I followed you to your door, and so made sure that I was really an object of interest to the celebrated Mr. Sherlock Holmes. Then I, rather imprudently, wished you good night, and started for the Temple to see my husband.

"We both thought the best resource was flight, when pursued by so formidable an antagonist; so you will find the nest empty when you call to-morrow. As to the photograph, your client may rest in peace. I love and am loved by a better man than he. The King may do what he will without hindrance from one whom he has cruelly wronged. I keep it only to safeguard myself, and to preserve a weapon which will always secure me from any steps which he might take in the future. I leave a photograph which he might care to possess; and I remain, dear Mr. Sherlock Holmes, very truly yours,

"IRENE NORTON, née ADLER."

"What a woman—oh, what a woman!" cried the King of Bohemia, when we had all three read this epistle. "Did I not tell you how quick and resolute she was? Would she not have made an admirable queen? Is it not a pity that she was not on my level?"

"From what I have seen of the lady, she seems, indeed, to be on a very different level to your Majesty," said Holmes coldly. "I am sorry that I have not been able to bring your Majesty's business to a more successful conclusion."

"On the contrary, my dear sir," cried the King. "Nothing could be more successful. I know that her word is inviolate. The photograph is now as safe as if it were in the fire."

"I am glad to hear your Majesty say so."

"I am immensely indebted to you. Pray tell me in what way I can reward you. This ring——." He slipped an emerald snake ring from his finger, and held it out upon the palm of his hand.

"Your Majesty has something which I should value even more highly," said Holmes.

"You have but to name it."

"This photograph!"

The King stared at him in amazement.

"Irene's photograph!" he cried. "Certainly, if you wish it."

"I thank your Majesty. Then there is no more to be done in the matter. I have the honour to wish you a very good morning." He bowed, and, turning away without observing the hand which the King had stretched out to him, he set off in my company for his chambers.

And that was how a great scandal threatened to affect the kingdom of Bohemia, and how the best plans of Mr. Sherlock Holmes were beaten by a woman's wit. He used to make merry over the cleverness of women, but I have not heard him do it of late. And when he speaks of Irene Adler, or when he refers to her photograph, it is always under the honourable title of *the* woman.

THE RED-HEADED LEAGUE

By Arthur Conan Doyle

"The Red-Headed League" is the second of The Strand *magazine Sherlock Holmes stories (August 1891), of which the author wrote some two dozen before wearying of the character and deciding to kill him off in "The Final Problem" (December 1893). Conan Doyles' object in doing this was to move on to what he thought of as more serious fiction. He had already published* The White Company, *a historical novel, in 1891, and for a new Strand series in 1894–1895 he created the character of Brigadier Étienne Gerard, an adventurous Frenchman with whom he hoped to replace Sherlock Holmes in the public's affection. He also wrote a prizefighting novel,* Rodney Stone *(1896), and in 1900 published a history of the Boer War that is still a standard work on the subject. In the end, however, pressure from readers and publishers forced him to revive the characters of Holmes and his friend and biographer Dr. Watson, and the books that followed include* The Hound of the Baskervilles *(1902) and* The Return of Sherlock Holmes *(1905), a short story collection. In all, Conan Doyle wrote four novels and fifty six stories about the detective.*

I had called upon my friend, Mr. Sherlock Holmes, one day in the autumn of last year, and found him in deep conversation with a very stout, florid-faced, elderly gentleman, with fiery red hair. With an apology for my intrusion, I was about to withdraw, when Holmes pulled me abruptly into the room, and closed the door behind me.

"You could not possibly have come at a better time, my dear Watson," he said cordially.

"I was afraid that you were engaged."

"So I am. Very much so."

"Then I can wait in the next room."

"Not at all. This gentleman, Mr. Wilson, has been my partner and helper in many of my most successful cases, and I have no doubt that he will be of the utmost use to me in yours also."

The stout gentleman half rose from his chair, and gave a bob of greeting, with a quick little questioning glance from his small, fat-encircled eyes.

"Try the settee," said Holmes, relapsing into his armchair, and putting his fingertips together, as was his custom when in judicial moods. "I know, my dear Watson, that you share my love of all that is bizarre and outside the conventions and humdrum routine of every-day life. You have shown your relish for it by the enthusiasm which has prompted you to chronicle, and, if you will excuse my saying so, somewhat to embellish so many of my own little adventures."

"Your cases have indeed been of the greatest interest to me," I observed.

"You will remember that I remarked the other day, just before we went into the very simple problem presented by Miss Mary Sutherland, that for strange effects and extraordinary combinations we must go to life itself, which is always far more daring than any effort of the imagination."

"A proposition which I took the liberty of doubting."

"You did, Doctor, but none the less you must come round to my view, for otherwise I shall keep on piling fact upon fact on you, until your reason breaks down under them and acknowledges me to be right. Now, Mr. Jabez Wilson here has been good enough to call upon me this morning, and to begin a narrative which promises to be one of the most singular which I have listened to for some time. You have heard me remark that the strangest and most unique things are very often connected not with the larger but with the smaller crimes, and occasionally, indeed, where there is room for doubt whether any positive crime has been committed. As far as I have heard it, it is impossible for me to say whether the present case is an instance of crime or not, but the course of events is certainly among the most singular that I have ever listened to. Perhaps, Mr. Wilson, you would have the great kindness to recommence your narrative. I ask you, not merely because my friend Dr. Watson has not heard the opening part, but also because the peculiar nature of the story makes me anxious to have every possible detail from your lips. As a rule, when I have heard some slight indication of the course of events I am able to guide myself by the thousands of other similar cases which occur to my memory. In the present instance I am forced to admit that the facts are, to the best of my belief, unique."

The portly client puffed out his chest with an appearance of some little pride, and pulled a dirty and wrinkled newspaper from the inside pocket of his greatcoat. As he glanced down the advertisement column, with his head thrust forward, and the paper flattened out upon his knee, I took a good look at the man, and endeavoured after the fashion of my companion to read the indications which might be presented by his dress or appearance.

I did not gain very much, however, by my inspection. Our visitor bore every mark of being an average commonplace British tradesman, obese, pompous, and slow. He wore rather baggy grey shepherd's check trousers, a not overclean black frockcoat, unbuttoned in the front, and a drab waistcoat with a heavy brassy Albert chain, and a square pierced bit of metal dangling down as an ornament. A frayed top hat and a faded brown overcoat with a wrinkled velvet collar lay upon a chair beside him. Altogether, look as I would, there was nothing remarkable about the man save his blazing red head, and the expression of extreme chagrin and discontent upon his features.

Sherlock Holmes' quick eye took in my occupation, and he shook his head with a smile as he noticed my questioning glances. "Beyond the obvious facts that he has at some time done manual labour, that he takes snuff, that he is a Freemason, that he has been in China, and that he has done a considerable amount of writing lately, I can deduce nothing else."

Mr. Jabez Wilson started up in his chair, with his forefinger upon the paper, but his eyes upon my companion.

"How, in the name of good fortune, did you know all that, Mr. Holmes?" he asked. "How did you know, for example, that I did manual labour. It's as true as gospel, for I began as a ship's carpenter."

"Your hands, my dear sir. Your right hand is quite a size larger than your left. You have worked with it, and the muscles are more developed."

"Well, the snuff, then, and the Freemasonry?"

"I won't insult your intelligence by telling you how I read that, especially as, rather against the strict rules of your order, you use an arc and compass breastpin."

"Ah, of course, I forgot that. But the writing?"

"What else can be indicated by that right cuff so very shiney for five inches, and the left one with the smooth patch near the elbow where you rest it upon the desk."

"Well, but China?"

"The fish which you have tattooed immediately above your right wrist could only have been done in China. I have made a small study of tattoo marks, and have even contributed to the literature of the subject. That trick of staining the fishes' scales of a delicate pink is quite peculiar to China. When, in addition, I see a Chinese coin hanging from your watch-chain, the matter becomes even more simple."

Mr. Jabez Wilson laughed heavily. "Well, I never!" said he. "I thought at first that you had done something clever, but I see that there was nothing in it after all."

"I begin to think, Watson," said Holmes, "that I made a mistake in explaining 'Omne ignotum pro magnifico,' you know, and my poor little reputation, such as it is, will suffer shipwreck if I am so candid. Can you not find the advertisement, Mr. Wilson?"

"Yes, I have got it now," he answered, with his thick, red finger planted half-way down the column. "Here it is. This is what began it all. You just read it for yourself, sir."

"I took the paper from him, and read as follows:—

"TO THE RED-HEADED LEAGUE. On account of the bequest of the late Ezekiah Hopkins, of Lebanon, Penn., U.S.A., there is now another vacancy open which entitles a member of the League to a salary of four pounds a week for purely nominal services. All red-headed men who are sound in body and mind, and above the age of twenty-one years, are eligible. Apply in person on Monday, at eleven o'clock, to Duncan Ross, at the offices of the League, 7, Pope's-court, Fleet-street."

"What on earth does this mean?" I ejaculated, after I had twice read over the extraordinary announcement.

Holmes chuckled, and wriggled in his chair, as was his habit when in high spirits. "It is a little off the beaten track, isn't it?" said he. "And now, Mr. Wilson, off you go at scratch, and tell us all about yourself, your household, and the effect which this advertisement had upon your fortunes. You will first make a note, Doctor, of the paper and the date."

"It is *The Morning Chronicle*, of April 27, 1890. Just two months ago."

"Very good. Now, Mr. Wilson?"

"Well, it is just as I have been telling you, Mr. Sherlock Holmes," said Jabez Wilson, mopping his forehead, "I have a small pawnbroker's business at Coburg-square, near the City. It's not a very large affair, and of late years it has not done more than just give me a living. I used to be able to keep two assistants, but now I only keep one; and I would have a job to pay him, but that he is willing to come for half wages, so as to learn the business."

"What is the name of this obliging youth?" asked Sherlock Holmes.

"His name is Vincent Spaulding, and he's not such a youth either. It's hard to say his age. I should not wish a smarter assistant, Mr. Holmes; and I know very well that he could better himself, and earn twice what I am able to give him. But after all, if he is satisfied, why should I put ideas in his head?"

"Why, indeed? You seem most fortunate in having an *employé* who comes under the full market price. It is not a common experience among employers in this age. I don't know that your assistant is not as remarkable as your advertisement."

"Oh, he has his faults, too," said Mr. Wilson. "Never was such a fellow for photography. Snapping away with a camera when he ought to be improving his mind, and then diving down into the cellar like a rabbit into its hole to develop his pictures. That is his main fault; but, on the whole, he's a good worker. There's no vice in him."

"He is still with you, I presume?"

"Yes, sir. He and a girl of fourteen, who does a bit of simple cooking, and keeps the place clean—that's all I have in the house, for I am a widower, and never had any family. We live very quietly, sir, the three of us; and we keep a roof over our heads, and pay our debts, if we do nothing more.

"The first thing that put us out was that advertisement. Spaulding, he came down into the office just this day eight weeks with this very paper in his hand, and he says:—

"'I wish to the Lord, Mr. Wilson, that I was a red-headed man.'

"'Why that?' I asks.

"'Why,' says he, 'here's another vacancy on the League of the Red-headed Men. It's worth quite a little fortune to any man who gets it, and I understand that there are more vacancies than there are men, so that the trustees are at their wits' end what to do with the money. If my hair would only change colour, here's a nice little crib all ready for me to step into.'

"'Why, what is it, then?' I asked. You see, Mr. Holmes, I am a very stay-at-home man, and, as my business came to me instead of my having to go to it, I was often weeks on end without putting my foot over the door-mat. In that way I didn't know much of what was going on outside, and I was always glad of a bit of news.

"'Have you never heard of the League of the Red-headed Men?' he asked, with his eyes open.

"'Never.'

"'Why, I wonder at that, for you are eligible yourself for one of the vacancies.'

"'And what are they worth?' I asked.

"'Oh, merely a couple of hundred a year, but the work is slight, and it need not interfere very much with one's other occupations.'

"Well, you can easily think that that make me prick up my ears, for the business has not been over good for some years, and an extra couple of hundred would have been very handy.

"'Tell me all about it,' said I.

"'Well,' said he, showing me the advertisement, 'you can see for yourself that the League has a vacancy, and there is the address where you should apply for particulars. As far as I can make out, the League was founded by an American millionaire, Ezekiah Hopkins, who was very peculiar in his ways. He was himself red-headed, and he had a great sympathy for all red-headed men; so, when he died, it was found that he had left his enormous fortune in the hands of trustees, with instructions to apply the interest to the providing of easy berths to men whose hair is of that colour. From all I hear it is splendid pay, and very little to do.'

"'But,' said I, 'there would be millions of red-headed men who would apply.'

"'Not so many as you might think,' he answered. 'You see it is really confined to Londoners, and to grown men. This American had started from London when he was young, and he wanted to do the old town a good turn. Then, again, I have heard it is no use your applying if your hair is light red, or dark red, or anything but real, bright, blazing, fiery red. Now, if you cared to apply, Mr. Wilson, you would just walk in; but perhaps it would hardly be worth your while to put yourself out of the way for the sake of a few hundred pounds.'"

"Now, it is a fact, gentlemen, as you may see for yourselves, that my hair is of a very full and rich tint, so that it seemed to me that, if there was to be any competition in the matter, I stood as good a chance as any man that I had ever met. Vincent Spaulding seemed to know so much about it that I thought he might prove useful, so I just ordered him to put up the shutters for the day, and to come right away with me.

He was very willing to have a holiday, so we shut the business up, and started off for the address that was given us in the advertisement.

"I never hope to see such a sight as that again, Mr. Holmes. From north, south, east, and west every man who had a shade of red in his hair had tramped into the City to answer the advertisement. Fleet-street was choked with red-headed folk, and Pope's-court look like a coster's orange barrow. I should not have thought there were so many in the whole country as were brought together by that single advertisement. Every shade of colour they were—straw, lemon, orange, brick, Irish-setter, liver, clay; but, as Spaulding said, there were not many who had the real vivid flame-coloured tint. When I saw how many were waiting, I would have given it up in despair; but Spaulding would not hear of it. How he did it I could not imagine, but he pushed and pulled and butted until he got me through the crowd, and right up to the steps which led to the office. There was a double stream upon the stair, some going up in hope, and some coming back dejected; but we wedged in as well as we could, and soon found ourselves in the office."

"Your experience has been a most entertaining one," remarked Holmes, as his client paused and refreshed his memory with a huge pinch of snuff. "Pray continue your very interesting statement."

"There was nothing in the office but a couple of wooden chairs and a deal table, behind which sat a small man, with a head that was even redder than mine. He said a few words to each candidate as he came up, and then he always managed to find some fault in them which would disqualify them. Getting a vacancy did not seem to be such a very easy matter after all. However, when our turn came, the little man was much more favourable to me than to any of the others, and he closed the door as we entered, so that he might have a private word with us.

"'This is Mr. Jabez Wilson,' said my assistant, 'and he is willing to fill a vacancy in the League.'

"'And he is admirably suited for it,' the other answered. 'He has every requirement. I cannot recall when I have seen anything so fine.' He took a step backwards, cocked his head on one side, and gazed at my hair until I felt quite bashful. Then suddenly he plunged forward, wrung my hand, and congratulated me warmly on my success.

"'It would be injustice to hesitate,' said he. 'You will, however, I am sure, excuse me for taking an obvious precaution.' With that he seized my hair in both his hands, and tugged until I yelled with the pain. 'There is water in your eyes,' said he, as he released me. 'I perceive that all is as it should be. But we have to be careful, for we have twice been deceived by wigs and once by paint. I could tell you tales of cobbler's wax which would disgust you with human nature.' He stepped over to the window, and shouted through it at the top of his voice that the vacancy was filled. A groan of disappointment came up from below, and the folk all trooped away in different directions, until there was not a red head to be seen except my own and that of the manager.

"'My name,' said he, 'is Mr. Duncan Ross, and I am myself one of the pensioners upon the fund left by our noble benefactor. Are you a married man, Mr. Wilson? Have you a family?'

"I answered that I had not.

"His face fell immediately.

"'Dear me!' he said, gravely, 'that is very serious indeed! I am sorry to hear you say that. The fund was, of course, for the propagation and spread of the redheads as well as for their maintenance. It is exceedingly unfortunate that you should be a bachelor.'

"My face lengthened at this, Mr. Holmes, for I thought that I was not to have the vacancy after all; but, after thinking it over for a few minutes, he said that it would be all right.

"'In the case of another,' said he, 'the objection might be fatal, but we must stretch a point in favour of a man with such a head of hair as yours. When shall you be able to enter upon your new duties?'

"'Well, it is a little awkward, for I have a business already,' said I.

"'Oh, never mind about that, Mr. Wilson!' said Vincent Spaulding. 'I shall be able to look after that for you.'

"'What would be the hours?' I asked.

"'Ten to two.'

"Now a pawnbroker's business is mostly done of an evening, Mr. Holmes, especially Thursday and Friday evening, which is just before pay-day; so it would suit me very well to earn a little in the mornings. Besides, I knew that my assistant was a good man, and that he would see to anything that turned up.

"'That would suit me very well,' said I. 'And the pay?'

"'Is four pounds a week.'

"'And the work?'

"'Is purely nominal.'

"'What do you call purely nominal?'

"'Well, you have to be in the office, or at least in the building, the whole time. If you leave, you forfeit your whole position for ever. The will is very clear upon that point. You don't comply with the conditions if you budge from the office during that time.'

"'It's only four hours a day, and I should not think of leaving,' said I.

"'No excuse will avail,' said Mr. Duncan Ross, 'neither sickness, nor business, not anything else. There you must stay, or you lose your billet.'

"'And the work?'

"'Is to copy out the "Encyclopaedia Britannica." There is the first volume of it in that press. You must find your own ink, pens, and blotting-paper, but we provide this table and chair. Will you be ready to-morrow?'

"'Certainly,' I answered.

"'Then, good-bye, Mr. Jabez Wilson, and let me congratulate you once more on the important position which you have been fortunate enough to gain.' He bowed me out of the room, and I went home with my assistant, hardly knowing what to say or do, I was so pleased at my own good fortune.

"Well, I thought over the matter all day, and by evening I was in low spirits again; for I had quite persuaded myself that the whole affair must be some great hoax or fraud, though what its object might be I could not imagine. It seemed altogether past belief that anyone could make such a will, or that they would pay such a sum for doing anything so simple as copying out the 'Encyclopaedia Britannica.' Vincent Spaulding did what he could to cheer me up, but by bedtime I had reasoned myself out of the whole thing. However, in the morning I determined to have a look at it anyhow, so I bought a penny bottle of ink, and with a quill pen, and seven sheets of foolscap paper, I started off for Pope's-court.

"Well, to my surprise and delight everything was as right as possible. The table was set out ready for me, and Mr. Duncan Ross was there to see that I got fairly to work. He started me off upon the letter A, and then he left me; but he would drop in from time to time to see that all was right with me. At two o'clock he bade me good-day, complimented me upon the amount that I had written, and locked the door of the office after me.

"This went on day after day, Mr. Holmes, and on Saturday the manager came in and planked down four golden sovereigns for my week's work. It was the same next week, and the same the week after. Every morning I was there at ten, and every afternoon I left at two. By degrees Mr. Duncan Ross took to coming in only once of a morning, and then, after a time, he did not come in at all. Still, of course, I never dared to leave the room for an instant, for I was not sure when he might come, and the billet was such a good one, and suited me so well, that I would not risk the loss of it.

"Eight weeks passed away like this, and I had written about Abbots, and Archery, and Armour, and Architecture, and Attica, and hoped with diligence that I might get on to the Bs before very long. It cost me something in foolscap, and I had pretty nearly filled a shelf with my writings. And then suddenly the whole business came to an end."

"To an end?"

"Yes, sir. And no later than this morning. I went to my work as usual at ten o'clock, but the door was shut and locked, with a little square of cardboard hammered on to the middle of the panel with a tack. Here it is, and you can read for yourself."

He held up a piece of white cardboard, about the size of a sheet of notepaper. It read in this fashion:—

"THE RED-HEADED LEAGUE
IS
DISSOLVED.
Oct. 9, 1890."

Sherlock Holmes and I surveyed this curt announcement and the rueful face behind it, until the comical side of the affair so completely toppled every other consideration that we both burst out into a roar of laughter.

"I cannot see that there is anything very funny," cried our client, flushing up to the roots of his flaming head. "If you can do nothing better than laugh at me, I can go elsewhere."

"No, no," cried Holmes, shoving him back into the chair from which he had half risen. "I really wouldn't miss your case for the world. It is most refreshingly unusual. But there is, if you will excuse my saying so, something just a little funny about it. Pray what steps did you take when you found the card upon the door?"

"I was staggered, sir. I did not know what to do. Then I called at the offices round, but none of them seemed to know anything about it. Finally, I went to the landlord, who is an accountant living on the ground floor, and I asked him if he could tell me what had become of the Red-headed League. He said that he had never heard of any such body. Then I asked him who Mr. Duncan Ross was. He answered that the name was new to him."

"'Well,' said I, 'the gentleman at No. 4.'"

"'What, the red-headed man?'"

"'Yes.'"

"'Oh,' said he, 'his name was William Morris. He was a solicitor, and was using my room as a temporary convenience until his new premises were ready. He moved out yesterday.'"

"'Where could I find him?'"

"Oh, at his new offices. He did tell me the address. Yes, 17, King Edward-street, near St. Paul's.'"

"I started off, Mr. Holmes, but when I got to that address it was a manufactory of artificial kneecaps, and no one in it had ever heard of either Mr. William Morris, or Mr. Duncan Ross."

"And what did you do then?" asked Holmes.

"I went home to Saxe-Coburg-square, and I took the advice of my assistant. But he could not help me in any way. He could only say that if I waited I should hear by post. But that was not quite good enough, Mr. Holmes. I did not wish to lose such a place without a struggle, so, as I had heard that you were good enough to give advice to poor folk who were in need of it, I came right away to you."

"And you did very wisely," said Holmes. "Your case is an exceedingly remarkable one, and I shall be happy to look into it. From what you have told me I think that it is possible that graver issues hang from it than might at first sight appear."

"Grave enough!" said Mr. Jabez Wilson. "Why, I have lost four pounds a week."

"As far as you are personally concerned," remarked Holmes, "I do not see that you have any grievance against this extraordinary league. On the contrary, you are, as I understand, richer by some thirty pounds, to say nothing of the minute knowledge which you have gained on every subject which comes under the letter A. You have lost nothing by them."

"No, sir. But I want to find out about them, and who they are, and what their object was in playing this prank—if it was a prank—upon me. It was a pretty expensive joke for them, for it cost them two and thirty pounds."

"We shall endeavour to clear up these points for you. And, first, one or two questions, Mr. Wilson. This assistant of yours who first called your attention to the advertisement—how long had he been with you?"

"About a month then."

"How did he come?"

"In answer to an advertisement."

"Was he the only applicant?"

"No, I had a dozen."

"Why did you pick him?"

"Because he was handy, and would come cheap."

"At half wages, in fact."

"Yes."

"What is he like, this Vincent Spaulding?"

"Small, stout-built, very quick in his ways, no hair on his face, though he's not short of thirty. Has a white splash of acid upon his forehead."

Holmes sat up in his chair in considerable excitement. "I thought as much," said he. "Have you ever observed that his ears are pierced for earrings?"

"Yes, sir. He told me that a gipsy had done it for him when he was a lad."

"Hum!" said Holmes, sinking back in deep thought. "He is still with you?"

"Oh yes, sir; I have only just left him."

"And has your business been attended to in your absence?"

"Nothing to complain of, sir. There's never much to do of a morning."

"That will do, Mr. Wilson. I shall be happy to give you an opinion upon the subject in the course of a day or two. Today is Saturday, and I hope that by Monday we may come to a conclusion."

"Well, Watson," said Holmes, when our visitor had left us, "what do you make of it all?"

"I make nothing of it," I answered, frankly. "It is a most mysterious business."

"As a rule," said Holmes, "the more bizarre a thing is the less mysterious it proves to be. It is your commonplace, featureless crimes which are really puzzling, just as a commonplace face is the most difficult to identify. But I must be prompt over this matter."

"What are you going to do then?" I asked.

"To smoke," he answered. "It is quite a three pipe problem, and I beg that you won't speak to me for fifty minutes." He curled himself up in his chair, with his thin knees drawn up to his hawk-like nose, and there he sat with his eyes closed and his black clay pipe thrusting out like the bill of some strange bird. I had come to the conclusion that he had dropped asleep, and indeed was nodding myself, when he suddenly sprang out of his chair with the gesture of a man who has made up his mind, and put his pipe down upon the mantelpiece.

"Sarasate plays at the St. James's Hall this afternoon," he remarked. "What do you think, Watson? Could your patients spare you for a few hours?"

"I have nothing to do to-day. My practice is never very absorbing."

"Then, put on your hat, and come. I am going through the City first, and we can have some lunch on the way. I observe that there is a good deal of German music on the programme, which is rather more to my taste than Italian or French. It is introspective, and I want to introspect. Come along!"

We travelled by the Underground as far as Aldersgate; and a short walk took us to Saxe-Coburg-square, the scene of the singular story which we had listened to in the morning. It was a pokey, little, shabby-genteel place, where four lines of dingy two-storied brick houses looked out into a small railed-in enclosure, where a lawn of weedy grass, and a few clumps of faded laurel bushes made a hard fight against a smoke-laden and uncongenial atmosphere. Three gilt balls and a brown board with "JABEZ WILSON" in white letters, upon a corner house, announced the place where our red-headed client carried on his business. Sherlock Holmes stopped in front of it with his head on one side, and looked it all over, with his eyes shining brightly between puckered lids. Then he walked slowly up the street, and then down again to the corner, still looking keenly at the houses. Finally he returned to the pawnbroker's, and, having thumped vigorously upon the pavement with his stick two or three times, he went up to the door and knocked. It was instantly opened by a bright-looking, clean-shaven young fellow, who asked him to step in.

"Thank you," said Holmes, "I only wished to ask you how you would go from here to the Strand."

"Third right, fourth left," answered the assistant promptly, closing the door.

"Smart fellow, that," observed Holmes as we walked away. "He is, in my judgment, the fourth smartest man in London, and for daring I am not sure that he has not a claim to be third. I have known something of him before."

"Evidently," said I, "Mr. Wilson's assistant counts for a good deal in this mystery of the Red-headed League. I am sure that you inquired your way merely in order that you might see him."

"Not him."

"What then?"

"The knees of his trousers."

"And what did you see?"

"What I expected to see."

"Why did you beat the pavement?"

"My dear Doctor, this is a time for observation, not for talk. We are spies in an enemy's country. We know something of Saxe-Coburg-square. Let us now explore the parts which lie behind it."

The road in which we found ourselves as we turned round the corner from the retired Saxe-Coburg-square presented as great a contrast to it as the front of a picture does to the back. It was one of the main arteries which convey the traffic of the City to the north and west. The roadway was blocked with the immense stream of commerce flowing in a double tide inwards and outwards, while the footpaths were black with the hurrying swarm of pedestrians. It was difficult to realise as we looked at the line of fine shops and stately business premises that they really abutted on the other side upon the faded and stagnant square which we had just quitted.

"Let me see," said Holmes, standing at the corner, and glancing along the line, "I should like just to remember the order of the houses here. It is a hobby of mine to have an exact knowledge of London. There is Mortimer's, the tobacconist, the little newspaper shop, the Coburg branch of the City and Suburban Bank, the Vegetarian Restaurant, and McFarlane's carriage-building depot. That carries us right on to the other block. And now, Doctor, we've done our work, so it's time we had some play. A sandwich, and a cup of coffee, and then off to violin-land, where all is sweetness, and delicacy, and harmony, and there are no red-headed clients to vex us with their conundrums."

My friend was an enthusiastic musician, being himself not only a very capable performer, but a composer of no ordinary merit. All the afternoon he sat in the stalls wrapped in the most perfect happiness, gently waving his long thin fingers in time to the music, while his gently smiling face and his languid dreamy eyes were as unlike those of Holmes the sleuth-hound; Holmes the relentless, keen-witted, ready-handed criminal agent, as it was possible to conceive. In his singular character the dual nature alternately asserted itself, and his extreme exactness and astuteness represented, as I have often thought, the reaction against the poetic and contemplative mood which occasionally predominated in him. The swing of his nature took him from extreme languor to devouring energy; and, as I knew well, he was never so truly formidable as when for days on end, he had been lounging in his armchair amid his improvisations and his black-letter editions. Then it was that the lust of the chase would suddenly come upon him, and that his brilliant reasoning power would rise to the level of intuition, until those who were unacquainted with his methods would look askance at him as on a man whose knowledge was not that of other mortals. When I saw him that afternoon so enwrapped in the music at St. James's Hall I felt that an evil time might be coming upon those whom he had set himself to hunt down.

"You want to go home, no doubt, Doctor," he remarked, as we emerged.

"Yes, it would be as well."

134

"And I have some business to do which will take some hours. This business at Coburg-square is serious."

"Why serious?"

"A considerable crime is in contemplation. I have every reason to believe that we shall be in time to stop it. But to-day being Saturday rather complicates matters. I shall want your help to-night."

"At what time?"

"Ten will be early enough."

"I shall be at Baker-street at ten."

"Very well. And, I say, Doctor! there may be some little danger, so kindly put your army revolver in your pocket." He waved his hand, turned on his heel, and disappeared in an instant among the crowd.

I trust that I am not more dense than my neighbours, but I was always oppressed with a sense of my own stupidity in my dealings with Sherlock Holmes. Here I had heard what he had heard, I had seen what he had seen, and yet from his words it was evident that he saw clearly not only what had happened, but what was about to happen, while to me the whole business was still confused and grotesque. As I drove home to my house in Kensington I thought over it all, from the extraordinary story of the red-headed copier of the "Encyclopædia" down to the visit to Saxe-Coburg-square, and the ominous words with which he had parted from me. What was this nocturnal expedition, and why should I go armed? Where were we going, and what were we to do? I had the hint from Holmes that this smooth-faced pawnbroker's assistant was a formidable man—a man who might play a deep game. I tried to puzzle it out, but gave it up in despair, and set the matter aside until night should bring an explanation.

It was a quarter past nine when I started from home and made my way across the Park, and so through Oxford-street to Baker-street. Two hansoms were standing at the door, and, as I entered the passage, I heard the sound of voices from above. On entering his room, I found Holmes in animated conversation with two men, one of whom I recognised as Peter Jones, the official police agent; while the other was a long, thin, sad-faced man, with a very shiny hat and oppressively respectable frock-coat.

"Ha! our party is complete," said Holmes, buttoning up his pea-jacket, and taking his heavy hunting crop from the rack. "Watson, I think you know Mr. Jones, of Scotland-yard? Let me introduce you to Mr. Merryweather, who is to be our companion in to-night's adventure."

"We're hunting in couples again, Doctor, you see," said Jones, in his consequential way. "Our friend here is a wonderful man for starting a chase. All he wants is an old dog to help him to do the running down."

"I hope a wild goose may not prove to be the end of our chase," observed Mr. Merryweather, gloomily.

"You may place considerable confidence in Mr. Holmes, sir," said the police agent, loftily. "He has his own little methods, which are, if he won't mind my saying so, just a little too theoretical and fantastic, but he has the markings of a detective in him. It is not too much to say that once or twice, as in that business of the Sholto murder and the Agra treasure, he has been more nearly correct than the official force."

"Oh, if you say so, Mr. Jones, it is all right!" said the stranger, with deference. "Still, I confess that I miss my rubber. It is the first Saturday night for seven-and-twenty years that I have not had my rubber."

"I think you will find," said Sherlock Holmes, "that you will play for a higher stake to-night than you have ever done yet, and that the play will be more exciting. For you, Mr. Merryweather, the stake will be some thirty thousand pounds; and for you, Jones, it will be the man upon whom you wish to lay your hands."

"John Clay, the murderer, thief, smasher and forger. He's a young man, Mr. Merryweather, but he is at the head of his profession, and I would rather have my bracelets on him than on any criminal in London. He's a remarkable man, is young John Clay. His grandfather was a Royal Duke, and he himself has been to Eton and Oxford. His brain is as cunning as his fingers, and though we meet signs of him at every turn, we never know where to find the man himself. He'll crack a crib in Scotland one week, and be raising money to build an orphanage in Cornwall the next. I've been on his track for years, and have never set eyes on him yet."

"I hope that I may have the pleasure of introducing you to-night. I've had one or two little turns also with Mr. John Clay, and I agree with you that he is at the head of his profession. It is past ten, however, and quite time that we started. If you two will take the first hansom, Watson and I will follow in the second."

Sherlock Holmes was not very communicative during the long drive, and lay back in the cab humming the tunes which he had heard in the afternoon. We rattled through an endless labyrinth of gas-lit streets until we emerged into Farringdon-street.

"We are close there now," my friend remarked. "This fellow Merryweather is a bank director and personally interested in the matter. I thought it as well to have Jones with us also. He is not a bad fellow, though an absolute imbecile in his profession. He has one positive virtue. He is as brave as a bulldog, and as tenacious as a lobster if he gets his claws upon anyone. Here we are, and they are waiting for us."

We had reached the same crowded thoroughfare in which we had found ourselves in the morning. Our cabs were dismissed, and, following the guidance of Mr. Merryweather, we passed down a narrow passage, and through a side door, which he opened for us. Within there was a small corridor, which ended in a very massive iron gate. This also was opened, and led down a flight of winding stone steps, which terminated at another formidable gate. Mr. Merryweather stopped to light a lantern, and then conducted us down a dark, earth-smelling passage, and so, after opening a third door, into a huge vault or cellar, which was piled all round with crates and massive boxes.

"You are not very vulnerable from above," Holmes remarked, as he held up the lantern and gazed about him.

"Nor from below," said Mr. Merryweather, striking his stick upon the flags which lined the floor. "Why, dear me, it sounds quite hollow!" he remarked, looking up in surprise.

"I must really ask you to be a little more quiet," said Holmes, severely. "You have already imperilled the whole success of our expedition. Might I beg that you would have the goodness to sit down upon one of those boxes, and not to interfere?"

The solemn Mr. Merryweather perched himself upon a crate, with a very injured expression upon his face, while Holmes fell upon his knees upon the floor, and, with the lantern and a magnifying lens, began to examine minutely the cracks between the stones. A few seconds sufficed to satisfy him, for he sprang to his feet again, and put his glass in his pocket.

"We have at least an hour before us," he remarked, "for they can hardly take any steps until the good pawnbroker is safely in bed. Then they will not lose a minute, for the sooner they do their work the longer time they will have for their escape. We are at present, Doctor—as no doubt you have divined—in the cellar of the City branch of one of the principal London banks. Mr. Merryweather is the chairman of directors, and he will explain to you that there are reasons why the more daring criminals of London should take a considerable interest in this cellar at present."

"It is our French gold," whispered the director. "We have had several warnings that an attempt might be made upon it."

"Your French gold?"

"Yes. We had occasion some months ago to strengthen our resources, and borrowed, for that purpose, thirty thousand napoleons from the Bank of France. It has become known that we have never had occasion to unpack the money, and that it is still lying in our cellar. The crate upon which I sit contains two thousand napoleons packed between layers of lead foil. Our reserve of bullion is much larger at present than is usually kept in a single branch office, and the directors have had misgivings upon the subject."

"Which were very well justified," observed Holmes. "And now it is time that we arranged our little plans. I expect that within an hour matters will come to a head. In the meantime, Mr. Merryweather, we must put the screen over that dark lantern."

"And sit in the dark?"

"I am afraid so. I had brought a pack of cards in my pocket, and I thought that, as we were a *partie carrée*, you might have your rubber after all. But I see that the enemy's preparations have gone so far that we cannot risk the presence of a light. And, first of all, we must choose our positions. These are daring men, and, though we shall take them at a disadvantage they may do us some harm, unless we are careful. I shall stand behind this crate, and do you conceal yourselves behind those. Then, when I flash a light upon them, close in swiftly. If they fire, Watson, have no compunction about shooting them down."

I placed my revolver, cocked, upon the top of the wooden case behind which I crouched. Holmes shot the slide across the front of his lantern, and left us in pitch darkness—such an absolute darkness as I have never before experienced. The smell of hot metal remained to assure us that the light was still there, ready to flash out at a moment's notice. To me, with my nerves worked up to a pitch of expectancy, there was something depressing and subduing in the sudden gloom, and in the cold, dank air of the vault.

"They have but one retreat," whispered Holmes. "That is back through the house into Saxe-Coburg-square. I hope that you have done what I asked you, Jones?"

"I have an inspector and two officers waiting at the front door."

"Then we have stopped all the holes. And now we must be silent and wait."

What a time it seemed! From comparing notes afterwards it was but an hour and a quarter, yet it appeared to me that the night must have almost gone, and the dawn be breaking above us. My limbs were weary and stiff, for I feared to change my position, yet my nerves were worked up to the highest pitch of tension, and my hearing was so acute that I could not only hear the gentle breathing of my companions, but I could distinguish the deeper, heavier inbreath of the bulky Jones from the thin sighing note of the bank director. From my position I could look over the case in the direction of the floor. Suddenly my eyes caught the glint of a light.

At first it was but a lurid spark upon the stone pavement. Then it lengthened out until it became a yellow line, and then, without any warning or sound, a gash seemed to open and a hand appeared, a white, almost womanly hand, which felt about in the centre of the little area of light. For a minute or more the hand, with its writhing fingers, protruded out of the floor. Then it was withdrawn as suddenly as it appeared, and all was dark again save the single lurid spark, which marked a chink between the stones.

Its disappearance, however, was but momentary. With a rending, tearing sound, one of the broad, white stones turned over upon its side, and left a square, gaping hole, through which streamed the light of a lantern. Over the edge there peeped a clean-cut, boyish face, which looked keenly about it, and then, with a hand on either side of the aperture, drew itself shoulder high and waist high, until one knee rested upon the edge. In another instant he stood at the side of the hole, and was hauling after him a companion, lithe and small like himself, with a pale face and a shock of very red hair.

"It's all clear," he whispered. "Have you the chisel and the bags. Great Scott! Jump, Archie, jump, and I'll swing for it!"

Sherlock Holmes had sprung out and seized the intruder by the collar. The other dived down the hole, and I heard the sound of rending cloth as Jones clutched at his skirts. The light flashed upon the barrel of a revolver, but Holmes' hunting crop came down on the man's wrist, and the pistol clinked upon the stone floor.

"It's no use, John Clay," said Holmes blandly, "You have no chance at all."

"So I see," the other answered, with the utmost coolness. "I fancy that my pal is all right, though I see you have got his coat-tails."

"There are three men waiting for him at the door," said Holmes.

"Oh, indeed. You seem to have done the thing very completely. I must compliment you."

"And I you," Holmes answered. "Your red-headed idea was very new and effective."

"You'll see your pal again presently," said Jones. "He's quicker at climbing down holes than I am. Just hold out while I fix the derbies."

"I beg that you will not touch me with your filthy hands," remarked our prisoner, as the handcuffs clattered upon his wrists. "You may not be aware that I have royal blood in my veins. Have the goodness also when you address me always to say 'sir' and 'please.'"

"All right," said Jones, with a stare and a snigger. "Well, would

139

you please, sir, march upstairs, where we can get a cab to carry your highness to the police-station."

"That is better," said John Clay, serenely. He made a sweeping bow to the three of us, and walked quietly off in the custody of the detective.

"Really, Mr. Holmes," said Mr. Merryweather, as we followed them from the cellar, "I do not know how the bank can thank you or repay you. There is no doubt that you have detected and defeated in the most complete manner one of the most determined attempts at bank robbery that have ever come within my experience."

"I have had one or two little scores of my own to settle with Mr. John Clay," said Holmes, "I have been at some small expense over this matter, which I shall expect the bank to refund, but beyond that I am amply repaid by having had an experience which is in many ways unique, and by hearing the very remarkable narrative of the Red-headed League."

"You see, Watson," he explained, in the early hours of the morning, as we sat over a glass of whiskey and soda in Baker-street, "it was perfectly obvious from the first that the only possible object of this rather fantastic business of the advertisement of the League, and the copying of the 'Encyclopædia,' must be to get this not over-bright pawnbroker out of the way for a number of hours every day. It was a curious way of managing it, but really it would be difficult to suggest a better. The method was no doubt suggested to Clay's ingenious mind by the colour of his accomplice's hair. The four pounds a week was a lure which must draw him, and what was it to them, who were playing for thousands? They put in the advertisement, one rogue has the temporary office, the other rogue incites the man to apply for it, and together they manage to secure his absence every morning in the week. From the time that I heard of the assistant having come for half wages, it was obvious to me that he had some strong motive for securing the situation."

"But how could you guess what the motive was?"

"Had there been women in the house, I should have suspected a mere vulgar intrigue. That, however, was out of the question. The man's business was a small one, and there was nothing in his house which could account for such elaborate preparations, and such an expenditure as they were at. It must then be something out of the house. What could it be? I thought of the assistant's fondness for photography, and his trick of vanishing into the cellar. The cellar! There was the end of this tangled clue. Then I made inquiries as to this mysterious assistant, and found that I had to deal with one of the coolest and most daring criminals in London. He was doing something in the cellar—something which took many hours a day for months on end. What could it be, once more? I could think of nothing save that he was running a tunnel to some other building.

"So far I had got when we went to visit the scene of action. I surprised you by beating upon the pavement with my stick. I was ascertaining whether the cellar stretched out in front or behind. It was not in front. Then I rang the bell, and, as I hoped, the assistant answered it. We have had some skirmishes, but we had never set eyes upon each other before. I hardly looked at his face. His knees were what I wished to see. You must yourself have remarked how worn, wrinkled, and stained they were. They spoke of those hours of burrowing. The only remaining point was what they were burrowing for. I walked round the corner, saw that the City and Suburban Bank abutted on our friend's premises, and felt that I had solved my problem. When you drove home after the concert I called upon Scotland Yard, and upon the chairman of the bank directors, with the result that you have seen."

"And how could you tell that they would make their attempt to-night?" I asked.

"Well, when they closed their League offices that was a sign that they cared no longer about Mr. Jabez Wilson's presence, in other words, that they had completed their tunnel. But it was essential that they should use it soon as it might be discovered, or the bullion might be removed. Saturday would suit them better than any other day, as it would give them two days for their escape. For all these reasons I expected them to come to-night."

"You reasoned it out beautifully," I exclaimed in unfeigned admiration. "It is so long a chain, and yet every link rings true."

"It saved me from ennui," he answered, yawning. "Alas! I already feel it closing in upon me. My life is spent in one long effort to escape from the commonplaces of existence. These little problems help me to do so."

"And you are a benefactor of the race," said I.

He shrugged his shoulders. "Well, perhaps, after all, it is of some little use," he remarked. "'L'homme c'est rien—l'œuvre c'est tout,' as Gustave Flaubert wrote to Georges Sand."

THE ADVENTURE OF THE SPECKLED BAND

By Arthur Conan Doyle

Conan Doyle was not satisfied merely to write about detectives and their work but, at various times, actually involved himself in criminal cases. Once he managed to free a young student wrongly convicted of horse maiming by proving that the supposed culprit was nearly blind and could not have committed the crime. On another occasion, he rescued a man who had been falsely imprisoned for eighteen years by showing that two important witnesses had given perjured testimony. Paradoxically, the creator of Sherlock Holmes, one of the greatest proponents of logic and scientific analysis in all of literature, was himself, especially in his last years, an enthusiastic believer in spiritualism. He toured much of the English-speaking world in quest of converts and died firmly believing that he would be able to communicate with those he left behind. "The Adventure of the Speckled Band," originally published in The Strand magazine in February 1892 and later reprinted as the eighth story in The Adventures of Sherlock Holmes, itself combines a certain atmosphere of gothic supernaturalism with a purely rational explanation of its mystery. The indispensible edition of the Holmes stories is William S. Baring-Gould's The Annotated Sherlock Holmes (New York: Potter, 1967). For more about the author see John Dickson Carr's The Life of Sir Arthur Conan Doyle (New York: Harper & Brothers, 1949) and Hesketh Pearson's Conan Doyle: His Life and Art (New York: Walker, 1961).

In glancing over my notes of the seventy-odd cases in which I have, during the last eight years, studied the methods of my friend, Sherlock Holmes, I find many tragic, some comic, a large number merely strange, but none commonplace; for, working as he did rather for the love of his art than for the acquirement of wealth, he refused to associate himself with any investigation which did not tend toward the unusual, and even the fantastic. Of all these varied cases, however, I cannot recall any which presented more singular features than that which was associated with the well-known Surrey family of the Roylott of Stoke Moran. The events in question occurred in the early days of my association with Holmes, when we were sharing rooms as bachelors in Baker Street. It is possible that I might have placed them upon record before, but a promise of secrecy was made by the untimely death of the lady to whom the pledge was given. It is perhaps as well that the facts should now come to light, for I have reasons to know that there are widespread rumors as to the death of Dr. Grimesby Roylott which tend to make the matter even more terrible than the truth.

It was early in April in the year '83 that I woke one morning to find Sherlock Holmes standing, fully dressed, by the side of my bed. He was a late riser as a rule, and as the clock on the mantel-piece showed me that it was only a quarter past seven, I blinked up at him in some surprise, and perhaps just a little resentment, for I was myself regular in my habits.

"Very sorry to knock you up, Watson," said he, "but it's the common lot this morning. Mrs. Hudson has been knocked up; she retorted upon me; and I on you."

"What is it, then—a fire?"

"No; a client. It seems that a young lady has arrived in a considerable state of excitement, who insists upon seeing me. She is waiting now in the sitting-room. Now, when young ladies wander about the metropolis at this hour of the morning, and knock sleepy people up out of their beds, I presume that it is something very pressing which they have to communicate. Should it prove to be an interesting case, you would, I am sure, wish to follow it from the outset. I thought, at any rate, that I should call you and give you the chance."

"My dear fellow, I would not miss it for anything."

I had no keener pleasure than in following Holmes in his professional investigations, and in admiring the rapid deductions, as swift as intuitions, and yet always founded on a logical basis, with which he unraveled the problems which were submitted to him. I rapidly threw on my clothes, and was ready in a few minutes to accompany my friend down to the sitting-room. A lady dressed in black and heavily veiled, who had been sitting in the window, rose as we entered.

"Good-morning, madam," said Holmes, cheerily. "My name is Sherlock Holmes. This is my intimate friend and associate, Dr. Watson, before whom you can speak as freely as before myself. Ha!—I am glad to see that Mrs. Hudson has had the good sense to light the fire. Pray draw up to it, and I shall order you a cup of hot coffee, for I observe that you are shivering."

"It is not cold which makes me shiver," said the woman, in a low voice, changing her seat as requested.

"What then?"

"It is fear, Mr. Holmes. It is terror." She raised her veil as she spoke, and we could see that she was indeed in a pitiable state of agitation, her face all drawn and gray, with restless, frightened eyes, like those of some hunted animal. Her features and figure were those of a woman of thirty, but her hair was shot with premature gray, and her expression was weary and haggard. Sherlock Holmes ran her over with one of his quick, all-comprehensive glances.

"You must not fear," said he, soothingly, bending forward and patting her forearm. "We shall soon set matters right, I have no doubt. You have come in by train this morning, I see."

"You know me, then?"

"No, but I observe the second half of a return ticket in the palm of your left glove. You must have started early, and yet you had a good drive in a dog-cart, along heavy roads, before you reached the station."

The lady gave a violent start, and stared in bewilderment at my companion.

"There is no mystery, my dear madam," said he, smiling. "The left arm of your jacket is spattered with mud in no less than seven places. The marks are perfectly fresh. There is no vehicle save a dog-cart which throws up mud in that way, and then only when you sit on the left-hand side of the driver."

"Whatever your reasons may be, you are perfectly correct," said she. "I started from home before six, reached Leatherhead at twenty past, and came in by the first train to Waterloo. Sir, I can stand this strain no longer; I shall go mad if it continues. I have no one to turn to—none, save only one, who cares for me, and he, poor fellow, can be of little aid. I have heard of you, Mr. Holmes; I have heard of you from Mrs. Farintosh, whom you helped in the hour of her sore need. It was from her that I had your address. Oh, sir, do you not think that you could help me, too, and at least throw a little light through the dense darkness which surrounds me? At present it is out of my power to reward you for your services, but in a month or six weeks I shall be married, with the control of my own income, and then at least you shall not find me ungrateful."

Holmes turned to his desk, and unlocking it, drew out a small casebook, which he consulted.

"Farintosh," said he. "Ah, yes, I recall the case; it was concerned with an opal tiara. I think it was before your time, Watson. I can only say, madam, that I shall be happy to devote the same care to your case as I did to that of your friend. As to reward, my profession is its own reward; but you are at liberty to defray whatever expenses I may be put to, at the time which suits you best. And now I beg that you will lay before us everything that may help us in forming an opinion upon the matter."

"Alas!" replied our visitor, "the very horror of my situation lies in the fact that my fears are so vague, and my suspicions depend so entirely upon small points, which might seem trivial to another, that even he to whom of all others I have a right to look for help and advice, looks upon all that I tell him about it as the fancies of a nervous woman. He does not say so, but I can read it from his soothing answers and averted eyes. But I have heard, Mr. Holmes, that you can see deeply into the manifold wickedness of the human heart. You may advise me how to walk amid the dangers which encompass me."

"I am all attention, madam."

"My name is Helen Stoner, and I am living with my step-father, who is the last survivor of one of the oldest Saxon families in England, the Roylotts of Stoke Moran, on the western border of Surrey."

Holmes nodded his head. "The name is familiar to me," said he.

"The family was at one time among the richest in England, and the estates extended over the borders into Berkshire in the north, and Hampshire in the west. In the last century, however, four successive heirs were of a dissolute and wasteful disposition, and the family ruin was eventually completed by a gambler in the days of the Regency. Nothing was left save a few acres of ground, and the two-hundred-year-old house, which is itself crushed under a heavy mortgage. The last squire dragged out his existence there, living the horrible life of an aristocratic pauper; but his only son, my step-father, seeing that he must adapt himself to the new conditions, obtained an advance from a relative, which enabled him to take a medical degree, and went out to Calcutta, where, by his professional skill and his force of character, he established a large practice. In a fit of anger, however, caused by some robberies which had been perpetrated in the house, he beat his native butler to death, and narrowly escaped a capital sentence. As it was, he suffered a long term of imprisonment, and afterward returned to England a morose and disappointed man.

"When Dr. Roylott was in India he married my mother, Mrs. Stoner, the young widow of Major-General Stoner, of the Bengal Artillery. My sister Julia and I were twins, and we were only two years old at the time of my mother's remarriage. She had a considerable sum of money—not less than 1,000 pounds a year—and this she bequeathed to Dr. Roylott entirely while we resided with him, with a provision that a certain annual sum should be allowed to each of us in the event of our marriage. Shortly after our return to England my mother died—she was killed eight years ago in a railway accident near Crewe. Dr. Roylott then abandoned his attempts to establish himself in practice in London, and took us to live with him in the old ancestral house at Stoke Moran. The money which my mother had left was enough for all our wants, and there seemed to be no obstacle to our happiness.

"But a terrible change came over our step-father about this time. Instead of making friends and exchanging visits with our neighbors, who had at first been overjoyed to see a Roylott of Stoke Moran back in the old family seat, he shut himself up in his house, and seldom came out save to indulge in ferocious quarrels with whoever might cross his path. Violence of temper approaching to mania has been hereditary in the men of the family, and in my step-father's case it had, I believe, been increased by his long residence in the tropics. A series of disgraceful brawls took place, two of which ended in the police-court, until at last he became the terror of the village, and the folks would fly at his approach, for he is a man of immense strength, and absolutely uncontrollable in his anger.

"Last week he hurled the local blacksmith over a parapet into a stream; and it was only by paying over all the money which I could gather together that I was able to avert another public exposure. He had no friends at all save the wandering gypsies, and he would give these vagabonds leave to encamp upon the few acres of bramble-covered land which represent the family estate, and would accept in return the hospitality of their tents, wandering away with them sometimes for weeks on end. He has a passion also for Indian animals, which are sent over to him by a correspondent, and he has at this moment a cheetah and a baboon, which wander freely over the grounds, and are feared by the villagers almost as much as their master.

"You can imagine from what I say that my poor sister Julia and I had no great pleasure in our lives. No servant would stay with us, and for a long time we did all the work of the house. She was but thirty at the time of her death, and yet her hair had already begun to whiten, even as mine has."

"Your sister is dead, then?"

"She died just two years ago, and it is of her death that I wish to speak to you. You can understand that, living the life which I have described, we were little likely to see anyone of our own age and position. We had, however, an aunt, my mother's maiden sister, Miss Honoria Westphail, who lives near Harrow, and we were occasionally allowed to pay short visits at this lady's house. Julia went there at Christmas two years ago, and met there a half-pay major of marines, to whom she became engaged. My step-father learned of the engagement when my sister returned, and offered no objection to the marriage; but within a fortnight of the day which had been fixed for the wedding, the terrible event occurred which has deprived me of my only companion."

Sherlock Holmes had been leaning back in his chair with his eyes closed and his head sunk in a cushion, but he half opened his lids now and glanced at his visitor.

"Pray be precise as to details," said he.

"It is easy for me to be so, for every event of that dreadful time is seared into my memory. The manorhouse is, as I have already said, very old, and only one wing is now inhabited. The bedrooms in this wing are on the ground floor, the sitting-rooms being in the central block of the buildings. Of these bedrooms the first is Dr. Roylott's, the second my sister's, and the third my own. There is no communication between them, but they all open out into the same corridor. Do I make myself plain?"

"Perfectly so."

"The windows of the three rooms open out upon the lawn. That fatal night Dr. Roylott had gone to his room early, though we knew that he had not retired to rest, for my sister was troubled by the smell of the strong Indian cigars which it was his custom to smoke. She left her room, therefore, and came into mine, where she sat for some time, chatting about her approaching wedding. At eleven o'clock she rose to leave me, but she paused at the door and looked back.

"'Tell me, Helen,' said she, 'have you ever heard any one whistle in the dead of the night?'

"'Never,' said I.

"'I suppose that you could not possibly whistle, yourself, in your sleep?'

"'Certainly not. But why?'

"'Because during the last few nights I have always, about three in the morning, heard a low, clear whistle. I am a light sleeper, and it has awakened me. I cannot tell where it came from—perhaps from the next room, perhaps from the lawn. I thought that I would just ask you whether you had heard it.'

"'No, I have not. It must be those wretched gypsies in the plantation.'

"'Very likely. And yet if it were on the lawn, I wonder that you did not hear it also.'

"'Ah, but I sleep more heavily than you.'

"'Well, it is of no great consequence, at any rate.' She smiled back at me, closed my door, and a few moments later I heard her key turn in the lock."

"Indeed," said Holmes. "Was it your custom always to lock yourselves in at night?"

"Always."

"And why?"

"I think that I mentioned to you that the doctor kept a cheetah and a baboon. We had no feeling of security unless our doors were locked."

"Quite so. Pray proceed with your statement."

"I could not sleep that night. A vague feeling of impending misfortune impressed me. My sister and I, you will recollect, were twins, and you know how subtle are the links which bind two souls which are so closely allied. It was a wild night. The wind was howling outside, and the rain was beating and splashing against the windows. Suddenly, amid all the hubbub of the gale, there burst forth the wild scream of a terrified woman. I knew that it was my sister's voice. I sprang from my bed, wrapped a shawl round me, and rushed into the corridor. As I opened my door I seemed to hear a low whistle, such as my sister described, and a few moments later a clanging sound, as if a mass of metal had fallen. As I ran down the passage my sister's door was unlocked, and revolved slowly upon its hinges. I stared at it horror-stricken, not knowing what was about to issue from it. By the light of the corridor-lamp I saw my sister appear at the opening, her face blanched with terror, her hands groping for help, her whole figure swaying to and fro like that of a drunkard. I ran to her and threw my arms round her, but at that moment her knees seemed to give way and she fell to the ground. She writhed as one who is in terrible pain, and her limbs were dreadfully convulsed. At first I thought that she had not recognized me, but as I bent over her, she suddenly shrieked out, in a voice which I shall never forget: 'Oh, my God! Helen! It was the band! The speckled band!' There was something else which she would fain have said, and she stabbed with her finger into the air in the direction of the doctor's room, but a fresh convulsion seized her and choked her words. I rushed out, calling loudly for my step-father, and I met him hastening from his room in his dressing-gown. When he reached my sister's side she was unconscious, and though he poured brandy down her throat and sent for medical aid from the village, all efforts were in vain, for she slowly sank and died without having recovered her consciousness. Such was the dreadful end of my beloved sister."

"One moment," said Holmes; "are you sure about this whistle and metallic sound? Could you swear to it?"

"That was what the county coroner asked me at the inquiry. It is my strong impression that I heard it, and yet, among the crash of the gale and the creaking of an old house, I may possibly have been deceived."

"Was your sister dressed?"

"No, she was in her night-dress. In her right hand was found the charred stump of a match, and in her left a match-box."

"Showing that she had struck a light and looked about her when the alarm took place. That is important. And what conclusions did the coroner come to?"

"He investigated the case with great care, for Dr. Roylott's conduct had long been notorious in the county, but he was unable to find any satisfactory cause of death. My evidence showed that the door had been fastened upon the inner side, and the windows were blocked by old-fashioned shutters with broad iron bars, which were secured every night. The walls were carefully sounded, and were shown to be quite solid all round, and the flooring was also thoroughly examined, with the same result. The chimney is wide, but is barred up by four large staples. It is certain, therefore, that my sister was quite alone when she met her end. Besides, there were no marks of violence upon her."

"How about poison?"

"The doctors examined her for it, but without success."

"What do you think that this unfortunate lady died of, then?"

"It is my belief that she died of pure fear and nervous shock, though what it was that frightened her I cannot imagine."

"Were there gypsies in the plantation at the time?"

"Yes, there are nearly always some there."

"Ah, and what did you gather from this allusion to a band—a speckled band?"

"Sometimes I have thought that it was merely the wild talk of delirium, sometimes that it may have referred to some band of people, perhaps to these very gypsies in the plantation. I do not know whether the spotted handkerchiefs which so many of them wear over their heads might have suggested the strange adjective which she used."

Holmes shook his head like a man who is far from being satisfied.

"These are very deep waters," said he; "pray go on with your narrative."

"Two years have passed since then, and my life had been until lately lonelier than ever. A month ago, however, a dear friend, whom I have known for many years, has done me the honor to ask my hand in marriage. His name is Armitage—Percy Armitage—the second son of Mr. Armitage, of Crane Water, near Reading. My step-father has offered no opposition to the match, and we are to be married in the course of the spring. Two days ago some repairs were started in the west wing of the building, and my bedroom wall has been pierced, so that I have had to move into the chamber in which my sister died, and to sleep in the very bed in which she slept.

"Imagine, then, my thrill of terror when last night, as I lay awake, thinking over her terrible fate, I suddenly heard in the silence of the night the low whistle which had been the herald of her own death. I sprang up and lit the lamp, but nothing was to be seen in the room. I was too shaken to go to bed again, however; so I dressed, and as soon as it was daylight I slipped down, got a dog-cart at the 'Crown Inn,' which is opposite, and drove to Leatherhead, from whence I have come on this morning with the one object of seeing you and asking your advice."

"You have done wisely," said my friend. "But have you told me all?"

"Yes, all."

"Miss Roylott, you have not. You are screening your step-father."

"Why, what do you mean?"

For answer Holmes pushed back the frill of black lace which fringed the hand that lay upon our visitor's knee. five little livid spots, the marks of four fingers and a thumb, were printed upon the white wrist.

"You have been cruelly used," said Holmes.

The lady colored deeply and covered over her injured wrist. "He is a hard man," she said, "and perhaps he hardly knows his own strength."

There was a long silence, during which Holmes leaned his chin upon his hands and stared into the crackling fire.

"This is a very deep business," he said, at last. "There are a thousand details which I should desire to know before I decide upon our course of action. Yet we have not a moment to lose. If we were to come to Stoke Moran today, would it be possible for us to see over these rooms without the knowledge of your step-father?"

"As it happens, he spoke of coming into town today upon some most important business. It is probable that he will be away all day, and that there would be nothing to disturb you. We have a housekeeper now, but she is old and foolish, and I could easily get her out of the way."

"Excellent. You are not averse to this trip, Watson?"

"By no means."

"Then we shall both come. What are you going to do yourself?"

"I have one or two things which I would wish to do now that I am in town. But I shall return by the twelve o'clock train, so as to be there in time for your coming."

"And you may expect us early in the afternoon. I have myself some small business matters to attend to. Will you not wait and breakfast?"

"No, I must go. My heart is lightened already since I have confided my trouble to you. I shall look forward to seeing you again this afternoon." She dropped her thick black veil over her face and glided from the room.

"And what do you think of it all, Watson?" asked Sherlock Holmes, leaning back in his chair.

"It seems to me to be a most dark and sinister business."

"Dark enough and sinister enough."

"Yet if the lady is correct in saying that the flooring and walls are sound, and that the door, window, and chimney are impassable, then her sister must have been undoubtedly alone when she met her mysterious end."

"What becomes, then, of these nocturnal whistles, and what of the very peculiar words of the dying woman?"

"I cannot think."

"When you combine the ideas of whistles at night, the presence of a band of gypsies who are on intimate terms with this old doctor, the fact that we have every reason to believe the doctor has an interest in preventing his step-daughter's marriage, the dying allusion to a band, and, finally, the fact that Miss Helen Stoner heard a metallic clang, which might have been caused by one of those metal bars which secured the shutters falling back into its place, I think that there is good ground to think that the mystery may be cleared along those lines."

"But what, then, did the gypsies do?"

"I cannot imagine."

"I see many objections to any such theory."

"And so do I. It is precisely for that reason that we are going to Stoke Moran this day. I want to see whether the objections are fatal, or if they may be explained away. But what, in the name of the devil!"

The ejaculation had been drawn from my companion by the fact that our door had been suddenly dashed open, and that a huge man had framed himself in the aperture. His costume was a peculiar mixture of the professional and of the agricultural, having a black top-hat, a long frock-coat, and a pair of high gaiters, with a hunting-crop swinging in his hand. So tall was he that his hat actually brushed the cross-bar of the doorway, and his breadth seemed to span it across from side to side. A large face, seared with a thousand wrinkles, burned yellow with the sun, and marked with every evil passion, was turned from one to the other of us, while his deep-set, bile-shot eyes, and his high, thin, fleshless nose, gave him somewhat the resemblance to a fierce old bird of prey.

"Which of you is Holmes?" asked this apparition.

"My name, sir; but you have the advantage of me," said my companion, quietly.

"I am Dr. Grimesby Roylott, of Stoke Moran."

"Indeed, doctor," said Holmes, blandly. "Pray take a seat."

"I will do nothing of the kind. My step-daughter has been here. I have traced her. What has she been saying to you?"

"It is a little cold for the time of year," said Holmes.

"What has she been saying to you?" screamed the old man, furiously.

"But I have heard that the crocuses promise well," continued my companion, imperturbably.

"Ha! You put me off, do you?" said our new visitor, taking a step forward and shaking his hunting-crop. "I know you, you scoundrel! I have heard of you before. You are Holmes, the meddler."

My friend smiled.

"Holmes, the busybody!"

His smile broadened.

"Holmes, the Scotland-yard Jack-in-office!"

Holmes chuckled heartily. "Your conversation is most entertaining," said he. "When you go out, close the door, for there is a decided draught."

"I will go when I have said my say. Don't you dare to meddle with my affairs. I know that Miss Stoner has been here. I traced her! I am a dangerous man to fall foul of! See here." He stepped swiftly forward, seized the poker, and bent it into a curve with his huge brown hands.

"See that you keep yourself out of my grip," he snarled; and hurling the twisted poker into the fireplace, he strode out of the room.

"He seems a very amiable person," said Holmes, laughing. "I am not quite so bulky, but if he had remained I might have shown him that my grip was not much more feeble than his own." As he spoke he picked up the steel poker, and with a sudden effort straightened it out again.

"Fancy his having the insolence to confound me with the official detective force! This incident gives zest to our investigation, however, and I only trust that our little friend will not suffer from her imprudence in allowing this brute to trace her. And now, Watson, we shall order breakfast, and afterward I shall walk down to Doctors' Commons, where I hope to get some data which may help us in this matter."

It was nearly one o'clock when Sherlock Holmes returned from his excursion. He held in his hand a sheet of blue paper, scrawled over with notes and figures.

"I have seen the will of the deceased wife," said he. "To determine its exact meaning I have been obliged to work out the present prices of the investments with which it is concerned. The total income, which at the time of the wife's death was little short of 1,100 pounds, is now, through the fall in agricultural prices, not more than 750 pounds. Each daughter can claim an income of 250 pounds, in case of marriage. It is evident, therefore, that if both girls had married, this beauty would have had a mere pittance, while even one of them would cripple him to a very serious intent. My morning's work has not been wasted, since it has proved that he had the very strongest motives for standing in the way of anything of the sort. And now, Watson, this is too serious for dawdling, especially as the old man is aware that we are interesting ourselves in his affairs; so if you are ready, we shall call a cab and drive to Waterloo. I should be very much obliged if you would slip your revolver into your pocket. An Eley's No. 2 is an excellent argument with gentlemen who can twist steel pokers into knots. That and a toothbrush are, I think, all that we need."

At Waterloo, we were fortunate in catching a train for Leatherhead, where we hired a trap at the station inn, and drove for four or five miles through the lovely Surrey lanes. It was a perfect day, with a bright sun and a few fleecy clouds in the heavens. The trees and wayside hedges were just throwing out their first green shoots, and the air was full of the pleasant smell of the moist earth. To me at least there was a strange contrast between the sweet promise of the spring and the sinister quest upon which we were engaged. My companion sat in front of the trap, his arms folded, his hat pulled down over his eyes, and his chin sunk upon his breast, buried in the deepest thought. Suddenly, however, he started, tapped me on the shoulder, and pointed over the meadows. ·

"Look there!" said he.

A heavily timbered park stretched up in a gentle slope, thickening into a grove at the highest point. From amid the branches there jutted out the gray gables and high roof-tree of a very old mansion.

"Stoke Moran?" said he.

"Yes, sir, that be the house of Dr. Grimesby Roylott," remarked the driver.

"There is some building going on there," said Holmes; "that is where we are going."

"There's the village," said the driver, pointing to a cluster of roofs some distance to the left; "but if you want to get to the house, you'll find it shorter to get over this stile, and so by the foot-path over the fields. There it is, where the lady is walking."

"And the lady, I fancy, is Miss Stoner," observed Holmes, shading his eyes. "Yes, I think we had better do as you suggest."

We got off, paid our fare, and the trap rattled back on its way to Leatherhead.

"I thought it as well," said Holmes, as we climbed the stile, "that this fellow should think we had come here as architects or on some definite business. It may stop his gossip. Good-afternoon, Miss Stoner. You see that we have been as good as our word."

Our client of the morning had hurried forward to meet us with a face which spoke her joy. "I have been waiting so eagerly for you!" she cried, shaking hands with us warmly. "All has turned out splendidly. Dr. Roylott has gone to town, and it is unlikely that he will be back before evening."

"We have had the pleasure of making the doctor's acquaintance," said Holmes, and in a few words he sketched out what had occurred. Miss Stoner turned white to the lips as she listened.

"Good heavens!" she cried, "he has followed me, then."

"So it appears."

"He is so cunning that I never know when I am safe from him. What will he say when he returns?"

"He must guard himself, for he may find that there is some one more cunning than himself upon his track. You must lock yourself up from him tonight. If he is violent, we shall take you away to your aunt's at Harrow. Now, we must make the best use of our time, so kindly take us at once to the rooms which we are to examine."

The building was of gray, lichen-blotched stone, with a high central portion, and two curving wings, like the claws of a crab, thrown out on each side. In one of these wings the windows were broken, and blocked with wooden boards, while the roof was partly caved in, a picture of ruin. The central portion was in little better repair, but the right-hand block was comparatively modern, and the blinds in the windows, with the blue smoke curling up from the chimneys, showed that this was where the family resided. Some scaffolding had been erected against the end wall, and the stone-work had been broken into, but there were no signs of any workmen at the moment of our visit. Holmes walked slowly up and down the ill-trimmed lawn, and examined with deep attention the outsides of the windows.

"This, I take it, belongs to the room in which you used to sleep, the center one to your sister's, and the one next to the main building to Dr. Roylott's chamber?"

"Exactly so. But I am now sleeping in the middle one."

"Pending the alterations, as I understand. By-the-way, there does not seem to be any very pressing need for repairs at that end wall."

"There were none. I believe that it was an excuse to move me from my room."

"Ah! that is suggestive. Now, on the other side of this narrow wing runs the corridor from which these three rooms open. There are windows in it, of course?"

"Yes, but very small ones. Too narrow for any one to pass through."

"As you both locked your doors at night, your rooms were unapproachable from that side. Now, would you have the kindness to go into your room and bar your shutters."

Miss Stoner did so, and Holmes, after a careful examination through the open window, endeavored in every way to force the shutter open, but without success. There was no slit through which a knife could be passed to raise the bar. Then with his lens he tested the hinges, but they were of solid iron, built firmly into the massive masonry. "Hum!" said he, scratching his chin in some perplexity; "my theory certainly presents some difficulties. No one could pass these shutters if they were bolted. Well, we shall see if the inside throws any light upon the matter."

A small side door led into the whitewashed corridor from which the three bedrooms opened. Holmes refused to examine the third chamber, so we passed at once to the second, that in which Miss Stoner was now sleeping, and in which her sister had met with fate. It was a homely little room, with a low ceiling and a gaping fireplace, after the fashion of old country-houses. A brown chest of drawers stood in one corner, a narrow white-counterpaned bed in another, and a dressing-table on the left-hand side of the window. These articles, with two small wicker-work chairs, made up all the furniture in the room, save for a square of Wilton carpet in the center. The boards round and the paneling of the walls were of brown, worm-eaten oak, so old and discolored that it may have dated from the original building of the house. Holmes drew one of the chairs into a corner and sat silent, while his eyes traveled round and round and up and down, taking in every detail of the apartment.

"Where does that bell communicate with?" he asked, at last, pointing to a thick bell-rope which hung down beside the bed, the tassel actually lying upon the pillow.

"It goes to the housekeeper's room."

"It looks newer than the other things?"

"Yes, it was only put there a couple of years ago."

"Your sister asked for it, I suppose?"

"No, I never heard of her using it. We used always to get what we wanted for ourselves."

"Indeed, it seemed unnecessary to put so nice a bell-pull there. You will excuse me for a few minutes while I satisfy myself as to this floor." He threw himself down upon his face with his lens in his hand, and crawled swiftly backward and forward, examining minutely the cracks between the boards. Then he did the same with the wood-work with which the chamber was paneled. Finally he walked over to the bed, and spent some time in staring at it, and in running his eye up and down the wall. Finally he took the bell-rope in his hand and gave it a brisk tug.

"Why, it's a dummy," said he.

"Won't it ring?"

"No, it is not even attached to a wire. This is very interesting. You can see now that it is fastened to a hook just above where the opening for the ventilator is."

"How very absurd! I never noticed that before."

"Very strange!" muttered Holmes, pulling at the rope. "There are one or two very singular points about this room. For example, what a fool a builder must be to open a ventilator into another room, when, with the same trouble, he might have communicated with the outside air!"

"That is also quite modern," said the lady.

"Done about the same time as the bell-rope?" remarked Holmes.

"Yes, there were several little changes carried out about that time."

"They seem to have been of a most interesting character—dummy bell-ropes, and ventilators which do not ventilate. With your permission, Miss Stoner, we shall now carry our researches into the inner apartment."

Dr. Grimesby Roylott's chamber was larger than that of his step-daughter, but was as plainly furnished. A camp-bed, a small wooden shelf full of books, mostly of a technical character, an arm-chair beside the bed, a plain wooden chair against the wall, a round table, and a large iron safe were the principal things which met the eye.

Holmes walked slowly round and examined each and all of them with the keenest interest.

"What's in here?" he asked, tapping the safe.

"My step-father's business papers."

"Oh, you have seen inside, then?"

"Only once, some years ago. I remember that it was full of papers."

"There isn't a cat in it, for example?"

"No. What a strange idea!"

"Well, look at this!" He took up a small saucer of milk which stood on the top of it.

"No; we don't keep a cat. But there is a cheetah and a baboon."

"Ah, yes, of course! Well, a cheetah is just a big cat, and yet a saucer of milk does not go very far in satisfying its wants, I dare say. There is one point which I should wish to determine." He squatted down in front of the wooden chair, and examined the seat of it with the greatest attention.

"Thank you. That is quite settled," said he, rising and putting his lens in his pocket. "Hello!—Here is something interesting!"

The object which had caught his eye was a small doglash hung on one corner of the bed. The lash, however, was curled upon itself, and tied so as to make a loop of whip-cord.

"What do you make of that, Watson?"

"It's a common enough lash. But I don't know why it should be tied."

"That is not quite so common, is it? Ah, me! it's a wicked world, and when a clever man turns his brains to crime it is the worst of all. I think that I have seen enough now, Miss Stoner, and with your permission we shall walk out upon the lawn."

I had never seen my friend's face so grim or his brow so dark as it was when we turned from the scene of this investigation. We had walked several times up and down the lane, neither Miss Stoner nor myself liking to break in upon his thoughts before he roused himself from his reverie.

"It is very essential, Miss Stoner," said he, "that you should absolutely follow my advice in every respect."

"I shall most certainly do so."

"The matter is too serious for any hesitation. Your life may depend upon your compliance."

"I assure you that I am in your hands."

"In the first place, both my friend and I must spend the night in your room."

Both Miss Stoner and I gazed at him in astonishment.

"Yes, it must be so. Let me explain. I believe that that is the village inn over there?"

"Yes, that is the 'Crown.'"

"Very good. Your windows would be visible from there?"

"Certainly."

"You must confine yourself to your room, on pretense of a head-ache, when your step-father comes back. Then when you hear him retire for the night, you must open the shutters of your window, undo the hasp, put your lamp there as a signal to us, and then withdraw quietly with everything which you are likely to want into the room which you used to occupy. I have no doubt that, in spite of the repairs, you could manage there for one night."

"Oh, yes, easily."

"The rest you will leave in our hands."

"But what will you do?"

"We shall spend the night in your room, and we shall investigate the cause of this noise which has disturbed you."

"I believe, Mr. Holmes, that you have already made up your mind," said Miss Stoner, laying her hand upon my companion's sleeve.

"Perhaps I have."

"Then, for pity's sake, tell me what was the cause of my sister's death."

"I should prefer to have clearer proofs before I speak."

"You can at least tell me whether my own thought is correct, and if she died from some sudden fright."

"No, I do not think so. I think that there was probably some more tangible cause. And now, Miss Stoner, we must leave you, for if Dr. Roylott returned and saw us, our journey would be in vain. Goodbye, and be brave, for if you will do what I have told you, you may rest assured that we shall soon drive away the dangers that threaten you."

Sherlock Holmes and I had no difficulty in engaging a bedroom and sitting-room at the "Crown Inn." They were on the upper floor, and from our window we could command a view of the avenue gate, and of the inhabited wing of Stoke Moran Manor-House. At dusk we saw Dr. Grimesby Roylott drive past, his huge form looming up beside the little figure of the lad who drove him. The boy had some slight difficulty in undoing the heavy iron gates, and we heard the hoarse roar of the doctor's voice, and saw the fury with which he shook his clenched fists at him. The trap drove on, and a few minutes later we saw a sudden light spring up among the trees as the lamp was lit in one of the sitting-rooms.

"Do you know, Watson," said Holmes, as we sat together in the gathering darkness, "I have really some scruples as to taking you to-night. There is a distinct element of danger."

"Can I be of assistance?"

"Your presence might be invaluable."

"Then I shall certainly come."

"It is very kind of you."

"You speak of danger. You have evidently seen more in these rooms than was visible to me."

"No, but I fancy that I may have deduced a little more. I imagine that you saw all that I did."

"I saw nothing remarkable save the bell-rope, and what purpose that could answer I confess is more than I can imagine."

"You saw the ventilator, too?"

"Yes, but I do not think that it is such a very unusual thing to have a small opening between two rooms. It was so small that a rat could hardly pass through."

"I knew that we should find a ventilator before ever we came to Stoke Moran."

"My dear Holmes!"

"Oh, yes, I did. You remember in her statement she said that her sister could smell Dr. Roylott's cigar. Now, of course, that suggested at once that there must be a communication between the two rooms. It could only be a small one, or it would have been remarked upon at the coroner's inquiry. I deduced a ventilator."

"But what harm can there be in that?"

"Well, there is at least a curious coincidence of dates. A ventilator is made, a cord is hung, and a lady who sleeps in the bed dies. Does not that strike you?"

"I cannot as yet see any connection."

"Did you observe anything very peculiar about that bed?"

"No."

"It was clamped to the floor. Did you ever see a bed fastened like that before?"

"I cannot say that I have."

"The lady could not move her bed. It must always be in the same relative position to the ventilator and to the rope—for we may call it, since it was clearly never meant for a bell-pull."

"Holmes," I cried, "I seem to see dimly what you are hinting at! We are only just in time to prevent some subtle and horrible crime."

"Subtle enough and horrible enough. When a doctor does go wrong, he is the first of criminals. He has nerve, and he has knowledge. Palmer and Pritchard were among the heads of their profession. This man strikes even deeper; but I think, Watson, that we shall be able to strike deeper still. But we shall have horrors enough before the night is over; for goodness' sake let us have a quiet pipe, and turn our minds for a few hours to something more cheerful."

About nine o'clock the light among the trees was extinguished, and all was dark in the direction of the Manor-House. Two hours passed slowly away, and then, suddenly, just at the stroke of eleven, a single bright light shone out in front of us.

"That is our signal," said Holmes, springing to his feet; "it comes from the middle window."

As we passed out he exchanged a few words with the landlord, explaining that we were going on a late visit to an acquaintance, and that it was possible that we might spend the night there. A moment later we were out on the dark road, a chill wind blowing in our faces, and one yellow light twinkling in front of us through the gloom to guide us on our somber errand.

There was little difficulty in entering the grounds, for unrepaired breaches gaped in the park wall. Making our way among the trees, we reached the lawn, crossed it, and were about to enter through the window, when out from a clump of laurel-bushes there darted what seemed to be a hideous and distorted child, who threw itself upon the grass with writhing limbs, and then ran swiftly across the lawn into the darkness.

"My God!" I whispered; "did you see it?"

Holmes was for the moment as startled as I. His hand closed like a vise upon my wrist in his agitation. Then he broke into a low laugh, and put his lips to my ear.

"It is a nice household," he murmured. "That is the baboon."

I had forgotten the strange pets which the doctor affected. There was a cheetah, too; perhaps we might find it upon our shoulders at any moment. I confess that I felt easier in my mind when, after following Holmes' example and slipping off my shoes, I found myself inside the bedroom. My companion noiselessly closed the shutters, moved the lamp onto the table, and cast his eyes round the room. All was as we had seen it in the daytime. Then creeping up to me and making a trumpet of his hand, he whispered into my ear again so gently that it was all that I could do to distinguish the words:

"The least sound would be fatal to our plans."

I nodded to show that I had heard.

"We must sit without light. He would see it through the ventilator."

I nodded again.

"Do not go asleep; your very life may depend on it. Have your pistol ready in case we should need it. I will sit on the side of the bed, and you in that chair."

I took out my revolver and laid it on the corner of the table.

Holmes had brought up a long, thin cane, and this he placed upon the bed beside him. By it he laid the box of matches and the stump of a candle. Then he turned down the lamp, and we were left in darkness.

How shall I ever forget that dreadful vigil? I could not hear a sound, not even the drawing of a breath, and yet I knew that my companion sat open-eyed, within a few feet of me, in the same state of nervous tension in which I was myself. The shutters cut off the least ray of light, and we waited in absolute darkness. From outside came the occasional cry of a night-bird, and once at our very window a long-drawn, cat-like whine, which told us that the cheetah was indeed at liberty. Far away we could hear the deep tones of the parish clock, which boomed out every quarter of an hour. How long they seemed, those quarters! Twelve struck, and one and two and three, and still we sat waiting silently for whatever might befall.

Suddenly there was the momentary gleam of a light up in the direction of the ventilator, which vanished immediately, but was succeeded by a strong smell of burning oil and heated metal. Some one in the next room had lit a dark-lantern. I heard a gentle sound of movement, and then all was silent once more, though the smell grew stronger. For half an hour I sat with straining ears. Then suddenly another sound became audible—a very gentle, soothing sound, like that of a small jet of steam escaping continually from a kettle. The instant that we heard it, Holmes sprang from the bed, struck a match, and lashed furiously with his cane at the bell-pull.

"You see it, Watson?" he yelled. "You see it?"

But I saw nothing. At the moment when Holmes struck the light I heard a low, clear whistle, but the sudden glare flashing into my weary eyes made it impossible for me to tell what it was at which my friend lashed so savagely. I could, however, see that his face was deadly pale, and filled with horror and loathing.

He had ceased to strike, and was gazing up at the ventilator, when suddenly there broke from the silence of the night the most horrible cry

161

to which I have ever listened. It swelled up louder and louder, a hoarse yell of pain and fear and anger all mingled in the one dreadful shriek. They say that away down in the village, and even in the distant parsonage, that cry raised the sleepers from their beds. It struck cold to our hearts, and I stood gazing at Holmes, and he at me, until the last echoes of it had died away into the silence from which it rose.

"What can it mean?" I gasped.

"It means that it is all over," Holmes answered. "And perhaps, after all, it is for the best. Take your pistol, and we will enter Dr. Roylott's room."

With a grave face he lit the lamp and led the way down the corridor. Twice he struck at the chamber door without any reply from within. Then he turned the handle and entered, I at his heels, with the cocked pistol in my hand.

It was a singular sight which met our eyes. On the table stood a dark-lantern with the shutter half open, throwing a brilliant beam of light upon the iron safe, the door of which was ajar. Beside this table, on the wooden chair, sat Dr. Grimesby Roylott, clad in a long gray dressing gown, his bare ankles protruding beneath, and his feet thrust into red heelless Turkish slippers. Across his lap lay the short stock with the long lash which we had noticed during the day. His chin was cocked upward and his eyes were fixed in a dreadful, rigid stare at the corner of the ceiling. Round his brow he had a peculiar yellow band, with brownish speckles, which seemed to be bound tightly round his head. As we entered he made neither sound nor motion.

"The band! the speckled band!" whispered Holmes.

I took a step forward. In an instant his strange headgear began to move, and there reared itself from among his hair the squat diamond-shaped head and puffed neck of a loathsome serpent.

"It is a swamp adder!" cried Holmes; "the deadliest snake in India. He has died within ten seconds of being bitten. Violence does, in truth, recoil upon the violent, and the schemer falls into the pit which he digs for another. Let us thrust this creature back into its den, and we can then remove Miss Stoner to some place of shelter, and let the county police know what has happened."

As he spoke he drew the dog-whip swiftly from the dead man's lap, and, throwing the noose round the reptile's neck, he drew it from its horrid perch, and carrying it at arm's-length, threw it into the iron safe, which he closed upon it.

Such are the true facts of the death of Dr. Grimesby Roylott, of Stoke Moran. It is not necessary that I should prolong a narrative which has already run to too great a length, by telling how we broke the sad news to the terrified girl, how we conveyed her by the morning train to the care of her good aunt at Harrow, of how the slow process of official inquiry came to the conclusion that the doctor met his fate while indiscreetly playing with a dangerous pet. The little which I had yet to learn of the case was told me by Sherlock Holmes as we traveled back next day.

"I had," said he, "come to an entirely erroneous conclusion, which shows, my dear Watson, how dangerous it always is to reason from insufficient data. The presence of the gypsies, and the use of the word 'band,' which was used by the poor girl, no doubt explain the appearance which she had caught a hurried glimpse of by the light of her match, were sufficient to put me upon an entirely wrong scent. I can only claim the merit that I instantly reconsidered my position when, however, it became clear to me that whatever danger threatened an occupant of the room could not come either from the window or the door. My attention was speedily drawn, as I have already remarked to you, to this ventilator, and to the bell-rope which hung down to the bed. The discovery that this was a dummy, and that the bed was clamped to the floor, instantly gave rise to the suspicion that the rope was there as bridge for something passing through the hole and coming to the bed. The idea of a snake instantly occurred to me, and when I coupled it with my knowledge that the doctor was furnished with a supply of creatures from India, I felt that I was probably on the right track. The idea of using a form of poison which could not possibly be discovered by any chemical test was just such a one as would occur to a clever and ruthless man who had had an Eastern training. The rapidity with which such a poison would take effect would also, from his point of view, be an advantage. It would be a sharp-eyed coroner, indeed, who could distinguish the two little dark punctures which would show where the poison fangs had done their work. Then I thought of the whistle. Of course he must recall the snake before the morning light revealed it to the victim. He had trained it, probably by the use of the milk which we saw, to return to him when summoned. He would put it through this ventilator at the hour that he thought best, with the certainty that it would crawl down the rope and land on the bed. It might not bite the occupant, perhaps she might escape every night for a week, but sooner or later she must fall a victim.

"I had come to these conclusions before ever I had entered his room. An inspection of his chair showed me that he had been in the habit of standing on it, which of course would be necessary in order that he should reach the ventilator. The sight of the safe, the saucer of milk, and the loop of whip-cord were enough to finally dispel any doubts

163

which may have remained. The metallic clang heard by Miss Stoner was obviously caused by her step-father hastily closing the door of his safe upon its terrible occupant. Having once made up my mind, you know the steps which I took in order to put the matter to the proof. I heard the creature hiss, as I have no doubt that you did also, and I instantly lit the light and attacked it."

"With the result of driving it through the ventilator."

"And also with the result of causing it to turn upon its master at the other side. Some of the blows of my cane came home, and roused its snakish temper, so that it flew upon the first person it saw. In this way I am no doubt indirectly responsible for Dr. Grimesby Roylott's death, and I cannot say that it is likely to weigh very heavily upon my conscience."

CHAPTER IV

MORE GREAT DETECTIVES

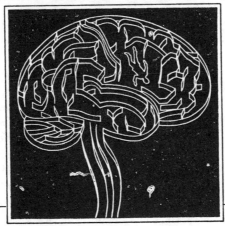

THE PROBLEM OF CELL 13

By Jacques Futrelle

Jacques Futrelle (1875–1912), despite his French Huguenot name, was an American writer born in Georgia. For a time, he worked as a newspaperman in Richmond, Virginia, the city in which Poe once held an editorial position on the Southern Literary Messenger. *Futrelle also served briefly as a theatrical manager before moving to Boston and joining the staff of the* Boston American, *in whose pages much of his fiction first appeared. That fiction includes many detective short stories featuring such now-forgotten sleuths as Fred Boyd, Dr. Spence, and Garron and Louis Harding, and several mystery novels, most notably* The Diamond Master *(1909) and* My Lady's Garter *(1912). The character for which Futrelle is best remembered today, however, is undoubtedly Professor Augustus S.F.X. Van Dusen, otherwise known as The Thinking Machine, one of the most cerebral and purely analytic of all detectives. Van Dusen appears in some forty-five stories, the best known of which is "The Problem of Cell 13," originally serialized in the* Boston American *from October 30 to November 5, 1905 and since widely anthologized. Futrelle's premature death aboard the* Titanic *abruptly ended the career of one of America's most creative mystery writers. For more stories about Professor Van Dusen, see Best "Thinking Machine" Detective Stories (New York: Dover, 1973) and Great Cases of The Thinking Machine (New York: Dover, 1976), both edited and with introductions by E. F. Bleiler.*

Practically all those letters remaining in the alphabet after Augustus S. F. X. Van Dusen was named were afterwards acquired by that gentleman in the course of a brilliant scientific career, and, being honorably acquired, were tacked on to the other end. His name, therefore, taken with all that belonged to it, was a wonderfully imposing structure. He was a Ph.D., an LL.D., an F.R.S., an M.D., and an M.D.S. He was also some other things—just what he himself couldn't say—through recognition of his ability by various foreign educational and scientific institutions.

In appearance he was no less striking than in nomenclature. He was slender with the droop of the student in his thin shoulders and the pallor of a close, sedentary life on his clean-shaven face. His eyes wore a perpetual, forbidding squint—the squint of a man who studies little things—and when they could be seen at all through his thick spectacles, were mere slits of watery blue. But above his eyes was his most striking feature. This was a tall, broad brow, almost abnormal in height and width, crowned by a heavy shock of bushy, yellow hair. All these things conspired to give him a peculiar, almost grotesque, personality.

Professor Van Dusen was remotely German. For generations his ancestors had been noted in the sciences; he was the logical result, the master mind. First and above all he was a logician. At least thirty-five years of the half-century or so of his existence had been devoted exclusively to proving that two and two always equal four, except in unusual cases, where they equal three or five, as the case may be. He stood broadly on the general proposition that all things that start must go somewhere, and was able to bring the concentrated mental force of his forefathers to bear on a given problem. Incidentally it may be remarked that Professor Van Dusen wore a No. 8 hat.

The world at large had heard vaguely of Professor Van Dusen as The Thinking Machine. It was a newspaper catch-phrase applied to him at the time of a remarkable exhibition at chess; he had demonstrated then that a stranger to the game might, by the force of inevitable logic, defeat a champion who had devoted a lifetime to its study. The Thinking Machine! Perhaps that more nearly described him than all his honorary initials, for he spent week after week, month after month, in the seclusion of his small laboratory from which had gone forth thoughts that staggered scientific associates and deeply stirred the world at large.

It was only occasionally that The Thinking Machine had visitors, and these were usually men who, themselves high in the sciences, dropped in to argue a point and perhaps convince themselves. Two of these men, Dr Charles Ransome and Alfred Fielding, called one evening to discuss some theory which is not of consequence here.

"Such a thing is possible," delcared Dr Ransome emphatically, in the course of the conversation.

"Nothing is impossible," declared The Thinking Machine with equal emphasis. He always spoke petulantly. "The mind is master of all things. When science fully recognizes that fact a great advance will have been made."

"How about the airship?" asked Dr Ransome.

"That's not impossible at all," asserted The Thinking Machine. "It will be invented some time. I'd do it myself, but I'm busy."

Dr Ransome laughed tolerantly.

"I've heard you say such things before," he said. "But they mean nothing. Mind may be master of matter, but it hasn't yet found a way to apply itself. There are some things that can't be *thought* out of existence, or rather which would not yield to any amount of thinking."

"What, for instance?" demanded The Thinking Machine.

Dr Ransome was thoughtful for a moment as he smoked.

"Well, say prison walls," he replied. "No man can *think* himself out of a cell. If he could, there would be no prisoners."

"A man can so apply his brain and ingenuity that he can leave a cell, which is the same," snapped The Thinking Machine.

Dr Ransome was slightly amused.

"Let's suppose a case," he said, after a moment. "Take a cell where prisoners under sentence of death are confined—men who are desperate and, maddened by fear, would take any chance to escape—suppose you were locked in such a cell. Could you escape?"

"Certainly," declared The Thinking Machine.

"Of course," said Mr Fielding, who entered the conversation for the first time, "You might wreck the cell with an explosive—but inside, a prisoner, you couldn't have that."

"There would be nothing of that kind," said The Thinking Machine. "You might treat me precisely as you treated prisoners under sentence of death, and I would leave the cell."

"Not unless you entered it with tools prepared to get out," said Dr Ransome.

The Thinking Machine was visibly annoyed and his blue eyes snapped.

"Lock me in any cell in any prison anywhere at any time, wearing only what is necessary, and I'll escape in a week," he declared, sharply.

Dr Ransome sat up straight in the chair, interested. Mr Fielding lighted a new cigar.

"You mean you could actually *think* yourself out?" asked Dr Ransome.

"I would get out," was the response.

"Are you serious?"

"Certainly I am serious."

Dr Ransome and Mr Fielding were silent for a long time.

"Would you be willing to try it?" asked Mr Fielding, finally.

"Certainly," said Professor Van Dusen, and there was a trace of irony in his voice. "I have done more asinine things than that to convince other men of less important truths."

The tone was offensive and there was an under-current strongly resembling anger on both sides. Of course it was an absurd thing, but Professor Van Dusen reiterated his willingness to undertake the escape and it was decided upon.

"To begin now," added Dr Ransome.

"I'd prefer that it begin to-morrow," said The Thinking Machine, "because—"

"No, now," said Mr Fielding, flatly. "You are arrested, figuratively, of course, without any warning locked in a cell with no chance to communicate with friends, and left there with identically the same care and attention that would be given to a man under sentence of death. Are you willing?"

"All right, now, then," said The Thinking Machine, and he arose.

"Say, the death-cell in Chisholm Prison."

"The death-cell in Chisholm Prison."

"And what will you wear?"

"As little as possible," said The Thinking Machine. "Shoes, stockings, trousers and a shirt."

"You will permit yourself to be searched, of course?"

"I am to be treated precisely as all prisoners are treated," said The Thinking Machine. "No more attention and no less."

There were some preliminaries to be arranged in the matter of obtaining permission for the test, but all three were influential men and everything was done satisfactorily by telephone, albeit the prison commissioners, to whom the experiment was explained on purely scientific grounds, were sadly bewildered. Professor Van Dusen would be the most distinguished prisoner they had ever entertained.

When The Thinking Machine had donned those things which he was to wear during his incarceration he called the little old woman who was his housekeeper, cook and maid-servant all in one.

"Martha," he said, "it is now twenty-seven minutes past nine o'clock. I am going away. One week from to-night, at half-past nine, these gentlemen and one, possibly two, others will take supper with me here. Remember Dr Ransome is very fond of artichokes."

The three men were driven to Chisholm Prison, where the Warden was awaiting them, having been informed of the matter by telephone. He understood merely that the eminent Professor Van Dusen was to be his prisoner, if he could keep him, for one week; that he had committed no crime, but that he was to be treated as all other prisoners were treated.

"Search him," instructed Dr Ransome.

The Thinking Machine was searched. Nothing was found on him; the pockets of the trousers were empty; the white, stiff-bosomed shirt had no pocket. The shoes and stockings were removed, examined, then replaced. As he watched all these preliminaries—the rigid search and noted the pitiful, childlike physical weakness of the man, the colourless face, and the thin, white hands—Dr Ransome almost regretted his part in the affair.

"Are you sure you want to do this?" he asked.

"Would you be convinced if I did not?" inquired The Thinking Machine in turn.

"No."

"All right. I'll do it."

What sympathy Dr Ransome had was dissipated by the tone. It nettled him, and he resolved to see the experiment to the end; it would be a stinging reproof to egotism.

"It will be impossible for him to communicate with anyone outside?" he asked.

"Absolutely impossible," replied the warden. "He will not be permitted writing materials of any sort."

"And your jailers, would they deliver a message from him?"

"Not one word, directly or indirectly," said the warden. "You may rest assured of that. They will report anything he might say or turn over to me anything he might give them."

"That seems entirely satisfactory," said Mr Fielding, who was frankly interested in the problem.

"Of course, in the event he fails," said Dr Ransome, "and asks for his liberty, you understand you are to set him free?"

"I understand," replied the warden.

The Thinking Machine stood listening, but had nothing to say until this was all ended, then:

"I should like to make three small requests. You may grant them or not, as you wish."

"No special favours, now," warned Mr Fielding.

"I am asking none," was the stiff response. "I would like to have some tooth powder—buy it yourself to see that it is tooth powder—and I should like to have one five-dollar and two ten-dollar bills."

Dr Ransome, Mr Fielding and the warden exchanged astonished glances. They were not surprised at the request for tooth powder, but were at the request for money.

"Is there any man with whom our friend would come in contact that he could bribe with twenty-five dollars?" asked Dr Ransome of the warden.

"Not for twenty-five hundred dollars," was the positive reply.

"Well, let him have them," said Mr Fielding. "I think they are harmless enough."

"And what is the third request?" asked Dr Ransome.

"I should like to have my shoes polished."

Again the astonished glances were exchanged. This last request was the height of absurdity, so they agreed to it. These things all being attended to, The Thinking Machine was led back into the prison from which he had undertaken to escape.

"Here is Cell 13," said the warden, stopping three doors down the steel corridor. "This is where we keep condemned murderers. No one can leave it without my permission; and no one in it can communicate with the outside. I'll stake my reputation on that. It's only three doors back of my office and I can readily hear any unusual noise."

"Will this cell do, gentlemen?" asked The Thinking Machine. There was a touch of irony in his voice.

"Admirably," was the reply.

The heavy steel door was thrown open, there was a great scurrying and scampering of tiny feet, and The Thinking Machine passed into the gloom of the cell. Then the door was closed and double locked by the warden.

"What is that noise in there?" asked Dr Ransome, through the bars.

"Rats—dozens of them," replied The Thinking Machine, tersely.

The three men, with final good-nights, were turning away when The Thinking Machine called:

"What time is it exactly, warden?"

"Eleven seventeen," replied the warden.

"Thanks. I will join you gentlemen in your office at half-past eight

171

o'clock one week from tonight," said The Thinking Machine.

"And if you do not?"

"There is no 'if' about it."

II

Chisholm Prison was a great, spreading structure of granite, four stories in all, which stood in the centre of acres of open space. It was surrounded by a wall of solid masonry eighteen feet high, and so smoothly finished inside and out as to offer no foothold to a climber, no matter how expert. Atop of this fence, as a further precaution, was a five-foot fence of steel rods, each terminating in a keen point. This fence in itself marked an absolute deadline between freedom and imprisonment, for, even if a man escaped from his cell, it would seem impossible for him to pass the wall.

The yard, which on all sides of the prison building was twenty-five feet wide, that being the distance from the building to the wall, was by day an exercise ground for those prisoners to whom was granted the boon of occasional semi-liberty. But that was not for those in Cell 13. At all times of the day there were armed guards in the yard, four of them, one patrolling each side of the prison building.

By night the yard was almost as brilliantly lighted as by day. On each of the four sides was a great arc light which rose above the prison wall and gave to the guards a clear sight. The lights, too, brightly illuminated the spiked top of the wall. The wires which fed the arc lights ran up the side of the prison building on insulators and from the top storey led out to the poles supporting the arc lights.

All these things were seen and comprehended by The Thinking Machine, who was only enabled to see out of his closely barred cell window by standing on his bed. This was on the morning following his incarceration. He gathered, too, that the river lay over there beyond the wall somewhere, because he heard faintly the pulsation of a motor boat and high up in the air saw a river bird. From that same direction came the shouts of boys at play and the occasional crack of a batted ball. He knew then that between the prison wall and the river was an open space, a playground.

Chisholm Prison was regarded as absolutely safe. No man had ever escaped from it. The Thinking Machine, from his perch on the bed, seeing what he saw, could readily understand why. The walls of the cell, though built, he judged, twenty years before, were perfectly solid, and the window bars of new iron had not a shadow of rust on them. The window itself, even with the bars out, would be a difficult mode of egress because it was small.

Yet, seeing these things, The Thinking Machine was not discouraged. Instead, he thoughtfully squinted at the great arc light—there was bright sunlight now—and traced with his eyes the wire which led from it to the building. That electric wire, he reasoned, must come down the side of the building not a great distance from his cell. That might be worth knowing.

Cell 13 was on the same floor with the offices of the prison—that is, not in the basement, nor yet upstairs. There were only four steps up to the office floor, therefore the level of the floor must be only three or four feet above the ground. He couldn't see the ground directly beneath his window, but he could see it further out toward the wall. It would be an easy drop from the window. Well and good.

Then The Thinking Machine fell to remembering how he had come to the cell. First, there was the outside guard's booth, a part of the wall. There were two heavily barred gates, both of steel. At this gate was one man always on guard. He admitted persons to the prison after much clanking of keys and locks, and let them out when ordered to do so. The warden's office was in the prison building, and in order to reach that official from the prison yard one had to pass a gate of solid steel with only a peep-hole in it. Then coming from that inner office to Cell 13, where he was now, one must pass a heavy wooden door and two steel doors into the corridors of the prison; and always there was the double-locked door of Cell 13 to reckon with.

There were then, The Thinking Machine recalled, seven doors to be overcome before one could pass from Cell 13 into the outer world, a free man. But against this was the fact that he was rarely interrupted. A jailer appeared at his cell door at six in the morning with a breakfast of prison fare; he would come again at noon, and again at six in the afternoon. At nine o'clock at night would come the inspection tour. That would be all.

"It's admirably arranged, this prison system," was the mental tribute paid by The Thinking Machine. "I'll have to study it a little when I get out. I had no idea there was such great care exercised in the prisons."

There was nothing, positively nothing, in his cell, except his iron bed, so firmly put together that no man could tear it to pieces save with sledges or a file. He had neither of these. There was not even a chair, or a small table, or a bit of tin or crockery. Nothing! The jailer stood by when he ate, then took away the wooden spoon and bowl which he had used.

One by one these things sank into the brain of The Thinking Machine. When the last possibility had been considered he began an examination of his cell. From the roof, down the walls on all sides, he examined the stones and the cement between them. He stamped over the floor carefully time after time, but it was cement, perfectly solid. After the examination he sat on the edge of the iron bed and was lost in thought for a long time. For Professor Augustus S.F.X. Van Dusen, The Thinking Machine, had something to think about.

He was disturbed by a rat, which ran across his foot, then scampered away into a dark corner of the cell, frightened at its own daring. After a while The Thinking Machine, squinting steadily into the darkness of the corner where the rat had gone, was able to make out in the gloom many little beady eyes staring at him. He counted six pair, and there were perhaps others; he didn't see very well.

Then The Thinking Machine, from his seat on the bed, noticed for the first time the bottom of his cell door. There was an opening there of two inches between the steel bar and the floor. Still looking steadily at this opening, The Thinking Machine backed suddenly into the corner where he had seen the beady eyes. There was a great scampering of tiny feet, several squeaks of frightened rodents, and then silence.

None of the rats had gone out the door, yet there were none in the cell. Therefore there must be another way out of the cell, however small. The Thinking Machine, on hands and knees, started a search for this spot, feeling in the darkness with his long, slender fingers.

At last his search was rewarded. He came upon a small opening in the floor, level with the cement. It was perfectly round and somewhat larger than a silver dollar. This was the way the rats had gone. He put his fingers deep into the opening; it seemed to be a disused drainage pipe and was dry and dusty.

Having satisfied himself on this point, he sat on the bed again for an hour, then made another inspection of his surroundings through the small cell window. One of the outside guards stood directly opposite, beside the wall, and happened to be looking at the window of Cell 13 when the head of The Thinking Machine appeared. But the scientist didn't notice the guard.

Noon came and the jailer appeared with the prison dinner of repulsively plain food. At home The Thinking Machine merely ate to live; here he took what was offered without comment. Occasionally he spoke to the jailer who stood outside the door watching him.

"Any improvements made here in the last few years?" he asked.

174

"Nothing particularly," replied the jailer. "New wall was built four years ago."

"Anything done to the prison proper?"

"Painted the woodwork outside, and I believe about seven years ago a new system of plumbing was put in."

"Ah!" said the prisoner. "How far is the river over there?"

"About three hundred feet. The boys have a baseball ground between the wall and the river."

The Thinking Machine had nothing further to say just then, but when the jailer was ready to go he asked for some water.

"I get very thirsty here," he explained. "Would it be possible for you to leave a little water in a bowl for me?"

"I'll ask the warden," replied the jailer, and he went away.

Half an hour later he returned with water in a small earthenware bowl.

"The warden says you may keep this bowl," he informed the prisoner. "But you must show it to me when I ask for it. If it is broken, it will be the last."

"Thank you," said The Thinking Machine. "I shan't break it."

The jailer went on about his duties. For just the fraction of a second it seemed that The Thinking Machine wanted to ask a question, but he didn't.

Two hours later this same jailer, in passing the door of Cell 13, heard a noise inside and stopped. The Thinking Machine was down on his hands and knees in a corner of the cell, and from that same corner came several frightened squeaks. The jailer looked on interestedly.

"Ah, I've got you," he heard the prisoner say.

"Got what?" he asked, sharply.

"One of these rats," was the reply. "See?" And between the scientist's long fingers the jailer saw a small gray rat struggling. The prisoner brought it over to the light and looked at it closely. "It's a water rat," he said.

"Ain't you got anything better to do than to catch rats?" asked the jailer.

"It's disgraceful that they should be here at all," was the irritated reply. "Take this one away and kill it. There are dozens more where it came from."

The jailer took the wriggling, squirmy rodent and flung it down on the floor violently. It gave one squeak and lay still. Later he reported the incident to the warden, who only smiled.

Still later that afternoon the outside armed guard on Cell 13 side of the prison looked up again at the window and saw the prisoner looking out. He saw a hand raised to the barred window and then something white fluttered to the ground, directly under the window of Cell 13. It was a little roll of linen, evidently of white shirting material, and tied around it was a five-dollar bill. The guard looked up at the window again, but the face had disappeared.

With a grim smile he took the little linen roll and the five-dollar bill to the warden's office. There together they deciphered something which was written on it with a queer sort of ink, frequently blurred. On the outside was this:

"Finder of this please deliver to Dr Charles Ransome."

"Ah," said the warden, with a chuckle. "Plan of escape number one has gone wrong." Then, as an afterthought: "But why did he address it to Dr Ransome?"

"And where did he get the pen and ink to write with?" asked the guard.

The warden looked at the guard and the guard looked at the warden. There was no apparent solution of that mystery. The warden studied the writing carefully, then shook his head.

"Well, let's see what he was going to say to Dr Ransome," he said at length, still puzzled, and he unrolled the inner piece of linen.

"Well, if that—what—what do you think of that?" he asked, dazed.

The guard took the bit of linen and read this:

"*Epa cseot d'net niiy awe htto n'si sih. 'T.'*"

III

The warden spent an hour wondering what sort of a cipher it was, and half an hour wondering why his prisoner should attempt to communicate with Dr Ransome, who was the cause of him being there. After this the warden devoted some thought to the question of where the prisoner got writing materials, and what sort of writing materials he had. With the idea of illuminating this point, he examined the linen again. It was a torn part of a white shirt and had ragged edges.

Now it was possible to account for the linen, but what the prisoner had use to write with was another matter. The warden knew it would have been impossible for him to have either pen or pencil, and, besides, neither pen nor pencil had been used in this writing. What, then? The warden decided to personally investigate. The Thinking Machine was his prisoner; he had orders to hold his prisoners; if this one sought to escape by sending cipher messages to persons outside, he would stop it,

176

as he would have stopped it in the case of any othe prisoner.

The warden went back to Cell 13 and found The Thinking Machine on his hands and knees on the floor, engaged in nothing more alarming than catching rats. The prisoner heard the warden's step and turned to him quickly.

"It's disgraceful," he snapped, "these rats. There are scores of them."

"Other men have been able to stand them." said the warden. "Here is another shirt for you—let me have the one you have on."

"Why?" demanded The Thinking Machine, quickly. His tone was hardly natural, his manner suggested actual perturbation.

"You have attempted to communicate with Dr Ransome," said the warden severely. "As my prisoner, it is my duty to put a stop to it."

The Thinking Machine was silent for a moment.

"All right," he said, finally, "Do your duty."

The warden smiled grimly. The prisoner arose from the floor and removed the white shirt, putting on instead a striped convict shirt the warden had brought. The warden took the white shirt eagerly, and then and there compared the pieces of linen on which was written the cipher with certain torn places in the shirt. The Thinking Machine looked on curiously.

"The guard brought *you* those, then?" he asked.

"He certainly did," replied the warden triumphantly. "And that ends your first attempt to escape."

The Thinking Machine watched the warden as he, by comparison, established to his own satisfaction that only two pieces of linen had been torn from the white shirt.

"What did you write this with?" demanded the warden.

"I should think it a part of your duty to find out," said The Thinking Machine, irritably.

The warden started to say some harsh things, then restrained himself and made a minute search of ·the cell and of the prisoner instead. He found absolutely nothing; not even a match or toothpick which might have been used for a pen. The same mystery surrounded the fluid with which the cipher had been written. Although the warden left Cell 13 visibly annoyed, he took the torn shirt in triumph.

"Well, writing notes on a shirt won't get him out, that's certain," he told himself with some complacency. He put the linen scraps into his desk to await developments. "If that man escapes from that cell I'll—hang it—I'll resign."

On the third day of his incarceration The Thinking Machine openly attempted to bribe his way out. The jailer had brought his dinner and was leaning against the barred door, waiting, when The Thinking Machine began the conversation.

"The drainage pipes of the prison lead to the river, don't they?" he asked.

"Yes," said the jailer.

"I suppose they are very small?"

"Too small to crawl through, if that's what you're thinking about," was the grinning response.

There was silence until The Thinking Machine finished his meal. Then:

"You know I'm not a criminal, don't you?"

"Yes."

"And that I've a perfect right to be freed if I demand it?"

"Yes."

"Well, I came here believing that I could make my escape," said the prisoner, and his squint eyes studied the face of the jailer. "Would you consider a financial reward for aiding me to escape?"

The jailer, who happened to be an honest man, looked at the slender, weak figure of the prisoner, at the large head with its mass of yellow hair, and was almost sorry.

"I guess prisons like these were not built for the likes of you to get out of," he said, at last.

"But would you consider a proposition to help me get out?" the prisoner insisted, almost beseechingly.

"No," said the jailer, shortly.

"Five hundred dollars," urged The Thinking Machine. "I am not a criminal."

"No," said the jailer.

"A thousand?"

"No," again said the jailer, and he started away hurriedly to escape further temptation. Then he turned back. "If you should give me ten thousand dollars I couldn't let you out. You'd have to pass through seven doors, and I only have the keys to two."

Then he told the warden all about it.

"Plan number two fails," said the warden, smiling grimly. "First a cipher, then bribery."

When the jailer was on his way to Cell 13 at six o'clock, again bearing food to The Thinking Machine, he paused, startled by the unmistakable scrape, scrape of steel against steel. It stopped at the sound of his steps, then craftily the jailer, who was beyond the prisoner's range of vision, resumed his tramping, the sound being apparently that of a man going away from Cell 13. As a matter of fact he was in the same spot.

After a moment there came again the steady scrape, scrape, and the jailer crept cautiously on tip-toes to the door and peered between the bars. The Thinking Machine was standing on the iron bed working at the bars of the little window. He was using a file, judging from the backward and forward swing of his arms.

Cautiously the jailer crept back to the office, summoned the warden in person, and they returned to Cell 13 on tip-toes. The steady scrape was still audible. The warden listened to satisfy himself and then suddenly appeared at the door.

"Well?" he demanded, and there was a smile on his face.

The Thinking Machine glanced back from his perch on the bed and leaped suddenly to the floor, making frantic efforts to hide something. The warden went in, with hand extended.

"Give it up," he said.

"No," said the prisoner, sharply.

"Come, give it up," urged the warden. "I don't want to have to search you again."

"No," repeated the prisoner.

"What was it, a file?" asked the warden.

The Thinking Machine was silent and stood squinting at the warden with something very nearly approaching disappointment on his face—nearly, but not quite. The warden was almost sympathetic.

"Plan number three fails, eh?" he asked, good-naturedly. "Too bad, isn't it?"

The prisoner didn't say.

"Search him," instructed the warden.

The jailer searched the prisoner carefully. At last, artfully concealed in the waist band of the trousers, he found a piece of steel about two inches long, with one side curved like a half moon.

"Ah," said the warden, as he received it from the jailer. "From your shoe heel," and he smiled pleasantly.

The jailer continued his search and on the other side of the trouser's waist band found another piece of steel identical with the first. The edges showed where they had been worn against the bars of the window.

"You couldn't saw a way through those bars with these, said the warden.

"I could have," said The Thinking Machine firmly.

"In six months, perhaps," said the warden, good-naturedly.

179

The warden shook his head slowly as he gazed into the slightly flushed face of his prisoner.

"Ready to give it up?" he asked.

"I haven't started yet," was the prompt reply.

Then came another exhaustive search of the cell. Carefully the two men went over it, finally turning out the bed and searching that. Nothing. The warden in person climbed upon the bed and examined the bars of the window where the prisoner had been sawing. When he looked he was amused.

"Just made it a little bright by hard rubbing," he said to the prisoner, who stood looking on with a somewhat crestfallen air. The warden grasped the iron bars in his strong hands and tried to shake them. They were immovable, set firmly in the solid granite. He examined each in turn and found them all satisfactory. Finally he climbed down from the bed.

"Give it up, professor," he advised.

The Thinking Machine shook his head and the warden and jailer passed on again. As they disappeared down the corridor The Thinking Machine sat on the edge of the bed with his head in his hands.

"He's crazy to try to get out of that cell," commented the jailer.

"Of course he can't get out," said the warden. "But he's clever. I would like to know what he wrote that cipher with."

•　　•　　•

It was four o'clock next morning when an awful, heartracking shriek of terror resounded through the great prison. It came from a cell, somewhere about the centre, and its tone told a tale of horror, agony, terrible fear. The warden heard and with three of his men rushed into the long corridor leading to Cell 13.

IV

As they ran there came again that awful cry. It died away in a sort of wail. The white faces of prisoners appeared at cell doors upstairs and down, staring out wonderingly, frightened.

"It's that fool in Cell 13," grumbled the warden.

He stopped and stared in as one of the jailers flashed a lantern. "That fool in Cell 13" lay comfortably on his cot, flat on his back with his mouth open, snoring. Even as they looked there came again the piercing cry, from somewhere above. The warden's face blanched a

180

little as he started up the stairs. There on the top floor he found a man in Cell 43, directly above Cell 13, but two floors higher, cowering in a corner of his cell.

"What's the matter?" demanded the warden.

"Thank God you've come," exclaimed the prisoner, and he cast himself against the bars of his cell.

"What is it?" demanded the warden again.

He threw open the door and went in. The prisoner dropped on his knees and clasped the warden about the body. His face was white with terror, his eyes were widely distended, and he was shuddering. His hands, icy cold, clutched at the warden's.

"Take me out of this cell, please take me out," he pleaded.

"What's the matter with you, anyhow?" insisted the warden impatiently.

"I heard something—something," said the prisoner, and his eyes roved nervously around the cell.

"What did you hear?"

"I—I can't tell you," stammered the prisoner. Then, in a sudden burst of terror: "Take me out of this cell—put me anywhere—but take me out of here."

The warden and the three jailers exchanged glances.

"Who is this fellow? What's he accused of?" asked the warden.

"Joseph Ballard," said one of the jailers. "He's accused of throwing acid in a woman's face. She died from it."

"But they can't prove it," gasped the prisoner. "They can't prove it. Please put me in some other cell."

He was still clinging to the warden, and that official threw his arms off roughly. Then for a time he stood looking at the cowering wretch, who seemed possessed of all the wild, unreasoning terror of a child.

"Look here, Ballard," said the warden, finally, "if you heard anything, I want to know what it was. Now tell me."

"I can't, I can't," was the reply. He was sobbing.

"Where did it come from?"

"I don't know. Everywhere—nowhere. I just heard it."

"What was it—a voice?"

"Please don't make me answer," pleaded the prisoner.

"You must answer," said the warden, sharply.

"It was a voice—but—but it wasn't human," was the sobbing reply.

"Voice, but not human?" repeated the warden, puzzled.

"It sounded muffled and—and far away—and ghostly," explained the man.

"Did it come from inside or outside the prison?"

"It didn't seem to come from anywhere—it was just here, here, everywhere. I heard it. I heard it."

For an hour the warden tried to get the story, but Ballard had become suddenly obstinate and would say nothing—only pleaded to be placed in another cell, or to have one of the jailers remain near him until daylight. These requests were gruffly refused.

"And see here," said the warden, in conclusion, "if there's any more of this screaming I'll put you in a padded cell."

Then the warden went his way, a sadly puzzled man. Ballard sat at his cell door until daylight, his face, drawn and white with terror, pressed against the bars, and looking out into the prison with wide, staring eyes.

That day, the fourth since the incarceration of The Thinking Machine, was enlivened considerably by the volunteer prisoner, who spent most of his time at the little window of his cell. He began proceedings by throwing another piece of linen down to the guard, who picked it up dutifully and took it to the warden. On it was written:

"Only three days more."

The warden was in no way surprised at what he read; he understood that The Thinking Machine meant only three days more of his imprisonment, and he regarded the note as a boast. But how was the thing written? Where had The Thinking Machine found this new piece of linen? Where? How? He carefully examined the linen. It was white, of fine texture, shirting material. He took the shirt which he had taken and carefully fitted the two original pieces of the linen to the torn places. This third piece was entirely superfluous; it didn't fit anywhere, and yet it was unmistakably the same goods.

"And where—where does he get anything to write with?" demanded the warden of the world at large.

Still later on the fourth day The Thinking Machine, through the window of his cell, spoke to the armed guard outside.

"What day of the month is it?" he asked.

"The fifteenth," was the answer.

The Thinking Machine made a mental astronomical calculation and satisfied himself that the moon would not rise until after nine o'clock that night. Then he asked another question:

"Who attends to those arc lights?"

"Man from the company."

"You have no electricians in the building?"

"No."

"I should think you could save money if you had your own man."

"None of my business," replied the guard.

The guard noticed The Thinking Machine at the cell window frequently during that day, but always the face seemed listless and there was a certain wistfulness in the squint eyes behind the glasses. After a while he accepted the presence of the leonine head as a matter of course. He had seen other prisoners do the same thing; it was the longing for the outside world.

That afternoon, just before the day guard was relieved, the head appeared at the window again, and The Thinking Machine's hand held something out between the bars. It fluttered to the ground and the guard picked it up. It was a five-dollar bill.

"That's for you," called the prisoner.

As usual, the guard took it to the warden. That gentleman looked at it suspiciously; he looked at everything that came from Cell 13 with suspicion.

"He said it was for me," explained the guard.

"It's a sort of tip, I suppose," said the warden. "I see no particular reason why you shouldn't accept—"

Suddenly he stopped. He had remembered that The Thinking Machine had gone into Cell 13 with one five-dollar bill and two ten-dollar bills; twenty-five dollars in all. Now a five-dollar bill had been tied around the first pieces of linen that came from the cell. The warden still had it, and to convince himself he took it out and looked at it. It was five dollars; yet here was another five dollars, and The Thinking Machine had only had ten-dollar bills.

"Perhaps somebody changed one of the bills for him," he thought at last, with a sigh of relief.

But then and there he made up his mind. He would search Cell 13 as a cell was never before searched in this world. When a man could write at will, and change money, and do other wholly inexplicable things, there was something radically wrong with his prison. He planned to enter the cell at night—three o'clock would be an excellent time. The Thinking Machine must do all the weird things he did sometime. Night seemed the most reasonable.

Thus it happened that the warden stealthily descended upon Cell 13 that night at three o'clock. He paused at the door and listened. There was no sound save the steady, regular breathing of the prisoner. The keys unfastened the double locks with scarcely a clank, and the warden entered, locking the door behind him. Suddenly he flashed his dark-lantern in the face of the recumbent figure.

If the warden had planned to startle The Thinking Machine he was mistaken, for that individual merely opened his eyes quietly, reached for his glasses and inquired, in a most matter-of-fact tone:

"Who is it?"

It would be useless to describe the search that the warden made. It was minute. Not one inch of the cell or the bed was overlooked. He found the round hole in the floor, and with a flash of inspiration thrust his thick fingers into it. After a moment of fumbling there he drew up something and looked at it in the light of his lantern.

"Ugh!" he exclaimed.

The thing he had taken out was a rat—a dead rat. His inspiration fled as a mist before the sun. But he continued the search. The Thinking Machine, without a word, arose and kicked the rat out of the cell into the corridor.

The warden climbed on the bed and tried the steel bars on the tiny window. They were perfectly rigid; every bar of the door was the same.

Then the warden searched the prisoner's clothing, beginning at the shoes. Nothing hidden in them! Then the trousers' waist band. Still nothing! Then the pockets of the trousers. From one side he drew out some paper money and examined it.

"Five one-dollar bills," he gasped.

"That's right," said the prisoner.

"But the—you had two tens and a five—what the—how do you do it?"

"That's my business," said The Thinking Machine.

"Did any of my men change this money for you—on your word of honour?"

The Thinking Machine paused just a fraction of a second.

"No," he said.

"Well, do you make it?" asked the warden. He was prepared to believe anything.

"That's my business," again said the prisoner.

The warden glared at the eminent scientist fiercely. He felt—he knew—that this man was making a fool of him, yet he didn't know how. If he were a real prisoner he would get the truth—but, then, perhaps, those inexplicable things which had happened would not have been brought before him so sharply. Neither of the men spoke for a long time, then suddenly the warden turned fiercely and left the cell, slamming the door behind him. He didn't dare to speak, then.

He glanced at the clock. It was ten minutes to four. He had hardly settled himself in bed when again came that heart-breaking shriek through the prison. With a few muttered words, which, while not elegant, were highly expressive, he relighted his lantern and rushed

184

through the prison again to the cell on the upper floor.

Again Ballard was crushing himself against the steel door, shrieking, shrieking at the top of his voice. He stopped only when the warden flashed his lamp in the cell.

"Take me out, take me out," he screamed. "I did it, I did it, I killed her. Take it away."

"Take what away?" asked the warden.

"I threw the acid in her face—I did it—I confess. Take me out of here."

Ballard's condition was pitiable; it was only an act of mercy to let him out into the corridor. There he crouched in a corner, like an animal at bay, and clasped his hands to his ears. It took half an hour to calm him sufficiently for him to speak. Then he told incoherently what had happened. On the night before at four o'clock he had heard a voice—a sepulchral voice, muffled and wailing in tone.

"What did it say?" asked the warden, curiously.

"Acid—acid— acid!" gasped the prisoner. "It accused me. Acid! I threw the acid, and the woman died. Oh!" It was a long shuddering wail of terror.

"Acid?" echoed the warden, puzzled. The case was beyond him.

"Acid. That's all I heard—that one word, repeated several times. There were other things, too, but I didn't hear them."

"That was last night, eh?" asked the warden. "What happened to-night—what frightened you just now?"

"It was the same thing," gasped the prisoner. "Acid—acid— acid!" He covered his face with his hands and sat shivering. "It was acid I used on her, but I didn't mean to kill her. I just heard the words. It was something accusing me—accusing me." He mumbled, and was silent.

"Did you hear anything else?"

"Yes—but I couldn't understand—only a little bit—just a word or two."

"Well, what was it?"

"I heard 'acid' three times, then I heard a long, moaning sound, then—then—I heard 'No. 8 hat.' I heard that twice."

"No. 8 hat," repeated the warden. "What the devil—No. 8 hat? Accusing voices of conscience have never talked about No. 8 hats, so far as I ever heard."

"He's insane," said one of the jailers, with an air of finality.

"I believe you," said the warden. "He must be. He probably heard something and got frightened. He's trembling now. No. 8 hat! What the——"

When the fifth day of The Thinking Machine's imprisonment rolled around the warden was wearing a hunted look. He was anxious for the end of the thing. He could not help but feel that his distinguished prisoner had been amusing himself. And if this were so, The Thinking Machine had lost none of his sense of humour. For on this fifth day he flung down another linen note to the outside guard, bearing the words; "Only two days more." Also he flung down half a dollar.

Now the warden knew—he *knew*—that the man in Cell 13 didn't have any half dollars—he *couldn't* have any half dollars, no more than he could have pen and ink and linen, and yet he did have them. It was a condition, not a theory; that is one reason why the warden was wearing a hunted look.

That ghastly, uncanny thing, too, about "Acid" and "No. 8 hat" clung to him tenaciously. They didn't mean anything, of course, merely the ravings of an insane murderer who had been driven by fear to confess his crime, still there were so many things that "didn't mean anything" happening in the prison now since The Thinking Machine was there.

On the sixth day the warden received a postal stating that Dr Ransome and Mr Fielding would be at Chisholm Prison on the following evening, Thursday, and in the event Professor Van Dusen had not yet escaped—and they presumed he had not because they had not heard from him—they would meet him there.

"In the event he had not yet escaped!" The warden smiled grimly. Escaped!

The Thinking Machine enlivened this day for the warden with three notes. They were on the usual linen and bore generally on the appointment at half-past eight o'clock Thursday night, which appointment the scientist had made at the time of his imprisonment.

On the afternoon of the seventh day the warden passed Cell 13 and glanced in. The Thinking Machine was lying on the iron bed, apparently sleeping lightly. The cell appeared precisely as it always did from a casual glance. The warden would swear that no man was going to leave it between that hour—it was then four o'clock—and half-past eight o'clock that evening.

On his way back past the cell the warden heard the steady breathing again, and coming close to the door looked in. He wouldn't have done so if The Thinking Machine had been looking, but now—well, it was different.

A ray of light came through the high window and fell on the face of the sleeping man. It occurred to the warden for the first time that his prisoner appeared haggard and weary. Just then The Thinking Machine stirred slightly and the warden hurried on up the corridor guiltily. That evening after six o'clock he saw the jailer.

"Everything all right in Cell 13?" he asked.

"Yes, sir," replied the jailer. "He didn't eat much, though."

It was with a feeling of having done his duty that the warden received Dr Ransome and Mr Fielding shortly after seven o'clock. He intended to show them the linen notes and lay before them the full story of his woes, which was a long one. But before this came to pass the guard from the river side of the prison yard entered the office.

"The arc light on my side of the yard won't light," he informed the warden.

"Confound it, that man's a hoodoo," thundered the official. "Everything has happened since he's been here."

The guard went back to his post in the darkness, and the warden 'phoned to the electric light company.

"This is Chisholm Prison," he said through the 'phone. "Send three or four men down here quick, to fix an arc light."

The reply was evidently satisfactory, for the warden hung up the receiver and passed out into the yard. While Dr Ransome and Mr Fielding sat waiting the guard at the outer gate came in with a special delivery letter. Dr Ransome happened to notice the address, and, when the guard went out, looked at the letter more closely.

"By George!" he exclaimed.

"What is it?" asked Mr Fielding.

Silently the doctor offered the letter. Mr Fielding examined it closely.

"Coincidence," he said. "It must be."

It was nearly eight o'clock when the warden returned to his office. The electricians had arrived in a wagon, and were now at work. The warden pressed the buzz-button communicating with the man at the outer gate in the wall.

"How many electricians came in?" he asked, over the short 'phone. "Four? Three workmen in jumpers and overall and the manager? Frock coat and silk hat? All right. Be certain that only four go out. That's all."

He turned to Dr Ransome and Mr Fielding.

"We have to be careful here—particularly," and there was broad sarcasm in his tone, "since we have scientists locked up."

The warden picked up the special delivery letter carelessly, and then began to open it.

187

"When I have read this I want to tell you gentlemen something about how—Great Caesar!" he ended, suddenly, as he glanced at the letter. He sat with mouth open, motionless, from astonishment.

"What is it?" asked Mr Fielding.

"A special delivery letter from Cell 13," gasped the warden. "An invitation to supper."

"What?" and the two others arose, unanimously.

The warden sat dazed, staring at the letter for a moment, then called sharply to a guard outside in the corridor.

"Run down to Cell 13 and see if that man's in there."

The guard went as directed, while Dr Ransome and Mr Fielding examined the letter.

"It's Van Dusen's handwriting; there's no question of that," said Dr Ransome. "I've seen too much of it."

Just then the buzz on the telephone from the outer gate sounded, and the warden, in a semi-trance, picked up the receiver.

"Hello! Two reporters, eh? Let 'em come in." He turned suddenly to the doctor and Mr Fielding. "Why, the man *can't* be out. He must be in his cell."

Just at that moment the guard returned.

"He's still in his cell, sir," he reported. "I saw him. He's lying down."

"There, I told you so," said the warden, and he breathed freely again. "But how did he mail that letter?"

There was a rap on the steel door which led from the jail yard into the warden's office.

"It's the reporters," said the warden. "Let them in," he instructed the guard; then to the other two gentlemen: "Don't say anything about this before them, because I'd never hear the last of it."

The door opened, and the two men from the front gate entered.

"Good-evening, gentlemen," said one. That was Hutchinson Hatch; the warden knew him well.

"Well?" demanded the other, irritably, "I'm here."

That was The Thinking Machine.

He squinted belligerently at the warden, who sat with mouth agape. For the moment that official had nothing to say. Dr Ransome and Mr Fielding were amazed, but they didn't know what the warden knew. They were only amazed; he was paralyzed. Hutchinson Hatch, the reporter, took in the scene with greedy eyes.

"How—how—how did you do it?" gasped the warden, finally.

"Come back to the cell," said The Thinking Machine, in the irritated voice which his scientific associates knew so well.

188

The warden, still in a condition bordering on trance, led the way.
"Flash your light in there," directed The Thinking Machine.

The warden did so. There was nothing unusual in the appearance of the cell, and there—there on the bed lay the figure of The Thinking Machine. Certainly! There was the yellow hair! Again the warden looked at the man beside him and wondered at the strangeness of his own dreams.

With trembling hands he unlocked the cell door and The Thinking Machine passed inside.

"See here," he said.

He kicked at the steel bars in the bottom of the cell door and three of them were pushed out of place. A fourth broke off and rolled away in the corridor.

"And here, too," directed the erstwhile prisoner as he stood on the bed to reach the small window. He swept his hand across the opening and every bar came out.

"What's this in the bed?" demanded the warden, who was slowly recovering.

"A wig," was the reply. "Turn down the cover."

The warden did so. Beneath it lay a large coil of strong rope, thirty feet or more, a dagger, three files, ten feet of electric wire, a thin, powerful pair of steel pliers, a small tack hammer with its handle, and—and a Derringer pistol.

"How did you do it?" demanded the warden.

"You gentlemen have an engagement to supper with me at half-past nine o'clock," said The Thinking Machine. "Come on, or we shall be late."

"But how did you do it?" insisted the warden.

"Don't ever think you can hold any man who can use his brain," said The Thinking Machine. "Come on; we shall be late."

VI

It was an impatient supper party in the rooms of Professor Van Dusen and a somewhat silent one. The guests were Dr Ransome, Albert Fielding, the warden, and Hutchinson Hatch, reporter. The meal was served to the minute, in accordance with Professor Van Dusen's instructions of one week before; Dr Ransome found the artichokes delicious. At last the supper was finished and The Thinking Machine turned full on Dr Ransome and squinted at him fiercely.

189

"Do you believe it now?" he demanded.

"I do," replied Dr Ransome.

"Do you admit that it was a fair test?"

"I do."

With the others, particularly the warden, he was waiting anxiously for the explanation.

"Suppose you tell us how—" began Mr Fielding.

"Yes, tell us how," said the warden.

The Thinking Machine readjusted his glasses, took a couple of preparatory squints at his audience, and began the story. He told it from the beginning logically; and no man ever talked to more interested listeners.

"My agreement was," he began, "to go into a cell, carrying nothing except what was necessary to wear, and to leave that cell within a week. I had never seen Chisholm Prison. When I went into the cell I asked for tooth powder, two ten and one five-dollar bills, and also to have my shoes blacked. Even if these requests had been refused it would not have mattered seriously. But you agreed to them.

"I knew there would be nothing in the cell which you thought I might use to advantage. So when the warden locked the door on me I was apparently helpless, unless I could turn three seemingly innocent things to use. They were things which would have been permitted any prisoner under sentence of death, were they not, warden?"

"Tooth powder and polished shoes, but not money," replied the warden.

"Anything is dangerous in the hands of a man who knows how to use it," went on The Thinking Machine. "I did nothing that first night but sleep and chase rats." He glared at the warden. "When the matter was broached I knew I could do nothing that night, so suggested next day. You gentlemen thought I wanted time to arrange an escape with outside assistance, but this was not true. I knew I could communicate with whom I pleased, when I pleased."

The warden stared at him a moment, then went on smoking solemnly.

"I was aroused next morning at six o'clock by the jailer with my breakfast," continued the scientist. "He told me dinner was at twelve and supper at six. Between these times, I gathered I would be pretty much to myself. So immediately after breakfast I examined my outside surroundings from my cell window. One look told me it would be useless to try to scale the wall, even should I decide to leave my cell by the window, for my purpose was to leave not only the cell, but the prison. Of course, I could have gone over that wall, but it would have

190

taken me longer to lay my plans that way. Therefore, for the moment, I dismissed all idea of that.

"From this first observation I knew the river was on that side of the prison, and that there was also a playground there. Subsequently these surmises were verified by a keeper. I knew then one important thing—that anyone might approach the prison wall from that side if necessary without attracting any particular attention. That was well to remember. I remembered it.

"But the outside thing which most attracted my attention was the feed wire to the arc light, which ran within a few feet—probably three or four—of my cell window. I knew that would be valuable in the event I found it necessary to cut off that arc light."

"Oh, you shut it off tonight, then?" asked the warden.

"Having learned all I could from that window," resumed The Thinking Machine, without heeding the interruption, "I considered the idea of escaping through the prison proper. I recalled just how I had come into the cell, which I knew would be the only way. Seven doors lay between me and the outside. So, also for the time being, I gave up the idea of escaping that way. And I couldn't go through the solid granite walls of the cell."

The Thinking Machine paused for a moment and Dr Ransome lighted a new cigar. For several minutes there was silence, then the scientific jail-breaker went on:

"While I was thinking about these things a rat ran across my foot. It suggested a new line of thought. There were at least half a dozen rats in the cell—I could see their beady eyes. Yet I had noticed none come under the cell door. I frightened them purposely and watched the cell door to see if they went out that way. They did not, but they were gone. Obviously they went another way. Another way meant another opening.

"I searched for this opening and found it. It was an old drain pipe, long unused and partly choked with dirt and dust. But this was the way the rats had come. They came from somewhere. Where? Drain pipes usually lead outside prison grounds. This one probably led to the river, or near it. The rats must therefore come from that direction. If they came a part of the way, I reasoned that they came all the way, because it was extremely unlikely that a solid iron or lead pipe would have any hole in it except at the exit.

"When the jailer came with my luncheon he told me two important things, although he didn't know it. One was that a new system of plumbing had been put in the prison system seven years before; another that the river was only three hundred feet away. Then I knew positively that the pipe was a part of an old system; I knew, too, that it slanted generally toward the river. But did the pipe end in the water or on land?

"That was the next question to be decided. I decided it by catching several of the rats in the cell. My jailer was surprised to see me engaged in this work. I examined at least a dozen of them. They were perfectly dry; they had come through the pipe, and, most important of all, they were *not house rats, but field rats*. The other end of the pipe was on land, then, outside the prison walls. So far, so good.

"Then I knew that if I worked freely from this point I must attract the warden's attention in another direction. You see, by telling the warden that I had come there to escape you made the test more severe, because I had to trick him by false scents."

The warden looked up with a sad expression in his eyes.

"The first thing was to make him think I was trying to communicate with you, Dr Ransome. So I wrote a note on a piece of linen I tore from my shirt, addressed it to Dr Ransome, tied a five-dollar bill around it and threw it out of the window. I knew the guard would take it to the warden but I rather hoped the warden would send it as addressed. Have you that first linen note, warden?"

The warden produced the cipher.

"What the deuce does it mean, anyhow?" he asked.

"Read it backwards, beginning with the 'T' signature and disregard the division into words," instructed The Thinking Machine.

The warden did so.

"T-h-i-s, this," he spelled, studied it a moment, then read it off, grinning:

"This is not the way I intend to escape."

"Well, now what do you think o' that?" he demanded, still grinning.

"I knew that would attract your attention, just as it did," said The Thinking Machine, "and if you really found out what it was it would be a sort of gentle rebuke."

"What did you write it with?" asked Dr Ransome, after he had examined the linen and passed it to Mr Fielding.

"This," said the erstwhile prisoner, and he extended his foot. On it was the shoe he had worn in prison, though the polish was gone — scraped off clean. "The shoe blacking, moistened with water, was my ink; the metal tip of the shoe lace made a fairly good pen."

The warden looked up and suddenly burst into a laugh, half of relief, half of amusement.

"You're a wonder," he said, admiringly. "Go on."

"That precipitated a search of my cell by the warden, as I had intended," continued The Thinking Machine. "I was anxious to get the warden into the habit of searching my cell, so that finally, constantly finding nothing, he would get disgusted and quit. This at last happened, practically."

The warden blushed.

"He then took my white shirt away and gave me a prison shirt. He was satisfied that those two pieces of the shirt were all that was missing. But while he was searching my cell I had another piece of that same shirt, about nine inches square, rolled up into a small ball in my mouth."

"Nine inches of that shirt?" demanded the warden. "Where did it come from?"

"The bosoms of all stiff white shirts are of triple thickness," was the explanation. "I tore out the inside thickness, leaving the bosom only two thicknesses. I knew you wouldn't see it. So much for that."

There was a little pause, and the warden looked from one to another of the men with a sheepish grin.

"Having disposed of the warden for the time being by giving him something else to think about, I took my first serious step toward freedom," said Professor Van Dusen. "I knew, within reason, that the pipe led somewhere to the playground outside; I knew a great many boys played there; I knew that rats came into my cell from out there. Could I communicate with some one outside with these things at hand?

"First was necessary, I saw, a long and fairly reliable thread, so—but here," he pulled up his trouser legs and showed that the tops of both stockings, of fine, strong lisle, were gone. "I unravelled those—after I got them started it wasn't difficult—and I had easily a quarter of a mile of thread I could depend on.

"Then on half of my remaining linen I wrote, laboriously enough I assure you, a letter explaining my situation to this gentleman here," and he indicated Hutchinson Hatch. "I knew he would assist me—for the value of the newspaper story. I tied firmly to this linen letter a ten-dollar bill—there is no surer way of attracting the eye of anyone—and wrote on the linen: 'Finder of this deliver to Hutchinson Hatch, *Daily American*, who will give another ten dollars for the information.'

"The next thing was to get this note outside on that playground where a boy might find it. There were two ways, but I chose the best. I took one of the rats—I became adept in catching them—tied the linen and money firmly to one leg, fastened my lisle thread to another, and turned him loose in the drain pipe. I reasoned that the natural fright of the rodent would make him run until he was outside the pipe and then out on earth he would probably stop to gnaw off the linen and money.

"From the moment the rat disappeared into that dusty pipe I became anxious. I was taking so many chances. The rat might gnaw the string, of which I held one end; other rats might gnaw it; the rat might run out of the pipe and leave the linen and money where they would never be found; a thousand other things might have happened. So began some nervous hours, but the fact that the rat ran on until only a few feet of the string remained in my cell made me think he was outside the pipe. I had carefully instructed Mr Hatch what to do in case the note reached him. The question was: would it reach him?

"This done, I could only wait and make other plans in case this one failed. I openly attempted to bribe my jailer, and learned from him that he held the keys to only two of seven doors between me and freedom. Then I did something else to make the warden nervous. I took the steel supports out of the heels of my shoes and made a pretence of sawing the bars of my cell window. The warden raised a pretty row about that. He developed, too, the habit of shaking the bars of my cell window to see if they were solid. They were—then."

Again the warden grinned. He had ceased being astonished.

"With this one plan I had done all I could and could only wait to see what happened," the scientist went on. "I couldn't know whether my note had been delivered or even found, or whether the rat had gnawed it up. And I didn't dare to draw back through the pipe that one slender thread which connected me with the outside.

"When I went to bed that night I didn't sleep, for fear there would come the slight signal twitch at the thread which was to tell me that Mr Hatch had received the note. At half-past three o'clock, I judge, I felt this twitch, and no prisoner actually under sentence of death ever welcomed a thing more heartily."

The Thinking Machine stopped and turned to the reporter.

"You'd better explain just what you did," he said.

"The linen note was brought to me by a small boy who had been playing baseball," said Mr Hatch. "I immediately saw a big story in it, so I gave the boy another ten dollars, and got several spools of silk, some twine, and a roll of light, pliable wire. The professor's note suggested that I have the finder of the note show me just where it was picked up, and told me to make my search from there, beginning at two o'clock in the morning. If I found the other end of the thread I was to twitch it gently three times, then a fourth.

"I began the search with a small bulb electric light. It was an hour and twenty minutes before I found the end of the drain pipe, half hidden in weeds. The pipe was very large there, say twelve inches across. Then I found the end of the lisle thread, twitched it as directed and immediately I got an answering twitch.

"Then I fastened the silk to this and Professor Van Dusen began to pull it into his cell. I nearly had heart disease for fear the string would break. To the end of the silk I fastened the twine, and when that had been pulled in I tied on the wire. Then that was drawn into the pipe and we had a substantial line, which rats couldn't gnaw, from the mouth of the drain into the cell."

The Thinking Machine raised his hand and Hatch stopped.

"All this was done in absolute silence," said the scientist. "But when the wire reached my hand I could have shouted. Then we tried another experiment, which Mr Hatch was prepared for. I tested the pipe as a speaking tube. Neither of us could hear very clearly, but I dared not speak loud for fear of attracting attention in the prison. At last I made him understand what I wanted immediately. He seemed to have great difficulty in understanding when I asked for nitric acid, and I repeated the word 'acid' several times.

"Then I heard a shriek from a cell above me. I knew instantly that some one had overheard, and when I heard you coming, Mr Warden, I feigned sleep. If you had entered my cell at that moment the whole plan of escape would have ended there. But you passed on. That was the nearest I ever came to being caught.

"Having established this improvised trolley it is easy to see how I got things in the cell and made them disappear at will. I merely dropped them back into the pipe. You, Mr Warden, could not have reached the connecting wire with your fingers; they are too large. My fingers, you see, are longer and more slender. In addition I guarded the top of that pipe with a rat—you remember how."

"I remember," said the warden, with a grimace.

"I thought that if any one were tempted to investigate that hole the rat would dampen his ardour. Mr Hatch could not send me anything useful through the pipe until next night, although he did send me change for ten dollars as a test, so I proceeded with other parts of my plan. Then I evolved the method of escape, which I finally employed.

"In order to carry this out successfully it was necessary for the guard in the yard to get accustomed to seeing me at the cell window. I arranged this by dropping linen notes to him, boastful in tone, to make the warden believe, if possible, one of his assistants was communicating with the outside for me. I would stand at my window for hours gazing out, so the guard could see, and occasionally I spoke to him. In that way I learned that the prison had no electricians of its own, but was dependent upon the lighting company if anything should go wrong.

"That cleared the way to freedom perfectly. Early in the evening of the last day of my imprisonment, when it was dark, I planned to cut the feed wire which was only a few feet from my window, reaching it with an acid-tipped wire I had. That would make that side of the prison perfectly dark while the electricians were searching for the break. That would also bring Mr Hatch into the prison yard.

"There was only one more thing to do before I actually began the work of setting myself free. This was to arrange final details with Mr Hatch through our speaking tube. I did this within half an hour after the warden left my cell on the fourth night of my imprisonment. Mr Hatch again had serious difficulty in understanding me, and I repeated the word 'acid' to him several times, and later the words: 'Number eight hat' — that's my size — and these were the things which made a prisoner upstairs confess to murder, so one of the jailers told me next day. This prisoner heard our voices, confused of course, through the pipe, which also went to his cell. The cell directly over me was not occupied, hence no one else heard.

"Of course the actual work of cutting the steel bars out of the window and door was comparatively easy with nitric acid, which I got through the pipe in thin bottles, but it took time. Hour after hour on the fifth and sixth and seventh days the guard below was looking at me as I worked on the bars of the window with the acid on a piece of wire. I used the tooth powder to prevent the acid spreading. I looked away abstractedly as I worked and each minute the acid cut deeper into the metal. I noticed the jailers always tried the door by shaking the upper part, never the lower bars, therefore I cut the lower bars, leaving them hanging in place by thin strips of metal. But that was a bit of daredevilry. I could not have gone that way so easily."

The Thinking Machine sat silently for several minutes.

"I think that makes everything clear," he went on. "Whatever points I have not explained were merely to confuse the warden and jailers. These things in my bed I brought in to please Mr Hatch, who wanted to improve the story. Of course, the wig was necessary in my plan. The special delivery letter I wrote and directed in my cell with Mr Hatch's fountain pen, then sent it out to him and he mailed it. That's all, I think."

"But your actually leaving the prison grounds and then coming in through the outer gate to my office?" asked the warden.

"Perfectly simple," said the scientist. "I cut the electric light wire with acid, as I said, when the current was off. Therefore when the current was turned on the arc didn't light. I knew it would take some time to find out what was the matter and make repairs. When the guard

196

went to report to you the yard was dark, I crept out the window — it was a tight fit, too — replaced the bars by standing on a narrow ledge and remained in a shadow until the force of electricians arrived. Mr Hatch was one of them.

"When I saw him I spoke and he handed me a cap, a jumper and overalls, which I put on within ten feet of you, Mr Warden, while you were in the yard. Later Mr Hatch called me, presumably as a workman, and together we went out the gate to get something out of the wagon. The gate guard let us pass out readily as two workmen who had just passed in. We changed our clothing and reappeared, asking to see you. We saw you. That's all."

There was silence for several minutes. Dr Ransome was first to speak.

"Wonderful!" he exclaimed. "Perfectly amazing."

"How did Mr Hatch happen to come with the electricians?" asked Mr Fielding.

"His father is manager of the company," replied The Thinking Machine.

"But what if there had been no Mr Hatch outside to help?"

"Every prisoner has one friend outside who would help him escape if he could."

"Suppose — just suppose — there had been no old plumbing system there?" asked the warden, curiously.

"There were two other ways out," said The Thinking Machine, enigmatically.

Ten minutes later the telephone bell rang. It was a request for the warden.

"Light all right, eh?" the warden asked, through the 'phone. "Good. Wire cut beside Cell 13? Yes, I know. One electrician too many? What's that? Two came out?"

The warden turned to the others with a puzzled expression.

"He only let in four electricians, he has let out two and says there are three left."

"I was the odd one," said The Thinking Machine.

"Oh," said the warden. "I see." Then through the 'phone: "Let the fifth man go. He's all right."

THE ORACLE
OF THE DOG
By G. K. Chesterton

Gilbert Keith Chesterton (1874–1936) was a man with an enormous range of interests and talents. Today he is perhaps most widely known as the author of the Father Brown detective stories, but ironically, he himself thought rather little of this accomplishment. Instead he placed more emphasis on his achievements as an artist, a poet, a novelist, a journalist, and a commentator on literary, religious, political, economic, and social issues. As a boy, Chesterton was a poor student though he did show some early literary promise. For a time, he contemplated a career in art, but when at the urging of a friend he wrote a number of reviews for the Bookman, *he found himself embarked, almost casually, on a life of letters. He was also a popular public speaker, he and his friend Hilaire Belloc participating in a famous series of debates on socialism with George Bernard Shaw. Chesterton found in the mystery story genre a form which allowed him to express many of his most serious philosophical interests in an entertaining way. His most memorable detective creation is the Catholic priest Father Brown, modeled on Essex clergyman Father John O'Connor. But he also wrote about gentlemen sleuth Horne Fisher in* The Man Who Knew Too Much *(1922) and the allegorical detective force called Philosophical Policemen in the novel* The Man Who Was Thursday *(1908). "The Oracle of the Dog" appears as the third story in* The Incredulity of Father Brown *(1926), and all fifty-one Father Brown stories, originally published between 1911 and 1935, have been collected in* The Father Brown Omnibus *(1951). For discussions of various facets of the author's work, including the Father Brown stories, see* Chesterton: A Centennial Appraisal *(New York: Barnes and Noble, 1974), a collection of essays edited by John Sullivan.*

Yes," said Father Brown, "I always like a dog, so long as he isn't spelt backwards."

Those who are quick in talking are not always quick in listening. Sometimes even their brilliancy produces a sort of stupidity. Father Brown's friend and companion was a young man with a stream of ideas and stories, an enthusiastic young man named Fiennes, with eager blue eyes and blond hair that seemed to be brushed back, not merely with a hair-brush but with the wind of the world as he rushed through it. But he stopped in the torrent of his talk in a momentary bewilderment before he saw the priest's very simple meaning.

"You mean that people make too much of them?" he said. "Well, I don't know. They're marvellous creatures. Sometimes I think they know a lot more than we do."

Father Brown said nothing, but continued to stroke the head of the big retriever in a half-abstracted but apparently soothing fashion.

"Why," said Fiennes, warming again to his monologue, "there was a dog in the case I've come to see you about: what they call the 'Invisible Murder Case', you know. It's a strange story, but from my point of view the dog is about the strangest thing in it. Of course, there's the mystery of the crime itself, and how old Druce can have been killed by somebody else when he was all alone in the summer-house—"

The hand stroking the dog stopped for a moment in its rhythmic movement, and Father Brown said calmly: "Oh, it was a summer-house, was it?"

"I thought you'd read all about it in the papers," answered Fiennes. "Stop a minute; I believe I've got a cutting that will give you all the particulars." He produced a strip of newspaper from his pocket and handed it to the priest, who began to read it, holding it close to his blinking eyes with one hand while the other continued its half-conscious caresses of the dog. It looked like the parable of a man not letting his right hand know what his left hand did.

Many mystery stories, about men murdered behind locked doors and windows, and murderers escaping without means of entrance and exit, have come true in the course of the extraordinary events at Cranston on the coast of Yorkshire, where Colonel Druce was found stabbed from behind by a dagger that has entirely disappeared from the scene, and apparently even from the neighbourhood.

The summer-house in which he died was indeed accessible at one entrance, the ordinary doorway which looked down the central walk of the garden towards the house. But, by a combination of events almost to be called a coincidence, it appears that both the path and the entrance were watched during the crucial time, and there is a chain of witnesses who confirm each other. The summer-house stands at the extreme end of the garden, where there is no exit or entrance of any kind. The central garden path is a lane between two ranks of tall delphiniums, planted so close that any stray step off the path would leave its traces; and both path and plants run right up to the very mouth of the summer-house, so that no straying from that straight path could fail to be observed, and no other mode of entrance can be imagined.

Patrick Floyd, secretary of the murdered man, testified that he had been in a position to overlook the whole garden from the time when Colonel Druce last appeared alive in the doorway to the time when he was found dead; as he, Floyd, had been on the top of a step-ladder clipping the garden hedge. Janet Druce, the dead man's daughter, confirmed this, saying that she had sat on the terrace of the housing throughout that time and had seen Floyd at his work. Touching some part of the time, this is again supported by Donald Druce, her brother—who overlooked the garden—standing at his bedroom window in his dressing-gown, for he had risen late. Lastly, the account is consistent with that given by Dr Valentine; a neighbour, who called for a time to talk with Miss Druce on the terrace, and by the Colonel's solicitor, Mr. Aubrey Traill, who was apparently the last to see the murdered man alive—presumably with the exception of the murderer.

All are agreed that the course of events was as follows: About half past three in the afternoon, Miss Druce went down the path to ask her father when he would like tea; but he said he did not want any and was waiting to see Traill, his lawyer, who was to be sent to him in the summer-house. The girl then came away and met Traill coming down the path; she directed him to her father and he went in as directed. About half an hour afterwards he came out again, the Colonel coming with him to the door and showing himself to all appearance in health and even high spirits. He had been somewhat annoyed earlier in the day by his son's irregular hours, but seemed to recover his temper in a perfectly normal fashion, and had been rather markedly genial in receiving other visitors, including two of his nephews, who came over for the day. But as these were out walking during the whole period of the tragedy, they had no evidence to give. It is said, indeed, that the Colonel was not on very good terms with Dr Valentine, but that gentleman only had a brief interview with the daughter of the house, to whom he is supposed to be paying serious attentions.

Traill, the solicitor, says he left the Colonel entirely alone in the summer-house, and this is confirmed by Floyd's bird's-eye view of the garden, which showed nobody else passing the only entrance. Ten minutes later, Miss Druce again went down the garden and had not reached the end of the path when she saw her father, who was conspicuous by his white linen coat, lying in a heap on the floor. She uttered a scream which brought others to the spot, and on entering the place they found the Colonel lying dead beside his basket-chair, which was also upset. Dr Valentine, who was still in the immediate neighbourhood, testified that the wound was made by some sort of stiletto, entering under the shoulder-blade and piercing the heart. The police have searched the neighbourhood for such a weapon, but no trace of it can be found.

"So Colonel Druce wore a white coat, did he?" said Father Brown as he put down the paper.

"Trick he learnt in the tropics," replied Fiennes, with some wonder. "He'd had some queer adventures there, by his own account; and I fancy his dislike of Valentine was connected with the doctor coming from the tropics, too. But it's all an infernal puzzle. The account there is pretty accurate; I didn't see the tragedy, in the sense of the discovery; I was out walking with the young nephews and the dog—the dog I wanted to tell you about. But I saw the stage set for it as described; the straight lane between the blue flowers right up to the dark entrance, and the lawyer going down it in his blacks and his silk hat, and the red head of the secretary showing high above the green hedge as he worked on it with his shears. Nobody could have mistaken that red head at any distance; and if people say they saw it there all the time, you may be sure they did. This red-haired secretary, Floyd, is quite a character; a breathless bounding sort of fellow, always doing everybody's work as he was doing the gardener's. I think he is an American; he's certainly got the American view of life—what they call the view-point, bless 'em."

"What about the lawyer?" asked Father Brown.

There was a silence and then Fiennes spoke quite slowly for him. "Traill struck me as a singular man. In his fine black clothes he was almost foppish, yet you can hardly call him fashionable. For he wore a pair of long, luxuriant black whiskers such as haven't been seen since Victorian times. He had rather a fine grave face and a fine grave manner, but every now and then he seemed to remember to smile. And when he showed his white teeth he seemed to lose a little of his dignity, and there was something faintly fawning about him. It may have been only embarrassment, for he would also fidget with his cravat and his tie-pin, which were at once handsome and unusual, like himself. If I could think of anybody—but what's the good, when the whole thing's impossible? Nobody knows who did it. Nobody knows how it could be done. At least there's only one exception I'd make, and that's why I really mentioned the whole thing. The dog knows."

Father Brown sighed and then said absently: "You were there as a friend of young Donald, weren't you? He didn't go on your walk with you?"

"No," replied Fiennes smiling. "The young scoundrel had gone to bed that morning and got up that afternoon. I went with his cousins, two young officers from India, and our conversation was trivial enough. I remember the elder, whose name I think is Herbert Druce and who is an authority on horse-breeding, talked about nothing but a mare he had bought and the moral character of the man who sold her; while his brother Harry seemed to be brooding on his bad luck at Monte Carlo. I only mention it to show you, in the light of what happened on our walk, that there was nothing psychic about us. The dog was the only mystic in our company."

"What sort of a dog was he?" asked the priest.

"Same breed as that one," answered Fiennes. "That's what started me off on the story, your saying you didn't believe in believing in a dog. He's a big black retriever, named Nox, and a suggestive name, too; for I think what he did a darker mystery than the murder. You know Druce's house and garden are by the sea; we walked about a mile from it along the sands and then turned back, going the other way. We passed a rather curious rock called the Rock of Fortune, famous in the neighbourhood because it's one of those examples of one stone barely balanced on another, so that a touch would knock it over. It is not really very high but the hanging outline of it makes it look a little wild and sinister; at least it made it look so to me, for I don't imagine my jolly young companions were afflicted with the picturesque. But it may be that I was beginning to feel an atmosphere; for just then the question arose of whether it was time to go back to tea, and even then I think I had a premonition that time counted for a good deal in the business. Neither Herbert Druce nor I had a watch, so we called out to his brother, who was some paces behind, having stopped to light his pipe under the hedge. Hence it happened that he shouted out the hour, which was twenty past four, in his big voice through the glowing twilight; and somehow the loudness of it made it sound like the proclamation of something tremendous. His unconsciousness seemed to make it all the more so; but that was always the way with omens; and particular ticks of the clock were really very ominous things that afternoon. According to Dr Valentine's testimony, poor Druce had actually died just about half past four.

"Well, they said we needn't go home for ten minutes, and we walked a little farther along the sands, doing nothing in particular—throwing stones for the dog and throwing sticks into the sea for him to swim after. But to me the twilight seemed to grow oddly oppressive, and the very shadow of the top-heavy Rock of Fortune lay on me like a load. And then the curious thing happened. Nox had just brought back Herbert's walking-stick out of the sea and his brother had thrown his in also. The dog swam out again, but just about what must have been the stroke of the half-hour, he stopped swimming. He came back again on to the shore and stood in front of us. Then he suddenly threw up his head and sent up a howl or wail of woe—if ever I heard one in the world.

"'What the devil's the matter with the dog?' asked Herbert; but none of us could answer. There was a long silence after the brute's wailing and whining died away on the desolate shore; and then the silence was broken. As I live, it was broken by a faint and far-off shriek, like the shriek of a woman from beyond the hedges inland. We didn't know what it was then; but we knew afterwards. It was the cry the girl gave when she first saw the body of her father."

"You went back, I suppose," said Father Brown patiently. "What happened then?"

"I'll tell you what happened then," said Fiennes with a grim emphasis. "When we got back into that garden the first thing we saw was Traill, the lawyer; I can see him now with his black hat and black whiskers relieved against the perspective of the blue flowers stretching down to the summer-house, with the sunset and the strange outline of the Rock of Fortune in the distance. His face and figure were in shadow against the sunset; but I swear the white teeth were showing in his head and he was smiling.

"The moment Nox saw that man the dog dashed forward and stood in the middle of the path barking at him madly, murderously, volleying out curses that were almost verbal in their dreadful distinctness of hatred. And the man doubled up and fled along the path between the flowers."

Father Brown sprang to his feet with a startling impatience.

"So the dog denounced him, did he?" he cried. "The oracle of the dog condemned him. Did you see what birds were flying, and are you sure whether they were on the right hand or the left? Did you consult the augurs about the sacrifices? Surely you didn't omit to cut open the dog and examine his entrails. That is the sort of scientific test you heathen humanitarians seem to trust when you are thinking of taking away the life and honour of a man."

Fiennes sat gaping for an instant before he found breath to say: "Why, what's the matter with you? What have I done now?"

A sort of anxiety came back into the priest's eyes—the anxiety of a man who has run against a post in the dark and wonders for a moment whether he has hurt it.

"I'm most awfully sorry," he said with sincere distress. "I beg your pardon for being so rude; pray forgive me."

Fiennes looked at him curiously. "I sometimes think you are more of a mystery than any of the mysteries," he said. "But anyhow, if you don't believe in the mystery of the dog, at least you can't get over the mystery of the man. You can't deny that at the very moment when the beast came back from the sea and bellowed, his master's soul was driven

203

out of his body by the blow of some unseen power that no mortal man can trace or even imagine. And as for the lawyer—I don't go only by the dog—there are other curious details, too. He sruck me as a smooth, smiling, equivocal sort of person; and one of his tricks seemed like a sort of hint. You know the doctor and the police were on the spot very quickly; Valentine was brought back when walking away from the house, and he telephoned instantly. That, with the secluded house, small numbers, and enclosed space, made it pretty possible to search everybody who could have been near; and everybody was thoroughly searched—for a weapon. The whole house, garden, and shore were combed for a weapon. The disappearance of the dagger is almost as crazy as the disappearance of the man."

"The disappearance of the dagger," said Father Brown, nodding. He seemed to have become suddenly attentive.

"Well," continued Fiennes, "I told you that man Traill had a trick of fidgeting with his tie and tie-pin—especially his tie-pin. His pin, like himself, was at once showy and old-fashioned. It had one of those stones with concentric coloured rings that look like an eye; and his own concentration on it got on my nerves, as if he had been a Cyclops with one eye in the middle of his body. But the pin was not only large but long; and it occurred to me that his anxiety about its adjustment was because it was even longer than it looked; as long as a stiletto in fact."

Father Brown nodded thoughtfully, "Was any other instrument ever suggested?" he asked.

"There was another suggestion," answered Fiennes, "from one of the young Druces—the cousins, I mean. Neither Herbert nor Harry Druce would have struck one at first as likely to be of assistance in scientific detection; but while Herbert was really the traditional type of heavy Dragoon, caring for nothing but horses and being an ornament to the Horse Guards, his younger brother Harry had been in the Indian Police and knew something about such things. Indeed, in his own way he was quite clever; and I rather fancy he had been too clever; I mean he had left the police through breaking some red-tape regulations and taking some sort of risk and responsibility of his own. Anyhow, he was in some sense a detective out of work, and threw himself into this business with more than the ardour of an amateur. And it was with him that I had an argument about the weapon—an argument that led to something new. It began by his countering my description of the dog barking at Traill; and he said that a dog at his worst didn't bark, but growled."

"He was quite right there," observed the priest.

"This young fellow went on to say that, if it came to that, he'd heard Nox growling at other people before then; and among others at Floyd, the secretary. I retorted that his own argument answered itself; for the crime couldn't be brought home to two or three people, and least of all to Floyd, who was as innocent as a harum-scarum schoolboy, and had been seen by everybody all the time perched above the garden hedge with his fan of red hair as conspicuous as a scarlet cockatoo. 'I know there's difficulties anyhow,' said my colleague; 'but I wish you'd come with me down the garden a minute. I want to show you something I don't think any one else has seen.' This was on the very day of the discovery, and the garden was just as it had been. The step-ladder was still standing by the hedge, and just under the hedge my guide stopped and disentangled something from the deep grass. It was the sheers used for clipping the hedge, and on the point of one of them was a smear of blood."

There was a short silence, and then Father Brown said suddenly, "What was the lawyer there for?"

"He told us the Colonel sent for him to alter his will," answered Fiennes. "And, by the way, there was another thing about the business of the will that I ought to mention. You see, the will wasn't actually signed in the summer-house that afternoon."

"I suppose not," said Father Brown; "there would have to be two witnesses."

"The lawyer actually came down the day before and it was signed then; but he was sent for again next day because the old man had a doubt about one of the witnesses and had to be reassured."

"Who were the witnesses?" asked Father Brown.

"That's just the point," replied his informant eagerly, "the witnesses were Floyd, the secretary, and this Dr Valentine, the foreign sort of surgeon or whatever he is; and the two had a quarrel. Now I'm bound to say that the secretary is something of a busybody. He's one of those hot and headlong people whose warmth of temperament has unfortunately turned mostly to pugnacity and bristling suspicion; to distrusting people instead of to trusting them. That sort of red-haired red-hot fellow is always either universally credulous or universally incredulous; and sometimes both. He was not only a Jack-of-all-trades, but he knew better than all tradesmen. He not only knew everything, but he warned everybody against everybody. All that must be taken into account in his suspicions about Valentine; but in that particular case there seems to have been something behind it. He said the name of Valentine was not really Valentine. He said he had seen him elsewhere known by the name of De Villon. He said it would invalidate the will;

of course he was kind enough to explain to the lawyer what the law was on that point. They were both in a frightful wax."

Father Brown laughed. "People often are when they are to witness a will," he said; "for one thing, it means that they can't have any legacy under it. But what did Dr Valentine say? No doubt the universal secretary knew more about the doctor's name than the doctor did. But even the doctor might have some information about his own name."

Fiennes paused a moment before he replied.

"Dr Valentine took it in a curious way. Dr Valentine is a curious man. His appearance is rather striking but very foreign. He is young but wears a beard cut square; and his face is very pale, dreadfully pale and dreadfully serious. His eyes have a sort of ache in them, as if he ought to wear glasses, or had given himself a headache with thinking; but he is quite handsome and always very formally dressed, with a top hat and a dark coat and a little red rosette. His manner is rather cold and haughty, and he has a way of staring at you which is very disconcerting. When thus charged with having changed his name, he merely stared like a sphinx and then said with a little laugh that he supposed Americans had no names to change. At that I think the Colonel also got into a fuss and said all sorts of angry things to the doctor; all the more angry because of the doctor's pretensions to a future place in his family. But I shouldn't have thought much of that but for a few words that I happened to hear later, early in the afternoon of the tragedy. I don't want to make a lot of them, for they weren't the sort of words on which one would like, in the ordinary way, to play the eavesdropper. As I was passing out towards the front gate with my two companions and the dog, I heard voices which told me that Dr Valentine and Miss Druce had withdrawn for a moment in the shadow of the house, in an angle behind a row of flowering plants, and were talking to each other in passionate whisperings—sometimes almost like hissings; for it was something of a lovers' quarrel as well as a lovers' tryst. Nobody repeats the sort of things they said for the most part; but in an unfortunate business like this I'm bound to say that there was repeated more than once a phrase about killing somebody. In fact, the girl seemed to be begging him not to kill somebody, or saying that no provocation could justify killing anybody; which seems an unusual sort of talk to address to a gentleman who has dropped in to tea."

"Do you know," asked the priest, "whether Dr Valentine seemed to be very angry after the scene with the secretary and the Colonel—I mean about witnessing the will?"

"By all accounts," replied the other, "he wasn't half so angry as the secretary was. It was the secretary who went away raging after witnessing the will."

"And now," said Father Brown, "what about the will itself?"

"The Colonel was a very wealthy man, and his will was important. Traill wouldn't tell us the alteration at that stage, but I have since heard only this morning in fact—that most of the money was transferred from the son to the daughter. I told you that Druce was wild with my friend Donald over his dissipated hours."

"The question of motive has been rather over-shadowed by the question of method," observed Father Brown thoughtfully. "At that moment, apparently, Miss Druce was the immediate gainer by the death."

"Good God! What a cold-blooded way of talking," cried Fiennes, staring at him. "You don't really mean to hint that she—"

"Is she going to marry that Dr Valentine?" asked the other.

"Some people are against it," answered his friend. "But he is liked and respected in the place and is a skilled and devoted surgeon."

"So devoted a surgeon," said Father Brown, "that he had surgical instruments with him when he went to call on the young lady at teatime. For he must have used a lancet or something, and he never seems to have gone home."

Fiennes sprang to his feet and looked at him in a heat of inquiry. "You suggest he might have used the very same lancet—"

Father Brown shook his head. "All these suggestions are fancies just now," he said. "The problem is not who did it or what did it, but how it was done. We might find many men and even many tools—pins and shears and lancets. But how did a man get into the room? How did even a pin get into it?"

He was staring reflectively at the ceiling as he spoke, but as he said the last words his eye cocked in an alert fashion as if he had suddenly seen a curious fly on the ceiling.

"Well, what would you do about it?" asked the young man. "You have a lot of experience; what would you advise now?"

"I'm afraid I'm not much use," said Father Brown with a sigh. "I can't suggest very much without having ever been near the place or the people. For the moment you can only go on with local inquiries. I gather that your friend from the Indian Police is more or less in charge of your inquiry down there. I should run down and see how he is getting on. See what he's been doing in the way of amateur detection. There may be news already."

As his guests, the biped and the quadruped, disappeared, Father Brown took up his pen and went back to his interrupted occupation of planning a course of lectures on the Encyclical *Rerum Novarum*. The subject was a large one and he had to recast it more than once, so that he was somewhat similarly employed some two days later when the big black dog again came bounding into the room and sprawled all over him with enthusiasm and excitement. The master who followed the dog shared the excitement if not the enthusiasm. He had been excited in a less pleasant fashion, for his blue eyes seemed to start from his head and his eager face was even a little pale.

"You told me," he said abruptly and without preface, "to find out what Harry Druce was doing. Do you know what he's done?"

The priest did not reply, and the young man went on in jerky tones:

"I'll tell you what he's done. He's killed himself."

Father Brown's lips moved only faintly, and there was nothing practical about what he was saying—nothing that has anything to do with this story or this world.

"You give me the creeps sometimes," said Fiennes. "Did you—did you expect this?"

"I thought it possible," said Father Brown; "that was why I asked you to go and see what he was doing. I hoped you might not be too late."

"It was I who found him," said Fiennes rather huskily. "It was the ugliest and most uncanny thing I ever knew. I went down that old garden again, and I knew there was something new and unnatural about it besides the murder. The flowers still tossed about in blue masses on each side of the black entrance into the old grey summer-house; but to me the blue flowers looked like blue devils dancing before some dark cavern of the underworld. I looked all round, everything seemed to be in its ordinary place. But the queer notion grew on me that there was something wrong with the very shape of the sky. And then I saw what it was. The Rock of Fortune always rose in the background beyond the garden hedge and against the sea. The Rock of Fortune was gone."

Father Brown had lifted his head and was listening intently.

"It was as if a mountain had walked away out of a landscape or a moon fallen from the sky; though I knew, of course, that a touch at any time would have tipped the thing over. Something possessed me and I rushed down that garden path like the wind and went crashing through that hedge as if it were a spider's web. It was a thin hedge really, though its undisturbed trimness had made it serve all the purposes of a wall. On the shore I found the loose rock fallen from its pedestal; and poor Harry Druce lay like a wreck underneath it. One arm was thrown round it in a sort of embrace as if he had pulled it down on himself; and on the broad brown sands beside it, in large crazy lettering, he had scrawled the words: 'The Rock of Fortune falls on the Fool.'"

"It was the Colonel's will that did that," observed Father Brown. "The young man had staked everything on profiting himself by Donald's disgrace, especially when his uncle sent for him on the same day as the lawyer, and welcomed him with so much warmth. Otherwise he was done; he'd lost his police job; he was beggared at Monte Carlo. And he killed himself when he found he'd killed his kinsman for nothing."

"Here, stop a minute!" cried the staring Fiennes. "You're going too fast for me."

"Talking about the will, by the way," continued Father Brown calmly, "before I forget it, or we go on to bigger things, there was a simple explanation, I think, of all that business about the doctor's name. I rather fancy I have heard both names before somewhere. The doctor is really a French nobleman with the title of the Marquis de Villon. But he is also an ardent Republican and has abandoned his title and fallen back on the forgotten family surname. 'With your Citizen Riquetti you have puzzled Europe for ten days.'"

"What is that?" asked the young man blankly.

"Never mind," said the priest. "Nine times out of ten it is a rascally thing to change one's name; but this was a piece of fine fanaticism. That's the point of his sarcasm about Americans having no names—that is, no titles. Now in England the Marquis of Hartington is never called Mr Hartington; but in France the Marquis de Villon is called M. de Villon. So it might well look like a change of name. As for the talk about killing, I fancy that also was a point of French etiquette. The doctor was talking about challenging Floyd to a duel, and the girl was trying to dissuade him."

"Oh, I see," cried Fiennes slowly. "Now I understand what she meant."

"And what is that about?" asked his companion, smiling.

"Well," said the young man, "it was something that happened to me just before I found that poor fellow's body; only the catastrophe drove it out of my head. I suppose it's hard to remember a little romantic idyll when you've just come on top of a tragedy. But as I went down the lanes leading to the Colonel's old place I met his daughter walking with Dr Valentine. She was in mourning, of course, and he always wore black as if he were going to a funeral; but I can't say that their faces were very funereal. Never have I seen two people looking in their own way more respectably radiant and cheerful. They stopped and saluted me, and then she told me they were married and living in a little house on the outskirts of the town, where the doctor was continuing his practice. This rather surprised me, because I knew that her old father's will had left her his property; and I hinted at it delicately by saying I was going along to her father's old place and had half expected to meet her there. But she only laughed and said: 'Oh, we've given up all that. My husband doesn't like heiresses.' And I doscovered with some astonishment they really had insisted on restoring the property to poor Donald; so I hope he's had a healthy shock and will treat it sensibly. There was never much really the matter with him; he was very young and his father was not very wise. But it was in connexion with that that she said something I didn't understand at the time; but now I'm sure it must be as you say. She said with a sort of sudden and splendid arrogance that was entirely altruistic:

"'I hope it'll stop that red-haired fool from fussing any more about the will. Does he think my husband, who has given up a crest and a coronet as old as the Crusades for his principles, would kill an old man in a summer-house for a legacy like that?' Then she laughed again and said, 'My husband isn't killing anybody except in the way of business. Why, he didn't even ask his friends to call on the secretary.' Now, of course, I see what she meant."

"I see part of what she meant, of course," said Father Brown. "What did she mean exactly by the secretary fussing about the will?"

Fiennes smiled as he answered, "I wish you knew the secretary, Father Brown. It would be a joy to you to watch him make things hum, as he calls it. He made the house of mourning hum. He filled the funeral with all the snap and zip of the brightest sporting event. There was no holding him, after something had really happened. I've told you how he used to oversee the gardener as he did the garden, and how he instructed the lawyer in the law. Needless to say, he also instructed the surgeon in the practice of surgery; and as the surgeon was Dr Valentine. you may be sure it ended in accusing him of something worse than bad surgery. The secretary got it fixed in his red head that the doctor had committed the crime, and when the police arrived he was perfectly sublime. Need I say that he became, on the spot, the greatest of all amateur detectives? Sherlock Holmes never towered over Scotland Yard with more Titanic intellectual pride and scorn than Colonel Druce's private secretary over the police investigating Colonel Druce's death. I tell you it was a joy to see him. He strode about with an abstracted air, tossing his scarlet crest of hair and giving curt impatient replies. Of course it was his demeanour during these days that made Druce's daughter so wild with him. Of course he had a theory. It's just the sort of theory a man would have in a book; and Floyd is the sort of man who ought to be in a book. He'd be better fun and less bother in a book."

"What was his theory?" asked the other.

"Oh, it was full of pep," replied Fiennes gloomily. "It would have been glorious copy if it could have held together for ten minutes longer. He said the Colonel was still alive when they found him in the summer-house, and the doctor killed him with the surgical instrument on pretence of cutting the clothes."

"I see," said the priest. "I suppose he was lying flat on his face on the mud floor as a form of siesta."

"It's wonderful what hustle will do," continued his informant. "I believe Floyd would have got his great theory into the papers at any rate, and perhaps had the doctor attested, when all these things were blown sky high as if by dynamite by the discovery of that dead body lying under the Rock of Fortune. And that's what we come back to after all. I suppose the suicide is almost a confession. But nobody will ever know the whole story."

There was a silence, and then the priest said modestly: "I rather think I know the whole story."

Fiennes stared. "But look here," he cried; "how do you come to know the whole story, or to be sure it's the true story? You've been sitting here a hundred miles away writing a sermon; do you mean to tell me you really know what happened already? If you've really come to the end, where in the world do you begin? What started you off with your own story?"

Father Brown jumped up with a very unusual excitement and his first exclamation was like an explosion.

"The dog!" he cried. "The dog, of course! You had the whole story in your hands in the business of the dog on the beach, if you'd only noticed the dog properly."

Fiennes stared still more. "But you told me before that my feelings about the dog were all nonsense, and the dog had nothing to do with it."

"The dog had everything to do with it," said Father Brown, "as you'd have found out if you'd only treated the dog as a dog, and not as God Almighty judging the souls of men."

He paused in an embarrassed way for a moment, and then said, with a rather pathetic air of apology: "The truth is, I happen to be awfully fond of dogs. And it seemed to me that in all this lurid halo of dog superstitions nobody was really thinking about the poor dog at all. To begin with a small point, about his barking at the lawyer or growling at the secretary. You asked how I could guess things a hundred miles away; but honestly it's mostly to your credit, for you described people so well that I know the types. A man like Traill, who frowns usually and smiles suddenly, a man who fiddles with things, especially at his throat, is a nervous, easily embarrassed man. I shouldn't wonder if Floyd, the efficient secretary, is nervy and jumpy, too; those Yankee hustlers often are. Otherwise he wouldn't have cut his fingers on the shears and dropped them when he heard Janet Druce scream.

Now dogs hate nervous people. I don't know whether they make the dog nervous, too; or whether, being after all a brute, he is a bit of a bully; or whether his canine vanity (which is colossal) is simply offended at not being liked. But anyhow there was nothing in poor Nox protesting against those people, except that he disliked them for being afraid of him. Now I know you're awfully clever, and nobody of sense sneers at cleverness. But I sometimes fancy, for instance, that you are too clever to understand animals. Sometimes you are too clever to understand men, especially when they act almost as simply as animals. Animals are very literal; they live in a world of truisms. Take this case: a dog barks at a man and a man runs away from a dog. Now you do not seem to be quite simple enough to see the fact: that the dog barked because he disliked the man and the man fled because he was frightened of the dog. They had no other motives and they needed none; but you must read psychological mysteries into it and suppose the dog had super-normal vision, and was a mysterious mouthpiece of doom. You must suppose the man was running away, not from the dog but from the hangman. And yet, if you come to think of it, all this deeper psychology is exceedingly improbable. If the dog really could completely and consciously realize the murderer of his master he wouldn't stand yapping as he might at a curate at a tea-party; he's much more likely to fly at his throat. And on the other hand, do you really think a man who had hardened his heart to murder an old friend and then walk about smiling at the old friend's family, under the eyes of his old friend's daughter and post-mortem doctor—do you think a man like that would be doubled up by mere remorse because a dog barked? He might feel the tragic irony of it; it might shake his soul, like any other tragic trifle. But he wouldn't rush madly the length of a garden to escape from the only witness whom he knew to be unable to talk. People have a panic like that when they are frightened, not of tragic ironies, but of teeth. The whole thing is simpler than you can understand.

"But when we come to that business by the seashore, things are much more interesting. As you stated them, they were much more puzzling. I didn't understand that tale of the dog going in and out of the water; it didn't seem to me a doggy thing to do. If Nox had been very much upset about something else, he might possibly have refused to go after the stick at all. He'd probably go off nosing in whatever direction he suspected the mischief. But when once a dog is actually chasing a thing, a stone or a stick or a rabbit, my experience is that he won't stop for anything but the most peremptory command, and not always for that. That he should turn round because his mood changed seems to me unthinkable."

"But he did turn round," insisted Fiennes; "and came back without the stick."

"He came back without the stick for the best reason in the world," replied the priest. "He came back because he couldn't find it. He whined because he couldn't find it. That's the sort of thing a dog really does whine about. A dog is a devil of a ritualist. He is as particular about the precise routine of a game as a child about the precise repetition of a fairy-tale. In this case something had gone wrong with the game. He came back to complain seriously of the conduct of the stick. Never had such a thing happened before. Never had an eminent and distinguished dog been so treated by a rotten old walking-stick."

"Why, what had the walking-stick done?" inquired the young man.

"It had sunk," said Father Brown.

Fiennes said nothing, but continued to stare; and it was the priest who continued:

"It had sunk because it was not really a stick, but a rod of steel with a very thin shell of cane and a sharp point. In other words, it was a sword stick. I suppose a murderer never gets rid of a bloody weapon so oddly and yet so naturally as by throwing it into the sea for a retriever."

"I begin to see what you mean," admitted Fiennes; "but even if a sword-stick was used, I have no guess of how it was used."

"I had a sort of guess," said Father Brown, "right at the beginning when you said the word summer-house. And another when you said that Druce wore a white coat. As long as everybody was looking for a short dagger, nobody thought of it; but if we admit a rather long blade like a rapier, it's not so impossible."

He was leaning back, looking at the ceiling, and began like one going back to his own first thoughts and fundamentals.

"All that discussion about detective stories like the Yellow Room, about a man found dead in sealed chambers which no one could enter, does not apply to the present case, because it is a summer-house. When we talk of a Yellow Room, or any room, we imply walls that are really homogeneous and impenetrable. But a summer-house is not made like that; it is often made, as it was in this case, of closely interlaced but separate boughs and strips of wood, in which there are chinks here and there. There was one of them just behind Druce's back as he sat in his chair up against the wall. But just as the room was a summer-house, so the chair was a basket-chair. That also was a lattice of loopholes. Lastly, the summer-house was close up under the hedge; and you have just told me that it was really a thin hedge. A man standing outside it could easily see, amid a network of twigs and branches and canes, one white spot of the Colonel's coat as plain as the white of a target.

"Now, you left the geography a little vague; but it was possible to put two and two together. You said the Rock of Fortune was not really high; but you also said it could be seen dominating the garden like a mountain-peak. In other words, it was very near the end of the garden, though your walk had taken you a long way round to it. Also, it isn't likely the young lady really howled so as to be heard half a mile. She gave an ordinary involuntary cry, and yet you heard it on the shore. And among other interesting things that you told me, may I remind you that you said Harry Druce had fallen behind to light his pipe under a hedge."

Fiennes shuddered slightly. "You mean he drew his blade there and sent it through the hedge at the white spot. But surely it was a very odd chance and a very sudden choice. Besides, he couldn't be certain the old man's money had passed to him, and as a fact it hadn't."

Father Brown's face became animated.

"You misunderstand the man's character, " he said, as if he himself had known the man all his life. "A curious but not unknown type of character. If he had really *known* the money would come to him, I seriously believe he wouldn't have done it. He would have seen it as the dirty thing it was."

"Isn't that rather paradoxical?" asked the other.

"This man was a gambler," said the priest, "and a man in disgrace for having taken risks and anticipated orders. It was probably for something pretty unscrupulous, for every imperial police is more like a Russian secret police than we like to think. But he had gone beyond the line and failed. Now, the temptation of that type of man is to do a mad thing precisely because the risk will be wonderful in retrospect. He wants to say, 'Nobody but I could have seized that chance or seen that it was then or never. What a wild and wonderful guess it was, when I put all those things together; Donald in disgrace; and the lawyer being sent for; and Herbert and I sent for at the same time—and then nothing more but the way the old man grinned at me and shook hands. Anybody would say I was mad to risk it; but that is how fortunes are

214

made, by the man mad enough to have a little foresight.' In short, it is the vanity of guessing. It is the megalomania of the gambler. The more incongruous the coincidence, the more instantaneous the decision, the more likely he is to snatch the chance. The accident, the very triviality of the white speck and the hole in the hedge intoxicated him like a vision of the world's desire. Nobody clever enough to see such a combination of accidents could be cowardly enough not to use them! That is how the devil talks to the gambler. But the devil himself would hardly have induced that unhappy man to go down in a dull, deliberate way and kill an old uncle from whom he'd always had expectations. It would be too respectable."

He paused a moment, and then went on with a certain quiet emphasis.

"And now try to call up the scene, even as you saw it yourself. As he stood there, dizzy with his diabolical opportunity, he looked up and saw that strange outline that might have been the image of his own tottering soul; the one great crag poised perilously on the other like a pyramid on its point, and remembered that it was called the Rock of Fortune. Can you guess how such a man at such a moment would read such a signal? I think it strung him up to action and even to vigilance. He who would be a tower must not fear to be a toppling tower. Anyhow, he acted; his next difficulty was to cover his tracks. To be found with a sword-stick, let alone a blood-stained sword-stick, would be fatal in the search that was certain to follow. If he left it anywhere, it would be found and probably traced. Even if he threw it into the sea the action might be noticed, and thought noticeable—unless indeed he could think of some more natural way of covering the action. As you know, he did think of one, and a very good one. Being the only one of you with a watch, he told you it was not yet time to return, strolled a little farther, and started the game of throwing in sticks for the retriever. But how his eyes must have rolled darkly over all that desolate sea-shore before they alighted on the dog!"

Fiennes nodded, gazing thoughtfully into space. His mind seemed to have drifted back to a less practical part of the narrative.

"It's queer," he said, "that the dog really was in the story after all."

"The dog could almost have told you the story, if he could talk," said the priest. "All I complain of is that because he couldn't talk you made up his story for him, and made him talk with the tongues of men and angels. It's part of something I've noticed more and more in the modern world, appearing in all sorts of newspaper rumours and conversational catchwords; something that's arbitrary without being authoritative. People readily swallow the untested claims of this, that, or the other. It's drowning all your old rationalism and scepticism, it's coming in like a sea; and the name of it is superstition." He stood up abruptly, his face heavy with a sort of frown, and went on talking almost as if he were alone. "It's the first effect of not believing in God that you lose your common sense and can't see things as they are. Anything that anybody talks about, and says there's a good deal in it, extends itself indefinitely like a vista in a nightmare. And a dog is an omen, and a cat is a mystery, and a pig is a mascot, and a beetle is a scarab, calling up all the menagerie of polytheism from Egypt and old India; Dog Anubis and great green-eyed Pasht and all the holy howling Bulls of Bashan; reeling back to the bestial gods of the beginning, escaping into elephants and snakes and crocodiles; and all because you are frightened of four words: 'He was made Man.'"

The young man got up with a little embarrassment, almost as if he had overheard a soliloquy. He called to the dog and left the room with vague but breezy farewells. But he had to call the dog twice, for the dog had remained behind quite motionless for a moment, looking up steadily at Father Brown as the wolf looked at St Francis.

THE DOOMDORF MYSTERY

By Melville Davisson Post

Melville Davisson Post (1869–1930), author of the Uncle Abner mystery stories, set in early nineteenth-century back country Virginia, came himself from rural West Virginia where he graduated from the state university and for thirteen years practiced criminal and corporate law. He then became a highly successful magazine writer, noted for his skillful plots and for creating such characters as Randolph Mason, an unscrupulous attorney who was clever at finding legal loopholes for his equally unscrupulous clients, and Sir Henry Marquise and Monsieur Jonquelle, respectively a British and a French police detective. However, it is for Uncle Abner, the stern, Bible-quoting backwoods squire, magisterially protecting the innocent and exposing the guilty in his mountain community, that Post is best remembered. Abner and his narrator nephew, Martin, are featured in twenty-two stories, eighteen of which were collected in Uncle Abner, Master of Mysteries *(1918). "The Doomsdorf Mystery" originally appeared in* The Saturday Evening Post *(July 18, 1914) and was the initial work in the 1918 volume. All twenty-two stories, together with useful bibliographical and biographical information, can be found in* The Complete Uncle Abner *(Del Mar, Calif.: The Mystery Library, 1977), edited and with an introduction by Allen J. Hubin. For more about the author and his work see Charles A. Norton's* Melville Davisson Post: Man of Many Mysteries *(Bowling Green, Ohio: Popular Press, 1973).*

The pioneer was not the only man in the great mountains behind Virginia. Strange aliens drifted in after the Colonial wars. All foreign armies are sprinkled with a cockle of adventurers that take root and remain. They were with Braddock and La Salle, and they rode north out of Mexico after her many empires went to pieces.

I think Doomdorf crossed the seas with Iturbide when that ill-starred adventurer returned to be shot against a wall; but there was no Southern blood in him. He came from some European race remote and barbaric. The evidences were all about him. He was a huge figure of a man, with a black spade beard, broad, thick hands, and square, flat fingers.

He had found a wedge of land between the Crown's grant to Daniel Davisson and a Washington survey. It was an uncovered triangle not worth the running of the lines; and so, no doubt, was left out, a sheer rock standing up out of the river for a base, and a peak of the mountain rising northward behind it for an apex.

Doomdorf squatted on the rock. He must have brought a belt of gold pieces when he took to his horse, for he hired old Robert Steuart's slaves and built a stone house on the rock, and he brought the furnishings overland from a frigate in the Chesapeake; and then in the handfuls of earth, wherever a root would hold, he planted the mountain behind his house with peach trees. The gold gave out; but the devil is fertile in resources. Doomdorf built a log still and turned the first fruits of the garden into a hell-brew. The idle and the vicious came with their stone jugs, and violence and riot flowed out.

The government of Virginia was remote and its arm short and feeble; but the men who held the lands west of the mountains against the savages under grants from George, and after that held them against George himself, were efficient and expeditious. They had long patience, but when that failed they went up from their fields and drove the thing before them out of the land, like a scourge of God.

There came a day, then, when my Uncle Abner and Squire Randolph rode through the gap of the mountains to have the thing out with Doomdorf. The work of this brew, which had the odors of Eden and the impulses of the devil in it, could be borne no longer. The drunken Negroes had shot old Duncan's cattle and burned his haystacks, and the land was on its feet.

They rode alone, but they were worth an army of little men. Randolph was vain and pompous and given over to extravagance of words, but he was a gentleman beneath it, and fear was an alien and a stranger to him. And Abner was the right hand of the land.

It was a day in early summer and the sun lay hot. They crossed through the broken spine of the mountains and trailed along the river in the shade of the great chestnut trees. The road was only a path and the horses went one before the other. It left the river when the rock began to rise and, making a detour through the grove of peach trees, reached the house on the mountain side. Randolph and Abner got down, unsaddled their horses and turned them out to graze, for their business with Doomdorf would not be over in an hour. Then they took a steep path that brought them out on the mountain side of the house.

A man sat on a big red-roan horse in the paved court before the door. He was a gaunt old man. He sat bare-headed, the palms of his hands resting on the pommel of his saddle, his chin sunk in his black stock, his face in retrospection, the wind moving gently his great shock of voluminous white hair. Under him the huge red horse stood with his legs spread out like a horse of stone.

There was no sound. The door to the house was closed; insects moved in the sun; a shadow crept out from the motionless figure, and swarms of yellow butterflies maneuvered like an army.

Abner and Randolph stopped. They knew the tragic figure—a circuit rider of the hills who preached the invective of Isaiah as though he were the mouthpiece of a militant and avenging overlord; as though the government of Virginia were the awful theocracy of the Book of Kings. The horse was dripping with sweat and the man bore the dust and the evidences of a journey on him.

"Bronson," said Abner, "where is Doomdorf?"

The old man lifted his head and looked down at Abner over the pommel of the saddle.

"'Surely,'" he said, "'he covereth his feet in his summer chamber.'"

Abner went over and knocked on the closed door, and presently the white, frightened face of a woman looked out at him. She was a little, faded woman, with fair hair, a broad foreign face, but with the delicate evidences of gentle blood.

Abner repeated his question.

"Where is Doomdorf?"

"Oh, sir," she answered with a queer lisping accent, "he went to lie down in his south room after his midday meal, as his custom is; and I went to the orchard to gather any fruit that might be ripened." She hesitated and her voice lisped into a whisper: "He is not come out and I cannot wake him."

219

The two men followed her through the hall and up the stairway to the door.

"It is always bolted," she said, "when he goes to lie down." And she knocked feebly with the tips of her fingers.

There was no answer and Randolph rattled the doorknob.

"Come out, Doomdorf!" he called in his big, bellowing voice.

There was only silence and the echoes of the words among the rafters. Then Randolph set his shoulder to the door and burst it open.

They went in. The room was flooded with sun from the tall south windows. Doomdorf lay on a couch in a little offset of the room, a great scarlet patch on his bosom and a pool of scarlet on the floor.

The woman stood for a moment staring; then she cried out:

"At last I have killed him!" And she ran like a frightened hare.

The two men closed the door and went over to the couch. Doomdorf had been shot to death. There was a great ragged hole in his waistcoat. They began to look about for the weapon with which the deed had been accomplished, and in a moment found it—a fowling piece lying in two dogwood forks against the wall. The gun had just been fired; there was a freshly exploded paper cap under the hammer.

There was little else in the room—a loom-woven rag carpet on the floor; wooden shutters flung back from the windows; a great oak table, and on it a big, round, glass water bottle, filled to its glass stopper with raw liquor from the still. The stuff was limpid and clear as spring water; and, but for its pungent odor, one would have taken it for God's brew instead of Doomdorf's. The sun lay on it and against the wall where hung the weapon that had ejected the dead man out of life.

"Abner," said Randolph, "this is murder! The woman took that gun down from the wall and shot Doomdorf while he slept."

Abner was standing by the table, his fingers round his chin.

"Randolph," he replied, "what brought Bronson here?"

"The same outrages that brought us," said Randolph. "The mad old circuit rider has been preaching a crusade against Doomdorf far and wide in the hills."

Abner answered, without taking his fingers from about his chin:

"You think this woman killed Doomdorf? Well, let us go and ask Bronson who killed him."

They closed the door, leaving the dead man on his couch, and went down into the court.

The old circuit rider had put away his horse and got an ax. He had taken off his coat and pushed his shirtsleeves up over his long elbows. He was on his way to the still to destroy the barrels of liquor. He stopped when the two men came out, and Abner called to him.

"Bronson," he said, "who killed Doomdorf?"

"I killed him," replied the old man, and went on toward the still.

Randolph swore under his breath. "By the Almighty," he said, "everybody couldn't kill him!"

"Who can tell how many had a hand in it?" replied Abner.

"Two have confessed!" cried Randolph. "Was there perhaps a third? Did you kill him, Abner? And I too? Man, the thing is impossible!"

"The impossible," replied Abner, "looks here like the truth. Come with me, Randolph, and I will show you a thing more impossible than this."

They returned through the house and up the stairs to the room. Abner closed the door behind them.

"Look at this bolt," he said; "it is on the inside and not connected with the lock. How did the one who killed Doomdorf get into this room, since the door was bolted?"

"Through the windows," replied Randolph.

There were but two windows, facing the south, through which the sun entered. Abner led Randolph to them.

"Look!" he said. "The wall of the house is plumb with the sheer face of the rock. It is a hundred feet to the river and the rock is as smooth as a sheet of glass. But that is not all. Look at these window frames; they are cemented into their casement with dust and they are bound along their edges with cobwebs. These windows have not been opened. How did the assassin enter?"

"The answer is evident," said Randolph: "The one who killed Doomdorf hid in the room until he was asleep; then he shot him and went out."

"The explanation is excellent but for one thing," replied Abner: "How did the assassin bolt the door behind him on the inside of this room after he had gone out?"

Randolph flung out his arms with a hopeless gesture.

"Who knows?" he cried. "Maybe Doomdorf killed himself."

Abner laughed.

"And after firing a handful of shot into his heart he got up and put the gun back carefully into the forks against the wall!"

"Well," cried Randolph, "there is one open road out of this mystery. Bronson and this woman say they killed Doomdorf, and if they killed him they surely know how they did it. Let us go down and ask them."

"In the law court," replied Abner, "that procedure would be considered sound sense; but we are in God's court and things are managed there in a somewhat stranger way. Before we go let us find out, if we can, at what hour it was that Doomdorf died."

He went over and took a big silver watch out of the dead man's pocket. It was broken by a shot and the hands lay at one hour after noon. He stood for a moment fingering his chin.

"At one o'clock," he said. "Bronson, I think, was on the road to this place, and the woman was on the mountain among the peach trees."

Randolph threw back his shoulders.

"Why waste time in a speculation about it, Abner?" he said. "We know who did this thing. Let us go and get the story of it out of their own mouths. Doomdorf died by the hands of either Bronson or this woman."

"I could better believe it," replied Abner, "but for the running of a certain awful law."

"What law?" said Randolph. "Is it a statute of Virginia?"

"It is a statute," replied Abner, "of an authority somewhat higher. Mark the language of it: 'He that killeth with the sword must be killed with the sword.'"

He came over and took Randolph by the arm.

"Must! Randolph, did you mark particularly the word 'must'? It is a mandatory law. There is no room in it for the vicissitudes of chance or fortune. There is no way round that word. Thus, we reap what we sow and nothing else; thus, we receive what we give and nothing else. It is the weapon in our own hands that finally destroys us. You are looking at it now." And he turned him about so that the table and the weapon and the dead man were before him. "'He that killeth with the sword must be killed with the sword.' And now," he said, "let us go and try the method of the law courts. Your faith is in the wisdom of their ways."

They found the old circuit rider at work in the still, staving in Doomdorf's liquor casks, splitting the oak heads with his ax.

"Bronson," said Randolph, "how did you kill Doomdorf?"

The old man stopped and stood leaning on his ax.

"I killed him," replied the old man, "as Elijah killed the captains of Ahaziah and their fifties. But not by the hand of any man did I pray the Lord God to destroy Doomdorf, but with fire from heaven to destroy him."

He stood up and extended his arms.

"His hands were full of blood," he said. "With his abomination from these groves of Baal he stirred up the people to contention, to strife and murder. The widow and the orphan cried to heaven against him. 'I will surely hear their cry,' is the promise written in the Book.

222

The land was weary of him; and I prayed the Lord God to destroy him with fire from heaven, as he destroyed the Princes of Gomorrah in their palaces!"

Randolph made a gesture as of one who dismisses the impossible, but Abner's face took on a deep, strange look.

"With fire from heaven!" he repeated slowly to himself. Then he asked a question. "A little while ago," he said, "when we came, I asked you where Doomdorf was, and you answered me in the language of the third chapter of the Book of Judges. Why did you answer me like that, Bronson?—'Surely he covereth his feet in his summer chamber.'"

"The woman told me that he had not come down from the room where he had gone up to sleep," replied the old man, "and that the door was locked. And then I knew that he was dead in his summer chamber like Eglon, King of Moab."

He extended his arm toward the south.

"I came here from the Great Valley," he said, "to cut down these groves of Baal and to empty out this abomination; but I did not know that the Lord had heard my prayer and visited His wrath on Doomdorf until I was come up into these mountains to his door. When the woman spoke I knew it." And he went away to his horse, leaving the ax among the ruined barrels.

Randolph interrupted.

"Come, Abner," he said; "this is wasted time. Bronson did not kill Doomdorf."

Abner answered slowly in his deep, level voice:

"Do you realize, Randolph, how Doomdorf died?"

"Not by fire from heaven, at any rate," said Randolph.

"Randolph," replied Abner, "are you sure?"

"Abner," cried Randolph, "you are pleased to jest, but I am in deadly earnest. A crime has been done here against the state. I am an officer of justice and I propose to discover the assassin if I can."

He walked away toward the house and Abner followed, his hands behind him and his great shoulders thrown loosely forward, with a grim smile about his mouth.

"It is no use to talk with the mad old preacher," Randolph went on. "Let him empty out the liquor and ride away. I won't issue a warrant against him. Prayer may be a handy implement to do a murder with, Abner, but it is not a deadly weapon under the statutes of Virginia. Doomdorf was dead when old Bronson got here with his Scriptural jargon. This woman killed Doomdorf. I shall put her to an inquisition."

223

"As you like," replied Abner. "Your faith remains in the methods of the law courts."

"Do you know of any better methods?" said Randolph.

"Perhaps," replied Abner, "when you have finished."

Night had entered the valley. The two men went into the house and set about preparing the corpse for burial. They got candles, and made a coffin, and put Doomdorf in it, and straightened out his limbs, and folded his arms across his shot-out heart. Then they set the coffin on benches in the hall.

They kindled a fire in the dining room and sat down before it, with the door open and the red firelight shining through on the dead man's narrow, everlasting house. The woman had put some cold meat, a golden cheese and a loaf on the table. They did not see her, but they heard her moving about the house; and finally, on the gravel court outside, her step and the whinny of a horse. Then she came in, dressed as for a journey. Randolph sprang up.

"Where are you going?" he said.

"To the sea and a ship," replied the woman. Then she indicated the hall with a gesture. "He is dead and I am free."

There was a sudden illumination in her face. Randolph took a step toward her. His voice was big and harsh.

"Who killed Doomdorf?" he cried.

"I killed him," replied the woman. "It was fair!"

"Fair!" echoed the justice. "What do you mean by that?"

The woman shrugged her shoulders and put out her hands with a foreign gesture.

"I remember an old, old man sitting against a sunny wall, and a little girl, and one who came and talked a long time with the old man, while the little girl plucked yellow flowers out of the grass and put them into her hair. Then finally the stranger gave the old man a gold chain and took the little girl away." She flung out her hands. "Oh, it was fair to kill him!" She looked up with a queer, pathetic smile.

"The old man will be gone by now," she said; "but I shall perhaps find the wall there, with the sun on it, and the yellow flowers in the grass. And now, may I go?"

It is a law of the story-teller's art that he does not tell a story. It is the listener who tells it. The story-teller does but provide him with the stimuli.

Randolph got up and walked about the floor. He was a justice of the peace in a day when that office was filled only by the landed gentry, after the English fashion; and the obligations of the law were strong on him. If he should take liberties with the letter of it, how could the weak and the evil be made to hold it in respect? Here was this woman before him a confessed assassin. Could he let her go?

Abner sat unmoving by the hearth, his elbow on the arm of his chair, his palm propping up his jaw, his face clouded in deep lines. Randolph was consumed with vanity and the weakness of ostentation, but he shouldered his duties for himself. Presently he stopped and looked at the woman, wan, faded like some prisoner of legend escaped out of fabled dungeons into the sun.

The firelight flickered past her to the box on the benches in the hall, and the vast, inscrutable justice of heaven entered and over-came him.

"Yes," he said. "Go! There is no jury in Virginia that would hold a woman for shooting a beast like that." And he thrust out his arm, with the fingers extended toward the dead man.

The woman made a little awkward curtsy.

"I thank you, sir." Then she hesitated and lisped, "But I have not shoot him."

"Not shoot him!" cried Randolph. "Why, the man's heart is riddled!"

"Yes, sir," she said simply, like a child. "I kill him, but have not shoot him."

Randolph took two long strides toward the woman.

"Not shoot him!" he repeated. "How then, in the name of heaven, did you kill Doomdorf?" And his big voice filled the empty places of the room.

"I will show you, sir," she said.

She turned and went away into the house. Presently she returned with something folded up in a linen towel. She put it on the table between the loaf of bread and the yellow cheese.

Randolph stood over the table, and the woman's deft fingers undid the towel from round its deadly contents; and presently the thing lay there uncovered.

It was a little crude model of a human figure done in wax with a needle thrust through the bosom.

Randolph stood up with a great intake of the breath.

"Magic! By the eternal!"

"Yes, sir," the woman explained, in her voice and manner of a child. "I have to try to kill him many times—oh, very many times!—with witch words which I have remember; but always they fail. Then, at last, I make him in wax, and I put a needle through his heart; and I kill him very quickly."

It was as clear as daylight, even to Randolph, that the woman was innocent. Her little harmless magic was the pathetic effort of a child to kill a dragon. He hesitated a moment before he spoke, and then he decided like the gentleman he was. If it helped the child to believe that her enchanted straw had slain the monster—well, he would let her believe it.

"And now, sir, may I go?"

Randolph looked at the woman in a sort of wonder.

"Are you not afraid," he said, "of the night and the mountains, and the long road?"

"Oh no, sir," she replied simply. "The good God will be everywhere now."

It was an awful commentary on the dead man—that this strange half-child believed that all the evil in the world had gone out with him; that now that he was dead, the sunlight of heaven would fill every nook and corner.

It was not a faith that either of the two men wished to shatter, and they let her go. It would be daylight presently and the road through the mountains to the Chesapeake was open.

Randolph came back to the fireside after he had helped her into the saddle, and sat down. He tapped on the hearth for some time idly with the iron poker; and then finally he spoke.

"This is the strangest thing that ever happened," he said. "Here's a mad old preacher who thinks that he killed Doomdorf with fire from Heaven, like Elijah the Tishbite; and here is a simple child of a woman who thinks she killed him with a piece of magic of the Middle Ages— each as innocent of his death as I am. And, yet, by the eternal, the beast is dead!"

He drummed on the hearth with the poker, lifting it up and letting it drop through the hollow of his fingers.

"Somebody shot Doomdorf. But who? And how did he get into and out of that shut-up room? The assassin that killed Doomdorf must have gotten into the room to kill him. Now, how did he get in?" He spoke as to himself; but my uncle sitting across the hearth replied:

"Through the window."

"Through the window!" echoed Randolph. "Why, man, you yourself showed me that the window had not been opened, and the precipice below it a fly could hardly climb. Do you tell me now that the window was opened?"

"No," said Abner, "it was never opened."

Randolph got on his feet.

"Abner," he cried, "are you saying that the one who killed Doomdorf climbed the sheer wall and got in through a closed window, without disturbing the dust or the cobwebs on the window frame?"

My uncle looked Randolph in the face.

"The murderer of Doomdorf did even more," he said. "That assassin not only climbed the face of that precipice and got in through the closed window, but he shot Doomdorf to death and got out again through the closed window without leaving a single track or trace behind, and without disturbing a grain of dust or a thread of a cobweb."

Randolph swore a great oath.

"The thing is impossible!" he cried. "Men are not killed today in Virginia by black art or a curse of God."

"By black art, no," replied Abner; "but by the curse of God, yes. I think they are."

Randolph drove his clenched right hand into the palm of his left.

"By the eternal!" he cried. "I would like to see the assassin who could do a murder like this, whether he be an imp from the pit or an angel out of Heaven."

"Very well," replied Abner, undisturbed. "When he comes back tomorrow I will show you the assassin who killed Doomdorf."

When day broke they dug a grave and buried the dead man against the mountain among his peach trees. It was noon when that work was ended. Abner threw down his spade and looked up at the sun.

"Randolph," he said, "let us go and lay an ambush for this assassin. He is on the way here."

And it was a strange ambush that he laid. When they were come again into the chamber where Doomdorf died he bolted the door; then he loaded the fowling piece and put it carefully back on its rack against the wall. After that he did another curious thing: He took the blood-stained coat, which they had stripped off the dead man when they had prepared his body for the earth, put a pillow in it and laid it on the couch precisely where Doomdorf had slept. And while he did these things Randolph stood in wonder and Abner talked:

"Look you, Randolph. . . . We will trick the murderer. . . . We will catch him in the act."

Then he went over and took the puzzled justice by the arm.

"Watch!" he said. "The assassin is coming along the wall!"

But Randolph heard nothing, saw nothing. Only the sun entered. Abner's hand tightened on his arm.

"It is here! Look!" And he pointed to the wall.

Randolph, following the extended finger, saw a tiny brilliant disk of light moving slowly up the wall toward the lock of the fowling piece. Abner's hand became a vise and his voice rang as over metal.

"'He that killeth with the sword must be killed with the sword,' It

is the water bottle, full of Doomdorf's liquid, focusing the sun. . . . .
And look, Randolph, how Bronson's prayer was answered!"

The tiny disk of light traveled on the plate of the lock.

"It is fire from heaven!"

The words rang above the roar of the fowling piece, and Randolph saw the dead man's coat leap up on the couch, riddled by the shot. The gun, in its natural position on the rack, pointed to the couch standing at the end of the chamber, beyond the offset of the wall, and the focused sun had exploded the percussion cap.

Randolph made a great gesture, with his arm extended.

"It is a world," he said, "filled with the mysterious joinder of accident!"

"It is a world," replied Abner, "filled with the mysterious justice of God!"

THE COIN
OF DIONYSIUS

By Ernest Bramah

Ernest Bramah (1868–1942) was born Ernest Brammah Smith in
Manchester, England. He left school early to try his hand at agriculture,
but his efforts produced nothing salable except a book about his experiences called English Farming and Why I Turned It Up. He next
became a journalist, working in editorial positions on a number of
magazines before deciding to devote full time to free-lance writing. In his
own day, he was best known as the author of several books about Kai
Lung, a professional storyteller in Old China whose seemingly authentic
adventures suggested to some readers that Bramah had spent time in the
Orient. The writer's retiring and finally reclusive life, however, has
never been well documented, and in later years there were even rumors
that his name was merely the pseudonym of another even better known
literary figure. Bramah is particularly remembered today as the creator of
Max Carrados, the first blind fictional detective, of whose affliction the
author once remarked that it "impelled him to develop those senses which
in most of us lie half dormant and practically unused. Thus you will
understand that while he may be at a disadvantage when you are at an
advantage, he is at an advantage when you are at a disadvantage." An
elegance of style and deft irony are features of the Carrados stories, three
collections of which were published over a period of thirteen years. "The
Coin of Dionysius" is from the first of these volumes, Max Carrados
(1914), and reflects the author's scholarly interest in numismatics. Best
Max Carrados Detective Stories was issued in 1972 by Dover.

It was eight o'clock at night and raining, scarcely a time when a business so limited in its clientele as that of a coin dealer could hope to attract any customer, but a light was still showing in the small shop that bore over its window the name of Baxter, and in the even smaller office at the back the proprietor himself sat reading the latest *Pall Mall*. His enterprise seemed to be justified, for presently the door bell gave its announcement, and throwing down his paper Mr. Baxter went forward.

As a matter of fact the dealer had been expecting someone and his manner as he passed into the shop was unmistakably suggestive of a caller of importance. But at the first glance towards his visitor the excess of deference melted out of his bearing, leaving the urbane, self-possessed shopman in the presence of the casual customer.

"Mr. Baxter, I think?" said the latter. He had laid aside his dripping umbrella and was unbuttoning overcoat and coat to reach an inner pocket. "You hardly remember me, I suppose? Mr. Carlyle—two years ago I took up a case for you——"

"To be sure. Mr. Carlyle, the private detective——"

"Inquiry agent," corrected Mr. Carlyle precisely.

"Well," smiled Mr. Baxter, "for that matter I am a coin dealer and not an antiquarian or a numismatist. Is there anything in that way that I can do for you?"

"Yes," replied his visitor; "it is my turn to consult you." He had taken a small wash-leather bag from the inner pocket and now turned something carefully out upon the counter. "What can you tell me about that?"

The dealer gave the coin a moment's scrutiny.

"There is no question about this," he replied. "It is a Sicilian tetradrachm of Dionysius."

"Yes, I know that—I have it on the label out of the cabinet. I can tell you further that it's supposed to be one that Lord Seastoke gave two hundred and fifty pounds for at the Brice sale in '94."

"It seems to me that you can tell me more about it than I can tell you," remarked Mr. Baxter. "What is it that you really want to know?"

"I want to know," replied Mr. Carlyle, "whether it is genuine or not."

"Has any doubt been cast upon it?"

"Certain circumstances raised a suspicion—that is all."

The dealer took another look at the tetradrachm through his magnifying glass, holding it by the edge with the careful touch of an expert.

Reprinted from *Max Carrados* by Ernest Bramah. Used with permission of the Estate of the late Ernest Bramah.

Then he shook his head slowly in a confession of ignorance.

"Of course I could make a guess——"

"No, don't," interrupted Mr. Carlyle hastily. "An arrest hangs on it and nothing short of certainty is any good to me."

"Is that so, Mr. Carlyle?" said Mr. Baxter, with increased interest. "Well, to be quite candid, the thing is out of my line. Now if it was a rare Saxon penny or a doubtful noble I'd stake my reputation on my opinion, but I do very little in the classical series."

Mr. Carlyle did not attempt to conceal his disappointment as he returned the coin to the bag and replaced the bag in the inner pocket.

"I had been relying on you," he grumbled reproachfully. "Where on earth am I to go now?"

"There is always the British Museum."

"Ah, to be sure, thanks. But will anyone who can tell me be there now?"

"Now? No fear!" replied Mr. Baxter. "Go round in the morning——"

"But I must know to-night," explained the visitor, reduced to despair again. "To-morrow will be too late for the purpose."

Mr. Baxter did not hold out much encouragement in the circumstances.

"You can scarcely expect to find anyone at business now," he remarked. "I should have been gone these two hours myself only I happened to have an appointment with an American millionaire who fixed his own time." Something indistinguishable from a wink slid off Mr. Baxter's right eye. "Offmunson he's called, and a bright young pedigree-hunter has traced his descent from Offa, King of Mercia. So he—quite naturally—wants a set of Offas as a sort of collateral proof."

"Very interesting," murmured Mr. Carlyle, fidgeting with his watch. "I should love an hour's chat with you about your millionaire customers—some other time. Just now—look here, Baxter, can't you give me a line of introduction to some dealer in this sort of thing who happens to live in town? You must know dozens of experts."

"Why, bless my soul, Mr. Carlyle, I don't know a man of them away from his business," said Mr. Baxter, staring. "They may live in Park Lane or they may live in Petticoat Lane for all I know. Besides, there aren't so many experts as you seem to imagine. And the two best will very likely quarrel over it. You've had to do with 'expert witness,' I suppose?"

"I don't want a witness; there will be no need to give evidence. All I want is an absolutely authoritative pronouncement that I can act on. Is there no one who can really say whether the thing is genuine or not?"

Mr. Baxter's meaning silence became cynical in its implication as he continued to look at his visitor across the counter. Then he relaxed.

"Stay a bit; there is a man—an amateur—I remember hearing wonderful things about some time ago. They say he really does know."

"There you are," explained Mr. Carlyle, much relieved. "There always is someone. Who is he?"

"Funny name," replied Baxter. "Something Wynn or Wynn something." He craned his neck to catch sight of an important motor-car that was drawing to the kerb before his window. "Wynn Carrados! You'll excuse me now, Mr. Carlyle, won't you? This looks like Mr. Offmunson."

Mr. Carlyle hastily scribbled the name down on his cuff.

"Wynn Carrados, right. Where does he live?"

"Haven't the remotest idea," replied Baxter, referring the arrangement of his tie to the judgment of the wall mirror. "I have never seen the man myself. Now, Mr. Carlyle, I'm sorry I can't do any more for you. You won't mind, will you?"

Mr. Carlyle could not pretend to misunderstand. He enjoyed the distinction of holding open the door for the transatlantic representative of the line of Offa as he went out, and then made his way through the muddy streets back to his office. There was only one way of tracing a private individual at such short notice—through the pages of the directories, and the gentleman did not flatter himself by a very high estimate of his chances.

Fortune favoured him, however. He very soon discovered a Wynn Carrados living at Richmond, and, better still, further search failed to unearth another. There was, apparently, only one householder at all events of that name in the neighbourhood of London. He jotted down the address and set out for Richmond.

The house was some distance from the station, Mr. Carlyle learned. He took a taxicab and drove, dismissing the vehicle at the gate. He prided himself on his power of observation and the accuracy of the deductions which resulted from it—a detail of his business. "It's nothing more than using one's eyes and putting two and two together," he would modestly declare, when he wished to be deprecatory rather than impressive, and by the time he had reached the front door of "The Turrets" he had formed some opinion of the position and tastes of the man who lived there.

A man-servant admitted Mr. Carlyle and took in his card—his private card with the bare request for an interview that would not detain Mr. Carrados for ten minutes. Luck still favoured him; Mr. Carrados was at home and would see him at once. The servant, the hall through which they passed, and the room into which he was shown, all contributed something to the deductions which the quietly observant gentleman was half unconsciously recording.

"Mr. Carlyle," announced the servant.

The room was a library or study. The only occupant, a man of about Carlyle's own age, had been using a typewriter up to the moment of his visitor's entrance. He now turned and stood up with an expression of formal courtesy.

"It's very good of you to see me at this hour," apologised the caller.

The conventional expression of Mr. Carrados's face changed a little.

"Surely my man has got your name wrong?" he explained. "Isn't it Louis Calling?"

The visitor stopped short and his agreeable smile gave place to a sudden flash of anger or annoyance.

"No, sir," he replied stiffly. "My name is on the card which you have before you."

"I beg your pardon," said Mr. Carrados, with perfect good-humour. "I hadn't seen it. But I used to know a Calling some years ago—at St. Michael's."

"St. Michael's!" Mr. Carlyle's features underwent another change, no less instant and sweeping than before. "St. Michael's! Wynn Carrados? Good heavens! it isn't Max Wynn—old 'Winning' Wynn?"

"A little older and a little fatter—yes, replied Carrados. "I have changed my name you see."

"Extraordinary thing meeting like this," said his visitor, dropping into a chair and staring hard at Mr. Carrados. "I have changed more than my name. How did you recognize me?"

"The voice," replied Carrados. "It took me back to that little smoke-dried attic den of yours.where we——"

"My God!" exclaimed Carylyle bitterly, "don't remind me of what we were going to do in those days." He looked round the well-furnished, handsome room and recalled the other signs of wealth that he had noticed. "At all events, you seem fairly comfortable, Wynn."

"I am alternately envied and pitied," replied Carrados, with a placid tolerance of circumstance that seemed characteristic of him. "Still, as you say, I am fairly comfortable."

"Envied, I can understand. But why are you pitied?"

"Because I am blind," was the tranquil reply.

"Blind!" exclaimed Mr. Carlyle, using his own eyes superlatively. "Do you mean—literally blind?"

"Literally.   . . I was riding along a bridle-path through a wood about a dozen years ago with a friend. He was in front. At one point a twig sprang back—you know how easily a thing like that happens. It just flicked my eye—nothing to think twice about."

"And that blinded you?"

"Yes, ultimately. It's called amaurosis."

"I can scarcely believe it. You seem so sure and self-reliant. Your eyes are full of expression—only a little quieter than they used to be. I believe you were typing when I came. . . . Aren't you having me?"

"You miss the dog and the stick?" smiled Carrados. "No; it's a fact."

"What an awful affliction for you, Max. You were always such an impulsive, reckless sort of fellow—never quiet. You must miss such a fearful lot."

"Has anyone else recognized you?" asked Carrados quietly.

"Ah, that was the voice, you said," replied Carlyle.

"Yes; but other people heard the voice as well. Only I had no blundering, self-confident eyes to be hoodwinked."

"That's a rum way of putting it," said Carlyle. "Are your ears never hoodwinked, may I ask?"

"Not now. Nor my fingers. Nor any of my other senses that have to look out for themselves."

"Well, well," murmured Mr. Carlyle, cut short in his sympathetic emotions. "I'm glad you take it so well. Of course, if you find it an advantage to be blind, old man——" He stopped and reddened. "I beg your pardon," he concluded stiffly.

"Not an advantage perhaps," replied the other thoughtfully. "Still it has compensations that one might not think of. A new world to explore, new experiences, new powers awakening; strange new perceptions; life in the fourth dimension. But why do you beg my pardon, Louis?"

"I am an ex-solicitor, struck off in connexion with the falsifying of a trust account, Mr. Carrados," replied Carlyle, rising.

"Sit down, Louis," said Carrados suavely. His face, even his incredibly living eyes, beamed placid good-nature. "The chair on which you will sit, the roof above you, all the comfortable surroundings to which you have so amiably alluded, are the direct result of falsifying a trust account. But do I call you 'Mr. Carlyle' in consequence? Certainly not, Louis."

"I did not falsify the account," cried Carlyle hotly. He sat down however, and added more quietly: "But why do I tell you all this? I have never spoken of it before."

"Blindness invites confidence," replied Carrados. "We are out of the running—human rivalry ceases to exist. Besides, why shouldn't you? In my case the account *was* falsified."

"Of course that's all bunkum, Max" commented Carlyle. "Still, I appreciate your motive."

"Practically everything I possess was left to me by an American cousin, on the condition that I took the name of Carrados. He made his fortune by an ingenious conspiracy of doctoring the crop reports and unloading favourably in consequence. And I need hardly remind you that the receiver is equally guilty with the thief."

"But twice as safe. I know something of that, Max. . . . Have you any idea what my business is?"

"You shall tell me," replied Carrados.

"I run a private inquiry agency. When I lost my profession I had to do something for a living. This occurred. I dropped my name, changed my appearance and opened an office. I knew the legal side down to the ground and I got a retired Scotland Yard man to organize the outside work."

"Excellent!" cried Carrados. "Do you unearth many murders?"

"No," admitted Mr. Carlyle; "our business lies mostly on the conventional lines among divorce and defalcation."

"That's a pity," remarked Carrados. "Do you know, Louis, I always had a secret ambition to be a detective myself. I have even thought lately that I might still be able to do something at it if the chance came my way. That makes you smile?"

"Well, certainly, the idea——"

"Yes, the idea of a blind detective—the blind tracking the alert—"

"Of course, as you say, certain facilities are no doubt quickened," Mr. Carlyle hastened to add considerately, "but, seriously, with the exception of an artist, I don't suppose there is any man who is more utterly dependent on his eyes."

Whatever opinion Carrados might have held privately, his genial exterior did not betray a shadow of dissent. For a full minute he continued to smoke as though he derived an actual visual enjoyment from the blue sprays that travelled and dispersed across the room. He had already placed before his visitor a box containing cigars of a brand which that gentleman keenly appreciated but generally regarded as unattainable, and the matter-of-fact ease and certainty with which the blind man had brought the box and put it before him had sent a questioning flicker through Carlyle's mind.

"You used to be rather fond of art yourself, Louis," he remarked presently. "Give me your opinion of my latest purchase—the bronze

235

lion on the cabinet there." Then, as Carlyle's gaze went about the room, he added quickly: "No, not that cabinet—the one on your left."

Carlyle shot a sharp glance at his host as he got up, but Carrados's expression was merely benignly complacent. Then he strolled across to the figure.

"Very nice," he admitted. "Late Flemish, isn't it?"

"No, It is a copy of Vidal's 'Roaring Lion.'"

"Vidal?"

"A French artist." The voice became indescribably flat. "He, also, had the misfortune to be blind, by the way."

"You old humbug, Max!" shrieked Carlyle, "you've been thinking that out for the last five minutes." Then the unfortunate man bit his lip and turned his back towards his host.

"Do you remember how we used to pile it up on that obtuse ass Sanders, and then roast him?" asked Carrados, ignoring the half-smothered exclamation with which the other man had recalled himself.

"Yes," replied Carlyle quietly. "This is very good," he continued, addressing himself to the bronze again. "How ever did he do it?"

"With his hands."

"Naturally. But, I mean, how did he study his model?"

"Also with his hands. He called it 'seeing near.'"

"Even with a lion—handled it?"

"In such cases he required the services of a keeper, who brought the animal to bay while Vidal exercised his own particular gifts. . . . You don't feel inclined to put me on the track of a mystery, Louis?"

Unable to regard this request as anything but one of old Max's unquenchable pleasantries, Mr. Carlyle was on the point of making a suitable reply when a sudden thought caused him to smile knowingly. Up to that point, he had, indeed, completely forgotten the object of his visit. Now that he remembered the doubtful Dionysius and Baxter's recommendation he immediately assumed that some mistake had been made. Either Max was not the Wynn Carrados he had been seeking or else the dealer had been misinformed; for although his host was wonderfully expert in the face of his misfortune, it was inconceivable that he could decide the genuineness of a coin without seeing it. The opportunity seemed a good one of getting even with Carrados by taking him at his word.

"Yes," he accordingly replied, with crisp deliberation, as he re-crossed the room; "yes, I will, Max. Here is the clue to what seems to be a rather remarkable fraud." He put the tetradrachm into his host's hand. "What do you make of it?"

For a few seconds Carrados handled the piece with the delicate manipulation of his finger-tips while Carlyle looked on with a self-appreciative grin. Then with equal gravity the blind man weighed the coin in the balance of his hand. Finally he touched it with his tongue.

"Well?" demanded the other.

"Of course I have not much to go on, and if I was more fully in your confidence I might come to another conclusion——"

"Yes, yes," interposed Carlyle, with amused encouragement.

"Then I should advise you to arrest the parlourmaid, Nina Brun, communicate with the police authorities of Padua for particulars of the career of Helene Brunesi, and suggest to Lord Seastoke that he should return to London to see what further depredations have been made in his cabinet."

Mr. Carlyle's groping hand sought and found a chair, on to which he dropped blankly. His eyes were unable to detach themselves for a single moment from the very ordinary spectacle of Mr. Carrados's mildly benevolent face, while the sterilized ghost of his now forgotten amusement still lingered about his features.

"Good heavens!" he managed to articulate, "how do you know?"

"Isn't that what you wanted of me?" asked Carrados suavely.

"Don't humbug, Max," said Carlyle severely. "This is no joke." An undefined mistrust of his own powers suddenly possessed him in the presence of this mystery. "How do you come to know of Nina Brun and Lord Seastoke?"

"You are a detective, Louis," replied Carrados. "How does one know these things? By using one's eyes and putting two and two together."

Carlyle groaned and flung out an arm petulantly.

"Is it all bunkum, Max? Do you really see all the time—though that doesn't go very far towards explaining it."

"Like Vidal, I see very well—at close quarters," replied Carrados, lightly running a forefinger along the inscription on the tetradrachm. "For longer range I keep another pair of eyes. Would you like to test them?"

Mr. Carlyle's assent was not very gracious; it was, in fact, faintly sulky. He was suffering the annoyance of feeling distinctly unimpressive in his own department; but he was also curious.

"The bell is just behind you, if you don't mind," said his host. "Parkinson will appear. You might take note of him while he is in."

The man who had admitted Mr. Carlyle proved to be Parkinson.

"This gentleman is Mr. Carlyle, Parkinson," explained Carrados the moment the man entered. "You will remember him for the future?"

Parkinson's apologetic eye swept the visitor from head to foot, but so lightly and swiftly that it conveyed to that gentleman the comparison of being very deftly dusted.

"I will endeavour to do so, sir," replied Parkinson, turning again to his master.

"I shall be at home to Mr. Carlyle whenever he calls. That is all."

"Very well, sir."

"Now, Louis," remarked Mr. Carrados briskly, when the door had closed again, "you have had a good opportunity of studying Parkinson. What is he like?"

"In what way?"

"I mean as a matter of description. I am a blind man—I haven't seen my servant for twelve years—what idea can you give me of him? I asked you to notice."

"I know you did, but your Parkinson is the sort of man who has very little about him to describe. He is the embodiment of the ordinary. His height is about average——"

"Five feet nine," murmured Carrados. "Slightly above the mean."

"Scarcely noticeably so. Clean-shaven. Medium brown hair. No particularly marked features. Dark eyes. Good teeth."

"False," interposed Carrados. "The teeth—not the statement."

"Possibly," admitted Mr. Carlyle. "I am not a dental expert and I had no opportunity of examining Mr. Parkinson's mouth in detail. But what is the drift of all this?"

"His clothes?"

"Oh, just the ordinary evening dress of a valet. There is not much room for variety in that."

"You noticed, in fact, nothing special by which Parkinson could be identified?"

"Well, he wore an unusually broad gold ring on the little finger of the left hand."

"But that is removable. And yet Parkinson has an ineradicable mole—a small one, I admit—on his chin. And you a human sleuth-hound. Oh, Louis!"

"At all events," retorted Carlyle, writhing a little under this good-humoured satire, although it was easy enough to see in it Carrados's affectionate intention—"at all events, I dare say I can give as good a description of Parkinson as he can give of me."

"That is what we are going to test. Ring the bell again."

"Seriously?"

"Quite. I am trying my eyes against yours. If I can't give you fifty out of a hundred I'll renounce my private detectorial ambition for ever."

238

"It isn't quite the same," objected Carlyle, but he rang the bell.

"Come in and close the door, Parkinson," said Carrados when the man appeared. "Don't look at Mr. Carlyle again—in fact, you had better stand with your back towards him, he won't mind. Now describe to me his appearance as you observed it."

Parkinson tendered his respectful apologies to Mr. Carlyle for the liberty he was compelled to take, by the deferential quality of his voice.

"Mr. Carlyle, sir, wears patent leather boots of about size seven and very little used. There are five buttons, but on the left boot one button—the third up—is missing, leaving loose threads and not the more usual metal fastener. Mr. Carlyle's trousers, sir, are of a dark material, a dark grey line of about a quarter of an inch width on a darker ground. The bottoms are turned permanently up and are, just now, a little muddy, if I may say so."

"Very muddy," interposed Mr. Carlyle generously. "It is a wet night, Parkinson."

"Yes, sir; very unpleasant weather. If you will allow me, sir, I will brush you in the hall. The mud is dry now, I notice. Then, sir," continued Parkinson, reverting to the business in hand, "there are dark green cashmere hose. A curb-pattern key-chain passes into the left-hand trouser pocket."

From the visitor's nether garments the photographic-eyed Parkinson proceeded to higher ground, and with increasing wonder Mr. Carlyle listened to the faithful catalogue of his possessions. His fetter-and-link albert of gold and platinum was minutely described. His spotted blue ascot, with its gentlemanly pearl scarfpin, was set forth, and the fact that the buttonhole in the left lapel of his morning coat showed signs of use was duly noted. What Parkinson saw he recorded, but he made no deductions. A handkerchief carried in the cuff of the right sleeve was simply that to him and not an indication that Mr. Carlyle was, indeed, left-handed.

But a more delicate part of Parkinson's undertaking remained. He approached it with a double cough.

"As regards Mr. Carlyle's personal appearance, sir——"

"No, enough!" cried the gentleman concerned hastily. "I am more than satisfied. You are a keen observer, Parkinson."

"I have trained myself to suit my master's requirements, sir," replied the man. He looked towards Mr. Carrados, received a nod and withdrew.

Mr. Carlyle was the first to speak.

"That man of yours would be worth five pounds a week to me, Max," he remarked thoughtfully. "But, of course——"

"I don't think that he would take it," replied Carrados, in a voice of equally detached speculation. "He suits me very well. But you have the chance of using his services—indirectly."

"You still mean that—seriously?"

"I notice in you a chronic disinclination to take me seriously, Louis. It is really—to an Englishman—almost painful. Is there something inherently comic about me or the atmosphere of The Turrets?"

"No, my friend," replied Mr. Carlyle, "but there is something essentially prosperous. That is what points to the improbable. Now what is it?"

"It might be merely a whim, but it is more than that," replied Carrados. "It is, well, partly vanity, partly *ennui*, partly"—certainly there was something more nearly tragic in his voice than comic now—"partly hope."

Mr. Carlyle was too tactful to pursue the subject.

"Those are three tolerable motives," he acquiesced. "I'll do anything you want, Max, on one condition."

"Agreed. And it is?"

"That you tell me how you knew so much of this affair." He tapped the silver coin which lay on the table near them. "I am not easily flabbergasted," he added.

"You won't believe that there is nothing to explain—that it was purely second-sight?"

"No," replied Carlyle tersely: "I won't."

"You are quite right. And yet the thing is very simple."

"They always are—when you know," soliloquised the other. "That's what makes them so confoundedly difficult when you don't."

"Here is this one then. In Padua, which seems to be regaining its old reputation as the birth place of spurious antiques, by the way, there lives an ingenious craftsman named Pietro Stelli. This simple soul, who possesses a talent not inferior to that of Cavino at his best, has for many years turned his hand to the not unprofitable occupation of forging rare Greek and Roman coins. As a collector and student of certain Greek colonials and a specialist in forgeries I have been familiar with Stelli's workmanship for years. Latterly he seems to have come under the influence of an international crook called—at the moment—Dompierre, who soon saw a way of utilizing Stelli's genius on a royal scale. Helene Brunesi, who in private life is—and really is, I believe—Madame Dompierre, readily lent her services to the enterprise."

"Quite so," nodded Mr. Carlyle, as his host paused.

"You see the whole sequence, of course?"

"Not exactly—not in detail," confessed Mr. Carlyle.

"Dompierre's idea was to gain access to some of the most celebrated cabinets of Europe and substitute Stelli's fabrications for the
genuine coins. The princely collection of rarities that he would thus
amass might be difficult to dispose of safely, but I have no doubt that he
had matured his plans. Helene, in the person of Nina Brun, an Angli-
cised French parlourmaid—a part which she fills to perfection—was to
obtain wax impressions of the most valuable pieces and to make the
exchange when the counterfeits reached her. In this way it was obviously hoped that the fraud would not come to light until long after
the real coins had been sold, and I gather that she has already done her
work successfully in general houses. Then, impressed by her excellent
references and capable manner, my housekeeper engaged her, and for a
few weeks she went about her duties here. It was fatal to this detail of
the scheme, however, that I have the misfortune to be blind. I am told
that Helene has so innocently angelic a face as to disarm suspicion, but
I was incapable of being impressed and that good material was thrown
away. But one morning my material fingers—which, of course, knew
nothing of Helene's angelic face—discovered an unfamiliar touch
about the surface of my favourite Euclideas, and, although there was
doubtless nothing to be seen, my critical sense of smell reported that
wax had been recently pressed against it. I began to make discreet
inquiries and in the meantime my cabinets went to the local bank for
safety. Helene countered by receiving a telegram from Angiers, calling
her to the death-bed of her aged mother. The aged mother succumbed;
duty compelled Helene to remain at the side of her stricken patriarchal
father, and doubtless The Turrets was written off the syndicate's operations as a bad debt."

"Very intersting," admitted Mr. Carlyle; "but at the risk of seeming obtuse"—his manner had become delicately chastened—"I must
say that I fail to trace the inevitable connexion between Nina Brun and
this particular forgery—assuming that it is a forgery."

"Set your mind at rest about that, Louis," replied Carrados. "It is a
forgery, and it is a forgery that none but Pietro Stelli could have
achieved. That is the essential connexion. Of course, there are acces-
sories. A private detective coming urgently to see me with a notable
tetradrachm in his pocket, which he announces to be the clue to a
remarkable fraud—well, really, Louis, one scarcely needs to be blind to
see through that."

"And Lord Seastoke? I suppose you happened to discover that
Nina Brun had gone there?"

"No, I cannot claim to have discovered that, or I should certainly
have warned him at once when I found out—only recently—about the

gang. As a matter of fact, the last information I had of Lord Seastoke was a line in yesterday's *Morning Post* to the effect that he was still at Cairo. But many of these pieces——" He brushed his finger almost lovingly across the vivid chariot race that embellished the reverse of the coin, and broke off to remark: "You really ought to take up the subject, Louis. You have no idea how useful it might prove to you some day."

"I really think I must," replied Carlyle grimly. "Two hundred and fifty pounds the original of this cost, I believe."

"Cheap, too; it would make five hundred pounds in New York to-day. As I was saying, many are literally unique. This gem by Kimon is—here is his signature, you see; Peter is particularly good at letter-ing—and as I handled the genuine tetradrachm about two years ago, when Lord Seastoke exhibited it at a meeting of our society in Albe-marle Street, there is nothing at all wonderful in my being able to fix the locale of your mystery. Indeed, I feel that I ought to apologize for it all being so simple."

"I think," remarked Mr. Carlyle, critically examining the loose threads on his left boot, "that the apology on that head would be more appropriate from me."

CHAPTER V

THE GOLDEN AGE

UNCLE MELEAGER'S WILL

By Dorothy L. Sayers

Dorothy Leigh Sayers (1893–1957) was born in Oxford where her father was headmaster of a school. She was a precocious and scholarly child, learning Latin at the age of seven and later graduating with high honors in medieval literature from Somerville College, Oxford, in 1915. During the next three years, she published two volumes of poetry, much of it devoted to religious subjects, and then, to earn a living, she became a copywriter for an advertising agency. At the same time she began working on a series of stylish and erudite detective stories about Lord Peter Wimsey, an eccentric aristocrat interested in rare books, music, and crime. The Peter Wimsey novels include Whose Body? *(1923),* Clouds of Witness *(1926),* Strong Poison *(1930),* Murder Must Advertise *(1933), which was based in part on the author's own experiences as a copywriter, and* The Nine Tailors *(1934). In addition there are twenty-one Peter Wimsey short stories, "The Fascinating Problem of Uncle Meleager's Will" appearing in the volume called* Lord Peter Views the Body *(1928). Dorothy Sayers also edited and prepared introductions for three highly regarded mystery story anthologies, and with Robert Eustace wrote her one non-Wimsey detective novel,* The Documents in the Case *(1930). As successful as she was with her detective fiction, the author was grateful when she no longer had to write it. "I did the Peter Wimsey books when I was young and had no money," she once remarked. "I made some money, and then stopped writing novels and began to write what I had always wanted to write." This included two books about Dante and a translation of* The Divine Comedy. *All the Peter Wimsey short stories are available in* Lord Peter *(New York: Avon/Equinox, 1972), edited by James Sandoe. For more about the author see Janet Hitchman's* Such a Strange Lady *(New York: Harper & Row, 1975).*

You look a little worried, Bunter," said his lordship kindly to his manservant. "Is there anything I can do?"

The valet's face brightened as he released his employer's grey trousers from the press.

"Perhaps your lordship could be so good as to think," he said hopefully, "of a word in seven letters with S in the middle, meaning two."

"Also," suggested Lord Peter thoughtlessly.

"I beg your lordship's pardon. T-w-o. And seven letters."

"Nonsense!" said Lord Peter. "How about that bath?"

"It should be just about ready, my lord."

Lord Peter Wimsey swung his mauve silk legs lightly over the edge of the bed and stretched appreciatively. It was a beautiful June that year. Through the open door he saw the delicate coils of steam wreathing across a shaft of yellow sunlight. Every step he took into the bathroom was a conscious act of enjoyment. In a husky light tenor he carolled a few bars of "Maman, dites-moi." Then a thought struck him, and he turned back.

"Bunter!"

"My lord?"

"No bacon this morning. Quite the wrong smell."

"I was thinking of buttered eggs, my lord."

"Excellent. Like primroses. The Beaconsfield touch," said his lordship approvingly.

His song died into a rapturous crooning as he settled into the verbena-scented water. His eyes roamed vaguely over the pale blue-and-white tiles of the bathroom walls.

Mr. Bunter had retired to the kitchen to put the coffee on the stove when the bell rang. Surprised, he hastened back to the bedroom. It was empty. With increased surprise, he realized that it must have been the bathroom bell. The words "heart-attack" formed swiftly in his mind, to be displaced by the still more alarming thought. "No soap." He opened the door almost nervously.

"Did you ring, my lord?" he demanded of Lord Peter's head, alone visible.

"Yes," said his lordship abruptly. "Ambsace."

"I beg your lordship's pardon?"

"The Fascinating Problem of Uncle Meleager's Will" from Lord Peter by Dorothy L. Sayers. Copyright 1928 by Dorothy Leigh Sayers Fleming. Reprinted by permission of Harper & Row, Publishers, Inc.

"Ambsace. Word of seven letters. Meaning two. With S in the middle. Two aces. Ambsace."

Bunter's expression became-beautified.

"Undoubtedly correct," he said, pulling a small sheet of paper from his pocket, and entering the word upon it in pencil. "I am extremely obliged to your lordship. In that case the 'indifferent cook in six letters ending with *red*' must be Alfred."

Lord Peter waved a dismissive hand.

On re-entering his bedroom, Lord Peter was astonished to see his sister Mary seated in his own particular chair and consuming his buttered eggs. He greeted her with a friendly acerbity, demanding why she should look him up at that unearthly hour.

"I'm riding with Freddy Arbuthnot," said her ladyship, "as you might see by my legs, if you were really as big a Sherlock as you make out."

"Riding," replied her brother, "I had already deduced, though I admit that Freddy's name was not writ large, to my before-breakfast eye, upon the knees of your breeches. But why this visit?"

"Well, because you were on the way," said Lady Mary, "and I'm booked up all day and I want you to come and dine at the Soviet Club with me tonight."

"Good God, Mary, why? You know I hate the place. Cooking's beastly, the men don't shave, and the conversation gets my goat. Besides, last time I went there, your friend Goyles plugged me in the shoulder. I thought you'd chucked the Soviet Club."

"It isn't me. It's Hannah Marryat."

"What, the intense young woman with the badly bobbed hair and the brogues?"

"Well, she's never been able to afford a good hairdresser. That's just what I want your help about."

"My dear child, I can't cut her hair for her. Bunter might. He can do most things."

"Silly. No. But she's got—that is, she used to have—an uncle, the very rich, curmudgeony sort, you know, who never gave anyone a penny. Well, he's dead, and they can't find his will."

"Perhaps he didn't make one."

"Oh, yes, he did. He wrote and told her so. But the nasty old thing hid it, and it can't be found."

"Is the will in her favour?"

"Yes."

"Who's the next-of-kin?"

"She and her mother are the only members of the family left."

"Well, then, she's only got to sit tight and she'll get the goods."

"No—because the horrid old man left two wills, and, if she can't find the latest one, they'll prove the first one. He explained that to her carefully."

"Oh, I see. H'm. By the way, I thought the young woman was a Socialist."

"Oh, she is. Terrifically so. One really can't help admiring her. She has done some wonderful work—"

"Yes, I dare say. But in that case I don't see why she need be so keen on getting uncle's dollars."

Mary began to chuckle.

"Ah! but that's where Uncle Meleager—"

"Uncle *what?*"

"Meleager. That's his name, Meleager Finch."

"Oh!"

"Yes—well, that's where he's been so clever. Unless she finds the new will, the old will comes into force and hands over every penny of the money to the funds of the Primrose League."

Lord Peter gave a little yelp of joy.

"Good for Uncle Meleager! But, look here, Polly, I'm a Tory, if anything. I'm certainly not a Red. Why should I help to snatch the good gold from the Primrose Leaguers and hand it over to the Third International? Uncle Meleager's a sport. I take to Uncle Meleager."

"Oh, but Peter, I really don't think she'll do that with it. Not at present, anyway. They're awfully poor, and her mother ought to have some frightfully difficult operation or something, and go and live abroad, so it really is ever so important they should get the money. And perhaps Hannah wouldn't be quite so Red if she'd ever had a bean of her own. Besides, you could make it a condition of helping her that she should go and get properly shingled at Bresil's."

"You are a very cynically-minded person," said his lordship. "However, it would be fun to have a go at Uncle M. Was he obliging enough to give any clues for finding the will?"

"He wrote a funny sort of letter, which we can't make head or tail of. Come to the club tonight and she'll show it to you."

"Right-ho! Seven o'clock do? And we could go on and see a show afterwards. Do you mind clearing out now? I'm going to get dressed."

Amid a deafening babble of voices in a low-pitched cellar, the Soviet Club meets and dines. Ethics and sociology, the latest vortices of the Whirligig school of verse, combine with the smoke of countless cigarettes to produce an inspissated atmosphere, through which flat, angular mural paintings dimly lower upon the revellers. There is painfully little room for the elbows, or indeed for any part of one's body. Lord Peter—his feet curled under his chair to avoid the stray kicks of the heavy brogues opposite him—was acutely conscious of an unbecoming attitude and an over-heated feeling about the head. He found it difficult to get any response from Hannah Marryat. Under her heavy, ill-cut fringe her dark eyes gloomed somberly at him. At the same time he received a strong impression of something enormously vital. He had a sudden fancy that if she were set free from self-defensiveness and the importance of being earnest, she would exhbit unexpected powers of enjoyment. He was interested, but oppressed. Mary, to his great relief, suggested that they should have their coffee upstairs.

They found a quiet corner with comfortable chairs.

"Well, now," said Mary encouragingly.

"Of course you understand," said Miss Marryat mournfully, "that if it were not for the monstrous injustice of Uncle Meleager's other will, and mother being so ill, I shouldn't take any steps. But when there is £250,000, and the prospect of doing real good with it—"

"Naturally," said Lord Peter, "it isn't the money you care about, as the dear old bromide says, it's the principle of the thing. Right you are! Now supposin' we have a look at Uncle Meleager's letter."

Miss Marryat rummaged in a very large handbag and passed the paper over.

This was Uncle Meleager's letter, dated from Siena twelve months previously.

My dear Hannah, When I die—which I propose to do at my own convenience and not at that of my family—you will at last discover my monetary worth. It is, of course, considerably less than you had hoped, and quite fails, I assure you, adequately to represent my actual worth in the eyes of the discerning. I made my will yesterday, leaving the entire sum, such as it is, to the Primrose League—a body quite as fatuous as any other in our preposterous state, but which has the advantage of being peculiarly obnoxious to yourself. This will will be found in the safe in the library.

I am not, however, unmindful of the fact that your mother is my sister, and you and she my only surviving relatives. I shall accordingly amuse myself by drawing up today a second will, superseding the other and leaving the money to you.

I have always held that woman is a frivolous animal. A woman who pretends to be serious is wasting her time and spoiling her appearance. I consider that you have wasted your time to a really shocking extent. Accordingly, I intend to conceal this will, and that in such a manner that you will certainly never find it unless by the exercise of a sustained frivolity.

I hope you will contrive to be frivolous enough to become the heiress of your affectionate

Uncle Meleager

"Couldn't we use that letter as proof of the testator's intention, and fight the will?" asked Mary anxiously.

"'Fraid not," said Lord Peter. "You see, there's no evidence here that the will was ever actually drawn up. Though I suppose we could find the witnesses."

"We've tried," said Miss Marryat, "but, as you see, Uncle Meleager was travelling abroad at the time, and he probably got some obscure people in some obscure Italian town to witness it for him. We advertised, but got no answer."

"H'm. Uncle Meleager doesn't seem to have left things to chance. And, anyhow, wills are queer things, and so are the probate and divorce wallahs. Obviously the thing to do is to find the other will. Did the clues he speaks of turn up among his papers?"

"We hunted through everything. And, of course, we had the whole house searched from top to bottom for the will. But it was quite useless."

"You've not destroyed anything, of course. Who were the executors of the Primrose League Will?"

"Mother and Mr. Sands, Uncle Meleager's solicitor. The will left mother a silver teapot for her trouble."

"I like Uncle Meleager more and more. Anyhow, he did the sporting thing. I'm beginnin' to enjoy this case like anything. Where did Uncle Meleager hang out?"

"It's an old house down at Dorking. It's rather quaint. Somebody had a fancy to build a little Roman villa sort of thing there, with a veranda behind, with columns and a pond in the front hall, and statues. It's very decent there just now, though it's awfully cold in the winter, with all those stone floors and stone stairs and the sky light over the hall! Mother said perhaps you would be very kind and come down and have a look at it."

"I'd simply love to. Can we start tomorrow? I promise you we'll be frivolous enough to please even Uncle Meleager, if you'll do your bit, Miss Marryat. Won't we, Mary?"

"Rather! And, I say, hadn't we better be moving if we're going to the Pallambra?"

"I never go to music halls," said Miss Marryat ungraciously.

"Oh, but you must come tonight," said his lordship persuasively. "It's so frivolous. Just think how it would please Uncle Meleager."

Accordingly, the next day found the party, including the indispensable Mr. Bunter, assembled at Uncle Meleager's house. Pending the settlement of the will question, there had seemed every reason why

Mr. Finch's executrix and next-of-kin should live in the house, thus providing every facility for what Lord Peter called the "Treasures hunt." After being introduced to Mrs. Marryat, who was an invalid and remained in her room, Lady Mary and her brother were shown over the house by Miss Marryat, who explained to them how carefully the search had been conducted. Every paper had been examined, every book in the library scrutinized page by page, the walls and chimneys tapped for hiding-places, the boards taken up, and so forth, but with no result.

"Y'know," said his lordship, "I'm sure you've been going the wrong way to work. My idea is, old Uncle Meleager was a man of his word. If he said frivolous, he meant really frivolous. Something beastly silly. I wonder what it was."

He was still wondering when he went up to dress. Bunter was putting studs in his shirt. Lord Peter gazed thoughtfully at him, and then inquired:

"Are any of Mr. Finch's old staff still here?"

"Yes, my lord. The cook and the housekeeper. Wonderful old gentleman they say he was, too. Eighty-three, but as up to date as you please. Had his wireless in his bedroom, and enjoyed the Savoy bands every night of his life. Followed his politics, and was always ready with the details of the latest big law-cases. If a young lady came to see him, he'd like to see she had her hair shingled and the latest style in fashions. They say he took up crosswords as soon as they came in, and was remarkably quick at solving them, my lord, and inventing them. Took a ten-pound prize in the *Daily Yell* for one, and was wonderfully pleased to get it, they say, my lord, rich as he was."

"Indeed."

"Yes, my lord. He was a great man for acrostics before that, I understood them to say, but, when crosswords came in, he threw away his acrostics and said he liked the new game better. Wonderfully adaptable, if I may say so, he seems to have been for an old gentleman."

"Was he, by Jove?" said his lordship absently, and then, with sudden energy:

"Bunter, I'd like to double your salary, but I suppose you'd take it as an insult."

The conversation bore fruit at dinner.

"What," inquired his lordship, "happened to Uncle Meleager's crosswords?"

"Crosswords?" said Hannah Marryat, knitting her heavy brows. "Oh, those puzzle things! Poor old man, he went mad over them. He had every newspaper sent him, and in his last illness he'd be trying to fill the wretched things in. It was worse than his acrostics and his

250

jig-saw puzzles. Poor old creature, he must have been senile, I'm afraid. Of course, we looked through them, but there wasn't anything there. We put them all in the attic."

"The attic for me," said Lord Peter.

"And for me," said Mary. "I don't believe there was anything senile about Uncle Meleager."

The evening was warm, and they had dined in the little viridarium at the back of the house, with its tall vases and hanging baskets of flowers and little marble statues.

"Is there an attic here?" said Peter. "It seems such a—well, such an un-Attic thing to have in a house like this."

"It's just a horrid poky little hole over the porch," said Miss Marryat, rising and leading the way. "Don't tumble into the pond, will you? It's a great nuisance having it there, especially at night. I always tell them to leave a light on."

Lord Peter glanced into the miniature impluvium, with its tiling of red, white, and black marble.

"That's not a very classic design," he observed.

"No. Uncle Meleager used to complain about it and say he must have it altered. There was a proper one once, I believe, but it got damaged, and the man before Uncle Meleager had it replaced by some local idiot. He built three bay windows out of the dining-room at the same time, which made it very much lighter and pleasanter, of course, but it looks awful. Now, this tiling is all right; uncle put that in himself."

She pointed to a mosaic dog at the threshold with the motto, "Cave canem," and Lord Peter recognized it as a copy of a Pompeian original.

A narrow stair brought them to the "attic," where the Wimseys flung themselves with enthusiasm upon a huge heap of dusty old newspapers and manuscripts. The latter seemed the likelier field, so they started with them. They consisted of a quantity of cross-words in manuscript—presumably the children of Uncle Meleager's own brain. The square, the list of definitions, and the solution were in every case neatly pinned together. Some (early efforts, no doubt) were childishly simple, but others were difficult, with allusive or punning clues; some of the ordinary newspaper type, others in the form of rhymed distichs. They scrutinized the solutions closely, and searched the definitions for acrostics or hidden words, unsuccessfully for a long time.

"This one's a funny one," said Mary, "nothing seems to fit. Oh! It's two pinned together. No, it isn't—yes, it is—it's only been pinned up wrong. Peter, have you seen the puzzle belonging to these clues anywhere?"

"What one's that?"

"Well, it's numbered rather funnily, with Roman and Arabic numerals, and it starts off with a thing that hasn't got any numbers at all:

'Truth, poor girl, was nobody's daughter;
She took off her clothes and jumped into the water.'"

"Frivolous old wretch!" said Miss Marryat.

"Friv—here, gimme that!" cried Lord Peter. "Look here, I say, Miss Marryat, you oughtn't to have overlooked this."

"I thought it just belonged to that other square."

"Not it. It's different. I believe it's our thing. Listen:

'Your expectation to be rich
Here will reach its highest pitch.'

That's one for you, Miss Marryat. Mary, hunt about. We *must* find the square that belongs to this."

But, though they turned everything upside-down, they could find no square with Roman and Arabic numerals.

"Hang it all!" said Peter, "it must be made to fit one of these others. Look! I know what he's done. He's just taken a fifteen-letter square, and numbered it with Roman figures one way and Arabic the other. I bet it fits into that one it was pinned up with."

But the one it was pinned up with turned out to have only thirteen squares.

"Dash it all," said his lordship, "we'll have to carry the whole lot down, and work away at it till we find the one it *does* fit."

He snatched up a great bundle of newspapers, and led the way out. The others followed, each with an armful. The search had taken some time, and the atrium was in semi-darkness.

"Where shall I take them?" asked Lord Peter, calling back over his shoulder.

"Hi!" cried Mary; and, "Look where you're going!" cried her friend.

They were too late. A splash and a flounder proclaimed that Lord Peter had walked, like Johnny Head-in-Air, over the edge of the impluvium, papers and all.

"You ass!" said Mary.

His lordship scrambled out, spluttering, and Hannah Marryat suddenly burst out into the first laugh Peter had ever heard her give.

"Truth, they say, was nobody's daughter;
She took off her clothes and fell into the water,"'

she proclaimed.

"Well, I couldn't take my clothes off with you here, could I?" grumbled Lord Peter. "We'll have to fish out the papers. I'm afraid they've got a bit damp."

Miss Marryat turned on the lights, and they started to clear the basin.

"Truth, poor girl—" began Lord Peter, and suddenly, with a little shriek, began to dance on the marble edge of the impluvium.

"One, two, three, four, five, six—"

"Quite, quite demented," said Mary. "How shall I break it to mother?"

"Thirteen, fourteen, *fifteen!*" cried his lordship, and sat down, suddenly and damply, exhausted by his own excitement.

"Feeling better?" asked his sister acidly.

"I'm well. I'm all right. Everything's all right. I *love* Uncle Meleager. Fifteen squares each way. Look at it. *Look* at it. The truth's in the water. Didn't he say so? Oh, frabjous day! Calloo! callay! I chortle. Mary, what became of those definitions?"

"They're in your pocket, all damp," said Mary.

Lord Peter snatched them out hurriedly.

"It's all right, they haven't run," he said. "Oh, *darling* Uncle Meleager. Can you drain the impluvium, Miss Marryat, and find a bit of charcoal. Then I'll get some dry clothes on and we'll get down to it. Don't you see? *There's* your missing crossword square—on the floor of the impluvium!"

It took, however, some time to get the basin emptied, and it was not till next morning that the party, armed with sticks of charcoal, squatted down in the empty impluvium to fill in Uncle Meleager's crossword on the marble tiles. Their first difficulty was to decide whether the red squares counted as stops or had to be filled in, but after a few definitions had been solved, the construction of the puzzle grew apace. The investigators grew steadily hotter and more thickly covered with charcoal, while the attentive Mr. Bunter hurried to and fro between the atrium and the library, and the dictionaries piled upon the edge of the impluvium.

Here was Uncle Meleager's crossword square:

Truth, poor girl, was nobody's daughter;
She took off her clothes and jumped into the water.

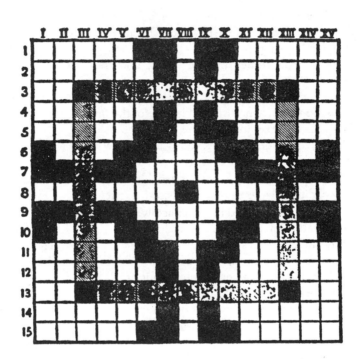

ACROSS

I.1   Foolish or wise, yet one remains alone,
'Twixt Strength and Justice on a heavenly throne.

XI.1   O to what ears the chink of gold was sweet;
The greed for treasure brought him but defeat.

"That's a hint to us," said Lord Peter.

I.2   One drop of vinegar to two of oil
Dresses this curly head sprung from the soil.

X.2	Nothing itself, it needs but little more
	To be that nothingness the Preacher saw.
I.3	Dusty though my fellows be,
	We are a kingly company.
IV.3	Have your own will, though here, I hold,
	The new is *not* a patch upon the old.
XIV.3	Any loud cry could do as well,
	Or so the poet's verses tell.
I.4	This is the most unkindest cut of all,
	Except your skill be mathematical.
X.4	Little and hid from mortal sight.
	I darkly work to make all light.
I.5	The need for this (like that it's cut off short)
	The building of a tower to humans taught.
XI.5	'More than mind discloses and more than men believe'
	(A definition by a man whom Pussyfoot doth grieve).
II.6	Backward observe her turn her way,
	The way of wisdom, wise men say.
VII.6	Grew long ago by river's edge
	Where grows today the common sedge.
XII.6	One of three by which, they say,
	You'll know the Cornishmen alway.
VI.7	Blow upon blow; five more the vanquished Roman shows
	And if the foot slip one, on crippled feet one goes.
I.8	By this Jew's work the whole we find,
	In a glass clearly, darkly in the mind.
IX.8	Little by little see it grow
	Till cut off short by hammer-blow.
VI.9	Watch him go, heel and toe,
	Across the wide Karroo!
II.10	In expectation to be rich
	Here you reach the highest pitch.
VII.10	Of this, concerning nothing, much—
	Too often do we hear of such!
XII.10	O'er land and sea, passing on deadly wings,
	Pain to the strong, to weaklings death it brings.
I.11	Requests like these, however long they be,
	Stop just too soon for common courtesy.
XI.11	Caesar, the living dead salute thee here,
	Facing for thy delight tooth, claw, and spear.
I.12	One word had served, but he in ranting vein
	'Lend me your ears' must mouth o'er Caesar slain.

X.12   Helical circumvolution
             Adumbrates correct solution.
I.13   One that works for Irish men
             Both by word and deed and pen.

"That's an easy one," said Miss Marryat.

IV.13   Seven out of twelve this number makes complete
             As the sun journeys on from seat to seat.
XIV.13   My brothers play with planets; Cicero,
             Master of words, my master is below.
I.14   Free of her jesses let the falcon fly,
             With sight undimmed into the azure sky.
X.14   And so you dine with Borgia? Let me lend
             You this as a precaution, my poor friend.
I.15   Friendship carried to excess
             Got him in a horrid mess.
XI.15   Smooth and elastic and, I guess
             The dearest treasure you possess.

DOWN

1.I   If step by step the Steppes you wander through
             Many of those in this, of these in those you'll view.

"Bunter," said Lord Peter, "bring me a whisky-and-soda!"

11.I   If me without my head you do,
             Then generously my head renew,
             Or put it to my hinder end—
             Your cheer it shall not mar nor mend.
1.II   Quietly, quietly, 'twixt edge and edge,
             Do this unto the thin end of the wedge.
10.II   'Something that hath a reference to my state?'
             Just as you like, it shall be written straight.
1.III   When all is read, then give the world its due,
             And never need the world read this of you.

"That's a comfort," said Lady Mary. "It shows we're on the right lines."

4.III   Sing *Nunc Dimittis* and *Magnificat*—
             But look a little farther back than that.
14.III   Here in brief epitome
             Attribute of royalty.

1.IV   Lo! at a glance
       The Spanish gipsy and her dance.
10.IV Bring me skin and a needle or a stick—
       A needle does it slowly, a stick does it quick.
1.V   It was a brazen business when
       King Phalaris made these for men.
11.V   This king (of whom not much is known)
       By Heaven's mercy was o'erthrown.
2.VI   'Bid συ και ημ συ farewell?' Nay, in this
       The sterner Roman stands by that which is.
7.VI   This the termination is
       Of many minds' activities.
12.VI I mingle on Norwegian shore,
       With ebbing water's backward roar.
6.VIII I stand a ladder to renown,
       Set 'twixt the stars and Milan town.
1.VIII Highest and lowliest both to me lay claim,
       The little hyssop and the king of fame.

"That makes that point about the squares clear," said Mary.
"I think it's even more significant," said her brother.

9.VIII This sensible old man refused to tread
       The path to Hades in a youngster's stead.
6.IX   Long since, at Nature's call, they let it drop,
       Thoughtlessly thoughtful for our next year's crop.
2.X   To smallest words great speakers greatness give;
       Here Rome propounded her alternative.
7.X   We heap up many with toil and trouble,
       And find that the whole of our gain is a bubble.
12.X   Add it among the hidden things—
       A fishy tale to light it brings.
1.XI   'Lions,' said a Gallic critic, 'are not these.'
       Benevolent souls—they'd made your heart's blood freeze.
11.XI An epithet for husky fellows,
       That stands, all robed in greens and yellows.
1.XII Whole without holes behold me here,
       My meaning should be wholly clear.
10.XII Running all around, never setting foot to floor,
       If there isn't one in this room, there may be one next door.
1.XIII Ye gods! think also of that goddess' name
       Whose might two hours on end the mob proclaim.

4.XIII	The Priest uplifts his voice on high,
	The choristers make their reply.
14.XIII	When you've guessed it, with one voice
	You'll say it was a golden choice.
1.XIV	Shall learning die amid a war's alarms?
	I, at my birth, was clasped in iron arms.
10.XIV	At sunset see the labourer now
	Loose all his oxen from the plough.
1.XV	Without a miracle it cannot be—
	At this point, Solver, bid him pray for thee!
11.XV	Two thousand years ago and more
	(Just as we do today),
	The Romans saw these distant lights—
	But, oh! how hard the way!

The most remarkable part of the search—or so Lord Peter thought—was its effect on Miss Marryat. At first she hovered disconsolately on the margin, aching with wounded dignity, yet ashamed to dissociate herself from people who were toiling so hard and so cheerfully in her cause.

"I think that's so-and-so," Mary would say hopefully.

And her brother would reply enthusiastically, "Holed it in one, old lady. Good for you! We've got it this time, Miss Marryat"—and explain it.

And Hannah Marryat would say with a snort:

"That's just the childish kind of joke Uncle Meleager *would* make."

Gradually, however, the fascination of seeing the squares fit together caught her, and, when the first word appeared which showed that the searchers were definitely on the right track, she lay down flat on the floor and peered over Lord Peter's shoulder as he grovelled below, writing letters in charcoal, rubbing them out with his handkerchief and mopping his heated face, till the Moor of Venice had nothing on him in the matter of blackness. Once, half scornfully, half timidly, she made a suggestion; twice, she made a suggestion; the third time she had an inspiration. The next minute she was down in the mêlée, crawling over the tiles, flushed and excited, wiping important letters out with her knees as fast as Peter could write them in, poring over the pages of Roget, her eyes gleaming under her tumbled black fringe.

Hurried meals of cold meat and tea sustained the exhausted party, and towards sunset Peter, with a shout of triumph, added the last letter to the square.

258

They crawled out and looked at it.

"All the words can't be clues," said Mary. "I think it must be just those four."

"Yes, undoubtedly. It's quite clear. We've only got to look it up. Where's a Bible?"

Miss Marryat hunted it out from the pile of reference books. "But that isn't the name of a Bible book," she said. "It's those things they have at evening service."

"That's all you know," said Lord Peter. "I was brought up religious, I was. It's Vulgate, that's what that is. You're quite right, of course, but, as Uncle Meleager says, we must 'look a little farther back than that'. Here you are. Now, then."

"But it doesn't say what chapter."

"So it doesn't. I mean, nor it does."

"And, anyhow, all the chapters are too short."

"Damn! Oh! Here, suppose we just count right on from the beginning—one, two, three—"

"Seventeen in chapter one, eighteen, nineteen—this must be it."

Two fair heads and one dark one peered excitedly at the small print, Bunter hovering decorously on the outskirts.

O my dove, that art in the clefts of the rock, in the covert of the steep place.

"Oh, dear!" said Mary, disappointed, "that does sound rather hopeless. Are you sure you've counted right? It might mean anything."

Lord Peter scratched his head.

"This is a bit of a blow," he said. "I don't like Uncle Meleager half as much as I did. Old beast!"

"After all our work!" moaned Mary.

"It must be right," cried Miss Marryat. "Perhaps there's some kind of anagram in it. We can't give up now!"

"Bravo!" said Lord Peter. "That's the spirit. 'Fraid we're in for another outburst of frivolity, Miss Marryat."

"Well, it's been great fun," said Hannah Marryat.

"If you will excuse me," began the deferential voice of Bunter.

"I'd forgotten you, Bunter," said his lordship. "Of course you can put us right—you always can. Where have we gone wrong?"

"I was about to observe, my lord, that the words you mention do not appear to agree with my recollection of the passage in question. In my mother's Bible, my lord, it ran, I fancy, somewhat differently."

Lord Peter closed the volume and looked at the back of it.

"Naturally," he said, "you are right again, of course. This is a Revised Version. It's your fault, Miss Marryat. You *would* have a Revised Version. But can we imagine Uncle Meleager with one? No. Bring me Uncle Meleager's Bible."

"Come and look in the library," cried Miss Marryat, snatching him by the hand and running. "Don't be so dreadfully calm."

On the centre of the library table lay a huge and venerable Bible—reverend in age and tooled leather binding. Lord Peter's hands caressed it, for a noble old book was like a song to his soul. Sobered by its beauty, they turned the yellow pages over:

In the clefts of the rocks, in the secret places of the stairs.

"Miss Marryat," said his lordship, "if your Uncle's will is not concealed in the staircase, then—well, all I can say is, he's played a rotten trick on us," he concluded lamely.

"Shall we try the main staircase, or the little one up to the porch?"

"Oh, the main one, I think. I hope it won't mean pulling it down. No. Somebody would have noticed if Uncle Meleager had done anything drastic in that way. It's probably quite a simple hiding-place. Wait a minute. Let's ask the housekeeper."

Mrs. Meakers was called, and perfectly remembered that about nine months previously Mr. Finch had pointed out to her a "kind of a crack like" on the under surface of the staircase, and had had a man in to fill it up. Certainly, she could point out the exact place. There was the mark of the plaster filling quite clear.

"Hurray!" cried Lord Peter. "Bunter—a chisel or something. Uncle Meleager, Uncle Meleager, we've *got* you! Miss Marryat, I think yours should be the hand to strike the blow. It's your staircase, you know—at least, if we find the will, so if any destruction has to be done it's up to you."

Breathless they stood round, while with a few blows the new plaster flaked off, disclosing a wide chink in the stonework. Hannah Marryat flung down hammer and chisel and groped in the gap.

"There's something," she gasped. "Lift me up; I can't reach. Oh, it is! it is! it *is* it!" And she withdrew her hand, grasping a long, sealed envelope, bearing the superscription:

POSITIVELY THE LAST WILL AND TESTAMENT OF
MELEAGER FINCH

Miss Marryat gave a yodel of joy and flung her arms round Lord Peter's neck.

Mary executed a joy-dance. "I'll tell the world," she proclaimed. "Come and tell mother!" cried Miss Marryat.

Mr. Bunter interposed.

"Your lordship will excuse me," he said firmly, "but your lordship's face is all over charcoal."

"Black but comely," said Lord Peter, "but I submit to your reproof. How clever we've all been. How topping everything is. How rich you are going to be. How late it is and how hungry I am. Yes, Bunter, I will wash my face. Is there anything else I can do for anybody while I feel in the mood?"

"If your lordship would be so kind," said Mr. Bunter, producing a small paper from his pocket, "I should be grateful if you could favour me with a South African quadruped in six letters, beginning with Q."

THE SOLUTION

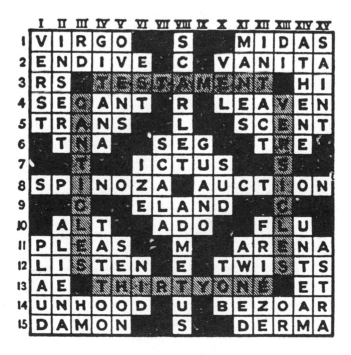

THE MAD TEA PARTY

By Ellery Queen

Ellery Queen is the joint pseudonym of two cousins, Frederic Dannay (1905–) and Manfred Bennington Lee (1905–1971), as well as being the name of the famous detective character created by the two authors. The cousins were both holding advertising jobs in New York City when in 1928 they collaborated on their first detective novel, The Roman Hat Mystery, *and entered it in a contest then being sponsored by McClure's magazine. The manuscript won the $7,500 first prize, and though McClure's went bankrupt before the money could be awarded, the novel itself was brought out the following year in book form by the Frederick A. Stokes Co., inaugurating one of the most significant careers in the history of the genre. A long series of novels featuring the always brilliant and (in the earlier books) sometimes arrogant Ellery Queen followed, notably* The Chinese Orange Mystery *(1934),* Calamity Town *(1942), and the controversial* And On the Eighth Day *(1964). In addition, there have been several volumes of short stories, including* The Adventures of Ellery Queen *(1934), in which "The Adventure of the Mad Tea Party" appears as the last work. Under the pseudonym Barnaby Ross, the partners have also published four novels about detective Drury Lane. In the Ellery Queen collaboration, the editorial and bibliographical duties have been performed chiefly by Dannay, whose activities have made him the single most influential figure in American detective fiction circles. His landmark anthologies and bibliographies include* 101 Years' Entertainment *(1941) and* Queen's Quorum *(1951); in addition,* Ellery Queen's Mystery Magazine, *which he has edited since its founding in 1941, has, in Anthony Boucher's words, "published every important crime writer who ever wrote a short story." For more about Ellery Queen the writer and the detective see Francis M. Nevins, Jr.'s* Royal Bloodline *(Bowling Green, Ohio: Popular Press, 1974).*

The tall young man in the dun raincoat thought that he had never seen such a downpour. It gushed out of the black sky in a roaring flood, gray-gleaming in the feeble yellow of the station lamps. The red tails of the local from Jamaica had just been drowned out in the west. It was very dark beyond the ragged blur of light surrounding the little railroad station, and unquestionably very wet. The tall young man shivered under the eaves of the platform roof and wondered what insanity had moved him to venture into the Long Island hinterland in such wretched weather. And where, damn it all, was Owen?

He had just miserably made up his mind to seek out a booth, telephone his regrets, and take the next train back to the City, when a lowslung coupé came splashing and snuffling out of the darkness, squealed to a stop, and a man in chauffeur's livery leaped out and dashed across the gravel for the protection of the eaves.

"Mr. Ellery Queen?" he panted, shaking out his cap. He was a blond young man with a ruddy face and sun-squinted eyes.

"Yes," said Ellery with a sigh. Too late now.

"I'm Millan, Mr. Owen's chauffeur, sir," said the man. "Mr. Owen's sorry he couldn't come down to meet you himself. Some guests—This way, Mr. Queen."

He picked up Ellery's bag and the two of them ran for the coupé. Ellery collapsed against the mohair in an indigo mood. Damn Owens and his invitations! Should have known better. Mere acquaintance, when it came to that. One of J.J.'s questionable friends. People were always pushing so. Put him up on exhibition, like a trained seal. Come, come, Rollo; here's a juicy little fish for you! . . . Got vicarious thrills out of listening to crime yarns. Made a man feel like a curiosity. Well, he'd be drawn and quartered if they got him to mention crime once! But then Owen had said Emmy Willowes would be there, and he'd always wanted to meet Emmy. Curious woman, Emmy, from all the reports. Daughter of some blueblood diplomat who had gone to the dogs—in this case, the stage. Stuffed shirts, her tribe, probably. Atavi! There were some people who still lived in mediæval . . . Hmm. Owen wanted him to see "the house." Just taken a month ago. Ducky, he'd said. "Ducky!" The big brute . . .

The coupé splashed along in the darkness, its headlights revealing only remorseless sheets of speckled water and occasionally a tree, a house, a hedge.

From *The Adventures of Ellery Queen*, Frederick A. Stokes Company, copyright 1933, 1934. Reprinted by permission of the author and the author's agents, Scott Meredith Literary Agency, Inc., 845 Third Avenue, New York, NY 10022.

263

Millan cleared his throat. "Rotten weather, isn't it, sir. Worst this spring."

Ah, the conversational chauffeur! thought Ellery with an inward groan. "Pity the poor sailor on a night like this," he said piously.

"Ha, ha," said Millan. "Isn't it the truth, though. You're a little late, aren't you, sir? That was the eleven-fifty. Mr. Owen told me this morning you were expected tonight on the nine-twenty."

"Detained," murmured Ellery, wishing he were dead.

"A case, Mr. Queen?" asked Millan eagerly, rolling his squinty eyes.

Even he, O Lord. . . . "No, no. My father had his annual attack of elephantiasis. Poor Dad! We thought for a bad hour there that it was the end."

The chauffeur gaped. Then, looking puzzled, he returned his attention to the soggy pelted road. Ellery closed his eyes with a sigh of relief.

But Millan's was a persevering soul, for after a moment of silence he grinned—true, a trifle dubiously—and said: "Lots of excitement at Mr. Owen's tonight, sir. You see, Master Jonathan—"

"Ah," said Ellery, starting a little. Master Jonathan, eh? Ellery recalled him as a stringy, hot-eyed brat in the indeterminate years between seven and ten who possessed a perfectly fiendish ingenuity for making a nuisance of himself. Master Jonathan. . . . He shivered again, this time from apprehension. He had quite forgotten Master Jonathan.

"Yes, sir, Jonathan's having a birthday party tomorrow, sir—ninth, I think—and Mr. and Mrs. Owen've rigged up something special." Millan grinned again, mysteriously. "Something very special, sir. It's a secret, y'see. The kid—Master Jonathan doesn't know about it yet. Will he be surprised!"

"I doubt it, Millan," groaned Ellery, and lapsed into a dismal silence which not even the chauffeur's companionable blandishments were able to shatter.

Richard Owen's "ducky" house was a large rambling affair of gables and ells and colored stones and bright shutters, set at the terminal of a winding driveway flanked by soldierly trees. It blazed with light and the front door stood ajar.

"Here we are, Mr. Queen!" cried Millan cheerfully, jumping out and holding the door open. "It's only a hop to the porch; you won't get wet, sir."

Ellery descended and obediently hopped to the porch. Millan

fished his bag out of the car and bounded up the steps. "Door open 'n' everything," he grinned. "Guess the help are all watchin' the show."

"Show?" gasped Ellery with a sick feeling at the pit of his stomach. Millan pushed the door wide open. "Step in, step in, Mr. Queen. I'll go get Mr. Owen. . . . They're rehearsing, y'see. Couldn't do it while Jonathan was up, so they had to wait till he'd gone to bed. It's for tomorrow, y'see. And he was very suspicious; they had an awful time with him—"

"I can well believe that," mumbled Ellery. Damn Jonathan and all his tribe! He stood in a small foyer looking upon a wide brisk living room, warm and attractive. "So they're putting on a play. Hmm. . . . Don't bother, Millan; I'll just wander in and wait until they've finished. Who am I to clog the wheels of Drama?"

"Yes, sir," said Millan with a vague disappointment; and he set down the bag and touched his cap and vanished in the darkness outside. The door closed with a click curiously final, shutting out both rain and night.

Ellery reluctantly divested himself of his drenched hat and raincoat, hung them dutifully in the foyer closet, kicked his bag into a corner, and sauntered into the living room to warm his chilled hands at the good fire. He stood before the flames soaking in heat, only half-conscious of the voices which floated through one of the two open doorways beyond the fireplace.

A woman's voice was saying in odd childish tones: "No, please go on! I won't interrupt you again. I dare say there may be *one*."

"Emmy," thought Ellery, becoming conscious very abruptly. "What's going on here?" He went to the first doorway and leaned against the jamb.

An astonishing sight. They were all—as far as he could determine—there. It was a large bookish room done in the modern manner. The farther side has been cleared and a home-made curtain, manufactured out of starchy sheets and a pulley, stretched across the room. The curtain was open, and in the cleared space there was a long table covered with a white cloth and with cups and saucers and things on it. In an armchair at the head of the table sat Emmy Willowes, whimsically girlish in a pinafore, her gold-brown hair streaming down her back, her slim legs sheathed in white stockings, and black pumps with low heels on her feet. Beside her sat an apparition, no less: a rabbity creature the size of a man, his huge ears stiffly up, an enormous bow tie at his furry neck, his mouth clacking open and shut as human sounds came from his throat. Beside the hare there was another apparition: a creature with an amiably rodent little face and slow sleepy movements.

And beyond the little one, who looked unaccountably like a dormouse, sat the most remarkable of the quartet—a curious creature with shaggy eyebrows and features reminiscent of George Arliss's, at his throat a dotted bow tie, dressed Victorianwise in a quaint waistcoat, on his head an extraordinary tall cloth hat in the band of which was stuck a placard reading: "For This Style 10/6."

The audience was composed of two women: an old lady with pure white hair and the stubbornly sweet facial expression which more often than not conceals a chronic acerbity; and a very beautiful young woman with full breasts, red hair, and green eyes. Then Ellery noticed that two domestic heads were stuck in another doorway, gaping and giggling decorously.

"The mad tea party," thought Ellery, grinning. "I might have known, with Emmy in the house. Too good for that merciless brat!"

"They were learning to draw," said the little dormouse in a high-pitched voice, yawning and rubbing its eye, "and they drew all manner of things—everything that begins with an M—".

"Why not an M?" demanded the woman-child.

"Why not?" snapped the hare, flapping his ears indignantly.

The dormouse began to doze and was instantly beset by the top-hatted gentleman, who pinched him so roundly that he awoke with a shriek and said: "—that begins with an M, such as mousetraps, and the moon, and memory, and muchness—you know you say things are 'much of a muchness'—did you ever see such a thing as a drawing of a muchness?"

"Really, now you ask me," said the girl, quite confused, "I don't think—"

"Then you shouldn't talk," said the Hatter tartly.

The girl rose in open disgust and began to walk away, her white legs twinkling. The dormouse fell asleep and the hare and the Hatter stood up and grasped the dormouse's little head and tried very earnestly to push it into the mouth of a monstrous teapot on the table.

And the little girl cried, stamping her right foot: "At any rate I'll never go *there* again. It's the stupidest tea party I was ever at in all my life!"

And she vanished behind the curtain; an instant later it swayed and came together as she operated the rope of the pulley.

"Superb," drawled Ellery, clapping his hands. "*Brava*, Alice. And a couple of *bravi* for the zoölogical characters, Messrs. Dormouse and March Hare, not to speak of my good friend the Mad Hatter."

The Mad Hatter goggled at him, tore off his hat, and came running across the room. His vulterine features under the make-up were both good-humoured and crafty; he was a stoutish man in his prime, a faintly cynical and ruthless prime. "Queen! When on earth did you come? What held you up?"

"Family matter. Millan did the honors. Owen, that's your natural costume, I'll swear. I don't know what ever possessed you to go into Wall Street. You were born to be the Hatter."

"Think so?" chuckled Owen, pleased. "I guess I always did have a yen for the stage; that's why I backed Emmy Willowes's *Alice* show. Here, I want you to meet the gang. Mother," he said to the white-haired old lady, "May I present Mr. Ellery Queen. Laura's mother, Queen—Mrs. Mansfield." The old lady smiled a sweet, sweet smile; but Ellery noticed that her eyes were very sharp. "Mrs. Gardner," continued Owen, indicating the buxom young woman with the red hair and green eyes. "Believe it or not, she's the wife of that hairy Hare over there. Ho, ho, ho!"

There was something a little brutal in Owen's laughter. Ellery bowed to the beautiful woman and said quickly: "Gardner? You're not the wife of Paul Gardner, the architect?"

"Guilty," said the March Hare in a cavernous voice; and he removed his head and disclosed a lean face with twinkling eyes. "How are you, Queen? I haven't seen you since I testified for your father in that Schultz murder case in the Village."

They shook hands. "Surprise," said Ellery. "This *is* nice. Mrs. Gardner, you have a clever husband. He set the defense by their respective ears with his expert testimony in that case."

"Oh, I've always said Paul is a genius," smiled the red-haired woman. She had a queer husky voice. "But he won't believe me. He thinks I'm the only one in the world who doesn't appreciate him."

"Now, Carolyn," protested Gardner with a laugh; but the twinkle had gone out of his eyes and for some odd reason he glanced at Richard Owen.

"Of course you remember Laura," boomed Owen, taking Ellery forcibly by the arm. "That's the Dormouse. Charming little rat, isn't she?"

Mrs. Mansfield lost her sweet expression for a fleeting instant; very fleeting indeed. What the Dormouse thought about being publicly characterized as a rodent, however charming, by her husband was concealed by the furry little head; when she took it off she was smiling. She was a wan little woman with tired eyes and cheeks that had already begun to sag.

"And this," continued Owen with the pride of a stock raiser exhibiting a prize milch cow, "is the one and only Emmy. Emmy, meet Mr.

267

Queen, that murder-smelling chap I've been telling you about. Miss Willowes."

"You see us, Mr. Queen," murmured the actress, "in character. I hope you aren't here on a professional visit? Because if you are, we'll get into mufti at once and let you go to work. I know *I've* a vicariously guilty conscience. If I were to be convicted of every mental murder I've committed, I'd need the nine lives of the Cheshire Cat. Those damn' critics—"

"The costume," said Ellery, not looking at her legs, "is most fetching. And I think I like you better as Alice." She made a charming Alice; she was curved in her slimness, half boy, half girl. "Whose idea was this, anyway?"

"I suppose you think we're fools or nuts," chuckled Owen. "Here, sit down, Queen. Maud!" he roared. "A cocktail for Mr. Queen. Bring some more fixin's." A frightened domestic head vanished. "We're having a dress rehearsal for Johnny's birthday party tomorrow; we've invited all the kids of the neighborhood. Emmy's brilliant idea; she brought the costumes down from the theatre. You know we closed Saturday night."

"I hadn't heard. I thought *Alice* was playing to S.R.O."

"So it was. But our lease at the Odeon ran out and we've our engagements on the road to keep. We open in Boston next Wednesday."

Slim-legged Maud set a pinkish liquid concoction before Ellery. He sipped slowly, succeeding in not making a face.

"Sorry to have to break this up," said Paul Gardner, beginning to take off his costume. "But Carolyn and I have a bad trip before us. And then tomorrow . . . The road must be an absolute washout."

"Pretty bad," said Ellery politely, setting down his three-quarters-full glass.

"I won't hear of it," said Laura Owen. Her pudgy little Dormouse's stomach gave her a peculiar appearance, tiny and fat and sexless. "Driving home in this storm! Carolyn, you and Paul must stay over."

"It's only four miles, Laura," murmured Mrs. Gardner.

"Nonsense, Carolyn! More like forty on a night like this," boomed Owen. His cheeks were curiously pale and damp under the makeup. "That's settled! We've got more room than we know what to do with. Paul saw to that when he designed this development."

"That's the insidious part of knowing architects socially," said Emmy Willowes with a grimace. She flung herself in a chair and tucked her long legs under her. "You can't fool 'em about the number of available guest rooms."

"Don't mind Emmy," grinned Owen. "She's the Peck's Bad Girl of show business: no manners at all. Well, well! This is great. How's about a drink, Paul?"

"No, thanks."

"You'll have one, won't you, Carolyn? Only good sport in the crowd." Ellery realized with embarrassment that his host was, under the jovial glaze of the exterior, drunk.

Mrs. Gardner raised her heavily-lidded green eyes to Owen's. "I'd love it, Dick." They stared with frank hunger at each other. Mrs. Owen suddenly smiled and turned her back, struggling with her cumbersome costume.

And, just as suddenly, Mrs. Mansfield rose and smiled her unconvincing sweet smile and said in her sugary voice to no one in particular: "*Will* you all excuse me? It's been a trying day, and I'm an old woman. . . . Laura, my darling." She went to her daughter and kissed the lined, averted forehead.

Everybody murmured something; including Ellery, who had a headache, a slow pinkish fire in his vitals, and a consuming wishfulness to be far, far away.

Mr. Ellery Queen came to with a start and a groan. He turned over in bed, feeling very poorly. He had dozed in fits since one o'clock, annoyed rather than soothed by the splash of the rain against the bedroom windows. And now he was miserably awake, attacked by an inexplicable insomnia. He sat up and reached for his wrist watch, which was ticking thunderously away on the night table beside his bed. By the radium hands he saw that it was five past two.

He lay back, tucking his palms behind his head and stared into the half-darkness. The mattress was deep and downy, as one had a right to expect of the mattress of a plutocrat, but it did not rest his restless bones. The house was cosy, but it did not comfort him. His hostess was thoughtful, but uncomfortably woebegone. His host was a disturbing force, like the storm. His fellow guests; Master Jonathan snuffling away in his junior bed—Ellery was positive that Master Jonathan snuffled. . . .

At two-fifteen he gave up the battle and, rising, turned on the light and got into his dressing gown and slippers. That there was no book or magazine on or in the night table he had ascertained before retiring. Shocking hospitality! Sighing, he went to the door and opened it and peered out. A small night light glimmered at the landing down the hall. Everything was quiet.

And suddenly he was attacked by the strangest diffidence. He definitely did not want to leave the bedroom.

Analyzing the fugitive fear, and arriving nowhere, Ellery sternly reproached himself for an imaginative fool and stepped out into the hall. He was not habitually a creature of nerves, nor was he psychic; he laid the blame to lowered physical resistance due to fatigue, lack of sleep. This was a nice house with nice people in it. It was like a man, he thought, saying: "Nice doggie, nice doggie," to a particularly fearsome beast with slavering jaws. That woman with the sea-green eyes. Put to sea in a sea-green boat. Or was it pea-green. . . . "No room! No room!" . . . "There's plenty of room," said Alice indignantly. . . . And Mrs. Mansfield's smile did make you shiver.

Berating himself bitterly for the ferment his imagination was in, he went down the carpeted stairs to the living room.

It was pitch-dark and he did not know where the light switch was. He stumbled over a hassock and stubbed his toe and cursed silently. The library should be across from the stairs, next to the fireplace. He strained his eyes toward the fireplace, but the last embers had died. Stepping warily, he finally reached the fireplace wall. He groped about in the rain-splattered silence, searching for the library door. His hand met a cold knob, and he turned the knob rather noisily and swung the door open. His eyes were oriented to the darkness now and he had already begun to make out in the mistiest black haze the unrecognizable outlines of still objects.

The darkness from beyond the door however struck him like a blow. It was darker darkness. . . . He was about to step across the sill when he stopped. It was the wrong room. Not the library at all. How he knew he could not say, but he was sure he had pushed open the door of the wrong room. Must have wandered orbitally to the right. Lost men in the dark forest. . . . He stared intently straight before him into the absolute, unrelieved blackness, sighed, and retreated. The door shut noisily again.

He groped along the wall to the left. A few feet. . . . There it was! The very next door. He paused to test his psychic faculties. No, all's well. Grinning, he pushed open the door, entered boldly, fumbled on the nearest wall for the switch, found it, pressed. The light flooded on to reveal, triumphantly, the library.

The curtain was closed, the room in disorder as he had last seen it before being conducted upstairs by his host.

He went to the built-in bookcases, scanned several shelves, hesitated between two volumes, finally selected *Huckleberry Finn* as blithe reading on a dour night, put out the light, and felt his way back across the living room to the stairway. Boots tucked under his arm, he began to climb the stairs. There was a footfall from the landing above. He looked up. A man's dark form was silhouetted below the tiny landing light.

"Owen?" whispered a dubious male voice.

Ellery laughed. "It's Queen, Gardner. Can't you sleep, either?"

He heard the man sigh with relief. "Lord, no! I was just coming downstairs for something to read. Carolyn—my wife's asleep, I guess, in the room adjoining mine. How she can sleep—! There's something in the air tonight."

"Or else you drank too much," said Ellery cheerfully, mounting the stairs.

Gardner was in pajamas and dressing gown, his hair mussed. "Didn't drink at all to speak of. Must be this confounded rain. My nerves are all shot."

"Something in that. Hardy believed, anyway, in the Greek unities. . . . If you can't sleep, you might join me for a smoke in my room, Gardner."

"You're sure I won't be—"

"Keeping me up? Nonsense. The only reason I fished about downstairs for a book was to occupy my mind with something. Talk's infinitely better than Huck Finn, though he does help at times. Come on."

They went to Ellery's room and Ellery produced cigarettes and they relaxed in chairs and chatted over tobacco about Inspector Queen, old books, and the price of green cheese until the early dawn began struggling to emerge from behind the fine gray wet bars of the rain outside. Then Gardner went yawning back to his room and Ellery fell into a heavy, uneasy slumber.

He was on the rack in a tall room of the Inquisition and his left arm was being torn out of his shoulder socket. The pain was almost pleasant. Then he awoke to find Millan's ruddy face in broad daylight above him, his blond hair tragically dishevelled. He was jerking at Ellery's arm for all he was worth.

"Mr. Queen!" he was crying. "Mr. Queen! For God's sake, wake up!"

Ellery sat up quickly, startled. "What's the matter, Millan?"

"Mr. Owen, sir. He's—he's gone!"

Ellery sprang out of bed. "What d'ye mean, man?"

"Disappeared, Mr. Queen. We—we can't find him. Just gone. Mrs. Owen is all—"

"You go downstairs, Millan," said Ellery calmly stripping off his pajama coat, "and pour yourself a drink. Please tell Mrs. Owen not to do anything until I come down. And nobody's to leave or telephone. You understand?"

"Yes, sir," said Millan in a low voice, and blundered off.

Ellery dressed like a firearm, splashed his face, spat water, adjusted his necktie, and ran downstairs. He found Laura Owen in a crumpled négligé on the sofa, sobbing. Mrs. Mansfield was patting her daughter's shoulder. Master Jonathan Owen was scowling at his grandmother, Emmy Willowes silently smoked a cigarette, and the Gardners were pale and quiet by the gray-washed windows.

"Mr. Queen," said the actress quickly. "It's a drama, hot off the script. At least Laura Owen thinks so. Won't you assure her that it's all probably nothing?"

"I can't do that," smiled Ellery, "until I learn the facts. Owen's gone? How? When?"

"Oh, Mr. Queen," choked Mrs. Owen, raising a tear-stained face. "I know something—something dreadful's happened. I had a feeling—You remember last night, after Richard showed you to your room?"

"Yes."

"Then he came back downstairs and said he had some work to do in his den for Monday, and told me to go to bed. Everybody else had gone upstairs. The servants, too. I warned him not to stay up too late and I went up to bed. I—I was exhausted, and I fell right asleep—"

"You occupy one bedroom, Mrs. Owen?"

"Yes. Twin beds. I fell asleep and didn't wake up until a half-hour ago. Then I saw—" She shuddered and began to sob again. Her mother looked helpless and angry. "His bed hadn't been slept in. His clothes—the ones he'd taken off when he got into the costume—were still where he had left them on the chair by his bed. I was shocked, and ran downstairs; but he was gone. . . ."

"Ah," said Ellery queerly. "Then, as far as you know, he's still in that Mad Hatter's rig? Have you looked over his wardrobe? Are any of his regular clothes missing?"

"No, no; they're all there. Oh, he's dead. I know he's dead."

"Laura, dear, please," said Mrs. Mansfield in a tight quavery voice.

"Oh, Mother, it's too horrible—"

"Here, here," said Ellery. "No hysterics. Was he worried about anything? Business, for instance?"

"No, I'm sure he wasn't. In fact, he said only yesterday things were picking up beautifully. And he isn't—isn't the type to worry, anyway."

"Then it probably isn't amnesia. He hasn't had a shock of some sort recently?"

"No, no."

"No possibility, despite the costume, that he went to his office?"

"No. He never goes down Saturdays."

Master Jonathan slammed his fists into the pockets of his Eton jacket and said bitterly: "I bet he's drunk again. Makin' Mamma cry. I hope he *never* comes back."

"Jonathan!" screamed Mrs. Mansfield. "You go up to your room this very minute, do you hear, you nasty boy? This minute!"

No one said anything; Mrs. Owen continued to sob; so Master Jonthan thrust out his lower lip, scowled at his grandmother with unashamed dislike, and stamped upstairs.

"Where," said Ellery with a frown, "was your husband when you last saw him, Mrs. Owen? In this room?"

"In his den," she said with difficulty. "He went in just as I went upstairs. I saw him go in. That door, there." She pointed to the door at the right of the library door. Ellery started; it was the door to the room he had almost blundered into during the night in his hunt for the library.

"Do you think—" began Carolyn Gardner in her husky voice, and stopped. Her lips were dry, and in the gray morning light her hair did not seem so red and her eyes did not seem so green. There was, in fact, a washed-out look about her, as if all the fierce vitality within her had been quenched by what had happened.

"Keep out of this Carolyn," said Paul Gardner harshly. His eyes were red-rimmed from lack of sleep.

"Come, come," murmured Ellery, "we may be, as Miss Willowes has said, making a fuss over nothing at all. If you'll excuse me . . . I'll have a peep at the den."

He went into the den, closing the door behind him, and stood with his back squarely against the door. It was a small room, so narrow that it looked long by contrast; it was sparsely furnished and seemed a business-like place. There was a simple neatness about its desk, a modern severity about its furnishings that were reflections of the direct, brutal character of Richard Owen. The room was as trim as a pin; it was almost ludicrous to conceive of its having served as the scene of a crime.

Ellery gazed long and thoughtfully. Nothing out of place, so far as he could see; and nothing, at least peceptible to a stranger, added.

Then his eyes wavered and fixed themselves upon what stood straight before him. That *was* odd. . . . Facing him as he leaned against the door there was a bold naked mirror set flush into the opposite wall and reaching from floor to ceiling—a startling feature of the room's decorations. Ellery's lean figure, and the door behind him, were perfectly reflected in the sparkling glass. And there, above . . . In the mirror he saw, above the reflection of the door against which he was leaning, the reflection of the face of a modern electric clock. In the dingy grayness of the light there was a curious lambent quality about its dial. . . . He pushed away from the door and turned and stared up. It was a chromium-and-onyx clock, about a foot in diameter.

He opened the door and beckoned Millan, who had joined the silent group in the living room. "Have you a stepladder?"

Millan brought one. Ellery shut the door firmly, mounted the ladder, and examined the clock. Its electric outlet was behind, concealed from view. The plug was in the socket, as he saw at once. The clock was going; the time—he consulted his wristwatch—was reasonably accurate. But then he cupped his hands as best he could to shut out what light there was and stared hard and saw that the numerals and the hands, as he had suspected, were radium-painted. They glowed faintly.

He descended, opened the door, gave the ladder into Millan's keeping, and sauntered into the living room. They looked up at him trustfully.

"Well," said Emmy Willowes with a light shrug, "has the Master Mind discovered the all-important clue? Don't tell us that Dickie Owen is out playing golf at the Meadowbrook links in that Mad Hatter's get-up!"

"Well, Mr. Queen?" asked Mrs. Owen anxiously.

Ellery sank into an armchair and lighted a cigarette. "There's something curious in there. Mrs. Owen, did you get this house furnished?"

She was puzzled. "Furnished? Oh, no. We bought it, you know; brought all our own things."

"Then the electric clock above the door in the den is yours?"

"The clock?" They all stared at him. "Why, of course. What has that—"

"Hmm," said Ellery. "That clock has a disappearing quality, like the Cheshire Cat—since we may as well continue being Carrollish, Miss Willowes."

"But what can the clock possibly have to do with Richard's being gone?" asked Mrs. Mansfield with asperity.

Ellery shrugged. "*Je n'sais.* The point is that a little after two this morning, being unable to sleep, I ambled downstairs to look for a book. In the dark I blundered to the door of the den, mistaking it for the library door. I opened it and looked in. But I saw nothing, you see."

"But how could you, Mr. Queen?" said Mrs. Gardner in a small voice; her breasts heaved. "If it was dark—"

"That's the curious part of it," drawled Ellery. "I *should* have seen something *because* it was so dark, Mrs. Gardner."

"But—"

"The clock over the door."

"Did you go in?" murmured Emmy Willowes, frowning. "I can't say I understand. The clock's above the door, isn't it?"

"There is a mirror facing the door," explained Ellery absently, "and the fact that it was so dark makes my seeing nothing quite remarkable. Because that clock has luminous hands and numerals. Consequently I should have seen their reflected glow very clearly indeed in that pitch darkness. But I didn't, you see. I saw literally nothing at all."

They were silent, bewildered. Then Gardner muttered: "I still don't see—You mean something, somebody was standing in front of the mirror, obscuring the reflection of the clock?"

"Oh, no. The clock's above the door—a good seven feet or more from the floor. The mirror reaches to the ceiling. There isn't a piece of furniture in that room seven feet high, and certainly we may dismiss the possibility of an intruder seven feet or more tall. No, no, Gardner. It does seem as if the clock wasn't above the door at all when I looked in."

"Are you sure, young man," snapped Mrs. Mansfield, "that you know what you're talking about? I thought we were concerned with my son-in-law's absence. And how on earth could the clock not have been there?"

Ellery closed his eyes. "Fundamental. *It was moved from its position.* Wasn't above the door when I looked in. After I left, it was returned."

"But why on earth," murmured the actress, "should anyone want to move a mere clock from a wall, Mr. Queen? That's almost as nonsensical as some of the things in *Alice.*"

"That," said Ellery, "is the question I'm propounding to myself. Frankly I don't know." Then he opened his eyes. "By the way, has anyone seen the Mad Hatter's hat?"

Mrs. Owen shivered. "No, that—that's gone, too."

"You've looked for it?"

"Yes. Would you like to look yours—"

"No, no, I'll take your word for it, Mrs. Owen. Oh, yes. Your husband has no enemies?" He smiled. "That's the routine question,

275

Miss Willowes. I'm afraid I can't offer you anything startling in the way of technique."

"Enemies? Oh, I'm sure not," quavered Mrs. Owen. "Richard was—is strong and—and sometimes rather curt and contemptuous, but I'm sure no one would hate him enough to—to kill him." She shivered again and drew the silk of her négligé closer about her plump shoulders.

"Don't say that, Laura," said Mrs. Mansfield sharply. "I do declare, you people are like children! It probably has the simplest explanation."

"Quite possible," said Ellery in a cheerful voice. "It's the depressing weather, I suppose. . . . There! I believe the rain's stopped." They dully looked out the windows. The rain had perversely ceased, and the sky was growing brighter. "Of course," continued Ellery, "there are certain possibilities. It's conceivable—I say conceivable, Mrs. Owen—that your husband has been . . . well, kidnaped. Now, now, don't look so frightened. It's a theory only. The fact that he has disappeared in the costume does seem to point to a very abrupt—and therefore possibly enforced—departure. You haven't found a note of some kind? Nothing in your letter box? The morning mail—"

"Kidnaped," whispered Mrs. Owen feebly.

"Kidnaped?" breathed Mrs. Gardner, and bit her lip. But there was a brightness in her eye, like the brightness of the sky outdoors.

"No note, no mail," snapped Mrs. Mansfield. "Personally, I think this is ridiculous. Laura, this is your house, but I think I have a duty. . . . You should do one of two things. Either take this seriously and telephone the *regular* police, or forget all about it. *I'm* inclined to believe Richard got befuddled—he *had* a lot to drink last night, dear—and wandered off drunk somewhere. He's probably sleeping it off in a field somewhere and won't come back with anything worse than pneumonia."

"Excellent suggestion," drawled Ellery. "All except for the summoning of the *regular* police, Mrs. Mansfield. I assure you I possess— er—*ex officio* qualifications. Let's not call the police and say we did. If there's any explaining to do—afterward—I'll do it. Meanwhile, I suggest we try to forget all this unpleasantness and wait. If Mr. Owen hasn't returned by nightfall, we can go into conference and decide what measures to take. Agreed?"

"Sounds reasonable," said Gardner disconsolately. "May I—" he smiled and shrugged—"this *is* exciting!—telephone my office, Queen?"

"Lord, yes."

Mrs. Owen shrieked suddenly, rising and tottering toward the stairs. "Jonathan's birthday party! I forgot all about it! And all those children invited—What *will* I say?"

"I suggest," said Ellery in a sad voice, "that Master Jonathan is indisposed, Mrs. Owen. Harsh, but necessary. You might phone all the potential spectators of the mad tea party and voice your regrets." And Ellery rose and wandered into the library.

It was a depressing day for all the lightening skies and the crisp sun. The morning wore on and nothing whatever happened. Mrs. Mansfield firmly tucked her daughter into bed, made her swallow a small dose of Luminal from a big bottle in the medicine chest, and remained with her until she dropped off to exhausted sleep. Then the old lady telephoned to all and sundry the collective Owen regrets over the unfortunate turn of events. Jonathan *would* have to run a fever when . . . Master Jonathan, apprised later by his grandmother of the *débâcle*, sent up a healthy howl of anguish that caused Ellery, poking about downstairs in the library, to feel prickles slither up and down his spine. It took the combined labors of Mrs. Mansfield, Millan, the maid, and the cook to pacify the Owen hope. A five-dollar bill ultimately restored a rather strained *entente*. . . . Emmy Willowes spent the day serenely reading. The Gardners listlessly played gin-rummy.

Luncheon was a dismal affair. No one spoke in more than monosyllables.

During the afternoon they wandered about, restless. Even the actress began to show signs of tension: she consumed innumerable cigarettes and cocktails and lapsed into almost sullen silence. No word came; the telephone rang only once, and then it was merely the local confectioner protesting the cancellation of the ice cream order. Ellery spent most of the afternoon in mysterious activity in the library and den. What he was looking for remained his secret. At five o'clock he emerged from the den, rather gray of face. There was a deep crease between his brows. He went out onto the porch and leaned against a pillar, sunk in thought. The gravel was dry; the sun had quickly sopped up the rain. When he went back into the house it was already dusk and growing darker each moment with the swiftness of the country nightfall.

There was no one about; the house was quiet, its miserable occupants having retired to their rooms. Ellery sought a chair. He buried his face in his hands and thought for long minutes, completely still.

And then at last something happened to him and he went to the foot of the stairs and listened. No sound. He tiptoed back, reached for the telephone, and spent the next fifteen minutes in low-voiced, earnest conversation with someone in New York. When he had finished, he went upstairs to his room.

An hour later, while the others were downstairs gathering for dinner, he slipped down the rear stairway and out of the house unobserved even by the cook in the kitchen. He spent some time in the thick darkness of the grounds.

How it happened Ellery never knew. He felt its effects soon after dinner; and on retrospection he recalled that the others, too, had seemed drowsy at approximately the same time. It was a late dinner and a cold one, Owen's disappearance apparently having disrupted the culinary organization as well; so that it was not until a little after eight that the coffee—Ellery was certain later it had been the coffee—was served by the trim-legged maid. The drowsiness came on less than half an hour later. They were seated in the living room, chatting dully about nothing at all. Mrs. Owen, pale and silent, had gulped her coffee thirstily; had called for a second cup, in fact. Only Mrs. Mansfield had been belligerent. She had been definitely of a mind, it appeared, to telephone the police. She had great faith in the local constabulary of Long Island, particularly in one Chief Naughton, the local prefect; and she left no doubt in Ellery's mind of *his* incompetency. Gardner had been restless and a little rebellious; he had tinkered with the piano in the alcove. Emmy Willowes had drawn herself into a slant-eyed shell, no longer amused and very, very quiet. Mrs. Gardner had been nervous. Jonathan, packed off screaming to bed. . . .

It came over their senses like a blanket of snow. Just a pleasant sleepiness. The room was warm, too, and Ellery rather hazily felt perspiration on his forehead. He was half-gone before his dulled brain sounded a warning note. And then, trying in panic to rise, to use his muscles, he felt himself slipping, slipping into unconsciousness, his body as leaden and remote as Vega. His last conscious thought, as the room whirled dizzily before his eyes and he saw blearily the expressions of his companions, was that they had all been drugged. . . .

The dizziness seemed merely to have taken up where it had left off. Specks danced before his closed eyes and somebody was hammering petulantly at his temples. Then he opened his eyes and saw glittering sun fixed upon the floor at his feet. Good God, all night. . . .

He sat up groaning and feeling his head. The others were sprawled in various attitudes of labored-breathing coma about him—without exception. Someone—his aching brain took it in dully; it was Emmy Willowes—stirred and sighed. He got to his feet and stumbled toward a portable bar and poured himself a stiff, nasty drink of Scotch. Then, with his throat burning, he felt unaccountably better; and he went to the actress and pummeled her gently until she opened her eyes.

"What—when—"

"Drugged," croaked Ellery. "The crew of us. Try to revive these people, Miss Willowes, while I scout about a bit. And see if anyone's shamming."

He wove his way a little uncertainly, but with purpose, toward the rear of the house. Groping, he found the kitchen. And there were the trim-legged maid and Millan and the cook unconscious in chairs about the kitchen table over cold cups of coffee. He made his way back to the living room, nodded at Miss Willowes working over Gardner at the piano, and staggered upstairs. He discovered Master Jonathan's bedroom after a short search; the boy was still sleeping—a deep natural sleep punctuated by nasal snuffles. Lord, he *did* snuffle! Groaning, Ellery visited the lavatory adjoining the master bedroom. After a little while he went downstairs and into the den. He came out almost at once, haggard and wild-eyed. He took his hat from the foyer closet and hurried outdoors into the warm sunshine. He spent fifteen minutes poking about the grounds; the Owen house was shallowly surrounded by timber and seemed isolated as a Western ranch. . . . When he returned to the house, looking grim and disappointed, the others were all conscious, making mewing little sounds and holding their heads like scared children.

"Queen, for God's sake," began Gardner hoarsely.

"Whoever it was used that Luminal in the lavatory upstairs," said Ellery, flinging his hat away and wincing at a sudden pain in his head. "The stuff Mrs. Mansfield gave Mrs. Owen yesterday to make her sleep. Except that almost the whole of that large bottle was used. Swell sleeping draught! Make yourselves comfortable while I conduct a little investigation in the kitchen. I think it was the Java." But when he returned he was grimacing. "No luck. *Madame la Cuisiniére*, it seems, had to visit the bathroom at one period; Millan was out in the garage looking at the cars; and the maid was off somewhere, doubtless primping. Result: our friend the Luminalist had an opportunity to pour most of the powder from the bottle into the coffeepot. Damn!"

"I *am* going to call the police!" cried Mrs. Mansfield hysterically, striving to rise. "We'll be murdered in our beds, next thing we know! Laura, I positively insist—"

"Please, please, Mrs. Mansfield," said Ellery wearily. "No heroics. And you would be of greater service if you went into the kitchen and checked the insurrection that's brewing there. The two females are on the verge of packing, I'll swear."

Mrs. Mansfield bit her lip and flounced off. They heard her no longer sweet voice raised in remonstrance a moment later.

"But, Queen," protested Gardner, "we can't go unprotected—"

"What I want to know in my infantile way," drawled Emmy Willowes from pale lips, "is who did it, and why. That bottle upstairs . . . It looks uncomfortably like one of us, doesn't it?"

Mrs. Gardner gave a little shriek. Mrs. Owen sank back into her chair.

"One of us?" whispered the red-haired woman.

Ellery smiled without humor. Then his smile faded and he cocked his head toward the foyer. "What was that?" he snapped.

They turned, terror-stricken, and looked. But there was nothing to see. Ellery strode toward the front door.

"What is it now, for heaven's sake?" faltered Mrs. Owen.

"I thought I heard a sound—" He flung the door open. The early morning sun streamed in. Then they saw him stoop and pick up something from the porch and rise and look swiftly about outside. But he shook his head and stepped back, closing the door.

"Package," he said with a frown. "I *thought* someone . . ."

They looked blankly at the brown-paper bundle in his hands. "Package?" asked Mrs. Owen. Her face lit up. Oh, it may be from Richard!" And then the light went out to be replaced by fearful pallor. "Oh, do you think—?"

"It's addressed," said Ellery slowly, "to you, Mrs. Owen. No stamp, no postmark, written in pencil in disguised block letters. I think I'll take the liberty of opening this, Mrs. Owen." He broke the feeble twine and tore away the wrapping of the crude parcel. And then he frowned even more deeply. For the package contained only a pair of large men's shoes, worn at the heels and soles—sport Oxfords in tan and white.

Mrs. Owen rolled her eyes, her nostrils quivering with nausea. "Richard's!" she gasped. And she sank back, half-fainting.

"Indeed?" murmured Ellery. "How interesting. Not, of course, the shoes he wore Friday night. You're positive they're his, Mrs. Owen?"

"Oh, he *has* been kidnaped!" quavered Mrs. Mansfield from the rear doorway. "Isn't there a note, b-blood . . ."

"Nothing but the shoes. I doubt the kidnap theory now, Mrs. Mansfield. These weren't the shoes Owen wore Friday night. When did you see these last, Mrs. Owen?"

280

She moaned: "In his wardrobe closet upstairs only yesterday afternoon."

"There. You see?" said Ellery cheerfully. "Probably stolen from the closet while we were all unconscious last night. And now returned rather spectacularly. So far, you know, there's been no harm done. I'm afraid," he said with severity, "we're nursing a viper at our bosoms."

But they did not laugh. Miss Willowes said strangely: "Very odd. In fact, insane, Mr. Queen. I can't see the slightest purpose in it."

"Nor I at the moment. Somebody's either playing a monstrous prank, or there's a devilishly clever and warped mentality behind all this." He retrieved his hat and made for the door.

"Wherever are you going?" gasped Mrs. Gardner.

"Oh, out for a thinking spell under God's blue canopy. But remember," he added quietly, "that's a privilege reserved to detectives. No one is to set foot outside this house."

He returned an hour later without explanation.

At noon they found the second package. It was a squarish parcel wrapped in the same brown paper. Inside there was a cardboard carton, and in the carton, packed in crumpled tissue paper, there were two magnificent toy sailing boats such as children race on summer lakes. The package was addressed to Miss Willowes.

"This is getting dreadful," murmured Mrs. Gardner, her full lips trembling. "I'm all goose pimples."

"I'd feel better," muttered Miss Willowes, "if it was a bloody dagger, or something. Toy boats!" She stepped back and her eyes narrowed. "Now, look here, good people, I'm as much a sport as anybody, but a joke's a joke and I'm just a bit fed up on this particular one. Who's manœuvering these monkeyshines?"

"Joke," snarled Gardner. He was white as death. "It's the work of a madman, I tell you!"

"Now, now," murmured Ellery, staring at the green-and-cream boats. "We shan't get anywhere this way. Mrs. Owen, have you ever seen these before?"

Mrs. Owen, on the verge of collapse, mumbled: "Oh, my good dear God. Mr. Queen, I don't— Why, they're—they're Jonathan's!"

Ellery blinked. Then he went to the foot of the stairway and yelled: "Jonny! Come down here a minute."

Master Jonathan descended sluggishly, sulkily. "What you want?" he asked in a cold voice.

"Come here, son." Master Jonathan came with dragging feet. "When did you see these boats of yours last?"

"Boats!" shrieked Master Jonathan, springing into life. He pounced on them and snatched them away, glaring at Ellery. "My boats! Never seen such a place. My boats! You stole 'em!"

"Come, come," said Ellery, flushing, "be a good little man. When did you see them last?"

"Yest'day! In my toy chest! My boats! Scan'lous," hissed Master Jonathan, and fled upstairs, hugging his boats to his scrawny breast.

"Stolen at the same time," said Ellery helplessly. "By thunder, Miss Willowes, I'm almost inclined to agree with you. By the way, who bought those boats for your son, Mrs. Owen?"

"H-his father."

"Damn," said Ellery for the second time that impious Sunday, and he sent them all on a search of the house to ascertain if anything else were missing. But no one could find that anything had been taken.

It was when they came down from upstairs that they found Ellery regarding a small white envelope with puzzlement.

"Now what?" demanded Gardner wildly.

"Stuck in the door," he said thoughtfully. "Hadn't noticed it before. This *is* a queer one."

It was a rich piece of stationery, sealed with blue wax on the back and bearing the same penciled scrawl, this time addressed to Mrs. Mansfield.

The old lady collapsed in the nearest chair, holding her hand to her heart. She was speechless with fear.

"Well," said Mrs. Gardner huskily, "open it."

Ellery tore open the envelope. His frown deepened. "Why," he muttered, "there's nothing at all inside!"

Gardner gnawed his fingers and turned away, mumbling. Mrs. Gardner shook her head like a dazed pugilist and stumbled toward the bar for the fifth time that day. Emmy Willowes's brow was dark as thunder.

"You know," said Mrs. Owen almost quietly, "that's Mother's stationery."

Ellery muttered: "Queerer and queerer. I *must* get this organized. . . . The shoes are a puzzler. The toy boats might be construed as a gift; yesterday was Jonathan's birthday; the boats are his—a distorted practical joke. . . ." He shook his head. "Doesn't wash. And this third—an envelope without a letter in it. That would seem to point to the envelope as the important thing. But the envelope's the property of Mrs. Mansfield. The only other thing—ah, the wax!" He scanned the blue blob on the back narrowly, but it bore no seal insignia of any kind.

282

"That," said Mrs. Owen again in the quiet unnatural voice, "looks like our wax, too, Mr. Queen, from the library."

Ellery dashed away, followed by a troubled company. Mrs. Owen went to the library desk and opened the top drawer.

"Was it here?" asked Ellery quickly.

"Yes," she said, and then her voice quivered. "I used it only Friday when I wrote a letter. Oh, good . . ."

There was no stick of wax in the drawer.

And while they stared at the drawer, the front doorbell rang.

It was a market basket this time, lying innocently on the porch. In it, nestling crisp and green, were two large cabbages.

Ellery shouted for Gardner and Millan, and himself led the charge down the steps. They scattered, searching wildly through the brush and woods surrounding the house. But they found nothing. No sign of the bell ringer, no sign of the ghost who had cheerfully left a basket of cabbages at the door as his fourth odd gift. It was as if he were made of smoke and materialized only for the instant he needed to press his impalpable finger to the bell.

They found the women huddled in a corner of the living room, shivering and white-lipped. Mrs. Mansfield, shaking like an aspen, was at the telephone ringing for the local police. Ellery started to protest, shrugged, set his lips, and stooped over the basket.

There was a slip of paper tied by string to the handle of the basket. The same crude pencil scrawl. . . . "Mr. Paul Gardner."

"Looks," muttered Ellery, "as if you're elected, old fellow, this time."

Gardner stared as if he could not believe his eyes. "Cabbages!"

"Excuse me," said Ellery curtly. He went away. When he returned he was shrugging. "From the vegetable bin in the outside pantry, says Cook. She hadn't thought to look for missing *vegetables*, she told me with scorn."

Mrs. Mansfield was babbling, excitedly over the telephone to a sorely puzzled officer of the law. When she hung up she was red as a newborn baby. "That will be *quite* enough of this crazy nonsense, Mr. Queen!" she snarled. And then she collapsed in a chair and laughed hysterically and shrieked: "Oh, I knew you were making the mistake of your life when you married that beast, Laura!" and laughed again like a madwoman.

The law arrived in fifteen minutes, accompanied by a howling siren and personified by a stocky, brick-faced man in chief's stripes and a gangling young policeman.

"I'm Naughton," he said shortly. "What the devil's goin' on here?"

Ellery said: "Ah, Chief Naughton. I'm Queen's son—Inspector Richard Queen of Centre Street. How d'ye do?"

"Oh!" said Naughton. He turned on Mrs. Mansfield sternly. "Why didn't you say Mr. Queen was here, Mrs. Mansfield? You ought to know—"

"Oh, I'm sick of the lot of you!" screamed the old lady. "Non-sense, nonsense from the instant, this week-end began! First that awful actress-woman there, in her short skirt and legs and things, and then this—this—"

Naughton rubbed his chin. "Come over here, Mr. Queen, where we can talk like human beings. What the deuce happened?"

Ellery with a sigh told him. As he spoke, the Chief's face grew redder and redder. "You mean you're serious about this business?" he rumbled at last. "It sounds plain crazy to me. Mr. Owen's gone off his nut and he's playing jokes on you people. Good God, you can't take this thing serious!"

"I'm afraid," murmured Ellery, "we must. . . . What's that? By heaven, if that's another manifestation of our playful ghost—!" And he dashed toward the door while Naughton gaped and pulled it open, to be struck by a wave of dusk. On the porch lay the fifth parcel, a tiny one this time.

The two officers darted out of the house, flashlights blinking and probing. Ellery picked up the packet with eager fingers. It was addressed in the now familiar scrawl to Mrs. Paul Gardner. Inside were two identically shaped objects: chessmen, kings. One was white and the other was black.

"Who plays chess here?" he drawled.

"Richard," shrieked Mrs. Owen. "Oh, my God, I'm going mad!"

Investigation proved that the two kings from Richard Owen's chess-set were gone.

The local officers came back, rather pale, and panting. They had found no one outside. Ellery was silently studying the two chessmen.

"Well?" said Naughton, drooping his shoulders.

"Well," said Ellery quietly. "I have the most brilliant notion, Naughton. Come here a moment." He drew Naughton aside and began to speak rapidly in a low voice. The others stood limply about, twitch-ing with nervousness. There was no longer any pretense of self-control. If this was a joke, it was a ghastly one indeed. And Richard Owen looming in the background . . .

The Chief blinked and nodded. "You people," he said shortly, turning to them, "get into that library there." They gaped. "I mean it! The lot of you. This tomfoolery is going to stop right now."

"But, Naughton," gasped Mrs. Mansfield, "it couldn't be any of us who sent those things. Mr. Queen will tell you we weren't out of his sight today—"

"Do as I say, Mrs. Mansfield," snapped the officer.

They trooped, puzzled, into the library. The policeman rounded up Millan, the cook, the maid, and went with them. Nobody said anything; nobody looked at anyone else. Minutes passed; a half-hour; an hour. There was silence of the grave from beyond the door to the living room. They strained their ears. . . .

At seven-thirty the door was jerked open and Ellery and the Chief glowered in on them. "Everybody out," said Naughton shortly. "Come on, step on it."

"Out?" whispered Mrs. Owen. "Where? Where is Richard? What—"

The policeman herded them out. Ellery stepped to the door of the den and pushed it open and switched on the light and stood aside.

"Will you please come in here and take seats," he said dryly; there was a tense look on his face and he seemed exhausted.

Silently, slowly, they obeyed. The policeman dragged in extra chairs from the living room. They sat down. Naughton drew the shades. The policeman closed the door and set his back against it.

Ellery said tonelessly: "In a way this has been one of the most remarkable cases in my experience. It's been unorthodox from every angle. Utterly nonconforming. I think, Miss Willowes, the wish you expressed Friday night has come true. You're about to witness a slightly cock-eyed exercise in criminal ingenuity."

"Crim—" Mrs. Gardner's full lips quivered. "You mean—there's been a crime?"

"Quiet," said Naughton harshly.

"Yes," said Ellery in gentle tones, "there has been a crime. I might say—I'm sorry to say, Mrs. Owen—a major crime."

"Richard's d—"

"Im sorry." There was a little silence. Mrs. Owen did not weep; she seemed dried out of tears. "Fantastic," said Ellery at last. "Look here." He sighed. "The crux of the problem was the clock. The Clock That Wasn't Where It Should Have Been, the clock with the invisible face. You remember I pointed out that, since I hadn't seen the reflection of the luminous hands in that mirror there, the clock must have been moved. That was a tenable theory. But it wasn't the *only* theory."

"Richard's dead," said Mrs. Owen, in a wondering voice.

"Mr. Gardner," continued Ellery quickly, "pointed out one possibility: that the clock may still have been over this door, but that something or someone may have been standing in front of the mirror. I told you why that was impossible. But," and he went suddenly to the tall mirror, "there was still another theory which accounted for the fact that I hadn't seen the luminous hands' reflection. And that was: that when I opened the door in the dark and peered in and saw nothing, the clock was still there but the *mirror* wasn't!"

Miss Willowes said with a curious dryness: "But how could that be, Mr. Queen? That—that's silly."

"Nothing is silly, dear lady, until it is proved so. I said to myself: How could it be that the mirror wasn't there at that instant? It's apparently a solid part of the wall, a built-in section in this modern room." Something glimmered in Miss Willowes's eyes. Mrs. Mansfield was staring straight before her, hands clasped tightly in her lap. Mrs. Owen was looking at Ellery with glazed eyes, blind and deaf. "Then," said Ellery with another sigh, "there was the very odd nature of the packages which have been descending upon us all day like manna from heaven. I said this was a fantastic affair. Of course it must have occurred to you that someone was trying desperately to call our attention to the secret of the crime."

"Call our at—" began Gardner, frowning.

"Precisely. Now, Mrs. Owen," murmured Ellery softly, "the first package was addressed to you. What did it contain?" She stared at him without expression. There was a dreadful silence. Mrs. Mansfield suddenly shook her, as if she had been a child. She started, smiled vaguely; Ellery repeated the question.

And she said, almost brightly: "A pair of Richard's sport Oxfords."

He winced. "In a word, *shoes*. Miss Willowes," and despite her nonchalance she stiffened a little, "you were the recipient of the second package. And what did that contain?"

"Jonathan's toy boats," she murmured.

"In a word, again—*ships*. Mrs. Mansfield, the third package was sent to you. It contained what, precisely?"

"Nothing." She tossed her head. "I still think this is the purest drivel. Can't you see you're driving my daughter—all of us—insane? Naughton, are you going to permit this farce to continue? If you know what's happened to Richard, for goodness' sake tell us!"

"Answer the question," said Naughton with a scowl.

"Well," she said defiantly, "a silly envelope, empty, and sealed with our own wax."

"And again in a word," drawled Ellery, "*sealing-wax*. Now, Gard-

286

ner, to you fell the really whimsical fourth bequest. It was—?"

"Cabbage," said Gardner with an uncertain grin.

"Caggages, my dear chap; there were two of them. And finally, Mrs. Gardner, you received what?"

"Two chessmen," she whispered.

"No, no. Not just two chessmen, Mrs. Gardner. Two *kings*." Ellery's gray eyes glittered. "In other words, in the order named we were bombarded with gifts . . ." he paused and looked at them, and continued softly, "'*of shoes and ships and sealing-wax, of cabbages and kings*.'"

There was the most extraordinary silence. Then Emmy Willowes gasped: "'The Walrus and the Carpenter.' *Alice's Adventures in Wonderland!*"

"I'm ashamed of you, Miss Willowes. Where precisely does Tweedledee's Walrus speech come in Carroll's duology?"

A great light broke over her eager features. "*Through the Looking Glass!*"

"*Through the Looking Glass*," murmured Ellery in the crackling silence that followed. "And do you know what the subtitle of *Through the Looking Glass* is?"

She said in an awed voice: "*And What Alice Found There*."

"A perfect recitation, Miss Willowes. We were instructed, then, to go through the looking glass and, by inference, find something on the other side connected with the disappearance of Richard Owen. Quaint idea, eh?" He leaned forward and said brusquely: "Let me revert to my original chain of reasoning. I said that a likely theory was that the mirror didn't reflect the luminous hands because the mirror wasn't there. But since the wall at any rate is solid, the mirror itself must be movable to have been shifted out of place. How was this possible? Yesterday I sought for two hours to find the secret of that mirror—or should I say . . . looking glass?" Their eyes went with horror to the tall mirror set in the wall, winking back at them in the glitter of the bulbs. "And when I discovered the secret, I looked *through the looking glass* and what do you suppose I—a clumsy Alice, indeed!—found there?"

No one replied.

Ellery went swiftly to the mirror, stood on tiptoe, touched something, and something happened to the whole glass. It moved forward as if on hinges. He hooked his fingers in the crack and pulled. The mirror, like a door, swung out and away, revealing a shallow closet-like cavity.

The women with one breath screamed and covered their eyes.

The stiff figure of the Mad Hatter, with Richard Owen's unmistakable features, glared out at them—a dead, horrible, baleful glare.

Paul Gardner stumbled to his feet, choking and jerking at his collar. His eyes bugged out of his head. "O-O-Owen," he gasped. "Owen. He *can't* be here. I b-b-buried him myself under the big rock behind the house in the woods. Oh, my God." And he smiled a dreadful smile and his eyes turned over and he collapsed in a faint on the floor.

Ellery sighed. "It's all right now, De Vere," and the Mad Hatter moved and his features ceased to resemble Richard Owen's magically. "You may come out now. Admirable bit of statuary histrionics. And it turned the trick, as I thought it would. There's your man, Mr. Naughton. And if you'll question Mrs. Gardner, I believe you'll find that she's been Owen's mistress for some time. Gardner obviously found it out and killed him. Look out—there *she* goes, too!"

"What I can't understand," murmured Emmy Willowes after a long silence late that night, as she and Mr. Ellery Queen sat side by side in the local bound for Jamaica and the express for Pennsylvania Station, "Is—" She stopped helplessly. "I can't understand so many things, Mr. Queen."

"It was simple enough," said Ellery wearily, staring out the window at the rushing dark countryside.

"But who is that man—that De Vere?"

"Oh, he! A Thespian acquaintance of mine temporarily 'at liberty.' He's an actor—does character bits. You wouldn't know him, I suppose. You see, when my deductions had led me to the looking glass and I examined it and finally discovered its secret and opened it, I found Owen's body lying there in the Hatter costume—"

She shuddered. "Much too realistic drama to my taste. Why didn't you announce your discovery at once?"

"And gain what? There wasn't a shred of evidence against the murderer. I wanted time to think out a plan to make the murderer give himself away. I left the body there—"

"You mean to sit there and say you knew Gardner did it all the time?" she demanded, frankly skeptical.

He shrugged. "Of course. The Owens had lived in that house barely a month. The spring on that compartment is remarkably well concealed; it probably would never be discovered unless you knew it existed and were looking for it. But I recalled that Owen himself had remarked Friday night that Gardner had designed 'this development.' I had it then, naturally. Who more likely than the architect to know the secret of such a hidden closet? Why he designed and had built a secret panel I don't know; I suppose it fitted into some architectural whim of his. So it had to be Gardner, you see." He gazed thoughtfully at the dusty ceiling of the car. "I reconstructed the crime easily enough. After we retired Friday night Gardner came down to have it out with Owen about Mrs. Gardner—a lusty wench, if I ever saw one. They had words; Gardner killed him. It must have been an unpremeditated crime. His first impulse was to hide the body. He couldn't take it out Friday night in that awful rain without leaving traces on his night clothes. Then he remembered the panel behind the mirror. The body would be safe enough there, he felt, until he could remove it, when the rain stopped and the ground dried, to a permanent hiding place; dig a grave, or whatnot. . . . He was stowing the body away in the closet when I opened the door of the den; that was why I didn't see the reflection of the clock. Then, while I was in the library, he closed the mirror door and dodged upstairs. I came out quickly, though, and he decided to brazen it out; even pretended he thought I might be 'Owen' coming up.

"At any rate, Saturday night he drugged us all, took the body out, buried it, and came back and dosed himself with the drug to make his part as natural as possible. He didn't know I had found the body behind the mirror Saturday afternoon. When, Sunday morning, I found the body gone, I knew of course the reason for the drugging. Gardner by buring the body in a place unknown to anyone—without leaving, as far as he knew, even a clue to the fact that murder had been committed at all—was naturally doing away with the primary piece of evidence in any murder case . . . the *corpus delicti*. . . . Well, I found the opportunity to telephone De Vere and instruct him in what he had to do. He dug up the Hatter's costume somewhere, managed to get a photo of Owen from a theatrical office, came down here. . . . We put him in the closet while Naughton's man was detaining you people in the library. You see, I had to build up suspense, make Gardner give himself away, break down his moral resistance. He had to be forced to disclose where he had buried the body; and he was the only one who could tell us. It worked."

The actress, regarded him sidewise out of her clever eyes. Ellery sighed moodily, glancing away from her slim legs outstretched to the opposite seat. "But the most puzzling thing of all," she said with a pretty frown. "Those perfectly fiendish and fantastic packages. Who sent them, for heaven's sake?"

Ellery did not reply for a long time. Then he said drowsily, barely audible above the clatter of the train: "You did, really."

"*I?*" She was so startled that her mouth flew open.

"Only in a manner of speaking," murmured Ellery, closing his eyes. "Your idea about running a mad tea party out of *Alice* for Master Jonathan's delectation—the whole pervading spirit of the Reverend Dodgson—started a chain of fantasy in my own brain, you see. Just opening the closet and saying that Owen's body had been there, or even getting De Vere to act as Owen, wasn't enough. I had to prepare Gardner's mind psychologically, fill him with puzzlement first, get him to realize after a while where the gifts with their implications were leading. . . . Had to torture him, I suppose. It's a weakness of mine. At any rate, it was an easy matter to telephone my father, the Inspector; and he sent Sergeant Velie down and I managed to smuggle all those things I'd filched from the house out into the woods behind and hand good Velie what I had. . . . He did the rest, packaging and all."

She sat up and measured him with a severe glance. "Mr. Queen! Is that cricket in the best detective circles?"

He grinned sheepishly. "Drama, Miss Willowes. You ought to be able to understand that. Surround a murderer with things he doesn't understand, bewilder him, get him mentally punch-drunk, and then spring the knock-out blow, the crusher. . . . Oh, it was devilish clever of me, I admit."

She regarded him for so long and in such silence and with such supple twisting of her boyish figure that he stirred uncomfortably. "And what, if I may ask," he said lightly, "brings that positively lewd expression to your Peter Pannish face? You must be feeling—"

"As Alice would say," she said softly, leaning a little toward him, "curiouser and curiouser."

CRIME
IN THE RUE
SAINTE-CATHERINE

By Georges Simenon

Georges Joseph Christian Simenon (1903–) was born into a struggling middle-class family in Liege, Belgium and at sixteen was forced to leave school in order to earn a living. He took a variety of jobs, first as a baker's apprentice, then as a clerk in a bookstore, and finally as a reporter on the local newspaper where for three years he had his own column. At the same time, he began writing short stories and novels, completing one book in ten days and publishing it in 1920 when he was still only seventeen. After his military service, Simenon went to Paris in 1923 and embarked on one of the most prolific careers in the history of fiction, producing forty novels in a single year. In 1929 he wrote The Strange Case of Peter the Lett, *the first of his detective novels featuring Jules Maigret, a warm-hearted, pipe-smoking, intuitive officer of French police, and followed this up with eighteen more Maigret books in as many months, including* The Crossroad Murders *(1931) and* The Sailors' Rendezvous *(1931). The Maigret stories were immediately popular in France and were soon being read in translation all over the world, but Simenon had meanwhile abandoned the character in order to write more serious fiction and did not return to him until the early 1940s. Between that time and 1973, when he announced that he was giving up writing because of poor health, Simenon continued to produce both novels and short stories about Maigret. The only appearances in the United States of the latter were frequently in the pages of* Ellery Queen's Mystery Magazine, *where "Crime in the Rue Ste. Catherine" was published in January 1970. Two books about Simenon and his work are Thomas Narcejac's* The Art of Simenon *(London: Routledge & Kegan Paul, 1952), and John Raymond's* Simenon in Court *(New York: Harcourt, Brace & World, 1969). See also* The Short Cases of Inspector Maigret *(New York: Doubleday, 1959).*

A fine, cold drizzle was falling, and it was dark. The only light was toward the end of the street, near the barracks, where at half-past five the trumpets had sounded, and now you could hear the noise of horses being taken to be watered. There the dimly lit rectangle of a window could be seen: someone getting up early, or perhaps a sick person who had been awake all night.

The rest of the street was asleep. A wide quiet street, newish with houses all much the same, one- or at the most two-storied, such as are found in the suburbs of most big provincial towns.

The whole district was new, devoid of mystery; its inhabitants were quiet and unassuming—employees, traveling salesmen; people of limited means, peaceable widows.

Inspector Maigret, coat collar turned up, stood pressed into the corner of the entrance to the boys' school; he was waiting, watch in hand and smoking his pipe.

At a quarter to six precisely, the bells of the parish church rang out behind him, and he knew it was, as the boy had said, the "first stroke" of the six o'clock Mass.

The chimes were still reverberating in the damp air when he heard, or rather sensed, the jarring outburst of an alarm clock in the house opposite. It lasted only a few seconds. In the dark the child's hand must already have stretched out from the warmth of his bed and gropingly turned off the alarm. A few seconds later the attic window on the second floor lit up.

It was happening exactly as the boy had said. He was the first to get up, noiselessly, in the still-sleeping house. Now he must be throwing on his clothes, his socks, splashing water on his face and hands, running a comb through his hair. As for his shoes, he had stated, "I carry them downstairs and put them on the bottom step in order not to wake my parents."

It had been the same every day, winter and summer, for almost two years, since Justin had started as altar boy at the six o'clock mass at the hospital.

He had also told them: "The hospital clock is always three or four minutes behind the parish church."

And the Chief Inspector had proof of this. The day before, at the flying squad to which he had been assigned for some months, his Inspectors had shrugged at these detailed stories of bells and first strokes and second strokes. But Maigret, perhaps because he too had served as

Reprinted by permission of the author from *Ellery Queen's Mystery Magazine*, January 1970. Copyright © 1970 by Georges Simenon.

altar boy for a long time, had not found them laughable.

The parish bells first, at a quarter to six. Then Justin's alarm clock in the attic where he slept. Then, after a few minutes' interval, the higher-pitched, more silvery chimes of the hospital chapel, which made one think of convent bells.

Maigret was still holding his watch in his hand. The child took just a little more than four minutes to dress. His light went out. He must have been groping his way downstairs, still trying not to wake his parents. Sitting down on the bottom step and putting on his shoes, taking his coat and cap from the bamboo hatstand that stood on the right in the hallway.

The door opened. The youngster closed it without a sound, looked anxiously up and down the street, then saw the bulky silhouette of the Inspector approaching.

"I was afraid you wouldn't be there," the boy said. And he started off, walking fast. He was a little fellow of twelve, fair, thin, already self-willed.

"You want me to do just the same as the other days, don't you? I always walk quickly. At first it was to see how many minutes it would take me, and then in winter, when it's dark, I'm afraid. In a month from now, at this time, it'll begin to get light."

He took the first street on the right, another quiet street, rather shorter, which opened out on a square planted round with elm trees and crossed diagonally by streetcar tracks.

Maigret noticed minute details that brought back his own childhood. First, the youngster kept away from the houses as he walked, no doubt because he was afraid someone might step out of the shadow of a doorway. Then, to cross the square, he kept clear of the trees in the same way, for a man could have been hiding behind them.

In fact, he was a pretty brave little chap, as, for two winters, in all weathers, sometimes in thick fog or moonless dark, he had been going along the same route every morning all alone.

"When we get to the middle of the rue Sainte-Catherine," the boy said, "you'll hear the second stroke of the Mass from the parish church."

"What time does the first streetcar go past?"

"Six o'clock. I've only seen it two or three times when I was late. Once my alarm didn't go off. Another time I went back to sleep. That's why I always jump out of bed when it goes off."

A wan little face in the rainy darkness, eyes that still retained some of the stupor of sleep, a thoughtful expression with only the slightest hint of fear.

"I shan't go on serving at Mass. It's only because you insisted that I came today."

They turned left on to the rue Sainte-Catherine where, as in all the other streets in the district, there was a lamp every fifty yards or so, each throwing a pool of light. Between these the child unconsciously walked more quickly than when he was crossing each reassuring circle of lamplight.

The distant noises of the barracks could still be heard. Lights were coming on in some of the windows. Someone was walking somewhere in a cross street.

"When you got to the corner of the street you didn't see anything?"

That was the critical point, for the rue Sainte-Catherine was quite straight and deserted. With the pavements straight as a die, and street-lamps at regular intervals, there was not enough shadow between them for one to miss seeing, even at a hundred yards, two men having a row.

"Perhaps I wasn't looking where I was going. I was talking to myself, I remember. I often do in the morning when I'm going this way, talk away to myself under my breath . . . I wanted to ask my mother something when I got home and I was repeating to myself what I was going to say to her."

"What did you want to say to her?"

"For a long time I've wanted a bike. I've already saved up one hundred francs out of what I get for the Masses."

It may have been just an impression, but it seemed to Maigret that the child was keeping farther out from the houses. He even stepped off the pavement, then got onto it a little farther on.

"Here it is. Listen—that's the second stroke chiming at the parish church."

Meanwhile Maigret was trying, quite unconscious of the absurdity, to penetrate into that world that was the boy's world each morning.

"I must have raised my head. You know, like when one is running without looking and one finds oneself up against a wall . . . It was right at this spot." He pointed to the line on the pavement that separated the shadow from the light of a streetlamp, in which the fine rain was dancing like luminous dust.

"First I noticed there was a man stretched out, and he seemed so big that I'd have sworn he took up the whole width of the pavement."

That was impossible, for the pavement was about eight feet wide.

"I don't know what I did exactly. I must have swerved out of the way. I didn't run off right away because I saw the knife in his chest, with a thick brown horn handle—I noticed it because my Uncle Henri has a knife almost the same and he told me it was stag's horn. I'm sure the man was dead."

"Why?"

"I don't know. He looked dead."

"His eyes were closed?"

"I didn't notice his eyes. I don't know any more. But I had a feeling he was dead. It all happened very quickly, as I told you yesterday in your office. But I had to repeat the same things so many times all day yesterday that I'm mixed up. Especially when I feel no one believes me."

"And the other man?"

"When I looked up I saw there was someone a little farther on, perhaps fifteen feet or so away. Someone with very bright eyes. He looked at me for a second, and started to run. It was the murderer."

"How d'you know?"

"Because he ran off as fast as he could."

"Which direction?"

"Straight down there."

"Towards the barracks, in fact?"

"Yes."

It was true that Justin had been questioned at least ten times the previous day. Before Maigret's arrival at the office, the other Inspectors had even made a sort of game of it. But not once had the boy changed the smallest detail.

"What did you do?"

"I started to run, too. It's difficult to explain . . . I think it was when I saw the man running away that I felt frightened. And then I ran as fast as I could."

"In the opposite direction?"

"Yes."

"You didn't think of calling for help?"

"No. I was too scared. Most of all I was afraid my legs would suddenly give out, for I couldn't feel them any longer. I ran back as far as the place du Congrès. I took the other street. It also leads to the hospital, but the long way round."

"Let's go on."

Bells again, high-pitched bells, the chapel ones. After another fifty yards or so there was a crossroads and on the left were the loopholed walls of the barracks, on the right a vast dimly-lit doorway surmounted by the greenish dial of a clock.

It was three minutes to six.

"I'm a minute late. Yesterday, in spite of everything I got here on time because I ran."

In the middle of the oak door there was a heavy knocker, which the boy raised. The din echoed through the porch. A slippered porter came to open up, let Justin through, and placed himself in Maigret's path, looking at him with suspicion. "What is it?"

"Police."

"You've got your identification?"

You crossed a porch, where the first hospital odors greeted you; then, through a second door, you found yourself in a vast courtyard full of outbuildings. Far away in the shadows you could make out the white headdresses of the nuns on their way to the chapel.

"Why didn't you say anything to the porter yesterday?"

"I don't know. I was hurrying to get there."

Maigret could understand that. For the boy it wasn't the lodge with its distrustful, grumpy porter that was a haven, or this cold court-yard where stretchers were borne silently past. It was the warm sacristy, near the chapel, where one of the sisters was lighting the altar candles.

There were two poles, in fact, for the boy each morning and he went from one to the other in a dizzy rush—his room under the roof, from which the ringing of the alarm clock dragged him, and, at the other end of a sort of void filled only with the chimes of the bells, the sacristy of the chapel.

"You're coming in with me?"

"Yes."

Justin seemed put out, or rather shocked, no doubt at the idea of this Inspector, who was perhaps an unbeliever, penetrating into his sacred world. Maigret could understand now why the child had the courage to get up so early every morning and overcome his fears.

The chapel was warm and cosy. Already the patients in their gray-blue uniforms, some with their heads bandaged, some with their arms in slings, some on crutches, were lined up on the seats in the nave. In the gallery the sisters formed up like a uniform troupe, and all the white coifs dipped at the same time in mystic reverence.

"Follow me."

They had to go up a few steps, pass near the altar, where the candles were already burning. On the right there was a dark-paneled sacristy, a tall bony priest who was finishing putting on his vestments, a lace-trimmed surplice that was ready for the boy, and a nun busy filling the altar vessels.

It was only at this point, the day before, that Justin, panting, his throat dry and his legs shaky, had come to a halt. It was here he had cried out, "A man has just been killed in the rue Sainte-Catherine."

A small clock set into the paneling showed six o'clock exactly. Bells were ringing again; they were less distinct inside than out. Justin said to the nun who was helping him with his surplice, "It's the police Inspector."

Maigret stood there while the child, preceding the chaplain, shook out the folds of his red cassock and hurried toward the altar steps.

The vestry nun had said "Justin is a good little boy. Very devout. He has never told us a lie. Sometimes he hasn't turned up to serve the Mass. He could have pretended he was sick. But no, he admitted quite openly that he couldn't bear to get up because it was too cold, or because he had had nightmares during the night and was feeling tired."

And the chaplain, Mass over, had looked at the Inspector with eyes as bright as those of a stained-glass saint, and said, "Why should you think this child would make up such a story?"

Maigret knew now what had happened in the hospital chapel. How Justin's teeth had chattered and how, at the end of his tether, he had a fit of hysterics. Mass mustn't be held up, so the sacristy nun warned the Sister Superior, and took the place of the child, who meanwhile was being fussed over in the vestry.

It was ten minutes before the Sister Superior thought of informing the police. She had to go through the chapel. Everybody felt something was afoot. At the local headquarters the desk sergeant could not understand.

"What? Sister Superior? Superior to what?"

So she repeated gently in her convent voice that a crime had been committed in the rue Sainte-Catherine. And the police had found nothing, neiher victim nor, of course, murderer . . .

As he did every day, Justin had gone to school at half-past eight as if nothing had happened, and he was in class when Inspector Besson, a chunky little man who looked like a boxer and played the tough guy, had come for him at half-past nine, when the report had reached the flying squad.

Poor boy, for two hours in a gloomy office that reeked of pipe smoke and the stove that didn't draw, he had been questioned, not as a witness but like a suspect. One after the other, three Inspectors— Besson, Thiberge, and Vallin—had tried to make him waver in his story.

And then, for good measure, his mother had followed the child. She waited in the anteroom, crying and sniffing by turn and telling everyone, "We're honest people. We've never had any trouble with the police."

Maigret, who had been working late the night before on a narcotics case, hadn't arrived in his office until around eleven.

"What's this?" he had asked on seeing the boy, dry-eyed, and looking with his skinny legs for all the world like an indignant little cock.

"A brat who's trying to make fools of us. He says he saw a corpse in the street—he even saw the murderer who ran away at his approach. But a streetcar passed along the same street four minutes later and the driver saw nothing. The street is a quiet one, and nobody heard anything. Furthermore, when the police were called, a quarter of an hour later, by some nun or other, there was absolutely nothing on the pavement, not the least speck of blood."

"Come into my office, son."

Maigret was the first person who had spoken civilly to Justin that morning, the first to treat him like a grownup and not like some brat with a vivid imagination.

Maigret had made him repeat his story, simply and quietly, without interrupting and without taking notes.

"You're going to go on serving Mass at the hospital?"

"No. I never want to go there again. I'm too scared."

But it was a heavy sacrifice. The child was certainly devout, he certainly responded to the poetry of early Mass in the warm, rather mysterious atmosphere of the chapel. And, besides, he was paid for these Masses, not much, but enough to let him put aside a little nest egg. And he did so long enough to have the bicycle his parents couldn't afford to give him.

"I'm going to ask you to go there once again. Only once. Tomorrow morning."

"I wouldn't dare to walk that way."

"I'll come with you. I'll wait for you in front of your house. And you'll do exactly the same as all the other times."

And that was how Maigret had found himself all alone at seven in the morning at the hospital entrance, in a district that the day before he knew only from having passed through by streetcar or automobile.

An icy drizzle was still falling from the sky, which was now a watery green. Eventually it soaked into the Inspector's coat and he sneezed twice. There were several people passing by, coat collars turned up and hands in pockets; at the butchers' and grocers' the shutters were being opened.

It was the most ordinary, peaceful district you could possibly imagine. Only with the greatest difficulty could you conceive of two men, even two drunks, having a row at five or six in the morning on the pavement of the rue Sainte-Catherine.

But then there was the sequel. According to the boy's statement, at his approach the murderer had run off, and it had then been five to six. Now, at six, the first streetcar went by and the driver insisted he had seen nothing. Of course, he could have had his attention distracted, could have been looking in the opposite direction.

But at five past six, two police constables who were coming off their beat had walked along that very same pavement. And *they* had seen nothing.

At seven or eight minutes past six, a cavalry officer who lived three houses away from the spot Justin had pointed out had left home as he did every morning to go to the barracks. *He* hadn't seen anything, either.

Finally, at six twenty, the constables had cycled from the district police station and *they* had found no trace of the victim.

Had someone come meanwhile and removed the body in a car or truck? Soberly and without any fuss, Maigret had set out to envisage all the possibilities, and this one had turned out to be as false as the others. There was a sick woman at Number 42 in the street, and her husband had been up with her all night. He was quite positive.

"We can hear all the noises from outside. I was paying special attention as my wife, who is in great pain, is upset by the slightest noise. Wait a moment . . . It was the streetcar that woke her, just as she had dropped off. I can tell you that no car went past before seven that morning. The first thing to go by was the dustcart."

"And you heard nothing else?"

"There was a sound of running at one point."

"Before the streetcar?"

"Yes, for my wife was sleeping. I was getting myself a cup of coffee."

"One person running?"

"More like two."

"You don't know in which direction?"

"The blind was down. As it makes a noise when you pull it up, I didn't look out."

That was the only evidence in support of Justin's story.

There was a bridge about two hundred yards away, and the constable on duty had not seen any car passing. One would have to suppose that only a few minutes after running away the murderer had come back, heaved his victim onto his shoulders, and carried him off heaven knows where—and all without attracting any attention.

There was worse to come. There was evidence that made people shrug off the child's story. The place he had pointed out was situated just across from 61. Inspector Thiberge had called there the day before, and Maigret, who left nothing to chance, was now ringing there in his turn.

It was a newish house of red brick, with three steps up to the varnished pitch-pine door on which a polished brass letterbox shone. It was only a quarter past seven, but from what he had heard, the Inspector knew he could safely present himself at that hour.

A withered old woman, with a hairy upper lip, first opened a spyhole in the door and parleyed with him before letting him into a hall fragrant with the aroma of freshly made coffee. "I'll find out if the Judge will see you."

The house was occupied by a retired member of the judiciary, who was said to have a private income; he lived there alone with his servant.

There was a sound of whispering in the front room, which would normally have been the drawing room. Then the old woman came out and said spitefully, "Come in, but wipe your feet, please. This isn't a stable."

It wasn't a drawing room—it wasn't like anything one normally imagines. The room, which was fairly large, was something of a bedroom, study, library, and even attic, for it was heaped with the most unexpected objects.

"You're coming to look for the corpse?" a voice sneered, and made the Inspector start.

As there was a bed in the room he had quite naturally looked in that direction, but it was empty. The voice came from the corner of the fireplace where a thin old man was sunk in the depths of an armchair, a rug around his legs.

"Take your coat off. I love heat, and you won't be able to stand it for long in here."

That was so. The old man, who had a pair of tongs within reach, was doing his best to produce the biggest blaze possible from a log fire.

"I thought that, since my day, the police had made some progress and had learned to distrust the evidence of children. Children and young girls, they're the most dangerous witnesses, and when I was a Judge—"

He was wearing a thick dressing gown, and, despite the temperature in the room, around his neck there was a scarf as wide as a shawl.

"So it was right opposite my house that the crime is supposed to have been committed, eh? And you, if I'm not mistaken, are the famous Chief Inspector Maigret, whom they've been good enough to send to our town to reorganize the flying squad?" His voice grated. He was a nasty old man, aggressive and full of savage irony.

"Well, my dear Inspector, unless you accuse me of being in league with the murderer I regret to inform you, as I already told your colleague yesterday, you're on the wrong track.

"As you've no doubt been told, old men need very little sleep. And there are some people who manage with very little all their lives. That was the case with Erasmus, for instance, and also with a gentleman known by the name of Voltaire." His glance moved complacently to the library shelves stacked up to the ceiling with books.

"I could quote you many other cases you would know equally little about. But, to be brief, it is so in my own case. I pride myself on not having slept more than three hours a night in the last fifteen years. As, for the last ten, my legs have refused to support me and, in any case, I have no curiosity about the places where they could take me, I spend my days and my nights in this room which, as you can see, looks straight out onto the street.

"From four in the morning I sit in this chair, wide-awake, believe me. I could show you the book in which I was immersed this morning, but as it's a Greek philosopher I suppose that wouldn't interest you. However, if any event of the kind described by your over-imaginative boy had taken place beneath my window, I can assure you I would have noticed it. My legs may have failed, as I told you, but my hearing is as good as ever.

"Besides, I am still curious enough by nature to take an interest in all that happens in the street, and if it amuses you I can tell at what time every housewife in the neighborhood passes my window on her way to the shops."

He looked at Miagret with a triumphant smile.

"So you're accustomed to hear young Justin going past?" the Inspector asked with saintly sweetness.

"Naturally."

"Hear and see him?"

"I don't understand."

"For more than half the year—for almost two-thirds, it's light at six in the morning. And the child served at Mass in summer as well as winter."

"I used to see him pass."

"Seeing that it was such a regular daily occurrence, like the first streetcar, you must have been expecting it."

"What do you mean?"

"For example, when a factory whistle in the neighborhood goes off every day at the same time, or when a person passes by your window as regular as clockwork, you naturally say to yourself, 'There, it's such-and-such a time.' If one day the whistle doesn't sound, you say to yourself, 'It must be Sunday.' If the person doesn't go past, you wonder, 'What can have happened to him? Is he ill?'"

The Judge's eyes were watching Maigret narrowly. He gave the impression of resenting Maigret's lecture.

"I know all that," he muttered, cracking his fingerjoints. "I was a Judge before you joined the force."

"When the altar boy went past—"

"I heard him, if that's what you want to make me admit!"

"And if he didn't go past?"

"I could happen to notice it. But I could also happen not to notice it. As in the case of the whistle you were speaking of just now: one is not struck by the absence of the whistle every Sunday."

"And yesterday?" Maigret might have been mistaken but he had the impression that the old Judge scowled; there was in his look something sulky, something fiercely shut in. But then old people often sulk just like children, and sometimes show the same childish stubbornness.

"Yesterday?"

"Yes, yesterday." There was no reason for the Judge to repeat the question except to give himself more time.

"I didn't notice anything."

"You didn't notice if he passed?"

"No."

"Or if he didn't pass?"

"No." Still the same frank and seemingly triumphant "No."

"No tramping of feet, no thud of a falling body, no gasping?"

"Nothing at all."

"Thank you."

"Pray don't mention it."

"Seeing that you were a magistrate, I obviously need not ask if you are ready to repeat your evidence under oath?"

"Whenever you want me to." And the old man said that with a sort of gleeful impatience.

"I must apologize for having disturbed you, sir."

The old servant must have been standing outside the door, for she was right on the threshold to show the Inspector out and close the door behind him.

Maigret had a strange feeling as he stepped out again into the everyday life of that calm suburban street, where the housewives were beginning to make their way to the shops and children could be seen going to school. It seemed to him that he had just been hoaxed, and yet the Judge had not been lying—except for one omission. He had the impression, too, that at one point he had been on the verge of discovering something very odd, very subtle, and very unexpected; at that moment it would have taken only a little effort to bring it off, but he had been incapable of doing it.

In his mind's eye he saw the boy again; he saw the old man again. He tried to see some connection between the two.

He stood on the edge of the pavement, slowly filling his pipe. Then as he had not yet had breakfast, not even a cup of coffee on getting up, and his drenched overcoat was clinging to his shoudlers, he went to the corner of the place du Congrès and waited for a streetcar to take him back.

The mass of sheets and blankets heaved like a sea swell, an arm emerged, a red face appeared, shining with sweat; then a surly voice grumbled out, "Pass me the thermometer."

Madame Maigret was sewing by the window where she had drawn back the lace curtain to be able to see despite the twilight; she rose with a sign and switched on the light. "I thought you were asleep. It's not half an hour since you took your temperature."

Resigned, knowing from experience that it was useless to thwart her great bear of a husband, she shook the thermometer, then slid it between his lips. He found time to ask, "Nobody's come?"

"You should know, as you haven't been alseep."

He must have dropped off, however, even if it was only for a few minutes. It was that wretched carillon that kept dragging him out of his torpor and bringing him to the surface again.

It wasn't their own home. As his assignment in this provincial town was to last about six months, and as Madame Maigret could not bear the thought of her husband eating in restaurants for such a long period, she had gone with him, and they had rented a furnished apartment in the center of the town.

It was too bright for their liking with its floral wallpapers and bargain-basement furniture, and the bed that groaned under the Inspector's weight. But at least they had chosen a quiet street where, as the landlady, Madame Danse, said, not even a cat went by.

What the landlady hadn't said was that, the ground floor being occupied by a dairy, a stale smell of cheese hung about the whole house. Nor had she mentioned—and Maigret had just found out, for it was the first time he had spent the day in bed there—that the door of the dairy below was fitted not with a bell of the usual kind but with a strange apparatus of metal tubes that slowly jangled out a carillon each time a customer entered.

"How much?"

"101½."

"A little while ago it was 101."

"It'll be 102 later."

He was furious. He was always bad-tempered when he was ill, and he glowered at Madame Maigret with deep resentment for she insisted on not going out just when he would have loved to have a smoke.

It was still raining, still the same fine rain that streaked the windows, falling silently, drearily down, and giving one the feeling of being in an aquarium. The electric-light bulb, hanging unshaded at the end of its cord, gave out a harsh light. You could picture street upon street, equally empty, where the windows lit up one after the other, and people went to and fro in their cages like fish in a bowl.

"You're going to have another cup of herb tea."

That would be about the tenth since midday, and he would have to sweat out all that tepid water into his sheets, turning them in the long run into a damp compress.

He must have caught this chill or cold while he was waiting for the boy in the cold morning rain on the school doorstep, or perhaps later while he was roaming round the street. He had hardly got back at ten o'clock to his office at the flying squad headquarters and embarked on his normal ritual of poking the stove when he started to shiver. Then he felt too hot. His eyelids began to sting, and when he looked into the scrap of mirror in the cloakroom he saw his eyes were swollen and moist.

Besides, his pipe didn't taste the same, always a sure sign.

"Look here, Besson, if by chance I don't come in this afternoon you'll go on with the inquiries on this affair of the altar boy."

And Besson, who always thought he knew better than anyone else, said, "You really think, Chief, that there is anything there that a good hiding wouldn't put a stop to?"

"All the same you'll have the rue Sainte-Catherine watched by one of your colleagues—by Vallin, for instance."

"In case the corpse comes back to lie down in front of the Judge's house?"

The start of his chill left Maigret too much under the weather to rise to that. He continued heavily giving instructions. "Give me a list of all the people living in the street. As it isn't a very long one, that won't be too much work."

"Shall I question the boy again?"

"No."

From then on he had been feverish; he could feel the drops of sweat break out on his skin one after the other; he had a stale taste in his mouth, and he kept longing to sink into sleep; but when he did it was only to hear immediately the ridiculous carillon of the brass tubes in the dairy.

He hated being ill because it humiliated him and also because Madame Maigret kept a fierce watch on him to prevent him smoking his pipe. If only there had been something she should go and buy at the pharmacist's! But she had taken care to bring the contents of a full medicine cabinet with her from home.

He hated being ill, and yet there were moments when it was almost voluptuous, moments when, on closing his eyes, his years dropped away and he relived his childhood. Then there would come before him the face of young Justin, pale and strong for his years. All that morning's images returned to his memory, no longer with the precision of everyday reality, no longer in the dry light of things that one sees, but with the peculiar intensity of things that one feels.

For instance, he could have described in almost every detail that attic room he had not been in — the iron bed, the alarm clock on the bedside table, the child stretching out his hand, dressing noiselessly, with every gesture the same as always . . .

The same as always — that was it. That seemed to him important as evidence, as truth. When for two years at a fixed time one serves at Mass, one's actions become absolutely automatic.

The first chimes at a quarter to six . . . the alarm . . . the higher-pitched chapel bells . . . the shoes at the bottom of the stairs . . . the door opening on the cold breath of the morning town.

"You know, Madame Maigret, he's never read a detective story." Ever since they had once done so as a joke they had called each other Maigret and Madame Maigret, and now they had almost forgotten that they had first names like everyone else.

"He doesn't read the papers either."

"You should try to get to sleep."

With a last look at his pipe, lying on the black marble of the mantelpiece, he closed his eyes.

"I questioned his mother for a long time. She's a good woman, but far too easily upset by the police."

"Go to sleep."

He was silent for a little while. His breathing became louder, as if he was about to drop off. "She said he'd never seen a corpse. That's something one avoids showing children."

"What's that to do with it?"

"He told me the corpse was so big it seemed to span the pavement. That's exactly the impression you do get from a dead body on the ground. A dead body always looks bigger than a living man. You understand?"

"I don't see why you are worrying about it. Besson's taking care of all that."

"Besson doesn't believe in it."

"In what?"

"In the dead man."

"Would you like me to turn off the light?"

Despite his protests she got up on a chair and put some oiled paper round the bulb in order to lessen the glare.

"Try to sleep for an hour, and then I'll give you a fresh cup of herb tea. You're not sweating enough."

"D'you think if I just took a puff or two at my pipe—?"

"Are you mad?"

She went into the kitchen to look at the vegetable broth; he could hear her padding about. All the time in front of his eyes he saw the same stretch of the rue Sainte-Catherine, with streetlamps every fifty yards.

"The Judge claims he didn't hear anything."

"What are you saying?"

"I bet you they loathe each other."

"Who are you talking about?" Her voice came from the other end of the kitchen. "Can't you see I'm busy?"

"The Judge and the altar boy . . . They've never spoken to each other, but I bet you anything they loathe each other. You know, very old people, especially those who live alone, come to be just like children. Justin went by every morning, and every morning the old Judge was there by the window. He looks like a screech owl."

"I don't know what you mean."

She stood there framed in the doorway, a steaming ladle in her hand.

"Try to follow. The Judge claims he didn't hear anything, and it's too serious for me to suspect him of lying."

"I should hope so!"

"Only he doesn't dare to say that he did or didn't hear Justin go by yesterday morning."

"Perhaps he fell asleep again."

"No . . . He doesn't dare to lie, so he is deliberately vague about it. But the husband in Number 42, who was sitting up with his sick wife, heard running in the street."

He kept coming back to that. Sharpened by the fever, his thoughts went round in circles.

"But what could have happened to the corpse?" Madame Maigret's objection showed all the sound sense of a middle-aged woman. "Anyway, don't think about it any more. Besson knows his job—you've often said so yourself."

Discouraged, he sank under the blankets, and tried hard to fall asleep, but it wasn't long before he was thinking again of the altar boy, his legs white against the black socks.

"There's something wrong—" he worried.

"What're you saying? Something wrong? You feel worse? You want me to call the doctor?"

Madame Maigret put down her ladle.

No. He was starting from zero all over again, obstinately. He was setting out again from the entry of the boy's school, crossing the place du Congrès. "There! It's here something goes wrong—"

First because the Judge hadn't heard anything. Unless one were to accuse him of giving false testimony, it was difficult to accept that there could have been a fight under his window, a few feet away, that a man could have started running in the direction of the barracks while the altar boy rushed off in the other direction without the Judge hearing any of it at all.

"I say, Madame Maigret—"

"What is it now?"

"Suppose they both ran off in the same direction?"

Madame Maigret sighed, picked up her sewing, and settled down dutifully to listen to this monologue interspersed with the hoarse breathing of her husband.

"For one thing, it's more logical—"

"What's more logical?"

"That they should both run off in the same direction. But, in this case, it was not in the direction of the barracks."

"You mean the boy chased the murderer?"

"No. It's the murderer who would have chased the boy."

"What for, as he didn't kill him?"

"To make him keep quiet, for instance."

"But he didn't manage, as the child has told his story."

"Or to prevent him saying something, giving away some detail. Listen, Madame Maigret—"

"What do you want?"

"I know you'll start by refusing, but it's absolutely essential. Pass me my pipe and my tobacco. Just a few puffs. I have the impression that I'm on the point of understanding—that in a few minutes, if I don't lose the thread—"

She went over for the pipe on the mantelpiece; with a sign of resignation she held it out to him. "I knew you'd find a good excuse. Anyway, this evening, whether you like it or not, I'm going to make you a mustard plaster."

As luck would have it, there was no telephone in the apartment. You had to go down to the dairy where the instrument was behind the counter.

"You are going to go downstairs, Madame Maigret, and you will call Besson. It's seven o'clock; maybe he's still at the office. If not, call the Café du Centre; he'll be playing billiards there with Thiberge."

"I'm to ask him to come round?"

"To bring me over as quickly as possible not the list of everybody who lives on the street, but a list of the tenants of the houses on the left-hand side, and only between the place du Congrès and the Judge's house."

"Try at least not to get uncovered."

She had hardly started going downstairs when he got himself out of bed, hurried barefoot to his tobacco pouch to fill the pipe, then lay down again, all innocence, in the bed.

Through the thin floorboards he could hear a voice murmuring, the voice of Madame Maigret at the telephone. He smoked with relish, in little greedy puffs, although his throat was very sore. In front of him raindrops slid slowly down the black windowpanes, and that reminded him afresh of his young days and the childhood illnesses when his mother brought him caramel custard in bed.

Madame Maigret came up again, puffing a little, glanced round the room to see if anything was wrong, but didn't think of the pipe.

"He'll be here in about an hour."

"I must ask you to do something else, Madame Maigret. You must get dressed—" She gave him a suspicious look. "You will go to young Justin's house and you will ask his parents' permission to bring him to me. Be nice to him. If I sent one of the Inspectors, he would be sure to frighten him, and the boy's already too inclined to stiffen up. You will simply tell him that I would like to chat with him for a few minutes."

"And if his mother wants to come with him?"

"Get out of it as best you can. I don't want the mother."

He was all alone, hot, sweaty, deep down in the bed, with his pipe sticking out from the bedclothes and emitting a light cloud of smoke. When he closed his eyes he kept seeing the corner of the rue Sainte-Catherine; he was no longer Maigret the Chief Inspector—he was the altar boy, hurrying along, going the same way every morning at the same time, speaking to himself under his breath to keep up his courage.

He turned the corner of the rue Sainte-Catherine . . .

"Mother, I would like you to buy me a bike—" The boy was practising the speech he would make to his mother when he got home from the hospital. But it must have been more complex than that. The child would surely think up some more subtle approaches.

"You know, Mother, if I had a bike, I could—"

Or perhaps: "I've already saved up one hundred francs. If you would lend me the rest—I promise to pay it back out of the money I get for the Masses—I could—"

The corner of the rue Sainte-Catherine . . . A few moments before the parish church bells sound the second stroke . . . and there were only another hundred and fifty meters of black, empty street to go in order to touch the reassuring door of the hospital . . . A few strides between the pools of light from the streetlamps.

And later the boy would say, "I looked up, and I saw—"

The whole problem was there. The Judge lived almost exactly halfway up the street, equidistant from the place du Congrès and the barracks corner, and he had neither seen nor heard anything.

The sick woman's husband, the man at Number 42, lived nearer the place du Congrès, on the right side of the street, and he had heard the hurrying footsteps of a man running.

Yet, five minutes later, there was neither corpse nor wounded man on the pavement. And neither car nor truck had passed. The constable on duty at the bridge, the other policemen in the district who were on their beats at different places, none of them had seen anything unusual—like, for example, a man carrying another on his back.

His temperature must have been rising, but Maigret no longer thought of consulting the thermometer. It was just like his childhood: when he was ill it seemed to him that his mother, leaning over him, seemed so big that she filled the house.

There was this body lying across the pavement—so big because it was dead, with a brown-handled knife in its chest.

And behind it a man standing a few yards away, a man with very bright eyes, who had started to run—

To run in the direction of the barracks, while Justin took to his heels and fled in the opposite direction.

"There!"

There what? Maigret had said the word aloud as if it contained the solution to the problem—as if it *were* the solution to the problem. He was smiling with satisfaction as he drew on his pipe in voluptuous little puffs.

Drunks are like that. Truths suddenly become evident to them which they are incapable of explaining and which fade away as soon as they sober up.

It was there that was something false! And, in his fever, it was exactly at the point that Miagret located the jarring detail.

"Justin didn't make it up—"

His fear, his panic, when he had arrived at the hospital weren't put on. Nor had he made up the body that looked too long lying on the pavement. And there was at least one person in the street who had heard running.

What was it, then, that the sneering Judge had said? "Are you still pinning your faith on the evidence of children?"

At all events, something of the sort. Yet it was the Judge who was wrong. Children are incapable of creating a story out of nothing, because truths are not built out of nothing—there must be some basis. Children distort the facts, perhaps, but they do not invent them.

There! Again that satisfied "there" that Maigret repeated at each stage, as if congratulating himself—

There had been a corpse on the pavement—

And, doubtless, there had been a man nearby. He might even have had bright eyes.

And someone had run away.

And the old Judge, Maigret would have sworn, was not the man to lie in so many words.

Maigret was hot. He was drenched; nevertheless, he emerged from the sheets to go and fill a last pipe before Madame Maigret returned. While he was up he took the opportunity of opening the cupboard and taking a large gulp from a bottle of rum. Too bad if his temperature did rise a little that night, but everything would be tied up.

And it would be a very pretty piece of work—an anything but orthodox inquiry conducted while tucked up in his bed. That was something Madame Maigret would be quite incapable of appreciating.

The Judge hadn't lied, and yet he must have done his utmost to dig at the boy he hated, as two children of the same age can hate one another.

The customers were getting fewer downstairs, for the preposterous door chimes were rining less often. No doubt the dairyman, his wife, and their daughter, pink as a ham, were at dinner in the rear of the shop.

Footsteps on the pavement. Coming up the stairs. Stumbling footsteps, like a child's. Madame Maigret opened the door and pushed young Justin in in front of her, his thick navy-blue woolen jacket sparkling with little pearls of rain. He smelled like a wet dog.

"Wait a minute, sonny, I'll take off your jacket."

"I can do it myself."

Another suspicious look from Madame Maigret. Obviously she could not believe that this was still the same pipeful. She may even have suspected the rum.

"Sit down, Justin," said the Inspector, pointing to a chair.

"Thanks. I'm not tired."

"I've had you brought here to have a friendly little chat. What were you busy at?"

"My arithmetic homework."

"So in spite of what you've been through, you've been to school?"

"Why shouldn't I have gone?"

He was a proud little fellow.

He had drawn himself up again to his full height. Perhaps the Inspector too, lying there in bed, seemed to him to be bigger and longer?

"Madame Maigret, be so kind as to go and take a look at the broth in the kitchen and close the door."

This done, he winked at the boy.

"Pass me my tobacco pouch. It's on the mantelpiece. And the pipe that should be in my overcoat pocket. Yes, the one hanging behind the door. Thank you, son. Were you frightened when my wife came to fetch you?"

"No." He said it with pride.

"Have things been difficult for you?"

"Only because everyone keeps saying I'm making it up."

"And you aren't making it up, are you?"

"There was a dead man on the pavement and another who—"

"Hush!"

"What?"

"Not so fast. Sit down."

"I'm not tired."

"You've already said so, but it makes *me* tired to watch you."

He sat down on the chair, right on the edge, and his feet didn't touch the ground. His legs swung and his knees stuck out bare between his short trousers and his socks.

"What prank have you played on the Judge?"

A rapid instinctive reaction. "I've never done anything to him."

"You know which Judge I'm talking about?"

"The one's who's always at his window. He looks like an owl."

"I should have said a screech owl. What's going on between you?"

"I've never spoken to him."

"What's been going on between you?"

"In winter I never saw him, because his curtains were drawn when I passed."

"But in summer?"

"I stuck out my tongue at him."

"Why?"

"Because he looked at me as if he was laughing at me; he would start snickering to himself while he watched me."

"You've often stuck out your tongue at him?"

"Every time I saw him."

"And he?"

"He'd give a nasty laugh. I thought it was because I served at Mass and because he was an unbeliever."

"So it was he who was lying."

"What did he say?"

"That nothing happened outside his house yesterday morning as he would have noticed."

The lad stared intently at Maigret, then lowered his head.

"He was lying, wasn't he?"

"There was a corpse with a knife in its chest on the pavement."

"I know."

"How do you know?"

"I know because it's true," said Maigret softly. "Pass me the matches. I've let my pipe go out."

"Are you too hot?"

"It's nothing. A chill."

"You caught it this morning?"

"That's possible. Sit down."

He came suddenly alert and called, "Madame Maigret! Would you go downstairs. I think that's Besson who's just arrived and I don't want him to come up till I've finished. You keep him company downstairs. My friend Justin will call you."

He said once more to his young companion, "Sit down. It's true, too, that you both ran away."

"I told you it was true."

"And I'm sure of it. Go and see that there's nobody at the door and it's closed tightly."

The boy went, not understanding, but imbued with the importance of his acts and movements.

"You know, Justin, you're a good little fellow."

"Why d'you say that?"

"The corpse is true, the man who ran is true."

The boy raised his head once again and Maigret saw that his lip was trembling.

"And the Judge, who didn't lie, because a Judge wouldn't dare to lie, didn't tell the whole truth."

The room was redolent of Maigret's cold, rum, and tobacco. The smell of the vegetable broth wafted in under the door from the kitchen, and it was still raining silver drops on the black windowpanes. Outside, the street was deserted. Was it still a man and a child who found themselves face to face? Or two men? Or two children?

Maigret's head felt heavy, his eyes were watering. His pipe had a strange sickly taste that he did not find unpleasant, and he remembered the odors of the hospital, the chapel, and the sacristy.

"The Judge didn't tell the whole truth because he wanted to torment you. And you, you didn't tell the whole truth, either. Now I won't have you crying—it's not worth letting the whole world know what's going on between the two of us at this moment. You understand, Justin?"

The boy nodded. "If what you told us hadn't happened at all, the husband at Number 42 would not have heard running."

"I didn't make it up."

"Exactly. But if it happened as you said, the Judge could not have said that he didn't hear anything. And if the murderer had run in the direction of the barracks, the old man could not have sworn that nobody ran past his house."

The child didn't move; he was staring fixedly at his toes.

"Basically, the Judge was honest when he dared not say that you had gone past his house yesterday morning. But he could perhaps have said that you didn't pass. That is the truth—because you ran away in the opposite direction. No doubt he was also being truthful when he claimed that no man had run past on the pavement outside his window For the man didn't go off in *that* direction."

"What do you know about it?" He had stiffened and was staring wide-eyed at Maigret, just as he must have stared the day before at the murderer or the victim.

"Because, inevitably, the man rushed off in the same direction as you, which explains how the husband at 42 heard him pass. Knowing that you had seen him, that you had seen the corpse, that you could get him caught, he ran *after* you."

"If you tell my mother—"

"Shush. I've no wish to say anything at all to your mother or anyone else. You see, Justin, my boy, I'm going to talk to you like a man. A murderer with enough intelligence and coolness to make a corpse disappear in a few minutes without leaving the slightest trace would not have been so stupid as to let you run away after what you had seen."

"I don't know."

"But I do. It's my business to know. The most difficult thing is not killing a man: it's getting rid of him afterwards—and this fellow contrived a magnificent disappearance. He disappeared even though you saw him and you saw the murderer. In other words, the latter was a very strong man. And a very strong man risking his neck would not have let you get away like that."

"I didn't know—"

"What didn't you know?"

"I didn't know it was so serious."

"It isn't at all serious, as the whole thing has now been put right."

"You've arrested him?" There was temendous hope in the way he spoke.

"He will no doubt be arrested very shortly. Sit still."

"I won't move."

"First of all, if the scene had taken place in front of the Judge's— that's to say, halfway up the street—you'd have noticed it from farther away, and you'd have had time to run away. That's the only mistake the murderer made, cunning as he was."

"How did you guess?"

"I didn't guess—I too was an altar boy, and I served at the six o'clock Mass. You wouldn't have gone almost a hundred yards down the street without looking in front of you. Therefore the corpse was nearer, much nearer, almost at the corner of the street."

"Five houses farther on."

"You were thinking of something else—your bicycle—and you probably walked twenty yards without seeing anything."

"You can't possibly know."

"And when you saw it you ran towards the place du Congrès to reach the hospital by the other way. The man ran behind you."

"I thought I was going to die of fright."

"He put his hand on your shoulder?"

"He grabbed my shoulders with both his hands. I thought he was going to throttle me."

"He told you to say—"

The child was crying, but not sobbing. He was ashen pale, and the tears were rolling slowly down his cheeks. "If you tell my mother she'll be at me about it all my life. She's always at me."

"He told you to say that it had all happened farther along?"

"Yes."

"In front of the Judge's?"

"It was I who thought of the Judge's house—because of sticking out my tongue at him. He only said towards the other end of the street. And to say that he ran away in the direction of the barracks."

"And it just missed being the perfect crime, for nobody believed you, seeing that there was no murderer or corpse or trace of any kind, and the whole thing seemed impossible."

"But you?"

"Me? I don't count. It's pure chance that I have been an altar boy and then that I've had a fever today. What did he promise you?"

"He told me that if I didn't say what he wanted he would surely find me wherever I went, in spite of the police, and he'd cut my throat like a chicken."

"And then?"

"He asked me what I'd like to have."

"And you replied. 'A bike.'"

"How did you know that?"

"I keep telling you, I was an altar boy myself."

"And you wanted a bike?"

"That and a lot of things that I'd never had. Why did you say he had bright eyes?"

"I don't know. I didn't see his eyes. He wore thick glasses. But I didn't want them to find him."

"Because of the bike."

"Perhaps. You're going to tell my mother, aren't you?"

"Neither your mother nor anyone else. We're pals, aren't we, you and I? Now, pass me my tobacco again and don't tell Madame Maigret I've smoked three pipefuls while we've been here. You see, grownups don't always tell the whole truth, either. What door was it in front of, Justin?"

"The yellow house next to the pork butcher's."

"Go and find my wife."

"Where is she?"

"Downstairs with Inspector Besson, who was so unkind to you."

"And is he going to arrest me?"

"Open the closet. There's a pair of trousers hanging there."

"What am I to do?"

"In the left-hand pocket you'll find a wallet."

"I've got it."

"In the wallet there are some visiting cards."

"You want them?"

"Give me one. And the pen on the table as well."

And Maigret took it and wrote on the card beside his name: *Credit for one bicycle.*

"Come in, Besson."

Madame Maigret threw a glance at the opaque cloud of smoke that encircled the light veiled with oiled paper, and rushed toward the kitchen from which there came a smell of burning.

As for Besson, taking the chair the boy had just got out of, he said, "I have the list you wanted me to draw up. I had better tell you straight away—"

"That it's no use. Who lives at Number 40?"

"One moment." He consulted his notes. "Wait . . . 40. The house has only one tenant."

"I thought as much."

"Oh?" A brief uneasy glance toward the child. "A foreigner, a dealer in precious stones. Name of Fross."

And from the depths of the pillows on which he now reclined, Maigret's voice rose in a nonchalant manner. "A receiver."

"What did you say, Chief?"

"A receiver. And also, perhaps, head of a gang."

"I don't understand."

"Doesn't matter. Be so kind, Besson, as to pass me the bottle of rum that's in the wall cupboard. Quickly before Madame Maigret arrives. I bet my temperature's 102—the sheets will have to be changed twice tonight. Fross . . . Get a search warrant from the Examining Magistrate—no, at this hour of night that'll take time, for he's sure to be out playing bridge somewhere. Have you had dinner? I'm waiting for my broth. There are some blank warrants in my desk. Fill one out Search the place. You're bound to find the corpse even if it means knocking down a cellar wall."

Poor Besson was looking anxiously at his Chief and then at the child, who was waiting good as gold in the corner.

316

"Do it quickly, old chap. If he knows the lad came here this evening you'll find the bird has flown. He's a smart one, you'll see."

And indeed he was. While the flying squad were ringing his bell he was trying to make his getaway over the courtyard walls. It took all night to lay hands on him—he was finally caught on the rooftops—while other detectives were searching the house for hours before they found the corpse buried in the cellar.

Obviously a case of settling an old score. Some fellow, dissatisfied with the boss and feeling cheated, had gone and badgered him at his house in the early hours of the morning; Fross had felled him on the doorstep, never thinking an altar boy would be coming round the corner at that moment.

"How much?" Maigret had no longer courage to look at the thermometer himself.

"102."

"You're not cheating?" He knew that she was cheating and that he had a higher temperature, but he didn't care. It was blissfully good to sink into unconsciousness like this, to let himself slip quickly, dizzily away into a world that was hazy but terribly real—a world where an altar boy who looked like the young Maigret of other days was running desperately down the street, thinking he was going to be strangled or that he was going to get a nickel-plated bicycle.

"What are you saying?" asked Madame Maigret, who stood waiting with a hot mustard plaster for his neck in her plump hands.

Meanwhile he was mumbling vaguely like a feverish child, speaking of the "first stroke" and the "second stroke."

"I'm going to be late—"

"Late for what?"

"For Mass. The sister . . ."

He couldn't manage the word *sacristine*. "The . . . sister—"

Finally, with a large compress round his neck, he fell asleep and dreamed of the Mass in his village church, of Marie Titin whose inn he used to run past because he was afraid.

"Afraid of what?"

"All the same, I got him—"

"Who?"

"The Judge."

It was so complicated to explain . . . The Judge looked like someone in his village, someone he had stuck out his tongue at . . . The

317

blacksmith? No . . . it was the father-in-law of the woman at the bakery. It didn't matter. Someone he didn't like . . .

It was the Judge who had cheated in order to get his own back on the altar boy. He had said he had not heard footsteps running *past* his house. He hadn't said that he had heard the sound of a chase *in the other direction*. Old men have a second childhood. They squabble with children—just like children . . .

Maigret was content, despite everything. He had cheated over the three pipefuls—no, four. There was a fine strong taste of tabacco in his mouth, and he could sink into sleep . . .

And tomorrow, because he had a chill, Madame Maigret would make him caramel custard.

CHAPTER VI

THE BLACK MASK SCHOOL

THE HOUSE
IN TURK STREET

By Dashiell Hammett

Samuel Dashiell Hammett (1894–1961), the most important and influential contributor to the Black Mask style of detective fiction, was born in Maryland, dropped out of school when he was only thirteen, and held a number of odd jobs before going to work for the Pinkerton National Detective Agency. Starting in Baltimore and later moving to San Francisco, Hammett remained a Pinkerton operative for eight years and then during World War I entered the army where he served as a sergeant until being hospitalized with tuberculosis. After the war he returned to the Pinkertons, but his health again collapsed and, following another period in the hospital, he began to write advertising copy for a living. At the same time he started to produce detective short stories, drawing heavily on his own Pinkerton experiences to create the Continental Op, a tough, nameless San Francisco agency investigator whose adventures appeared in the pages of Black Mask magazine during the 1920s and helped to form the so-called hard-boiled school of mystery writing. Hammett also published two novels about the Op, Red Harvest (1929) and The Dain Curse (1929), as well as The Maltese Falcon (1930), featuring private detective Sam Spade. During his last thirty years, the writer lived with playwright Lillian Hellman and produced no fiction, although he became deeply involved in a number of political and social causes. He finally succumbed to the combined effects of tuberculosis and alcoholism. "The House in Turk Street," originally published in the April 15, 1924 issue of Black Mask, was reprinted first by Ellery Queen in Hammett Homicides (1947) and later in The Continental Op (New York: Random House, 1974), a selection of stories edited and with an introduction by Steven Marcus. Also see The Big Knockover (New York: Random House, 1966), a collection edited by Lillian Hellman, Joe Gores' novel Hammett (New York: Putnam, 1975), recreating Hammett's early years as a writer in San Francisco, and the City of San Francisco magazine (November 4, 1975), largely devoted to Hammett.

I had been told that the man for whom I was hunting lived in a certain Turk Street block, but my informant hadn't been able to give me his house number. Thus it came about that late one rainy afternoon I was canvassing this certain block, ringing each bell, and reciting a myth that went like this:

"I'm from the law office of Wellington and Berkeley. One of our clients—an elderly lady—was thrown from the rear platform of a street car last week and severely injured. Among those who witnessed the accident was a young man whose name we don't know. But we have been told that he lives in this neighborhood." Then I would describe the man I wanted, and wind up: "Do you know of anyone who looks like that?"

All down one side of blocks the answers were: "No," "No," "No."

I crossed the street and started on the other side. The first house: "No." The second: "No." The third. The fourth. The fifth—

No one came to the door in answer to my first ring. After a while, I rang again. I had just decided that no one was at home, when the knob turned slowly and a little old woman opened the door. She was a very fragile little old woman, with a piece of gray knitting in one hand, and faded eyes that twinkled pleasantly behind goldrimmed spectacles. She wore a stiffly starched apron over a black dress.

"Good evening," she said in a thin friendly voice. "I hope you didn't mind waiting. I always have to peep out to see who's there before I open the door—an old woman's timidity."

"Sorry to disturb you," I apologized. "But—"

"Won't you come in, please?"

"No; I just want a little information. I won't take much time."

"I wish you would come in," she said, and then added with mock severity, "I'm sure my tea is getting cold."

She took my damp hat and coat, and I followed her down a narrow hall to a dim room, where a man got up as we entered. He was old too, and stout, with a thin white beard that fell upon a white vest that was as stiffly starched as the woman's apron.

"Thomas," the little fragile woman told him; "this is Mr.—"

"Tracy," I said, because that was the name I had given the other residents of the block; but I came as near blushing when I said it as I have in fifteen years. These folks weren't made to be lied to.

Their name, I learned, was Quarre; and they were an affectionate old couple. She called him "Thomas" every time she spoke to him, rolling the name around in her mouth as if she liked the taste of it. He called her "my dear" just as frequently, and twice he got up to adjust a cushion more comfortably to her frail back.

I had to drink a cup of tea with them and eat some little spiced cookies before I could get them to listen to a question. Then Mrs. Quarre made little sympathetic clicking sounds with her tongue and teeth, while I told about the elderly lady who had fallen off a street car. The old man rumbled in his beard that it was "a damn shame," and gave me a fat cigar.

Finally I got away from the accident, and described the man I wanted.

"Thomas," Mrs. Quarre said, "isn't that the young man who lives in the house with the railing—the one who always looks so worried?"

The old man stroked his snowy beard and pondered for a moment.

"But, my dear," he rumbled at last, "hasn't he got dark hair?"

She beamed upon her husband. "Thomas is so observant," she said with pride. "I had forgotten; but the young man I spoke of does have dark hair, so he couldn't be the one."

The old man then suggested that one who lived in the block below might be my man. They discussed this one at some length before they decided that he was too tall and too old. Mrs. Quarre suggested another. They discussed that one, and voted against him. Thomas offered a candidate; he was weighed and discarded. They chattered on.

Darkness settled. The old man turned on a light in a tall lamp that threw a soft yellow circle upon us and left the rest of the room dim. The room was a large one, and heavy with the thick hangings and bulky horsehair furniture of a generation ago. I didn't expect to get any information here; but I was comfortable, and the cigar was a good one. Time enough to go out into the drizzle when I had finished my smoke.

Something cold touched the nape of my neck.

"Stand up!"

I didn't stand up: I couldn't. I was paralyzed. I sat and blinked at the Quarres.

And looking at them, I knew that something cold *couldn't* be against the back of my neck; a harsh voice *couldn't* have ordered me to stand up. It wasn't possible!

Mrs. Quarre still sat primly upright against the cushions her husband had adjusted to her back; her eyes still twinkled with friendliness behind her glasses. The old man still stroked his white beard, and let cigar smoke drift unhurriedly from his nostrils.

They would go on talking about the young men in the neighborhood who might be the man I wanted. Nothing had happened. I had dozed.

"Get up!" The cold thing against my neck jabbed deep into the flesh.

I stood up. "Frisk him," the harsh voice came from behind.

The old man carefully laid his cigar down, came to me, and ran his hands over my body. Satisfied that I was unarmed, he emptied my pockets, dropping the contents upon the chair that I had just left.

"That's all," he told the man behind me, and returned to his chair.

"Turn around, you!" the harsh voice ordered.

I turned and faced a tall, gaunt, raw-boned man of about my own age, which is thirty-five. He had an ugly face—hollow-cheeked, bony, and spattered with big pale freckles. His eyes were of a watery blue, and his nose and chin stuck out abruptly. "Know me?" he asked.

"No."

"You're a liar!"

I didn't argue the point; he was holding a gun in one big freckled hand.

"You're going to know me pretty well before you're through with me," this big ugly man threatened. "You're going to—"

"Hook!" a voice came from a portièred doorway—the doorway through which the ugly man had no doubt crept up behind me. "Hook, come here!" The voice was feminine—young, clear, and musical.

"What do you want?" the ugly man called over his shoulder.

"*He's* here."

"All right!" He turned to Thomas Quarre. "Keep this joker safe."

From somewhere among his whiskers, his coat, and his stiff white vest, the old man brought out a big black revolver, which he handled with no signs of unfamiliarity.

The ugly man swept up the things that had been taken from my pockets, and carried them through the portières with him.

Mrs. Quarre smiled up at me. "Do sit down, Mr. Tracy," she said.

I sat.

Through the portières a new voice came from the next room; a drawling baritone voice whose accent was unmistakably British; cultured British. "What's up, Hook?" this voice was asking.

The harsh voice of the ugly man:

"Plenty's up, I'm telling you! They're on to us! I started out a while ago; and as soon as I got to the street, I seen a man I knowed on the other side. He was pointed out to me in Philly five-six years ago. I don't know his name, but I remember his mug—he's a Continental

Detective agency man. I came back in right away, and me and Elvira watched him out of the window. He went to every house on the other side of the street, asking questions or something. Then he came over and started to give this side a whirl, and after a while he rings the bell. I tell the old woman and her husband to get him in, stall him along, and see what he says for himself. He's got a song and dance about looking for a guy what seen an old woman bumped by a street car—but that's the bunk! He's gunning for us. I went in and stuck him up just now. I meant to wait till you come, but I was scared he'd get nervous and beat it."

The British voice: "You shouldn't have shown yourself to him. The others could have taken care of him."

Hook: "What's the diff? Chances is he knows us all anyway: But supposing he didn't, what diff does it make?"

The drawling British voice: "It may make a deal of difference. It was stupid."

Hook, blustering: "Stupid, huh? You're always bellyaching about other people being stupid. To hell with you, I say! Who does all the work? Who's the guy that swings all the jobs? Huh? Where—"

The young feminine voice: "Now, Hook, for God's sake don't make that speech again. I've listened to it until I know it by heart!"

A rustle of papers, and the British voice: "I say, Hook, you're correct about his being a detective. Here is an identification card."

The feminine voice from the next room: "Well, what's to be done? What's our play?"

Hook: "That's easy to answer. We're going to knock this sleuth off!"

The feminine voice: "And put our necks in the noose?"

Hook, scornfully: "As if they ain't there if we don't! You don't think this guy ain't after us for the L.A. job, do you?"

The British voice: "You're an ass, Hook, and a quite hopeless one. Suppose this chap is interested in the Los Angeles affair, as is probable; what then? He is a Continental operative. Is it likely that his organization doesn't know where he is? Don't you think they know he was coming up here? And don't they know as much about us—chances are—as he does? There's no use killing him. That would only make matters worse. The thing to do is to tie him up and leave him here. His associates will hardly come looking for him until tomorrow."

My gratitude went out to the British voice! Somebody was in my favor, at least to the extent of letting me live. I hadn't been feeling very cheerful these last few minutes. Somehow, the fact that I couldn't see these people who were deciding whether I was to live or die, made my plight seem all the more desperate. I felt better now, though far from gay; I had confidence in the drawling British voice; it was the voice of a man who habitually carries his point.

Hook, bellowing: "Let me tell you something, brother: that guy's going to be knocked off! That's flat! I'm taking no chances. You can jaw all you want to about it, but I'm looking out for my own neck and it'll be a lot safer with that guy where he can't talk. That's flat."

The feminine voice, disgustedly: "Aw, Hook, be reasonable!"

The British voice, still drawling, but dead cold: "There's no use reasoning with you, Hook, you've the instincts and the intellect of a troglodyte. There is only one sort of language that you understand; and I'm going to talk that language to you, my son. If you are tempted to do anything silly between now and the time of our departure, just say this to yourself two or three times: 'If he dies, I die.' Say it as if it were out of the Bible—because it's that true."

There followed a long space of silence, with a tenseness that made my not particularly sensitive scalp tingle.

When, at last, a voice cut the silence, I jumped as if a gun had been fired; though the voice was low and smooth enough.

It was the British voice, confidently victorious, and I breathed again.

"We'll get the old people away first," the voice was saying. "You take charge of our guest, Hook. Tie him up while I get the bonds, and we'll be gone in less than half an hour."

The portières parted and Hook came into the room—a scowling Hook whose freckles had a greenish tinge against the sallowness of his face. He pointed a revolver at me, and spoke to the Quarres, short and harsh:

"He wants you." They got up and went into the next room.

Hook, meanwhile, had stepped back to the doorway, still menacing me with his revolver; and pulled loose the plush ropes that were around the heavy curtains. Then he came around behind me, and tied me securely to the highbacked chair; my arms to the chair's arms, my legs to the chair's legs, my body to the chair's back and seat; and he wound up by gagging me with the corner of a cushion that was too well-stuffed.

As he finished lashing me into place, and stepped back to scowl at me, I heard the street door close softly, and then light footsteps ran back and forth overhead.

Hook looked in the direction of those footsteps, and his little watery blue eyes grew cunning. "Elvira!" he called softly.

The portières bulged as if someone had touched them, and the musical feminine voice came through. "What?"

"Come here."

"I'd better not. He wouldn't—"

"Damn him!" Hook flared up. "Come here!"

She came into the room and into the circle of light from the tall lamp; a girl in her early twenties, slender and lithe, and dressed for the street, except that she carried her hat in one hand. A white face beneath a bobbed mass of flame-colored hair. Smoke-gray eyes that were set too far apart for trustworthiness—though not for beauty—laughed at me; and her red mouth laughed at me, exposing the edges of little sharp animal-teeth. She was as beautiful as the devil, and twice as dangerous.

She laughed at me—a fat man, all trussed up with red plush rope, and with the corner of a green cushion in my mouth—and she turned to the ugly man. "What do you want?"

He spoke in an undertone, with a furtive glance at the ceiling, above which soft steps still padded back and forth.

"What say we shake him?"

Her smoke-gray eyes lost their merriment and became calculating.

"There's a hundred thousand he's holding—a third of it's mine. You don't think I'm going to take a Mickey Finn on that, do you?"

"Course not! Supposing we get the hundred-grand?"

"How?"

"Leave it to me, kid; leave it to me! If I swing it, will you go with me? You know I'll be good to you."

She smiled contemptuously, I thought—but he seemed to like it.

"You're whooping right you'll be good to me," she said. "But listen, Hook: we couldn't get away with it—not unless you *get him*. I know him! I'm not running away with anything that belongs to him unless he is fixed so that he can't come after it."

Hook moistened his lips and looked around the room at nothing. Apparently he didn't like the thought of tangling with the owner of the British drawl. But his desire for the girl was too strong for his fear.

"I'll do it!" he blurted. "I'll get him! Do you mean it, kid? If I get him, you'll go with me?"

She held out her hand. "It's a bet," she said and he believed her.

His ugly face grew warm and red and utterly happy, and he took a deep breath and straightened his shoulders. In his place, I might have believed her myself—all of us have fallen for that sort of thing at one time or another—but sitting tied up on the side-lines, I knew that he'd have been better off playing with a gallon of nitro than with this baby.

She was dangerous! There was a rough time ahead for Hook!

"This is the lay—" Hook began, and stopped, tongue-tied.

A step had sounded in the next room.

Immediately the British voice came through the portières, and there was exasperation to the drawl now:

"This is really too much! I can't"—he said *reahly* and *cawnt*— "leave for a moment without having things done all wrong. Now just what got into you, Elvira, that you must go in and exhibit yourself to our detective?"

Fear flashed into her smoke-gray eyes, and out again, and she spoke airily. "Don't be altogether yellow," she said. "Your precious neck can get along all right without so much guarding."

The portières parted, and I twisted my head around as far as I could get it for my first look at this man who was responsible for my still being alive. I saw a short fat man, hatted and coated for the street, and carrying a tan traveling bag in one hand.

Then his face came into the yellow circle of light, and I saw that it was a Chinese face. A short fat Chinese, immaculately clothed in garments that were as British as his accent.

"It isn't a matter of color," he told the girl—and I understood now the full sting of her jibe; "it's simply a matter of ordinary wisdom."

His face was a round yellow mask, and his voice was the same emotionless drawl that I had heard before; but I knew that he was as surely under the girl's sway as the ugly man—or he wouldn't have let her taunt bring him into the room. But I doubted that she'd find this Anglicized Oriental as easily handled as Hook.

"There was no particular need," the Chinese was still talking, "for this chap to have seen any of us." He looked at me now for the first time, with little opaque eyes that were like two black seeds. "It's quite possible that he didn't know any of us, even by description. This showing ourselves to him is the most arrant sort of nonsense."

"Aw, hell, Tai!" Hook blustered. "Quit your bellyaching, will you? What's the diff? I'll knock him off, and that takes care of that!"

The Chinese set down his tan bag and shook his head.

"There will be no killing," he drawled, "or there will be quite a bit of killing. You don't mistake my meaning, do you, Hook?"

Hook didn't. His Adam's apple ran up and down with the effort of his swallowing and behind the cushion that was choking me, I thanked the yellow man again.

Then this red-haired she-devil put her spoon in the dish.

"Hook's always offering to do things that he has no intention of doing," she told the Chinese.

Hook's ugly face blazed red at this reminder of his promise to get the Chinese, and he swallowed again, and his eyes looked as if nothing would have suited him better than an opportunity to crawl under something. But the girl had him; her influence was stronger than his cowardice.

He suddenly stepped close to the Chinese, and from his advantage of a full head in height scowled down into the round yellow face.

"Tai," the ugly man snarled; "you're done. I'm sick and tired of all this dog you put on—acting like you was a king or something. I'm going to—"

He faltered, and his words faded away into silence. Tai looked up at him with eyes that were as hard and black and inhuman as two pieces of coal. Hook's lips twitched and he flinched away a little.

I stopped sweating. The yellow man had won again. But I had forgotten the red-haired she-devil. She laughed now—a mocking laugh that must have been like a knife to the ugly man.

A bellow came from deep in his chest, and he hurled one big fist into the round blank face of the yellow man.

The force of the punch carried Tai all the way across the room, and threw him on his side in one corner.

But he had twisted his body around to face the ugly man even as he went hurtling across the room—a gun was in his hand before he went down—and he was speaking before his legs had settled upon the floor—and his voice was a cultured British drawl.

"Later," he was saying: "we will settle this thing that is between us. Just now you will drop your pistol and stand very still while I get up."

Hook's revolver—only half out of his pocket when the Oriental had covered him—thudded to the rug. He stood rigidly still while Tai got to his feet, and Hook's breath came out noisily, and each freckle stood ghastily out against the dirty scared white of his face.

I looked at the girl! There was contempt in the eyes with which she looked at Hook, but no disappointment.

Then I made a discovery: *something had changed in the room near her!*

I shut my eyes and tried to picture that part of the room as it had been before the two men had clashed: Opening my eyes suddenly, I had the answer.

On the table beside the girl had been a book and some magazines. They were gone now. Not two feet from the girl was the tan bag that Tai had brought into the room. Suppose the bag had held the bonds from the Los Angeles job that they had mentioned. It probably had.

What then? It probably now held the book and magazines that had been on the table. The girl had stirred up the trouble between the two men to distract their attention while she made a switch. Where would the loot be, then? I didn't know, but I suspected that it was too bulky to be on the girl's slender person.

Just beyond the table was a couch, with a wide red cover that went all the way down to the floor. I looked from the couch to the girl. She was watching me, and her eyes twinkled with a flash of mirth as they met mine coming from the couch. The couch it was!

By now the Chinese had pocketed Hook's revolver, and was talking to him: "If I hadn't a dislike for murder, and didn't think that you will perhaps be of some value to Elvira and me in effecting our departure, I should certainly relieve us of the handicap of your stupidity now. But I'll give you one more chance. I would suggest, however, that you think carefully before you give way to any more of your violent impulses." He turned to the girl. "Have you been putting foolish ideas in our Hook's head?"

She laughed. "Nobody could put any kind in it."

"Perhaps you're right," he said, and then came over to test the lashings about my arms and body.

Finding them satisfactory, he picked up the tan bag, and held out the gun he had taken from the ugly man a few minutes before.

"Here's your revolver, Hook, now try to be sensible. We may as well go now. The old man and his wife will do as they were told. They are on their way to a city that we needn't mention by name in front of our friend here, to wait for us and their share of the bonds. Needless to say, they will wait a long while—they are out of it now. But between ourselves there must be no more treachery. If we're to get clear, we must help each other."

According to the best dramatic rules, these folks should have made sarcastic speeches to me before they left, but they didn't. They passed me without even a farewell look, and went out of sight into the darkness of the hall.

Suddenly the Chinese was in the room again, running tiptoe—an open knife in one hand, a gun in the other. This was the man I had been thanking for saving my life! He bent over me.

The knife moved on my right side, and the rope that held that arm slackened its grip. I breathed again, and my heart went back to beating.

"Hook will be back," Tai whispered, and was gone.

On the carpet, three feet in front of me, lay a revolver.

The street door closed, and I was alone in the house for a while.

You may believe that I spent that while struggling with the red

329

plush ropes that bound me. Tai had cut one length, loosening my right arm somewhat and giving my body more play, but I was far from free. And his whispered "Hook will be back" was all the spur I needed to throw my strength against my bonds.

I understood now why the Chinese had insisted so strongly upon my life being spared. *I was the weapon with which Hook was to be removed!* The Chinese figured that Hook would make some excuse as soon as they had reached the street, slip back into the house, knock me off, and rejoin his confederates. If he didn't do it on his own initiative, I suppose the Chinese would suggest it.

So he had put a gun within reach and had loosened my ropes as much as he could, not to have me free before he himself got away.

This thinking was a side-issue. I didn't let it slow up my efforts to get loose. The *why* wasn't important to me just now—the important thing was to have that revolver in my hand when the ugly man came back.

Just as the front door opened, I got my right arm completely free, and plucked the strangling cushion from my mouth. The rest of my body was still held by the ropes—held loosely—but held.

I threw myself, chair and all, forward, breaking the fall with my free arm. The carpet was thick. I went down on my face, with the heavy chair atop me, all doubled up, but my right arm was free of the tangle, and my right hand grasped the gun. The dim light hit upon a man hurrying into the room—a glint of metal in his hand.

I fired.

He caught both hands to his belly, bent double, and slid out across the carpet.

That was over. But that was far from being all. I wrenched at the plush ropes that held me, while my mind tried to sketch what lay ahead.

The girl had switched the bonds, hiding them under the couch—there was no question of that. She had intended coming back for them before I had time to get free. But Hook had come back first, and she would have to change her plan. What more likely than that she would now tell the Chinese that Hook had made the switch? What then? There was only one answer: Tai would come back for the bonds—both of them would come. Tai knew that I was armed now, but they had said that the bonds represented a hundred thousand dollars. That would be enough to bring them back!

I kicked the last rope loose and scrambled to the couch. The bonds were beneath it: four thick bundles, done up with heavy rubber bands. I tucked them under one arm, and went over to the man who was dying near the door. His gun was under one of his legs. I pulled it out, stepped over him, and went into the dark hall. Then I stopped to consider.

The girl and the Chinese would split to tackle me. One would come in the front door and the other in the rear. That would be the safest way for them to handle me. My play, obviously, was to wait just inside one of those doors for them. It would be foolish for me to leave the house. That's exactly what they would be expecting at first—and they would be lying in ambush.

Decidedly, my play was to lie low within sight of this front door and wait until one of them came through it—as one of them surely would, when they had tired of waiting for me to come out.

Toward the street door, the hall was lighted with the glow that filtered through the glass from the street lights. The stairway leading to the second-story threw a triangular shadow across part of the hall—a shadow that was black enough for any purpose. I crouched low in this three-cornered slice of night, and waited.

I had two guns: the one the Chinese had given me, and the one I had taken from Hook. I had fired one shot; that would leave me eleven still to use—unless one of the weapons had been used since it was loaded. I broke the gun Tai had given me, and in the dark ran my fingers across the back of the cylinder. My fingers touched *one* shell—under the hammer. Tai had taken no chances; he had given me one bullet—the bullet with which I had dropped Hook.

I put the gun down on the floor, and examined the one I had taken from Hook. It was *empty*. The Chinese had taken no chances at all. He had emptied Hook's gun before returning it to him after their quarrel.

I was in a hole! Alone, unarmed, in a strange house that would presently hold two who were hunting me—and that one of them was a woman didn't soothe me any—she was none the less deadly on that account.

For a momemt I was tempted to make a dash for it; the thought of being out in the street again was pleasant; but I put the idea away. That would be foolishness, and plenty of it. Then I remembered the bonds under my arm. They would have to be my weapon; and if they were to serve me, they would have to be concealed.

I slipped out of my triangular shadow and went up the stairs. Thanks to the street lights, the upstairs rooms were not too dark for me to move around. Around and around I went through the rooms, hunting for a place to hide the bonds. But when suddenly a window rattled, as if from the draught created by the opening of an outside door somewhere, I still had the loot in my hands.

There was nothing to do now but to chuck them out of a window and trust to luck. I grabbed a pillow from a bed, stripped off the white case, and dumped the bonds into it. Then I leaned out of an already open window and looked down into the night, searching for a desirable dumping place: I didn't want the bonds to land on anything that would make a racket.

And, looking out of the window, I found a better hiding place. The window opened into a narrow court, on the other side of which was a house of the same sort as the one I was in. That house was of the same height as this one, with a flat tin roof that sloped down the other way. The roof wasn't far from me—not too far to chuck the pillow case. I chucked it. It disappeared over the edge of the roof and crackled softly on the tin.

Then I turned on all the lights in the room, lighted a cigarette (we all like to pose a little now and then), and sat down on the bed to await my capture. I might have stalked my enemies through the dark house, and possibly have nabbed them; but most likely I would simply have succeeded in getting myself shot. And I don't like to be shot.

The girl found me.

She came creeping up the hall, an automatic in each hand, hesitated for an instant outside the door, and then came in on the jump. And when she saw me sitting peacefully on the side of the bed, her eyes snapped scornfully at me, as if I had done something mean. I suppose she thought I should have given her an opportunity to shoot.

"I got him, Tai," she called, and the Chinese joined us.

"What did Hook do with the bonds?" he asked point blank.

I grinned into his round yellow face and led my ace.

"Why don't you ask the girl?"

His face showed nothing, but I imagined that his fat body stiffened a little within its fashionable British clothing. That encouraged me, and I went on with my little lie that was meant to stir things up.

"Haven't you rapped to it," I asked, "that they were fixing up to ditch you?"

"You dirty liar!" the girl screamed, and took a step toward me.

Tai halted her with an imperative gesture. He stared through her with his opaque black eyes, and as he stared the blood slid out of his face. She had this fat yellow man on her string, right enough, but he wasn't exactly a harmless toy.

"So that's how it is?" he said slowly, to no one in particular. Then to me: "Where did they put the bonds?"

The girl went close to him and her words came out tumbling over each other:

"Here's the truth of it, Tai, so help me God! I switched the stuff myself. Hook wasn't in it. I was going to run out on both of you. I stuck them under the couch downstairs, but they're not there now. That's the God's truth!"

He was eager to believe her, and her words had the ring of truth to them. And I knew that—in love with her as he was—he'd more readily forgive her treachery with the bonds than he would forgive her for planning to run off with Hook; so I made haste to stir things up again.

"Part of that is right enough," I said. "She did stick the bonds under the couch—but Hook was in on it. They fixed it up between them while you were upstairs. He was to pick a fight with you, and during the argument she was to make the switch, and that is exactly what they did.

I had him! As she wheeled savagely toward me, he stuck the muzzle of an automatic in her side—a smart jab that checked the angry words she was hurling at me.

"I'll take your guns, Elvira," he said, and took them.

"Where are the bonds now?" he asked me.

I grinned. "I'm not with you, Tai. I'm against you."

"I don't like violence," he said slowly, "and I believe you are a sensible person. Let us traffic, my friend."

"You name it," I suggested.

"Gladly! As a basis for our bargaining, we will stipulate that you have hidden the bonds where they cannot be found by anyone else; and that I have you completely in my power, as the shilling shockers used to have it."

"Reasonable enough," I said; "go on."

"The situation, then, is what gamblers call a standoff. Neither of us has the advantage. As a detective, you want us; but we have you. As thieves, we want the bonds; but you have them. I offer you the girl in exchange for the bonds, and that seems to me an equitable offer. It will give me the bonds and a chance to get away. It will give you no small degree of success in your task as a detective. Hook is dead. You will have the girl. All that will remain is to find me and the bonds again— by no means a hopeless task. You will have turned a defeat into half a victory, with an excellent chance to make it a complete one."

"How do I know that you'll give me the girl?"

He shrugged. "Naturally, there can be no guarantee. But, knowing that she planned to desert me for the swine who lies dead below, you can't imagine that my feelings for her are the most friendly. Too, if I take her with me, she will want a share in the loot."

I turned the lay-out over in my mind.

"This is the way it looks to me," I told him at last. "You aren't a killer. I'll come through alive no matter what happens. All right, why should I swap? You and the girl will be easier to find again than the bonds, and they are the most important part of the job anyway. I'll hold on to them, and take my chances on finding you folks again. Yes, I'm playing it safe."

"No, I'm not a killer," he said, very softly; and he smiled the first smile I had seen on his face. It wasn't a pleasant smile: and there was something in it that made you want to shudder. "But I am other things, perhaps, of which you haven't thought. But this talking is to no purpose. Elvira!"

The girl came obediently forward.

"You will find sheets in one of the bureau drawers," he told her. "Tear one or two of them into strips strong enough to tie up our friend securely."

The girl went to the bureau. I wrinkled my head, trying to find a not too disagreeable answer to the question in my mind. The answer that came first wasn't nice: *torture*.

Then a faint sound brought us all into tense motionlessness.

The room we were in had two doors: one leading into the hall, the other into another bedroom. It was through the hall door that the faint sound had come—the sound of creeping feet.

Swiftly, silently, Tai moved backward to a position from which he could watch the hall door without losing sight of the girl and me—and the gun poised like a live thing in his fat hand was all the warning we needed to make no noise.

The faint sound again, just outside the door.

The gun in Tai's hand seemed to quiver with eagerness.

Through the other door—the door that gave to the next room— popped Mrs. Quarre, an enormous cocked revolver in her thin hand.

"Let go it, you nasty heathen," she screeched.

Tai dropped his pistol before he turned to face her, and he held his hands up high—all of which was very wise.

Thomas Quarre came through the hall door then; he also held a cocked revolver—the mate of his wife's—though, in front of his bulk, his didn't look so enormously large.

I looked at the old woman again, and found little of the friendly fragile one who had poured tea and chatted about the neighbors. This was a witch if there ever was one—a witch of the blackest, most malignant sort. Her little faded eyes were sharp with ferocity, her withered lips were taut in a wolfish snarl, and her thin body fairly quivered with hate.

"I knew it," she was shrilling. "I told Tom as soon as we got far enough away to think things over. I knew it was a frame-up! I knew this supposed detective was a pal of yours! I knew it was just a scheme to beat Thomas and me out of our shares! Well, I'll show you, you yellow monkey! Where are them bonds? Where are they?"

The Chinese had recovered his poise, if he had ever lost it.

"Our stout friend can tell you perhaps," he said. "I was about to extract the information from him when you so—ah—dramatically arrived."

"Thomas, for goodness sakes don't stand there dreaming," she snapped at her husband, who to all appearances was still the same mild old man who had given me an excellent cigar. "Tie up this Chinaman! I don't trust him an inch, and I won't feel easy until he's tied up."

I got up from my seat on the side of the bed, and moved cautiously to a spot that I thought would be out of the line of fire if the thing I expected happened.

Tai had dropped the gun that had been in his hand, but he hadn't been searched. The Chinese are a thorough people; if one of them carries a gun at all, he usually carries two or three or more. One gun had been taken from Tai, and if they tried to truss him up without frisking him, there was likely to be fireworks. So I moved to one side.

Fat Thomas Quarre went phlegmatically up to the Chinese to carry out his wife's orders—and bungled the job perfectly.

He put his bulk between Tai and the old woman's gun.

Tai's hands moved. An automatic was in each.

Once more Tai ran true to racial form. When a Chinese shoots he keeps on until his gun is empty.

When I yanked Tai over backward by his fat throat, and slammed him to the floor, his guns were still barking metal; and they clicked empty as I got a knee on one of his arms. I didn't take any chances. I worked on his throat until his eyes and tongue told me that he was out of things for a while. Then I looked around.

Thomas Quarre was against the bed, plainly dead, with three round holes in his starched white vest.

Across the room, Mrs. Quarre lay on her back. Her clothes had somehow settled in place around her fragile body, and death had given her once more the gentle friendly look she had worn when I first saw her.

The red-haired girl Elvira was gone.

Presently Tai stirred, and after taking another gun from his clothes, I helped him sit up. He stroked his bruised throat with one fat hand and looked cooly around the room.

"Where's Elvira?" he asked.

"Got away—for the time being."

He shrugged. "Well, you can call it a decidedly successful operation. The Quarres and Hook dead; the bonds and I in your hands."

"Not so bad," I admitted, "but will you do me a favor?"

"If I may."

"Tell me what the hell this is all about!"

"All about?" he asked.

"Exactly! From what you people have let me overhear, I gather that you pulled some sort of job in Los Angeles that netted you a hundred-thousand-dollars' worth of bonds; but I can't remember any recent job of that size down there."

"Why, that's preposterous!" he said with what, for him, was almost wild-eyed amazement. "Preposterous! Of course you know all about it!"

"I do not! I was trying to find a young fellow named Fisher who left his Tacoma home in anger a week or two ago. His father wants him found on the quiet, so that he can come down and try to talk him into going home again. I was told that I might find Fisher in this block of Turk Street, and that's what brought me down here."

He didn't believe me. He never believed me. He went to the gallows thinking me a liar.

When I got out into the street again (and Turk Street was a lovely place when I came free into it after my evening in that house!) I bought a newspaper that told me most of what I wanted to know.

A boy of twenty—a messenger in the employ of a Los Angeles stock and bond house—had disappeared two days before, while on his way to a bank with a wad of bonds. That same night this boy and a slender girl with bobbed red hair had registered at a hotel in Fresno as *J. M. Riordan and wife*. The next morning the boy had been found in his room—murdered. The girl was gone. The bonds were gone.

That much the paper told me. During the next few days, digging up a little here and a little there, I succeeded in piecing together most of the story.

The Chinese—whose full name was Tai Choon Tau—had been the brains of the mob. Their game had been a variation of the always-reliable badger game. Tai would pick out some youth who was messenger or runner for a banker or broker—one who carried either cash or negotiable securities in large quantities.

The girl Elvira would then *make* this lad, get him all fussed up over her—which shouldn't have been very hard for her—and then lead him gently around to running away with her and whatever he could grab in the way of his employer's bonds or currency.

Wherever they spent the first night of their flight, there Hook would appear—foaming at the mouth and loaded for bear. The girl would plead and tear her hair and so forth, trying to keep Hook—in his rôle of irate husband—from butchering the youth. Finally she would succeed, and in the end the youth would find himself without either girl or the fruits of his thievery.

Sometimes he had surrendered to the police. Two we found had committed suicide. The Los Angeles lad had been built of tougher stuff than the others. He had put up a fight, and Hook had had to kill him. You can measure the girl's skill in her end of the game by the fact that not one of the half dozen youths who had been trimmed had said the least thing to implicate her; and some of them had gone to great trouble to keep her out of it.

The house in Turk Street had been the mob's retreat, and, that it might be always a safe one, they had not worked their game in San Francisco. Hook and the girl were supposed by the neighbors to be the Quarres' son and daughter—and Tai was the Chinese cook. The Quarres' benign and respectable appearances had also come in handy when the mob had securities to be disposed of.

The Chinese went to the gallows. We threw out the widest and finest-meshed of dragnets for the red-haired girl; and we turned up girls with bobbed red hair by the scores. But the girl Elvira was not among them.

I promised myself that some day . . .

I'LL BE WAITING

By Raymond Chandler

Raymond Chandler (1888–1959) was born in Chicago but was educated in England where for a time he worked as a free-lance journalist. During World War I he joined a Canadian regiment and afterwards settled in Los Angeles where he established himself as a successful oil company executive. With the collapse of the industry in the Depression, however, Chandler turned to the writing of pulp fiction and published his first Black Mask story in 1933. During the next several years he became a regular contributor to this and other magazines of the period, writing a number of novelettes about detectives called Carmody and Malvern and Mallory before developing the now famous character of Philip Marlowe. Marlowe, a thoughtful, well-educated man of honor in a hard-boiled world, is the detective described by Chandler in his 1944 essay, "The Simple Art of Murder," and is the central figure in a series of novels generally agreed to contain the author's best work. These include The Big Sleep (1939), Farewell, My Lovely (1940), and The Lady in the Lake (1943). In 1954, The Long Goodbye won the Mystery Writers of America's Edgar for the best novel of the year. Chandler's health declined after the death of his wife in 1954, alcohol became a serious problem for him, and he published only one more book before his own death five years later. "I'll Be Waiting" originally appeared in The Saturday Evening Post, October 14, 1939, and has since been reprinted in The Simple Art of Murder (Boston: Houghton Mifflin, 1950). For more information about Chandler and his work see Philip Durham's Down These Mean Streets a Man Must Go: Raymond Chandler's Knight (Chapel Hill: University of North Carolina Press, 1963). See also Raymond Chandler Speaking (Boston: Houghton Mifflin, 1962), selected Chandler correspondence edited by Dorothy Gardiner and Katherine Sorely Walker, and Frank MacShane's The Life of Raymond Chandler (New York: Dutton, 1976).

At one o'clock in the morning, Carl, the night porter, turned down the last of three table lamps in the main lobby of the Windermere Hotel. The blue carpet darkened a shade or two and the walls drew back into remoteness. The chairs filled with shadowy loungers. In the corners were memories like cobwebs.

Tony Reseck yawned. He put his head on one side and listened to the frail, twittery music from the radio room beyond a dim arch at the far side of the lobby. He frowned. That should be his radio room after one A.M. Nobody should be in it. That red-haired girl was spoiling his nights.

The frown passed and a miniature of a smile quirked at the corners of his lips. He sat relaxed, a short, pale, paunchy, middle-aged man with long, delicate fingers clasped on the elk's tooth on his watch chain; the long delicate fingers of a sleight-of-hand artist, fingers with shiny, molded nails and tapering first joints, fingers a little spatulate at the ends. Handsome fingers. Tony Reseck rubbed them gently together and there was peace in his quiet sea-gray eyes.

The frown came back on his face. The music annoyed him. He got up with a curious litheness, all in one piece, without moving his clasped hands from the watch chain. At one moment he was leaning back relaxed, and the next he was standing balanced on his feet, perfectly still, so that the movement of rising seemed to be a thing perfectly perceived, an error of vision. . . .

He walked with small, polished shoes delicately across the blue carpet and under the arch. The music was louder. It contained the hot, acid blare, the frenetic, jittering runs of a jam session. It was too loud. The red-haired girl sat there and stared silently at the fretted part of the big radio cabinet as though she could see the band with its fixed professional grin and the sweat running down its back. She was curled up with her feet under her on a davenport which seemed to contain most of the cushions in the room. She was tucked among them carefully, like a corsage in the florist's tissue paper.

She didn't turn her head. She leaned there, one hand in a small fist on her peach-colored knee. She was wearing lounging pajamas of heavy ribbed silk embroidered with black lotus buds.

"You like Goodman, Miss Cressy?" Tony Reseck asked.

The girl moved her eyes slowly. The light in there was dim, but the violet of her eyes almost hurt. They were large, deep eyes without a

From *The Simple Art of Murder* by Raymond Chandler, Houghton Mifflin, 1950.
Used by permission of the publisher.

trace of thought in them. Her face was classical and without expression. She said nothing.

Tony smiled and moved his fingers at his sides, one by one, feeling them move. "You like Goodman, Miss Cressy?" he repeated gently.

"Not to cry over," the girl said tonelessly.

Tony rocked back on his heels and looked at her eyes. Large, deep, empty eyes. Or were they? He reached down and muted the radio.

"Don't get me wrong," the girl said. "Goodman makes money, and a lad that makes legitimate money these days is a lad you have to respect. But this jitterbug music gives me the backdrop of a beer flat. I like something with roses in it."

"Maybe you like Mozart," Tony said.

"Go on, kid me," the girl said.

"I wasn't kidding you, Miss Cressy. I think Mozart was the greatest man that ever lived—and Toscanini is his prophet."

"I thought you were the house dick." She put her head back on a pillow and stared at him through her lashes.

"Make me some of that Mozart," she added.

"It's too late," Tony sighed. "You can't get it now."

She gave him another long lucid glance. "Got the eye on me, haven't you, flatfoot?" She laughed a little, almost under her breath. "What did I do wrong?"

Tony smiled his toy smile. "Nothing, Miss Cressy. Nothing at all. But you need some fresh air. You've been five days in this hotel and you haven't been outdoors. And you have a tower room."

She laughed again. "Make me a story about it. I'm bored."

"There was a girl here once had your suite. She stayed in the hotel a whole week, like you. Without going out at all, I mean. She didn't speak to anybody hardly. What do you think she did then?"

The girl eyed him gravely. "She jumped her bill."

He put his long delicate hand out and turned it slowly, fluttering the fingers, with an effect almost like a lazy wave breaking. "Unh-uh. She sent down for her bill and paid it. Then she told the hop to be back in half an hour for her suitcases. Then she went out on her balcony."

The girl leaned forward a little, her eyes still grave, one hand capping her peach-colored knee. "What did you say your name was?"

"Tony Reseck."

"Sounds like a hunky."

"Yeah," Tony said. "Polish."

"Go on, Tony."

"All the tower suites have private balconies, Miss Cressy. The walls of them are too low for fourteen stories above the street. It was a

340

dark night, that night, high clouds." He dropped his hand with a final gesture, a farewell gesture. "Nobody saw her jump. But when she hit, it was like a big gun going off."

"You're making it up, Tony." Her voice was a clean dry whisper of sound.

He smiled his toy smile. His quiet sea-gray eyes seemed almost to be smoothing the long waves of her hair. "Eve Cressy," he said musingly. "A name waiting for lights to be in."

"Waiting for a tall dark guy that's no good, Tony. You wouldn't care why. I was married to him once. I might be married to him again. You can make a lot of mistakes in just one lifetime." The hand on her knee opened slowly until the fingers were strained back as far as they would go. Then they closed quickly and tightly, and even in that dim light the knuckles shone like the little polished bones. "I played him a low trick once. I put him in a bad place—without meaning to. You wouldn't care about that either. It's just that I owe him something."

He leaned over softly and turned the knob on the radio. A waltz formed itself dimly on the warm air. A tinsel waltz, but a waltz. He turned the volume up. The music gushed from the loudspeaker in a swirl of shadowed melody. Since Vienna died, all waltzes are shadowed.

The girl put her hand on one side and hummed three or four bars and stopped with a sudden tightening of her mouth.

"Eve Cressy," she said. "It was in lights once. At a bum night club. A dive. They raided it and the lights went out."

He smiled at her almost mockingly. "It was no dive while you were there, Miss Cressy . . . That's the waltz the orchestra always played when the old porter walked up and down in front of the hotel entrance, all swelled up with his medals on his chest. *The Last Laugh.*[1] Emil Jannings.[2] You wouldn't remember that one, Miss Cressy."

"'Spring, Beautiful Spring,'" she said. "No, I never saw it."

He walked three steps away from her and turned. "I have to go upstairs and palm doorknobs. I hope I didn't bother you. You ought to go to bed now. It's pretty late."

The tinsel waltz stopped and a voice began to talk. The girl spoke through the voice. "You really thought something like that—about the balcony?"

He nodded. "I might have," he said softly. "I don't any more."

"No chance, Tony." Her smile was a dim lost leaf. "Come and talk to me some more. Redheads don't jump, Tony. They hang on—and wither."

---

[1] *The Last Laugh.* A German silent film (1924).
[2] *Emil Jannings.* A distinguished German actor who starred in *The Last Laugh.*

He looked at her gravely for a moment and then moved away over the carpet. The porter was standing in the archway that led to the main lobby. Tony hadn't looked that way yet, but he knew somebody was there. He always knew if anybody was close to him. He could hear the grass grow, like the donkey in *The Blue Bird*.[3]

The porter jerked his chin at him urgently. His broad face above the uniform collar looked sweaty and excited. Tony stepped up close to him and they went together through the arch and out to the middle of the dim lobby.

"Trouble?" Tony asked wearily.

"There's a guy outside to see you, Tony. He won't come in. I'm doing a wipe-off on the plate glass of the doors and he comes up beside me, a tall guy. 'Get Tony,' he says, out of the side of his mouth."

Tony said: "Uh-huh," and looked at the porter's pale blue eyes. "Who was it?"

"Al, he said to say he was."

Tony's face became as expressionless as dough. "Okey." He started to move off.

The porter caught his sleeve. "Listen, Tony. You got any enemies?"

Tony laughed politely, his face still like dough.

"Listen, Tony." The porter held his sleeve tightly. "There's a big black car down the block, the other way from the hacks. There's a guy standing beside it with his foot on the running board. This guy that spoke to me, he wears a dark-colored, wrap-around overcoat with a high collar turned up against his ears. His hat's way low. You can't hardly see his face. He says, 'Get Tony,' out of the side of his mouth. You ain't got any enemies, have you, Tony?"

"Only the finance company," Tony said. "Beat it."

He walked slowly and a little stiffly across the blue carpet, up the three shallow steps to the entrance lobby with the three elevators on one side and the desk on the other. Only one elevator was working. Beside the open doors, his arms folded, the night operator stood silent in a neat blue uniform with silver facings. A lean, dark Mexican named Gomez. A new boy, breaking in on the night shift.

The other side was the desk, rose marble, with the night clerk leaning on it delicately. A small neat man with a wispy reddish mustache and cheeks so rosy they looked roughed. He stared at Tony and poked a nail at his mustache.

Tony pointed a stiff index finger at him, folded the other three

---

[3] *The Blue Bird*. A play by Maurice Maeterlinck (1908). The play was made into a silent movie in 1916 and was remade in 1940.

fingers tight to his palm, and flicked his thumb up and down on the stiff finger. The clerk touched the other side of his mustache and looked bored.

Tony went on past the closed and darkened newsstand and the side entrance to the drugstore, out to the brassbound plate-glass doors. He stopped just inside them and took a deep, hard breath. He squared his shoulders, pushed the doors open and stepped out into the cold damp night air.

The street was dark, silent. The rumble of traffic on Wilshire, two blocks away, had no body, no meaning. To the left were two taxis. Their drivers leaned against a fender, side by side, smoking. Tony walked the other way. The big dark car was a third of a block from the hotel entrance. Its lights were dimmed and it was only when he was almost up to it that he heard the gentle sound of its engine turning over.

A tall figure detached itself from the body of the car and strolled toward him, both hands in the pockets of the dark overcoat with the high collar. From the man's mouth a cigarette tip glowed faintly, a rusty pearl.

They stopped two feet from each other.

The tall man said, "Hi, Tony. Long time no see."

"Hello, Al. How's it going?"

"Can't complain." The tall man started to take his right hand out of his overcoat pocket, then stopped and laughed quietly. "I forgot. Guess you don't want to shake hands."

"That don't mean anything," Tony said. "Shaking hands. Monkeys can shake hands. What's on your mind, Al?"

"Still the funny little fat guy, eh, Tony?"

"I guess." Tony winked his eyes tight. His throat felt tight.

"You like your job back there?"

"It's a job."

Al laughed his quiet laugh again. "You take it slow, Tony. I'll take it fast. So it's a job and you want to hold it. Oke. There's a girl named Eve Cressy flopping in your quiet hotel. Get her out. Fast and right now."

"What's the trouble?"

The tall man looked up and down the street. A man behind in the car coughed lightly. "She's hooked with a wrong number. Nothing against her personal, but she'll lead trouble to you. Get her out, Tony. You got maybe an hour."

"Sure," Tony said aimlessly, without meaning.

Al took his hand out of his pocket and stretched it against Tony's chest. He gave him a light, lazy push. "I wouldn't be telling you just for the hell of it, little fat brother. Get her out of there."

"Okey," Tony said, without any tone in his voice.

The tall man took back his hand and reached for the car door. He opened it and started to slip in like a lean black shadow.

Then he stopped and said something to the men in the car and got out again. He came back to where Tony stood silent, his pale eyes catching a little dim light from the street.

"Listen, Tony. You always kept your nose clean. You're a good brother, Tony."

Tony didn't speak.

Al leaned toward him, a long urgent shadow, the high collar almost touching his ears. "It's trouble business, Tony. The boys won't like it, but I'm telling you just the same. This Cressy was married to a lad named Johnny Ralls. Ralls is out of Quentin two, three days, or a week. He did a three-spot for manslaughter. The girl put him there. He ran down an old man one night when he was drunk, and she was with him. He wouldn't stop. She told him to go in and tell it, or else. He didn't go in. So the Johns come for him."

Tony said, "That's too bad."

"It's kosher, kid. It's my business to know. This Ralls flapped his mouth in stir about how the girl would be waiting for him when he got out, all set to forgive and forget, and he was going straight to her."

Tony said, "What's he to you?" His voice had a dry, stiff crackle, like thick paper.

Al laughed. "The trouble boys want to see him. He ran a table at a spot on the Strip and figured out a scheme. He and another guy took the house for fifty grand. The other lad coughed up, but we still need Johnny's twenty-five. The trouble boys don't get paid to forget."

Tony looked up and down the dark street. One of the taxi drivers flicked a cigarette stub in a long arc over the top of one of the cabs. Tony watched it fall and spark on the pavement. He listened to the quiet sound of the big car's motor.

"I don't want any part of it," he said. "I'll get her out."

Al backed away from him, nodding. "Wise kid. How's mom these days?"

"Okey," Tony said.

"Tell her I was asking for her."

"Asking for her isn't anything," Tony said.

Al turned quickly and got into the car. The car curved lazily in the middle of the block and drifted back toward the corner. Its lights went up and sprayed on a wall. It turned a corner and was gone. The linger-

344

ing smell of its exhaust drifted past Tony's nose. He turned and walked back to the hotel and into it. He went along to the radio room.

The radio still muttered, but the girl was gone from the davenport in front of it. The pressed cushions were hollowed out by her body. Tony reached down and touched them. He thought they were still warm. He turned the radio off and stood there, turning a thumb slowly in front of his body, his hand flat against his stomach. Then he went back through the lobby toward the elevator bank and stood beside a majolica jar of white sand. The clerk fussed behind a pebbled-glass screen at one end of the desk. The air was dead.

The elevator bank was dark. Tony looked at the indicator of the middle car and saw that it was at 14.

"Gone to bed," he said under his breath.

The door of the porter's room beside the elevators opened and the little Mexican night operator came out in street clothes. He looked at Tony with a quiet sidewise look out of eyes the color of dried-out chestnuts.

"Good night, boss."

"Yeah," Tony said absently.

He took a thin dappled cigar out of his vest pocket and smelled it. He examined it slowly, turning it around in his neat fingers. There was a small tear along the side. He frowned at that and put the cigar away.

There was a distant sound and the hand on the indicator began to steal around the bronze dial. Light glittered up in the shaft and the straight line of the car floor dissolved the darkness below. The car stopped and the doors opened, and Carl came out of it.

His eyes caught Tony's with a kind of jump and he walked over to him, his head on one side, a thin shine along his pink upper lip.

"Listen, Tony."

Tony took his arm in a hard swift hand and turned him. He pushed him quickly, yet somehow casually, down the steps to the dim main lobby and steered him into a corner. He let go of the arm. His throat tightened again, for no reason he could think of.

"Well?" he said darkly. "Listen to what?"

The porter reached into a pocket and hauled out a dollar bill. "He gimme this," he said loosely. His glittering eyes looked past Tony's shoulder at nothing. They winked rapidly. "Ice and ginger ale."

"Don't stall," Tony growled.

"Guy in Fourteen-B," the porter said.

"Lemme smell your breath."

The porter leaned toward him obediently.

"Liquor," Tony said harshly.

345

"He gimme a drink."

Tony looked down at the dollar bill. "Nobody's in Fourteen-B. Not on my list," he said.

"Yeah. There is." The porter licked his lips and his eyes opened and shut several times. "Tall dark guy."

"All right," Tony said crossly. "All right. There's a tall dark guy in Fourteen-B and he gave you a buck and a drink. Then what?"

"Gat under his arm," Carl said, and blinked.

Tony smiled, but his eyes had taken on the lifeless glitter of thick ice. "You take Miss Cressy up to her room?"

Carl shook his head. "Gomez. I saw her go up."

"Get away from me," Tony said between his teeth. "And don't accept any more drinks from the guests."

He didn't move until Carl had gone back into his cubbyhole by the elevators and shut the door. Then he moved silently up the three steps and stood in front of the desk, looking at the veined rose marble, the onyx pen set, the fresh registration card on its leather frame. He lifted a hand and smacked it down hard on the marble. The clerk popped out from behind the glass screen like a chipmunk coming out of its hole.

Tony took a flimsy out of his breast pocket and spread it on the desk. "No Fourteen-B on this," he said in a bitter voice.

The clerk wisped politely at his mustache. "So sorry. You must have been out to supper when he checked in."

"Who?"

"Registered as James Watterson, San Diego." The clerk yawned.

"Ask for anybody?"

The clerk stopped in the middle of the yawn and looked at the top of Tony's head. "Why yes. He asked for a swing band. Why?"

"Smart, fast and funny," Tony said. "If you like 'em that way." He wrote on his flimsy and stuffed it back into his pocket. "I'm going upstairs and palm doorknobs. There's four tower rooms you ain't rented yet. Get up on your toes, son. You're slipping."

"I made out," the clerk drawled, and completed his yawn. "Hurry back, pop. I don't know how I'll get through the time."

"You could shave that pink fuzz off your lip," Tony said, and went across to the elevators.

He opened up a dark one and lit the dome light and shot the car up to fourteen. He darkened it again, stepped out and closed the doors. This lobby was smaller than any other, except the one immediately below it. It had a single blue-paneled door in each of the walls other than the elevator wall. On each door was a gold number and letter with a gold wreath around it. Tony walked over to 14A and put his ear to the panel. He heard nothing. Eve Cressy might be in bed asleep, or in the bathroom, or out on the balcony. Or she might be sitting there in the room, a few feet from the door, looking at the wall. Well, he wouldn't expect to be able to hear her sit and look at the wall. He went over to 14B and put his ear to that panel. This was different. There was a sound in there. A man coughed. It sounded somehow like a solitary cough. There were no voices. Tony pressed the small nacre button beside the door.

Steps came without hurry. A thickened voice spoke through the panel. Tony made no answer, no sound. The thickened voice repeated the question. Lightly, maliciously, Tony pressed the bell again.

Mr. James Watterson, of San Diego, should now open the door and give forth noise. He didn't. A silence fell beyond that door that was like the silence of a glacier. Once more Tony put his ear to the wood. Silence utterly.

He got out a master key on a chain and pushed it delicately into the lock of the door. He turned it, pushed the door inward three inches and withdrew the key. Then he waited.

"All right," the voice said harshly. "Come in and get it."

Tony pushed the door wide and stood there, framed against the light from the lobby. The man was tall, black-haired, angular and white-faced. He held a gun. He held it as though he knew about guns.

"Step right in," he drawled.

Tony went in through the door and pushed it shut with his shoulder. He kept his hands a little out from his sides, the clever fingers curled and slack. He smiled his quiet little smile.

"Mr. Watterson?"

"And after that what?"

"I'm the house detective here."

"It slays me."

The tall, white-faced, somehow handsome and somehow not handsome man backed slowly into the room. It was a large room with a low balcony around two sides of it. French doors opened out on the little private open-air balcony that each of the tower rooms had. There was a grate set for a log fire behind a paneled screen in front of a cheerful davenport. A tall misted glass stood on a hotel tray beside a deep, cozy chair. The man backed toward this and stood in front of it. The large, glistening gun drooped and pointed at the floor.

"It slays me," he said. "I'm in the dump an hour and the house copper gives me the buzz. Okey, sweetheart, look in the closet and bathroom. But she just left."

"You didn't see her yet," Tony said.

The man's bleached face filled with unexpected lines. His thickened voice edged toward a snarl. "Yeah? Who didn't I see yet?"

"A girl named Eve Cressy."

The man swallowed. He put his gun down on the table beside the tray. He let himself down into the chair backwards, stiffly, like a man with a touch of lumbago. Then he leaned forward and put his hands on his kneecaps and smiled brightly between his teeth. "So she got here, huh? I didn't ask about her yet. I'm a careful guy. I didn't ask yet."

"She's been here five days," Tony said. "Waiting for you. She hasn't left the hotel a minute."

The man's mouth worked a little. His smile had a knowing tilt to it. "I got delayed a little up north," he said smoothly. "You know how it is. Visiting old friends. You seem to know a lot about my business, copper."

"That's right, Mr. Ralls."

The man lunged to his feet and his hand snapped at the gun. He stood leaning over, holding it on the table, staring. "Dames talk too much," he said with a muffled sound in his voice as though he held something soft between his teeth and talked through it.

"Not dames, Mr. Ralls."

"Huh?" The gun slithered on the hard wood of the table. "Talk it up, copper. My mind reader just quit."

"Not dames, guys. Guys with guns."

The glacier silence fell between them again. The man straightened his body out slowly. His face was washed clean of expression, but his eyes were haunted. Tony leaned in front of him, a shortish plump man with a quiet, pale, friendly face and eyes as simple as forest water.

"They never run out of gas—those boys," Johnny Ralls said, and licked at his lip. "Early and late, they work. The old firm never sleeps."

"You know who they are?" Tony said softly.

"I could maybe give nine guesses. And twelve of them would be right."

"The trouble boys," Tony said, and smiled a brittle smile.

"Where is she?" Johnny Ralls asked harshly.

"Right next door to you."

The man walked to the wall and left his gun lying on the table. He stood in front of the wall, studying it. He reached up and gripped the grillwork of the balcony railing. When he dropped his hand and turned, his face had lost some of its lines. His eyes had a quieter glint. He moved back to Tony and stood over him.

"I've got a stake," he said. "Eve sent me some dough and I built it up with a touch I made up north. Case dough, what I mean. The trouble boys talk about twenty-five grand." He smiled crookedly. "Five C's I can count. I'd have a lot of fun making them believe that, I would."

"What did you do with it?" Tony asked indifferently.

"I never had it, copper. Leave that lay. I'm the only guy in the world that believes it. It was a little deal that I got suckered on."

"I'll believe it," Tony said.

"They don't kill often. But they can be awful tough."

"Mugs," Tony said with a sudden bitter contempt. "Guys with guns. Just mugs."

Johnny Ralls reached for his glass and drained it empty. The ice cubes tinkled softly as he put it down. He picked his gun up, danced it on his palm, then tucked it, nose down, into an inner breast pocket. He stared at the carpet.

"How come you're telling me this, copper?"

"I thought maybe you'd give her a break."

"And if I wouldn't?"

"I kind of think you will," Tony said.

Johnny Ralls nodded quietly. "Can I get out of here?"

"You could take the service elevator to the garage. You could rent a car. I can give you a card to the garage man."

"You're a funny little guy," Johnny Ralls said.

Tony took out a worn ostrich-skin billfold and scribbled on a printed card. Johnny Ralls read it, and stood holding it, tapping it against a thumbnail.

"I could take her with me," he said, his eyes narrow.

"You could take a ride in a basket too," Tony said. "She's been here five days, I told you. She's been spotted. A guy I know called me up and told me to get her out of here. Told me what it was all about. So I'm getting you out instead."

"They'll love that," Johnny Ralls said. "They'll send you violets."

"I'll weep about it on my day off."

Johnny Ralls turned his hand over and stared at the palm. "I could see her, anyway. Before I blow. Next door to here, you said?"

Tony turned on his heel and started for the door. He said over his shoulder, "Don't waste a lot of time, handsome. I might change my mind."

The man said, almost gently: "You might be spotting me right now, for all I know."

Tony didn't turn his head. "That's a chance you have to take."

He went on to the door and passed out of the room. He shut it carefully, silently, looked once at the door of 14A and got into his dark

349

elevator. He rode it down to the linen-room floor and got out to remove the basket that held the service elevator open at that floor. The door slid quietly shut. He held it so that it made no noise. Down the corridor, light came from the open door of the housekeeper's office. Tony got back into his elevator and went on down to the lobby.

The little clerk was out of sight behind his pebbled-glass screen, auditing accounts. Tony went through the main lobby and turned into the radio room. The radio was on again, soft. She was there, curled on the davenport again. The speaker hummed to her, a vague sound so low that what it said was as wordless as the murmur of trees. She turned her head slowly and smiled at him.

"Finished palming doorknobs? I couldn't sleep worth a nickel. So I came down again. Okey?"

He smiled and nodded. He sat down in a green chair and patted the plump brocade arms of it. "Sure, Miss Cressy."

"Waiting is the hardest kind of work, isn't it? I wish you'd talk to that radio. It sounds like a pretzel being bent."

Tony fiddled with it, got nothing he liked, set it back where it had been.

"Beer-parlor drunks are all the customers now."

She smiled at him again.

"I don't bother you being here, Miss Cressy?"

"I like it. You're a sweet little guy, Tony."

He looked stiffly at the floor and a ripple touched his spine. He waited for it to go away. It went slowly. Then he sat back, relaxed again, his neat fingers clasped on his elk's tooth. He listened. Not to the radio—to far-off, uncertain things menacing things. And perhaps to just the safe whir of wheels going away into a strange night.

"Nobody's all bad," he said out loud.

The girl looked at him lazily. "I've met two or three I was wrong on, then."

He nodded. "Yeah," he admitted judiciously. "I guess there's some that are."

The girl yawned and her deep violet eyes half closed. She nestled back into the cushions. "Sit there for a while, Tony. Maybe I could nap."

"Sure. Not a thing for me to do. Don't know why they pay me."

She slept quickly and with complete stillness, like a child. Tony hardly breathed for ten minutes. He just watched her, his mouth a little open. There was a quiet fascination in his limpid eyes, as if he was looking at an altar.

Then he stood up with infinite care and padded away under the arch to the entrance lobby and the desk. He stood at the desk listening for a little while. He heard a pen rustling out of sight. He went around the corner to the row of house phones in little glass cubbyholes. He lifted one and asked the night operator for the garage.

It rang three or four times and then a boyish voice answered: "Windermere Hotel. Garage speaking."

"This is Tony Reseck. That guy Watterson I gave a card to. He leave?"

"Sure, Tony. Half a hour almost. Is it your charge?"

"Yeah," Tony said. "My party. Thanks. Be seein' you."

He hung up and scratched his neck. He went back to the desk and slapped a hand on it. The clerk wafted himself around the screen with his greeter's smile in place. It dropped when he saw Tony.

"Can't a guy catch up on his work?" he grumbled.

"What's the professional rate on Fourteen-B?"

The clerk stared morosely. "There's no professional rate in the tower."

"Make one. The fellow left already. Was there only an hour."

"Well, well," the clerk said airily. "So the personality didn't click tonight. We get a skip-out."

"Will five bucks satisfy you?"

"Friend of yours?"

"No. Just a drunk with delusions of grandeur and no dough."

"Guess we'll have to let it ride, Tony. How did he get out?"

"I took him down the service elevator. You was asleep. Will five bucks satisfy you?"

"Why?"

The worn ostrich-skin wallet came out and a weedy five slipped across the marble. "All I could shake him for," Tony said loosely.

The clerk took the five and looked puzzled. "You're the boss," he said, and shrugged. The phone shrilled on the desk and he reached for it. He listened and then pushed it toward Tony. "For you."

Tony took the phone and cuddled it close to his chest. He put his mouth close to the transmitter. The voice was strange to him. It had a metallic sound. Its syllables were meticulously anonymous.

"Tony? Tony Reseck?"

"Talking."

"A message from Al. Shoot?"

Tony looked at the clerk. "Be a pal," he said over the mouthpiece. The clerk flicked a narrow smile at him and went away. "Shoot," Tony said into the phone.

"We had a little business with a guy in your place. Picked him up

351

scramming. Al had a hunch you'd run him out. Tailed him and took him to the curb. Not so good. Backfire."

Tony held the phone very tight and his temples chilled with the evaporation of moisture. "Go on," he said. "I guess there's more."

"A little. The guy stopped the big one. Cold. Al—Al said to tell you goodbye."

Tony leaned hard against the desk. His mouth made a sound that was not speech.

"Get it?" The metallic voice sounded impatient, a little bored. "This guy had him a rod. He used it. Al won't be phoning anybody any more."

Tony lurched at the phone, and the base of it shook on the rose marble. His mouth was a hard dry knot.

The voice said: "That's as far as we go, bub. G'night." The phone clicked dryly, like a pebble hitting a wall.

Tony put the phone down in its cradle very carefully, so as not to make any sound. He looked at the clenched palm of his left hand. He took a handkerchief out and rubbed the palm softly and straightened the fingers out with his other hand. Then he wiped his forehead. The clerk came around the screen again and looked at him with glinting eyes.

"I'm off Friday. How about lending me that phone number?"

Tony nodded at the clerk and smiled a minute frail smile. He put his handkerchief away and patted the pocket he had put it in. He turned and walked away from the desk, across the entrance lobby, down the three shallow steps, along the shadowy reaches of the main lobby, and so in through the arch to the radio room once more. He walked softly, like a man moving in a room where somebody is very sick. He reached the chair he had sat in before and lowered himself into it inch by inch. The girl slept on, motionless, in that curled-up looseness achieved by some women and all cats. Her breath made no slightest sound against the vague murmur of the radio.

Tony Reseck leaned back in the chair and clasped his hands on his elk's tooth and quietly closed his eyes.

MURDER AT THE AUTOMAT

By Cornell Woolrich

Cornell George Hopley-Woolrich (1903–1968) led a life as dark and strange as any he depicted in his more than 250 short stories and novels. His childhood was a painfully rootless one, divided between travel in Latin America with his father, a civil engineer, and hotel living in New York with his socially prominent mother. He wrote his first novel, a romantic story called Cover Charge, during a six-week illness when he could not attend classes at Columbia College, and a year later he won a $10,000 prize for a second romantic novel. While in Hollywood in 1929, Woolrich married but within a few weeks was separated from his wife and returned to New York to share a hotel apartment with his mother. From this time on Woolrich was very nearly a recluse, rarely leaving the hotel room in which he wrote the literally hundreds of short stories of suspense and psychological terror which he published under either his own name or the pseudonym William Irish. He also wrote a number of novels including The Bride Wore Black (1940), Phantom Lady (1942), and, as George Hopley, The Night Has a Thousand Eyes (1945). The last years of the man whom Otto Penzler has called "possibly the finest mystery writer of the twentieth century" were particularly bitter and lonely ones, marred by illness and alcoholism. At his death, Woolrich left a nearly $1-million estate to establish a scholarship at Columbia University in his mother's name. Many of Woolrich's stories first appeared in such period pulp magazines as Detective Fiction Weekly and Black Mask. "Murder at the Automat" was published in 1937 in Dime Detective and was reprinted in Nightwebs (New York: Harper & Row, 1971), a selection of Woolrich fiction edited by Francis M. Nevins, Jr. A 1965 collection with a foreword by Ellery Queen is called The Ten Faces of Cornell Woolrich (New York: Simon & Schuster).

Nelson pushed through the revolving-door at twenty to one in the morning, his squadmate, Sarecky, in the compartment behind him. They stepped clear and looked around. The place looked funny. Almost all the little white tables had helpings of food on them, but no one was at them eating. There was a big black crowd ganged up over in one corner, thick as bees and sending up a buzz. One or two were standing up on chairs, trying to see over the heads of the ones in front, rubbering like a flock of cranes.

The crowd burst apart, and a cop came through. "Now, stand back. Get away from this table, all of you," he was saying. "There's nothing to see. The man's dead—that's all."

He met the two dicks halfway between the crowd and the door. "Over there in the corner," he said unnecessarily. "Indigestion, I guess." He went back with them.

They split the crowd wide open again, this time from the outside. In the middle of it was one of the little white tables, a dead man in a chair, an ambulance doctor, a pair of stretcher-bearers, and the automat manager.

"He gone?" Nelson asked the interne.

"Yep. We got here too late." He came closer so the mob wouldn't overhear. "Better send him down to the morgue and have him looked at. I think he did the Dutch. There's a white streak on his chin, and a half-eaten sandwich under his face spiked with some more of it, whatever it is. That's why I got in touch with you fellows. Good night," he wound up pleasantly and elbowed his way out of the crowd, the two stretcher-bearers tagging after him. The ambulance clanged dolorously outside, swept its fiery headlights around the corner, and whined off.

Nelson said to the cop: "Go over to the door and keep everyone in here, until we get the three others that were sitting at this table with him."

The manager said: "There's a little balcony upstairs. Couldn't he be taken up there, instead of being left down here in full sight like this?"

"Yeah, pretty soon," Nelson agreed, "but not just yet."

He looked down at the table. There were four servings of food on it, one on each side. Two had barely been touched. One had been finished and only the soiled plates remained. One was hidden by the

"Murder at the Automat" from *Dime Detective*, August 1937. Copyright ©1937 by Popular Publications, Inc. Renewed 1964 by Popular Publications, Inc. Reprinted by permission of Chase Manhattan Bank, N.A., executors of the estate of Cornell Woolrich.

prone figure sprawled across it, one arm out, the other hanging limply down toward the floor.

"Who was sitting here?" said Nelson, pointing to one of the unconsumed portions. "Kindly step forward and identify yourself." No one made a move. "No one," said Nelson, raising his voice, "gets out of here until we have a chance to question the three people that were at this table with him when it happened."

Someone started to back out of the crowd from behind. The woman who had wanted to go home so badly a minute ago, pointed accusingly. "He was—that man there! I remember him distinctly. He bumped into me with his tray just before he sat down."

Sarecky went over, took him by the arm, and brought him forward again. "No one's going to hurt you," Nelson said, at sight of his pale face. "Only don't make it any tougher for yourself than you have to."

"I never even saw the guy before," wailed the man, as if he had already been accused of murder, "I just happened to park my stuff at the first vacant chair I—" Misery liking company, he broke off short and pointed in turn. "He was at the table, too. Why doncha hold him, if you're gonna hold me?"

"That's just what we're going to do," said Nelson dryly. "Over here, you," he ordered the new witness. "Now, who was eating spaghetti on the right here? As soon as we find that out, the rest of you can go home."

The crowd looked around indignantly in search of the recalcitrant witness that was the cause of detaining them all. But this time no one was definitely able to single him out. A white-uniformed busman finally edged forward and said to Nelson: "I think he musta got out of the place right after it happened. I looked over at this table a minute before it happened, and he was already through eating, picking his teeth and just holding down the chair."

"Well, he's not as smart as he thinks he is," said Nelson. "We'll catch up with him, whether he got out or didn't. The rest of you clear out of here now. And don't give fake names and addresses to the cop at the door, or you'll be making trouble for yourselves."

The place emptied itself like magic, self-preservation being stronger than curiosity in most people. The two table-mates of the dead man, the manager, the staff, and the two dicks remained inside.

An assistant medical examiner arrived, followed by two men with the usual basket, and made a brief preliminary investigation. While this was going on, Nelson was questioning the two witnesses, the busman, and the manager. He got an illuminating composite picture.

The man was well known to the staff by sight, and was considered an eccentric. He always came in at the same time each night, just before closing time, and always helped himself to the same snack—coffee and a bologna sandwich. It hadn't varied for six months now. The remnants that the busman removed from where the man sat each time, were always the same. The manager was able to corroborate this. He, the dead man, had raised a kick one night about a week ago, because the bologna-sandwich slots had all been emptied before he came in. The manager had had to remind him that it's first come, first served, at an automat, and you can't reserve your food ahead of time. The man at the change-booth, questioned by Nelson, added to the old fellow's reputation for eccentricity. Other, well-dressed people came in and changed a half-dollar, or at the most a dollar bill. He, in his battered hat and derelict's overcoat, never failed to produce a ten and sometimes even a twenty.

"One of these misers, eh?" said Nelson. "They always end up behind the eight-ball, one way or another."

The old fellow was removed, also the partly consumed sandwich. The assistant examiner let Nelson know: "I think you've got something here, brother. I may be wrong, but that sandwich was loaded with cyanide."

Sarecky, who had gone through the man's clothes, said: "The name was Leo Avram, and here's the address. Incidentally, he had seven hundred dollars, in C's, in his right shoe and three hundred in his left. Want me to go over there and nose around?"

"Suppose I go," Nelson said. "You stay here and clean up."

"My pal," murmured the other dick dryly.

The waxed paper from the sandwich had been left lying under the chair. Nelson picked it up, wrapped it in a paper-napkin, and put it in his pocket. It was only a short walk from the automat to where Avram lived, an outmoded, walk-up building, falling to pieces with neglect.

Nelson went into the hall and there was no such name listed. He thought at first Sarecky had made a mistake, or at least been misled by whatever memorandum it was he had found that purported to give the old fellow's address. He rang the bell marked *Superintendent*, and went down to the basement-entrance to make sure. A stout blond woman in an old sweater and carpet-slippers came out.

"Is there anyone named Avram living in this building?"

"That's my husband—he's the superintendent. He's out right now, I expect him back any minute."

Nelson couldn't understand, himself, why he didn't break it to her then and there. He wanted to get a line, perhaps, on the old man's surroundings while they still remained normal. "Can I come in and wait a minute?" he said.

"Why not?" she said indifferently.

She led him down a barren, unlit basement-way, stacked with empty ashcans, into a room green-yellow with a tiny bud of gaslight. Old as the building upstairs was, it had been wired for electricity, Nelson had noted. For that matter, so was this basement down here. There was a cord hanging from the ceiling ending in an empty socket. It had been looped up out of reach. "The old bird sure was a miser," thought Nelson. "Walking around on one grand and living like this!" He couldn't help feeling a little sorry for the woman.

He noted to his further surprise that a pot of coffee was boiling on a one-burner gas stove over in the corner. He wondered if she knew that he treated himself away from home each night. "Any idea where he went?" he asked, sitting down in a creaking rocker.

"He goes two blocks down to the automat for a bite to eat every night at this time," she said.

"How is it," he asked curiously, "he'll go out and spend money like that, when he could have coffee right here where he lives with you?"

A spark of resentment showed in her face, but a defeated resentment that had long turned to resignation. She shrugged. "For himself, nothing's too good. He goes there because the light's better, he says. But for me and the kids, he begrudges every penny."

"You've got kids, have you?"

"They're mine, not his," she said dully.

Nelson had already caught sight of a half-grown girl and a little boy peeping shyly out at him from another room. "Well," he said, getting up, "I'm sorry to have to tell you this, but your husband had an accident a little while ago at the automat, Mrs. Avram. He's gone."

The weary stolidity on her face changed very slowly. But it did change—to fright. "Cyanide—what's that?" she breathed, when he'd told her.

"Did he have any enemies?"

She said with utter simplicity. "Nobody loved him. Nobody hated him that much, either."

"Do you know of any reason he'd have to take his own life?"

"Him? Never! He held on tight to life, just like he did to his money."

There was some truth in that, the dick had to admit. Misers seldom commit suicide.

The little girl edged into the room fearfully, holding her hands behind her. "Is—is he dead, Mom?"

The woman just nodded, dry-eyed.

"Then, can we use this now?" She was a holding a fly-blown electric bulb in her hands.

Nelson felt touched, hard-boiled dick though he was. "Come down to headquarters tomorrow, Mrs. Avram. There's some money there you can claim. G'night." He went outside and clanged the basement-gate shut after him. The windows alongside him suddenly bloomed feebly with electricity, and the silhouette of a woman standing up on a chair was outlined against them.

"It's a funny world," thought the dick with a shake of his head, as he trudged up to sidewalk-level.

It was now two in the morning. The automat was dark when Nelson returned there, so he went down to headquarters. They were questioning the branch-manager and the unseen counterman who prepared the sandwiches and filled the slots from the inside.

Nelson's captain said: "They've already telephoned from the chem lab that the sandwich is loaded with cyanide crystals. On the other hand, they give the remainder of the loaf that was used, the leftover bologna from which the sandwich was prepared, the breadknife, the cutting-board, and the scraps in the garbage-receptacle—all of which we sent over there—a clean bill of health. There was clearly no slip-up or carelessness in the automat pantry. Which means that cyanide got into that sandwich on the consumer's side of the apparatus. He committed suicide or was deliberately murdered by one of the other customers."

"I was just up there," Nelson said. "It wasn't suicide. People don't worry about keeping their light bills down when they're going to take their own lives."

"Good psychology," the captain nodded. "My experience is that miserliness is simply a perverted form of self-preservation, an exaggerated clinging to life. The choice of method wouldn't be in character, either. Cyanide's expensive, and it wouldn't be sold to a man of Avram's type, just for the asking. It's murder, then. I think it's highly important you men bring in whoever the fourth man at that table was tonight. Do it with the least possible loss of time."

A composite description of him, pieced together from the few scraps that could be obtained from the busman and the other two at the table, was available. He was a heavy-set dark-complected man, wearing a light-tan suit. He had been the first of the four at the table, and already through eating, but had lingered on. Mannerisms—had kept looking back over his shoulder, from time to time, and picking his

358

teeth. He had had a small black satchel, or sample-case, parked at his feet under the table. Both survivors were positive on this point. Both had stubbed their toes against it in sitting down, and both had glanced to the floor to see what it was.

Had he reached down toward it at any time, after their arrival, as if to open it or take anything out of it?

To the best of their united recollections — no.

Had Avram, *after* bringing the sandwich to the table, gotten up again and left it unguarded for a moment?

Again, no. In fact the whole thing had been over with in a flash. He had noisily unwrapped it, taken a huge bite, swallowed without chewing, heaved convulsively once or twice, and fallen prone across the tabletop.

"Then it must have happened right outside the slot — I mean the inserting of the stuff — and not at the table, at all," Sarecky told Nelson privately. "Guess he laid it down for a minute while he was drawing his coffee."

"Absolutely not!" Nelson contradicted. "You're forgetting it was all wrapped up in wax-paper. How could anyone have opened, then closed it again, without attracting his attention? And if we're going to suspect the guy with the satchel — and the cap seems to want us to — he was already *at* the table and all through eating when Avram came over. How could he know ahead of time which table the old guy was going to select?"

"Then how did the stuff get on it? Where did it come from?" the other dick asked helplessly.

"It's little things like that we're paid to find out," Nelson reminded him dryly.

"Pretty large order, isn't it?"

"You talk like a layman. You've been on the squad long enough by now to know how damnably unescapable little habits are, how impossible it is to shake them off, once formed. The public at large thinks detective work is something miraculous like pulling rabbits out of a silk-hat. They don't realize that no adult is a free agent — that they're tied hand and foot by tiny, harmless little habits, and held helpless. This man has a habit of taking a snack to eat at midnight in a public place. He has a habit of picking his teeth after he's through, of lingering on at the table, of looking back over his shoulder aimlessly from time to time. Combine that with a stocky build, a dark complexion, and you have him! What more d'ya want — a spotlight trained on him?"

It was Sarecky, himself, in spite of his misgivings, who picked him

359

up forty-eight hours later in another automat, sample-case and all, at nearly the same hour as the first time, and brought him in for questioning! The busman from the former place, and the two customers, called in, identified him unhesitatingly, even if he was now wearing a gray suit.

His name, he said, was Alexander Hill, and he lived at 215 Such-and-such a street.

"What business are you in?" rapped out the captain.

The man's face got livid. His Adam's apple went up and down like an elevator. He could barely articulate the words. "I'm—I'm a salesman for a wholesale drug concern," he gasped terrifiedly.

"Ah!" said two of his three questioners expressively. The sample-case, opened, was found to contain only tooth-powders, aspirins, and headache remedies.

But Nelson, rummaging through it, thought: "Oh, nuts, it's too pat. And he's too scared, too defenseless, to have really done it. Came in here just now without a bit of mental build-up prepared ahead of time. The real culprit would have been all primed, all rehearsed, for just this. Watch him go all to pieces. The innocent ones always do."

The captain's voice rose to a roar. "How is it everyone else stayed in the place that night, but you got out in such a hurry?"

"I—I don't know. It happened so close to me, I guess I—I got nervous."

That wasn't necessarily a sign of guilt; Nelson was thinking. It was his duty to take part in the questioning, so he shot out at him: "You got nervous, eh? What reason d'you have for getting nervous? How'd *you* know it wasn't just a heart attack or malnutrition—unless you were the cause of it?"

He stumbled badly over that one. "No! No! I don't handle that stuff! I don't carry anything like that—"

"So you know what it was? How'd you know? We didn't tell you," Sarecky jumped on him.

"I—I read it in the papers next morning," he wailed.

Well, it had been in all of them, Nelson had to admit.

"You didn't reach out in front of you—toward him—for anything that night? You kept your hands to yourself?" Then, before he could get a word out, *"What about sugar?"*

The suspect went from bad to worse: "I don't use any!" he whimpered.

Sarecky had been just waiting for that. "Don't lie to us!" he yelled, and swung at him. "I watched you for ten full minutes tonight before I went over and tapped your shoulder. You emptied half the container into your cup!" His fist hit him a glancing blow on the side of the jaw, knocked him and the chair he was sitting on both off-balance. Fright was making the guy sew himself up twice as badly as before.

"Aw, we're just barking up the wrong tree," Nelson kept saying to himself. "It's just one of those fluke coincidences. A drug salesman happens to be sitting at the same table where a guy drops from cyanide poisoning!" Still, he knew that more than one guy had been strapped into the chair just on the strength of such a coincidence and nothing more. You couldn't expect a jury not to pounce on it for all it was worth.

The captain took Nelson out of it at this point, somewhat to his relief, took him aside and murmured: "Go over there and give his place a good cleaning while we're holding him here. If you can turn up any of that stuff hidden around there, that's all we need. "He'll break down like a stack of cards." He glanced over at the cowering figure in the chair. "We'll have him before morning," he promised.

"That's what I'm afraid of," thought Nelson, easing out. "And then what'll we have? Exactly nothing." He wasn't the kind of a dick that would have rather had a wrong guy than no guy at all, like some of them. He wanted the right guy—or none at all. The last he saw of the captain, he was stripping off his coat for action, more as a moral threat than a physical one, and the unfortunate victim of circumstances was wailing, "I didn't do it, I didn't do it," like a record with a flaw in it.

Hill was a bachelor and lived in a small, one-room flat on the upper West Side. Nelson let himself in with the man's own key, put on the lights, and went to work. In half an hour, he had investigated the place upside-down. There was not a grain of cyanide to be found, nor anything beyond what had already been revealed in the sample-case. This did not mean, of course, that he couldn't have obtained some either through the firm he worked for, or some of the retail druggists whom he canvassed. Nelson found a list of the latter and took it with him to check over the following day.

Instead of returning directly to headquarters, he detoured on an impulse past the Avram house, and, seeing a light shining in the basement windows, went over and rang the bell.

The little girl came out, her brother behind her. "Mom's not in," she announced.

"She's out with Uncle Nick," the boy supplied.

His sister whirled on him. "She told us not to tell anybody that, didn't she!"

Nelson could hear the instructions as clearly as if he'd been in the room at the time, "If that man comes around again, don't you tell him I've gone out with Uncle Nick, now!"

Children are after all very transparent. They told him most of what he wanted to know without realizing they were doing it. "He's not really your uncle, is he?"

A gasp of surprise. "How'd you know that?"

"Your ma gonna marry him?"

They both nodded approvingly. "He's gonna be out new Pop."

"What was the name of your real Pop—the one before the last?"

"Edwards," they chorused proudly.

"What happened to him?"

"He died."

"In Dee-troit," added the little boy.

He only asked them one more question. "Can you tell me his full name?"

"Albert J. Edwards," they recited.

He gave them a friendly push. "All right, kids, go back to bed."

He went back to headquarters, sent a wire to the Bureau of Vital Statistics in Detroit, on his own hook. They were still questioning Hill down to the bone, meanwhile, but he hadn't caved in yet. "Nothing," Nelson reported. "Only this account-sheet of where he places his orders."

"I'm going to try framing him with a handful of bicarb of soda, or something—pretend we got the goods on him. I'll see if that'll open him up," the captain promised wrathfully. "He's not the push-over I expected. You start in at seven this morning and work your way through this list of retail druggists. Find out if he ever tried to contract them for any of that stuff."

Meanwhile, he had Hill smuggled out the back way to an outlying precinct, to evade the statute governing the length of time a prisoner can be held before arraignment. They didn't have enough of a case against him to arraign him, but they weren't going to let him go.

Nelson was even more surprised than the prisoner at what he caught himself doing. As they stood Hill up next to him in the corridor, for a minute, waiting for the Black Maria, he breathed over his shoulder, "Hang on tight, or you're sunk!"

The man acted too far gone even to understand what he was driving at.

Nelson was present the next morning when Mrs. Avram showed up to claim the money, and watched her expression curiously. She had the same air of weary resignation as the night he had broken the news

362

to her. She accepted the money from the captain, signed for it, turned apathetically away, holding it in her hand. The captain, by prearrangement, had pulled another of his little tricks—purposely withheld one of the hundred-dollar bills to see what her reaction would be.

Halfway to the door, she turned in alarm, came hurrying back. "Gentlemen, there must be a mistake! There's—there's a hundred-dollar bill here on top!" She shuffled through the roll hastily. "They're all hundred-dollar bills!" she cried out aghast. "I knew he had a little money in his shoes—he slept with them under his pillow at nights—but I thought maybe, fifty, seventy dollars—"

"There was a thousand in his shoes," said the captain, "and another thousand stitched all along the seams of his overcoat."

She let the money go, caught the edge of the desk he was sitting behind with both hands, and slumped draggingly down it to the floor in a dead faint. They had to hustle in with a pitcher of water to revive her.

Nelson impatiently wondered what the heck was the matter with him, what more he needed to be convinced she hadn't known what she was coming into? And yet, he said to himself, how are you going to tell a real faint from a fake one? They close their eyes and they flop, and which is it?

He slept three hours, and then he went down and checked at the wholesale-drug concern Hill worked for. The firm did not handle cyanide or any other poisonous substance, and the man had a very good record there. He spent the morning working his way down the list of retail druggists who had placed their orders through Hill, and again got nowhere. At noon he quit and went back to the automat where it had happened—not to eat but to talk to the manager. He was really working on two cases simultaneously—an official one for his captain and a private one of his own. The captain would have had a fit if he'd known it.

"Will you lemme have that busman of yours, the one we had down at headquarters the other night? I want to take him out of here with me for about half an hour."

"You're the Police Department," the manager smiled acquiescently.

Nelson took him with him in his streetclothes. "You did a pretty good job of identifying Hill, the fourth man at that table," he told him. "Naturally, I don't expect you to remember every face that was in there that night. Especially with the quick turnover there is in an automat. However, here's what you do. Go down this street here to Number One-twenty-one—you can see it from here. Ring the superintendent's

363

bell. You're looking for an apartment, see? But while you're at it, you take a good look at the woman you'll see, and then come back and tell me if you remember seeing her face in the automat that night or any other night. Don't stare now—just size her up."

It took him a little longer than Nelson had counted on. When he finally rejoined the dick around the corner, where the latter was waiting, he said: "Nope, I've never seen her in our place, that night or any other, to my knowledge. But don't forget—I'm not on the floor every minute of the time. She could have been in and out often without my spotting her."

"But not," thought Nelson, "without Avram seeing her, if she went anywhere near him at all." She hadn't been there, then. That was practically certain. "What took you so long?" he asked him.

"Funny thing. There was a guy there in the place with her that used to work for us. He remembered me right away."

"Oh, yeah?" The dick drew up short. "Was *he* in there that night?"

"Naw, he quit six months ago. I haven't seen him since."

"What was he, sandwich-maker?"

"No, busman like me. He cleaned up the tables."

Just another coincidence, then. But, Nelson reminded himself, if one coincidence was strong enough to put Hill in jeopardy, why should the other be passed over as harmless? Both cases—his and the captain's—now had their coincidences. It remained to be seen which was just that—a coincidence and nothing more—and which was the McCoy.

He went back to headquarters. No wire had yet come from Detroit in answer to his, but he hadn't expected any this soon—it took time. The captain, bulldog-like, wouldn't let Hill go. They had spirited him away to still a third place, were holding him on some technicality or other that had nothing to do with the Avram case. The bicarbonate of soda trick hadn't worked, the captain told Nelson ruefully.

"Why?" the dick wanted to know. "Because he caught on just by looking at it that it wasn't cyanide—is that it? I think that's an important point, right there."

"No, he thought it was the stuff all right. But he hollered blue murder it hadn't come out of his room."

"Then if he doesn't know the difference between cyanide and bicarb of soda at sight, doesn't that prove he didn't put any on that sandwich?"

The captain gave him a look. "Are you for us or against us?" he wanted to know acidly. "You go ahead checking that list of retail druggists until you find out where he got it. And if we can't dig up any other motive, unhealthy scientific curiosity will satisfy me. He wanted to study the effects at first hand, and picked the first stranger who came along."

"Sure, in an automat—the most conspicuous, crowded public eating-place there is. The one place where human handling of the food is reduced to a minimum."

He deliberately disobeyed orders, a thing he had never done before—or rather, postponed carrying them out. He went back and commenced a one-man watch over the basement-entrance of the Avram house.

In about an hour, a squat, foreign-looking man came up the steps and walked down the street. This was undoubtedly "Uncle Nick," Mrs. Avram's husband-to-be, and former employee of the automat. Nelson tailed him effortlessly on the opposite side, boarded the same bus he did a block below, and got off at the same stop. "Uncle Nick" went into a bank, and Nelson into a cigar-store across the way that had transparent telephone booths commanding the street through the glass front.

When he came out again, Nelson didn't bother following him any more. Instead, he went into the bank himself. "What'd that guy do— open an account just now? Lemme see the deposit-slip."

He had deposited a thousand dollars cash under the name of Nicholas Krassin, half of the sum Mrs. Avram had claimed at headquarters only the day before. Nelson didn't have to be told that this by no means indicated Krassin and she had had anything to do with the old man's death. The money was rightfully hers as his widow, and, if she wanted to divide it with her groom-to-be, that was no criminal offense. Still, wasn't there a stronger motive here than the "unhealthy scientific curiosity" the captain had pinned on Hill? The fact remained that she wouldn't have had possession of the money had Avram still been alive. It would have still been in his shoes and coat-seams where she couldn't get at it.

Nelson checked Krassin at the address he had given at the bank, and, somewhat to his surprise, found it to be on the level, not fictitious. Either the two of them weren't very bright, or they were innocent. He went back to headquarters at six, and the answer to his telegram to Detroit had finally come. "Exhumation order obtained as per request stop Albert J. Edwards deceased January 1936 stop death certificate gives cause fall from steel girder while at work building under construction stop—autopsy—"

Nelson read it to the end, folded it, put it in his pocket without changing his expression.

"Well, did you find out anything?" the captain wanted to know.

"No, but I'm on the way to," Nelson assured him, but he may have been thinking of that other case of his own, and not the one they were all steamed up over. He went out again without saying where.

He got to Mrs. Avram's at quarter to seven, and rang the bell. The little girl came out to the basement-entrance. At sight of him, she called out shrilly, but without humorous intent, "Ma, that man's here again."

Nelson smiled a little and walked back to the living-quarters. A sudden hush had fallen thick enough to cut with a knife. Krassin was there again, in his shirt-sleeves, having supper with Mrs. Avram and the two kids. They not only had electricity now but a midget radio as well, he noticed. You can't arrest people for buying a midget radio. It was silent as a tomb, but he let the back of his hand brush it, surreptitiously, and the front of the dial was still warm from recent use.

"I'm not butting in, am I?" he greeted them cheerfully.

"N-no, sit down," said Mrs. Avram nervously. "This is Mr. Krassin, a friend of the family. I don't know your name—"

"Nelson."

Krassin just looked at him watchfully.

The dick said: "Sorry to trouble you. I just wanted to ask you a couple questions about your husband. About what time was it he had the accident?"

"You know better than I," she objected. "You were the one came here and told me."

"I don't mean Avram, I mean Edwards, in Detroit—the riveter that fell off the girder."

Her face went a little gray, as if the memory were painful. Krassin's face didn't change color, but only showed considerable surprise.

"About what time of day?" he repeated.

"Noon," she said almost inaudibly.

"Lunch-time," said the dick softly, as if to himself. "Most workmen carry their lunch from home in a pail—" He looked at her thoughtfully. Then he changed the subject, wrinkled up his nose appreciatively. "That coffee smells good," he remarked.

She gave him a peculiar, strained smile. "Have a cup, Mr. Detective," she offered. He saw her eyes meet Krassin's briefly.

"Thanks, don't mind if I do," drawled Nelson.

She got up. Then, on her way to the stove, she suddenly flared out at the two kids for no apparent reason: "What are you hanging around here for? Go to bed. Get out of here now, I say!" She banged the door shut on them, stood before it with her back to the room for a minute. Nelson's sharp ears caught the faint but unmistakable click of a key.

She turned back again, purred to Krassin: "Nick, go outside and take a look at the furnace, will you, while I'm pouring Mr. Nelson's coffee? If the heat dies down, they'll all start complaining from upstairs right away. Give it a good shaking up."

The hairs at the back of Nelson's neck stood up a little as he watched the man get up and sidle out. But he'd asked for the cup of coffee, himself.

He couldn't see her pouring it—her back was turned toward him again as she stood over the stove. But he could hear the splash of the hot liquid, see her elbow-motions, hear the clink of the pot as she replaced it. She stayed that way a moment longer, after it had been poured, with her back to him—less than a moment, barely thirty seconds. One elbow moved slightly. Nelson's eyes were narrow slits. It was thirty seconds too long, one elbow-motion too many.

She turned, came back, set the cup down before him. "I'll let you put your own sugar in, yes?" she said almost playfully. "Some like a lot, some like a little." There was a disappearing ring of froth in the middle of the black steaming liquid.

Outside somewhere, he could hear Krassin raking up the furnace.

"Drink it while it's still hot," she urged.

He lifted it slowly to his lips. As the cup went up, her eyelids went down. Not all the way, not enough to completely shut out sight, though.

He blew the steam away. "Too hot—burn my mouth. Gotta give it a minute to cool," he said. "How about you—ain't you having any? I couldn't drink alone. Ain't polite."

"I had mine," she breathed heavily, opening her eyes again. "I don't think there's any left."

"Then I'll give you half of this."

Her hospitable alarm was almost overdone. She all but jumped back in protest. "No, no! Wait, I'll look. "Yes, there's more, there's plenty!"

He could have had an accident with it while her back was turned a second time, upset it over the floor. Instead, he took a kitchen-match out of his pocket, broke the head off short with his thumbnail. He threw the head, not the stick, over on top of the warm stove in front of which she was standing. It fell to one side of her, without making any noise, and she didn't notice it. If he'd thrown stick and all, it would have clicked as it dropped and attracted her attention.

367

She came back and sat down opposite him. Krassin's footsteps could be heard shuffling back toward them along the cement corridor outside.

"Go ahead. Don't be bashful—drink up," she encouraged. There was something ghastly about her smile, like a death's-head grinning across the table from him.

The match-head on the stove, heated to the point of combustion, suddenly flared up with a little spitting sound and a momentary gleam. She jumped a little, and her head turned nervously to see what it was. When she looked back again, he already had his cup to his lips. She raised hers, too, watching him over the rim of it. Krassin's footfalls had stopped somewhere just outside the room door, and there wasn't another sound from him, as if he were standing there, waiting.

At the table, the cat-and-mouse play went on a moment longer. Nelson started swallowing with a dry constriction of the throat. The woman's eyes, watching him above her cup, were greedy half-moons of delight. Suddenly, her head and shoulders went down across the table with a bang, like her husband's had at the automat that other night, and the crash of the crushed cup sounded from underneath her.

Nelson jumped up watchfully, throwing his chair over. The door shot open, and Krassin came in, with an ax in one hand and an empty burlap-bag in the other.

"I'm not quite ready for cremation yet," the dick gritted, and threw himself at him.

Krassin dropped the superfluous burlap-bag, the ax flashed up overhead. Nelson dipped his knees, down in under it before it could fall. He caught the shaft with one hand, midway between the blade and Krassin's grip, and held the weapon teetering in mid-air. With his other fist he started imitating a hydraulic drill against his assailant's teeth. Then he lowered his barrage suddenly to solar-plexus level, sent in two bodyblows that caved his opponent in—and that about finished it.

Out in the wilds of Corona, an hour later, in a sub-basement locker-room, Alexander Hill—or at least what was left of him—was saying: "And you'll lemme sleep if I do? And you'll get it over real quick, send me up and put me out of my misery?"

"Yeah, yeah!" said the haggard captain, flicking ink out of a fountain pen and jabbing it at him. "Why dincha do this days ago, make it easier for us all?"

"Never saw such a guy," complained Sarecky, rinsing his mouth with water over in a corner.

"What's that man signing?" exploded Nelson's voice from the

stairs.

"Whaddye think he's signing?"snarled the captain. "And where you been all night, incidentally?"

"Getting poisoned by the same party that croaked Avram!" He came the rest of the way down, and Krassin walked down alongside at the end of a short steel link.

"Who's this guy?" they both wanted to know.

Nelson looked at the first prisoner, in the chair. "Take him out of here a few minutes, can't you?" he requested. "He don't have to know all our business."

"Just like in the story-books," muttered Sarecky jealously. "One-Man Nelson walks in at the last minute and cops all the glory."

A cop led Hill upstairs. Another cop brought down a small brown-paper parcel at Nelson's request. Opened, it revealed a small tin that had once contained cocoa. Nelson turned it upside down and a few threads of whitish substance spilled lethargically out, filling the close air of the room with a faint odor of bitter almonds.

"There's your cyanide," he said. "It came off the shelf above Mrs. Avram's kitchen-stove. Her kids, who are being taken care of at headquarters until I can get back there, will tell you it's roach-powder and they were warned never to go near it. She probably got it in Detroit, way back last year."

"She did it!" said the captain. "How could she? It was on the automat-sandwich, not anything he ate at home. She wasn't at the automat that night, she was home, you told us that yourself."

"Yeah, she was at home, but she poisoned him at the automat just the same. Look, it goes like this." He unlocked his manacle, refastened his prisoner temporarily to a plumbing-pipe in the corner. He took a paper-napkin out of his pocket, and, from within that, the carefully preserved waxpaper wrapper the death-sandwich had been done in.

Nelson said: "This has been folded over twice, once on one side, once on the other. You can see that, yourself. Every crease in it is double-barreled. Meaning what? The sandwich was taken out, doctored, and rewrapped. Only, in her hurry, Mrs. Avram slipped up and put the paper back the other way around.

"As I told Sarecky already, there's death in little habits. Avram was a miser. Bologna is the cheapest sandwich that automat sells. For six months straight, he never bought any other kind. This guy here used to work there. He knew at what time the slots were refilled for the last time. He knew that that was just when Avram always showed up. And, incidentally, the old man was no fool. He didn't go there because the light was better—he went there to keep from getting poisoned at

369

home. Ate all his meals out.

"All right, so what did they do? They got him, anyway—like this. Krassin, here, went in, bought a bologna sandwich, and took it home to her. She spiked it, rewrapped it, and, at eleven-thirty, he took it back there in his pocket. The sandwich-slots had just been refilled for the last time. They wouldn't put any more in till next morning. There are three bologna-slots. He emptied all three, to make sure the victim wouldn't get any but the lethal sandwich. After they're taken out, the glass slides remain ajar. You can lift them and reach in without inserting a coin. He put his death-sandwich in, stayed by it so no one else would get it. The old man came in. Maybe he's near sighted and didn't recognize Krassin. Maybe he didn't know him at all—I haven't cleared that point up yet. Krassin eased out of the place. The old man is a miser. He sees he can get a sandwich for nothing, thinks something went wrong with the mechanism, maybe. He grabs it up twice as quick as anyone else would have. There you are.

"What was in his shoes is the guy's motive. As for her, that was only partly her motive. She was a congenital killer, anyway, outside of that. He would have married her, and it would have happened to him in his turn some day. She got rid of her first husband, Edwards, in Detroit that way. She got a wonderful break. He ate the poisoned lunch she'd given him way up on the crossbeams of a building under construction, and it looked like he'd lost his balance and toppled to his death. They exhumed the body and performed an autopsy at my request. This telegram says they found traces of cyanide poisoning even after all this time.

"I paid out rope to her tonight, let her know I was onto her. I told her her coffee smelled good. Then I switched cups on her. She's up there now, dead. I can't say that I wanted it that way, but it was me or her. You never would have gotten her to the chair, anyway. She was unbalanced of course, but not the kind that's easily recognizable. She'd have spent a year in an institution, been released, and gone out and done it all over again. It grows on 'em, gives 'em a feeling of power over their fellow human beings.

"This louse, however, is *not* insane. He did it for exactly one thousand dollars and no cents—and he knew what he was doing from first to last. So I think he's entitled to a chicken-and-ice-cream-dinner in the death-house, at the state's expense."

"The Sphinx," growled Sarecky under his breath, shrugging into his coat. "Sees all, knows all, keeps all to himself."

"Who stinks?" corrected the captain, misunderstanding. "If anyone does, it's you and me. He brought home the bacon!"

THE
SLEEPING DOG
By Ross Macdonald

*Ross Macdonald is the pseudonym of Kenneth Millar (1915–), a native
Californian who spent his early years in Canada where he studied at the
University of Western Ontario. Later, he earned a Ph. D. in English
Literature at the University of Michigan and taught there for a time
before entering the navy during World War II. Macdonald began
publishing mystery novels in 1944, in part inspired by the success in the
field of his wife, Margaret Millar, and he adopted his pseudonym to avoid
any confusion of his work with hers. In 1949 he introduced his detective
character Lew Archer in the novel* The Moving Target *and has been
writing about him almost exclusively ever since in such books as* The
Drowning Pool *(1950),* The Far Side of the Dollar *(1965), and*
The Underground Man *(1971). Of the introspective and philosophical
Archer and his origins Macdonald has said: "In some ways he is me. I'm
not Archer exactly but Archer is me. That is, his points of view and
reactions are more or less mine. There is no point in writing about a
central character unless he reflects the author's philosophy." Since the
late 1960s, Macdonald has come to be considered a serious American
novelist, one who uses but transcends the detective story form, and he is
particularly praised for his withering though compassionate depiction of
the Southern California scene. "The Sleeping Dog," one of a number of
Lew Archer short stories, develops this theme. It was originally published
in 1965 and was reprinted in the January 1976 issue of* Ellery Queen's
Mystery Magazine *together with a brief interview. For further discus-
sion of the author and his work see Elmer Pry's "Lew Archer's 'Moral
Landscape'" in* Dimensions of Detective Fiction *(Bowling Green,
Ohio: Popular Press, 1976) and Macdonald's own "The Writer as
Detective Hero" in* The Mystery Writer's Art *(Bowling Green, Ohio:
Popular Press, 1970).*

T he day after her dog disappeared, Fay Hooper called me early. Her normal voice was like waltzing violins, but this morning the violins were out of tune. She sounded as though she'd been crying.

"Otto's gone."

Otto was her one-year-old German shepherd.

"He jumped the fence yesterday afternoon and ran away. Or else he was kidnaped—dognaped, I suppose is the right word to use."

"What makes you think that?"

"You know, Otto, Mr. Archer—how loyal he was. He wouldn't deliberately stay away from me overnight, not under his own power. There must be thieves involved."

She caught her breath. "I realize searching for stolen dogs isn't your métier. But you *are* a detective, and I thought, since we knew one another . . ."

She allowed her voice to suggest, ever so chastely, that we might get to know one another better.

I liked the woman. I liked the dog, I liked the breed. I was taking my own German shepherd pup to obedience school, which is where I met Fay Hooper. Otto and she were the handsomest and most expensive members of the class.

"How do I get to your place?"

She lived in the hills north of Malibu, she said, on the far side of the county line. If she wasn't home when I got there, her husband would be.

On my way out I stopped at the dog school in Pacific Palisades to talk to the man who ran it, Fernando Rambeau. The kennels behind the house burst into clamor when I knocked on the front door. Rambeau boarded dogs as well as trained them

A dark-haired girl looked out and informed me that her husband was feeding the animals. "Maybe I can help," she added doubtfully, and then she let me into a small living room.

I told her about the missing dog. "It would help if you called the vets and animal shelters and gave them a description," I said.

"We've already been doing that. Mrs. Hooper was on the phone to Fernando last night." She sounded vaguely resentful. "I'll get him."

Setting her face against the continuing noise, she went out the back door. Rambeau came in with her, wiping his hands on a rag. He was a square-shouldered Canadian with a curly black beard that failed to conceal his youth. Over the beard, his intense dark eyes peered at me warily, like an animal's sensing trouble.

Rambeau handled dogs as if he loved them. He wasn't quite so patient with human beings. His current class was only in its third week, but he was already having dropouts. The man was loaded with explosive feeling, and it was close to the surface now.

"I'm sorry about Mrs. Hooper and her dog. They were my best pupils. He was, anyway. But I can't drop everything and spend the next week looking for him."

"Nobody expects that. I take it you've had no luck with your contacts."

"I don't have such good contacts. Marie and I, we just moved down here last year, from British Columbia."

"That was a mistake," his wife said from the doorway.

Rambeau pretended not to hear her. "Anyway, I know nothing about dog thieves." With both hands he pushed the possibility away from him. "If I hear any word of the dog I'll let you know, naturally. I've got nothing against Mrs. Hooper."

His wife gave him a quick look. It was one of those revealing looks which said, among other things, that she loved him and didn't know if he loved her, and she was worried about him. She caught me watching her and lowered her eyes. Then she burst out, "Do you think somebody killed the dog?"

"I have no reason to think so."

"Some people shoot dogs, don't they?"

"Not around here," Rambeau said. "Maybe back in the bush someplace." He turned to me with a sweeping explanatory gesture. "These things make her nervous and she gets wild ideas. You know Marie is a country girl—"

"I am not. I was born in Chilliwack." Flinging a bitter look at him, she left the room.

"Was Otto shot?" I asked Rambeau.

"Not that I know of. Listen, Mr. Archer, you're a good customer, but I can't stand here talking all day. I've got twenty dogs to feed."

They were still barking when I drove up the coast highway out of hearing. It was nearly 40 miles to the Hoopers' mailbox, and another mile up a black-top lane which climbed the side of a canyon to the gate. On both sides of the heavy wire gate, which had a new combination padlock on it, a hurricane fence, eight feet high and topped with barbed wire, extended out of sight. Otto would have to be quite a jumper to clear it. So would I.

The house beyond the gate was low and massive, made of

fieldstone and steel and glass. I honked at it and waited. A man in blue bathing trunks came out of the house with a shotgun. The sun glinted on its twin barrels and on the man's bald head and round, brown, burnished belly. He walked quite slowly, a short heavy man in his sixties, scuffling along in huaraches. The flabby brown shell of fat on him jiggled lugubriously.

When he approached the gate, I could see the stiff gray pallor under his tan, like stone showing under varnish. He was sick, or afraid, or both. His mouth was profoundly discouraged.

"What do you want?" he said over the shotgun.

"Mrs. Hooper asked me to help find her dog. My name is Lew Archer."

He was not impressed. "My wife isn't here, and I'm busy. I happen to be following soy-bean futures rather closely."

"Look here, I've come quite a distance to lend a hand. I met Mrs. Hooper at dog school and—"

Hooper uttered a short savage laugh. "That hardly constitutes an introduction to either of us. You'd better be on your way right now."

"I think I'll wait for your wife."

"I think you won't." He raised the shotgun and let me look into its close-set, hollow, round eyes. "This is my property all the way down to the road, and you're trespassing. That means I can shoot you if I have to."

"What sense would that make? I came out here to help you."

"You can't help me." He looked at me through the wire gate with a kind of pathetic arrogance, like a lion that had grown old in captivity. "Go away."

I drove back down to the road and waited for Fay Hooper. The sun slid up the sky. The inside of my car turned oven-hot. I went for a walk down the canyon. The brown September grass crunched under my feet. Away up on the far side of the canyon an earth mover that looked like a crazy red insect was cutting the ridge to pieces.

A very fast black car came up the canyon and stopped abruptly beside me. A gaunt man in a wrinkled brown suit climbed out, with his hand on his holster, told me that he was Sheriff Carlson, and asked me what I was doing there. I told him.

He pushed back his wide cream-colored hat and scratched at his hairline. The pale eyes in his sun-fired face were like clouded glass inserts in a brick wall.

"I'm surprised Mr. Hooper takes that attitude. Mrs. Hooper just came to see me in the courthouse. But I can't take you up there with me if Mr. Hooper says no."

374

"Why not?"

"He owns most of the county and holds the mortgage on the rest of it. Besides," he added with careful logic, "Mr. Hooper is a friend of mine."

"Then you better get him a keeper."

The sheriff glanced around uneasily, as if the Hoopers' mailbox might be bugged. "I'm surprised he has a gun, let alone threatening you with it. He must be upset about the dog."

"He didn't seem to care about the dog."

"He does, though. *She* cares, so *he* cares," Carlson said.

"What did she have to tell you?"

"She can talk to you herself. She should be along any minute. She told me that she was going to follow me out of town."

He drove his black car up the lane. A few minutes later Fay Hooper stopped her Mercedes at the mailbox. She must have seen the impatience on my face. She got out and came toward me in a little run, making noises of dismayed regret.

Fay was in her late thirties and fading slightly, as if a light frost had touched her pale gold head, but she was still a beautiful woman. She turned the gentle force of her charm on me.

"I'm dreadfully sorry," she said. "Have I kept you waiting long?"

"Your husband did. He ran me off with a shotgun."

Her gloved hand lighted on my arm, and stayed. She had an electric touch, even through layers of cloth.

"That's terrible. I had no idea that Allan still had a gun."

Her mouth was blue behind her lipstick, as if the information had chilled her to the marrow. She took me up the hill in the Mercedes. The gate was standing open, but she didn't drive in right away.

"I might as well be perfectly frank," she said without looking at me. "Ever since Otto disappeared yesterday, there's been a nagging question in my mind. What you've just told me raises the question again. I was in town all day yesterday so that Otto was alone here with Allan when—when it happened."

The values her voice gave to the two names made it sound as if Allan were the dog and Otto the husband.

"When what happened, Mrs. Hooper?" I wanted to know.

Her voice sank lower. "I can't help suspecting that Allan shot him. He's never liked any of my dogs. The only dogs he appreciates are hunting dogs—and he was particularly jealous of Otto. Besides, when I got back from town, Allan was getting the ground ready to plant some roses. He's never enjoyed gardening, particularly in the heat. We have professionals to do our work. And this really isn't the time of year to put in a bed of roses."

"You think your husband was planting a dog?" I asked.

"If he was, I have to know." She turned toward me, and the leather seat squeaked softly under her movement. "Find out for me, Mr. Archer. If Allan killed my beautiful big old dog, I couldn't stay with him."

"Something you said implied that Allan used to have a gun or guns, but gave them up. Is that right?"

"He had a small arsenal when I married him. He was an infantry officer in the war and a big-game hunter in peacetime. But he swore off hunting years ago."

"Why?"

"I don't really know. We came home from a hunting trip one fall and Allan sold all his guns. He never said a word about it to me but it was the fall after the war ended, and I always thought that it must have had something to do with the war."

"Have you been married so long?"

"Thank you for that question." She produced a rueful smile. "I met Allan during the war, the year I came out, and I knew I'd met my fate. He was a very powerful person."

"And a very wealthy one."

She gave me a flashing, haughty look and stepped so hard on the accelerator that she almost ran into the sheriff's car parked in front of the house. We walked around to the back, past a free-form swimming pool that looked inviting, into a walled garden. A few Greek statues stood around in elegant disrepair. Bees murmured like distant bombers among the flowers.

The bed where Allan Hooper had been digging was about five feet long and three feet wide, and it reminded me of graves.

"Get me a spade," I said.

"Are you going to dig him up?"

"You're pretty sure he's in there, aren't you, Mrs. Hooper?"

"I guess I am."

From a lath house at the end of the garden she fetched a square-edged spade. I asked her to stick around.

I took off my jacket and hung it on a marble torso where it didn't look too bad. It was easy digging in the newly worked soil. In a few minutes I was two feet below the surface, and the ground was still soft and penetrable.

The edge of my spade struck something soft but not so penetrable. Fay Hooper heard the peculiar dull sound it made. She made a dull

376

sound of her own. I scooped away more earth. Dog fur sprouted like stiff black grass at the bottom of the grave.

Fay got down on her knees and began to dig with her lacquered fingernails. Once she cried out in a loud harsh voice, "Dirty murderer!"

Her husband must have heard her. He came out of the house and looked over the stone wall. His head seemed poised on top of the wall, hairless and bodiless, like Humpty-Dumpty. He had that look on his face, of not being able to be put together again.

"I didn't kill your dog, Fay. Honest to God, I didn't."

She didn't hear him. She was talking to Otto. "Poor boy, poor boy," she said. "Poor, beautiful boy."

Sheriff Carlson came into the garden. He reached down into the grave and freed the dog's head from the earth. His large hands moved gently on the great wedge of the skull.

Fay knelt beside him in torn and dirty stockings. "What are you doing?"

Carlson held up a red-tipped finger. "Your dog was shot through the head, Mrs. Hooper, but it's no shotgun wound. Looks to me more like a deer rifle."

"I don't even own a rifle," Hooper said over the wall. "I haven't owned one for nearly twenty years. Anyway, I wouldn't shoot your dog."

Fay scrambled to her feet. She looked ready to climb the wall. "Then why did you bury him?"

His mouth opened and closed.

"Why did you buy a shotgun without telling me?"

"For protection."

"Against my dog?"

Hooper shook his head. He edged along the wall and came in tentatively through the gate. He had on slacks and a short-sleeved yellow jersey which somehow emphasized his shortness and his fatness and his age.

"Mr. Hooper had some threatening calls," the sheriff said. "Somebody got hold of his unlisted number. He was just telling me about it now."

"Why didn't you tell me, Allan?"

"I didn't want to alarm you. You weren't the one they were after, anyway. I bought a shotgun and kept it in my study."

"Do you know who they are?"

"No. I make enemies in the course of business, especially the farming operations. Some crackpot shot your dog, gunning for me. I heard a shot and found him dead in the driveway."

"But how could you bury him without telling me?"

Hooper spread his hands in front of him. "I wasn't thinking too well. I felt guilty, I suppose, because whoever got him was after me. And I didn't want you to see him dead. I guess I wanted to break it to you gently."

"This is gently?"

"It's not the way I planned it. I thought if I had a chance to get you another pup—"

"No one will ever take Otto's place."

Allan Hooper stood and looked at her wistfully across the open grave, as if he would have liked to take Otto's place. After a while the two of them went into the house.

Carlson and I finished digging Otto up and carried him out to the sheriff's car. His inert blackness filled the trunk from side to side.

"What are you going to do with him, Sheriff?" I asked.

"Get a vet I know to recover the slug in him. Then if we nab the sniper we can use ballistics to convict him."

"You're taking this just as seriously as a real murder, aren't you?" I observed.

"They want me to," he said with a respectful look toward the house.

Mrs. Hooper came out carrying a white leather suitcase which she deposited in the back seat of her Mercedes.

"Are you going someplace?" I asked her.

"Yes, I am." She didn't say where.

Her husband, who was watching her from the doorway, didn't speak. The Mercedes went away. He closed the door. Both of them had looked sick.

"She doesn't seem to believe he didn't do it. Do you, Sheriff?"

Carlson jabbed me with his forefinger. "Mr. Hooper is no liar. If you want to get along with me, get that through your head. I've known Mr. Hooper for over twenty years—served under him in the war—and I never heard him twist the truth."

"I'll have to take your word for it. What about those threatening phone calls? Did he report them to you before today?"

"No."

"What was said on the phone?"

"He didn't tell me."

"Does Hooper have any idea who shot the dog?"

"Well, he did say he saw a man slinking around outside the fence. He didn't get close enough to the guy to give me a good description, but he did make out that he had a black beard."

378

"There's a dog trainer in Pacific Palisades named Rambeau who fits the description. Mrs. Hooper has been taking Otto to his school."

"Rambeau?" Carlson said with interest.

"Fernando Rambeau. He seemed pretty upset when I talked to him this morning."

"What did he say?"

"A good deal less than he knows, I think. I'll talk to him again."

Rambeau was not at home. My repeated knocking was answered only by the barking of the dogs. I retreated up the highway to a drive-in where I ate a torpedo sandwich. When I was on my second cup of coffee, Marie Rambeau drove by in a pickup truck. I followed her home.

"Where's Fernando?" I asked.

"I don't know. I've been out looking for him."

"Is he in a bad way?"

"I don't know how you mean."

"Emotionally upset."

"He has been ever since that woman came into the class."

"Mrs. Hooper?"

Her head bobbed slightly.

"Are they having an affair?"

"They better not be." Her small red mouth looked quite implacable. "He was out with her night before last. I heard him make the date. He was gone all night, and when he came home he was on one of his black drunks and he wouldn't go to bed. He sat in the kitchen and drank himself glassy-eyed." She got out of the pickup facing me. "Is shooting a dog a very serious crime?"

"It is to me, but not to the law. It's not like shooting a human being."

"It would be to Fernando. He loves dogs the way other people love human beings. That included Otto."

"But he shot him."

Her head drooped. I could see the straight white part dividing her black hair. "I'm afraid he did. He's got a crazy streak and it comes out in him when he drinks. You should have heard him in the kitchen yesterday morning. He was moaning and groaning about his brother."

"His brother?"

"Fernando had an older brother, George, who died back in Canada after the war. Fernando was just a kid when it happened and it was a big loss to him. His parents were dead, too, and they put him in a foster home in Chilliwack. He still has nightmares about it."

"What did his brother die of?"

379

"He never told me exactly, but I think he was shot in some kind of hunting accident. George was a guide and packer in the Fraser River valley below Mount Robson. That's where Fernando comes from, the Mount Robson country. He won't go back, on account of what happened to his brother."

"What did he say about his brother yesterday?" I asked.

"That he was going to get his revenge for George. I got so scared I couldn't listen to him. I went out and fed the dogs. When I came back in, Fernando was loading his deer rifle. I asked him what he was planning to do, but he walked right out and drove away."

"May I see the rifle?"

"It isn't in the house. I looked for it after he left today. He must have taken it with him again. I'm so afraid that he'll kill somebody."

"What's he driving?"

"Our car. It's an old blue Meteor sedan."

Keeping an eye out for it, I drove up the highway to the Hoopers' canyon. Everything there was very peaceful. Too peaceful. Just inside the locked gate, Allan Hooper was lying face down on his shotgun. I could see small ants in single file trekking across the crown of his bald head.

I got a hammer out of the trunk of my car and used it to break the padlock. I lifted his head. His skin was hot in the sun, as if death had fallen on him like a fever. But he had been shot neatly between the eyes. There was no exit wound; the bullet was still in his head. Now the ants were crawling on my hands.

I found my way into the Hoopers' study, turned off the stuttering teletype, and sat down under an elk head to telephone the courthouse. Carlson was in his office.

"I have bad news, Sheriff. Allan Hooper's been shot."

I heard him draw in his breath quickly. "Is he dead?"

"Extremely dead. You better put out a general alarm for Rambeau."

Carlson said with gloomy satisfaction, "I already have him."

"You have him?"

"That's correct. I picked him up in the Hoopers' canyon and brought him in just a few minutes ago." Carlson's voice sank to a mournful mumble. "I picked him up a little too late, I guess."

"Did Rambeau do any talking?"

"He hasn't had a chance to yet. When I stopped his car, he piled out and threatened me with a rifle. I clobbered him one good."

I went outside to wait for Carlson and his men. A very pale afternoon moon hung like a ghost in the sky. For some reason it made

380

me think of Fay. She ought to be here. It occurred to me that possibly she had been.

I went and looked at Hooper's body again. He had nothing to tell me. He lay as if he had fallen from a height, perhaps all the way from the moon.

They came in a black county wagon and took him away. I followed them inland to the county seat, which rose like a dusty island in a dark green lake of orange groves. We parked in the courthouse parking lot, and the sheriff and I went inside.

Rambeau was under guard in a second-floor room with barred windows. Carlson said it was used for interrogation. There was nothing in the room but an old deal table and some wooden chairs. Rambeau sat hunched forward on one of them, his hands hanging limp between his knees. Part of his head had been shaved and plastered with bandages.

"I had to cool him with my gun butt," Carlson said. "You're lucky I didn't shoot you—you know that, Fernando?"

Rambeau made no response. His black eyes were set and dull.

"Had his rifle been fired?"

"Yeah. Chet Scott is working on it now. Chet's my identification lieutenant and he's a bear on ballistics." The sheriff turned back to Rambeau. "You might as well give us a full confession, boy. If you shot Mr. Hooper and his dog, we can link the bullets to your gun. You know that."

Rambeau didn't speak or move.

"What did you have against Mr. Hooper?" Carlson said.

No answer. Rambeau's mouth was set like a trap in the thicket of his beard.

"Your older brother," I said to him, "was killed in a hunting accident in British Columbia. Was Hooper at the other end of the gun that killed George?"

Rambeau didn't answer me, but Carlson's head came up. "Where did you get that, Archer?"

"From a couple of things I was told. According to Rambeau's wife, he was talking yesterday about revenge for his brother's death. According to Fay Hooper, her husband swore off guns when he came back from a hunting trip after the war. Would you know if that trip was to British Columbia?"

"Yeah. Mr. Hooper took me and the wife with him."

"Whose wife?"

"Both our wives."

"To the Mount Robson area?"

"That's correct. We went up after elk."

"And did he shoot somebody accidentally?"

"Not that I know of. I wasn't with him all the time, understand. He often went out alone, or with Mrs. Hooper," Carlson replied.

"Did he use a packer named George Rambeau?"

"I wouldn't know. Ask Fernando here."

I asked Fernando. He didn't speak or move. Only his eyes had changed. They were wet and glistening-black, visible parts of a grief that filled his head like a dark underground river.

The questioning went on and produced nothing. It was night when I went outside. The moon was slipping down behind the dark hills. I took a room in a hotel and checked in with my answering service in Hollywood.

About an hour before, Fay Hooper had called me from a Las Vegas hotel. When I tried to return the call, she wasn't in her room and didn't respond to paging. I left a message for her to come home, that her husband was dead.

Next, I called R.C.M.P. headquarters in Vancouver to ask some questions about George Rambeau. The answers came over the line in clipped Canadian tones. George and his dog had disappeared from his cabin below Red Pass in the fall of 1945. Their bodies hadn't been recovered until the following May, and by that time they consisted of parts of the two skeletons. These included George Rambeau's skull, which had been pierced in the right front and left rear quadrants by a heavy-caliber bullet. The bullet had not been recovered. Who fired, or when, or why, had never been determined. The dog, a husky, had also been shot through the head.

I walked over to the courthouse to pass the word to Carlson. He was in the basement shooting gallery with Lieutenant Scott, who was firing test rounds from Fernando Rambeau's .30/30 repeater.

I gave them the official account of the accident. "But since George Rambeau's dog was shot, too, it probably wasn't an accident," I said.

"I see what you mean," Carlson said. "It's going to be rough, spreading all this stuff out in court about Mr. Hooper. We have to nail it down, though."

I went back to my hotel and to bed, but the process of nailing down the case against Rambeau continued through the night. By morning Lieutenant Scott had detailed comparisons set up between the test-fired slugs and the ones dug out of Hooper and the dog.

I looked at his evidence through a comparison microscope. It left no doubt in my mind that the slugs that killed Allan Hooper and the dog, Otto, had come from Rambeau's gun.

But Rambeau still wouldn't talk, even to phone his wife or ask for a lawyer.

"We'll take you out to the scene of the crime," Carlson said. "I've cracked tougher nuts than you, boy."

We rode in the back seat of his car with Fernando handcuffed between us. Lieutenant Scott did the driving. Rambeau groaned and pulled against his handcuffs. He was very close to the breaking point, I thought.

It came a few minutes later when the car turned up the lane past the Hoopers' mailbox. He burst into sudden fierce tears as if a pressure gauge in his head had broken. It was strange to see a bearded man crying like a boy. "I don't want to go up there."

"Because you shot him?" Carlson said.

"I shot the dog. I confess I shot the dog," Rambeau said.

"And the man?"

"No!" he cried. "I never killed a man. Mr. Hooper was the one who did. He followed my brother out in the woods and shot him."

"If you knew that," I said, "why didn't you tell the Mounties years ago?"

"I didn't know it then. I was seven years old. How would I under-stand? When Mrs. Hooper came to our cabin to be with my brother, how would I know it was a serious thing? Or when Mr. Hooper asked me if she had been there? I didn't know he was her husband. I thought he was her father checking up. I knew I shouldn't have told him—I could see it in his face the minute after—but I didn't understand the situation till the other night, when I talked to Mrs. Hooper."

"Did she know that her husband had shot George?"

"She didn't even know George had been killed. They never went back to the Fraser River after nineteen forty-five. But when we put our facts together, we agreed he must have done it. I came out here next morning to get even. The dog came out to the gate. It wasn't real to me—I'd been drinking most of the night—it wasn't real to me until the dog went down. I shot him. Mr. Hooper shot my dog. But when he came out of the house himself, I couldn't pull the trigger. I yelled at him and ran away."

"What did you yell?" I said.

"The same thing I told him on the telephone: 'Remember Mount Robson.'"

A yellow cab, which looked out of place in the canyon, came over the ridge above us. Lieutenant Scott waved it to a stop. The driver said he'd just brought Mrs. Hooper home from the airport and wanted to know if that constituted a felony. Scott waved him on.

"I wonder what she was doing at the airport," Carlson said.

"Coming home from Vegas. She tried to call me from there last night. I forgot to tell you."

"You don't forget important things like that," Carlson said.

"I suppose I wanted her to come home under her own power."

"In case she shot her husband?"

"More or less."

"She didn't. Fernando shot him, didn't you, boy?"

"I shot the dog. I am innocent of the man." He turned to me. "Tell her that. Tell her I am sorry about the dog. I came out here to surrender the gun and tell her yesterday. I don't trust myself with guns."

"With darn good reason," Carlson said. "We know you shot Mr. Hooper. Ballistic evidence doesn't lie."

Rambeau screeched in his ear, "You're a liar! You're all liars!"

Carlson swung his open hand against the side of Rambeau's face. "Don't call me names, little man."

Lieutenant Scott spoke without taking his eyes from the road. "I wouldn't hit him, Chief. You wouldn't want to damage our case."

Carlson subsided, and we drove on up to the house. Carlson went in without knocking. The guard at the door discouraged me from following him.

I couldn't hear Fay's voice on the other side of the door, too low to be understood. Carlson said something to her.

"Get out! Get out of my house, you killer!" Fay cried out sharply.

Carlson didn't come out. I went in instead. One of his arms was wrapped around her body, the other hand was covering her mouth. I got his Adam's apple in the crook of my left arm, pulled him away from her, and threw him over my left hip. He went down clanking and got up holding his revolver.

He should have shot me right away. But he gave Fay Hooper time to save my life.

She stepped in front of me. "Shoot me, Mr. Carlson. You might as well. You shot the one man I ever cared for."

"Your husband shot George Rambeau, if that's who you mean. I ought to know. I was there." Carlson scowled down at his gun and replaced it in his holster.

Lieutenant Scott was watching him from the doorway.

"You were there?" I said to Carlson. "Yesterday you told me Hooper was alone when he shot Rambeau."

"He was. When I said I was there, I meant in the general neighborhood."

"Don't believe him," Fay said. "He fired the gun that killed

384

George, and it was no accident. The two of them hunted George down in the woods. My husband planned to shoot him himself, but George's dog came at him and he had to dispose of it. By that time George had drawn a bead on Allan. Mr. Carlson shot him. It was hardly a coincidence that the next spring Allan financed his campaign for sheriff."

"She's making it up," Carlson said. "She wasn't within ten miles of the place."

"But you were, Mr. Carlson, and so was Allan. He told me the whole story yesterday, after we found Otto. Once that happened, he knew that everything was bound to come out. I already suspected him, of course, after I talked to Fernando. Allan filled in the details himself. He thought, since he hadn't killed George personally, I would be able to forgive him. But I couldn't. I left him and flew to Nevada, intending to divorce him. I've been intending to for twenty years."

Carlson said, "Are you sure you didn't shoot him before you left?"

"How could she have?" I said. "Ballistics don't lie, and the ballistic evidence says he was shot with Fernando's rifle. Nobody had access to it but Fernando—and you. You stopped him on the road and knocked him out, took his rifle, and used it to kill Hooper. You killed him for the same reason that Hooper buried the dog—to keep the past buried. You thought Hooper was the only witness to the murder of George Rambeau. But by that time Mrs. Hooper knew about it, too."

"It wasn't murder. It was self-defense, just like in the war. Anyway, you'll never hang it on me."

"We don't have to. We'll hang Hooper on you. How about it, Lieutenant?"

Scott nodded grimly, not looking at his chief. I relieved Carlson of his gun. He winced, as if I were amputating part of his body. He offered no resistance when Scott took him out to the car.

I stayed behind for a final word with Fay. "Fernando asked me to tell you he's sorry for shooting your dog."

"We're both sorry." She stood with her eyes down, as if the past was swirling visibly around her feet. I'll talk to Fernando later. Much later."

"There's one coincidence that bothers me. How did you happen to take your dog to his school?"

"I happened to see his sign, and Fernando Rambeau isn't a common name. I couldn't resist going there. I had to know what had happened to George. I think perhaps Fernando came to California for the same reason."

"Now you both know," I said.

CHAPTER VII

THE LIMITS OF DETECTION

THE
ABSENT-MINDED
COTERIE

By Robert Barr

Robert Barr (1850–1912) was born in Scotland but as a young child was taken to Canada where he was educated and became headmaster of a school in Windsor, Ontario before he was twenty. He later turned to newspaper reporting in Detroit, sometimes encountering considerable danger in quest of stories, and in his early thirties went back to Great Britain. There he edited several publications, helped establish The Idler, for a time an extremely successful magazine, and wrote a number of widely popular short stories. These include a parody of Sherlock Holmes called "The Great Pegram Mystery," published under the pseudonym Luke Sharp and later brought out in the volume The Face and the Mask (1894), and eight tales about his best known creation, French detective Eugène Valmont, collected in 1906 under the title The Triumphs of Eugène Valmont. Ellery Queen has called Valmont "the literary forefather of [Agatha Christie's] Hercule Poirot" and has written of "The Absent-Minded Coterie" that were it the only story about detective Valmont, "he would still be immortal."

I well remember the November day when I first heard of the Summer-trees case, because there hung over London a fog so thick that two or three times I lost my way, and no cab was to be had at any price. The few cabmen then in the streets were leading their animals slowly along, making for their stables. It was one of those depressing London days which filled me with ennui and a yearning for my own clear city of Paris, where, if we are ever visited by a slight mist, it is at least clean, white vapor, and not this horrible London mixture saturated with suffocating carbon. The fog was too thick for any passer to read the contents bills of the newspapers plastered on the pavement, and as there were probably no races that day the newsboys were shouting what they considered the next most important event—the election of an American President. I bought a paper and thrust it into my pocket. It was late when I reached my flat, and, after dining there, which was an unusual thing for me to do, I put on my slippers, took an easy-chair before the fire, and began to read my evening journal. I was distressed to learn that the eloquent Mr. Bryan had been defeated. I knew little about the silver question, but the man's oratorical powers had appealed to me, and my sympathy was aroused because he owned many silver mines, and yet the price of the metal was so low that apparently he could not make a living through the operation of them. But, of course, the cry that he was a plutocrat, and a reputed millionaire over and over again, was bound to defeat him in a democracy where the average voter is exceedingly poor and not comfortably well-to-do, as is the case with our peasants in France. I always took great interest in the affairs of the huge republic to the West, having been at some pains to inform myself accurately regarding its politics; and although, as my readers know, I seldom quote anything complimentary that is said of me, nevertheless, an American client of mine once admitted that he never knew the true inwardness—I think that was the phrase he used—of American politics until he heard me discourse upon them. But then, he added, he had been a very busy man all his life.

I had allowed my paper to slip to the floor, for in very truth the fog was penetrating even into my flat, and it was becoming difficult to read, notwithstanding the electric light. My man came in, and announced that Mr. Spenser Hale wished to see me, and, indeed, any night, but especially when there is rain or fog outside, I am more pleased to talk with a friend than to read a newspaper.

"Mon Dieu, my dear Monsieur Hale, it is a brave man you are to venture out in such a fog as is abroad tonight."

"Ah, Monsieur Valmont," said Hale with pride, "you cannot raise a fog like this in Paris!"

"No. There you are supreme," I admitted, rising and saluting my visitor, then offering him a chair.

"I see you are reading the latest news," he said, indicating my newspaper. "I am very glad that man Bryan is defeated. Now we shall have better times."

I waved my hand as I took my chair again. I will discuss many things with Spenser Hale, but not American politics; he does not understand them. It is a common defect of the English to suffer complete ignorance regarding the internal affairs of other countries.

"It is surely an important thing that brought you out on such a night as this. The fog must be very thick in Scotland Yard."

This delicate shaft of fancy completely missed him, and he answered stolidly:

"It's thick all over London, and, indeed, throughout most of England."

"Yes, it is," I agreed, but he did not see that either.

Still, a moment later, he made a remark which, if it had come from some people I know, might have indicated a glimmer of comprehension.

"You are a very, very clever man, Monsieur Valmont, so all I need say is that the question which brought me here is the same as that on which the American election was fought. Now, to a countryman, I should be compelled to give further explanation, but to you, monsieur, that will not be necessary."

There are times when I dislike the crafty smile and partial closing of the eyes which always distinguishes Spenser Hale when he places on the table a problem which he expects will baffle me. If I said he never did baffle me, I would be wrong, of course, for sometimes the utter simplicity of the puzzles which trouble him leads me into an intricate involution entirely unnecessary in the circumstances.

I pressed my finger tips together, and gazed for a few moments at the ceiling. Hale had lit his black pipe, and my silent servant placed at his elbow the whisky and soda, then tiptoed out of the room. As the door closed my eyes came from the ceiling to the level of Hale's expansive countenance.

"Have they eluded you?" I asked quietly.

"Who?"

"The coiners."

Hale's pipe dropped from his jaw, but he managed to catch it before it reached the floor. Then he took a gulp from the tumbler.

"That was just a lucky shot," he said.

"*Parfaitement*," I replied carelessly.

"Now, own up, Valmont, wasn't it?"

I shrugged my shoulders. A man cannot contradict a guest in his own house.

"Oh, stow that!" cried Hale impolitely. He is a trifle prone to strong and even slangy expressions when puzzled. "Tell me how you guessed it."

"It is very simple, *mon ami*. The question on which the American election was fought is the price of silver, which is so low that it has ruined Mr. Bryan, and threatens to ruin all the farmers of the West who possess silver mines on their farms. Silver troubled America, *ergo* silver troubles Scotland Yard.

"Very well; the natural inference is that some one has stolen bars of silver. But such a theft happened three months ago, when the metal was being unloaded from a German steamer at Southampton, and my dear friend Spenser Hale ran down the thieves very cleverly as they were trying to dissolve the marks off the bars with acid. Now crimes do not run in series, like the numbers in roulette at Monte Carlo. The thieves are men of brains. They say to themselves, 'What chance is there successfully to steal bars of silver while Mr. Hale is at Scotland Yard?' Eh, my good friend?"

"Really, Valmont," said Hale, taking another sip, "sometimes you almost persuade me that you have reasoning powers."

"Thanks, comrade. Then it is not a *theft* of silver we have now to deal with. But the American election was fought on the *price* of silver. If silver had been high in cost, there would have been no silver question. So the crime that is bothering you arises through the low price of silver, and this suggests that it must be a case of illicit coinage, for there the low price of the metal comes in. You have, perhaps, found a more subtle illegitimate act going forward than heretofore. Some one is making your shillings and your half crowns from real silver, instead of from baser metal, and yet there is a large profit which has not hitherto been possible through the high price of silver. With the old conditions you were familiar, but this new element sets at naught all your previous formulas. That is how I reasoned the matter out."

"Well, Valmont, you have hit it, I'll say that for you; you have hit it. There is a gang of expert coiners who are putting out real silver money, and making a clear shilling on the half crown. We can find no trace of the coiners, but we know the man who is shoving the stuff."

"That ought to be sufficient," I suggested.

"Yes, it should, but it hasn't proved so up to date. Now I came tonight to see if you would do one of your French tricks for us, right on the quiet."

"What French trick, Monsieur Spenser Hale?" I inquired with some asperity, forgetting for the moment that the man invariably became impolite when he grew excited.

"No offense intended," said this blundering officer, who really is a good-natured fellow, but always puts his foot in it, and then apologizes. "I want some one to go through a man's house without a search warrant, spot the evidence, let me know, and then we'll rush the place before he has time to hide his tracks."

"Who is this man, and where does he live?"

"His name is Ralph Summertrees, and he lives in a very natty little *bijou* residence, as the advertisements call it, situated in no less a fashionable street than Park Lane."

"I see. What has aroused your suspicions against him?"

"Well, you know, that's an expensive district to live in; it takes a bit of money to do the trick. This Summertrees has no ostensible business, yet every Friday he goes to the United Capital Bank in Piccadilly, and deposits a bag of swag, usually all silver coin."

"Yes; and this money?"

"This money, so far as we can learn, contains a good many of these new pieces which never saw the British Mint."

"It's not all the new coinage, then?"

"Oh, no, he's a bit too artful for that! You see, a man can go round London, his pockets filled with new-coined five-shilling pieces, buy this, that, and the other, and come home with his change in legitimate coins of the realm—half crowns, florins, shillings, sixpences, and all that."

"I see. Then why don't you nab him one day when his pockets are stuffed with illegitimate five-shilling pieces?"

"That could be done, of course, and I've thought of it, but, you see, we want to land the whole gang. Once we arrested him, without knowing where the money came from, the real coiners would take flight."

"How do you know he is not the real coiner himself?"

Now poor Hale is as easy to read as a book. He hesitated before answering this question, and looked confused as a culprit caught in some dishonest act.

"You need not be afraid to tell me," I said soothingly, after a pause. "You have had one of your men in Mr. Summertrees' house, and so learned that he is not the coiner. But your man has not succeeded in getting you evidence to incriminate other people."

"You've about hit it again, Monsieur Valmont. One of my men has been Summertrees' butler for two weeks, but, as you say, he has found no evidence."

"Is he still butler?"

"Yes."

"Now tell me how far you have got. You know that Summertrees deposits a bag of coin every Friday in the Piccadilly Bank, and I suppose the bank has allowed you to examine one or two of the bags."

"Yes, sir, they have, but, you see, banks are very difficult to treat with. They don't like detectives bothering round, and while they do not stand out against the law, still they never answer any more questions than they're asked, and Mr. Summertrees has been a good customer at the United Capital for many years."

"Haven't you found out where the money comes from?"

"Yes, we have; it is brought there night after night by a man who looks like a respectable city clerk, and he puts it into a large safe, of which he holds the key, this safe being on the ground floor, in the dining room."

"Haven't you followed the clerk?"

"Yes. He sleeps in the Park Lane house every night and goes up in the morning to an old curiosity shop in Tottenham Court Road, where he stays all day, returning with his bag of money in the evening."

"Why don't you arrest and question him?"

"Well, Monsieur Valmont, there is just the same objection to his arrest as to that of Summertrees himself. We could easily arrest both, but we have not the slightest evidence against either of them, and then, although we put the go-betweens in clink, the worst criminals of the lot would escape."

"Nothing suspicious about the old curiosity shop?"

"No. It appears to be perfectly regular."

"This game has been going on under your noses for how long?"

"For about six weeks."

"Is Summertrees a married man?"

"No."

"Are there any women servants in the house?"

"No, except that three charwomen come in every morning to do up the rooms."

"Of what is his household comprised?"

"There is the butler, then the valet, and last the French cook."

"Ah," cried I, "the French cook! This case interests me. So Summertrees has succeeded in completely disconcerting your man. Has he prevented him going from top to bottom of the house?"

"Oh, no! He has rather assisted him than otherwise. On one

occasion he went to the safe, took out the money, had Podgers—that's my chap's name—help him to count it, and then actually sent Podgers to the bank with the bag of coin."

"And Podgers has been all over the place?"

"Yes."

"Saw no signs of a coining establishment?"

"No. It is absolutely impossible that any coining can be done there. Besides, as I tell you, that respectable clerk brings him the money."

"I suppose you want me to take Podgers's position?"

"Well, Monsieur Valmont, to tell you the truth, I would rather you didn't. Podgers has done everything a man can do, but I thought if you got into the house, Podgers assisting, you might go through it night after night at your leisure."

"I see. That's just a little dangerous in England. I think I should prefer to assure myself the legitimate standing of being amiable Podger's successor. You say that Summertrees has no business?"

"Well, sir, not what you might call a business. He is by way of being an author, but I don't count that any business."

"Oh, an author, is he? When does he do his writing?"

"He locks himself up most of the day in his study."

"Does he come out for lunch?"

"No; he lights a little spirit lamp inside, Podgers tells me, and makes himself a cup of coffee, which he takes with a sandwich or two."

"That's rather frugal fare for Park Lane."

"Yes, Monsieur Valmont, it is, but he makes it up in the evening, when he has a long dinner, with all them foreign kickshaws you people like, done by his French cook."

"Sensible man! Well, Hale, I see I shall look forward with pleasure to making the acquaintance of Mr. Summertrees. Is there any restriction on the going and coming of your man Podgers?"

"None in the least. He can get away either night or day."

"Very good, friend Hale; bring him here tomorrow, as soon as our author locks himself up in his study, or rather I should say, as soon as the respectable clerk leaves for Tottenham Court Road, which I should guess, as you put it, is about half an hour after his master turns the key of the room in which he writes."

"You are quite right in that guess, Valmont. How did you hit it?"

"Merely a surmise, Hale. There is a good deal of oddity about that Park Lane house, so it doesn't surprise me in the least that the master gets to work earlier in the morning than the man. I have also a suspicion that Ralph Summertrees knows perfectly well what the estimable Podgers is there for."

"What makes you think that?"

"I can give no reason except that my opinion of the acuteness of Summertrees has been gradually rising all the while you were speaking, and at the same time my estimate of Podgers's craft has been as steadily declining. However, bring the man here tomorrow, that I may ask him a few questions."

Next day, about eleven o'clock, the ponderous Podgers, hat in hand, followed his chief into my room. His broad, impassive, immobile, smooth face gave him rather more the air of a genuine butler than I had expected, and this appearance, of course, was enhanced by his livery. His replies to my questions were those of a well-trained servant who will not say too much unless it is made worth his while. All in all, Podgers exceeded my expectations, and really my friend Hale had some justification for regarding him, as he evidently did, a triumph in his line.

"Sit down, Mr. Hale, and you, Podgers."

The man disregarded my invitation, standing like a statue until his chief made a motion; then he dropped into a chair. The English are great on discipline.

"Now, Mr. Hale, I must first congratulate you on the make-up of Podgers. It is excellent. You depend less on artificial assistance than we do in France, and in that I think you are right."

"Oh, we know a bit over here, Monsieur Valmont!" said Hale, with pardonable pride.

"Now then, Podgers, I want to ask you about this clerk. What time does he arrive in the evening?"

"At prompt six, sir."

"Does he ring, or let himself in with a latchkey?"

"With a latchkey, sir."

"How does he carry the money?"

"In a little locked leather satchel, sir, flung over his shoulder."

"Does he go direct to the dining room?"

"Yes, sir."

"Have you seen him unlock the safe, and put in the money?"

"Yes, sir."

"Does the safe unlock with a word or a key?"

"With the key, sir. It's one of the old-fashioned kind."

"Then the clerk unlocks his leather money bag?"

"Yes, sir."

"That's three keys used within as many minutes. Are they separate or in a bunch?"

"In a bunch, sir."

"Did you ever see your master with this bunch of keys?"

"No, sir."

"You saw him open the safe once, I am told?"

"Yes, sir."

"Did he use a separate key, or one of a bunch?"

Podgers slowly scratched his head, then said:

"I don't just remember, sir."

"Ah, Podgers, you are neglecting the big things in that house! Sure you can't remember?"

"No, sir."

"Once the money is in the safe locked up, what does the clerk do?"

"Goes to his room, sir."

"Where is this room?"

"On the third floor, sir."

"Where do you sleep?"

"On the fourth floor with the rest of the servants, sir."

"Where does the master sleep?"

"On the second floor, adjoining his study."

"The house consists of four stories and a basement, does it?"

"Yes, sir."

"I have somehow arrived at the suspicion that it is a very narrow house. Is that true?"

"Yes, sir."

"Does the clerk ever dine with your master?"

"No, sir. The clerk don't eat in the house at all, sir."

"Does he go away before breakfast?"

"No, sir."

"No one takes breakfast to his room?"

"No, sir."

"What time does he leave the house?"

"At ten o'clock, sir."

"When is breakfast served?"

"At nine o'clock, sir."

"At what hour does your master retire to his study?"

"At half past nine, sir."

"Locks the door on the inside?"

"Yes, sir."

"Never rings for anything during the day?"

"Not that I know of, sir."

"What sort of a man is he?"

Here Podgers was on familiar ground, and he rattled off a description minute in every particular.

"What I meant was, Podgers, is he silent, or talkative, or does he get angry? Does he seem furtive, suspicious, anxious, terrorized, calm, excitable, or what?"

"Well, sir, he is by way of being very quiet, never has much to say for hisself; never saw him angry or excited."

"Now, Podgers, you've been at Park Lane for a fortnight or more. You are a sharp, alert, observant man. What happens there that strikes you as unusual?"

"Well, I can't exactly say, sir" replied Podgers, looking rather helplessly from his chief to myself, and back again.

"Your professional duties have often compelled you to enact the part of butler before, otherwise you wouldn't do it so well. Isn't that the case?"

Podgers did not reply, but glanced at his chief. This was evidently a question pertaining to the service, which a subordinate was not allowed to answer. However, Hale said at once:

"Certainly. Podgers has been in dozens of places."

"Well, Podgers, just call to mind some of the other households where you have been employed, and tell me any particulars in which Mr. Summertrees's establishment differs from them."

Podgers pondered a long time.

"Well, sir, he do stick to writing pretty close."

"Ah, that's his profession, you see, Podgers. Hard at it from half past nine till toward seven, I imagine?"

"Yes, sir."

"Anything else, Podgers? No matter how trivial."

"Well, sir, he's fond of reading, too; leastways, he's fond of newspapers."

"When does he read?"

"I never seen him read 'em, sir; indeed, so far as I can tell, I never knew the papers to be opened, but he takes them all in, sir."

"What, all the morning papers?"

"Yes, sir, and all the evening papers, too."

"Where are the morning papers placed?"

"On the table in his study, sir."

"And the evening papers?"

"Well, sir, when the evening papers come, the study is locked.

They are put on a side table in the dining room, and he takes them upstairs with him to his study."

"This has happened every day since you've been there?"

"Yes, sir."

"You reported that very striking fact to your chief, of course?"

"No, sir, I don't think I did," said Podgers, confused.

"You should have done so. Mr. Hale would have known how to make the most of a point so vital."

"Oh, come now, Valmont," interrupted Hale, "You're chaffing us! Plenty of people take in all the papers!"

"I think not. Even clubs and hotels subscribe to the leading journals only. You said *all*, I think, Podgers?"

"Well, *nearly* all, sir."

"But which is it? There's a vast difference."

"He takes a good many, sir."

"How many?"

"I don't just know, sir."

"That's easily found out, Valmont," cried Hale, with some impatience, "if you think it really important."

"I think it so important that I'm going back with Podgers myself. You can take me into the house, I suppose, when you return?"

"Oh, yes, sir!"

"Coming back to these newspapers for a moment, Podgers. What is done with them?"

"They are sold to the ragman, sir, once a week."

"Who takes them from the study?"

"I do, sir."

"Do they appear to have been read very carefully?"

"Well, no, sir; leastways, some of them seem never to have been opened, or else folded up very carefully again."

"Did you notice that extracts have been clipped from any of them?"

"No, sir."

"Does Mr. Summertrees keep a scrapbook?"

"Not that I know of, sir."

"Oh, the case is perfectly plain!" said I, leaning back in my chair, and regarding the puzzled Hale with that cherubic expression of self-satisfaction which I know is so annoying to him.

"*What's* perfectly plain?" he demanded, more gruffly perhaps than etiquette would have sanctioned.

"Summertrees is no coiner, nor is he linked with any band of coiners."

398

"What is he, then?"

"Ah, that opens another avenue of inquiry! For all I know to the contrary, he may be the most honest of men. On the surface it would appear that he is a reasonably industrious tradesman in Tottenham Court Road, who is anxious that there should be no visible connection between a plebeian employment and so aristocratic a residence as that in Park Lane."

At this point Spenser Hale gave expression to one of those rare flashes of reason which are always an astonishment to his friends.

"That is nonsense, Monsieur Valmont," he said; "the man who is ashamed of the connection between his business and his house is one who is trying to get into society, or else the women of his family are trying it, as is usually the case. Now Summertrees has no family. He himself goes nowhere, gives no entertainments, and accepts no invitations. He belongs to no club; therefore, to say that he is ashamed of his connection with the Tottenham Court Road shop is absurd. He is concealing the connection for some other reason that will bear looking into."

"My dear Hale, the Goddess of Wisdom herself could not have made a more sensible series of remarks. Now, *mon ami*, do you want my assistance, or have you enough to go on with?"

"Enough to go on with? We have nothing more than we had when I called on you last night."

"Last night, my dear Hale, you supposed this man was in league with coiners. Today you know he is not."

"I know you *say* he is not."

I shrugged my shoulders, and raised my eyebrows, smiling at him.

"It is the same thing, Monsieur Hale."

"Well, of all the conceited—" and the good Hale could get no farther.

"If you wish my assistance, it is yours."

"Very good. Not to put too fine a point upon it, I do."

"In that case, my dear Podgers, you will return to the residence of our friend Summertrees, and get together for me in a bundle all of yesterday's morning and evening papers that were delivered to the house. Can you do that, or are they mixed up on a heap in the coal cellar?"

"I can do it, sir. I have instructions to place each day's papers in a pile by itself in case they should be wanted again. There is always one week's supply in the cellar, and we sell the papers of the week before to the ragman."

"Excellent. Well, take the risk of abstracting one day's journals, and have them ready for me. I will call upon you at half past three o'clock exactly, and then I want you to take me upstairs to the clerk's bedroom in the third story, which I suppose is not locked during the daytime?"

"No, sir, it is not."

With this the patient Podgers took his departure. Spenser Hale rose when his assitant left.

"Anything further I can do?" he asked.

"Yes; give me the address of the shop in Tottenham Court Road. Do you happen to have about you one of those new five-shilling pieces which you believe to be illegally coined?"

He opened his pocket book, took out the bit of white metal, and handed it to me.

"I'm going to pass this off before evening," I said, putting it in my pocket, "and I hope none of your men will arrest me."

"That's all right," laughed Hale as he took his leave.

At half past three Podgers was waiting for me, and opened the front door as I came up the steps, thus saving me the necessity of ringing. The house seemed strangely quiet. The French cook was evidently down in the basement, and we had probably all the upper part to ourselves, unless Summertrees was in his study, which I doubted. Podgers led me directly upstairs to the clerk's room on the third floor, walking on tiptoe, with an elephantine air of silence and secrecy combined, which struck me as unnecessary

"I will make an examination of this room," I said. "Kindly wait for me down by the door of the study."

The bedroom proved to be of respectable size when one considers the smallness of the house. The bed was all nicely made up, and there were two chairs in the room, but the usual washstand and swing mirror were not visible. However, seeing a curtain at the farther end of the room, I drew it aside, and found, as I expected, a fixed lavatory in an alcove of perhaps four feet deep by five in width. As the room was about fifteen feet wide, this left two thirds of the space unaccounted for. A moment later I opened a door which exhibited a closet filled with clothes hanging on hooks. This left a space of five feet between the clothes closet and the lavatory. I thought at first that the entrance to the secret stairway must have issued from the lavatory, but examining the boards closely, although they sounded hollow to the knuckles, they were quite evidently plain match boarding, and not a concealed door. The entrance to the stairway, therefore, must issue from the clothes closet. The right-hand wall proved similar to the match boarding of the lavatory, so far as the casual eye or touch was concerned, but I saw at

400

once it was a door. The latch turned out to be somewhat ingeniously operated by one of the hooks which held a pair of old trousers. I found that the hook, if pressed upward, allowed the door to swing outward, over the stairhead. Descending to the second floor, a similar latch let me into a similar clothes closet in the room beneath. The two rooms were identical in size, one directly above the other, the only difference being that the lower-room door gave into the study, instead of into the hall, as was the case with the upper chamber.

The study was extremely neat, either not much used, or the abode of a very methodical man. There was nothing on the table except a pile of that morning's papers. I walked to the farther end, turned the key in the lock, and came out upon the astonished Podgers.

"Well, I'm blowed!" exclaimed he.

"Quite so," I rejoined; "you've been tiptoeing past an empty room for the last two weeks. Now, if you'll come with me, Podgers, I'll show you how the trick is done."

When he entered the study I locked the door once more, and led the assumed butler, still tiptoeing through force of habit, up the stair into the top bedroom, and so out again, leaving everything exactly as we found it. We went down the main stair to the front hall, and there Podgers had my parcel of papers all neatly wrapped up. This bundle I carried to my flat, gave one of my assistants some instructions, and left him at work on the papers.

I took a cab to the foot of Tottenham Court Road, and walked up that street till I came to J. Simpson's old curiosity shop. After gazing at the well-filled windows for some time, I stepped inside, having selected a little iron crucifix displayed behind the pane; the work of some ancient craftsman.

I knew at once from Podgers's description that I was waited upon by the veritable respectable clerk who brought the bag of money each night to Park Lane, and who, I was certain, was no other than Ralph Summertrees himself.

There was nothing in his manner differing from that of any other quiet salesman. The price of the crucifix proved to be seven-and-six, and I threw down a sovereign to pay for it.

"Do you mind the change being all in silver, sir?" he asked, and I answered without any eagerness, although the question aroused a suspicion that had begun to be allayed:

"Not in the least."

He gave me half a crown, three two-shilling pieces, and four separate shillings, all coins being well-worn silver of the realm, the undoubted inartistic product of the reputable British Mint. This seemed to dispose of the theory that he was palming off illegitimate money. He asked me if I were interested in any particular branch of antiquity, and I replied that my curiosity was merely general, and exceedingly amateurish, whereupon he invited me to look around. This I proceeded to do, while he resumed the addressing and stamping of some wrapped-up pamphlets which I surmised to be copies of his catalogue.

He made no attempt either to watch me or to press his wares upon me. I selected at random a little inkstand, and asked its price. It was two shillings, he said, whereupon I produced my fraudulent five-shilling piece. He took it, gave me the change without comment, and the last doubt about his connection with coiners flickered from my mind.

At this moment a young man came in who, I saw at once, was not a customer. He walked briskly to the farther end of the shop, and disappeared behind a partition which had one pane of glass in it that gave an outlook toward the front door.

"Excuse me a moment," said the shopkeeper, and he followed the young man into the private office.

As I examined the curious heterogeneous collection of things for sale, I heard the clink of coins being poured out on the lid of a desk or an uncovered table, and the murmur of voices floated out to me. I was now near the entrance of the shop, and by a sleight-of-hand trick, keeping the corner of my eye on the glass pane of the private office, I removed the key of the front door without a sound, and took an impression of it in wax, returning the key to its place unobserved. At this moment another young man came in, and walked straight past me into the private office. I heard him say:

"Oh, I beg pardon, Mr. Simpson! How are you, Rogers?"

"Hello, Macpherson," saluted Rogers, who then came out, bidding good night to Mr. Simpson, and departed, whistling, down the street, but not before he had repeated his phrase to another young man entering, to whom he gave the name of Tyrrel.

I noted these three names in my mind. Two others came in together, but I was compelled to content myself with memorizing their features, for I did not learn their names. These men were evidently collectors, for I heard the rattle of money in every case; yet here was a small shop, doing apparently very little business, for I had been within it for more than half an hour, and yet remained the only customer. If credit were given, one collector would certainly have been sufficient, yet five had come in, and had poured their contributions into the pile Summertrees was to take home with him that night.

I determined to secure one of the pamphlets which the man had been addressing. They were piled on a shelf behind the counter, but I had no difficulty in reaching across and taking the one on top, which I slipped into my pocket. When the fifth young man went down the street Summertrees himself emerged, and this time he carried in his hand the well-filled locked leather satchel, with the straps dangling. It was now approaching half past five, and I saw he was eager to close up and get away.

"Anything else you fancy, sir?" he asked me.

"No, or, rather, yes and no. You have a very interesting collection here, but it's getting so dark I can hardly see."

"I close at half past five, sir."

"Ah! in that case," I said, consulting my watch, "I shall be pleased to call some other time."

"Thank you, sir," replied Summertrees quietly, and with that I took my leave.

From the corner of an alley on the other side of the street I saw him put up the shutters with his own hands, then he emerged with overcoat on, and the money satchel slung across his shoulder. He locked the door, tested it with his knuckles, and walked down the street, carrying under one arm the pamphlets he had been addressing. I followed him at some distance, saw him drop the pamphlets into the box at the first post office he passed, and walk rapidly toward his house in Park Lane.

When I returned to my flat and called in my assistant, he said: "After putting to one side the regular advertisements of pills, soap, and what not, here is the only one common to all the newspapers, morning and evening alike. The advertisements are not identical, sir, but they have two points of similarity, or perhaps I should say three. They all profess to furnish a cure for absent-mindedness; they all ask that the applicant's chief hobby shall be stated, and they all bear the same address: Dr. Willoughby, in Tottenham Court Road."

"Thank you," said I, as he placed the scissored advertisements before me.

I read several of the announcements. They were all small, and perhaps that is why I had never noticed one of them in the newspapers, for certainly they were odd enough. Some asked for lists of absent-minded men, with the hobbies of each, and for these lists, prizes of from one shilling to six were offered. In other clippings Dr. Willoughby professed to be able to cure absent-mindedness. There were no fees and no treatment, but a pamphlet would be sent, which, if it did not benefit the receiver, could do no harm. The Doctor was unable to meet patients personally, nor could he enter into correspondence with them. The address was the same as that of the old curiosity shop in Tottenham

Court Road. At this juncture I pulled the pamphlet from my pocket, and saw it was entitled, "Christian Science and Absent-Mindedness," by Dr. Stamford Willoughby, and at the end of the article was the statement contained in the advertisements, that Dr. Willoughby would neither see patients nor hold any correspondence with them.

I drew a sheet of paper toward me, wrote to Dr. Willoughby, alleging that I was a very absent-minded man, and would be glad of his pamphlet, adding that my special hobby was the collecting of first editions. I then signed myself, "Alport Webster, Imperial Flats, London, W."

I may here explain that it is often necessary for me to see people under some other name than the well-known appellation of Eugène Valmont. There are two doors to my flat, and on one of these is painted, "Eugène Valmont"; on the other there is a receptacle, into which can be slipped a sliding panel bearing any *non de guerre* I choose. The same device is arranged on the ground floor, where the names of all the occupants of the building appear on the right-hand wall.

I sealed, addressed, and stamped my letter, then told my man to put out the name of Alport Webster, and if I did not happen to be in when any one called upon that mythical person, he was to make an appointment for me.

It was nearly six o'clock next afternoon when the card of Angus Macpherson was brought in to Mr. Alport Webster. I recognized the young man at once as the second who had entered the little shop, carrying his tribute to Mr. Simpsom the day before. He held three volumes under his arm, and spoke in such a pleasant, insinuating sort of way, that I knew at once he was an adept in his profession of canvasser.

"Will you be seated, Mr. Macpherson? In what can I serve you?"

He placed the three volumes, backs upward, on my table.

"Are you interested at all in first editions, Mr. Webster?"

"It is the one thing I am interested in," I replied; "but unfortunately they often run into a lot of money."

"That is true," said Macpherson sympathetically, "and I have here three books, one of which is an exemplification of what you say. This one costs a hundred pounds. The last copy that was sold by auction in London brought a hundred and twenty-three pounds. This next one is forty pounds, and the third ten pounds. At these prices I am certain you could not duplicate three such treasures in any bookshop in Britain."

I examined them critically, and saw at once that what he said was true. He was still standing on the opposite side of the table.

"Please take a chair, Mr. Macpherson. Do you mean to say you go round London with a hundred and fifty pounds' worth of goods under your arm in this careless way?"

The young man laughed.

"I run very little risk, Mr. Webster. I don't suppose anyone I meet imagines for a moment there is more under my arm than perhaps a trio of volumes I have picked up in the fourpenny box to take home with me."

I lingered over the volume for which he asked a hundred pounds, then said, looking across at him:

"How came you to be posessed of this book, for instance?"

He turned upon me a fine, open countenance, and answered without hesitation in the frankest possible manner:

"I am not in actual possession of it, Mr. Webster. I am by way of being a connoisseur in rare and valuable books myself, although, of course, I have little money with which to indulge in the collection of them. I am acquainted, however, with the lovers of desirable books in different quarters of London. These three volumes, for instance, are from the library of a private gentleman in the West End. I have sold many books to him, and he knows I am trustworthy. He wishes to dispose of them at something under their real value, and has kindly allowed me to conduct the negotiations. I make it my business to find out those who are interested in rare books, and by such trading I add considerably to my income."

"How, for instance, did you learn that I was a bibliophile?"

Mr. Macpherson laughed genially.

"Well, Mr. Webster, I must confess that I chanced it. I do that very often. I take a flat like this, and send in my card to the name on the door. If I am invited in, I ask the occupant the question I asked you just now: 'Are you interested in rare editions?' If he says no, I simply beg pardon and retire. If he says yes, then I show my wares."

"I see," said I, nodding. What a glib young liar he was, with that innocent face of his, and yet my next question brought forth the truth.

"As this is the first time you have called upon me, Mr. Macpherson, you have no objection to my making some further inquiry, I suppose. Would you mind telling me the name of the owner of these books in the West End?"

"His name is Mr. Ralph Summertrees, of Park Lane."

"Of Park Lane? Ah, indeed!"

"I shall be glad to leave the books with you, Mr. Webster, and if you care to make an appointment with Mr. Summertrees, I am sure he will not object to say a word in my favor."

"Oh, I do not in the least doubt it, and should not think of troubling the gentleman."

"I was going to tell you," went on the young man, "that I have a friend, a capitalist, who, in a way, is my supporter; for, as I said, I have little money of my own. I find it is often inconvenient for people to pay down any considerable sum. When, however, I strike a bargain, my capitalist buys the books, and I make an arrangement with my customer to pay a certain amount each week, and so even a large purchase is not felt, as I make the installments small enough to suit my client."

"You are employed during the day, I take it?"

"Yes, I am a clerk in the City."

Again we were in the blissful realms of fiction!

"Suppose I take this book at ten pounds, what installments should I have to pay each week?"

"Oh, what you like, sir. Would five shillings be too much?"

"I think not."

"Very well, sir; if you pay me five shillings now, I will leave the book with you, and shall have pleasure in calling this day week for the next installment."

I put my hand into my pocket, and drew out two half crowns, which I passed over to him.

"Do I need to sign any form or undertaking to pay the rest?"

The young man laughed cordially.

"Oh, no, sir, there is no formality necessary. You see, sir, this is largely a labor of love with me, although I don't deny I have my eye on the future. I am getting together what I hope will be a very valuable connection with gentlemen like yourself who are fond of books, and I trust some day that I may be able to resign my place with the insurance company and set up a choice little business of my own, where my knowledge of values in literature will prove useful."

And then, after making a note in a little book he took from his pocket, he bade me a most graceful good-by and departed, leaving me cogitating over what it all meant.

Next morning two articles were handed to me. The first came by post and was a pamphlet on "Christian Science and Absent-Mindedness," exactly similar to the one I had taken away from the old curiosity shop; the second was a small key made from my wax impression that would fit the front door of the same shop—a key fashioned by an excellent anarchist friend of mine in an obscure street near Holborn.

That night at ten o'clock I was inside the old curiosity shop, with a small storage battery in my pocket, and a little electric glowlamp at my buttonhole, a most useful instrument for either burglar or detective.

I had expected to find the books of the establishment in a safe, which, if it was similar to the one in Park Lane, I was prepared to open with the false keys in my possession, or to take an impression of the keyhole and trust to my anarchist friend for the rest. But to my amazement I discovered all the papers pertaining to the concern in a desk which was not even locked. The books, three in number, were the ordinary daybook, journal, and ledger referring to the shop; bookkeeping of the older fashion; but in a portfolio lay half a dozen foolscap sheets, headed, "Mr. Roger's List," "Mr. Macpherson's," "Mr. Tyrrel's," the names I had already learned, and three others. These lists contained in the first column, names; in the second column, addresses; in the third, sums of money; and then in the small, square places following were amounts ranging from two-and-sixpence to a pound. At the bottom of Mr. Macpherson's list was the name Alport Webster, Imperial Flats, £10; then in the small, square place, five shillings. These six sheets, each headed by a canvasser's name, were evidently the record of current collections, and the innocence of the whole thing was so apparent that, if it were not for my fixed rule never to believe that I am at the bottom of any case until I have come on something suspicious, I would have gone out empty-handed as I came in.

The six sheets were loose in a thin portfolio, but standing on a shelf above the desk were a number of fat volumes, one of which I took down, and saw that it contained similar lists running back several years. I noticed on Mr. Macpherson's current list the name of Lord Semptam, an eccentric old nobleman whom I knew slightly. Then turning to the list immediately before the current one the name was still there; I traced it back through list after list until I found the first entry, which was no less than three years previous, and there Lord Semptam was down for a piece of furniture costing fifty pounds, and on that account he had paid a pound a week for more than three years, totaling a hundred and seventy pounds at the least, and instantly the glorious simplicity of the scheme dawned upon me, and I became so interested in the swindle that I lit the gas, fearing my little lamp would be exhausted before my investigation ended, for it promised to be a long one.

In several instances the intended victim proved shrewder than old Simpson had counted upon, and the word "Settled" had been written on the line carrying the name when the exact number of installments was paid. But as these shrewd persons dropped out, others took their places, and Simpson's dependence on their absent-mindedness seemed to be justified in nine cases out of ten. His collectors were collecting long after the debt had been paid. In Lord Semptam's case, the payment had evidently become chronic, and the old man was giving away

407

his pound a week to the suave Macpherson two years after his debt had been liquidated.

From the big volume I detached the loose leaf, dated 1893, which recorded Lord Semptam's purchase of a carved table for fifty pounds, and on which he had been paying a pound a week from that time to the date of which I am writing, which was November, 1896. This single document, taken from the file of three years previous, was not likely to be missed, as would have been the case if I had selected a current sheet. I nevertheless made a copy of the names and addresses of Macpherson's present clients; then, carefully placing everything exactly as I had found it, I extinguished the gas, and went out of the shop, locking the door behind me. With the 1893 sheet in my pocket I resolved to prepare a pleasant little surprise for my suave friend Macpherson when he called to get his next installment of five shillings.

Late as was the hour when I reached Trafalgar Square, I could not deprive myself of the felicity of calling on Mr. Spenser Hale, who I knew was then on duty. He never appeared at his best during office hours, because officialism stiffened his stalwart frame. Mentally he was impressed with the importance of his position, and added to this he was not then allowed to smoke his big black pipe and terrible tobacco. He received me with the curtness I had been taught to expect when I inflicted myself upon him at his office. He greeted me abruptly with:

"I say, Valmont, how long do you expect to be on this job?"

"What job?" I asked mildly.

"Oh, you know what I mean: the Summertrees affair?"

"Oh, that!" I exclaimed, with surprise. "The Summertree case is already completed, of course. If I had known you were in a hurry, I should have finished up everything yesterday, but as you and Podgers, and I don't know how many more, have been at it sixteen or seventeen days, if not longer, I thought I might venture to take as many hours, as I am working entirely alone. You said nothing about haste, you know."

"Oh, come now, Valmont, that's a bit thick. Do you mean to say you have already got evidence against the man?"

"Evidence absolute and complete."

"Then who are the coiners?"

"My most estimable friend, how often have I told you not to jump at conclusions? I informed you when you first spoke to me about the matter that Summertrees was neither a coiner nor a confederate of coiners. I secured evidence sufficient to convict him of quite another offense, which is probably unique in the annals of crime. I have penetrated the mystery of the shop, and discovered the reason for all those suspicious actions which quite properly set you on his trail. Now I wish you to come to my flat next Wednesday night at a quarter to six, prepared to make an arrest."

"I must know whom I am to arrest, and on what counts."

"Quite so, *mon ami* Hale; I did not say you were to make an arrest, but merely warned you to be prepared. If you have time now to listen to the disclosures, I am quite at your service. I promise you there are some original features in the case. If, however, the present moment is inopportune, drop in on me at your convenience, previously telephoning so that you may know whether I am there or not, and thus your valuable time will not be expended purposelessly."

With this I presented to him my most courteous bow, and although his mystified expression hinted a suspicion that he thought I was chaffing him, as he would call it, official dignity dissolved somewhat, and he intimated his desire to hear all about it then and there. I had succeeded in arousing my friend Hale's curiosity. He listened to the evidence with perplexed brow, and at last ejaculated he would be blessed.

"This young man," I said, in conclusion, "will call upon me at six on Wednesday afternoon, to receive his second five shillings. I propose that you, in your uniform, shall be seated there with me to receive him, and I am anxious to study Mr. Macpherson's countenance when he realizes he has walked in to confront a policeman. If you will then allow me to cross-examine him for a few moments, not after the manner of Scotland Yard, with a warning lest he incriminate himself, but in the free and easy fashion we adopt in Paris, I shall afterwards turn the case over to you to be dealt with at your discretion."

"You have a wonderful flow of language Monsieur Valmont," was the officer's tribute to me. "I shall be on hand at a quarter to six on Wednesday."

"Meanwhile," said I, "kindly say nothing of this to any one. We must arrange a complete surprise for Macpherson. That is essential. Please make no move in the matter at all until Wednesday night." Spenser Hale, much impressed, nodded acquiescence, and I took a polite leave of him.

The question of lighting is an important one in a room such as mine, and electricity offers a good deal of scope to the ingenious. Of this fact I have taken full advantage. I can manipulate the lighting of my room so that any particular spot is bathed in brilliancy, while the rest of the space remains in comparative gloom, and I arranged the lamps so that the full force of their rays impinged against the door that Wednesday evening, while I sat on one side of the table in semidarkness and Hale sat on the other, with a light beating down on him from above which gave him the odd, sculptured look of a living statue of Justice, stern and triumphant. Any one entering the room would first be dazzled by the light, and next would see the gigantic form of Hale in the full uniform of his order.

When Angus Macpherson was shown into this room, he was quite visibly taken aback, and paused abuptly on the threshold, his gaze riveted on the huge policeman. I think his first purpose was to turn and run, but the door closed behind him, and he doubtless heard, as we all did, the sound of the bolt being thrust in its place, thus locking him in.

"I—I beg your pardon," he stammered, "I expected to meet Mr. Webster."

As he said this, I pressed the button under my table, and was instantly enshrouded with light. A sickly smile overspread the countenance of Macpherson as he caught sight of me, and he made a very creditable attempt to carry off the situation with nonchalance.

"Oh, there you are, Mr. Webster; I did not notice you at first."

It was a tense moment. I spoke slowly and impressively.

"Sir, perhaps you are not unacquainted with the name of Eugène Valmont."

He replied brazenly:

"I am sorry to say, sir, I never heard of the gentleman before."

At this came a most inopportune "Haw-haw" from that blockhead Spenser Hale, completely spoiling the dramatic situation I had elaborated with such thought and care. It is little wonder the English possess no drama, for they show scant appreciation of the sensational moments in life; they are not quickly alive to the lights and shadows of events.

"Haw-haw," brayed Spenser Hale, and at once reduced the emotional atmosphere to a fog of commonplace. However, what is a man to do? He must handle the tools with which it pleases Providence to provide him. I ignored Hale's untimely laughter.

"Sit down, sir," I said to Macpherson, and he obeyed.

"You have called on Lord Semptam this week," I continued sternly.

"Yes, sir."

"And collected a pound from him?"

"Yes, sir."

"In October, 1893, you sold Lord Semptam a carved antique table for fifty pounds?"

"Quite right, sir."

"When you were here last week you gave me Ralph Summertrees as the name of a gentleman living in Park Lane. You knew at the time that this man was your employer?"

Macpherson was now looking fixedly at me, and on this occasion made no reply. I went on calmly:

"You also knew that Summertrees, of Park Lane, was identical with Simpson, of Tottenham Court Road?"

"Well, sir," said Macpherson, "I don't exactly see what you're driving at, but it's quite usual for a man to carry on a business under an assumed name. There is nothing illegal about that."

"We will come to the illegality in a moment, Mr. Macpherson. You and Rogers and Tyrrel and three others are confederates of this man Simpson."

"We are in his employ; yes, sir, but no more confederates than clerks usually are."

"I think, Mr. Macpherson, I have said enough to show you that the game is what you call up. You are now in the presence of Mr. Spenser Hale, from Scotland Yard, who is waiting to hear your confession."

Here the stupid Hale broke in with his:

"And remember, sir, that anything you say will be—"

"Excuse me, Mr. Hale," I interrupted hastily, "I shall turn over the case to you in a very few moments, but I ask you to remember our compact, and to leave it for the present entirely in my hands. Now, Mr. Macpherson, I want your confession, and I want it at once."

"Confession? Confederates?" protested Macpherson, with admirably simulated surprise. "I must say you use extraordinary terms, Mr. — Mr. — What did you say the name was?"

"Haw-haw," roared Hale. "His name is Monsieur Valmont."

"I implore you, Mr. Hale, to leave this man to me for a very few moments. Now, Macpherson, what have you to say in your defense?"

"Where nothing criminal has been alleged, Monsieur Valmont, I see no necessity for defense. If you wish me to admit that somehow you have acquired a number of details regarding our business, I am perfectly willing to do so, and to subscribe to their accuracy. If you will be good enough to let me know of what you complain, I shall endeavor to make the point clear to you, if I can. There has evidently been some misapprehension, but for the life of me, without further explanation, I am as much in a fog as I was on my way coming here, for it is getting a little thick outside."

Macpherson certainly was conducting himself with great discretion, and presented, quite unconsciously, a much more diplomatic figure than my friend Spenser Hale, sitting stiffly opposite me. His tone was one of mild expostulation, mitigated by the intimation that all misunderstanding speedily would be cleared away. To outward view he

411

offered a perfect picture of innocence, neither protesting too much nor too little. I had, however, another surprise in store for him, a trump card, as it were, and I played it down on the table.

"There!" I cried with vim, "have you ever seen that sheet before?"

He glanced at it without offering to take it in his hand.

"Oh, yes," he said, "that has been abstracted from our file. It is what I call my visiting list."

"Come, come, sir," I cried sternly, "you refuse to confess, but I warn you we know all about it. You never heard of Dr. Willoughby, I suppose."

"Yes, he is the author of the silly pamphlet on Christian Science."

"You are in the right, Mr. Macpherson; on Christian Science and Absent-Mindedness."

"Possibly. I haven't read it for a long while."

"Have you ever met this learned doctor, Mr. Macpherson?"

"Oh, yes. Dr. Willoughby is the pen name of Mr. Summertrees. He believes in Christian Science and that sort of thing, and writes about it."

"Ah, really. We are getting your confession bit by bit, Mr. Macpherson. I think it would be better to be quite frank with us."

"I was just going to make the same suggestion to you, Monsieur Valmont. If you will tell me in a few words exactly what is your charge against either Mr. Summertrees or myself, I will know then what to say."

"We charge you, sir, with obtaining money under false pretenses, which is a crime that has landed more than one distinguished financier in prison."

Spenser Hale shook his fat forefinger at me, and said:

"Tut, tut, Valmont; we mustn't threaten, we mustn't threaten, you know"; but I went on without heeding him.

"Take, for instance, Lord Semptam. You sold him a table for fifty pounds, on the installment plan. He was to pay a pound a week, and in less than a year the debt was liquidated. But he is an absent-minded man, as all your clients are. That is why you came to me. I had answered the bogus Willoughby's advertisement. And so you kept on collecting and collecting for something more than three years. Now do you understand the charge?"

Mr. Macpherson's head, during this accusation, was held slightly inclined to one side. At first his face was clouded by the most clever imitation of anxious concentration of mind I had ever seen, and this was gradually cleared away by the dawn of awakening perception. When I had finished, an ingratiating smile hovered about his lips.

412

"Really, you know," he said, "that is rather a capital scheme. The absent-minded league, as one might call them. Most ingenious. Summertrees, if he had any sense of humor, which he hasn't, would be rather taken by the idea that his innocent fad for Christian Science had led him to be suspected of obtaining money under false pretenses. But, really, there are no pretensions about the matter at all. As I understand it, I simply call and receive the money through the forgetfulness of the persons on my list, but where I think you would have both Summertrees and myself, if there was anything in your audacious theory, would be an indictment for conspiracy. Still, I quite see how the mistake arises. You have jumped to the conclusion that we sold nothing to Lord Semptam except that carved table three years ago. I have pleasure in pointing out to you that his lordship is a frequent customer of ours, and has had many things from us at one time or another. Sometimes he is in our debt; sometimes we are in his. We keep a sort of running contract with him by which he pays us a pound a week. He and several other customers deal on the same plan, and in return, for an income that we can count upon, they get the first offer of anything in which they are supposed to be interested. As I have told you, we call these sheets in the office our visiting lists, but to make the visiting lists complete you need what we term our encyclopedia. We call it that because it is in so many volumes; a volume for each year, running back I don't know how long. You will notice little figures here from time to time above the amount stated on this visiting list. These figures refer to the page of the encyclopedia for the current year, and on that page is noted the new sale and the amount of it, as it might be set down, say, in a ledger."

"That is a very entertaining explanation, Mr. Macpherson. I suppose this encyclopedia, as you call it, is in the shop at Tottenham Court Road?"

"Oh, no, sir. Each volume of the encyclopedia is self-locking. These books contain the real secret of our business, and they are kept in the safe at Mr. Summertree's house in Park Lane. Take Lord Semptam's account, for instance. You will find, in faint figures under a certain date, 102. If you turn to page 102 of the encyclopedia for that year, you will then see a list of what Lord Semptam has bought, and the prices he was charged for them. It is really a very simple matter. If you will allow me to use your telephone for a moment, I will ask Mr. Summertrees, who has not yet begun dinner, to bring with him here the volume for 1893, and within a quarter of an hour you will be perfectly satisfied that everything is quite legitimate."

I confess that the young man's naturalness and confidence staggered me, the more so as I saw by the sarcastic smile on Hale's lips that he did not believe a single word spoken. A portable telephone stood on the table, and as Macpherson finished his explanation, he reached over and drew it toward him. Then Spenser Hale interfered.

"Excuse *me*," he said, "I'll do the telephoning. What is the call number of Mr. Summertrees?"

"One forty Hyde Park."

Hale at once called up Central, and presently was answered from Park Lane. We heard him say:

"Is this the residence of Mr. Summertrees? Oh, is that you, Podgers? Is Mr. Summertrees in? Very well. This is Hale. I am in Valmont's flat—Imperial Flats—you know. Yes, where you went with me the other day. Very well, go to Mr. Summertrees, and say to him that Mr. Macpherson wants the encyclopedia for 1893. Do you get that? Yes, encyclopedia. Oh, don't understand what it is. Mr. Macpherson. No, don't mention my name at all. Just say Mr. Macpherson wants the encyclopedia for the year 1893, and that you are to bring it. Yes, you may tell him that Mr. Macpherson is at Imperial Flats, but don't mention my name at all. Exactly. As soon as he gives you the book, get into a cab, and come here as quickly as possible with it. If Summertrees doesn't want to let the book go, then tell him to come with you. If he won't do that, place him under arrest, and bring both him and the book here. All right. Be as quick as you can; we're waiting."

Macpherson made no protest against Hale's use of the telephone; he merely sat back in his chair with a resigned expression on his face which, if painted on canvas, might have been entitled, "The Falsely Accused." When Hale rang off, Macpherson said:

"Of course you know your business best, but if your man arrests Summertrees, he will make you the laughingstock of London. There is such a thing as unjustifiable arrest, as well as getting money under false pretenses, and Mr. Summertrees is not the man to forgive an insult. And then, if you will allow me to say so, the more I think over your absent-minded theory the more absolutely grotesque it seems, and if the case ever gets into the newspapers, I am sure, Mr. Hale, you'll experience an uncomfortable half hour with your chiefs at Scotland Yard."

"I'll take the risk of that, thank you," said Hale stubbornly.

"Am I to consider myself under arrest?" inquired the young man.

"No, sir."

"Then, if you will pardon me, I shall withdraw. Mr. Summertrees will show you everything you wish to see in his books, and can explain his business much more capably than I, because he knows more about it; therefore, gentlemen, I bid you good night."

"No, you don't. Not just yet awhile," exclaimed Hale, rising to his feet simultaneously with the young man.

"Then I *am* under arrest," protested Macpherson.

"You're not going to leave this room until Podgers brings that book."

"Oh, very well," and he sat down again.

And now, as talking is dry work, I set out something to drink, a box of cigars, and a box of cigarettes. Hale mixed his favorite brew, but Macpherson, shunning the wine of his country, contented himself with a glass of plain mineral water, and lit a cigarette. Then he awoke my high regard by saying pleasantly, as if nothing had happened:

"While we are waiting, Monsieur Valmont, may I remind you that you owe me five shillings?"

I laughed, took the coin from my pocket, and paid him, where-upon he thanked me.

"Are you connected with Scotland Yard, Monsieur Valmont?" asked Macpherson, with the air of a man trying to make conversation to bridge over a tedious interval; but before I could reply Hale blurted out:

"Not likely!"

"You have no official standing as a detective, then, Monsieur Valmont?"

"None whatever," I replied quickly, thus getting in my oar ahead of Hale.

"That is a loss to our country," pursued this admirable young man, with evident sincerity.

I began to see I could make a good deal of so clever a fellow if he came under my tuition.

"The blunders of our police," he went on, "are something deplorable. If they would but take lessons in strategy, say, from France, their unpleasant duties would be so much more acceptably performed, with much less discomfort to their victims."

"France," snorted Hale in derision, "why, they call a man guilty there until he's proven innocent."

"Yes, Mr. Hale, and the same seems to be the case in Imperial Flats. You have quite made up your mind that Mr. Summertrees is guilty, and will not be content until he proves his innocence. I venture to predict that you will hear from him before long in a manner that may astonish you."

Hale grunted and looked at his watch. The minutes passed very slowly as we sat there smoking and at last even I began to get uneasy. Macpherson, seeing our anxiety, said that when he came in the fog was almost as thick as it had been the week before, and that there might be some difficulty in getting a cab. Just as he was speaking the door was unlocked from the outside, and Podgers entered, bearing a thick volume in his hand. This he gave to his superior, who turned over its pages in amazement, and then looked at the back, crying:

"*Encyclopedia of Sport, 1893!* What sort of a joke is this, Mr. Macpherson?"

There was a pained look on Mr. Macpherson's face as he reached forward and took the book. He said with a sigh:

"If you had allowed me to telephone, Mr. Hale, I should have made it perfectly plain to Summertrees what was wanted. I might have known this mistake was liable to occur. There is an increasing demand for out-of-date books of sport, and no doubt Mr. Summertrees thought this was what I meant. There is nothing for it but to send your man back to Park Lane and tell Mr. Summertrees that what we want is the locked volume of accounts for 1893, which we call the encyclopedia. Allow me to write an order that will bring it. Oh, I'll show you what I have written before your man takes it," he said, as Hale stood ready to look over his shoulder.

On my note paper he dashed off a request such as he had outlined, and handed it to Hale, who read it and gave it to Podgers.

"Take that to Summertrees, and get back as quickly as possible. Have you a cab at the door?"

"Yes, sir."

"Is it foggy outside?"

"Not so much, sir, as it was an hour ago. No difficulty about the traffic now, sir."

"Very well, get back as soon as you can."

Podgers saluted, and left with the book under his arm. Again the door was locked, and again we sat smoking in silence until the stillness was broken by the tinkle of the telephone. Hale put the receiver to his ear.

"Yes, this is the Imperial Flats. Yes. Valmont. Oh, yes; Macpherson is here. What? Out of what? Can't hear you. Out of print. What, the encyclopedia's out of print? Who is that speaking? Dr. Willoughby; thanks."

Macpherson rose as if he would go to the telephone, but instead (and he acted so quietly that I did not notice what he was doing until the thing was done) he picked up the sheet which he called his visiting list, and walking quite without haste, held it in the glowing coals of the fireplace until it disappeared in a flash of flame up the chimney. I sprang to my feet indignant, but too late to make even a motion toward saving

416

the sheet. Macpherson regarded us both with that self-depreciatory smile which had several times lighted his face.

"How dared you burn that sheet?" I demanded.

"Because, Monsieur Valmont, it did not belong to you; because you do not belong to Scotland Yard; because you stole it; because you had no right to it; and because you have no official standing in this country. If it had been in Mr. Hale's possession I should not have dared, as you put it, to destroy the sheet, but as this sheet was abstracted from my master's premises by you, an entirely unauthorized person, whom he would have been justified in shooting dead if he had found you housebreaking, and you had resisted him on his discovery, I took the liberty of destroying the document. I have always held that these sheets should not have been kept, for, as has been the case, if they fell under the scrutiny of so intelligent a person as Eugène Valmont, improper inferences might have been drawn. Mr. Summertrees, however, persisted in keeping them, but made this concession, that if I ever telegraphed him or telephoned him the word 'Encyclopedia,' he would at once burn these records, and he, on his part, was to telegraph or telephone to me 'The encyclopedia is out of print,' whereupon I would know that he had succeeded.

"Now, gentlemen, open this door, which will save me the trouble of forcing it. Either put me formally under arrest, or cease to restrict my liberty. I am very much obliged to Mr. Hale for telephoning, and I have no protest to so gallant a host as Monsieur Valmont is, because of the locked door. However, the farce is now terminated. The proceedings I have sat through were entirely illegal, and if you will pardon me, Mr. Hale, they have been a little too French to go down here in old England, or to make a report in the newspapers that would be quite satisfactory to your chiefs. I demand either my formal arrest or the unlocking of that door."

In silence I pressed a button, and my man threw open the door. Macpherson walked to the threshold, paused, and looked back at Spenser Hale, who sat there silent as a sphinx.

"Good evening, Mr. Hale."

There being no reply, he turned to me with the same ingratiating smile:

"Good evening, Monsieur Eugène Valmont," he said, "I shall give myself the pleasure of calling next Wednesday at six for my five shillings."

THE
CHOCOLATE BOX
By Agatha Christie

Agatha Mary Clarissa Miller Christie (1890–1976) was born in
Devon, England, the second daughter of a wealthy American father and
an English mother. Tutored at home until she was sixteen, she went for a
time to Paris to study singing but was too shy for a vocal career. Some
early attempts at writing were also unsuccessful. In 1914 she married
Col. Archibald Christie of the Royal Flying Corps, and while working at
a local hospital dispensary during the war, planned and wrote a mystery
novel for relaxation. The book, which took two years to complete and
which was rejected by several publishers before appearing in 1920, was
The Mysterious Affair at Styles featuring Belgian detective Hercule
Poirot. Encouraged by the sale of her book, the writer went on to produce
several more, including what may be her most famous detective novel,
The Murder of Roger Ackroyd (1926). It was at just this time, too,
that she suffered an attack of amnesia, apparently brought on by her
mother's recent death and the failure of her marriage, and she myste-
riously dropped from sight for ten days. Her sensational disappearance
was highly publicized and has never been fully explained. On her return,
she continued with her fiction, creating such other celebrated detective
characters as Miss Jane Marple and Tuppence and Tommy Beresford,
and producing the long series of superior novels, short stories, and plays
that have made her perhaps the most popular mystery writer of the
twentieth century. In 1930, after a divorce from her first husband, she
married archaeologist Max Mallowan, accompanying him every year to
the Middle East, where she particularly enjoyed writing. Among her best
known books are Murder on the Orient Express *(1934),* The
A.B.C. Murders *(1936),* And Then There Were None *(1939),*
The Body in the Library *(1942),* Curtain *(1975), and her first story*
collection, Poirot Investigates *(1924), in which "The Chocolate Box"*
appears as the final work. For more about the author see Derrick
Murdock's The Agatha Christie Mystery *(New York: Pagurian,*
1971) and Agatha Christie: First Lady of Crime *(New York: Holt,*
Rinehart and Winston, 1977), edited by H. R. F. Keating.

It was a wild night. Outside, the wind howled malevolently, and the rain beat against the windows in great gusts.

Poirot and I sat facing the hearth, our legs stretched out to the cheerful blaze. Between us was a small table. On my side of it stood some carefully brewed hot toddy; on Poirot's was a cup of thick, rich chocolate which I would not have drunk for a hundred pounds! Poirot sipped the thick brown mess in the pink china cup, and sighed with contentment.

"*Quelle belle vie!*" he murmured.

"Yes, it's a good old world," I agreed. "Here am I with a job, and a good job too! And here are you, famous——"

"Oh, *mon ami!*" protested Poirot.

"But you are. And rightly so! When I think back on your long line of successes, I am positively amazed. I don't believe you know what failure is!"

"He would be a droll kind of original who could say that!"

"No, but seriously, *have* you ever failed?"

"Innumerable times, my friend. What would you? *La bonne chance*, it cannot always be on your side. I have been called in too late. Very often another, working toward the same goal, has arrived there first. Twice have I been striken down with illness just as I was on the point of success. One must take the downs with the ups, my friend."

"I didn't quite mean that," I said. "I meant, had you ever been completely down and out over a case through your own fault?"

"Ah, I comprehend! You ask if I have ever made the complete prize ass of myself, as you say over here? Once, my friend—" A slow, reflective smile hovered over his face. "Yes, once I made a fool of myself."

He sat up suddenly in his chair.

"See here, my friend, you have, I know, kept a record of my little successes. You shall add one more story to the collection, the story of a failure!"

He leaned forward and placed a log on the fire. Then, after carefully wiping his hands on a little duster that hung on a nail by the fireplace, he leaned back and commenced his story.

That of which I tell you, (said M. Poirot), took place in Belgium many years ago. It was at the time of the terrible struggle in France between church and state. M. Paul Déroulard was a French deputy of note. It was an open secret that the portfolio of a Minister awaited him. He was among the bitterest of the anti-Catholic party, and it was certain that on his accession to power, he would have to face violent enmity. He was in many ways a peculiar man. Though he neither drank nor smoked, he was nevertheless not so scrupulous in other ways. You comprehend, Hastings, c' etait des femmes—toujours des femmes!

He had married some years earlier a young lady from Brussels who had brought him a substantial dot. Undoubtedly the money was useful to him in his career, as his family was not rich, though on the other hand he was entitled to call himself M. le Baron if he chose. There were no children of the marriage, and his wife died after two years—the result of a fall downstairs. Among the property which she bequeathed to him was a house on the Avenue Louise in Brussels.

It was in this house that his sudden death took place, the event coinciding with the resignation of the Minister whose portfolio he was to inherit. All the papers printed long notices of his career. His death, which had taken place quite suddenly in the evening after dinner, was attributed to heart-failure.

At that time, mon ami, I was, as you know, a member of the Belgian detective force. The death of M. Paul Déroulard was not particularly interesting to me. I am, as you also know, bon catholique, and his demise seemed to me fortunate.

It was some three days afterward, when my vacation had just begun, that I received a visitor at my own apartments—a lady, heavily veiled, but evidently quite young; and I perceived at once that she was a jeune fille tout à fait comme il faut.

"You are Monsieur Hercule Poirot?" she asked in a low sweet voice.

I bowed.

"Of the detective service?"

Again I bowed. "Be seated, I pray of you, mademoiselle," I said.

She accepted a chair and drew aside her veil. Her face was charming, though marred with tears, and haunted as though with some poignant anxiety.

"Monsieur," she said, "I understand that you are now taking a vacation. Therefore you will be free to take up a private case. You understand that I do not wish to call in the police."

I shook my head. "I fear what you ask is impossible, mademoiselle. Even though on vacation, I am still of the police."

She leaned forward. "Ecoutez, monsieur. All that I ask of you is to investigate. The result of your investigations you are at perfect liberty

420

to report to the police. If what I believe to be true *is* true, we shall need all the machinery of the law."

That placed a somewhat different complexion on the matter, and I placed myself at her service without more ado.

A slight color rose in her cheeks. "I thank you, monsieur. It is the death of M. Paul Déroulard that I ask you to investigate."

"*Comment?*" I exclaimed, surprised.

"Monsieur, I have nothing to go upon—nothing but my woman's instinct, but I am convinced—*convinced,* I tell you—that M. Déroulard did not die a natural death!"

"But surely the doctors——"

"Doctors may be mistaken. He was so robust, so strong. Ah, Monsieur Poirot, I beseech of you to help me——"

The poor child was almost beside herself. She would have knelt to me. I soothed her as best I could.

"I will help you, mademoiselle. I feel almost sure that your fears are unfounded, but we will see. First, I will ask you to describe to me the inmates of the house."

"There are the domestics, of course, Jeannette, Félicie, and Denise the cook. She has been there many years; the others are simple country girls. Also there is François, but he too is an old servant. Then there is Monsieur Déroulard's mother who lived with him, and myself. My name is Virginie Mesnard. I am a poor cousin of the late Madame Déroulard, M. Paul's wife, and I have been a member of their ménage for over three years. I have now described to you the household. There were also two guests staying in the house."

"And they were?"

"M. de Saint Alard, a neighbor of M. Déroulard's in France. Also an English friend, Mr. John Wilson."

"Are they still with you?"

"Mr. Wilson, yes, but M. de Saint Alard departed yesterday."

"And what is your plan, Mademoiselle Mesnard?"

"If you will present yourself at the house in half an hour's time, I will have arranged some story to account for your presence. I had better represent you to be connected with journalism in some way. I shall say you have come from Paris, and that you have brought a card of introduction from M. de Saint Alard. Madame Déroulard is very feeble in health, and will pay little attention to details."

On mademoiselle's ingenious pretext I was admitted to the house, and after a brief interview with the dead deputy's mother, who was a wonderfully imposing and aristrocratic figure, though obviously in failing health, I was made free of the premises.

I wonder, my friend (continued Poirot), whether you can possibly figure to yourself the difficulties of my task? Here was a man whose death had taken place three days previously. If there *had* been foul play, only one possibility was admittable—*poison!* And I had had no chance of seeing the body, and there was no possibility of examining, or analyzing, any medium in which the poison could have been administered. There were no clues, false or otherwise, to consider. Had the man been poisoned? Had he died a natural death? I, Hercule Poirot, with nothing to help me, had to decide.

First, I interviewed the domestics, and with their aid, I recapitulated the evening. I paid especial notice to the food at dinner, and the method of serving it. The soup had been served by M. Déroulard himself from a tureen. Next a dish of cutlets, then a chicken. Finally a compote of fruits. And all placed on the table, and served by Monsieur himself. The coffee was brought in a big pot to the dinner-table. Nothing there, *mon ami*—impossible to poison one without poisoning all!

After dinner Madame Déroulard had retired to her own apartments and Mademoiselle Virginie had accompanied her. The three men had adjourned to M. Déroulard's study. Here they had chatted amicably for some time, when suddenly, without any warning, the deputy had fallen heavily to the ground. M. de Saint Alard had rushed out and told François to fetch a doctor immediately. He said it was without doubt an apoplexy, explained the man. But when the doctor arrived, the patient was past help.

Mr. John Wilson, to whom I was presented by Mademoiselle Virginie, was what was known in those days as a regular John Bull Englishman, middle-aged and burly. His account, delivered in very British French, was substantially the same.

"Déroulard went very red in the face, and down he fell."

There was nothing further to be found out there. Next I went to the scene of the tragedy, the study, and was left alone there at my own request. So far there was nothing to support Mademoiselle Mesnard's theory. I could not but believe that it was a delusion on her part. Evidently she had entertained a romantic passion for the dead man which had not permitted her to take a normal view of the case. Nevertheless, I searched the study with meticulous care. It was just possible that a hypodermic needle might have been introduced into the dead man's chair in such a way as to allow of a fatal injection. The minute puncture it would cause was likely to remain unnoticed. But I could discover no sign to support that theory. I flung myself down in the chair with a gesture of despair.

"*Enfin*, I abandon it!" I said aloud. "There is not a clue anywhere! Everything is perfectly normal."

As I said the words, my eyes fell on a large box of chocolates standing on a table near by, and my heart gave a leap. It might not be a clue to M. Déroulard's death, but here at least was something that was *not* normal. I lifted the lid. The box was full, untouched; not a chocolate was missing—but that only made the peculiarity that had caught my eye more striking. For, see you, Hastings, while the box itself was pink, the lid was *blue*. Now, one often sees a blue ribbon on a pink box, and vice versa, but a box of one color, and a lid of another—no, decidedly—*ça ne se voit jamais!*

I did not as yet see that this little incident was of any use to me, yet I determined to investigate it as being out of the ordinary. I rang the bell for François, and asked him if his late master had been fond of sweets. A faint melancholy smile came to his lips.

"Passionately fond of them, monsieur. He would always have a box of chocolates in the house. He did not drink wine of any kind, you see."

"Yet this box has not been touched?" I lifted the lid to show him.

"Pardon, monsieur, but that was a new box purchased on the day of his death, the other being nearly finished."

"Then the other box was finished on the day of his death," I said slowly.

"Yes, monsieur, I found it empty in the morning and threw it away."

"Did M. Déroulard eat sweets at all hours of the day?"

"Usually after dinner, monsieur."

I began to see the light.

"François," I said, "you can be discreet?"

"If there is need, monsieur."

"*Bon!* Know, then, that I am of the police. Can you find me that other box?"

"Without doubt, monsieur. It will be in the dustbin."

He departed, and returned in a few minutes with a dust-covered object. It was the duplicate of the box I held, save for the fact that this time the box was *blue* and the lid was *pink*. I thanked François, recommended him once more to be discreet, and left the house in the Avenue Louise without more ado.

Next I called upon the doctor who had attended M. Déroulard. With him I had a difficult task. He entrenched himself prettily behind a wall of learned phraseology, but I fancied that he was not quite as sure about the case as he would like to be.

"There have been many cruious occurrences of the kind," he observed, when I managed to disarm him somewhat. "A sudden fit of anger, a violent emotion, — after a heavy dinner, *c'est entendu*, — then, with an access of rage, the blood flies to the head, and *pst!* — there you are!"

"But M. Déroulard had had no violent emotion."

"No? I made sure that he had been having a stormy altercation with M. de Saint Alard."

"Why should he?"

"*C' est évident!*" The doctor shrugged his shoulders. "Was not M. de Saint Alard a Catholic of the most fanatical? Their friendship was being ruined by this question of church and state. Not a day passed without discussions. To M. de Saint Alard, Déroulard appeared almost as Antichrist."

This was unexpected, and gave me food for thought.

"One more question, Doctor: would it be possible to introduce a fatal dose of poison into a chocolate?"

"It would be possible, I suppose," said the doctor slowly. "Pure prussic acid would meet the case if there were no chance of evaporation, and a tiny globule of anything might be swallowed unnoticed — but it does not seem a very likely supposition. A chocolate full of morphine or strychnine —" He made a wry face. "You comprehend, M. Poirot — one bite would be enough! The unwary one would not stand upon ceremony."

"Thank you, M. le Docteur."

I withdrew. Next I made inquiries of the chemists, especially those in the neighborhood of the Avenue Louise. It is good to be of the police. I got the information I wanted without any trouble. Only in one case could I hear of any poison having been supplied to the house in question. This was some eye drops of atropine sulphate for Madame Déroulard. Atropine is a potent poison, and for the moment I was elated, but the symptoms of atropine poisoning are closely allied to those of ptomaine, and bear no resemblance to those I was studying. Besides, the prescription was an old one. Madame Déroulard had suffered from cataract in both eyes for many years.

I was turning away discouraged when the chemist's voice called me back.

"*Un moment*, M. Poirot. I remember, the girl who brought that prescription, she said something about having to go on to the *English* chemist. You might try there."

I did. Once more enforcing my official status, I got the information I wanted. On the day before M. Déroulard's death they had made up a prescription for Mr. John Wilson. Not that there was any making up about it. They were simply little tablets of trinitrin. I asked if I might see some. He showed me them, and my heart beat faster—for the tiny tablets were of *chocolate*.

"It is a poison?" I asked.

"No, monsieur."

"Can you describe to me its effect?"

"It lowers the blood-pressure. It is given for some forms of heart trouble—angina pectoris for instance. It relieves the arterial tension. In arteriosclerosis——"

I interrupted him. "*Ma foi!* This rigmarole says nothing to me. Does it cause the face to flush?"

"Certainly it does."

"And supposing I ate ten—twenty of your little tablets, what then?"

"I should not advise you to attempt it," he replied dryly.

"And yet you say it is not poison?"

"There are many things not called poison which can kill a man," he replied as before.

I left the shop elated. At last, things had begun to march!

I now knew that John Wilson held the means for the crime—but what about the motive? He had come to Belgium on business, and had asked M. Déroulard, whom he knew slightly, to put him up. There was apparently no way in which Déroulard's death could benefit him. Moreover, I discovered by inquiries in England that he had suffered for some years from that painful form of heart disease known as angina. Therefore he had a genuine right to have those tablets in his possession. Nevertheless, I was convinced that someone had gone to the chocolate box, opening the full one first by mistake, and had abstracted the contents of the last chocolate; cramming in instead as many little trinitrin tablets as it would hold. The chocolates were large ones. Between twenty or thirty tablets, I felt sure, could have been inserted. But who had done this?

There were two guests in the house. John Wilson had the means. Saint Alard had the motive. Remember, he was a fanatic, and there is no fanatic like a religious fanatic. Could he, by any means, have got hold of John Wilson's trinitrin?

Another little idea came to me. Ah! You smile at my little ideas! Why had Wilson run out of trinitrin? Surely he would bring an adequate supply from England. I called once more at the house in the Avenue Louise. Wilson was out, but I saw the girl who did his room, Félicie. I demanded of her immediately whether it was not true that M.

425

Wilson had lost a bottle from his washstand some little time ago. The girl responded eagerly. It was quite true. She, Félicie, had been blamed for it. The English gentleman had evidently thought that she had broken it, and did not like to say so. Whereas she had never even touched it. Without doubt it was Jeannette—always nosing round where she had no business to be——

I calmed the flow of words, and took my leave. I knew now all that I wanted to know. It remained for me to prove my case. That, I felt, would not be easy. *I* might be sure that Saint Alard had removed the bottle of trinitrin from John Wilson's washstand, but to convince others, I would have to produce evidence. And I had none to produce!

Never mind. I *knew*—that was the great thing. You remember our difficulty in the Styles case, Hastings? There again, I *knew*—but it took me a long time to find the last link which made my chain of evidence against the murderer complete.

I asked for an interview with Mademoiselle Mesnard. She came at once. I demanded of her the address of M. de Saint Alard. A look of trouble came over her face.

"Why do you want it, monsieur?"

"Mademoiselle, it is necessary."

She seemed doubtful—troubled.

"He can tell you nothing. He is a man whose thoughts are not in this world. He hardly notices what goes on around him."

"Possibly, mademoiselle. Nevertheless, he was an old friend of M. Déroulard's. There may be things he can tell me—things of the past—old grudges—old love-affairs."

The girl flushed and bit her lip. "As you please—but—but—I feel sure now that I have been mistaken. It was good of you to accede to my demand, but I was upset—almost distraught at the time. I see now that there is no mystery to solve. Leave it, I beg of you, monsieur."

I eyed her closely.

"Mademoiselle," I said, "it is sometimes difficult for a dog to find a scent, but once he *has* found it, nothing on earth will make him leave it! That is if he is a good dog! And I, mademoiselle, I, Hercule Poirot, am a very good dog."

Without a word she turned away. A few minutes later she returned with the address written on a sheet of paper. I left the house. François was waiting for me outside. He looked at me anxiously.

"There is no news, monsieur?"

"None as yet, my friend."

"Ah! *Pauvre* Monsieur Déroulard!" he sighed. "I too was of his way of thinking. I do not care for priests. Not that I would say so in the

426

house. The women are all devout—a good thing perhaps. *Madame est très pieuse—et Mademoiselle Virginie aussi.*"

Mademoiselle Virginie? Was she "*très pieuse?*" Thinking of the tear-stained passionate face I had seen that first day, I wondered.

Having obtained the address of M. de Saint Alard, I wasted no time. I arrived in the neighborhood of his château in the Ardennes but it was some days before I could find a pretext for gaining admission to the house. In the end I did—how do you think—as a plumber, *mon ami!* It was the affair of a moment to arrange a neat little gas leak in his bedroom. I departed for my tools, and took care to return with them at an hour when I knew I should have the field pretty well to myself. What I was searching for, I hardly knew. The one thing needful, I could not believe there was any chance of finding. He would never have run the risk of keeping it.

Still when I found a little cupboard above the washstand locked, I could not resist the temptation of seeing what was inside it. The lock was quite a simple one to pick. The door swung open. It was full of old bottles. I took them up one by one with a trembling hand. Suddenly, I uttered a cry. Figure to yourself, my friend, I held in my hand a little phial with an English chemist's label. On it were the words: "*Trinitrin Tablets. One to be taken when required. Mr. John Wilson.*"

I controlled my emotion, closed the little cupboard, slipped the bottle into my pocket, and then continued to repair the gas leak! One must be methodical. Then I left the château, and took train for my own country as soon as possible. I arrived in Brussels late that night. I was writing out a report for the préfet in the morning, when a note was brought to me. It was from old Madame Déroulard, and it summoned me to the house in the Avenue Louise without delay.

Francois opened the door to me.

"Madame la Boronne is awaiting you."

He conducted me to her apartments. She sat in state in a large armchair. There was no sign of Mademoiselle Virginie.

"M. Poirot," said the old lady. "I have just learned that you are not what you pretend to be. You are a police officer."

"That is so, madame."

"You came here to inquire into the circumstances of my son's death?"

Again I replied: "That is so, madame."

"I should be glad if you would tell me what progress you have made."

I hesitated.

"First, I would like to know how you have learned all this, madame."

"From one who is no longer of this world."

Her words, and the brooding way she uttered them, sent a chill to my heart. I was incapable of speech.

"Therefore, monsieur, I would beg of you most urgently to tell me exactly what progress you have made in your investigation."

"Madame, my investigation is finished."

"My son?"

"Was killed deliberately."

"You know by whom?"

"Yes, madame."

"Who, then?"

"M. de Saint Alard."

The old lady shook her head.

"You are wrong. M. de Saint Alard is incapable of such a crime."

"The proofs are in my hands."

"I beg of you once more to tell me all."

This time I obeyed, going over each step that had led me to the discovery of the truth. She listened attentively. At the end she nodded her head.

"Yes, yes, it is all as you say, all but one thing. It was not M. de Saint Alard who killed my son. It was I, his mother."

I stared at her. She continued to nod her head gently.

"It is well that I sent for you. It is the providence of the good God that Virginie told me before she departed for the convent, what she had done. Listen, M. Poirot! My son was an evil man. He persecuted the church. He led a life of mortal sin. He dragged down other souls beside his own. But there was worse than that. As I came out of my room in this house one morning, I saw my daughter-in-law standing at the head of the stairs. She was reading a letter. I saw my son steal up behind her. One swift push, and she fell, striking her head on the marble steps. When they picked her up she was dead. My son was a murderer, and only I, his mother, knew it."

She closed her eyes for a moment. "You cannot conceive, monsieur, of my agony, my despair. What was I to do? Denounce him to the police? I could not bring myself to do it. It was my duty, but my flesh was weak. Besides, would they believe me? My eyesight had been failing for some time—they would say I was mistaken. I kept silence. But my conscience gave me no peace. By keeping silence I too was a murderer. My son inherited his wife's money. He flourished as the green bay tree. And now he was to have a Minister's portfolio. His persecution of the church would be redoubled. And there was Virginie. She, poor child, beautiful, naturally pious, was fascinated by him. He had a strange and terrible power over women. I saw it coming. I was powerless to prevent it. He had no intention of marrying her. The time came when she was ready to yield everything to him.

"Then I saw my path clear. He was my son. I had given him life. I was responsible for him. He had killed one woman's body, now he would kill another's soul! I went to Mr. Wilson's room, and took the bottle of tablets. He had once said laughingly that there were enough in it to kill a man! I went into the study and opened the big box of chocolates that always stood on the table. I opened a new box by mistake. The other was on the table also. There was just one chocolate left in it. That simplified things. No one ate chocolates except my son and Virginie. I would keep her with me that night. All went as I had planned——"

She paused, closing her eyes a minute then opened them again.

"M. Poirot, I am in your hands. They tell me I have not many days to live. I am willing to answer for my action before the good God. Must I answer for it on earth also?"

I hesitated. "But the empty bottle, madame," I said to gain time. "How came that into M. de Saint Alard's possession?"

When he came to say good-by to me, monsieur, I slipped it into his pocket. I did not know how to get rid of it. I am so infirm that I cannot move about much without help, and finding it empty in my rooms might have caused suspicion. You understand, monsieur,"—she drew herself up to her full height,—"it was with no idea of casting suspicion on M. de Saint Alard! I never dreamed of such a thing. I thought his valet would find an empty bottle and throw it away without question."

I bowed my head. "I comprehend, madame," I said.

"And your decision, monsieur?"

Her voice was firm and unfaltering, her head held as high as ever. I rose to my feet.

"Madame," I said, "I have the honor to wish you good day. I have made my investigations—and failed! The matter is closed."

He was silent for a moment, then said quietly: "She died just a week later. Mademoiselle Virginie passed through her novitiate, and duly took the veil. That, my friend, is the story. I must admit that I do not make a fine figure in it."

"But that was hardly a failure," I expostulated. "What else could you have thought under the circumstances?"

"Ah, *sacré, mon ami*," cried Poirot, becoming suddenly animated.

"Is it that you do not see? But I was thirty-six times an idiot! My gray cells, they functioned not at all. The whole time I had the true clue in my hands."

"What clue?"

"*The chocolate box!* Do you not see? Would anyone in possession of their full eyesight make such a mistake? I knew Madame Déroulard had cataract—the atropine drops told me that. There was only one person in the household whose eyesight was such that she could not see which lid to replace. It was the chocolate box that started me on the track, and yet up to the end I failed consistently to perceive its real significance!

"Also my psychology was at fault. Had M. de Saint Alard been the criminal, he would never have kept an incriminating bottle. Finding it was a proof of his innocence. I had learned already from Mademoiselle Virginie that he was absent-minded. Altogether it was a miserable affair that I have recounted to you there! Only to you have I told the story. You comprehend, I do not figure well in it! An old lady commits a crime in such a simple and clever fashion that I, Hercule Poirot, am completely deceived. *Sapristi!* it does not bear thinking of! Forget it. Or no—remember it, and if you think at any time that I am growing conceited—it is not likely, but it might arise."

I concealed a smile.

"*Eh bien*, my friend, you shall say to me, 'Chocolate box.' Is it agreed?"

"It's a bargain!"

"After all," said Poirot reflectively, "it was an experience! I, who have undoubtedly the finest brain in Europe at present, can afford to be magnanimous!"

"Chocolate box," I murmured gently.

"*Pardon, mon ami?*"

I looked at Poirot's innocent face, as he bent forward inquiringly, and my heart smote me. I had suffered often at his hands, but I, too, though not possessing the finest brain in Europe, could afford to be magnanimous!

"Nothing," I lied, and lit another pipe, smiling to myself.

DEATH AND THE COMPASS

By Jorge Luis Borges

Jorge Luis Borges (1900–), a major figure in twentieth-century litera-
ture, was born in Argentina. Delicate and short-sighted as a boy, he was
a precocious student, especially of English, and at the age of nine had
already published a translation of Oscar Wilde's "Happy Prince" in a
Buenos Aires newspaper. In 1914 he accompanied his family to Europe
where they spent the war years in Geneva and then moved to Madrid.
During this time, the young Borges continued his education, reading
fluently in Latin, Greek, English, French, and German and becoming
acquainted with the avant-garde artists and philosophers of his time. He
also began to write poetry and on his return to Argentina in 1921
founded a literary magazine. Like Chesterton, whose works he had read
in his father's library, Borges was attracted to the detective story form
because of the opportunity it gave him to express metaphysical ideas in a
dramatic way. Many of the works in Ficciones (1945), a volume of his
short stories, employ elements to be found in crime and mystery
literature, and of these, "Death and the Compass," with its many
references to Sherlock Holmes and Auguste Dupin, makes the most
direct use of such materials. Now nearly blind, Borges continues to live
and work in Argentina. Ficciones is available in a translation by
Anthony Kerrigan (New York: Grove, 1962). Also see J. M. Cohen's
Jorge Luis Borges (New York: Barnes and Nobel, 1974) for an
analysis of "Death and the Compass" and of Borges' writing generally.
Borges' own notes on his short fiction appear in Aleph and Other
Stories, edited and translated by Norman Thomas di Giovanni (New
York: Dutton, 1970).

Of the many problems which exercised the daring perspicacity of Lönnrot none was so strange—so harshly strange, we may say—as the staggered series of bloody acts which culminated at the villa of Triste-le-Roy, amid the boundless odor of the eucalypti. It is true that Erik Lönnrot did not succeed in preventing the last crime, but it is indisputable that he foresaw it. Nor did he, of course, guess the identity of Yarmolinsky's unfortunate assassin, but he did divine the secret morphology of the vicious series as well as the participation of Red Scharlach, whose alias is Scharlach the Dandy. This criminal (as so many others) had sworn on his honor to kill Lönnrot, but the latter had never allowed himself to be intimidated. Lönnrot thought of himself as a pure thinker, an Auguste Dupin, but there was something of the adventurer in him, and even of the gamester.

The first crime occurred at the Hôtel du Nord—that high prism that dominates the estuary whose waters are the colors of the desert. To this tower (which most manifestly unites the hateful whiteness of a sanitorium, the numbered divisibility of a prison, and the general appearance of a bawdy house) on the third day of December came the delegate from Podolsk to the Third Talmudic Congress, Doctor Marcel Yarmolinsky, a man of gray beard and gray eyes. We shall never know whether the Hôtel du Nord pleased him: he accepted it with the ancient resignation which had allowed him to endure three years of war in the Carpathians and three thousand years of oppression and pogroms. He was given a sleeping room on floor R, in front of the suite which the Tetrarch of Galilee occupied not without some splendor. Yarmolinsky supped, postponed until the following day an investigation of the unknown city, arranged upon a cupboard his many books and his few possessions, and before midnight turned off the light. (Thus declared the Tetrarch's chauffeur, who slept in an adjoining room.) On the fourth, at 11:03 A.M., there was a telephone call call for him from the editor of the *Yiddische Zeitung*; Doctor Yarmolinsky did not reply; he was found in his room, his face already a little dark, and his body, almost nude, beneath a large anachronistic cape. He was lying not far from the door which gave onto the corridor; a deep stab wound had split open his breast. In the same room, a couple of hours later, in the midst of journalists, photographers, and police, Commissioner Treviranus and Lönnrot were discussing the problem with equanimity.

"There's no need to look for a Chimera, or a cat with three legs,"

Treviranus was saying as he brandished an imperious cigar. "We all know that the Tetrarch of Galilee is the possessor of the finest sapphires in the world. Someone, intending to steal them, came in here by mistake. Yarmolinsky got up; the robber had to kill him. What do you think?"

"It's possible, but not interesting," Lönnrot answered. "You will reply that reality hasn't the slightest need to be of interest. And I'll answer you that reality may avoid the obligation to be interesting, but that hypotheses may not. In the hypothesis you have postulated, chance intervenes largely. Here lies a dead rabbi; I should prefer a purely rabbinical explanation; not the imaginary mischances of an imaginary robber."

Treviranus answered ill-humoredly:

"I am not interested in rabbinical explanations; I am interested in the capture of the man who stabbed this unknown person."

"Not so unknown," corrected Lönnrot. "Here are his complete works." He indicated a line of tall volumes: *A Vindication of the Cabala; An Examination of the Philosophy of Robert Fludd)* a literal translation of the *Sepher Yezirah; a Biography of the Baal Shem;* a *History of the Sect of the Hasidim;* a monograph (in German) on the Tetragrammaton; another, on the divine nomenclature of the Pentateuch. The Commissioner gazed at them with suspicion, almost with revulsion. Then he fell to laughing.

"I'm only a poor Christian," he replied. "Carry off all these moth-eaten classics if you like; I haven't got time to lose in Jewish superstitions."

"Maybe this crime belongs to the history of Jewish superstitions," murmured Lönnrot.

"Like Christianity," the editor of the *Yiddische Zeitung* dared to put in. He was a myope, an atheist, and very timid.

No one answered him. One of the agents had found inserted in the small typewriter a piece of paper on which was written the following inconclusive sentence.

The first letter of the Name has been spoken

Lönnrot abstained from smiling. Suddenly become a bibliophile—or Hebraist—he directed that the dead man's books be made into a parcel, and he carried them to his office. Indifferent to the police investigation, he dedicated himself to studying them. A large octavo volume revealed to him the teachings of Israel Baal Shem-Tob, founder of the sect of the Pious; another volume, the virtues and terrors of the

433

Tetragrammaton, which is the ineffable name of God; another, the thesis that God has a secret name, in which is epitomized (as in the crystal sphere which the Persians attribute to Alexander of Macedon) his ninth attribute, eternity—that is to say, the immediate knowledge of everything that will exist, exists, and has existed in the universe. Tradition numbers ninety-nine names of God; the Hebraists attribute this imperfect number to the magical fear of even numbers; the Hasidim reason that this hiatus indicates a hundredth name—the Absolute Name.

From this erudition he was distracted, within a few days, by the appearance of the editor of the *Yiddische Zeitung*. This man wished to talk of the assassination; Lönnrot preferred to speak of the diverse names of God. The journalist declared, in three columns, that the investigator Erik Lönnrot had dedicated himself to studying the names of God in order to "come up with" the name of the assassin. Lönnrot, habituated to the simplifications of journalism, did not become indignant. One of those shopkeepers who have found that there are buyers for every book came out with a popular edition of the *History of the Sect of the Hasidim*.

The second crime occurred on the night of the third of January, in the most deserted and empty corner of the capital's western suburbs. Toward dawn, one of the gendarmes who patrol these lonely places on horseback detected a man in a cape, lying prone in the shadow of an ancient paint shop. The hard visage seemed bathed in blood; a deep stab wound had split open his breast. On the wall, upon the yellow and red rhombs, there were some words written in chalk. The gendarme spelled them out. . . .

That afternoon Treviranus and Lönnrot made their way toward the remote scene of the crime. To the left and right of the automobile, the city disintegrated; the firmament grew larger and the houses meant less and less and a brick kiln or a poplar grove more and more. They reached their miserable destination: a final alley of rose-colored mud walls which in some way seemed to reflect the disordered setting of the sun. The dead man had already been identified. He was Daniel Simon Azevedo, a man of some fame in the ancient northern suburbs, who had risen from wagoner to political tough, only to degenerate later into a thief and even an informer. (The singular style of his death struck them as appropriate: Azevedo was the last representative of a generation of bandits who knew how to handle a dagger, but not a revolver.) The words in chalk were the following:

The second letter of the Name has been spoken

The third crime occurred on the night of the third of February. A little before one o'clock, the telephone rang in the office of Commissioner Treviranus. In avid secretiveness a man with a guttural voice spoke: he said his name was Ginzberg (or Ginsburg) and that he was disposed to communicate, for a reasonable remuneration, an explanation of the two sacrifices of Azevedo and Yarmolinsky. The discordant sound of whistles and horns drowned out the voice of the informer. Then the connection was cut off. Without rejecting the possibility of a hoax (it was carnival time), Treviranus checked and found he had been called from Liverpool House, a tavern on the Rue de Toulon—that dirty street where cheek by jowl are the peepshow and the milk store, the bordello and the women selling Bibles. Treviranus called back and spoke to the owner. This personage (Black Finnegan by name, an old Irish criminal who was crushed, annihilated almost, by respectability) told him that the last person to use the establishment's phone had been a lodger, a certain Gryphius, who had just gone out with some friends. Treviranus immediately went to Liverpool House, where Finnegan related the following facts. Eight days previously, Gryphius had taken a room above the saloon. He was a man of sharp features, a nebulous gray beard, shabbily clothed in black; Finnegan (who put the room to a use which Treviranus guessed) demanded a rent which was undoubtedly excessive; Gryphius immediately paid the stipulated sum. He scarcely ever went out; he dined and lunched in his room; his face was hardly known in the bar. On this particular night, he came down to telephone from Finnegan's office. A closed coupe stopped in front of the tavern. The driver did not move from his seat; several of the patrons recalled that he was wearing a bear mask. Two harlequins descended from the coupe; they were short in stature, and no one could fail to observe that they were very drunk. With a tooting of horns they burst into Finnegan's office; they embraced Gryphius, who seemed to recognize them but who replied to them coldly; they exchanged a few words in Yiddish—he, in a low guttural voice; they, in shrill, falsetto tones—and then the party climbed to the upstairs room. Within a quarter hour the three descended, very joyous; Gryphius, staggering, seemed as drunk as the others. He walked—tall, dazed—in the middle, between the masked harlequins. (One of the women in the bar remembered the yellow, red and green rhombs, the diamond designs.) Twice he stumbled; twice he was held up by the harlequins. Alongside the adjoining dock basin, whose water was rectangular, the trio got into the coupe and disappeared. From the running board, the last of the harlequins had scrawled an obscene figure and a sentence on one of the slates of the outdoor shed.

Treviranus gazed upon the sentence. It was nearly foreknowable. It read:

The last of the letters of the Name has been spoken

He examined, then, the small room of Gryphius-Ginzberg. On the floor was a violent star of blood; in the corners, the remains of some Hungarian-brand cigarettes; in a cabinet, a book in Latin—the *Philologus Hebraeo-Graecus* (1739) of Leusden—along with various manuscript notes. Treviranus studied the book with indignation and had Lönnrot summoned. The latter, without taking off his hat, began to read while the Commissioner questioned the contradictory witnesses to the possible kidnapping. At four in the morning they came out. In the tortuous Rue de Toulon, as they stepped on the dead serpentines of the dawn, Treviranus said:

"And supposing the story of this night were a sham?"

Erik Lönnrot smiled and read him with due gravity a passage (underlined) of the thirty-third dissertation of the *Philologus*:

*Dies Judaeorum incipit a solis occasu
usque ad solis occasum diei sequentis.*

"This means," he added, "that *the Hebrew day begins at sundown and lasts until the following sundown.*"

Treviranus attempted an irony.

"Is this fact the most worthwhile you've picked up tonight?"

"No. Of even greater value is a word Ginzberg used."

The afternoon dailies did not neglect this series of disappearances. *The Cross and the Sword* contrasted them with the admirable discipline and order of the last Eremitical Congress; Ernest Palast, writing in *The Martyr*, spoke out against "the intolerable delays in this clandestine and frugal pogrom, which has taken three months to liquidate three Jews"; the *Yiddische Zeitung* rejected the terrible hypothesis of an anti-Semitic plot, "even though many discerning intellects do not admit of any other solution to the triple mystery"; the most illustrious gunman in the South, Dandy Red Scharlach, swore that in his district such crimes as these would never occur, and he accused Commissioner Franz Treviranus of criminal negligence.

On the night of March first, the Commissioner received an imposing-looking, sealed envelope. He opened it: the envelope contained a letter signed Baruj Spinoza, and a detailed plan of the city, obviously torn from a Baedeker. The letter prophesied that on the third

436

of March there would *not* be a fourth crime, inasmuch as the paint shop in the West, the Tavern on the Rue de Toulon and the Hôtel du Nord were the "perfect vertices of an equilateral and mystic triangle"; the regularity of this triangle was made clear on the map with red ink. This agreement, *more geometrico*, Treviranus read with resignation, and sent the letter and map on to Lönnrot—who deserved such a piece of insanity.

Erik Lönnrot studied the documents. The three sites were in fact equidistant. Symmetry in time (the third of December, the third of January, the third of February); symmetry in space as well. . . . Of a sudden he sensed he was about to decipher the mystery. A set of calipers and a compass completed his sudden intuition. He smiled, pronounced the word "Tetragrammaton" (of recent acquisition), and called the Commissioner on the telephone. He told him:

"Thank you for the equilateral triangle you sent me last night. It has enabled me to solve the problem. Tomorrow, Friday, the criminals will be in jail, we can rest assured."

"In that case, they're not planning a fourth crime?"

"Precisely because they *are* planning a fourth crime can we rest assured."

Lönnrot hung up. An hour later he was traveling in one of the trains of the Southern Railways, en route to the abandoned villa of Triste-le-Roy. South of the city of our story there flows a blind little river filled with muddy water made disgraceful by floating scraps and garbage. On the further side is a manufacturing suburb where, under the protection of a chief from Barcelona, gunmen flourish. Lönnrot smiled to himself to think that the most famous of them—Red Scharlach—would have given anything to know of this clandestine visit. Azevedo had been a comrade of Scharlach's; Lönnrot considered the remote possibility that the fourth victim might be Scharlach himself. Then, he put aside the thought. . . . He had virtually deciphered the problem; the mere circumstances, or the reality (names, prison records, faces, judicial and penal proceedings), scarcely interested him now. Most of all he wanted to take a stroll, to relax from three months of sedentary investigation. He reflected on how the explanation of the crimes lay in an anonymous triangle and a dust-laden Greek word. The mystery seemed to him almost crystalline now; he was mortified to have dedicated a hundred days to it.

The train stopped at a silent loading platform. Lönnrot descended. It was one of those deserted afternoons which seem like dawn. The air over the muddy plain was damp and cold. Lönnrot set off across the fields. He saw dogs, he saw a wagon on a dead road, he saw the horizon, he saw a silvery horse drinking the crapulous water of a puddle. Dusk was falling when he saw the rectangular belvedere of the villa of Triste-le-Roy, almost as tall as the black eucalypti which surrounded it. He thought of the fact that only one more dawn and one more nightfall, an ancient splendor in the east, and another in the west separated him from the hour so much desired by the seekers of the Name.

A rust colored wrought-iron fence defined the irregular perimeter of the villa. The main gate was closed. Without much expectation of entering, Lönnrot made a complete circuit. In front of the insurmountable gate once again, he put his hand between the bars almost mechanically and chanced upon the bolt. The creaking of the iron surprised him. With laborious passivity the entire gate gave way.

Lönnrot advanced among the eucalypti, stepping amidst confused generations of rigid, broken leaves. Close up, the house on the estate of Triste-le-Roy was seen to abound in superfluous symmetries and in maniacal repetitions: a glacial Diana in one lugubrious niche was complemented by another Diana in another niche; one balcony was repeated by another balcony; double steps of stairs opened into a double balustrade. A two-faced Hermes cast a monstrous shadow. Lönnrot circled the house as he had the estate. He examined everything; beneath the level of the terrace he noticed a narrow shutter door.

He pushed against it: some marble steps descended to a vault. Versed now in the architect's preferences, Lönnrot divined that there would be a set of stairs on the opposite wall. He found them, ascended, raised his hands, and pushed up a trap door.

The diffusion of light guided him to a window. He opened it: a round, yellow moon outlined two stopped-up fountains in the melancholy garden. Lönnrot explored the house. He traveled through antechambers and galleries to emerge upon duplicate patios; several times he emerged upon the same patio. He ascended dust-covered stairways and came out into circular antechambers; he was infinitely reflected in opposing mirrors; he grew weary of opening or half-opening windows which revealed the same desolate garden outside, from various heights and various angles; inside, the furniture was wrapped in yellow covers and the chandeliers bound up with cretonne. A bedroom detained him; in the bedroom, a single rose in a porcelain vase—at the first touch the ancient petals fell apart. On the second floor, on the top story, the house seemed to be infinite and growing. *The house is not this large*, he thought. *It is only made larger by the penumbra, the symmetry, the mirrors, the years, my ignorance, the solitude.*

Going up a spiral staircase he arrived at the observatory. The evening moon shone through the rhomboid diamonds of the windows, which were yellow, red and green. He was brought to a halt by a stunning and dizzying recollection.

Two men of short stature, ferocious and stocky, hurled themselves upon him and took his weapon. Another man, very tall, saluted him gravely, and said:

"You are very thoughtful. You've saved us a night and a day."

It was Red Scharlach. His men manacled Lönnrot's hands. Lönnrot at length found his voice.

"Are you looking for the Secret Name, Scharlach?"

Scharlach remained standing, indifferent. He had not participated in the short struggle; he scarcely stretched out his hand to receive Lönnrot's revolver. He spoke; in his voice Lönnrot detected a fatigued triumph, a hatred the size of the universe, a sadness no smaller than that hatred.

"No," answered Scharlach. "I am looking for something more ephemeral and slippery, I am looking for Erik Lönnrot. Three years ago, in a gambling house on the Rue de Toulon, you arrested my brother and had him sent to prison. In the exchange of shots that night my men got me away in a coupe, with a police bullet in my chest. Nine days and nine nights I lay dying in this desolate, symmetrical villa; I was racked with fever, and the odious double-faced Janus who gazes toward the twilights of dusk and dawn terrorized my dreams and my waking. I learned to abominate my body, I came to feel that two eyes, two hands, two lungs are as monstrous as two faces. An Irishman attempted to convert me to the faith of Jesus; he repeated to me that famous axiom of the goyim: All roads lead to Rome. At night, my delirium nurtured itself on this metaphor: I sensed that the world was a labyrinth, from which it was impossible to flee, for all paths, whether they seemed to lead north or south, actually led to Rome, which was also the quadrilateral jail where my brother was dying and the villa of Triste-le-Roy. During those nights I swore by the god who sees from two faces, and by all the gods of fever and of mirrors, to weave a labyrinth around the man who had imprisoned my brother. I have woven it, and it holds: the materials are a dead writer on heresies, a compass, an eighteenth-century sect, a Greek word, a dagger, the rhombs of a paint shop.

"The first objective in the sequence was given me by chance. I had made plans with some colleagues—among them, Daniel Azevedo—to take the Tetrarch's sapphires. Azevedo betrayed us; with the money we advanced him he got himself inebriated and started on the job a day early. In the vastness of the hotel he got lost; at two in the morning he blundered into Yarmolinsky's room. The latter, harassed by insomnia, had set himself to writing. He was editing some notes, apparently, or writing an article on the Name of God; he had just written the words *The first letter of the Name has been spoken*. Azevedo enjoined him to be quiet; Yarmolinsky reached out his hand for the bell which would arouse all the hotel's forces; Azevedo at once stabbed him in the chest. It was almost a reflex action: half a century of violence had taught him that it was easiest and surest to kill. . . . Ten days later, I learned through the *Yiddische Zeitung* that you were perusing the writings of Yarmolinsky for the key to his death. For my part I read the *History of the Sect of the Hasidim*; I learned that the reverent fear of pronouncing the Name of God had given rise to the doctrine that this Name is all-powerful and mystic. I learned that some Hasidim, in search of this secret Name, had gone as far as to offer human sacrifices. . . . I knew you would conjecture that the Hasidim had sacrificed the rabbi; I set myself to justifying this conjecture.

"Marcel Yarmolinsky died on the night of December third; for the second sacrifice I selected the night of January third. Yarmolinsky died in the North; for the second sacrifice a place in the West was preferable. Daniel Azevedo was the inevitable victim. He deserved death; he was an impulsive person, a traitor; his capture could destroy the entire plan. One of our men stabbed him; in order to link his corpse to the other one I wrote on the paint shop diamonds *The second letter of the Name has been spoken*.

"The third 'crime' was produced on the third of February. It was as Treviranus must have guessed, a mere mockery, a simulacrum. I am Gryphius-Ginzberg-Ginsburg; I endured an interminable week (filled out with a tenuous false beard) in that perverse cubicle on the Rue de Toulon, until my friends spirited me away. From the running board one of them wrote on a pillar *The last of the letters of the Name has been spoken*. This sentence revealed that the series of crimes was *triple*. And the public thus understood it; nevertheless, I interspersed repeated signs that would allow you, Erik Lönnrot, the reasoner, to understand that it is *quadruple*. A portent in the North, others in the East and West, demand a fourth portent in the South; the Tetragrammaton—the name of God, JHVH—is made up of *four* letters; the harlequins and the paint shop sign suggested four points. In the manual of Leusden I underlined a certain passage: it manifested that the Hebrews calculate a day counting from dusk to dusk and that therefore the deaths occurred on the *fourth* day of each month. To Treviranus I sent the equilateral triangle. I sensed that you would supply the missing point. The point which would form a perfect rhomb, the point which fixes where death, exactly, awaits you. In order to attract you I have premeditated everything. Erik Lönnrot, so as to draw you to the solitude of Triste-le-Roy."

Lönnrot avoided Scharlach's eyes. He was looking at the trees and the sky divided into rhombs of turbid yellow, green and red. He felt a little cold, and felt, too, an impersonal, almost anonymous sadness. It was already night; from the dusty garden arose the useless cry of a bird. For the last time, Lönnrot considered the problem of symmetrical and periodic death.

"In your labyrinth there are three lines too many," he said at last. "I know of a Greek labyrinth which is a single straight line. Along this line so many philosophers have lost themselves that a mere detective might well do so too. Scharlach, when, in some other incarnation you hunt me, feign to commit (or do commit) a crime at A, then a second crime at B, eight kilometers from A, then a third crime at C, four kilometers from A and B, halfway enroute between the two. Wait for me later at D, two kilometers from A and C, halfway, once again, between both. Kill me at D, as you are now going to kill me at Triste-le-Roy."

"The next time I kill you," said Scharlach, "I promise you the labyrinth made of the single straight line which is invisible and everlasting."

He stepped back a few paces. Then, very carefully, he fired.

1942
—Translated by ANTHONY KERRIGAN